PRAISE FOR THIS NEW EDIT
ALEC FORBES OF HOWGLEN

"[In David Jack's translation of *Alec Forbes*]...the value of having the original Scottish and the English translation side by side [is that] both are charming. They enhance one another. At the beginning of the last century, Chesterton says MacDonald has yet to be discovered. In our century, it is finally starting to happen."
  Dale Ahlquist
  President of The American Chesterton Society
  Author of *G.K. Chesterton: The Apostle of Common Sense*

"While studying Victorian Literature in graduate school, I never once heard or saw the name of George MacDonald mentioned. Hence, when I first read *Alec Forbes of Howglen*, I experienced a sea-change--or perhaps "river-change" would better describe it. Amazed by the cogency and insight of the novel, I suddenly recognized why MacDonald's fiction should be taken seriously. Nevertheless, like Alec negotiating a flooded river, I struggled to stay afloat whenever streams of Scots dialogue flooded the text. David Jack's lovely translation of MacDonald's Doric has made these overwhelming passages navigable, allowing readers to baptize their imaginations without abandoning ship".
  Dr. Crystal Downing
  Former Co-director of the Marion E. Wade Center
  Author of six books about faith and culture

PRAISE FOR OTHER BOOKS IN THIS SERIES

"George MacDonald is one of the greatest and perhaps most forgotten writers of our modern world. This may in part be because of his frequent usage of Doric, the language of the North-Eastern Scots which is barely comprehensible to the rest of us. *Sir Gibbie* is an astonishingly beautiful book, filled with joy, love, devotion, adventure, and, at the same time, hardship. David Jack has now made it available to all with his two-columned technique, the English in the one column and the Doric in the other. I have already read and

enjoyed his earlier two works, *Robert Falconer* and *Castle Warlock*, and have no reservations at all in recommending *Sir Gibbie*."
    Douglas Gresham
    Stepson of C. S. Lewis
    Series Producer, *The Chronicles of Narnia*

"David Jack's translation of *Donal Grant*—the life of a former shepherd who has just finished a college education and wishes to tutor—brings the novel to life again, not least by his inspired translation of Scottish Doric dialect often used in the book. Having the translation and rich dialect in parallel columns carries the reader along. Donal's story is a sequel to MacDonald's beautiful and famous *Sir Gibbie*, which continues the thread of how an honest and good life lived out in a tried and greatly tested way can leaven the people and circumstances encountered. The resistance of good against evil is presented in ordinary life, making an extraordinary story centred on the power of pure goodness."
    Colin Duriez
    Author of *The Oxford Inklings* and *C S Lewis: A Biography of Friendship*

"For many readers, the use of the Doric dialect in MacDonald's Scottish writings has resulted in the misunderstanding, misinterpretation, or abandonment of these captivating novels altogether. In this edition of *Malcolm*, David Jack does a masterful job not only preserving the original meaning and nuance within his interpretation, but also respecting the original text by including it intact. This volume would be a welcome edition to any George MacDonald reader, scholar or layman alike.
    Dean Hardy
    Teacher of Christian Philosophy and Apologetics at Charlotte Christian School
    Author of *Waking the Dead: George MacDonald as Philosopher, Mystic, and Apologist*

Alec Forbes of Howglen

GEORGE MACDONALD

Translation by David Jack
Introduction by Dale Ahlquist
Illustrated by Carrie Stout*

*with one additional illustration by Arthur Hughes

This edition of *Alec Forbes of Howglen* is an independent production by David Jack, translator of the Scots-English editions of George MacDonald's Scottish novels.
theroomtoroam.com

George MacDonald's bookplate inside the front cover was adapted from the etching "Death's Door" by William Blake, to incorporate the words of the MacDonald family motto:
"Corage, God Mend Al."

Scots dialogue translated by David Jack
Translator's Preface by David Jack
Introduction by Dale Ahlquist
Cover art, design and interior illustrations by Carrie Stout (with one additional illustration by Arthur Hughes)
Interior design by Jessica Jack
All rights reserved.

ISBN: 978-1-7385314-7-9

MacDonald's Scottish Novels

David Elginbrod
Alec Forbes of Howglen
Robert Falconer
Malcolm
The Marquis of Lossie
Sir Gibbie
Castle Warlock
Donal Grant
What's Mine's Mine
The Elect Lady
Heather and Snow
Salted With Fire

GEORGE MACDONALD'S SCOTTISH NOVELS:
THE SCOTS-ENGLISH EDITIONS

"The man who loves the antique speech...of his childhood, and knows how to use it, possesses therein a certain kind of power over the hearts of men, which the most refined and perfect of languages cannot give, inasmuch as it has travelled farther from the original sources of laughter and tears."
 -Sir Gibbie

"George MacDonald writes of homely things and simple people who saw, in the stuff of a shepherd's cottage or a fisherman's arduous work on the cold sea, the love of God."
 -Elisabeth Elliot

"All his life he continued to love the rock from which he had been hewn. All that is best in his novels carries us back to that 'kaleyard' world of granite and heather, of bleaching greens beside burns that look as if they flowed not with water but with stout, to the thudding of wooden machinery, the oatcakes, the fresh milk, the pride, the poverty, and the passionate love of hard-won learning."
 -C S Lewis

"Among the many men of genius Scotland produced in the nineteenth century, there was only one...who really represented what Scottish religion should have been, if it had continued the colour of the Scottish medieval poetry. In his particular type of literary work, he did indeed realise the apparent paradox of a St. Francis of Aberdeen."
 -G K Chesterton

"While MacDonald's current reputation rests largely on his mythopoeic genius, the reader who would truly know him cannot afford to neglect the twelve novels set in his native Scotland. Full of the spiritual wisdom characterising all his work, there is a further element of oracular power drawn from the very soil itself, so strong was his bond to the land that reared him. As soon might we separate Dickens from London, Hardy from Wessex, or Tolstoy from the heart of Russia, as think of George MacDonald without picturing the Aberdeenshire he brought to life in these stories."
 -David Jack

CONTENTS

Acknowledgements   xv
Translator's Preface by David Jack   xvi
Introduction by Dale Ahlquist   xix
Alec Forbes of Howglen Cast of Characters   xxv

	PAGE
CHAPTER I.	1
CHAPTER II.	5
CHAPTER III.	9
CHAPTER IV.	13
CHAPTER V.	17
CHAPTER VI.	20
CHAPTER VII.	25
CHAPTER VIII.	31
CHAPTER IX.	38
CHAPTER X.	44
CHAPTER XI.	49
CHAPTER XII.	56
CHAPTER XIII.	64
CHAPTER XIV.	69
CHAPTER XV.	83
CHAPTER XVI.	87
CHAPTER XVII.	96
CHAPTER XVIII.	103
CHAPTER XIX.	111
CHAPTER XX.	114

CHAPTER XXI.	....	124
CHAPTER XXII.	....	139
CHAPTER XXIII.	....	148
CHAPTER XXIV.	....	154
CHAPTER XXV.	....	159
CHAPTER XXVI.	....	165
CHAPTER XXVII.	....	170
CHAPTER XXVIII.	....	174
CHAPTER XXIX.	....	180
CHAPTER XXX.	....	191
CHAPTER XXXI.	....	196
CHAPTER XXXII.	....	204
CHAPTER XXXIII.	....	213
CHAPTER XXXIV.	....	215
CHAPTER XXXV.	....	218
CHAPTER XXXVI.	....	221
CHAPTER XXXVII.	....	223
CHAPTER XXXVIII.	....	228
CHAPTER XXXIX.	....	235
CHAPTER XL.	....	247
CHAPTER XLI.	....	252
CHAPTER XLII.	....	260
CHAPTER XLIII.	....	265
CHAPTER XLIV.	....	270

CHAPTER XLV.	284
CHAPTER XLVI.	293
CHAPTER XLVII.	296
CHAPTER XLVIII.	304
CHAPTER XLIX.	307
CHAPTER L.	312
CHAPTER LI.	319
CHAPTER LII.	327
CHAPTER LIII.	333
CHAPTER LIV.	340
CHAPTER LV.	347
CHAPTER LVI.	354
CHAPTER LVII.	359
CHAPTER LVIII.	363
CHAPTER LIX.	374
CHAPTER LX.	379
CHAPTER LXI.	383
CHAPTER LXII.	386
CHAPTER LXIII.	392
CHAPTER LXIV.	401
CHAPTER LXV.	407
CHAPTER LXVI.	410
CHAPTER LXVII.	417
CHAPTER LXVIII.	429

CHAPTER LXIX.	....	437
CHAPTER LXX.	....	452
CHAPTER LXXI.	....	472
CHAPTER LXXII.	....	477
CHAPTER LXXIII.	....	479
CHAPTER LXXIV.	....	486
CHAPTER LXXV.	....	497
CHAPTER LXXVI.	....	503
CHAPTER LXXVII.	....	511
CHAPTER LXXVIII.	....	514
CHAPTER LXXIX.	....	520
CHAPTER LXXX.	....	534
CHAPTER LXXXI.	....	550
CHAPTER LXXXII.	....	556
CHAPTER LXXXIII.	....	567
CHAPTER LXXXIV.	....	581
CHAPTER LXXXV.	....	589
CHAPTER LXXXVI.	....	601
CHAPTER LXXXVII.	....	606
CHAPTER LXXXVIII.	....	611
CHAPTER LXXXIX.	....	618
CHAPTER XC.	....	625
CHAPTER XCI.	....	627
CHAPTER XCII.	....	635
CHAPTER XCIII.	....	643

ACKNOWLEDGEMENTS

George MacDonald's extensive use of Scots in several of his greatest novels has been a stumbling block for many potential readers. This series of Scots-English translations offers unique assistance to all who wish to read the original, unabridged texts (read by C.S. Lewis, G.K. Chesterton, et al.) by retaining, in its entirety, the authentic Scots speech, and placing a parallel English column alongside MacDonald's dialogue.

This new edition of *Alec Forbes of Howglen* is the ninth in the series, following on from *Robert Falconer, Castle Warlock, Sir Gibbie, Donal Grant, Malcolm, The Marquis of Lossie, What's Mine's Mine,* and *Salted With Fire*. It would not have been possible without help from the following contributors, to whom I would like to express my deepest thanks: my wife Jessica, for formatting the book's interior; Carrie Stout, for her stunning cover art and beautiful illustrations; Dale Ahlquist, for his expert and erudite introduction.

Source for the front cover quote: Gabelman, Daniel. "Nocturnal Anarchist, Mystic, and Fairytale King: G.K. Chesterton's Portrait of George MacDonald." *VII: Journal of the Marion E. Wade Center.* Vol. 28. Wheaton, IL: Marion E. Wade Center, 2011: 27-46

TRANSLATOR'S PREFACE
BY DAVID JACK

"I have read *Alec Forbes*, and am delighted with it, and I *very much* want to meet Annie Anderson in real life."
—Lewis Carroll, letter to
Mary MacDonald, Jan 22 1866

"It is in exactly the same sense in which we pity a man who has missed the whole of Keats or Milton, that we can feel compassion for the critic who has not...made the acquaintance of Mr. Cupples in the adventures of Alec Forbes."

—G K Chesterton,
George MacDonald and His Wife

A certain passage towards the end of *Alec Forbes* (which would later be echoed in C S Lewis' *The Weight of Glory*) tells of a universal and unquenchable human longing: a "formless idea of something at hand that keeps men and women striving to tear from the bosom of the world the secret of their own hopes." By that point in the story, both Annie Anderson and Alec Forbes, the two young people around whose fortunes this history revolves, have laid hold upon the secret, and their friend Mr Cupples is in a fair way of receiving it—or being received into it, which is perhaps a better way of expressing the same thing.

What this secret is, MacDonald is not long in showing us, and for Annie too the veil is lifted early—but Alec's enlightenment tarries. This may be one of the reasons that we are shown so much through Annie's eyes; from the opening scenes at the farm, to the seasons of light and shade engendered by her stays at Howglen and Bruce's spider-web of a shop. We are told in the first few chapters that she has the gift of sleep, and there is a corresponding reposefulness about her during her waking hours, which makes her fit to be admitted to life's secret whenever the time is ripe. "Those also serve who only stand and wait" says Milton, and Mr Cupples—though at one point deemed unfit company for the poet—shows he has read him to good purpose when he learns this lesson and would teach it to the striving Thomas Crann.

Indeed who better than these two to show, by contrast, the upward-tending nature of Annie's quiescence? For while it is true that Thomas has a glimpse into something outside the scope of her experience, it remains, for very eagerness and overstraining, but a glimpse: he can no more find the secret of life in his Calvinism than Cupples in his cups. But Annie, placidly steering her course like the boat that bears her name, "possesses her soul in patience" and enters into joy before either of the pair. To those who might urge that she is a touch too patient, I can only point triumphantly to the results: the combined Godsends of the cat to save her from the *rottans*, Mrs Forbes to deliver her from the Bruces, and Alec to take her out of the hand of their sons and Mr Malison.

Then in superabundance of blessing, there is the friendship of blind Tibbie Dyster, and, above all, the meeting of Annie and Cupples, the two most memorable characters among many within these pages. The contact of their souls I find inexpressibly moving, and while their paths converge somewhat late in the novel, it takes little imagination to picture the bookworm, who could only "breathe when he got next to the stars," being led by the orphan girl ever closer to the secret beyond those skyey regions. I am almost tempted, MacDonald-wise, to express a preference for their companionship over that of the young people (whose fate I will leave the reader to trace) but that each have their merits, and that, here as elsewhere, it is no doubt better to enjoy than to compare.

INTRODUCTION
BY DALE AHLQUIST

It begins like a murder mystery with a corpse on the first page. There is nothing like a dead body to capture and keep a reader's attention.

But before we consider the mystery of the exquisite novel Alec Forbes (without giving anything away), let us first consider the mystery of its author (trying to give away as much as possible).

To help us, we will call upon one of George MacDonald's greatest admirers, G.K. Chesterton. At the dawn of the 20th century when Chesterton appeared on the London literary scene, he wrote some deeply perceptive essays about MacDonald. He calls MacDonald "one of the three or four greatest men of 19th century Britain." So impressed was MacDonald's son Greville, that when he published his monumental biography of his father, he asked Chesterton to write the introduction.

Chesterton sees MacDonald as a poet who writes stories, "far too good a poet to be a good novelist in the highest sense," because novelists "look at humanity from a hundred standpoints," but the poet looks at it from one. He is not a detached or even cynical outsider looking in, but an insider completely intertwined into the lives of the people on the pages. Chesterton even sees MacDonald as someone who could be a character in one of his own fairy tales, and not a minor character, but "an elemental figure." He even goes so far as to say, "Macdonald enters fairyland like a citizen returning to his home."

MacDonald, according to Chesterton, is also a sage and a mystic. He compares him to a man who would "walk about the streets of some Greek or Eastern village with a long white beard, simply saying what he had to say." The sage is a sayer of things. George MacDonald, the man behind the stories, had something to say. "But, unfortunately for him – or, rather, unfortunately for us – the thing that he had to say was something not easily understood in this particular time." At the beginning of the last century, Chesterton says MacDonald has yet to be discovered. In our century, it is finally starting to happen.

Certainly one of MacDonald's most sagacious lines, one often quoted by Chesterton, comes from the novel *Donal Grant*: "God is easy to please and hard to satisfy." But it is also one of his most mystical lines.

A mystic, according to Chesterton, is one who does not hide mysteries but reveals them, who gives the rest of us a glimpse of a direct encounter with the divine. He includes MacDonald among the truest mystics because to him the supernatural was natural.

"True Mysticism will have nothing to do with vagueness. True Mysticism will have nothing to do with twilight. True Mysticism is entirely concerned with absolute things; not with twilight, but with the sacred black darkness and the sacred white sun. For to all good Mystics, from Plato downwards, absolute ideas, like those of light and darkness, are the real and interesting things. It must always be remembered that the only person in the world who can be really exact and definite is the Mystic. All sane materialism is avowedly agnostic and relative. The Evolutionist cannot be precise. The Positivist cannot be positive. But the Mystic believes that a rose is red with a fixed and sacred redness, and that a cucumber is green by a thundering decree of Heaven... And this great man has now gone deeper into a world of dreadful actuality, of a deepening and dreadful joy.

... melancholy is a frivolous thing compared with the seriousness of joy. Melancholy is negative, it has to do with trivialities like death: joy is positive and has to answer for the renewal and perpetuation of being. Melancholy is irresponsible; it could watch the universe fall to pieces: joy is responsible and upholds the universe in the void of space. This conception of the vigilance of the universal Power fills all Dr. Macdonald's novels with the unfathomable gravity of complete happiness, the gravity of a child at play."

Poet. Sage. Mystic.
"For the sea of summer ebbed away, and the rocky channels of the winter appeared, with its cold winds, its ghost-like mists, and the damps and shiverings that cling about the sepulchre in which Nature lies sleeping." Those are lines from a poet.

"The door into life generally opens behind us, and a hand is put forth which draws us in backwards." That is the sage.

"All the fairies and gnomes and goblins, yes, the great giants too, are only different sizes, shapes, and characters of children." That is the mystic.

And all are lines from the novel *Alec Forbes*.

This novel, as I said earlier, begins like a murder mystery. But it is soon established that there is no murder. However, there is still a mystery. We are drawn in. What is this story going to be about? And whose story is it? It seems that the main character is going to be the daughter of the dead man on the first page.

The character of Annie completely wins my heart when she opens Milton's *Paradise Lost* and after reading it a bit says, "I don't think this is the right book for me." Or rather, "I dinna think this is the richt buik for me." (That's the value of having the original Scottish and the English translation, side by side. Both are charming. They enhance one another.) Annie is sweet and innocent, and being such, of course needs to be rescued.

Our hero, Alec Forbes, is not introduced until several chapters into the book when his rescuing services are called upon. He will be the love interest of our heroine, but the story eventually becomes his and not hers, as we follow his travels and his tragedies and his triumphs.

But another character arriving very late in the action, almost steals the show. Mr. Cosmo Cupples is one of Mac-Donald's most beloved characters. He is something like Sam Weller, who arrives late in Dickens' *Pickwick Papers*, and becomes more of an audience favorite than the main character. Mr. Cupples (as his name even seems to suggest) is a split personality, part Greek scholar in the library, part dialect-speaking drunk in the street. Mr. Cupples is very aware of this "double existence" when he tells Alec: "I protest against being held responsible for anything that fellow Cupples may choose to say when I'm not at home." And he later bursts out: "Gin I cud but get a kick at that fellow Cupples! But I declare I canna help it" – as if the sodden and the sober versions of the same self could actually confront one another. It is hilarious. It is heartbreaking. It is mystical. But the comedy wins. Says Chesterton:

> "Anyone who has read Macdonald's novels will remember a sort of celestial wit in some of the dialogues, retorts that seem really like thunderbolts from heaven, such as . . . the perfect reply of Mr. Cupples, in Alec Forbes, to the man who objected to his carrying a foxglove on the Lord's Day. "It angert me sae to see the ill-faured thing growin' there on the Lord's Day, that I maist pulled it up by the root."

Chesterton, amazingly quoting from memory, manages to give the quotation in dialect. Almost. He mixes it up a bit with his own improvised translation.

Here's the original: ". . .it angert me sae to see the ill-faured thing positeevely growin' there upo' the Lord's day, that I pu'd it up 'maist by the reet. To think o' a weyd like that prankin' itsel' oot in its purple and its spots upo' the

Sawbath day! It canna ken what it's aboot. I'm only feared I left eneuch o' 't to be up again afore lang."

And here's David Jack's translation: "Well, you see, Mr Bruce, it angered me so to see the impudent thing positively growing there upon the Lord's day, that I pulled it up almost by the root. To think of a weed like that decking itself out in its purple and its spots upon the Sabbath day! It can't know what it's about. I'm only afraid I left enough of it to be up again before long."

Seldom has a mere flower seemed so important, even if only for an instant. Chesterton says that "a curious glow" pervades MacDonald's books: "the flowers seem like coloured flames broken loose from the flaming heart of the world: every bush of gorse is a burning bush, burning for the same cause as that of Moses."

Just as the narrator of Alec Forbes at one point steps out of the frame and says, "But I have wandered from Alec's thoughts into my own," it's hard to say where MacDonald's thoughts stop and Chesterton's begin, but when one great writer writes about another, it is not just worth reading, it leads to a greater prize for the reader. For me, I think Chesterton's most profound insight into MacDonald is the suggestion that MacDonald's novels are really the outer shells of his fairy tales, and that he "could write fairy-tales that made all experience a fairy-tale. He could give the real sense that every one had the end of an elfin thread that must at last lead them into Paradise."

ALEC FORBES OF HOWGLEN CAST OF CHARACTERS

THE FARM

ANNIE ANDERSON: an orphan girl, later brought up by the Bruces
MEG/MARGARET/MARGET ANDERSON: Annie's Aunt
BETTY: a servant
JAMES DOW/"DOOIE": A labourer at the farm, and later at Howglen

HOWGLEN

ALEC FORBES: the novel's hero, a schoolboy who befriends Annie
MRS FORBES: Alec's mother, a widow
MARY: the maid

THE BRUCES

ROBERT BRUCE: a greedy local shopkeeper
MRS BRUCE: Robert's wife
ROBERT BRUCE (JUNIOR): The Bruces' elder son
JOHNNIE BRUCE: The Bruces' younger son

THE MACWHAS

GEORGE MACWHA: the "wright" (carpenter)
WILLIE MACWHA/"CURLY": George's son, a friend of Alec and Annie's

GLAMERTON LOCALS

THOMAS CRANN: the stonemason
JEAN: Thomas' housekeeper
PETER WHAUP: the blacksmith
TIBBIE DYSTER: an elderly blind woman, befriended by Annie
MR COWIE: the parish church minister, also a friend of Annie's
MR TURNBULL: the pastor of the Independent ("Missionar") church
MURDOCH MALISON: the schoolmaster

CAST OF CHARACTERS, CONT'D

ANDREW TRUFFEY: an orphan boy, crippled by a beating from Malison
DIVOT, CADGER, SCRUMPIE, & LINKUM: schoolfriends of Alec's
"STUMPIN' STEENIE": the local policeman
ANDREW CONSTABLE: the clothier, a respected church elder
MRS CONSTABLE: Andrew's wife
ISIE CONSTABLE: their curious, old-fashioned young daughter

ABERDEEN

COSMO CUPPLES: Alec's fellow lodger, an eccentric, drunken scholar
MRS LESLIE: Alec and Mr Cupples' landlady (seldom named)
MR FRASER: A Professor of Greek at the university
KATE FRASER: the professor's niece, with whom Alec falls in love
PATRICK BEAUCHAMP: Alec's unprincipled rival for Kate's affections

MISCELLANEOUS

WATTIE SIM: the watchmaker
ROB GUDDLE: the barber
CHARLIE CHAPMAN: the wool-carder
REDFORD: the bookseller

CHAPTER I

The farm-yard was full of the light of a summer noontide. Nothing can be so desolately dreary as full strong sunlight can be. Not a living creature was to be seen in all the square inclosure, though cow-houses and stables formed the greater part of it, and one end was occupied by a dwelling-house. Away through the gate at the other end, far off in fenced fields, might be seen the dark forms of cattle; and on a road, at no great distance, a cart crawled along, drawn by one sleepy horse. An occasional weary low came from some imprisoned cow—or animal of the cow-kind; but not even a cat crossed the yard. The door of the barn was open, showing a polished floor, as empty, bright, and clean as that of a ball-room. And through the opposite door shone the last year's ricks of corn, golden in the sun.

Now, although a farm-yard is not, either in Scotland or elsewhere, the liveliest of places in ordinary, and still less about noon in summer, yet there was a peculiar cause rendering this one, at this moment, exceptionally deserted and dreary. But there were, notwithstanding, a great many more people about the place than was usual, only they were all gathered together in the ben-end, or best room of the house—a room of tolerable size, with a clean boarded floor, a mahogany table, black with age, and chairs of like material, whose wooden seats, and high, straight backs, were more suggestive of state than repose. Every one of these chairs was occupied by a silent man, whose gaze was either fixed on the floor, or lost in the voids of space. Each wore a black coat, and most of them were in black throughout. Their hard, thick, brown hands—hands evidently unused to idleness—grasped their knees, or, folded in each other, rested upon them. Some bottles and glasses, with a plate of biscuits, on a table in a corner, seemed to indicate that the meeting was not entirely for business purposes; and yet there were no signs of any sort of enjoyment. Nor was there a woman to be seen in the company.

Suddenly, at the open door, appeared a man whose shirt-sleeves showed very white against his other clothing which, like that of the rest, was of decent black. He addressed the assembly thus:

| "Gin ony o' ye want to see the corp, noo's yer time." | "If any of you want to see the body, now's your time." |

To this offer no one responded; and, with a slight air of discomfiture, for he was a busy man, and liked bustle, the carpenter turned on his heel, and re-ascended the narrow stairs to the upper room, where the corpse lay, waiting for its final dismission and courted oblivion.

"I reckon they've a' seen him afore," he remarked, as he rejoined his companion. "Puir fallow! He's unco worn. There'll no be muckle o' *him* to rise again."

"George, man, dinna jeest i' the face o' a corp," returned the other. "Ye kenna whan yer ain turn may come."

"It's no disrespeck to the deid, Thamas. That ye ken weel eneuch. I was only pityin' the worn face o' him, leukin up there atween the buirds, as gin he had gotten what he wanted sae lang, and was thankin' heaven for that same. I jist dinna like to pit the lid ower him."

"Hoot! hoot! Lat the Lord luik efter his ain. The lid o' the coffin disna hide frae his een."

"I reckon they've all seen him before," he remarked, as he rejoined his companion. "Poor fellow! He's worn to the bone. There won't be much of *him* to rise again."

"George, man, don't jest in the face of a corpse," returned the other. "You don't know when your own turn may come."

"It's no disrespect to the dead, Thomas. You know that well enough. I was only pitying the worn face of him, looking up there between the boards, as if he had got what he wanted so long, and was thanking heaven for that same. I just don't like to put the lid over him."

"Heavens, man! Let the Lord look after his own. The lid of the coffin doesn't hide from his eyes."

The last speaker was a stout, broad-shouldered man, a stonemason by trade, powerful, and somewhat asthmatic. He was regarded in the neighbourhood as a very religious man, but was more respected than liked, because his forte was rebuke. It was from deference to him that the carpenter had assumed a mental position generating a poetic mood and utterance quite unusual with him, for he was a jolly, careless kind of fellow, well-meaning and good-hearted.

So together they lifted the last covering of the dead, laid it over him, and fastened it down. And there was darkness about the dead; but he knew it not, because he was full of light. For this man was one who, all his life, had striven to be better.

Meantime, the clergyman having arrived, the usual religious ceremonial of a Scotch funeral—the reading of the Word and prayer—was going on below. This was all that gave the burial any sacred solemnity; for at the grave the Scotch terror of Popery forbids any observance of a religious character. The voice of the reader was heard in the chamber of death.

"The minister's come, Thamas.

"Come or gang," said Thomas, "it's muckle the same. The word itsel' oot o' his mou' fa's as deid as chaff upo' clay. Honest Jeames there'll rise ance mair; but never a word that man says, wi' the croon o' 's heid i' the how o' 's neck, 'll rise to beir witness o' his ministrations."

"Hoot, Thamas! It's no for the likes o' me to flee i' your face—but jist say a fair word for the livin' ower the deid, ye ken."

"Na, na. It's fair words maks foul wark; and the wrath o' the Almichty maun purge this toon or a' be dune. There's a heap o' graceless gaeins on in't; and that puir feckless body, the minister, never gies a pu' at the bridle o' salvation, to haud them aff o' the scaur o' hell."

"The minister's come, Thomas."

"Come or go," said Thomas, "it's much the same. The word itself falls from his mouth as dead as chaff upon clay. Honest James there'll rise once more; but never a word that man says, with the crown of his head in the how (*hollow*) of his neck, will rise to bear witness to his work."

"Heavens, Thomas! It's not for the likes of me to fly in your face—but just say a fair word for the living over the dead, you know."

"Na, na. It's fair words make foul work; and the wrath of the Almighty must purge this town in the end. There's a heap of wickedness goes on in it; and that poor feckless man, the minister, gives never a pull at the bridle of salvation, to keep them back from the cliff of hell."

The stone-mason generally spoke of the Almighty as if he were in a state of restrained indignation at the wrongs he endured from his children. If Thomas was right in this, then certainly he himself was one of his offspring. If he was wrong, then there was much well worth his unlearning.

The prayer was soon over, and the company again seated themselves, waiting till the coffin should be placed in the hearse, which now stood at the door.

"We'll jist draw the cork o' anither boatle," whispered a sharp-faced man to his neighbour.

And rising, he opened two bottles, and filled the glasses the second time with wine, red and

"We'll just draw the cork of another bottle," whispered a sharp-faced man to his neighbour.

And rising, he opened two bottles, and filled the glasses the second time with wine, red and white, which he handed to the minister first.

"Take a drop more, sir," he whispered in a coaxing, old-wivish tone; "it's a long road to the churchyard."

But the minister declining, most of the others followed his example. One after another they withdrew to the door, where the hearse was now laden with the harvest of the grave.

Falling in behind the body, they moved in an irregular procession from the yard. Outside, they were joined by several more in gigs and on horseback; and thus they crept, a curious train, away towards the resting-place of the dead.

It were a dreary rest, indeed, if that were their resting-place—on the side of a low hill, without tree or shrub to beautify it, or even the presence of an old church to seem to sanctify the spot. There was some long grass in it, though, clambering up as if it sought to bury the gravestones in their turn. And that long grass was a blessing. Better still, there was a sky overhead, in which men cannot set up any gravestones. But if any graveyard be the type of the rest expected by those left behind, it is no wonder they shrink from joining those that are away.

CHAPTER II

When the last man had disappeared, the women, like those of an eastern harem, began to come out. The first that entered the deserted room was a hard-featured, reproachful-looking woman, the sister of the departed. She instantly began to put the place in order, as if she expected her turn to come on the morrow. In a few moments more a servant appeared, and began to assist her. The girl had been crying, and the tears would still come, in spite of her efforts to repress them. In the vain attempt to dry her eyes with the corner of her apron, she nearly dropped one of the chairs, which she was simultaneously dusting and restoring to its usual place. Her mistress turned upon her with a kind of cold fierceness.

"Is that hoo ye shaw yer regaird to the deid, by brackin' the cheirs he left ahin' him? Lat sit, an' gang an' luik for that puir, doited thing, Annie. Gin it had only been the Almichty's will to hae ta'en her, an' left him, honest man!"

"Dinna daur to say a word again' the bairn, mem. The deid'll hear ye, an' no lie still."

"Supperstitious quean! Gang an' do as I tell ye this minute. What business hae ye to gang greetin aboot the hoose? He was no drap's bluid o' yours!"

"Is that how you show your regard for the dead, by breaking the chairs he left behind him? Let them be, and go and look for that poor, daft thing, Annie. If it had only been the Almighty's will to have taken her, and left him, honest man!"

"Don't dare to say a word against the child, ma'am. The dead'll hear you, and not lie still."

"Superstitious girl! Go and do as I tell you this minute. What business have you to go crying about the house? He was no drop's blood of yours!"

To this the girl made no reply, but left the room in quest of Annie. When she reached the door, she stood for a moment on the threshold, and, putting her hand over her eyes, shouted *"Annie!"* But, apparently startled at the sound of her own voice where the unhearing dead had so lately passed, she let the end of the call die away in a quaver, and, without repeating it, set off to find the missing child by the use of her eyes alone. First she went into the barn, and then through the barn into the stackyard, and then round the ricks one after another, and then into the cornloft; but all without avail. At length, as she was beginning to feel rather alarmed about the child, she arrived, in the progress of her search, at the door of one of the cow-houses. The moment she looked round the corner into the stall next the door, she stood stock-still, with her mouth wide open. This stall was occupied by a favourite cow—brown, with large white spots, called therefore *Brownie*. Her manger was full of fresh-cut grass; and half-buried in this grass, at one end of the manger, with her back against the wall, sat Annie, holding one of the ears of the hornless Brownie with one hand and stroking the creature's nose with the other.

She was a delicate child, about nine years old, with blue eyes, half full of tears, hair somewhere between dark and fair, gathered in a silk net, and a pale face, on which a faint moon-like smile was glimmering. The old cow continued to hold her nose to be stroked.

"Isn't Broonie a fine cow, Betty?" said the child, as the maid went on staring at her. "Poor Broonie! No one remembered me, and so I came to you, Broonie."

And she laid her cheek, white, smooth, and thin, against the broad, flat, hairy forehead of the friendly cow. Then turning again to Betty, she said—

"Don't tell auntie where I am, Betty. Let me be. I'm best here with Broonie."

Betty said never a word, but returned to her mistress.

"Where's the child, Betty? At some mischief or other, I'll be bound."

"Heavens! ma'am, the child's well enough. Children mustn't be followed like calves."

"Where is she?"

"I can't just downright exactly take upon me to say," answered Betty; "but I have no fear about her. She's a wise child."

"You're not the lassie's keeper, Betty. I see I must seek her myself.

"She laid her cheek...against the broad, flat, hairy forehead of the friendly cow."

mysel'. Ye're aidin' an' abettin' as usual."	You're aiding and abetting as usual."

So saying, Auntie Meg went out to look for her niece. It was some time before the natural order of her search brought her at last to the *byre*. By that time Annie was almost asleep in the grass, which the cow was gradually pulling away from under her. Through the open door the child could see the sunlight lying heavy upon the hot stones that paved the yard; but in here it was so dark-shadowy and cool, and the cow was such good, kindly company, and she was so safe hidden from auntie, as she thought—for no one had ever found her there before, and she knew Betty would not tell—that, as I say, she was nearly asleep with comfort, half-buried in Brownie's dinner.

But she was roused all at once to a sense of exposure and insecurity. She looked up, and at the same moment the hawk-nose of her aunt came round the *door-cheek*. Auntie's temper was none the better than usual that it had pleased the *Almichty* to take the brother whom she loved, and to leave behind the child whom she regarded as a painful responsibility. And now with her small, fierce eyes, and her big, thin nose—both red with suppressed crying—she did not dawn upon the sense of Annie as an embodiment of the maternity of the universe.

"Ye plaguesome brat!" cried Auntie; "there has Betty been seekin' ye, and I hae been seekin' ye, far an' near, i' the verra rottan-holes; an' here ye are, on yer ain father's buryin' day, that comes but ance—takin' up wi' a coo."	"You plaguesome brat!" cried Auntie; "there has Betty been seeking you, and I've been seeking you, far and near, in the very rat-holes; and here you are, on your own father's burying day, that comes but once—taking up with a cow."

But the causes of Annie's preference of the society of Brownie to that of Auntie might have been tolerably clear to an onlooker, without word spoken. For to Annie and her needs, notwithstanding the humble four-footedness of Brownie, there was in her large mild eyes, and her hairy, featureless face, all nose and no nose, more of the divine than in the human form of Auntie Meg. And there was something of an indignation quite human in the way the cow tossed her bound head and neck towards the woman that darkened the door, as if warning her off her premises. But without a word of reply, Annie rose, flung her arms around Brownie's head, kissed the white star on her forehead, disengaged herself from the grass, and got out of the manger. Auntie seized her hand with a rough action, but not ungentle grasp, and led her away to the house. The stones felt very hot to her little bare feet.

CHAPTER III

By this time the funeral was approaching the churchyard at a more rapid pace; for the pedestrians had dropped away one by one, on diverging roads, or had stopped and retraced their steps. But as they drew near the place, the slow trot subsided into a slow walk once more. To an English eye the whole mode would have appeared barbarous. But if the carved and gilded skulls and cross-bones on the hearse were ill-conceived, at least there were no awful nodding plumes to make death hideous with yet more of cloudy darkness; and one of the panels showed, in all the sunshine that golden rays could yield, the Resurrection of the Lord—the victory over the grave. And, again, when they stopped at the gate of the churchyard, they were the hands of friends and neighbours, and not those of cormorant undertakers and obscene mutes, that bore the dead man to his grave. And, once more, if the only rite they observed, when the body had settled into its place of decay, was the silent uncovering of the head, as a last token of respect and farewell, it may be suggested that the Church of England herself, in all her beautiful service, has no prayer for the departed soul, which cannot be beyond the need of prayer, as the longings that follow it into the region of the Unknown, are not beyond its comfort.

Before the grave was quite filled the company had nearly gone. Thomas Crann, the stone-mason, and George Macwha, the *wright*, alone remained behind, for they had some charge over the arrangements, and were now taking a share in covering the grave. At length the last sod was laid upon the mound, and stamped into its place, where soon the earth's broken surface would heal, as society would flow together again, closing over the place that had known the departed, and would know him no more. Then Thomas and George sat down, opposite to each other, on two neighbouring tombstones, and wiping their brows, gave each a sigh of relief, for the sun was hot and oppressive.

"Hech! It's a weary warl," said George.

"Ye hae no richt to say sae, George," answered Thomas, "for ye

"Hech![1] It's a weary world," said George.

"You have no right to say so, George," answered Thomas, "for

---

1 HECH (Scots): in this context, an expression of sorrow

hae never met it, an' foughten wi' 't. Ye hae never draan the soord o' the Lord and o' Gideon. Ye hae never broken the pitcher, to lat the lamp shine out, an' I doubt ye hae smo'red it by this time. And sae, whan the bridegroom comes, ye'll be ill-aff for a licht."

"Hoot, man! dinna speak sic awfu' things i' the verra kirkyard."

"Better hear them i' the kirkyard than at the closed door, George!"

"Weel, but," rejoined Macwha, anxious to turn the current of the conversation, which he found unpleasantly personal, "jist tell me honestly, Thamas Crann, do ye believe, wi' a' yer heart an' sowl, that the deid man—Gude be wi' him!—"

"No prayin' for the deid i' my hearin', George! As the tree falleth, so it shall lie."

"Weel! weel! I didna mean onything."

"That I verily believe. Ye seldom do!"

"But I jist want to speir," resumed George, with some asperity, getting rather nettled at his companion's persistent discourtesy, "gin ye believe that Jeames Anderson here, honest man, aneath our feet, crumblin' awa', as ye ken, and no ae spoke o' his wheel to the fore, or lang, to tell what his cart was like—do ye believe that his honest face will, ae day, pairt the mouls,

you've never met it, and fought with it. You've never drawn the sword of the Lord and of Gideon. You've never broken the pitcher, to let the lamp shine out, and I expect you've smothered it by now. And so, when the bridegroom comes, you'll be ill-off for a light."

"Heavens, man! don't speak such awful things in the very churchyard."

"Better hear them in the churchyard than at the closed door, George!"

"Well, but," rejoined Macwha, anxious to turn the current of the conversation, which he found unpleasantly personal, "just tell me honestly, Thomas Crann, do you believe, with all your heart and soul, that the dead man—God be with him!"

"No praying for the dead in my hearing, George! As the tree falleth, so it shall lie."

"Well! well! I didn't mean anything."

"That I verily believe. You seldom do!"

"But I just want to ask," resumed George, with some asperity, getting rather nettled at his companion's persistent discourtesy, "if you believe that James Anderson there, honest man, beneath our feet, crumbling away, as you know, and not one spoke of his wheel left, soon enough, to tell what his cart was like—do you believe that his honest face will, one day, part the earth, and come up again, just here, in the face of the light, the very same as it vanished when we put the lid over him? Do you believe that, Thomas Crann?"

"Na, na, George, man. You know little what you're busiest saying. It'll be a glorified body that he'll rise with. It's sown in dishonour and raised in glory. Heavens! you *are* ignorant, man!"

Macwha got more nettled still at his tone of superiority.

"Would it be a glorified wooden-leg he rose with, if he had been buried with a wooden-leg?" asked he.

"His own leg would be buried somewhere."

"Oh ay! no doubt. And it would come hopping over the Pacific, or the Atlantic, to join its original stump—wouldn't it? But supposing the man had been born *without* a leg—eh, Thomas?"

"George! George!" said Thomas, with great solemnity, "look you after your soul, and the Lord'll look after your body, legs and all! Man, you're not converted, and how can you understand the things of the spirit? Always jeering, and jeering!"

"Well! well! Thomas," rejoined Macwha, mollified in perceiving that he had not had altogether the worst in the tilt of words; "I would only take the liberty of thinking that, when He was about it, the Almighty might as well make a new body altogether, as go patching up up the auld ane. Sae I s' awa hame."

"Mind ye yer immortal pairt, George," said Thomas with a final thrust, as he likewise rose to go home with him on the box of the hearse.

"Gin the Lord tak's sic guid care o' the body, Thamas," retorted Macwha, with less of irreverence than appeared in his words, "maybe he winna objec' to gie a look to my puir soul as weel; for they say it's worth a hantle mair. I wish he wad, for he kens better nor me hoo to set aboot the job."

So saying, he strode briskly over the graves and out of the churchyard, leaving Thomas to follow as fast as suited his unwieldy strength.

the old one. So I'll be off home."

"Remember your immortal part, George," said Thomas with a final thrust, as he likewise rose to go home with him on the box of the hearse.

"If the Lord takes such good care of the body, Thomas," retorted Macwha, with less of irreverence than appeared in his words, "maybe he won't mind seeing to my poor soul as well; for they say it's worth much more. I wish he would, for he knows better than me how to set about the job."

So saying, he strode briskly over the graves and out of the churchyard, leaving Thomas to follow as fast as suited his unwieldy strength.

CHAPTER IV

Meantime another conversation was going on in one of the gigs, as it bore two of the company from the place of tombs, which will serve a little for the purposes of this history. One of the twain was a cousin of the deceased, already incidentally mentioned as taking some direction in the matter of refreshment. His name was no less than Robert Bruce. The other was called Andrew Constable, and was a worthy elder of the kirk.

"Weel, Robert," began the latter, after they had jogged on in silence for half a mile or so, "what's to be done wi' little Annie Anderson and her Auntie Meg, noo that the douce man's gane hame, an' left them theroot, as 't war?"

"They canna hae that muckle to the fore efter the doctor an' a' 's sattled for."

"It's no to be thought. It's lang sin' ever he wrought a day's darg."

"Jeames Dow luikit weel after the farmin', though."

"Nae doot. He's a guid servant that, to ony man he ca's master. But there canna be muckle siller to the fore."

A pause followed.

"What think ye noo, Andrew?" recommenced Bruce. "Ye're weel kent for an honest an' a langheided man. Do ye think that folk wad expec' onything o' me gin the warst cam to the warst?"

"Weel, Robert, I dinna think there's muckle guid in luikin' to

"Well, Robert," began the latter, after they had jogged on in silence for half a mile or so, "what's to be done with little Annie Anderson and her Auntie Meg, now that the douce (*quiet, sensible*) man's gone home, and left them outside, as it were?"

"They can't have that much left after they've settled with the doctor and all."

"It's not to be thought. It's long since ever he did a day's work."

"James Dow took good care of the farming, though."

"No doubt. He's a good servant, that, to any man he calls master. But there can't be much money left."

A pause followed.

"What do you think now, Andrew?" recommenced Bruce. "You're well known for an honest and a longheaded man. Do you think that folk would expect anything of me if the worst came to the worst?"

"Well, Robert, I don't think there's much good in looking to what folk might or might not expect of you."

"That's just what I was thinking myself; for, you see, I have a small family of my own to feed already."

"No doubt—no doubt. But—"

"Ay, ay; I know what you would say. I mustn't altogether disregard what folk think, 'cause there's the shop,; and if I once got—not to say a bad name, but just the wind of not being as considerate as I might have been, there's no saying but two or three might go by my door, and across to Jamie Mitchell's there."

"Do what's right, Robert Bruce, and so defy folk and fairy."

"Na, na, that won't *always* work. A man must take care of his own, else who's to do it?"

"Well," rejoined Andrew with a smile, for he understood Bruce well enough, although he pretended to have mistaken his meaning—"well, if the child falls to you, no doubt you'll have to take charge of her."

"I don't mean James Anderson's children—I mean my own children."

"Robert, whatever way you decide, I hope it may be such a decision as will let you cast your care upon *Him*."

"I know all about that, Andrew. But my opinion on that text is just this—that every vessel has to hold its fill, and what runs over may be ower may be committed to Him, for ye can haud it no langer. Them that winna tak tent 'll tak scathe. It's a sweer thochtless way to gang to the Almichty wi' ilka fash. Whan I'm driven to ane mair, that ane sall aye be Him. Ye min' the story about my namesake and the spidder?"

"Ay, weel eneuch," answered Andrew.

But he did not proceed to remark that he could see no connection between that story and the subject in hand, for Bruce's question did not take him by surprise, it being well understood that he was in the habit of making all possible and some impossible references to his great namesake. Indeed, he wished everybody to think, though he seldom ventured to assert it plainly, that he was lineally descended from the king. Nor did Andrew make further remark of any sort with regard to the fate of Annie or the duty of Bruce, for he saw that his companion wanted no advice—only some talk, and possibly some sympathy with his perplexity as to what the world might think of him. But with this perplexity Andrew could accord him very little sympathy indeed; for he could not take much interest in the buttressing of a reputation which he knew to be already quite undermined by widely-reported acts of petty meanness and selfishness. Nor was this fact much to be wondered at, if his principles were really those which he had so openly advocated. Indeed, Andrew knew well that it would be a bad day for poor Annie when she came under Bruce's roof, and therefore sincerely hoped that Auntie Meg might find some way of managing so as to avoid parting with the child; for he knew, too, that, though her aunt was fierce and hard, she had yet a warm spot somewhere about her heart.

Margaret Anderson had known perfectly well for some time that she and Annie must part before long. The lease of the farm would expire at the close of the autumn of next year; and as it had been rather a losing affair for some time, she had no inclination to request a renewal. When her brother's debts should be paid, there would not remain, even after the sale of the stock, more than a hundred and fifty pounds. For herself, she believed she must go into service—which would hurt her pride more than it would alter her position, for her hands had done far more of the necessary labour than those of the maid who assisted her. Indeed, in her proudest mood, she would have welcomed death rather than idleness. What was to become of Annie she did not yet see.

Meantime there remained for the child just a year more of the native farm, with all the varieties of life which had been so dear to her. Auntie Meg did not spare to put her in mind of the coming change; but it seemed to Annie so long in coming that it never would come. The impression was worn off by the daily attempt to deepen it, she gave herself up to the childish pleasures within her reach, without thinking of their approaching loss.

CHAPTER V

And why should Annie think of the future? The future was not: the present was—and full of delights. If she did not receive much tenderness from auntie, at least she was not afraid of her. The pungency of her temper was but as the salt and vinegar which brought out the true flavour of the other numberless pleasures around her. Were her excursions far afield, perched aloft on Dowie's shoulder, and holding on by the top of his head, or clinging to his back with her arms round his neck, at all the less delightful that auntie was scolding at home? They would have been less delightful if she had thought of the future; but she thought only of the present joy; or rather she took it as it came, and let it play upon her, without thinking about it at all. And if she was late for one of her meals, for Annie had no very correct sense of the lapse of time, and auntie had declared she should go fasting, it was yet not without her connivance that rosy-faced Betty got the child the best of everything that was at hand, and put cream in her milk, and butter on her oat cake, Annie managing to consume everything with satisfaction, notwithstanding the hurdy-gurdy accompaniment of her aunt's audible reflections. And Brownie was always friendly; ever ready on any serious emergency, when auntie's temper was still less placid than usual, to yield a corner of her manger for a refuge to the child. And the cocks and hens, even the peacock and the turkey-cock, knew her perfectly, and would come when she called them, if not altogether out of affection for her, at least out of hope in her bounty; and she had not yet arrived at the painful wisdom of beginning to question motives—a wisdom which misleads more than it guides. She loved *them*, and that was enough for her. And she would ride the horses to water, sitting sideways on their broad backs like a barefooted lady; for Dowie had such respect for his little mistress, as he called her, that he would never let her get astride "like a laddie," however much she wanted to do so. And when the morning was wet, and the sound of the flails came to her from the barn, she would watch for the moment when her aunt's back would be turned, and then scurry across the yard, like a mouse to its hole; for auntie's first impulse was always to oppose whatever Annie desired. Once in the barn, she would bury herself like a mole in the straw, and listen to the unfailing metronome of the flails, till she would fall so fast asleep as to awake only when her uncomfortable aunt, believing that at last the awful something or other *had* happened to the *royt*[1] lassie, dragged her out ignominiously by the heels. But the *royt* lassie was one of the gentlest of girls, what adventurousness she had being the result of faith, and not of hardihood.

And then came the delights of the harvest-field—soon to become great golden splendours to the memory. With the reapers she would remain from morning till night, sharing in their meals, and lightening their labour with her gentle frolic. Every day, after the noon-tide meal, she would go to sleep on the shady side of a *stook*, upon two or three sheaves which Dowie would lay down for her in a choice spot. Indeed the little mistress was very fond of sleep, and would go to sleep anywhere; this habit being indeed one of her aunt's chief grounds of complaint. For before hay-time, for instance, when the grass was long in the fields, if she came upon any place that took her fancy, she would tumble down at once, and show that she loved it by going to sleep upon it. Then it was no easy task to find her amidst the long grass that closed over her, as over a bird in its nest. But the fact was, this habit indicated a feebleness of constitution, to which sleep itself was the best restorative. And in the harvest-field, at least, no harm could come of it; for Dooie, as she always called him, watched her like a mother; so that sometimes when she awoke, she would find a second stook of ten sheaves, with a high-uplifted crowning pair above, built at right angles to the first, to shelter her from the sun which had peered round the corner, and would soon have stared her awake.

The only discomfort of the harvest-field was, that the sharp stubble forced her to wear shoes. But when the corn had all been carried home, and the potatoes had been dug up and heaped in warm pits against the winter, and the mornings and evenings grew cold, and, though still friendly to strong men and women, were rather too keen for delicate little Annie—she had to put on both shoes and stockings, which she did not like at all.

So with "gentle gliding," through a whole winter of ice and snow, through a whole spring of promises tardily fulfilled, through a summer of glory, and another autumn of harvest joy, the day drew on when they must leave the farm. And still to Annie it seemed as far off as ever.

---

[1] ROYT (Scots) wild, unruly

"After the noon-tide meal, she would go to sleep upon two or three sheaves..."

CHAPTER VI

One lovely evening in October, when the shadows were falling from the western sun, and the light that made them was as yellow as a marigold, and a keen little wind was just getting ready to come out and blow the moment the sun would be out of sight, Annie, who was helping to fasten up the cows for the night, drawing iron chains round their soft necks, saw a long shadow coming in at the narrow entrance of the yard. It came in and in; and was so long in coming in, that she began to feel as if it was something not quite *cannie*, and to fancy herself frightened. But, at length, she found that the cause of the great shadow was only a little man; and that this little man was no other than her father's cousin, Robert Bruce. Alas! how little a man may cast a great shadow!

He came up to Annie, and addressed her in the smoothest voice he could find, fumbling at the same time in his coat-pocket.

"Hoo are ye the nicht dawtie? Are ye verra weel? An' hoo's yer auntie?"

He waited for no reply to any of these questions, but went on.

"See what I hae brocht ye frae the chop."

So saying, he put into her hand about half-a-dozen *sweeties*, screwed up in a bit of paper. With this gift he left her, and walked on to the open door of the house, which, as a cousin, he considered himself privileged to enter unannounced even by a knock. He found the mistress of it in the kitchen, superintending the cooking of the supper.

"Hoo are ye the nicht, Marget?" he said, still in a tone of conciliatory

"How are you tonight pet? Are you very well? And how's your auntie?"

He waited for no reply to any of these questions, but went on.

"See what I've brought you from the shop."

So saying, he put into her hand about half-a-dozen *sweeties*, screwed up in a bit of paper. With this gift he left her, and walked on to the open door of the house, which, as a cousin, he considered himself privileged to enter unannounced even by a knock. He found the mistress of it in the kitchen, superintending the cooking of the supper.

"How are you tonight, Marget?" he said, still in a tone of conciliatory smoothness, through which, however, he could not prevent a certain hardness from cropping out plentifully. "You're busy as usual, I see. Well, the hand of the diligent maketh rich, you know."

"That portion of the Word must be of limited application, I think," returned Marget, as, withdrawing her hand from her cousin's, she turned again to the pot hanging over the fire. "No man dares to say that my hand has not been diligent; but God knows I'm none the richer."

"We mustn't repine, Marget. Right or wrong, it's the Lord's will."

"It's easy to you, Robert Bruce, with your money in the bank, to speak that way to a poor lone body like me, that must slave for my bread when I'm not so young as I might be. Not that I'm like to die of old age either."

"I haven't as much money in the bank as some folk may think; though what there is is safe enough. But I have a bonny business down there, and it might be better yet. It's just the land of Goshen, only it wants some more top-dressing."

"Take it from the bank, then, Robert."

"The bank! you say, Marget? I can't do that."

"And why not?"

"'Cause I'm just like the hens, Marget. If they don't see one egg in the nest, they have no heart to lay another. I daren't meddle with the bank."

"Weel, lat sit than; an' lay awa' at yer leisur'. Hoo's the mistress?"

"No that weel, and no that ill. The faimily's rather sair upo' her. But I canna haud her oot o' the chop for a' that. She's like mysel'—she wad aye be turnin' a bawbee. But what are ye gaein to do yersel', Marget?"

"I'm gaein to my uncle and aunt—auld John Peterson and his wife. They're gey and frail noo, and they want somebody to luik efter them."

"Than ye're weel provided for; Praise be thankit! Marget."

"Ow, ay; nae doot," replied Marget, with bitterness, of which Bruce took no notice.

"And what's to come o' the bairnie?" pursued he.

"I maun jist get some dacent auld body i' the toon to tak' her in, and lat her gang to the schuil. It's time. The auld fowk wadna pit up wi' her a week."

"And what'll that cost ye, Marget?"

"I dinna ken. But the lassie's able to pay for her ain upbringin'."

"It's no far 'at a hunner and fifty'll gang i' thae times, woman. An' it's a pity to tak frae the prencipal. She'll be merryin' some day."

"Ow, 'deed, maybe. Bairns will be fules."

"Weel, cud na ye pit it oot at five per cent., and there wad aye be something comin' o' 't? That wad be

"Well, let it be then; and lay away at your leisure. How's the mistress?"

"Not that well, and not that ill. The family's rather hard on her. But I can't keep her out of the shop for all that. She's like myself—she would always be earning a penny. But what are you going to do yourself, Marget?"

"I'm going to my uncle and aunt—old John Peterson and his wife. They're very old and frail now, and they want somebody to look after them."

"Then you're well provided for; Thank heaven! Marget."

"Oh, ay; no doubt," replied Marget, with bitterness, of which Bruce took no notice.

"And what's to come of the child?" pursued he.

"I'll just have to get some decent old body in the town to take her in, and let her go to the school. It's time. The old folk wouldn't put up with her a week."

"And what'll that cost you, Marget?"

"I don't know. But the lassie's able to pay for her own upbringing."

"It's not far that a hundred and fifty'll go in these times, woman. And it's a pity to take from the principal. She'll be marrying some day."

"Oh, indeed, she may. Children will be fools."

"Well, couldn't you put it out at five per cent, and there would always be something to come of it?

That would be seven pounds ten in the year, and the child might almost—not quite, but almost—be brought up upon that."

Margaret lifted her head and looked at him.

"And who would give five per cent. for her money when he can get it from the bank, on good security, for four and a half?"

"Just myself, Marget. The poor orphan has no one but you and me to look to; and I would willingly do that much for her. I'll tell you what—I'll give her five per cent. for her money; and for the interest, I'll take her in with my own children, and she'll have her meals with them, and go to school with them, and then—after a bit—we'll see what comes next."

To Margaret this seemed a very fair offer. It was known to all that the Bruce children were well-enough dressed for their station, and looked well-fed; and although Robert had the character of being somewhat mean, she did not regard that as the worst possible fault, or one likely to operate for the injury of the child. So she told her cousin that she would think about it; which was quite as much as he could have expected. He took his leave all but satisfied that he had carried his point, and not a little uplifted with his prospects.

For was it not a point worth carrying—to get both the money and the owner of it into his own hands? Not that he meant conscious dishonesty to Annie. He only rejoiced to think that he would thus satisfy any expectations that the public might have formed of him, and would enjoy besides a splendid increase of capital for his business; while he hoped to keep the girl upon less than the interest would come to. And then, if anything should happen to her—seeing she was not over vigorous—the result was worth waiting for; whereas—if she throve—he had sons growing up, one of whom might take a fancy to the heiress, and would have facilities for marrying her, &c. &c.; for Grocer Robert was as deep in his foresight and scheming as King Robert, the crowning triumph of whose intellect, in the eyes of his descendant, was the strewing of the caltrops on the field of Bannockburn.

But James Dow was *ill-pleased* when he heard of the arrangement—which was completed in due time. "For," said he, "I canna bide that Bruce. He's a naisty mean cratur. He wadna fling a bane till a dog, afore he had ta'en a pyke at it himsel'."[1] He agreed, however, with his mistress, that it would be better to keep Annie in ignorance of her destiny as long as possible; a consideration which sprung from the fact that her aunt, now that she was on the eve of parting with her, felt a little delicate growth of tenderness sprouting over the old stone wall of her affection for the child, owing its birth, in part, to the doubt whether she would be comfortable in her new home.

---

1   He wouldn't fling a bone to a dog, before he had taken a pick at it himself.

CHAPTER VII

A day that is fifty years off comes as certainly as if it had been in the next week; and Annie's feeling of infinite duration did not stop the sand-glass of Old Time. The day arrived when everything was to be sold by public *roup*. A great company of friends, neighbours, and acquaintances gathered; and much drinking of whisky-punch went on in the kitchen as well as in the room where, a few months before, the solemn funeral-assembly had met.

Little Annie speedily understood what all the bustle meant: that the day of desolation so long foretold by the Cassandra-croak of her aunt, had at length actually arrived, and that all the things she knew so well were vanishing from her sight for ever.

She was in the barn when the sound of the auctioneer's voice in the corn-yard made her look over the half-door and listen. Gradually the truth dawned upon her; and she burst into tears over an old rake which she had been accustomed to call hers, because she had always dragged it at hay-making. Then wiping her eyes hastily—for, partly from her aunt's hardness, she never could bear to be seen crying, even when a child—she fled to Brownie's stall, and burying herself in the manger, began weeping afresh. After a while, the fountain of tears was for the time exhausted, and she sat disconsolately gazing at the old cow feeding away, as if food were everything and a *roup* nothing at all, when footsteps approached the *byre*, and, to her dismay, two men, whom she did not know, came in, untied Brownie, and actually led her away from before her eyes. She still stared at the empty space where Brownie had stood,—stared like a creature stranded by night on the low coast of Death, before whose eyes in the morning the sea of Life is visibly ebbing away. At last she started up. How could she sit there without Brownie! Sobbing so that she could not breathe, she rushed across the yard, into the crowded and desecrated house, and up the stair to her own little room, where she threw herself on the bed, buried her eyes in the pillow, and, overcome with grief, fell fast asleep.

When she woke in the morning, she remembered nothing of Betty's undressing and putting her to bed. The dreadful day that was gone seemed only a dreadful dream, that had left a pain behind it. But when she went out, she found that yesterday would not stay amongst her dreams. Brownie's stall was empty. The horses were all gone, and many of the cattle. Those that remained looked like creatures forgotten. The pigs were gone, and most of the poultry. Two or three favourite hens were left, which auntie was going to take with her. But of all the living creatures she had loved, not one had been kept for Annie. Her life grew bitter with the bitterness of death.

In the afternoon, her aunt came up to her room, where she sat in tearful silence, and telling her that she was going to take her into the town, proceeded, without further explanation, to put all her little personal effects into an old hair-trunk, which Annie called her own. Along with some trifles that lay about the room, she threw into the bottom of the box about a dozen of old books, which had been on the chest of drawers since long before Annie could remember. She, poor child, let her do as she pleased, and asked no questions; for the shadow in which she stood was darkening, and she did not care what came next. For an hour the box stood on the floor like a coffin, and then Betty came, with red eyes and a red nose, and carried it downstairs. Then auntie came up again, dressed in her Sunday clothes. She put on Annie's best frock and bonnet—adorning the victim for sacrifice—at least, so Annie's face would have suggested—and led her down to the door. There stood a horse and cart. In the cart was some straw, and a sack stuffed with hay. As auntie was getting into the cart, Betty rushed out from somewhere upon Annie, caught her up, kissed her in a vehement and disorderly manner, and before her mistress could turn round in the cart, gave her into James Dow's arms, and vanished with strange sounds of choking. Dowie thought to put her in with a kiss, for he dared not speak; but Annie's arms went round his neck, and she clung to him sobbing—clung till she roused the indignation of auntie, at the first sound of whose voice, Dowie was free, and Annie lying in the cart, with her face buried in the straw. Dowie then mounted in front, with his feet on the shaft; the horse—one Annie did not know—started off gently; and she was borne away helpless to meet the unknown.

And the road was like the going. She had often been upon it before, but it had never looked as it did now. The first half-mile went through fields whose crops were gone. The stubble was sticking through the grass, and the potato stalks, which ought to have been gathered and burnt, lay scattered about all over the brown earth. Then came two miles of moorland country, high, and bleak, and barren, with hillocks of peat in all directions, standing beside the black holes whence they had been dug. These holes were full of dark water, frightful to look at; while along the side of the road went deep black ditches half-full of the same dark water. There was no danger of the cart getting into them, for the ruts were too deep to let the wheels out; but it jolted so dreadfully from side to side, as it crawled along, that Annie was afraid every other moment of being tilted into one of the frightful pools. Across the waste floated now and then the cry of a bird, but other sound there was none in this land of drearihead. Next came some scattered and ragged fields, the skirts of cultivation, which seemed to draw closer and closer together, while the soil grew richer and more hopeful, till, after two miles more, they entered the first straggling precincts of the grey market-town.

By this time the stars were shining clear in the cold, frosty sky, and candles or train-oil lamps were burning in most of the houses; for all these things took place long before gas had been heard of in those quarters. A few faces were pressed close to the window-panes as the cart passed; and some rather untidy women came to the house-doors to look. And they spoke one to another words which, though inaudible through the noise of the cart, were yet intelligible enough to Annie, with her own forebodings to interpret the expression of their faces.

"That'll be little Annie Anderson," they said. "She's gaein hame to bide wi' her cousin, Robert Bruce, up i' the Wast Wynd. Puir wee lassie!"

For, on the way, Annie had been informed of her destination.

"That'll be little Annie Anderson," they said. "She's going home to live with her cousin, Robert Bruce, up in the West Wynd. Poor wee lassie!"

For, on the way, Annie had been informed of her destination.

But she was too miserable already, because of leaving her old home, to care much to what new one she was going. Had it not been for the absorption of this grief, she could not have been indifferent to the prospect of going to live with her cousin, although her dislike to him had never assumed a more active form than that of wishing to get away from him, as often as he came near her.

The cart stopped at Bruce's shop-door. It looked a heavy door, although the upper half was of glass—in small panes. Dowie got down and went into the shop; and before he returned Annie had time to make some listless observations. The house was a low one, although of two stories, built of grey stone, and thatched. The heavy door was between two windows belonging to the shop, in each of which burned a single tallow candle, revealing to the gaze of Annie, in all the enhancing mystery of candlelight, what she could not but regard as a perfect mine of treasures. For besides calico and sugar, and all the multifarious stock in the combined trades of draper and grocer, Robert Bruce sold penny toys, and halfpenny picture-books, and all kinds of confectionery which had been as yet revealed to the belated generations of Glamerton.

But she had not to contemplate these wonders long from the outside; for Bruce came to the door, and, having greeted his cousin and helped her down, turned to take Annie. Dowie had been before him, however, and now held the pale child silent in his arms. He carried her into the shop, and set her down on a sack that stood outside the counter, leaning against it. He then went back to his horse's head.

The sack made no bad seat, for it was half-full of turnip-seed; and upon it Annie sat, and drearily surveyed the circumstances.

Auntie was standing in the middle of the shop. Bruce was holding the counter open, and inviting her to enter.

"Ye'll come in and tak a cup o' tay, efter yer journey, Marget?" said he.

"Na, I thank ye, Robert Bruce. Jeames and I maun jist turn and gae hame again. There's a hantle to look efter yet, and we maunna neglec' oor wark. The hoose-gear's a' to be roupit the morn."

Then turning to Annie, she said:

"Noo, Annie, lass, ye'll be a guid bairn, and do as ye're tell't. An' min' and no pyke the things i' the chop."

A smile of peculiar import glimmered over Bruce's face at the sound of this injunction. Annie made no reply, but stared at Mr Bruce, and sat staring.

"Good-bye to ye, Annie!" said her aunt, and roused her a little from her stupor.

She then gave her a kiss—the first, as far as the child knew, that

"You'll come in and have a cup of tea, after your journey, Margaret?" said he.

"Na, I thank you, Robert Bruce. James and I must be getting home again. There's a lot to be done yet, and we mustn't neglect our work. The furniture's all to be auctioned tomorrow."

Then turning to Annie, she said:

"Now, Annie, lass, you'll be a good girl, and do as you're told. And remember not to pyke (*pick at*) the things in the shop."

A smile of peculiar import glimmered over Bruce's face at the sound of this injunction. Annie made no reply, but stared at Mr Bruce, and sat staring.

"Good-bye to you, Annie!" said her aunt, and roused her a little from her stupor.

She then gave her a kiss—the first, as far as the child knew, that she had ever given her—and went out. Bruce followed her out, and Dowie came in. He took her up in his arms, and said:

"Good-bye to ye, my bonnie bairn. Be a guid lass, and ye'll be ta'en care o'. Dinna forget that. Min' and say yer prayers."

Annie kissed him with all her heart, but could not reply. He set her down again, and went out. She heard the harness rattle, and the cart go off. She was left sitting on the sack.

Presently Mr Bruce came in, and passing behind his counter, proceeded to make an entry in a book. It could have been no order from poor, homeless Margaret. It was, in fact, a memorandum of the day and the hour when Annie was set down on that same sack—so methodical was he! And yet it was some time before he seemed to awake to the remembrance of the presence of the child. Looking up suddenly at the pale, weary thing, as she sat with her legs hanging lifelessly down the side of the sack, he said—pretending to have forgotten her—

"Ow, bairn, are ye there yet?"

And going round to her, he set her on the floor, and leading her by the hand through the mysterious gate of the counter, and through a door behind it, called in a sharp decided tone:

"Mother, ye're wanted!"

Thereupon a tall, thin, anxious-looking woman appeared, wiping her hands in her apron.

"This is little Miss Anderson," said Bruce, "come to bide wi's. Gie her a biscuit, and tak' her up the stair till her bed."

As it was the first, so it was the last time he called her *Miss* Anderson, at least while she was one of his household.—Mrs Bruce took Annie by the hand in silence, and led her up two narrow stairs, into a small room with a skylight. There, by the shine of the far-off stars, she undressed her. But she forgot the biscuit; and, for the first time in her life, Annie went supperless to bed.

She lay for a while trying to fancy herself in Brownie's stall among the grass and clover, and so get rid of the vague fear she felt at being in a strange place without light, for she found it unpleasant not to know what was next her in the dark. But the fate of Brownie and of everything she had loved came back upon her; and the sorrow drove away the fear, and she cried till she could cry no longer, and then she slept. It is by means of sorrow, sometimes, that He gives his beloved sleep.

CHAPTER VIII

She woke early, rose, and dressed herself. But there was no water for her to wash with, and she crept down-stairs to look for help in this her first need. Nobody, however, was awake. She looked long and wistfully at the house-door, but seeing that she could not open it, she went back to her room. If she had been at home, she would soon have had a joyous good-morrow from the burst of fresh wind meeting her as she lifted the ready latch, to seek the companionship of yet earlier risers than herself; but now she was as lonely as if she had anticipated the hour of the resurrection, and was the little only one up of the buried millions. All that she had left of that home was her box, and she would have betaken herself to a desolate brooding over its contents; but it had not been brought up, and neither could she carry it up herself, nor would she open it in the kitchen where it stood. So she sat down on the side of her bed, and gazed round the room. It was a cheerless room. At home she had had chequered curtains to her bed: here there were none of any kind; and her eyes rested on nothing but bare rafters and boards. And there were holes in the roof and round the floor, which she did not like. They were not large, but they were dreadful. For they were black, nor did she know where they might go to. And she grew very cold.

At length she heard some noise in the house, and in her present mood any human noise was a sound of deliverance. It grew; was presently enriched by the admixture of baby-screams, and the sound of the shop-shutters being taken down; and at last footsteps approached her door. Mrs Bruce entered, and finding her sitting dressed on her bed, exclaimed:

"Ow! ye can dress yersel! can ye?"	"Oh! you can dress yourself! can you?"
"Ay, weel that," answered Annie, as cheerily as she could. "But," she added, "I want some water to wash mysel' wi'."	"Ay, easily," answered Annie, as cheerily as she could. "But," she added, "I want some water to wash myself with."
"Come doon to the pump, than," said Mrs Bruce.	"Come down to the pump, then," said Mrs Bruce.

Annie followed her to the pump, where she washed in a tub. She then ran dripping into the house for a towel, and was dried by the hands of Mrs Bruce in her dirty apron.—This mode of washing lasted till the first hoar-frost, after which there was a basin to be had in the kitchen, with plenty of water and not much soap.

By this time breakfast was nearly ready, and in a few minutes more, Mrs Bruce called Mr Bruce from the shop, and the children from the yard, and they all sat round the table in the kitchen—Mr Bruce to his tea and oat-cake and butter—Mrs Bruce and the children to badly-made oatmeal porridge and sky-blue milk. This quality of the milk was remarkable, seeing they had cows of their own. But then they sold milk. And if any customer had accused her of watering it, Mrs Bruce's best answer would have been to show how much better what she sold was than what she retained; for she put twice as much water in what she used for her own family—with the exception of the portion destined for her husband's tea, whose two graces were long and strong enough for a better breakfast. But then his own was good enough.

There were three children, two boys with great jaws—the elder rather older than Annie—and a very little baby. After Mr Bruce had prayed for the blessing of the Holy Spirit upon their food, they gobbled down their breakfasts with all noises except articulate ones. When they had finished—that is, eaten everything up—the Bible was brought; a psalm was sung, after a fashion not very extraordinary to the ears of Annie, or, indeed, of any one brought up in Scotland; a chapter was read—it happened to tell the story of Jacob's speculations in the money-market of his day and generation; and the *exercise* concluded with a prayer of a quarter of an hour, in which the God of Jacob especially was invoked to bless the Bruces, His servants, in their basket and in their store, and to prosper the labours of that day in particular. The prayer would have been longer, but for the click of the latch of the shop-door, which brought it to a speedier close than one might have supposed even Mr Bruce's notions of decency would have permitted. And almost before the *Amen* was out of his month, he was out of the kitchen.

When he had served the early customer, he returned, and sitting down, drew Annie towards him—between his knees, in fact, and addressed her with great solemnity.

"Noo, Annie," said he, "ye s' get the day to play yersel'; but ye maun gang to the school the morn. We can hae no idle fowk i' this hoose,

"Now, Annie," said he, "you'll get today to play by yourself; but you must go to school tomorrow. We can have no idle folk in this house, so we must have no words about it."

Annie was not one to make words about that or anything. She was only too glad to get away from him. Indeed the prospect of school, after what she had seen of the economy of her home, was rather enticing. So she only answered,

"Very well, sir. Will I go to-day?"

Whereupon, finding her so tractable, Mr Bruce added, in the tone of one conferring a great favour, and knowing that he did so,

"You can come into the shop for the day, and see what's going on. When you're a grown woman, you may be fit to stand behind the counter some day yourself—who knows?"

Robert Bruce regarded the shop as his Bannockburn, where all his enemies, namely customers, were to be defeated, that he might be enriched with their spoils. It was, therefore, a place of so great interest in his eyes, that he thought it must be interesting to everybody else. And, indeed, the permission did awake some ill-grounded expectations in the mind of Annie.

She followed him into the shop, and saw quite a fabulous wealth of good things around her; of which, however, lest she should put forth her hand and take, the militant eyes of Robert Bruce never ceased watching her, with quick-recurring glances, even while he was cajoling some customer into a doubtful purchase.

Long before dinner-time arrived, she was heartily sick of the monotony of buying and selling in which she had no share. Not even a picture-book was taken down from the window for her to look at; so that she soon ceased to admire even the picture-books—a natural result of the conviction that they belonged to a sphere above her reach. Mr Bruce, on the other hand, looked upon them as far below the notice of his children, although he derived a keen enjoyment from the transference, by their allurements, of the half-pence of other children from their pockets into his till.

"Nasty lying trash," he remarked, apparently for Annie's behoof, as he hung the fresh bait up in his window, after two little urchins, with *bawbees* (pennies) to spend, had bought a couple of the radiant results of literature and art combined. "Nasty lying trash—only fit for dirty lads and lassies."

He stood on the watch in his shop like a great spider that ate children; and his windows were his web.

They dined off salt herrings and potatoes—much better fare than bad porridge and watered milk. Robert Bruce the younger, who inherited his father's name and disposition, made faces at Annie across the table as often as he judged it prudent to run the risk of discovery; but Annie was too stupefied with the awful change to mind it much, and indeed required all the attention she had at command, for the arrest of herring bones on their way to her throat.

After dinner, business was resumed in the shop, with at least the resemblance of an increase of vigour, for Mrs Bruce went behind the counter, and gave her husband time to sit down at the desk to write letters and make out bills. Not that there was much of either sort of clerkship necessary; but Bruce, like Chaucer's Man of Law, was so fond of business, that he liked to seem busier than he was. As it happened to be a half-holiday, Annie was sent with the rest of the children into the garden to play up and down the walks.

"And remember," said Bruce, "to keep away from the dog."

In the garden Annie soon found herself at the mercy of those who had none.

It is marvellous what an amount of latent torment there is in boys, ready to come out the moment an object presents itself. It is not exactly cruelty. The child that tears the fly to pieces does not represent to himself the sufferings the insect undergoes; he merely yields to an impulse to disintegrate. So children, even ordinarily good children, are ready to tease any child who simply looks teasable, and so provokes the act. Now the Bruces were not good children, as was natural; and they despised

Annie because she was a girl, and because she had no self-assertion. If she had shown herself aggressively disagreeable, they would have made some attempt to conciliate her; but as it was, she became at once the object of a succession of spiteful annoyances, varying in intensity with the fluctuating invention of the two boys. At one time they satisfied themselves with making grimaces of as insulting a character as they could produce; at another they rose to the rubbing of her face with dirt, or the tripping up of her heels. Their persecution bewildered her, and the resulting stupefaction was a kind of support to her for a time; but at last she could endure it no longer, being really hurt by a fall, and ran crying into the shop, where she sobbed out,

"Please, sir, they winna lat me be."

"Dinna come into the chop wi' yer stories. Mak' it up amo' yersels."

"But they winna mak' it up."

Robert Bruce rose indignant at such an interruption of his high calling, and went out with the assumption of much parental grandeur. He was instantly greeted with a torrent of assurances that Annie had fallen, and then laid the blame upon them; whereupon he turned sternly to her, and said—

"Annie, gin ye tell lees, ye'll go to hell."

But paternal partiality did not prevent him from reading them also a lesson, though of a quite different tone.

"Mind, boys," he said, in a condescending whine, "that poor Annie has neither father nor mither; an' ye maun be kind till her."

He then turned and left them for the more important concerns within-doors; and the persecution recommenced, though in a somewhat mitigated form. The little wretches were perfectly unable to abstain from indulging in a pleasure of such intensity. Annie had indeed fallen upon evil days.

I am thus minute in my description of her first day, that my reader, understanding something similar of many following days, may be able to give due weight to the influence of other events, when, in due time, they come to be recorded. But I must not conclude the account without mentioning something which befell her at the close of the same day, and threatened to be productive of yet more suffering.

After *worship*, the boys crawled away to bed, half-asleep already; or, I should rather say, only half-awake from their prayers. Annie lingered.

"Can't you take off your own clothes, as well as put them on, Annie?" asked Mrs Bruce.

"Ay, well enough. Only I'd really like a bit of a candle," was Annie's trembling reply, for she had a sad foreboding instinct now.

"Candle! Na, na, child," answered Mrs Bruce. "You'll get no candle here. You would have the house in a flame about our ears. I can't afford candles. You can just make a candle of your hands, and feel your way up the two stairs. There's thirteen steps to the first, and twelve to the next."

With choking heart, but without reply, Annie went.

Groping her way up the steep ascent, she found her room without any difficulty. As it was again a clear, starlit night, there was light enough for her to find everything she wanted; and the trouble at her heart kept her imagination from being as active as it would otherwise have been, in recalling the terrible stories of ghosts and dead people with which she was far too familiar. She soon got into bed, and, as a precautionary measure, buried her head under the clothes before she began to say her prayers, which, under the circumstances, she had thought she might be excused for leaving till she had lain down. But her prayers were suddenly interrupted by a terrible noise of scrambling and scratching and scampering in the very room beside her.

"I tried to cry out," she said afterwards, "for I knew that it was rats; but my tongue bowed in my mouth for fear, and I couldn't speak one word."

The child's fear of rats amounted to a frenzied horror. She dared not move a finger. To get out of bed with those creatures running about the room was as impossible as it was to cry out. But her heart did what her tongue could not do—cried out with a great and bitter cry to one who was more ready to hear than Robert and Nancy Bruce. And what her heart cried was this:

"O God, protect me from the rats."

There was no need to send an angel from heaven in answer to this little one's prayer: the cat would do. Annie heard a scratch and a mew at the door. The rats made one frantic scramble and were still.

"It's pussy!" she cried, recovering the voice for joy that had failed her for fear.

Fortified by her arrival, and still more by the feeling that she was a divine messenger sent to succour her because she had prayed, she sprang out of bed, darted across the room, and opened the door to let her in. A few moments and she was fast asleep, guarded by God's angel, the cat, for whose entrance she took good care ever after to leave the door ajar.

There are ways of keeping the door of the mind also, ready as it is to fall to, ajar for the cat.

CHAPTER IX

"Now, Annie, put on your bonnet, and go to school with the rest; and be a good girrl."

This was the Bruce's parting address to Annie, before he left the kitchen for the shop, after breakfast and worship had been duly observed; and having just risen from his knees, his voice, as he stooped over the child, retained all the sanctity of its last occupation. It was a quarter to ten o'clock, and the school was some five minutes distant.

With a flutter of fearful hope, Annie obeyed. She ran upstairs, made herself as tidy as she could, smoothed her hair, put on her bonnet, and had been waiting a long time at the door when her companions joined her. It was very exciting to look forward to something that might not be disagreeable.

As they went, the boys got one on each side of her in a rather sociable manner. But they had gone half the distance and not a word had been spoken, when Robert Bruce, junior, opened the conversation abruptly.

"You'll get it!" he said, as if he had been brooding upon the fact for some time, and now it had broken out.

"What'll I get?" asked Annie timidly, for his tone had already filled her with apprehension.

"Such lickings," answered the little wretch, drawing back his lips till his canine teeth were fully disclosed, as if he gloated in a carnivorous sort of way over the prospect. "Won't she, Johnnie?"

"Ay she will," answered Johnnie, following his leader with confidence.

Annie's heart sank within her. The poor little heart was used to sinking now. But she said nothing, resolved, if possible, to avoid all occasion for "getting it."

Not another word was spoken before they reached the school, the door of which was not yet open. A good many boys and a few girls were assembled, waiting for the master, and filling the lane, at the end of which the school stood, with the sound of voices fluctuating through a very comprehensive scale. In general the school-door was opened a few minutes before the master's arrival, but on this occasion no one happened to have gone to his house to fetch the key, and the scholars had therefore to wait in the street. None of them took any notice of Annie; so she was left to study the outside of the school. It was a long, low, thatched building, of one story and a garret, with five windows to the lane, and some behind, for she could see light through. It had been a weaving-shop originally, full of hand-looms, when the trade in linen was more prosperous than it was now. From the thatch some of the night's frost was already dripping in slow clear drops. Past the door, which was in a line with the windows, went a gutter, the waters of which sank through a small grating a few steps further on. But there was no water running in it now.

Suddenly a boy cried out: "The maister's comin'!" and instantly the noise sunk to a low murmur. Looking up the lane, which rose considerably towards the other end, Annie saw the figure of the descending dominie.[1] He was dressed in what seemed to be black, but was in reality gray, almost as good as black, and much more thrifty. He came down the hill swinging his arms, like opposing pendulums, in a manner that made the rapid pace at which he approached like a long slow trot. With the door-key in his hand, already pointed towards the key-hole, he went right through the little crowd, which cleared a wide path for him, without word or gesture of greeting on either side. I might almost say he swooped upon the door, for with one hand on the key, and the other on the latch, he seemed to wrench it open the moment he touched it. In he strode, followed at the heels by the troop of boys, big and little, and lastly by the girls—last of all, at a short distance, by Annie, like a motherless lamb that followed the flock, because she did not know what else to do. She found she had to go down a step into a sunk passage or lobby, and then up another step, through a door on the left, into the school. There she saw a double row of desks, with a clear space down the middle between the rows. Each scholar was hurrying to his place at one

---

1   DOMINIE (Scots): schoolmaster

of the desks, where, as he arrived, he stood. The master already stood in solemn posture at the nearer end of the room on a platform behind his desk, prepared to commence the extempore prayer, which was printed in a kind of blotted stereotype upon every one of their brains. Annie had hardly succeeded in reaching a vacant place among the girls when he began. The boys were as still as death while the master prayed; but a spectator might easily have discovered that the chief good some of them got from the ceremony was a perfect command of the organs of sound; for the restraint was limited to those organs; and projected tongues, deprived of their natural exercise, turned themselves, along with winking eyes, contorted features, and a wild use of hands and arms, into the means of telegraphic despatches to all parts of the room, throughout the ceremony. The master, afraid of being himself detected in the attempt to combine prayer and vision, kept his "eyelids screwed together tight," and played the spy with his ears alone. The boys and girls, understanding the source of their security perfectly, believed that the eyelids of the master would keep faith with them, and so disported themselves without fear in the delights of dumb show.

As soon as the prayer was over they dropped, with no little noise and bustle, into their seats. But presently Annie was rudely pushed out of her seat by a hoydenish girl, who, arriving late, had stood outside the door till the prayer was over, and then entered unperceived during the subsequent confusion. Some little ones on the opposite form, however, liking the look of her, and so wishing to have her for a companion, made room for her beside them. The desks were double, so that the two rows at each desk faced each other.

"Bible-class come up," were the first words of the master, ringing through the room, and resounding awfully in Annie's ears.

A moment of chaos followed, during which all the boys and girls, considered capable of reading the Bible, were arranging themselves in one great crescent across the room in front of the master's desk. Each read a verse—neither more nor less—often leaving the half of a sentence to be taken up as a new subject in a new key; thus perverting what was intended as an assistance to find the truth into a means of hiding it—a process constantly repeated, and with far more serious results, when the words of truth fall, not into the hands of the incapable, but under the protection of the ambitious.

The chapter that came in its turn was one to be pondered over by the earnest student of human nature, not one to be blundered over by boys who had still less reverence for humanity than they had for Scripture.

It was a good thing that they were not the sacred fountains of the New Testament that were thus dabbled in—not, however, that the latter were considered at all more precious or worthy; as Saturday and the Shorter Catechism would show.

Not knowing the will of the master, Annie had not dared to stand up with the class, although she could read very fairly. A few moments after it was dismissed she felt herself overshadowed by an awful presence, and, looking up, saw, as she had expected, the face of the master bending down over her. He proceeded to question her, but for some time she was too frightened to give a rational account of her acquirements, the best of which were certainly not of a kind to be appreciated by the master, even if she had understood them herself sufficiently to set them out before him. For, besides her aunt, who had taught her to read, and nothing more, her only instructors had been Nature, with her whole staff, including the sun, moon, and wind; the grass, the corn, Brownie the cow, and her own faithful subject, Dowie. Still, it was a great mortification to her to be put into the spelling-book, which excluded her from the Bible-class. She was also condemned to follow with an uncut quill, over and over again, a single straight stroke, set her by the master. Dreadfully dreary she found it, and over it she fell fast asleep. Her head dropped on her outstretched arm, and the quill dropped from her sleeping fingers—for when Annie slept she all slept. But she was soon roused by the voice of the master. "Ann Anderson!" it called in a burst of thunder to her ear; and she awoke to shame and confusion, amidst the titters of those around her.

Before the morning was over she was called up, along with some children considerably younger than herself, to read and spell. The master stood before them, armed with a long, thick strap of horse-hide, prepared by steeping in brine, black and supple with constant use, and cut into fingers at one end, which had been hardened in the fire.

Now there was a little pale-faced, delicate-looking boy in the class, who blundered a good deal. Every time he did so the cruel serpent of leather went at him, coiling round his legs with a sudden, hissing swash. This made him cry, and his tears blinded him so that he could not even see the words which he had been unable to read before. But he still attempted to go on, and still the instrument of torture went swish-swash round his little thin legs, raising upon them, no doubt, plentiful blue wales, to be revealed, when he was undressed for the night, to the indignant eyes of pitying mother or aunt, who would yet send him back to the school the next morning without fail.

At length either the heart of the master was touched by the sight of his sufferings and repressed weeping, or he saw that he was compelling the impossible; for he stayed execution, and passed on to the next, who was Annie.

It was no wonder that the trembling child, who could read very fairly, should yet, after such an introduction to the ways of school, fail utterly in making anything like coherence of the sentence before her. What she would have done, had she been left to herself, would have been to take the little boy in her arms and cry too. As it was, she struggled mightily with her tears, and yet she did not read to much better purpose than the poor boy, who was still busy wiping his eyes with his sleeves, alternately, for he never had had a handkerchief. But being a new-comer, and a girl to boot, and her long frock affording no facilities for this kind of incentive to learning, she escaped for the time.

It was a dreadful experience of life, though, that first day at school. Well might the children have prayed with David—"Let us fall now into the hand of the Lord, for his mercies are great; and let us not fall into the hand of man." And well might the children at many another school respond with a loud *Amen!*

At one o'clock they were dismissed, and went home to dinner, to return at three.

In the afternoon she was set to make figures on a slate. She made figures till her back ached. The monotony of this occupation was relieved only by the sight of the execution of criminal law upon various offending boys; for, as must be already partially evident, the master was a hard man, with a severe, if not an altogether cruel temper, and a quite savage sense of duty. The punishment was mostly in the form of *pandies*,—blows delivered with varying force, but generally with the full swing of the *tag*, as it was commonly called, thrown over the master's shoulder, and brought down with the whole strength of his powerful right arm upon the outstretched hand of the culprit. But there were other modes of punishment, of which the restraints of art would forbid the description, even if it were possible for any writer to conquer his disgust so far as to attempt it.

Annie shivered and quaked. Once she burst out crying, but managed to choke her sobs, if she could not hide her tears.

A fine-looking boy, three or four years older than herself, whose open countenance was set off by masses of dark brown hair, was called up to receive chastisement, merited or unmerited as the case might be;

for such a disposition as that of Murdoch Malison must have been more than ordinarily liable to mistake. Justice, according to his idea, consisted in vengeance. And he was fond of justice. He did not want to punish the innocent, it is true; but I doubt whether the discovery of a boy's innocence was not a disappointment to him. Without a word of expostulation or defence, the boy held out his hand, with his arm at full length, received four stinging blows upon it, grew very red in the face, gave a kind of grotesque smile, and returned to his seat with the suffering hand sent into retirement in his trowsers-pocket. Annie's admiration of his courage as well as of his looks, though perhaps unrecognizable as such by herself, may have had its share with her pity in the tears that followed. Somehow or other, at all events, she made up her mind to bear more patiently the persecutions of the little Bruces, and, if ever her turn should come to be punished, as no doubt it would, whether she deserved it or not, to try to take the whipping as she had seen Alec Forbes take it. Poor Annie! If it should come to that—nervous organizations are so different!

At five, the school was dismissed for the day, not without another extempore prayer. A succession of jubilant shouts arose as the boys rushed out into the lane. Every day to them was a cycle of strife, suffering, and deliverance. Birth and death, with the life-struggle between, were shadowed out in it—with this difference, that the God of a corrupt Calvinism, in the person of Murdoch Malison, ruled that world, and not the God revealed in the man Christ Jesus. And most of them having felt the day more or less a burden, were now going home to heaven for the night.

Annie, having no home, was amongst the few exceptions. Dispirited and hopeless—a terrible condition for a child—she wondered how Alec Forbes could be so merry. But he had had his evil things, and they were over; while hers were all about her still. She had but one comfort left— that no one would prevent her from creeping up to her own desolate garret, which was now the dreary substitute for Brownie's stall. Thither the persecuting boys were not likely to follow her. And if the rats were in that garret, so was the cat; or at least the cat knew the way to it. There she might think in peace about some things about which she had never before seemed to have occasion to think.

CHAPTER X

Thus at home, if home it could be called, and at school, Annie's days passed—as most days pass—with family resemblance and individual difference wondrously mingled. She became interested in what she had to learn, if not from the manner in which it was presented to her comprehension, yet from the fact that she had to learn it. Happily or unhappily, too, she began to get used to the sight of the penal suffering of her schoolfellows. Nor had anything of the kind as yet visited her; for it would have been hard for even a more savage master than Mr Malison to find occasion, now that the first disabling influences had passed away, to punish the nervous, delicate, anxious little orphan, who was so diligent, and as quiet as a mouse that fears to awake a sleeping cat. She had a scared look too, that might have moved the heart of Malison even, if he had ever paid the least attention to the looks of children. For the absence of human companionship in bestial forms; the loss of green fields, free to her as to the winds of heaven, and of country sounds and odours; and an almost constant sense of oppression from the propinquity of one or another whom she had cause to fear, were speedily working sad effects upon her. The little colour she had died out of her cheek. Her face grew thin, and her blue eyes looked wistful and large out of their sulken cells. Not often were tears to be seen in them now, and yet they looked well acquainted with tears—like fountains that had been full yesterday. She never smiled, for there was nothing to make her smile.

But she gained one thing by this desolation: the thought of her dead father came to her, as it had never come before; and she began to love him with an intensity she had known nothing of till now. Her mother had died at her birth, and she had been her father's treasure; but in the last period of his illness she had seen less of him, and the blank left by his death had, therefore, come upon her gradually. Before she knew what it was, she had begun to forget. In the minds of children the grass grows very quickly over their buried dead. But now she learned what death meant, or rather what love had been; not, however, as an added grief: it comforted her to remember how her father had loved her; and she said her prayers the oftener, because they seemed to go somewhere near the place where her father was. She did not think of her father being where God was, but of God being where her father was.

The winter was drawing nearer too, and the days were now short and cold. A watery time began, and for many days together the rain kept falling without intermission. I almost think Annie would have died, but for her dead father to think about. On one of those rainy days, however, she began to find that it is in the nature of good things to come in odd ways. It had rained the whole day, not tamely and drizzingly, but in real earnest, dancing and rebounding from the pools, and raising a mist by the very "crash of water-drops." Now and then the school became silent, just to listen to the wide noise made by the busy cataract of the heavens, each drop a messenger of good, a sweet returning of earth's aspirations, in the form of Heaven's *Amen!* But the boys thought only of the fun of dabbling in the torrents as they went home; or the delights of net-fishing in the swollen and muddy rivers, when the fish no longer see their way, but go wandering about in perplexity, just as we human mortals do in a thick fog, whether of the atmosphere or of circumstance.

The afternoon was waning. It was nearly time to go; and still the rain was pouring and plashing around. In the gathering gloom there had been more than the usual amount of wandering from one part of the school to another, and the elder Bruce had stolen to a form occupied by some little boys, next to the one on which Annie sat with her back towards them. If it was not the real object of his expedition, at least he took the opportunity to give Annie a spiteful dig with his elbow; which, operating even more powerfully than he had intended, forced from her an involuntary cry. Now the master indulged in an occasional refinement of the executive, which consisted in this: he threw the *tawse* at the offender, not so much for the sake of hurting—although that, being a not infrequent result, may be supposed to have had a share in the intention—as of humiliating; for the culprit had to bear the instrument of torture back to the hands of the executioner. He threw the tawse at Annie, half, let us suppose, in thoughtless cruelty, half in evil jest. It struck her rather sharply, before she had recovered breath after the blow Bruce had given her. Ready to faint with pain and terror, she rose, pale as death, and staggered up to the master, carrying the tawse with something of the same horror she would have felt had it been a snake. With a grim smile, he sent her back to her seat. The moment she reached it her self-control gave way, and she burst into despairing, though silent tears. The desk was still shaking with her sobs, and some of the girls were still laughing at her grief, when a new occurrence attracted their attention. Through the noise of the falling rain a still louder rushing of water was heard, and the ears and eyes of all sought the source of the sound. Even Annie turned her wet cheeks and overflowing eyes languidly towards the door. Mr Malison went and opened it. A flood of brown water was pouring into the sunk passage already described. The grating by which the rain-torrent that flowed past the door should have escaped, had got choked, the stream had been dammed back, and in a few moments more the room itself would be flooded. Perceiving this, the master hastily dismissed his pupils.

There could be no better fun for most of the boys and some of the girls, than to wade through the dirty water. Many of the boys dashed through it at once, shoes and all; but some of the boys, and almost all the girls, took off their shoes and stockings. When Annie got a peep of the water, writhing and tumbling in the passage, it looked so ugly, that she shrunk from fording it, especially if she must go in with her bare feet. She could not tell what might be sweeping about in that filthy whirlpool. She was still looking at it as it kept rising, in pale perplexity and dismay, with the forgotten tears still creeping down her cheeks, when she was caught up from behind by a boy, who, with his shoes and stockings in one hand, now seated her on the other arm. She peeped timidly round to see who it was, and the brave brown eyes of Alec Forbes met hers, lighted by a kind, pitying smile. In that smile the cloudy sky of the universe gently opened, and the face of God looked out upon Annie. It gave her, for the moment, all that she had been dying for want of for many weeks—weeks long as years. She could not help it—she threw her arms round Alec Forbes's neck, laid her wet cheek against his, and sobbed as if her heart would break. She did not care for the Bruces, or the rats, or even the schoolmaster now. Alec clasped her tighter, and vowed in his heart that if ever that brute Malison lifted the tag to her, he would fly at his throat. He would have carried her all the way home, for she was no great weight; but as soon as they were out of the house Annie begged him to set her down so earnestly, that he at once complied, and, bidding her good night, ran home barefoot through the flooded roads.

The Bruces had gone on with the two umbrellas, one of which, more to her discomfort than protection, Annie had shared in coming to the school; so that she was very wet before she got home. But no notice was taken of the condition she was in; the consequence of which was a severe cold and cough, which however, were not regarded as any obstacles to her going to school the next day.

That night she lay awake for a long time, and when at last she fell asleep, she dreamed that she took Alec Forbes home to see her father—out the street and the long road; over the black moor, and through the fields; in at the door of the house, and up the stair to her father's room, where he lay in bed. And she told him how kind Alec had been to her, and how happy she was going to be now. And her father put his hand out of the bed, and laid it on Alec's head, and said: "Thank ye, Alec for being kind to my poor Annie." And then she cried, and woke crying—strange tears out of dreamland, half of delicious sorrow and half of trembling joy.

With what altered feelings she seated herself after the prayer, next day, and glanced round the room to catch a glimpse of her new friend! There he was, radiant as usual. He took no notice of her, and she had not expected that he would. But it was not long before he found out, now that he was interested in her, that her cousins were by no means friendly to her; for their seats were not far from the girl's quarter, and they took every sheltered opportunity of giving her a pinch or a shove, or of making vile grimaces at her.

In the afternoon, while she was busy over an addition sum which was more than usually obstinate, Robert came stealthily behind her, and, licking his hand, watched his opportunity, and rubbed the sum from her slate. The same moment he received a box on the ear, that no doubt filled his head with more noises than that of the impact. He yelled with rage and pain, and, catching sight of the administrator of justice as he was returning to his seat, bawled out in a tone of fierce complaint: "Sanny Forbes!"

"Alexander Forbes! come up," responded the voice of the master. Forbes not being a first-rate scholar, was not a favourite with him, for Mr Malison had no sense for what was fine in character or disposition. Had the name been that of one of his better Latin scholars, the cry of Bruce would most likely have passed unheeded.

"Hold up your hand," he said, without requesting or waiting for an explanation.

Alec obeyed. Annie gave a smothered shriek, and, tumbling from her seat, rushed up to the master. When she found herself face to face with the tyrant, however, not one word could she speak. She opened her mouth, but throat and tongue refused their offices, and she stood gasping. The master stared, his arm arrested in act to strike, and his face turned over his left shoulder, with all the blackness of his anger at Forbes lowering upon Annie. He stood thus for one awful moment, then motioning her aside with a sweep of his head, brought down the tawse upon the hand which Alec had continued to hold outstretched, with the vehemence of accumulated wrath. Annie gave a choking cry, and Alec, so violent was the pain, involuntarily withdrew his hand. But instantly, ashamed of his weakness, he presented it again, and received the remainder of his punishment without flinching. The master then turned to Annie; and finding her still speechless, gave her a push that nearly threw her on her face, and said,

"Go to your seat, Ann Anderson. The next time you do that I will punish you severely."

Annie sat down, and neither sobbed nor cried. But it was days before she recovered from the shock. Once, long after, when she was reading about the smothering of the princes in the Tower, the whole of the physical sensations of those terrible moments returned upon her, and she sprang from her seat in a choking agony.

CHAPTER XI

For some time neither of the Bruces ventured even to make a wry face at her in school; but their behaviour to her at home was only so much the worse.

Two days after the events recorded, as Annie was leaving the kitchen, after worship, to go up to bed, Mr Bruce called her.

"Annie Anderson," he said, "I want to speak to you."

Annie turned, trembling.

"I see you know what it's about," he went on, staring her full in the pale face, which grew paler as he stared. "You can't look me in the face. Where's the candy-sugar and the prunes? I know well enough where they are, and so do you."

"I know nothing about them," answered Annie, with a sudden revival of energy.

"Don't lie, Annie. It's bad enough to steal, without lying."

"I'm not lying," answered she, bursting into tears of indignation. "Who said that I took them?"

"That's nothing to the point. You wouldn't cry like that if you were innocent. I never missed anything before. And you know well enough there's an eye that sees all, and you can't hide from it."

Bruce could hardly have intended that it was by inspiration from on high that he had discovered the thief of his sweets. But he thought it better to avoid mentioning that the informer was his own son Johnnie. Johnnie, on his part, had thought it better not to mention that he had been incited to the act by his brother Robert. And Robert had thought it better not to mention that he did so partly to shield himself, and partly out of revenge for the box on the ear which Alec Forbes had given him. The information had been yielded to the inquisition of the parent, who said with truth that he had never missed anything before; although I suspect that a course of petty and cautious pilfering had at length passed the narrow bounds within which it could be concealed from the lynx eyes inherited from the kingly general. Possibly a bilious attack, which confined the elder boy to the house for two or three days, may have had something to do with the theft; but if Bruce had any suspicions of the sort, he never gave utterance to them.

"I don't want to hide from it," cried Annie. "God knows," she went on in desperation, "that I wouldn't touch a grain of salt without leave."

"It's a pity, Annie, that some folk don't get their own share of Mr Malison's tards." (*Tards* was considered a more dignified word than *tag*.) "I don't like to lick you myself, 'cause you're not my child; but I can hardly keep my hands off you."

It must not be supposed from this speech that Robert Bruce ever ventured to lay his hands on his own children. He was too much afraid of their mother, who, perfectly submissive and sympathetic in ordinary, would have flown into the rage of a hen with chickens if even her own husband had dared to chastise one of *her* children. The shop might be more Robert's than hers, but the children were more hers than Robert's.

Overcome with shame and righteous anger, Annie burst out in the midst of fresh tears:

"I wish Auntie would come and take me away! It's a bad house to be in."

These words had a visible effect upon Bruce. He expected a visit from Marget Anderson within a day or two; and he did not know what the effect of the representations of Annie might be. The use of her money had not been secured to him for any lengthened period—Dowie, anxious to take all precautions for his little mistress, having consulted a friendly lawyer on the subject, lest she should be left defenceless in the hands of a man of whose moral qualities Dowie had no exalted opinion. The sale having turned out better than had been expected, the sum committed to Bruce was two hundred pounds, to lose which now would be hardly less than ruin. He thought it better, therefore, not doubting Annie to be the guilty person, to count the few lumps of sugar he might lose, as an additional trifle of interest, and not quarrel with his creditor for extorting it. So with the weak cunning of his kind, he went to the shop, and bringing back a bit of sugar-candy, about the size of a pigeon's egg, said to the still weeping child:

"Dinna greit, Annie. I canna bide to see ye greitin'. Gin ye want a bittie o' sugar ony time, jist tell me, an' dinna gang helpin' yoursel'. That's a'. Hae."

"Don't cry, Annie. I can't bear to see you crying. If you want a bit of sugar any time, just tell me, and don't go helping yourself. That's all. Here."

He thrust the lump into Annie's hand; but she dropped it on the floor with disgust, and rushed up-stairs to her bed as fast as the darkness would let her: where, notwithstanding her indignation, she was soon fast asleep.

Bruce searched for the sugar-candy which she had rejected, until he found it. He then restored it to the drawer whence he had taken it—which he could find in the dark with perfect ease—resolving as he did so, to be more careful in future of offending little Annie Anderson.

When the day arrived upon which he expected Marget's visit, that being a Saturday, Bruce was on the watch the whole afternoon. From his shop-door he could see all along the street, and a good way beyond it; and being very quick-sighted, he recognized Marget at a great distance by her shawl, as she sat in a slow-nearing cart.

"Annie!" he called, opening the inner door, as he returned behind the counter.

Annie, who was up-stairs in her own room, immediately appeared.

"Annie," he said, "rin oot at the back door, and through the yard,

"Annie!" he called, opening the inner door, as he returned behind the counter.

Annie, who was up-stairs in her own room, immediately appeared.

"Annie," he said, "run out at the back door, and through the yard, and over to Laurie Lumley's, and tell him to come over to me at once. Don't come back without him. There's a good girl!"

He sent her upon this message, knowing well enough that the man had gone into the country that day, and that there was no one at his house who would be likely to know where he had gone. He hoped, therefore, that she would go and look for him in the town, and so be absent during her aunt's visit.

"Well, Marget," he said, with his customary greeting, in which the foreign oil sought to overcome the home-bred vinegar, "how are you today?"

"Oh! not that bad," answered Marget with a sigh.

"And how's Mr and Mistress Peterson?"

"Just fine. How's Annie coming on?"

"Not that bad. Just a bit wild."

He thought to please her by the remark, because she had been in the habit of saying so herself. But distance had made Annie dearer; and her aunt's nose took fire with indignation, as she replied:

"The lassie's well enough. *I* saw nothing of the sort about her. If you can't manage her, that's *your* fault."

Bruce was abashed, but not confounded. He was ready in a moment.

"I never knew any good come of being too hard on bairns," said he.

"She's as easy managed as a cow going home at night, only you need to let her know that you're there, you know."

"Oh! ay," said Marget, a little nonplussed in her turn.

"Would you like to see her?"

"What else did I come for?"

"Well, I'll go and look for her."

He went to the back door, and called aloud: "Annie, your auntie's here and wants to see you."

"She'll be here in a minute," he said to Marget, as he re-entered the shop.

After a little more desultory conversation, he pretended to be surprised that she she did not make her appearance, and going once more to the door, called her name several times. He then pretended to search for her in the garden and all over the house, and returned with the news that she was nowhere to be seen.

"She's afraid you're come to take her with you, and she's run away off somewhere. I'll send the laddies to look for her."

"Na, na, never mind. If she doesn't want to see me, I'm sure I needn't want to see her. I'll be heading down the town," said Margaret, her face growing very red as she spoke.

She bustled out of the shop, too angry with Annie to say farewell to Bruce. She had not gone far, however, before Annie came running out of a narrow close, almost into her aunt's arms. But there was no refuge for her there.

"You little hussy!" cried Margaret, seizing her by the shoulder, "why did you run away? I don't want you, you brat!"

"I didn't run away, auntie."

"Robert Bruce called you to come in, himself."

"He sent me himself to Laurie Lumley's to tell him to come to him at once."

Margaret could not make "head or tail" of it. But as Annie had never told her a lie, she could not doubt her. So taking time to think about it, she gave her some rough advice and a smooth penny, and went away on her errands. She was not long in coming to the conclusion that Bruce wanted to sunder her and the child; and this offended her so much, that she did not go near the shop for a long time. Thus Annie was forsaken, and Bruce had what he wanted.

He needed not have been so full of scheming, though. Annie never said a word to her aunt about their treatment of her. It is one of the marvels in the constitution of children, how much they will bear without complaining. Parents and guardians have no right to suppose that all is well in the nursery or school-room, merely from the fact that the children do not complain. Servants and tutors may be cruel, and children will be silent—partly, I presume, because they forget so soon.

But vengeance of a sort soon overtook Robert Bruce the younger; for the evil spirit in him, derived from no such remote ancestor as the king, would not allow him a long respite from evil-doing, even in school. He knew Annie better than his father, that she was not likely to complain of anything, and that the only danger lay in the chance of being discovered in the deed. One day when the master had left the room to confer with some visitor at the door, he spied Annie in the act of tying her shoe. Perceiving, as he believed, at a glance, that Alec Forbes was totally unobservant, he gave her an ignominious push from behind, which threw her out on her face in the middle of the floor. But Alec did catch sight of him in the very deed, was down upon him in a moment, and, having already proved that a box on the ear was of no lasting effect, gave him a downright good thrashing. He howled vigorously, partly from pain, partly in the hope that the same consequences as before would overtake Forbes; and therefore was still howling when Mr Malison re-entered.

"Robert Bruce, come up," bawled he, the moment he opened the door.

And Robert Bruce went up, and notwithstanding his protestations, received a second, and far more painful punishment from the master, who, perhaps, had been put out of temper by his visitor. But there is no good in speculating on that or any other possibility in the matter; for, as far at least as the boys could see, the master had no fixed principle as to the party on whom the punishment should fall. Punishment, in his eyes, was perhaps enough in itself. If he was capable of seeing that *punishment*, as he called it, falling on the wrong person, was not *punishment*, but only *suffering*, certainly he had not seen the value of the distinction.

If Bruce howled before, he howled tenfold now, and went home howling. Annie was sorry for him, and tried to say a word of comfort to him; but he repelled her advances with hatred and blows. As soon as he reached the shop he told his father that Forbes had beaten him without his having even spoken to him, which was as correct as it was untrue, and that the master had taken Forbes's part, and *licked* him over again, of which latter assertion there was proof enough on his person. Robert the elder was instantly filled with smouldering wrath, and from that moment hated Alec Forbes. For, like many others of low nature, he had yet some animal affection for his children, combined with an endless amount of partisanship on their behalf, which latter gave him a full right to the national motto of Scotland. Indeed, for nothing in the world but money, would he have sacrificed what seemed to him their interests.

A man must learn to love his children, not because they are his, but because they are *children*, else his love will be scarcely a better thing at last than the party-spirit of the faithful politician. I doubt if it will prove even so good a thing.

From this hatred to Alec Forbes came some small consequences at length. But for the present it found no outlet save in sneers and prophetic hints of an "ill hinner en'."[1]

---

1   A bad end.

CHAPTER XII

In her inmost heart Annie dedicated herself to the service of Alec Forbes. Nor was it long before she had an opportunity of helping him.

One Saturday the master made his appearance in black instead of white stockings, which was regarded by the scholars as a bad omen; and fully were their prognostications justified, on this occasion, at least. The joy of the half-holiday for Scotch boys and girls has a terrible weight laid in the opposite scale—I mean the other half of the day. This weight, which brings the day pretty much on a level with all other days, consists in a free use of the Shorter Catechism. This, of course, made them hate the Catechism, though I am not aware that that was of any great consequence, or much to be regretted. For my part, I wish the spiritual engineers who constructed it had, after laying the grandest foundation-stone that truth could afford them, glorified God by going no further. Certainly many a man would have enjoyed Him sooner, if it had not been for their work. But, alas! the Catechism was not enough, even of the kind. The tormentors of youth had gone further, and provided what they called Scripture proofs of the various assertions of the Catechism; a support of which it stood greatly in need. Alas! I say, for the boys and girls who had to learn these proofs, called texts of Scripture, but too frequently only morsels torn bleeding and shapeless from "the lovely form of the Virgin Truth!" For these tasks, combined with the pains and penalties which accompanied failure, taught them to dislike the Bible as well as the Catechism, and that was a matter of altogether different import.

Every Saturday, then, Murdoch Malison's pupils had to learn so many questions of the Shorter Catechism, with proofs from Scripture; and whoever failed in this task was condemned to imprisonment for the remainder of the day, or, at least, till the task should be accomplished. The imprisonment was sometimes commuted for chastisement—or finished off with it, when it did not suit the convenience of the master to enforce the full term of a school-day. Upon certain Saturdays, moreover, one in each month, I think, a repetition was required of all the questions and proofs that had been, or ought to have been, learned since the last observance of the same sort.

Now the day in question was one of these of accumulated labour, and Alec Forbes only succeeded in bringing proof of his inability for the task, and was in consequence condemned "to be keepit in"[1] —a trial hard enough for one whose chief delights were the open air and the active exertion of every bodily power.

Annie caught sight of his mortified countenance, the expression of which, though she had not heard his doom, so filled her with concern and indignation, that—her eyes and thoughts fixed upon him, at the other end of the class—she did not know when her turn came, but allowed the master to stand before her in bootless expectation. He did not interrupt her, but with a refinement of cruelty that ought to have done him credit in his own eyes, waited till the universal silence had at length aroused Annie to self-consciousness and a sense of annihilating confusion. Then, with a smile on his thin lips, but a lowering thunder-cloud on his brow, he repeated the question:

"What doth every sin deserve?"

Annie, bewildered, and burning with shame at finding herself the core of the silence—feeling as if her poor little spirit stood there naked to the scoffs and jeers around—could not recall a word of the answer given in the Catechism. So, in her bewilderment, she fell back on her common sense and experience, which, she ought to have known, had nothing to do with the matter in hand.

"What doth every sin deserve?" again repeated the tyrant.

"A lickin'," whimpered Annie, and burst into tears.

The master seemed much inclined to consider her condemned out of her own mouth, and give her a whipping at once; for it argued more than ignorance to answer *a whipping*, instead of *the wrath and curse of God*, &c., &c., as plainly set down in the Scotch Targum. But reflecting, perhaps, that she was a girl, and a little one, and that although it would be more gratification to him to whip her, it might be equal suffering to her to be *kept in*, he gave that side wave of his head which sealed the culprit's doom, and Annie took her place among the condemned, with a flutter of joy at her heart that Alec Forbes would not be left without a servant to wait upon him. A few more boys made up the unfortunate party, but they were all little ones, and so there was no companion for Forbes, who evidently felt the added degradation of being alone. The hour arrived; the school was dismissed; the master strode out, locking the door behind him; and the defaulters were left alone, to chew the bitter cud of ill-cooked Theology.

1   KEEPIT IN (Scots): kept in

For some time a dreary silence reigned. Alec sat with his elbows on his desk, biting his nails, and gnawing his hands. Annie sat dividing her silent attention between her book and Alec. The other boys were, or seemed to be, busy with their catechisms, in the hope of getting out as soon as the master returned. At length Alec took out his knife, and began, for very vacancy, to whittle away at the desk before him. When Annie saw that, she crept across to his form, and sat down on the end of it. Alec looked up at her, smiled, and went on with his whittling. Annie slid a little nearer to him, and asked him to hear her say her catechism. He consented, and she repeated the lesson perfectly.

"Now let me hear you, Alec," she said.

"Na, thank ye, Annie. I canna say't. And I wonna say't for a' the dominies in creation."

"But he'll lick ye, Alec; an' I canna bide it," said Annie, the tears beginning to fill her eyes.

"Weel, I'll try—to please you, Annie," said Alec, seeing that the little thing was in earnest.

How her heart bounded with delight! That great boy, so strong and so brave, trying to learn a lesson to please her!

But it would not do.

"I canna min' a word o' 't, Annie. I'm dreidfu' hungry, forbye. I was in a hurry wi' my brakfast the day. Gin I had kent what was comin', I wad hae laid in a better stock," he added, laughing rather drearily.

As he spoke he looked up; and his eyes wandered from one window to another for a few moments after he had ceased speaking.

"Na; it's no use," he resumed at last. "I hae eaten ower muckle for that, ony gait."

Annie was as pitiful over Alec's

hunger as any mother over her child's. She felt it pure injustice that he should ever be hungry. But, unable to devise any help, she could only say,

"I don't know what you mean, Alec."

"When I was no bigger than you, Annie, I could get through a smaller hole than that," answered he, and pointed to the open wooden pane in an upper corner of one of the windows; "but I've eaten too much since then."

And he laughed again; but it was again an unsuccessful laugh.

Annie sprang to her feet.

"If you could get through that hole once, I can get through it now, Alec. Just hold me up a bit. You *can* lift me, you know."

And she looked up at him shyly and gratefully.

"But what will you do when you *are* out, Annie?"

"Run home, and bring a loaf with me at once."

"But Rob Bruce'll see your head between your feet before he'll give you a loaf, or a mouthful of cakes either; and it's too far to run to my mother's. Murdoch would be back long before that."

"Just help me out, and leave the rest to me," said Annie, confidently. "If I don't bring a loaf of white bread, never trust me again."

The idea of the bread, always a rarity and consequent delicacy to

Scotch country boys, so early in the century as the date of my story, was too much for Alec's imagination. He jumped up, and put his head out of one of those open panes to reconnoitre. He saw a woman approaching whom he knew.

"I say, Lizzie," he called.

The woman stopped.

"Just stand there and pull this lassie out. We're all kept in together, and nearly famished."

"The Lord preserve us! I'll go for the key."

"Na, na; *we* would have to pay for that. Take her out—that's all we want."

"He's a bad man—that master of yours. I would go to see him hanged."

"Wait a bit; that'll come in good time," said Alec, pseudo-prophetically.

"Well I'll have a pull at his legs, to help him to judgement; for he'll be the death of one or two of you before long."

"Never mind Murder Malison. Will you take the lassie out?"

"That I will! Where is she?"

Alec jumped down and held her up to the open pane, not a foot square. He told her to put her arms through first. Then between them they got her head through, whereupon Lizzie caught hold of her—so low was the school-room—and dragged her out, and set her on her feet.

But alas, a window was broken in the process!

"Now, Annie," cried Alec, "never mind the window. Run."

She was off like a live bullet.

She scampered home prepared to encounter all dangers. The worst of them all to her mind was the danger of not succeeding, and of so breaking faith with Alec. She had sixpence of her own in coppers in her box,—the only difficulty was to get into the house and out again without being seen. By employing the utmost care and circumspection, she got in by the back or house door unperceived, and so up to her room. In a moment more the six pennies were in her hand, and she in the street; for she did not use the same amount of precaution in getting out again, not minding discovery so much now, if she could only have a fair start. No one followed her, however. She bolted into a baker's shop.

"A sixpenny-loaf," she panted out.

"Who wants it?" asked the baker's wife.

"There's the pennies," answered Annie, laying them on the counter.

The baker's wife gave her the loaf, with the biscuit which, from time immemorial, had always graced a purchase to the amount of sixpence; and Annie sped back to the school like a runaway horse to his stable.

As she approached, out popped the head of Alec Forbes. He had been listening for the sound of her feet. She held up the loaf as high as she could, and he stretched down as low as he could, and so their hands met on the loaf.

"Thank you, Annie," said Alec with earnestness. "I shan't forget this. How did you get it?"

"Never mind that. I didn't steal

it," answered Annie. "But I must get in again," she added, suddenly awaking to that difficult necessity, and looking up at the window above her head.

"I'm a predestined idiot!" said Alec, with an impious allusion to the Shorter Catechism, as he scratched his helpless head. "I never thought of that."

It was clearly impossible.

"You'll catch it," said one of the urchins to Annie, with his nose flattened against the window.

The roses of Annie's face turned pale, but she answered stoutly,

"Well! I care as little as the rest of you, I'm thinking."

By this time the "idiot" had made up his mind. He never could make up any other than a bull-headed mind.

"Run home, Annie," he said; "and if Murder offers to lay a finger upon you on Monday, *I'll* murder him. Faith! I'll kill him. Run home before he comes and catches you at the window."

"No, no, Alec," pleaded Annie.

"Hold your tongue," interrupted Alec, "and run, will you?"

Seeing he was quite determined, Annie, though loath to leave him, and in terror of what was implied in the threats he uttered against the master and might be involved in the execution of them, obeyed him and walked leisurely home, avoiding the quarters in which there was a chance of meeting her gaoler.

She found that no one had observed her former visit; the only remarks made being some *goody* ones about the disgrace of being kept in.

When Mr Malison returned to the school about four o'clock, he found all quiet as death. The boys appeared totally absorbed in *committing* the Shorter Catechism, as if the Shorter Catechism was a sin, which perhaps it was not. But, to his surprise, which he pretended to be considerably greater than it really was, the girl was absent.

"Where is Ann Anderson?" were the first words he condescended to utter.

"Gane hame," cried two of the little prisoners.

"Gone home!" echoed the master in a tone of savage incredulity; although not only was it plain that she was gone, but he must have known well enough, from former experience, how her escape had been effected.

"Yes," said Forbes; "it was me made her go. I put her out at the window. And I broke the window," he added, knowing that it must soon be found out, "but I'll get it mended on Monday."

Malison turned as white as a sheet with venomous rage. Indeed, the hopelessness of the situation had made Alec speak with too much nonchalance.

Anxious to curry favour, the third youngster now called out, "Sandy Forbes gart her gang an' fess a loaf o' white breid."[1]

Of this bread, the wretched informer had still some of the crumbs sticking to his jacket—so vitiating is the influence of a reign of terror. The bread was eaten, and the giver might be betrayed in the hope of gaining a little favour with the tyrant.

"Alexander Forbes, come up."

Beyond this point I will not here prosecute the narrative.

Alec bore his punishment with great firmness, although there were few beholders, and none of them worth considering. After he had spent his wrath, the master allowed them all to depart without further reference to the Shorter Catechism.

---

[1] "Sandy Forbes made her go and fetch a loaf of white bread."

CHAPTER XIII

The Sunday following was anything but a day of repose for Annie—she looked with such frightful anticipation to the coming Monday. Nor was the assurance with which Alec Forbes had sent her away, and which she was far from forgetting, by any means productive of unmingled consolation; for, in a conflict with such a power of darkness as Mr Malison, how could Alec, even if sure to be victorious as any knight of old story, come off without injury terrible and not to be contemplated! Yet, strange to tell—or was it really strange?—as she listened to the evening sermon, a sermon quietly and gently enforcing the fate of the ungodly, it was not with exultation at the tardy justice that would overtake such men as Murdoch Malison or Robert Bruce, nor yet with pity for their fate, that she listened; but with anxious heart-aching fear for her friend, the noble, the generous Alec Forbes, who withstood authority, and was therefore in danger of hell-fire. About her own doom, speculation was uninteresting.

The awful morning dawned. When she woke, and the thought of what she had to meet came back on her, though it could hardly be said to have been a moment absent all night long, she turned, not metaphorically, but physically sick. Yet breakfast time would come, and worship did not fail to follow, and then to school she must go. There all went on as usual for some time. The Bible-class was called up, heard, and dismissed; and Annie was beginning to hope that the whole affair was somehow or other wrapt up and laid by. She had heard nothing of Alec's fate after she had left him imprisoned, and except a certain stoniness in his look, which a single glance discovered, his face gave no sign. She dared not lift her eyes from the spelling-book before her, to look in the direction of the master. No murderer could have felt more keenly as if all the universe were one eye, and that eye fixed on him, than Annie.

Suddenly the awful voice resounded through the school, and the words it uttered—though even after she heard them it seemed too terrible to be true—were,

"Ann Anderson, come up."

For a moment she lost consciousness—or at least memory. When she recovered herself, she found herself standing before the master. His voice seemed to have left two or three unanswered questions somewhere in her head. What they were she had no idea. But presently he spoke again, and, from the tone, what he said was evidently the repetition of a question—probably put more than once before.

"Did you, or did you not, go out at the window on Saturday?"

She did not see that Alec Forbes had left his seat, and was slowly lessening the distance between them and him.

"Yes," she answered, trembling from head to foot.

"Did you, or did you not, bring a loaf of bread to those who were kept in?"

"Yes, sir."

"Where did you get it?"

"I bought it, sir."

"Where did you get the money?"

Of course every eye in the school was fixed upon her, those of her cousins sparkling with delight.

"I got it oot o' my ain kist (*own chest*), sir."

"Hold up your hand."

Annie obeyed, with a most pathetic dumb terror pleading in her face.

"Don't touch her," said Alec Forbes, stepping between the executioner and his victim. "You know well enough it was all my fault. I told you so on Saturday."

Murder Malison, as the boys called him, turned with the tawse over his shoulder, whence it had been on the point of swooping upon Annie, and answered him with a hissing blow over his down-bent head, followed by a succession of furious blows upon every part of his person, as it twisted and writhed and doubled; till, making no attempt at resistance, he was knocked down by the storm, and lay prostrate under the fierce lashes, the master holding him down with one foot, and laying on with the whole force of the opposite arm. At length Malison stopped, exhausted, and turning, white with rage, towards Annie, who was almost in a fit with agony, repeated the order:

"Hold up your hand."

But as he turned Alec bounded to his feet, his face glowing, and his eyes flashing, and getting round in front, sprang at the master's throat, just as the tawse was descending. Malison threw him off, and lifting his weapon once more, swept it with a stinging lash round his head and face. Alec, feeling that this was no occasion on which to regard the rules of fair fight, stooped his head, and rushed, like a ram, or a negro, full tilt against the pit of Malison's stomach, and doubling him up, sent him with a crash into the peat fire which was glowing on the hearth. In the attempt to save himself, he thrust his hand right into it, and Alec and Annie were avenged.

Alec rushed to drag him off the fire; but he was up before he reached him.

"Go home!" he bawled to the scholars generally, and sat down at his desk to hide his suffering.

For one brief moment there was silence. Then a tumult arose, a shouting, and holloing, and screeching, and the whole school rushed to the door, as if the devil had been after them to catch the hindmost. Strange uproar invaded the ears of Glamerton—strange, that is, at eleven o'clock in the forenoon of Monday—the uproar of jubilant freedom.

But the culprits, Annie and Alec, stood and stared at the master, whose face was covered with one hand, while the other hung helpless at his side. Annie stopped partly out of pity for the despot, and partly because Alec stopped. Alec stopped because he was the author of the situation—at least he never could give any better reason.

At length Mr Malison lifted his head, and made a movement towards his hat. He started when he saw the two standing there. But the moment he looked at them their courage failed them.

"Rin, Annie!" said Alec.

Away she bolted, and he after her, as well as he could, which was not with his usual fleetness by any means. When Annie had rounded a corner, not in the master's way home, she stopped, and looked back for Alec. He was a good many paces behind her; and then first she discovered the condition of her champion. For now that the excitement was over, he could scarcely walk, and evidence in kind was not wanting that from head to foot he must be one mass of wales and bruises. He put his hand on her shoulder to help him along, and made no opposition to her accompanying him as far as the gate of his mother's garden, which was nearly a mile from the town, on the further bank of one of the rivers watering the valley-plain in which Glamerton had stood for hundreds of years. Then she went slowly home, bearing with her the memory of the smile which, in spite of pain, had illuminated his tawse-waled cheeks, as she took her leave.

"Good-bye, dear Alec!" she had said.

"Good-bye, Annie dear," he had answered, with the smile; and she had watched him crawl into the house before she turned away.

When she got home, she saw at once, from the black looks of the Bruce, that the story, whether in its true shape or not, had arrived before her.

Nothing was said, however, till after worship; when Bruce gave her a long lecture, as impressive as the creature was capable of making it, on the wickedness and certain punishment of "takin' up wi' ill loons like Sandy Forbes, wha was brakin' his mither's hert wi' his baad behaviour." But he came to the conclusion, as he confided to his wife that night, that the lassie "was growin' hardent already;" probably from her being in a state of too great excitement from the events of the day to waste a tear upon his lecture; for, as she said in the hearing of the rottans, when she went up to bed, she *"didna care a flee for't."* But the moment she lay down she fell to weeping bitterly over the sufferings of Alec. She was asleep in a moment after, however. If it had not been for the power of sleeping that there was in the child, she must long before now have given way to the hostile influences around her, and died.

There was considerable excitement about the hearths of Glamerton, generally, in consequence of the news of the master's defeat carried home by the children. For, although it was amazing how little of the doings at school the children were in the habit of reporting—so little, indeed, that this account involved revelations of the character and proceedings of Mr Malison which appeared to many of the parents quite incredible—the present occurrence so far surpassed the ordinary, and had excited the beholders so much, that they could not be quiet about it. Various were the judgments elicited by the story. The religious portion of the community seemed to their children to side with the master; the worldly—namely, those who did not profess to be particularly religious—all sided with Alec Forbes; with the exception of a fish-cadger, who had one son, the plague of his life.

Amongst the religious, there was, at least, one exception, too; but he had no children of his own, and had a fancy for Alec Forbes. That exception was Thomas Crann, the stone-mason.

CHAPTER XIV

Thomas Crann was building a house; for he was both contractor—in a small way, it is true, not undertaking to do anything without the advance of a good part of the estimate—and day-labourer at his own job. Having arrived at the point in the process where the assistance of a carpenter was necessary, he went to George Macwha, whom he found at his bench, planing. This bench was in a work-shop, with two or three more benches in it, some deals set up against the wall, a couple of red cart-wheels sent in for repair, and the tools and materials of his trade all about. The floor was covered with shavings, or *spales*, as they are called by northern consent, which a poor woman was busy gathering into a sack. After a short and gruff greeting on the part of Crann, and a more cordial reply from Macwha, who ceased his labour to attend to his visitor, they entered on the business-question, which having been carefully and satisfactorily discussed, with the aid of various diagrams upon the half-planed deal, Macwha returned to his work, and the conversation took a more general scope, accompanied by the sounds of Macwha's busy instrument.

"A terrible laddie, that Sandy Forbes!" said the carpenter, with a sort of laugh in the *whishk* of his plane, as he threw off a splendid *spale*. "They say he's licked the schoolmaster, and nearly been the death of him."

"I've known worse laddies than Sandy Forbes," was Thomas's curt reply.

"Oh, surely! I know nothing against the laddie. He and our Willie are very close."

To this the sole answer Thomas gave was a grunt, and a silence of a few seconds followed before he spoke, reverting to the point from which they had started.

"I don't know but Alec might have committed a worse sin than thrashing the schoolmaster. He's a dour fellow, that Murdoch Malison, with his fair face and his harsh words. I expect the children have the worst of it in general. And for Alec I have great hopes. He comes of a good stock. His father, honest man, was one of the Lord's own, although he didn't make such a stand as, maybe, he ought to have done; and if his mother has been rather soft with him, and given him too long a tether, he'll come all right before long, for he's worth looking after."

"I don't quite understand you, Thomas."

"I don't think the Lord will lose hold of his father's son. He's not converted yet, but he's well worth converting, for there's good stuff in him."

Thomas did not consider how his common sense was running away with his theology. But Macwha was not the man to bring him to book on that score. His only reply lay in the careless *whishk whashk* of his plane. Thomas resumed:

"He just wants what you want, George Macwha."

"What's that, Thomas?" asked George, with a grim attempt at a smile, as if to say: "I know what's coming, but I'm not going to mind it."

"He just wants to be well shaken over the mouth of the pit. He must smell the brimstone of the everlasting burnings. He's none of your soft boards, that you can smooth with a swipe of your arm; he's a blue whinstone that's hard to dress, but once dressed, it stands the weather well. I like to work upon hard stone myself. None of your soft freestone, that you could cut with a knife, for me!"

"Well, I daresay you're right, Thomas."

"And, besides, they say he took all his own licks in silence, and flew at the master only when he was going to lick the poor orphan lassie—James Anderson's lassie, you know."

"Oh! ay. It's the same tale they all tell. I have no doubt it's true."

"Well, let him take it, then, and be thankful! for it's no more than was well spent on him."

With these conclusive words, Thomas departed. He was no sooner out of the shop, than out started, from behind the deal boards that stood against the wall, Willie, the eldest hope of the house of Macwha, a dusky-skinned, black-eyed, curly-headed, roguish-looking boy, Alec Forbes's companion and occasional accomplice. He was more mischievous than Alec, and sometimes led him into unforeseen scrapes; but whenever anything extensive had to be executed, Alec was always the leader.

"What are you hiding for, you rascal?" said his father. "What mischief have you been after now?"

"Nothing special," was Willie's cool reply.

"What made you hide, then?"

"Tom Crann never sees me, but he scolds me, and I don't like to be scolded, more than other folk."

"You get no more than you deserve, I expect," returned George. "Here, take the chisel, and cut that beading into lengths."

"I'm going over the water to ask after Alec," was the excusatory rejoinder.

"Ay, ay! pot and pan!—What ails Alec now?"

"Mr Malison's nearhand killed him. He hasn't been at the school these two days."

With these words Willie bolted from the shop, and set off at full speed. The latter part of his statement was perfectly true.

The day after the fight, Mr Malison came to the school as usual, but with his arm in a sling. To Annie's dismay, Alec did not make his appearance.

It had of course been impossible to conceal his corporal condition from his mother; and the heart of the widow so yearned over the suffering of her son, though no confession of suffering escaped Alec's lips, that she vowed in anger that he should never cross the door of that school again. For three or four days she held immovably to her resolution, much to Alec's annoyance, and to the consternation of Mr Malison, who feared that he had not only lost a pupil, but made an enemy. For Mr Malison had every reason for being as smooth-faced with the parents as he always was: he had ulterior hopes in Glamerton.

The clergyman was getting old, and Mr Malison was a licentiate of the Church; and although the people had no direct voice in the filling of the pulpit, it was very desirable that a candidate should have none but friends in the parish.

Mr Malison made no allusion whatever to the events of Monday, and things went on as usual in the school, with just one exception: for a whole week the tawse did not make its appearance. This was owing in part at least to the state of his hand; but if he had ever wished to be freed from the necessity of using the lash, he might have derived hope from the fact that somehow or other the boys were during this week no worse than usual. I do not pretend to explain the fact, and beg leave to refer it to occult meteorological influences.

As soon as school was over on that first day of Alec's absence, Annie darted off on the road to Howglen, where he lived, and never dropped into a walk till she reached the garden-gate. Fully conscious of the inferiority of her position, she went to the kitchen door. The door was opened to her knock before she had recovered breath enough to speak. The servant, seeing a girl with a shabby dress, and a dirty bonnet, from underneath which hung disorderly masses of hair—they would have *glinted* in the eye of the sun, but in the eye of the maid they looked only dusky and disreputable—for Annie was not kept so tidy on the interest of her money as she had been at the farm—the girl, I say, seeing this, and finding besides, as she thought, that Annie had nothing to say, took her for a beggar, and returning into the kitchen, brought her a piece of oat-cake, the common dole to the young mendicants of the time. Annie's face flushed crimson, but she said gently, having by this time got her runaway breath a little more under control,

"No, I thank ye; I'm no a beggar. I only wanted to ken hoo Alec was the day."

"Come in," said the girl, anxious to make some amends for her blunder, "and I'll tell the mistress."

Annie would gladly have objected, contenting herself with the maid's own account; but she felt rather than understood that there would be something undignified in refusing to face Alec's mother; so she followed the maid into the kitchen, and sat down on the edge of a wooden chair, like a perching bird, till she should return.

"Please, mem, here's a lassie wantin' to ken hoo Maister Alec is the day," said Mary, with the handle of the parlour door in her hand.

"That must be little Annie Anderson, mamma," said Alec, who was lying on the sofa very comfortable, considering what he had to lie upon.

It may be guessed at once that Scotch was quite discouraged at home.

Alec had told his mother all about the affair; and some of her friends from Glamerton, who likewise had sons at the school, had called and given their versions of the story, in which the prowess of Alec was made more of than in his own account. Indeed, all his fellow-scholars except the young Bruces, sung his praises aloud; for, whatever the degree of their affection for Alec, every one of them hated the master—a terrible thought for him, if he had been able to appreciate it; but I do not believe he had any suspicion of the fact that he was the centre of converging thoughts of revengeful dislike. So the mother was proud of her boy—far prouder than she was willing for him to see: indeed, she put on the guise of the offended proprieties as much as she could in his presence, thus making Alec feel like a culprit in hers, which was more than she intended, or would have liked, could she have peeped into his mind. So she could not help feeling some interest in Annie, and some curiosity to see her. She had known James Anderson, her father, and he had been her guest more than once when he had called upon business. Everybody had liked him; and this general approbation was owing to no lack of character, but to his genuine kindness of heart. So Mrs Forbes was prejudiced in Annie's favour—but far more by her own recollections of the father, than by her son's representations of the daughter.

"Tell her to come up, Mary," she said.

So Annie, with all the disorganization of school about her, was shown, considerably to her discomfort, into Mrs Forbes's dining-room.

There was nothing remarkable in the room; but to Annie's eyes it seemed magnificent, for carpet and curtains, sideboard and sofa, were luxuries altogether strange to her eyes. So she entered very timidly, and stood trembling and pale—for she rarely blushed except when angry—close to the door. But Alec scrambled from the sofa, and taking hold of her by both hands, pulled her up to his mother.

"There she is, mamma!" he said.

And Mrs Forbes, although her sense of the fitness of things was not gratified at seeing her son treat with such familiarity a girl so neglectedly attired, yet received her kindly and shook hands with her.

"How do you do, Annie?" she said.

"Quite well, I thank ye, mem," answered Annie, showing in her voice that she was overawed by the grand lady, yet mistress enough of her manners not to forget a pretty modest courtesy as she spoke.

"What's gaein' on at the school the day, Annie?" asked Alec.

"Naething by ordidar," answered Annie, the sweetness of her tones contrasting with the roughness of the dialect. "The maister's a hantle quaieter than usual. I fancy he's a' the better behaved for's brunt fingers. But, oh, Alec!"

And here the little maiden burst into a passionate fit of crying.

"What's the matter, Annie," said Mrs Forbes, as she drew her nearer, genuinely concerned at the child's tears.

"Oh! mem, ye didna see hoo the maister lickit him, or ye wad hae grutten yersel'."

Tears from some mysterious source sprang to Mrs Forbes's eyes. But at the moment Mary opened the door, and said—

"Here's Maister Bruce, mem, wantin' to see ye."

"Tell him to walk up, Mary."

"Oh! no, no, mem; dinna lat

"What's going on at the school today, Annie?" asked Alec.

"Naething (*nothing*) special," answered Annie, the sweetness of her tones contrasting with the roughness of the dialect. "The master's much quieter than usual. I fancy he's all the better behaved for his burnt fingers. But oh, Alec!"

And here the little maiden burst into a passionate fit of crying.

"What's the matter, Annie," said Mrs Forbes, as she drew her nearer, genuinely concerned at the child's tears.

"Oh! ma'am, you didn't see how the master licked him, or you would have cried yourself."

Tears from some mysterious source sprang to Mrs Forbes's eyes. But at the moment Mary opened the door, and said—

"Here's Mister Bruce, ma'am, wanting to see you."

"Tell him to walk up, Mary."

"Oh! no, no, ma'am; don't let

him come till I'm out of this. He'll take me with him," cried Annie.

Mary stood waiting the result.

"But you must go home, you know, Annie," said Mrs Forbes, kindly.

"Ay, but not with *him*," pleaded Annie.

From what Mrs Forbes knew of the manners and character of Bruce, she was not altogether surprised at Annie's reluctance. So, turning to the maid, she said—

"Have you told Mr Bruce that Miss Anderson is here?"

"Me tell him! No, ma'am. What's *his* business?"

"Mary, you forget yourself."

"Well, ma'am, I can't stand him."

"Hold your tongue, Mary," said her mistress, hardly able to restrain her own amusement, "and take the child into my room till he is gone. But perhaps he knows you are here, Annie?"

"He can't know that, ma'am. Sometimes he jumps at things, though, sharp enough."

"Well, well! We shall see."

So Mary led Annie away to the sanctuary of Mrs Forbes's bedroom.

But the Bruce was not upon Annie's track at all. His visit wants a few words of explanation.

Bruce's father had been a faithful servant to Mr Forbes's father, who held the same farm before his son, both having been what are called gentlemen-farmers. The younger Bruce, being anxious to set up a shop, had, for his father's sake, been assisted with money by the elder

Forbes. This money he had repaid before the death of the old man, who had never asked any interest for it. More than a few years had not passed before Bruce, who had a wonderful capacity for petty business, was known to have accumulated some savings in the bank. Now the younger Forbes, being considerably more enterprising than his father, had spent all his capital upon improvements—draining, fencing, and such like—when a younger brother, to whom he was greatly attached, applied to him for help in an emergency, and he had nothing of his own within his reach wherewith to aid him. In this difficulty he bethought him of Bruce, to borrow from whom would not involve the exposure of the fact that he was in any embarrassment, however temporary—an exposure very undesirable in a country town like Glamerton.

After a thorough investigation of the solvency of Mr Forbes, and a proper delay for consideration besides, Bruce supplied him with a hundred pounds upon personal bond, at the usual rate of interest, for a certain term of years. Mr Forbes died soon after, leaving his affairs in some embarrassment in consequence of his outlay. Mrs Forbes had paid the interest of the debt now for two years; but, as the rent of the farm was heavy, she found this additional trifle a burden. She had good reason, however, to hope for better times, as the farm must soon increase its yield. Mr Bruce, on his part, regarded the widow with somewhat jealous eyes, because he very much doubted whether, when the day arrived, she would be able to pay him the money she owed him. That day was, however, not just at hand. It was this diversion of his resources, and not the moral necessity for a nest-egg, as he had represented the case to Margaret Anderson, which had urged him to show hospitality to Annie Anderson and her little fortune.

So neither was it anxiety for the welfare of Alec that induced him to call on Mrs Forbes. Indeed if Malison had killed him outright, he would have been rather pleased than otherwise. But he was in the habit of reminding the widow of his existence by an occasional call, especially when the time approached for the half-yearly payment of the interest. And now the report of Alec's condition gave him a suitable pretext for looking in upon his debtor, without, as he thought, appearing too greedy after his money.

"Weel, mem, hoo are ye the day?" said he, as he entered, rubbing his hands.

"Quite well, thank you, Mr Bruce. Take a seat."

"Well, ma'am, how are you today?" said he, as he entered, rubbing his hands.

"Quite well, thank you, Mr Bruce. Take a seat."

"And how's Mr Alec?"

"There he is to answer for himself," said Mrs Forbes, looking towards the sofa.

"How are you, Mr Alec, after all this?" said Bruce, turning towards him.

"Quite well, thank you," answered Alec, in a tone that did not altogether please either of the listeners.

"I thought you had been rather sore, sir," returned Bruce, in an acid tone.

"I've got a wale or two, that's all," said Alec.

"Well, I hope it'll be a lesson to you."

"To Mr Malison, you should have said, Mr Bruce. I am perfectly satisfied, for my part."

His mother was surprised to hear him speak like a grown man, as well as annoyed at his behaviour to Bruce, in whose power she feared they might one day find themselves to their cost. But she said nothing. Bruce, likewise, was rather nonplussed. He grinned a smile and was silent.

"I hear you have taken James Anderson's daughter into your family now, Mr Bruce."

"Oh, ay, ma'am. There was nobody to look after the lassie; so, though I could hardly afford it, with my own small family coming up, I was just in a manner obliged to take her, James Anderson being a cousin of my own, you know, ma'am."

"Well, I am sure it was very kind of you and Mrs Bruce. How does the child get on?"

"Middling, ma'am, middling. She's just too fond of taking up with boys."

Here he glanced at Alec, with an expression of successful spite. He certainly had the best of it now.

Alec was on the point of exclaiming "That's a lie," but he had prudence enough to restrain himself, perceiving that the contradiction would have a better chance with his mother if he delayed its utterance till after the departure of Bruce. So, meantime, the subject was not pursued. A little desultory conversation followed, and the visitor departed, with a laugh from between his teeth as he took leave of Alec, which I can only describe as embodying an *I told you so* sort of satisfaction.

Almost as soon as he was out of the house the parlour-door opened, and Mary brought in Annie. Mrs Forbes's eyes were instantly fixed on her with mild astonishment, and something of a mother's tenderness awoke in her heart towards the little maid-child. What would she not have given for such a daughter! During Bruce's call, Mary had been busy with the child. She had combed and brushed her thick brown hair, and, taken with its exceeding beauty, had ventured on a stroke of originality no one would have expected of her: she had left it hanging loose on her shoulders. Any one would think such an impropriety impossible to a Scotchwoman. But then she had been handling the hair, and contact with anything alters so much one's theories about it. If Mary had found it so, instead of making it so, she would have said it was "no dacent." (*not decent*.) But the hair gave her its own theory before she had done with it, and this was the result. She had also washed her face and hands and neck, made the best she could of her poor, dingy dress, and put one of her own Sunday collars upon her.

Annie had submitted to it all without question; and thus adorned, Mary introduced her again to the dining-room. Before Mrs Forbes had time to discover that she was shocked, she was captivated by the pale, patient face, and the longing blue eyes, that looked at her as if the child felt that she ought to have been her mother, but somehow they had missed each other. They gazed out of the shadows of the mass of dark brown wavy hair that fell to her waist, and there was no more any need for Alec to contradict Bruce's calumny. But Mrs Forbes was speedily recalled to a sense of propriety by observing that Alec too was staring at Annie with a mingling of amusement, admiration, and respect.

"What have you been about, Mary?" she said, in a tone of attempted reproof. "You have made a perfect fright of the child. Take her away."

When Annie was once more brought back, with her hair restored to its net, silent tears of mortification were still flowing down her cheeks.—When Annie cried, the tears always rose and flowed without any sound or convulsion. Rarely did she sob even.—This completed the conquest of Mrs Forbes's heart. She drew the little one to her, and kissed her, and Annie's tears instantly ceased to rise, while Mrs Forbes wiped away those still lingering on her face. Mary then went to get the tea, and Mrs Forbes having left the room for a moment to recover that self-possession, the loss of which is peculiarly objectionable to a Scotchwoman, Annie was left seated on a footstool before the bright fire, the shadows from which were now dancing about the darkening room, and Alec lay on the sofa looking at her. There was no great occasion for his lying on the sofa, but his mother desired it, and Alec had at present no particular objection.

"I wadna like to be gran' fowk," mused Annie aloud, forgetting that she was not alone.

"We're no gran' fowk, Annie," said Alec.

"Ay are ye," returned Annie, persistently.

"Weel, what for wadna ye like it?"

"Ye maun be aye feared for blaudin' things."

"Mamma wad tell ye a different story," rejoined Alec laughing. "There's naething here to blaud."

Mrs Forbes returned. Tea was brought in. Annie comported herself like a lady, and, after tea, ran home with mingled feelings of pleasure and pain. For, notwithstanding her assertion that she would not like to be "gran' fowk," the kitchen fire, small and dull, the smelling shop, and her own dreary garret-room, did not seem more desirable from her peep into the warmth and comfort of the house at Howglen.

Questioned as to what had delayed her return from school, she told the truth; that she had gone to ask after Alec Forbes, and that they had kept her to tea.

"I told them that you ran after boys!" said Bruce triumphantly. Then stung with the reflection that *he* had not been asked to stay to tea, he added: "It's not for the likes of you, Annie, to go to gentlefolk's houses, making free where you're not wanted. So don't let me hear the like again."

But it was wonderful how Bruce's influence over Annie, an influence of distress, was growing gradually weaker. He could make her uncomfortable enough; but as to his opinion of her, she had almost reached the point of not caring a straw for that. And she had faith enough in Alec to hope that he would defend her from whatever Bruce might have said against her.

Whether Mary had been talking in the town, as is not improbable, about little Annie Anderson's visit to her mistress, and so the story of the hair came to be known, or not, I cannot tell; but it was a notable coincidence that a few days after, Mrs Bruce came to the back-door, with a great pair of shears in her hand, and calling Annie, said:

"Here, Annie! Your hair's too long. I'll have to clip it. It's giving you sore eyes."

"There's nothing the matter with my eyes," said Annie gently.

"Don't answer back. Sit down," returned Mrs Bruce, leading her into the kitchen.

Annie cared very little for her hair, and well enough remembered that Mrs Forbes had said it made a fright of her; so it was with no great reluctance that she submitted to the operation. Mrs Bruce chopped it short off all round. As, however, this permitted what there was of it to fall about her face, there being too little to confine in the usual prison of the net, her appearance did not bear such marks of deprivation, or, in other and Scotch words, "she didna luik sae dockit," (*didn't look as shorn*) as might have been expected.

Her wavy locks of rich brown were borne that night, by the careful hand of Mrs Bruce, to Rob Guddle, the barber. Nor was the hand less careful that brought back their equivalent in money. With a smile to her husband, half loving and half cunning, Mrs Bruce dropped the amount into the till.

CHAPTER XV

Although Alec Forbes was not a boy of quick receptivity as far as books were concerned, and therefore was no favourite with Mr Malison, he was not by any means a common or a stupid boy. His own eyes could teach him more than books could, for he had a very quick observation of things about him, both in what is commonly called nature and in humanity. He knew all the birds, all their habits, and all their eggs. Not a boy in Glamerton could find a nest quicker than he, or when found treated it with such respect. For he never took young birds, and seldom more than half of the eggs. Indeed he was rather an uncommon boy, having, along with more than the usual amount of activity even for a boy, a tenderness of heart altogether rare in boys. He was as familiar with the domestic animals and their ways of feeling and acting as Annie herself. Anything like cruelty he detested; and yet, as occasion will show, he could execute stern justice. With the world of men around him, he was equally conversant. He knew the characters of the simple people wonderfully well; and *took to* Thomas Crann more than to any one else, notwithstanding that Thomas would read him a long lecture sometimes. To these lectures Alec would listen seriously enough, believing Thomas to be right; though he could never make up his mind to give any after attention to what he required of him.

The first time Alec met Thomas after the affair with the dominie, was on the day before he was to go back to school; for his mother had yielded at last to his entreaties. Thomas was building an addition to a water-mill on the banks of the Glamour not far from where Alec lived, and Alec had strolled along thither to see how the structure was going on. He expected a sharp rebuke for his behaviour to Mr Malison, but somehow he was not afraid of Thomas, and was resolved to face it out. The first words Thomas uttered, however, were:

"Weel, Alec, can ye tell me what was the name o' King Dawvid's mither?"

"I can*not*, Thomas," answered Alec. "What was it?"

"Fin' ye that oot. Turn ower yer

"Well, Alec, can you tell me what was the name of King David's mother?"

"I can*not*, Thomas," answered Alec. "What was it?"

"Find that out. Turn over your

Bible. Have you been back to the school yet?"

"No. I'm going tomorrow."

"You're not going to strive with the master before night, are you?"

"I don't know," answered Alec. "Maybe he'll strive with me.—But you know, Thomas," he continued, defending himself from what he supposed Thomas was thinking, "King David himself killed the giant."

"Oh! ay; alright. I'm not referring to that. Maybe you did quite right. But take care, Alec—" here Thomas paused from his work, and turning towards the boy with a trowelful of mortar in his hand, spoke very slowly and solemnly—"take care that you bear no malice against the master. Justice itself, done for the sake of a private grudge, will bounce back upon the doer. I have little doubt the master'll be the better for it; but if you be the worse, it'll be a bad job, Alec, my man."

"I have no ill-will at him, Thomas."

"Well, just watch your own heart, and beware of that. I would advise you to try and please him a little more than usual. It's not that easy to the carnal man, but you know we ought to crucify the old man, with his affections and lusts."

"Well, I'll try," said Alec, to whom it was not nearly so difficult as Thomas imagined. His *man* apparently was not very old yet.

And he did try; and the master seemed to appreciate his endeavours, and to accept them as a peace-offering, thus showing that he really was the better for the punishment he had received.

It would be great injustice to Mr Malison to judge him by the feeling of the present day. It was the custom of the time and of the country to use the tawse unsparingly; for *law* having been, and still, in a great measure, being, the highest idea generated of the divine by the ordinary Scotch mind, it must be supported, at all risks even, by means of the leather strap. In the hands of a wise and even-tempered man, no harm could result from the use of this instrument of justice; but in the hands of a fierce-tempered and therefore changeable man, of small moral stature, and liable to prejudices and offence, it became the means of unspeakable injury to those under his care; not the least of which was the production, in delicate natures, of doubt and hesitancy, sometimes deepening into cowardice and lying.

Mr Malison had nothing of the childlike in himself, and consequently never saw the mind of the child whose person he was assailing with a battery of excruciating blows. A *man* ought to be able to endure grief suffering wrongfully, and be none the worse; but who dares demand that of a child? Well it is for such masters that even they are judged by the heart of a father, and not by the law of a king, that worst of all the fictions of an ignorant and low theology. And if they must receive punishment, at least it will not be the heartless punishment which they inflicted on the boys and girls under their law.

Annie began to be regarded as a protegée of Alec Forbes, and as Alec was a favourite with most of his schoolfellows, and was feared where he was not loved, even her cousins began to look upon her with something like respect, and mitigate their persecutions. But she did not therefore become much more reconciled to her position; for the habits and customs of her home were distasteful to her, and its whole atmosphere uncongenial. Nor could it have been otherwise in any house where the entire anxiety was, first, to make money, and next, not to spend it. The heads did not in the least know that they were unkind to her. On the contrary, Bruce thought himself a pattern of generosity if he gave her a scrap of string; and Mrs Bruce, when she said to inquiring gossips "The bairn's like ither bairns—she's weel eneuch,"[1] thought herself a pattern

---

1   "The child's like other children, she's well enough."

of justice or even of forbearance. But both were jealous of her, in relation to their own children; and when Mrs Forbes sent for her one Saturday, soon after her first visit, they hardly concealed their annoyance at the preference shown her by one who was under such great obligation to the parents of other children every way superior to her whose very presence somehow or other made them uncomfortable.

CHAPTER XVI

The winter drew on—a season as different from the summer in those northern latitudes, as if it belonged to another solar system. Cold and stormy, it is yet full of delight for all beings that can either romp, sleep, or think it through. But alas for the old and sickly, in poor homes, with scanty food and firing! Little children suffer too, though the gift of forgetfulness does for them what the gift of faith does for their parents—helps them over many troubles, besides tingling fingers and stony feet. There would be many tracks of those small feet in the morning snow, leading away across the fresh-fallen clouds from the house and cottage doors; for the barbarity of *morning-school*, that is, an hour and a half of dreary lessons before breakfast, was in full operation at Glamerton.

The winter came. One morning, all the children awoke, and saw a white world around them. Alec jumped out of bed in delight. It was a sunny, frosty morning. The snow had fallen all night, with its own silence, and no wind had interfered with the gracious alighting of the feathery water. Every branch, every twig, was laden with its sparkling burden of down-flickered flakes, and threw long lovely shadows on the smooth featureless dazzle below. Away, away, stretched the outspread glory, the only darkness in it being the line of the winding river. All the snow that fell on it vanished, as death and hell shall one day vanish in the fire of God. It flowed on, black through its banks of white. Away again stretched the shine to the town, where every roof had the sheet that was let down from heaven spread over it, and the streets lay a foot deep in yet unsullied snow, soon, like the story of the ages, to be trampled, soiled, wrought, and driven with human feet, till, at last, God's strong sun would wipe it all away.

From the door opening into this fairy-land, Alec sprang into the untrodden space, as into a new America. He had discovered a world, without even the print of human foot upon it. The keen air made him happy; and the face of nature, looking as peaceful as the face of a dead man dreaming of heaven, wrought in him jubilation and leaping. He was at the school door before a human being had appeared in the streets of Glamerton. Its dwellers all lay still under those sheets of snow, which seemed to hold them asleep in its cold enchantment.

Before any of his fellows made their appearance, he had kneaded and piled a great heap of snowballs, and stood by his pyramid, prepared for the offensive. He attacked the first that came, and soon there was a troop of boys pelting away at him. But with his store of balls at his foot, he was able to pay pretty fairly for what he received; till, that being exhausted, he was forced to yield the unequal combat. By-and-by the little ones gathered, with Annie amongst them; but they kept aloof, for fear of the flying balls, for the boys had divided into two equal parties, and were pelting away at each other. At length the woman who had charge of the school-room, having finished lighting the fire, opened the door, and Annie, who was very cold, made a run for it, during a lull in the fury of the battle.

"Stop," cried Alec; and the balling ceased, that Annie, followed by a few others, might pass in safety through the midst of the combatants. One boy, however, just as Annie was entering, threw a ball after her. He missed her, but Alec did not miss him; for scarcely was the ball out of his hand when he received another, right between his eyes. Over he went, amidst a shout of satisfaction.

When the master appeared at the top of the lane the fight came to a close; and as he entered the school, the group round the fire broke up and dispersed. Alec, having entered close behind the master, overtook Annie as she went to her seat, for he had observed, as she ran into the school, that she was lame—indeed limping considerably.

"What's the maitter wi' ye, Annie?" he said. "What gars ye hirple?"

"What's the matter with you, Annie?" he said. "What makes you limp?"

"Juno bitet me," answered Annie.

"Juno bit me," answered Annie.

"Ay! Verra weel!" returned Alec, in a tone that had more meaning than the words.

"Ay! Very well!" returned Alec, in a tone that had more meaning than the words.

Soon after the Bible-class was over, and they had all taken their seats, a strange quiet stir and excitement gradually arose, like the first motions of a whirlpool at the turn of the tide. The master became aware of more than the usual flitting to and fro amongst the boys, just like the coming and going which preludes the swarming of bees. But as he had little or no constructive power, he never saw beyond the symptoms. They were to him mere isolated facts, signifying present disorder.

"John Morison, go to your seat," he cried.

John went.

"Robert Rennie, go to your seat."

Robert went. And this continued till, six having been thus passed by, and a seventh appearing three forms from his own, the master, who seldom stood it so long, could stand it no longer. The *tag* was thrown, and a *licking* followed, making matters a little better from the master's point of view.

Now I will try to give, from the scholars' side, a peep of what passed.

As soon as he was fairly seated, Alec said in a low voice across the double desk to one of the boys opposite, calling him by his nickname,

"I say, Divot, do ye ken Juno?"

"Maybe no!" answered Divot. "But gin I dinna, my left leg dis."

"I thocht ye kent the shape o' her teeth, man. Jist gie Scrumpie there a dig i' the ribs."

"What are ye efter, Divot? I'll gie ye a cloot o' the lug," growled Scrumpie.

"Hoot man! The General wants ye."

The General was Alec's nickname.

"What is't, General?"

"Do ye ken Juno?"

"Hang the bitch! I ken her ower weel. She took her denner aff o' ane o' my hips, ae day last year."

"Jist creep ower to Cadger there, and speir gin he kens Juno. Maybe he's forgotten her."

"I say, Divot, do you know Juno?"

"Maybe not! answered Divot. "But if I don't, my left leg does."

"I thought you knew the shape of her teeth, man. Just give Scrumpie there a dig in the ribs."

"What do you want, Divot? I'll give you a smack on the ear," growled Scrumpie.

"Heavens, man! The General wants you."

The General was Alec's nickname.

"What is it, General?"

"Do you know Juno?"

"Hang the bitch! I know her too well. She took her lunch off one of my hips, one day last year."

"Just creep over to Cadger there, and ask if he knows Juno. Maybe he's forgotten her."

Cadger's reply was interrupted by the interference of the master, but a pantomimic gesture conveyed to the General sufficient assurance of the retentiveness of Cadger's memory in regard to Juno and her favours. Such messages and replies, notwithstanding more than one licking, kept passing the whole of the morning.

Now Juno was an animal of the dog kind, belonging to Robert Brace. She had the nose and the legs of a bull-dog, but was not by any means thorough-bred, and her behaviour was worse than her breed. She was a great favourite with her master, who ostensibly kept her chained in his back-yard for the protection of his house and property. But she was not by any means popular with the rising generation. For she was given to biting, with or without provocation, and every now and then she got loose—upon sundry of which occasions she had bitten boys. Complaint had been made to her owner, but without avail; for he only professed great concern, and promised she should not get loose again, which promise had been repeatedly broken. Various vows of vengeance had been made, and forgotten. But now Alec Forbes had taken up the cause of humanity and justice: for the brute had bitten Annie, and *she* could have given no provocation.

It was soon understood throughout the school that war was to be made upon Juno, and that every able-bodied boy must be ready when called out by the General. The minute they were dismissed, which, at this season of the year, took place at three o'clock, no interval being given for dinner, because there was hardly any afternoon, the boys gathered in a knot at the door.

"What are you going to do, General?" asked one.

"Kill her," answered Alec.

"How?"

"Stone her to death, lads, like the man that broke the Sabbath."

"Broken bones for broken skins—eh? Ay!"

"The damned horrid brute, to bite Annie Anderson!"

"But there's no stones to be had in the snow, General," said Cadger.

"You blockhead! You'll get more stones than you'll carry, I reckon, up on the side of the toll-road there. Nothing like road-metal!"

A confused chorus of suggestions and exclamations now arose, in the midst of which Willie Macwha, whose cognomen was Curly-pow, came up. He was not often the last in a conspiracy. His arrival had for the moment a sedative effect.

"Here's Curly! Here's Curly!"

"Well, is it all settled?" asked he.

"She's condemned, but not killed yet," said Grumpie.

"How are we to get at her?" asked Cadger.

"That's just the point," said Divot.

"We can hardly kill her in her own yard," suggested Houghie.

"Na. We must bide our time, and take her when she's at large," said the General.

"But who's to know that? and how are we to gather?" asked Cadger, who seemed both of a practical and a despondent turn of mind.

"Now, just hold your tongues, and listen to me," said Alec.

The excited assembly was instantly silent.

"The first thing," began Alec, "is to store plenty of ammunition."

"Ay, ay, General."

"Hold your tongues.—Where had we best stow the stones, Curly?"

"In our yard. They'll never be noticed there."

"That'll do. Some time tonight, you'll all carry what stones you can get—and make sure they're useful ones—to Curly's yard. He'll be looking out for you. And, I say, Curly, doesn't your roof-stone overlook most of the town?"

"Ay, General."

"You can see our house from it—can't you?"

"Ay."

"Weel, ye jist buy a twa three blue lichts. Hae ye ony bawbees?"

"Deil ane, General."

"Hae than, there's fower an' a bawbee for expenses o' the war."

"Thank ye, General."

"Ye hae an auld gun, haena' ye?"

"Ay have I; but she's nearhan' the rivin'."

"Load her to the mou', and lat her rive. We'll may be hear't. But haud weel oot ower frae her. Ye can lay a train, ye ken."

"I s' tak care o' that, General."

"Scrumpie, ye bide no that far frae the draigon's den. Ye jist keep yer ee—nae the crookit ane—upo' her ootgoins an' incomins; or raither, ye luik efter her comin oot, an' we'll a' luik efter her gaein in again. Jist mak a regiment o' yer ain to watch her, and bring ye word o' her proceedins. Ye can easy luik roun the neuk o' the back-yett, an' nobody be a hair the wiser. As sune as ever ye spy her lowse i' the yard be aff wi' ye to Willie Macwha. Syne, Curly, ye fire yer gun, and burn the blue lichts o' the tap o' the hoose; and gin I see or hear the signal, I'll be ower in seven minutes an' a half. Ilka ane o' ye 'at hears, maun luik efter the neist; and sae we'll a' gether at Curly's. Fess yer bags for the stanes, them 'at has bags."

"But gin ye dinna see or hear, for it's a lang road, General?" interposed Cadger.

"Well, just you buy a few blue lights. Have you any pennies?"

"I've none, General."

"Here then, there's four and a penny for expenses of the war."

"Thank you, General."

"You have an old gun, haven't you?"

"Ay, I have, but she's almost burst."

"Load her to the mouth, and let her burst. We'll maybe hear it. But keep well away from her. You can lay a train, you know."

"I'll take care of that, General."

"Scrumpie, you live not far from the dragon's den. You just keep your eye—not the crooked one—upon her outgoings and incomings; or rather, you look after her coming out, and we'll all look after her going in again. Just make a regiment of your own to watch her, and bring word of her proccedings. You can easily look round the corner of the back-gate, and nobody be a hair the wiser. As soon as ever you spy her loose in the yard, be off with you to Willie Macwha. Then, Curly, you fire your gun, and burn the blue lights on the top of the house; and if I see or hear the signal, I'll be over in seven minutes and a half. Every one of you that hears, must look after the next; and so we'll all gather at Curly's. Bring your bags for the stones, those that have bags."

"But if you don't see or hear, for it's a long road, General?" interposed Cadger.

"If I'm not at your yard, Curly, in seven and a half minutes, send Linkum after me. He's the only one of you that can run. It's all that he can do, but he does it well.—When Juno's once out, she's not in a hurry in again."

The boys separated and went home in a state of excitement, which probably, however, interfered very little with their appetites, seeing it was moderated in the mean time by the need and anticipation of their dinners.

The sun set now between two and three o'clock, and there were long forenights to favour the plot. Perhaps their hatred of the dog would not have driven them to such extreme measures, even although she had bitten Annie Anderson, had her master been a favourite, or even generally respected. But Alec knew well enough that the townsfolk were not likely to sympathize with Bruce on the ill-treatment of his cur.

When the dinner and the blazing fire had filled him so full of comfort that he was once more ready to encounter the cold, Alec could stay in the house no longer.

"Where are you going, Alec?" said his mother.

"Into the garden, mamma."

"What can you want in the garden—full of snow?"

"It's just the snow I want, mamma. It won't keep."

And, in another moment, he was under the clear blue night-heaven, with the keen frosty air blowing on his warm cheek, busy with a wheelbarrow and a spade, slicing and shovelling in the snow. He was building a hut of it, after the fashion of the Esquimaux hut, with a very thick circular wall, which began to lean towards its own centre as soon as it began to rise. This hut he had pitched at the foot of a flag-staff on the green—*lawn* would be too grand a word for the hundred square feet in front of his mother's house, though the grass which lay beneath the snowy carpet was very green and lovely grass, smooth enough for any lawn. In summer Alec had quite revelled in its greenness and softness, as he lay on it reading the *Arabian Nights* and the Ettrick Shepherd's stories: now it was "white with the whiteness of what is dead;" for is not the snow just dead water? The flag-staff he had got George Macwha to erect for him, at a very small outlay; and he had himself fitted it with shrouds and a cross-yard, and signal halliards; for he had always a fancy for the sea, and boats, and rigging of all sorts. And he had a great red flag, too, which he used to hoist on special occasions—on market-days and such like; and often besides when a good wind blew. And very grand it looked, as it floated in the tide of the wind.

Often he paused in his work, and turned—and oftener without raising himself he glanced towards the town; but no signal burned from the ridge of Curly's house, and he went on with his labour. When called in to tea, he gave a long wistful look townwards, but saw no sign. Out again he went, but no blue fire rejoiced him that night with the news that Juno was ranging the streets; and he was forced to go to bed at last, and take refuge from his disappointment in sleep.

The next day he strictly questioned all his officers as to the manner in which they had fulfilled their duty, and found no just cause of complaint.

"In future," he said to Curly, with the importance of one who had the affairs of boys and dogs upon his brain—so that his style rose into English—"in future, Curly, you may always know I am at home when you see the red flag flying from my flag-staff."

"That's o' sma' service, General, i' the lang forenichts. A body canna see freely so far."	"That's of small service, General, in the long forenights. You can't see quite so far."
"But Linkum wad see't fleein', lang or he wan to the yett."	"But Linkum would see it flying, long before he reached the gate."
"It wad flee nae mair nor a deid deuke i' this weather. It wad be frozen as stiff's a buird."	"It would fly no more than a dead duck in this weather. It would be frozen as stiff as a board."
"Ye gowk! Do ye think fowk wash their flags afore they hing them oot, like sarks or sheets? Dinna ye be ower clever, Curly, my man."	"You goose! Do you think folk wash their flags before they hang them out, like shirts or sheets? Don't you be too clever, Curly, my man."
Whereupon Curly shut up.	Whereupon Curly shut up.

*****

"What are you in such a state about, Alec?" asked his mother.

"Nothing very particular, mamma," answered Alec, ashamed of his want of self-command.

"You've looked out at the window twenty times in the last half-hour," she persisted.

"Curly promised to burn a blue light, and I wanted to see if I could see it."

Suspecting more, his mother was forced to be content with this answer.

But that night was also passed without sight or sound. Juno kept safe in her barrel, little thinking of the machinations against her in the wide snow-covered country around. Alec finished the Esquimaux hut, and the snow falling all night, the hut looked the next morning as if it had been there all the winter. As it seemed likely that a long spell of white weather had set in, Alec resolved to extend his original plan, and carry a long snow passage, or covered vault, from the lattice-window of a small closet, almost on a level with the ground, to this retreat by the flag-staff. He was hard at work in the execution of this project, on the third night, or rather late afternoon: they called it *forenight* there.

CHAPTER XVII

"What can that be, ma'am, away over the town there?" said Mary to her mistress, as in passing she peeped out of the window, the blind of which Alec had drawn up behind the curtain.

"What is it, Mary?"

"That's just what I don't know, ma'am. It can't be the rory-bories (*aurora borealis*), as Alec calls them. It's too blue.—It's out.—It's in again.—It's not canny.—And, preserve us all! it's cracking as well," cried Mary, as the subdued sound of a far-off explosion reached her.

This was of course no other than the roar of Curly's gun in the act of bursting and vanishing; for neither stock, lock, nor barrel was ever seen again. It left the world like a Norse king on his fire-ship. But, at the moment, Alec was too busy in the depths of his snow-vault to hear or see the signals.

By-and-by a knock came to the kitchen door. Mary went and opened it.

"Alec's at home, I know," said a rosy boy, almost breathless with past speed and present excitement.

"How do you know that, my man?" asked Mary.

"Cause the flag's flying. Where is he?"

"If you know so much about him already, you can just find him yourself!"

"The bitch is out!" panted Linkum.

But Mary shut the door.

"Here's a job!" said Linkum to himself. "I can't go through a shut door. And there's Juno with the run of the whole town. Devil take her!"

But at the moment he heard Alec whistling a favourite tune, as he shovelled away at the snow.

"General!" cried Linkum, in ecstasy.

"Here!" answered Alec, flinging his spade twenty feet from him, and bolting in the direction of the call. "Is it you, Linkum?"

"She's out, General."

"Devil have her, if ever she wins in again, the curst worrying brute! Did you go to Curly?"

"Ay, I did. He fired the gun, and burnt three blue lights, and waited seven minutes and a half; and then he sent me for you, General."

"*Confound* it," cried Alec, and tore through shrubbery and hedge, the nearest way to the road, followed by Linkum, who even at full speed was not a match for Alec. Away they flew like the wind, along the well-beaten path to the town, over the footbridge that crossed the Glamour, and full speed up the hill to Willie

Macwha, who, with a dozen or fifteen more, was anxiously waiting for the commander. They all had their book-bags, pockets, and arms filled with stones lately broken for mending the turnpike road, mostly granite, but partly whinstone and flint. One bag was ready filled for Alec.

"Noo," said the General, in the tone of Gideon of old, "gin ony o' ye be fleyt at the brute, jist gang hame."

"Ay! ay! General."

But nobody stirred, for those who were afraid had slunk away the moment they saw Alec coming up the hill, like the avenger of blood.

"Wha's watchin' her?"

"Doddles, Gapy, and Goat."

"Whaur was she last seen?"

"Takin' up wi' anither tyke on the squaure."

"Doddles 'll be at the pump, to tell whaur's the ither twa and the tyke."

"Come along, then. This is hoo ye're to gang. We maunna a' gang thegither. Some o' ye—you three—doon the Back Wynd; you sax, up Lucky Hunter's Close; and the lave by Gowan Street; an' first at the pump bides for the lave."

"Hoo are we to mak the attack, General?"

"I'll gie my orders as the case may demand," said Alec.

And away they shot.

The muffled sounds of the feet of the various companies as they

Macwha, who, with a dozen or fifteen more, was anxiously waiting for the commander. They all had their book-bags, pockets, and arms filled with stones lately broken for mending the turnpike road, mostly granite, but partly whinstone and flint. One bag was ready filled for Alec.

"Now," said the General, in the tone of Gideon of old, "if any of you be afraid of the brute, just go home."

"Ay! ay! General."

But nobody stirred, for those who were afraid had slunk away the moment they saw Alec coming up the hill, like the avenger of blood.

"Who's watching her?"

"Doddles, Gapy, and Goat."

"Where was she last seen?"

"Taking up with another dog on the square."

"Doddles'll be at the pump, keeping tabs on the other two and the dog."

"Come along, then. This is how you're to go. We mustn't all go together. Some of you—you three—down the Back Wynd; you six, up Lucky Hunter's Close; and the rest by Gowan Street; and first at the pump waits for the rest."

"How are we to make the attack, General?"

"I'll give my orders as the case may demand," said Alec.

And away they shot.

The muffled sounds of the feet of the various companies as they thundered past upon the snow, roused the old wives dozing over their knitting by their fires of spent oak-bark; and according to her temper would be the remark with which each startled dame turned again to her former busy quiescence:—"Some mischeef o' the loons!" "Some ploy o' the laddies!" "Some deevilry o' thae rascals frae Malison's school!"

They reached the square almost together, and found Doddles at the pump; who reported that Juno had gone down the inn-yard, and Gapey and Goat were watching her. Now she must come out to get home again, for there was no back-way; so by Alec's orders they dispersed a little to avoid observation, and drew gradually between the entrance of the inn-yard, and the way Juno would take to go home.

The town was ordinarily lighted at night with oil lamps, but moonlight and snow had rendered them for some time unnecessary.

"Here she is! Here she is!" cried several at once in a hissing whisper of excitement. "Lat at her!"

"Haud still!" cried Alec. "Bide till I tell ye. Dinna ye see there's Lang Tam's dog wi' her, an' he's done naething. Ye maunna punish the innocent wi' the guilty."

A moment after the dogs took their leave of each other, and Juno

thundered past upon the snow, roused the old wives dozing over their knitting by their fires of spent oak-bark; and according to her temper would be the remark with which each startled dame turned again to her former busy quiescence:—"Some mischief of the boys!" "Some ploy of the laddies!" "Some devilry of those rascals from Malison's school!"

They reached the square almost together, and found Doddles at the pump; who reported that Juno had gone down the inn-yard, and Gapey and Goat were watching her. Now she must come out to get home again, for there was no back-way; so by Alec's orders they dispersed a little to avoid observation, and drew gradually between the entrance of the inn-yard, and the way Juno would take to go home.

The town was ordinarily lighted at night with oil lamps, but moonlight and snow had rendered them for some time unnecessary.

"Here she is! Here she is!" cried several at once in a hissing whisper of excitement. "Let at her!"

"Keep still!" cried Alec. "Wait till I tell you. Don't you see there's Long Tam's dog with her, and he's done nothing. You mustn't punish the innocent with the guilty."

A moment after the dogs took their leave of each other, and Juno went, at a slow slouching trot, in the direction of her own street.

"Close in!" cried Alec.

Juno found her way barred in a threatening manner, and sought to pass meekly by.

"Let at her, boys!" cried the General.

A storm of stones was their answer to the order; and a howl of rage and pain burst from the animal. She turned; but found that she was the centre of a circle of enemies.

"Let at her! Keep at her!" bawled Alec.

And thick as hail the well-aimed stones flew from practised hands; though of course in the frantic rushes of the dog to escape, not half of them took effect. She darted first at one and then at another, snapping wildly, and meeting with many a kick and blow in return.

The neighbours began to look out at their shop-doors and their windows; for the boys, rapt in the excitement of the sport, no longer laid any restraint upon their cries. Andrew Constable, the clothier, from his shop-door; Rob Guddle, the barber, from his window, with his face shadowed by Annie's curls; Redford, the bookseller, from the top of the stairs that led to his shop; in short, the whole of the shopkeepers on the square of Glamerton were regarding this battle of odds. The half-frozen place looked half-alive. But none of the good folks cared much to interfere, for flying stones are not pleasant to encounter. And indeed they could not clearly make out what was the matter.—In a minute more, a sudden lull came over the hubbub. They saw all the group gather together in a murmuring knot.

The fact was this. Although cowardly enough now, the brute, infuriated with pain, had made a determined rush at one of her antagonists, and a short hand-to-teeth struggle was now taking place, during which the stoning ceased.

"She has a grip of my leg," said Alec quietly; "and I have a grip of her throat. Curly, put your hand in my coat-pocket, and take out the rope you'll find there."

Curly did as he was desired, and drew out a yard and a half of garden-line.

"Just put it with one single knot round her neck, and a few of you take hold at each end, and pull for your lives!"

They hauled with hearty vigour, Juno's teeth relaxed their hold of Alec's calf; in another minute her tongue was hanging out her mouth, and when they ceased the strain she lay limp on the snow. With a shout of triumph, they started off at full speed, dragging the brute by the neck through the street. Alec essayed to follow them; but found his leg too painful; and was forced to go limping home.

When the victors had run till they were out of breath, they stopped to confer; and the result of their conference was that in solemn silence they drew her home to the back gate, and finding all still in the yard, deputed two of their company to lay the dead body in its kennel.

Curly and Linkum drew her into the yard, tumbled her into her barrel, which they set up on end, undid the string, and left Juno lying neck and tail together in ignominious peace.

Before Alec reached home his leg had swollen very much, and was so painful that he could hardly limp along; for Juno had taken no passing snap, but a great strong mouthful. He concealed his condition from his mother for that night; but next morning his leg was so bad, that there was no longer a possibility of hiding the fact. To tell a lie would have been so hard for Alec, that he had scarcely any merit in not telling one. So there was nothing for it but confession. His mother scolded him to a degree considerably beyond her own sense of the wrong, telling him he would get her into disgrace in the town as the mother of a lawless son, who meddled with other people's property in a way little better than stealing.

"I fancy, mamma, a boy's legs are aboot as much his ain (*own*) property as the dog was Rob Bruce's. It's not the first time she's bitten half a dozen legs that were neither her own nor her master's."

Mrs Forbes could not well answer this argument; so she took advantage of the fact that Alec had, in the excitement of self-defence, lapsed into Scotch.

"Don't talk so vulgarly to me, Alec," she said; "keep that for your ill-behaved companions in the town."

"They are no worse than I am, mamma. *I* was at the bottom of it."

"I never said they were," she answered.

But in her heart she thought if they were not, there was little amiss with them.

CHAPTER XVIII

Alec was once more condemned to the sofa, and Annie had to miss him, and wonder what had become of him. She always felt safe when Alec was there, and when he was not she grew timid; although whole days would sometimes pass without either speaking to the other. But before the morning was over she learned the reason of his absence.

For about noon, when all was tolerably harmonious in the school, the door opened, and the face of Robert Bruce appeared, with gleaming eyes of wrath.

"Lord preserve us!" said Scrumpie to his next neighbour. "We're all in for such a hiding! Here's Rob Bruce! Who's gone and told him?"

But some of the gang of conspirators, standing in a class near the door, stared in horror. Amongst them was Curly. His companions declared afterwards that had it not been for the strength of the curl, his hair would have stood upright. For, following Bruce, led in fact by a string, came an awful apparition—Juno herself, a pitiable mass of caninity—looking like the resuscitated corpse of a dog that had been nine days buried, crowded with lumps, and speckled with cuts, going on three legs, and having her head and throat swollen to a size past recognition.

"She's not dead after all! Devil take her! for he's in her," said Doddles.

"We haven't killed her enough," said Curly.

"I told you, Curly! You had little business loosening the rope. She would have been as dead before the morning as Lucky Gordon's cat whose head you cut off," said Linkum.

"Eh! but she looks bonnie!" said Curly, trying to shake off his dismay. "Man, we'll have it all to do over again. Such fun!"

But he could not help looking a little rueful when Linkum expressed a wish that they were themselves well through with their share of the killing.

And now the storm began to break. The master had gone to the door and shaken hands with his visitor, glancing a puzzled interrogation at the miserable animal in the string, which had just shape enough left to show that it was a dog.

"I'm very sorry, Mister Malison, to come to you with my complaints," said Bruce; "but just look at the poor dumb animal! She couldn't come herself, and so I had to bring her. Stand still, you brute!"

For Juno having caught sight of some boy-legs, through a corner of one eye not quite *bunged up*, began to tug at the string with feeble earnestness—no longer, however, regarding the said legs as made for dogs to bite, but as fearful instruments of vengeance, in league with stones and cords. So the straining and pulling was all homewards. But her master had brought her as chief witness against the boys, and she must remain where she was.

"Eh, lass!" he said, hauling her back by the string; "if you had but the tongue of the prophet's ass, you would soon point out the rascals that harassed you and hurt

"Following Bruce...came an awful apparition—Juno herself, a pitiable mass of caninity..."

you like that. But here's the just judge that'll give you your rights, and that without fee or reward. —Mr Malison, she was one of the bonniest bitches you could set your eye upon—"

A smothered laugh gurgled through the room.

—"till some of your boys—no offence, sir—I know well enough they're not yours, nor a bit like you—some of your pupils, sir, have just driven the soul from her with stones."

"Where does the soul of a bitch live?" asked Goat, in a whisper, of his neighbour.

"Devil knows," answered Gapey; "if it isn't in the bottom of Rob Bruce's belly."

The master's wrath, ready enough to rise against boys and all their works, now showed itself in the growing redness of his face. This was not one of his worst passions—in them, he grew white—for the injury had not been done to himself.

"Can you tell me which of them did it?"

"No, sir. There must have been more than two or three at it, or she would have worried them. The best-natured beast in the town!"

"William Macwha," cried Malison.

"Here, sir."

"Come up."

Willie ascended to the august presence. He had made up his mind that, seeing so many had known all about it, and some of them had turned cowards, it would be of no service to deny the deed.

"Do you know anything about this cruelty to the poor dog, William?" said the master.

Willie gave a Scotchman's answer, which, while evasive, was yet answer and more.

"She bit me, sir."

"When? While you were stoning her?"

"No, sir. A month ago."

"You're a lying wretch, Willie MacWha, as you well know in your own conscience!" cried Bruce. "She's the quietest, kindliest beast that ever was whelped. See, sir; just look you here. She'll let me put my hand in her mouth, and take no more notice than if it was her own tongue."

Now whether it was that the said tongue was still swollen and painful, or that Juno, conscious of her own ill deserts, disapproved of the whole proceeding, I cannot tell; but the result of this proof of her temper was that she made her teeth meet through Bruce's hand.

"Damn the bitch!" he roared, snatching it away with the blood beginning to flow.

A laugh, not smothered this time, billowed and broke through the whole school; for the fact that Bruce should be caught swearing, added to the yet more delightful fact that Juno had bitten her master, was altogether too much.

"Eh! isn't it lucky we didn't kill her after all?" said Curly.

"Good doggie!" said another, patting his own knee, as if to entice her to come and be caressed.

"At him again, Juno!" said a third.

"I'll give her a treat the next time I see her," said Curly.

Bruce, writhing with pain, and mortified at the result of his ocular proof of Juno's incapability of biting, still more mortified at having so far forgotten himself as to utter an oath, and altogether discomfited by the laughter, turned away in confusion.

"It's all their fault, the bad boys! She never did the like before. They've ruined her temper," he said, as he left the school, following Juno, which was tugging away at the string as if she had been a blind man's dog.

"Well, what have you to say for yourself, William?" said Malison.

"She began it, sir."

This best of excuses would not, however, satisfy the master. The punishing mania had possibly taken fresh hold upon him. But he would put more questions first.

"Who besides you tortured the poor animal?"

Curly was silent. He had neither a very high sense of honour, nor any principles to come and go upon; but he had a considerable amount of devotion to his party, which is the highest form of conscience to be found in many.

"Tell me their names, sir?"

Curly was still silent.

But a white-headed urchin, whom innumerable whippings, not bribes, had corrupted, cried out in a wavering voice:

"Sanny Forbes was one of them; and he's not here, 'cause Juno worried him."

The poor creature gained little by his treachery; for the smallest of the conspirators fell on him when school was over, and gave him a thrashing, which he deserved more than ever one of Malison's.

But the effect of Alec's name on the master was talismanic. He changed his manner at once, sent Curly to his seat, and nothing more was heard of Juno or her master.

The opposite neighbours stared across, the next morning, in bewildered astonishment, at the place where the shop of Robert Bruce had been wont to invite the public to enter and buy. Had it been possible for an avalanche to fall like a thunderbolt from the heavens, they would have supposed that one had fallen in the night, and overwhelmed the house. Door and windows were invisible, buried with the rude pavement in front beneath a mass of snow. Spades and shovels in boys' hands had been busy for hours during the night, throwing it up against the house, the door having first been blocked up with a huge ball, which they had rolled in silence the whole length of the long street.

Bruce and his wife slept in a little room immediately behind the shop, that they might watch over their treasures; and Bruce's first movement in the morning was always into the shop to unbolt the door and take down the shutters. His astonishment when he looked upon a blank wall of snow may be imagined. He did not question that the whole town was similarly overwhelmed. Such a snow-storm had never been heard of before, and he thought with uneasy recollection of the oath he had uttered in the school-room; imagining for a moment that the whole of Glamerton lay overwhelmed by the divine wrath, because he had, under the agony of a bite from his own dog, consigned her to a quarter where dogs and children are not admitted. In his bewilderment, he called aloud:

"Nancy! Robbie! Johnnie! We're a' beeriet alive!"

"Preserve's a', Robert! what's happent?" cried his wife, rushing from the kitchen.

"I'm no beeriet, that I ken o'," cried Robert the younger, entering from the yard.

"Nancy! Robbie! Johnnie! We're all buried alive!"

"Preserve us all, Robert! what's happened?" cried his wife, rushing from the kitchen.

"I'm not buried, that I know of," cried Robert the younger, entering from the yard.

His father rushed to the back-door, and, to his astonishment and relief, saw the whole world about him. It was a private judgment, then, upon him and his shop. And so it was—a very private judgment. Probably it was the result of his meditations upon it, that he never after carried complaints to Murdoch Malison.

Alec Forbes had nothing to do with this revenge. But Bruce always thought he was at the bottom of it, and hated him the more. He disliked all *loons* (boys) but his own; for was not the spirit of *loons* the very antipodes to that of money-making? But Alec Forbes he hated, for he was the very antipode to Robert Bruce himself. Mrs Bruce always followed her husband's lead, being capable only of two devotions—the one to her husband and children, the other to the shop.—Of Annie they highly and righteously disapproved, partly because they had to feed her, and partly because she was friendly with Alec. This disapproval rose into dislike after their sons had told them that it was because Juno had bitten her that the boys of the school, with Alec for a leader, had served her as they had. But it was productive of no disadvantage to her; for it could not take any active form because of the money-bond between them, while its negative operation gave rise chiefly to neglect, and so left her more at liberty, to enjoy herself as she could after her own fashion.

For the rest of Juno's existence, the moment she caught sight of a boy she fled as fast as her four bow-legs would carry her, not daring even to let her tail stick out behind her, lest it should afford a handle against her.

CHAPTER XIX

When Annie heard that Alec had been bitten she was miserable. She knew his bite must be worse than hers, or he would not be kept at home. Might she not venture to go and see him again? The modesty of a maidenly child made her fear to intrude; but she could not constrain her feet from following the path to his house. And as it was very dusk, what harm could there be in going just inside the gate, and on to the green? Through the parlour windows she saw the fire burning bright, and a shadow moving across the walls and the ceiling; but she could not make up her mind to knock at the door, for she was afraid of Mrs Forbes, notwithstanding her kindness. So she wandered on—for here there was no dog—wondering what that curious long mound of snow, with the round heap at the end, by the flag-staff, could be? What could Alec have made it for? Examining it closely all along, she came to the end of it next the house, and looking round, saw that it was hollow. Without a moment's thought, for she had no fear of Alec, she entered. The passage was dark, but she groped her way, on and on, till she came to the cell at the end. Here a faint ghostly light glimmered; for Alec had cleared a small funnel upwards through the roof, almost to the outside, so that a thin light filtered through a film of snow. This light being reflected from the white surface of the cave, showed it all throbbing about her with a faint bluish white, ever and anon whelmed in the darkness and again glimmering out through its folds. She seated herself on a ledge of snow that ran all round the foundation. It was not so cold here as in the outer air, where a light frosty wind was blowing across the world of snow. And she had not sat long, before, according to her custom when left to herself, she fell fast asleep.

Meantime Alec, his mother having gone to the town, was sitting alone, finishing, by the light of the fire, the last of a story. At length the dreariness of an ended tale was about him, and he felt the inactivity to which he had been compelled all day no longer tolerable. He would go and see how his snow-chamber looked by candlelight. His mother had told him not to go out; but that, he reasoned, could hardly be called going out, when there was not more than a yard of open air to cross. So he got a candle, was out of the window in a moment, notwithstanding his lameness, and crept through the long vault of snow towards the inmost recess. As he approached the end he started. Could he believe his eyes? A figure was there—motionless—dead perhaps. He went on—he went in—and there he saw Annie, leaning against the white wall, with her white face turned up to the frozen ceiling. She might have been the frost-queen, the spirit that made the snow, and built the hut, and dwelt in it; for all the powers that vivify nature must be children. The popular imagination seems to have caught this truth, for all the fairies and gnomes and goblins, yes, the great giants too, are only different sizes, shapes, and characters of children. But I have wandered from Alec's thoughts into my own. He knew it was Annie, and no strange creature of the elements. And if he had not come, she might have slept on till her sleep was too deep for any voice of the world to rouse her.

It was, even then, with difficulty that he woke her. He took hold of her hands, but she did not move. He sat down, took her in his arms, spoke to her—got frightened and shook her, but she would not open her eyes. Her long dark eyelashes sloped still upon her white cheek, like the low branches of a cedar upon the lawn at its foot. But he knew she was not dead yet, for he could feel her heart beating. At length she lifted her eyelids, looked up in his face, gave a low happy laugh, like the laugh of a dreaming child, and was fast asleep again in a moment.

Alec hesitated no longer. He rose with her in his arms, carried her into the parlour, and laid her down on the rug before the fire, with a sofa-pillow under her head. There she might have her sleep out. When Mrs Forbes came home she found Alec reading, and Annie sleeping by the fireside. Before his mother had recovered from her surprise, and while she was yet staring at the lovely little apparition, Alec had the first word.

"Mamma!" he said, "I found her sleeping in my snow hut there; and if I had not brought her in, she would have been dead by this time."

"Poor little darling!" thought Mrs Forbes; but she was Scotch, and therefore she did not say it. But she stooped, and drew the child back from the fire, lest she should have her face scorched, and after making the tea, proceeded to put off her bonnet and shawl. By the time she had got rid of them, Annie was beginning to move, and Alec rose to go to her.

"Let her alone," said his mother. "Let her come to herself by degrees. Come to the table."

Alec obeyed. They could see that Annie had opened her eyes, and lay staring at the fire. What was she thinking about? She had fallen asleep in the snow-hut, and here she was by a bright fire!

"Annie, dear, come to your tea," were the first words she heard. She rose and went, and sat down at the table with a smile, taking it all as the gift of God, or a good dream, and never asking how she had come to be so happy.

CHAPTER XX

The spirit of mischief had never been so thoroughly aroused in the youth of Glamerton as it was this winter. The snow lay very deep, while almost every day a fresh fall added to its depth, and this rendered some of their winter-amusements impossible; while not many of them had the imagination of Alec Forbes to suggest new ones. At the same time the cold increased, and strengthened their impulses to muscular exertion.

"Those boys are just growing perfect devils," said Charlie Chapman, the wool-carder, as he bolted into his own shop, with the remains of a snowball melting down the back of his neck. "We must have another constable to keep them in order."

The existing force was composed of one long-legged, short-bodied, middle-aged man, who was so slow in his motions, apparently from the weight of his feet, which were always dragging behind him, that the boys called him Stumpin' Steenie (*dim. for "Stephen"*), and stood in no more awe of him than they did of his old cow—which, her owner being a widower, they called *Mrs Stephen*—when she went up the street, hardly able to waddle along for the weight of her udder. So there was some little ground for the wool-carder's remark. How much a second constable would have availed, however, is doubtful.

"I never saw such gallows-birds!" chimed in a farmer's wife who was standing in the shop. "They had a rope across the West Wynd in the snow, and down I came on my nose, as sure's your name's Charles Chapman—and more of my legs out of my coats, I suspect, than was altogether to my credit."

"I'm sure you can have no reason to be ashamed of your legs, goodwife," was the gallant rejoinder; to which their owner replied, with a laugh:

"They weren't made for public inspection, anyway."

"Heavens! Nobody saw them. I'm sure you didn't lie long! But those boys—they're just past all! Did you hear how they served Rob Bruce?"

"Faith! they tell me they all but buried him alive."

"Oh! ay. But it's a later story, the last."

"It's a pity there aren't a dozen or two of them in Abraham's bosom.—What did they do to him next?"

Here Andrew Constable dropped in, and Chapman turned towards him with the question:

"Did *you* hear, Mr Constable, what the boys did to Robert Bruce the night before last?"

"No. What was that? They have a spite at poor Rob, I believe."

"Well, it didn't look altogether like respect, I must admit.—I was standing at the counter of his shop waiting for an ounce of snuff; and Robert he was serving a child over the counter with a pennyworth of treacle, when, in a jiffey, there came such a blast, and a smoke fit to smother you, out of the fire, and the shop was full of smoke, before you could have put the point of one thumb upon the point of the other.

'Preserve us all!' cried Rob; but before he could say another word, through the house, shuffling in her slippers, comes Nancy, running, and opens the door with a screech: 'Preserve us all!' says she, 'Robert, the chimney's on fire!' And faith! between the two smokes, to sunder them, there was nothing but Nancy herself. The house was as full as it could hold, from cellar to garret, of the blackest smoke that ever crept out of coal. Out we ran, and it was a sight to see the man with his long neck looking up at the chimneys. But devil a spark came out of them—or smoke either, for that matter. It was easy to see what was amiss. The boys had been on the roof, and flung a handful of blasting powder down every smoking chimney, and then clapped a turf or a sod upon the mouth of it. None of them were in sight, but I doubt if any of them were far away. There was nothing for it but get a ladder, and just go up and take off the pot-lids. But eh! poor Robert was just ramping with rage! Not that he said much, for he hardly dared open his mouth for swearing; and Robert wouldn't swear, you know; but he was neither to hold nor bind."

"What laddies were they, Charles, do you know?" asked Andrew.

"There's a heap of them up to tricks. If I haven't the rheumatics screwing away between my shoulders tonight it won't be their faults;

their fau'ts; for as I cam' ower frae the ironmonger's there, I jist got a ba' i' the how o' my neck, 'at amaist sent me howkin' wi' my snoot i' the snaw. And there it stack, and at this preceese moment it's rinnin' doon the sma' o' my back as gin 't war a burnie doon a hillside. We maun hae mair constables!"

"Hoot! toot! Charles. Ye dinna want a constable to dry yer back. Gang to the gudewife wi' 't," said Andrew, "she'll gie ye a dry sark. Na, na. Lat the laddies work it aff. As lang's they haud their han's frae what doesna belang to them, I dinna min' a bit ploy noo and than. They'll no turn oot the waur men for a pliskie or twa."

for as I came over from the ironmonger's there, I just got a ball in the how (*hollow*) of my neck, that almost sent me digging with my snout in the snow. And there it stuck, and at this very moment it's running down the small of my back as if it were a stream down a hillside. We must have more constables!"

"Nonsense! Charles. You don't want a constable to dry your back. Go to the goodwife with it," said Andrew, "she'll give you a dry shirt. Na, na. Let the laddies work it off. As long as they keep their hands from what doesn't belong to them, I don't mind a wee frolic now and then. They won't turn out the worse men for a prank or two."

The fact was, none of the boys would have dreamed of interfering with Andrew Constable. Everybody respected him; not because he was an elder of the kirk, but because he was a good-tempered, kindly, honest man; or to sum up all in one word—*a douce child*—by which word *douce* is indicated every sort of propriety of behaviour—a virtue greatly esteemed by the Scotch. This adjective was universally applied to Andrew.

While Alec was confined to the house, he had been busy inventing all kinds of employments for the period of the snow. His lessons never occupied much of his thoughts, and no pains having yet been taken to discover in what direction his tastes inclined him, he had of course to cater for himself. The first day of his return, when school was over, he set off rejoicing in his freedom, for a ramble through the snow, still revolving what he was to do next; for he wanted some steady employment with an end in view. In the course of his solitary walk, he came to the Wan Water, the other river that flowed through the wide valley—and wan enough it was now with its snow-sheet over it! As he stood looking at its still, dead face, and lamenting that the snow lay too deep over the ice to admit of skating, by a sudden reaction, a summer-vision of the live water arose before him; and he thought how delightful it would be to go sailing down the sparkling ripples, with the green fields all about him, and the hot afternoon sun over his head. That would be better even than scudding along it on his skates. His next thought was at once an idea and a resolve. Why should he not build a boat? He *would* build a boat. He would set about it directly.—Here was work for the rest of the winter!

His first step must be to go home and have his dinner; his next—to consult George Macwha, who had been a ship-carpenter in his youth. He would run over in the evening before George should have dropped work, and commit the plan to his judgment.

In the evening, then, Alec reached the town, on his way to George Macwha. It was a still lovely night, clear and frosty, with—yes, there were—millions of stars overhead. Away in the north, the streamers were shooting hither and thither, with marvellous evanescence and re-generation. No dance of goblins could be more lawless in its grotesqueness than this dance of the northern lights in their ethereal beauty, shining, with a wild ghostly changefulness and feebleness, all colours at once; now here, now there, like a row of slender organ-pipes, rolling out and in and along the sky. Or they might have been the chords of some gigantic stringed instrument, which chords became visible only when mighty hands of music struck their keys and set them vibrating; so that, as the hands swept up and down the Titanic key-board, the chords themselves seemed to roll along the heavens, though in truth some vanished here and others appeared yonder. Up and down they darted, and away and back—and always in the direction he did not expect them to take. He thought he heard them crackle, and he stood still to listen; but he could not be sure that it was not the snow sinking and *crisping* beneath his feet. All around him was still as a world too long frozen: in the heavens alone was there motion. There this entrancing dance of colour and shape went on, wide beneath, and tapering up to the zenith! Truly there was revelry in heaven! One might have thought that a prodigal son had just got home, and that the music and the dancing had begun, of which only the far-off rhythmic shine could reach the human sense; for a dance in heaven might well show itself in colour to the eyes of men.—Alec went on till the lights from the windows of the town began to throw shadows across the snow. The street was empty. From end to end nothing moved but an occasional shadow. As he came near to Macwha's shop, he had to pass a row of cottages which stood with their backs to a steep slope. Here too all was silent as a frozen city.

But when he was about opposite the middle of the row, he heard a stifled laugh, and then a kind of muffled sound as of hurrying steps, and, in a moment after, every door in the row was torn open, and out bolted the inhabitants—here an old woman, halting on a stick as she came, there a shoemaker, with last and awl in his hands, here a tailor with his shears, and there a whole family of several trades and ages. Every one rushed into the middle of the road, turned right round and looked up. Then arose such a clamour of tongues, that it broke on the still air like a storm.

"What's ado, Betty?" asked Alec of a decrepit old creature, bent almost double with rheumatism, who was trying hard to see something or other in the air or on the roof of her cottage.

But before she could speak, the answer came in another form, addressing itself to his nose instead of his ears. For out of the cottages floated clouds of smoke, pervading the air with a variety of scents—of burning oak-bark, of burning leather-cuttings, of damp fire-wood and peat, of the cooking of red herrings, of the boiling of porridge, of the baking of oat-cake, &c., &c. Happily for all the inhabitants, "thae deevils o' loons" (*those devils of boys*) had used no powder here.

But the old woman, looking round when Alec spoke, and seeing that he was one of the obnoxious school-boys, broke out thus:

"Gang an' tak the divot aff o' my lum, Alec, there's a good laad! Ye sudna play sic tricks on puir auld bodies like me, near brackin' in twa wi' the rheumateeze. I'm jist greetin' wi' the reek i' my auld een."

And as she spoke she wiped her eyes with her apron.

"Go and take the turf off my chimney, Alec, there's a good lad! You shouldn't play such tricks on poor old bodies like me, near breaking in two with the rheumatics. I'm just crying with the smoke in my old eyes."

And as she spoke she wiped her eyes with her apron.

Alec did not wait to clear himself of an accusation so gently put, but was on the roof of Luckie Lapp's cottage before she had finished her appeal to his generosity. He took the "divot aff o' her lum" (*turf off her chimney*) and pitched it half way down the brae, at the back of the cottage. Then he scrambled from one chimney to the other, and went on pitching the sods down the hill. At length two of the inhabitants, who had climbed up at the other end of the row, met him, and taking him for a repentant sinner at best, made him prisoner, much to his amusement, and brought him down, protesting that it was too bad of gentle-folk's sons to persecute the poor in that way.

"I didn't do it," said Alec.
"Don't lie," was the curt rejoinder.
"I'm not lying."
"Who did it, then?"
"I can guess; and it shan't happen again, if I can help it."
"Tell us who did it, then."
"I won't say names."
"He's one of them."
"The foul thief take him! I'll give him a hiding," said a burly sutor (*shoemaker*) coming up. "Those boys aren't to be borne with any longer."
And he caught Alec by the arm.
"I didn't do it," persisted Alec.
"Who killed Rob Bruce's dog?" asked the sutor, squeezing Alec's arm to point the question.
"I did," answered Alec; "and I will do yours the same good turn, if he worries children."
"And quite right, too!" said the sutor's wife. "Let him go, Donal. I'm sure he's not one of them."
"Tell us all about it, then. How came you up there?"
"I went up to take the turf off Lucky Lapp's chimney. Ask her. Once up I thought I might give the rest of you a good turn, and this is all I get for it."
"Well, well! Come in and get warmed, then," said the shoemaker, convinced at last.
So Alec went in and had a chat with them, and then went on to George Macwha's.
The carpenter took to his scheme at once. Alec was a fair

hand at all sorts of tool-work; and being on the friendliest terms with Macwha, it was soon arranged that the keel should be laid in the end of the workshop, and that, under George's directions, and what help Willie chose to render, Alec should build his boat himself. Just as they concluded these preliminaries, in came Willie, wiping some traces of blood from his nose. He made a pantomimic gesture of vengeance at Alec.

"What have you been up to now, laddie?" asked his father.

"Alec's just given me a bloody nose," said Willie.

"How did that happen? You well deserved it, I have no doubt. Just give him another when he wants it, Alec."

"What do you mean, Curly?" asked Alec in amazement.

"That turf you threw off Luckie Lapp's roof," said Curly, "came right on the back of my head, as I lay on the hill, and drove the blood out at my nose. That's all. You'll pretend you didn't see me, no doubt."

"I say, Curly," said Alec, putting his arm round his shoulders, and leading him aside, "we must have no more of this kind of work. It's a damned shame! Do you see no difference between choking an ill-favoured cur and choking a poor widow's chimney?"

"It was only for fun."

"It's poor fun that both sides can't laugh at, Curly."

"Rob Bruce wasna lauchin' whan he brocht the bick to the schuil, nor yet whan he gaed hame again."

"That was nae fun, Curly. That was doonricht earnest."

"Weel, weel, Alec; say nae mair aboot it."

"No more I will. But gin I was you, Curly, I wad tak Lucky a seck o' spales the morn."

"I'll tak them the nicht, Alec.—Father, hae ye an auld seck ony gait?"

"There's ane up i' the laft. What want ye wi' a seck?"

But Curly was in the loft almost before the question had left his father's lips. He was down again in a moment, and on his knees filling the sack with shavings and all the chips he could find.

"Gie's a han' up wi't, Alec," he said.

And in a moment more Curly was off to Widow Lapp with his bag of firing.

"He's a fine chield that Willie o' yours, George," said Alec to the father. "He only wants to hae a thing weel pitten afore him, an' he jist acts upo' 't direckly."

"It's weel he maks a cronie o' you, Alec. There's a heap o' mischeef in him. Whaur's he aff wi thae spells?"

Alec told the story, much to the satisfaction of George, who could appreciate the repentance of his son; although he was "nane o' the

"Rob Bruce wasn't laughing when he brought the bitch to the school, nor yet when he went home again."

"That was no fun, Curly. That was downright earnest."

"Well, well, Alec; say no more about it."

"No more I will. But if I were you, Curly, I would take Lucky a sack of spales tomorrow."

"I'll take them tonight, Alec.—Father, have you an old sack anywhere?"

"There's one up in the loft. What do you want with a sack?"

But Curly was in the loft almost before the question had left his father's lips. He was down again in a moment, and on his knees filling the sack with shavings and all the chips he could find.

"Give me a hand up with it, Alec," he said.

And in a moment more Curly was off to Widow Lapp with his bag of firing.

"He's a fine lad that Willie of yours, George," said Alec to the father. "He only wants to have a thing put well before him, and he just acts upon it at once."

"It's well he makes a friend of you, Alec. There's a heap of mischief in him. Where's he off to with those spales?"

Alec told the story, much to the satisfaction of George, who could appreciate the repentance of his son; although he was "nane o' the unco guid"[1] himself. From that day he thought more of his son, and of Alec as well.

"Now, Curly," said Alec, as soon as he re-appeared with the empty sack, "your father's going to let me build a boat, and you must help me."

"What's the use of a boat in this weather?" said Curly.

"You blockhead!" returned his father; "you never look an inch before the point of your own nose. You wouldn't think of a boat before the spring; and faith! the summer would be over, and the water frozen again, before you had it built. Look at Alec there. He's worth ten of you."

"I know that every bit as well as you do, father. Just set us off with it, father."

"I can't attend to it just now; but I'll get you started with it tomorrow night."

So here was an end to the troubles of the townsfolks from the *loons*, and without any increase of the constabulary force; for Curly being withdrawn, there was no one else of sufficiently inventive energy to take the lead, and the loons ceased to be dangerous to the peace of the community. Curly soon had both his head and his hands quite occupied with boat-building.

---

1   NANE O' THE UNCO GUID (Scots): none of the rigidly righteous

CHAPTER XXI

Every afternoon, now, the moment dinner was over, Alec set off for the workshop, and did not return till eight o'clock, or sometimes later. Mrs Forbes did not at all relish this change in his habits; but she had the good sense not to interfere.

One day he persuaded her to go with him, and see how the boat was getting on. This enticed her into some sympathy with his new pursuit. For there was the boat—a skeleton it is true, and not nearly ready yet for the clothing of its planks, or its final skin of paint—yet an undeniable boat to the motherly eye of hope. And there were Alec and Willie working away before her eyes, doing their best to fulfil the promise of its looks. A little quiet chat she had with George Macwha, in which he poured forth the praises of her boy, did not a little, as well, to reconcile her to his desertion of her.

"Indeed, ma'am," said George, whose acquaintance with Scripture was neither extensive nor precise, "to my mind he's just a fulfilment of the prophecy, 'An old head upon young shoulders;' though I can't quite remember which of the lesser prophets it is that contains it."

But Mrs Forbes never saw a little figure, lying in a corner, half-buried in wood-shavings, and utterly unconscious of her presence, being fast asleep.

This was, of course, Annie Anderson, who having heard of the new occupation of her hero, had, one afternoon, three weeks before Mrs Forbes's visit, found herself at George's shop door, she hardly knew how. It seemed to her that she had followed her feet, and they had taken her there before she knew where they were going. Peeping in, she watched Alec and Willie for some time at their work, without venturing to show herself. But George, who came up behind her as she stood, and perceived her interest in the operations of the boys, took her by the hand, and led her in, saying kindly:

"Here's a new apprentice, Alec. She wants to learn boat-biggin."

"Ou! Annie, is that you, lassie? Come awa'," said Alec. "There's a fine heap o' spales ye can sit upo', and see what we're aboot."

And so saying he seated her on the shavings, and half-buried her with an armful more to keep her warm.

"Put to the door, Willie," he added. "She'll be cauld. She's no workin', ye see."

Whereupon Willie shut the door, and Annie found herself very comfortable indeed. There she sat, in perfect contentment, watching the progress of the boat—a progress not very perceptible to her inexperienced eyes, for the building of a boat is like the building of a city or the making of a book: it turns out a boat at last. But after she had sat for a good while in silence, she looked up at Alec, and said:

"Is there naething I can do to help ye, Alec?"

"Naething, Annie. Lassies canna saw or plane, ye ken. Ye wad tak' aff yer ain lugs in a jiffey."

Again she was silent for a long time; and then, with a sigh, she looked up and said:

"Alec, I'm so cauld!"

"I'll bring my plaid to row ye in the morn's nicht."

Annie's heart bounded for joy; for here was what amounted to an express invitation for to-morrow.

"But," Alec went on, "come wi' me, and we'll sune get ye warm again. Gie's yer han'."

"Nothing, Annie. Lassies can't saw or plane, you know. You would take off your own ears in a jiffey."

Again she was silent for a long time; and then, with a sigh, she looked up and said:

"Alec, I'm so cold!"

"I'll bring my plaid to wrap you in tomorrow night."

Annie's heart bounded for joy; for here was what amounted to an express invitation for to-morrow.

"But," Alec went on, "come with me, and we'll soon get you warm again. Give me your hand."

Annie gave Alec her hand; and he lifted her out of her heap of spales, and led her away. She never thought of asking where he was leading her. They had not gone far down the *close*, when a roaring sound fell upon her ear, growing louder and louder as they went on; till, turning a sharp corner, there they saw the smithy fire. The door of the smithy was open, and they could see the smith at work some distance off. The fire glowed with gathered rage at the impudence of the bellows blowing in its face. The huge smith, with one arm flung affectionately over the shoulder of the insulting party, urged it to the contest; while he stirred up the other to increased ferocity, by poking a piece of iron into the very middle of it. How the angry glare started out of it and stared all the murky *smiddy* in the face, showing such gloomy holes and corners in it, and such a lot of horse-shoes hung up close to the roof, ready to be fitted for unbelievable horse-wear; and making the smith's face and bare arms glow with a dusky red, like hot metal, as if he were the gnome-king of molten iron. Then he stooped, and took up some coal dust in a little shovel, and patted it down over the fire, and blew stronger than ever, and the sparks flew out with the rage of the fire. Annie was delighted to look at it; but there was a certain fierceness about the whole affair that made her shrink from going nearer; and she could not help feeling a little afraid of the giant smith in particular, with his brawny arms that twisted and tortured iron bars all day long,—and his black angry-looking face, that seemed for ever fighting with fire and stiff-necked metal. His very look into the forge-fire ought to have been enough to put it out of countenance. Perhaps that was why it was so necessary to keep blowing and poking at it. Again he stooped, caught up a great iron spoon, dipped it into a tub of water, and poured the spoonful on the fire—a fresh insult, at which it hissed and sputtered, like one of the fiery flying serpents of which she had read in her Bible—gigantic, dragon-like creatures to her imagination—in a perfect insanity of fury. But not the slightest motion of her hand lying in Alec's, indicated reluctance, as he led her into the shop, and right up to the wrathful man, saying:

"Peter Whaup, here's a lassie that's almost frozen to death with cold. Will you take her in and let her stand by your chimney-corner, and warm herself?"

"I'll do that, Alec. Come on in, my child. What do they call you?"

"Annie Anderson."

"Oh, ay! I know all about you well enough. You can leave her with me, Alec; I'll look after her."

"I must go back to my boat, Annie," said Alec, then, apologetically, "but I'll come in for you again."

So Annie was left with the smith, of whom she was not the least afraid, now that she had heard him speak. With his leathern apron, caught up in both hands, he swept a space on the front of the elevated hearth of the forge, clear of cinders and dust, and then, having wiped his hands on the same apron, lifted the girl as tenderly as if she had been a baby, and set her down on this spot, about a yard from the fire, on a level with it; and there she sat, in front of the smith, looking at the fire and the smith and the work he was about, in turns. He asked her a great many questions about herself and the Bruces, and her former life at home; and every question he asked he put in a yet kindlier voice. Sometimes he would stop in the middle of blowing, and lean forward with his arm on the handle of the bellows, and look full in the child's face till she had done answering him, with eyes that shone in the firelight as if the tears would have gathered, but could not for the heat.

"Ay! ay!" he would say, when she had answered him, and resume his blowing, slowly and dreamily. For this terrible smith's heart was just like his fire. He was a dreadful fellow for fighting and quarrelling when he got a drop too much, which was rather too often, if the truth must be told; but to this little woman-child his ways were as soft and tender as a woman's: he could burn or warm.

"And so you liked being at the farm best?" he said.

"Ay. But you see my father died—"

"I know that, my child. The Lord keep a grip of you!"

It was not often that Peter Whaup indulged in a pious ejaculation. But this was a genuine one, and may be worth recording for the sake of Annie's answer:

"I'm thinking he keeps a grip of us all, Mr Whaup."

And then she told him the story about the rats and the cat; for hardly a day passed just at this time without her not merely recalling it, but reflecting upon it. And the smith drew the back of his hand across both his eyes when she had done, and then pressed them both hard with the thumb and forefinger of his right hand, as if they ached, while his other arm went blowing away as if nothing was the matter but plenty of wind for the forge-fire. Then he pulled out the red-hot *gad*, or iron bar, which he seemed to have forgotten ever since Annie came in, and, standing with his back to her to protect her from the sparks, put it on his anvil, and began to lay on it, as if in a fury; while the sparks flew from his blows as if in mortal terror of the angry man that was pelting at the luminous glory laid thus submissive before him. In fact, Peter was attempting to hammer out more things than one, upon that *study* of his; for in Scotland they call a smith's anvil a study, so that he ranks with other artists in that respect. Then, as if anxious to hear the child speak yet again, he said, putting the iron once more in the fire, and proceeding to rouse the wrath of the coals:

"You knew James Dow, then?"

"Ay; very well. I knew Dooie as well as Broonie."

"Who was Broonie?"

"Oh! nobody but my own cow."

"And James was kind to you?"

To this question no reply followed; but Peter, who stood looking at her, saw her lips and the muscles of her face quivering an answer, which if uttered at all, could come only in sobs and tears.

But the sound of approaching steps and voices restored her equanimity, and a listening look gradually displaced the emotion on her countenance. Over the half-door of the shop appeared two men, each bearing on his shoulder the socks (*shares*) of two ploughs, to be sharpened, or set. The instant she saw them she tumbled off her perch, and before they had got the door opened was half way to it, crying, "Dooie! Dooie!" Another instant and she was lifted high in Dowie's arms.

"My little mistress!" exclaimed he, kissing her. "How did you come here?"

"I'm safe enough here, Dooie; don't be scared. I'll tell you all about it. Alec's in George MacWha's shop there."

"And who's Alec?" asked Dowie.

Leaving them now to their private communications, I will relate, for the sake of its result, what passed between James Dow's companion and the smith.

"The last time," said the youth, "that you set my sock, Peter Whaup, you turned it out just as soft as putty, and it wore out rather sooner."

"Heavens! man, you mistake. It wasn't the sock. It was the head that came behind it, and didn't know how to keep it off the stones."

"Ha! ha! ha! My head's not as soft as your own. It's not roasting all day like yours, till it's scorched and singed like a sheep's. Just give me a hold of the tongs, and I'll set my sock to my own mind."

Peter gave up the tongs at once, and the young fellow proceeded to put the share in the fire, and to work the bellows.

"You'll never make anything of it that way," said Peter, as he took the tongs from his hand, and altered the position of the share for him. "You would have it black upon one side, and white on the other. Go steady now, and don't blow the fire off the forge."

But when it came to the anvil part of the work, Peter found so many faults with the handling and the execution generally, that at length the lad threw down the tongs with a laugh and an oath intermingled, saying:

"You can make putty of it yourself, then, Peter.—You just remind me of the Waesome Carl."[1]

"What's that, Rory, man?"

"Oh! nothing but a wee song I came upon the other day in the corner of an old newspaper."

"Let's hear it," said Peter. "Sing it, Rory. You're better known for a good song than for setting socks."

"I can't sing it, for I don't know the tune. I only got a glimpse of it, as I tell you, in an old paper."

"Well, say it, then. You're as well known for a good memory, as a good song."

Without more preamble, Rory repeated, with appropriate gesture,

THE WAESOME CARL

There cam a man to oor toon en',
   An' a waesome carl was he;
Wi' a snubbert nose, an' a crookit mou',
   An' a cock in his left ee.

---

[1] WAESOME CARL (Scots): Woesome Man

And muckle he spied, and muckle he spak';
   But the burden o' his sang
Was aye the same, and ower again:
   There's nane o' ye a' but's wrang.
      Ye're a' wrang, and a' wrang,
        And a'thegither a' wrang;
        There's no a man aboot the toon,
        But's a'thegither a' wrang.

That's no the gait to bake the breid,
   Nor yet to brew the yill;
That's no the gait to haud the pleuch,
   Nor yet to ca the mill.
That's no the gait to milk the coo,
   Nor yet to spean the calf;
Nor yet to fill the girnel-kist—
   Ye kenna yer wark by half.
      Ye're a' wrang, &c.

The minister wasna fit to pray,
   And lat alane to preach;
He nowther had the gift o' grace,
   Nor yet the gift o' speech.
He mind 't him o' Balaam's ass,
   Wi' a differ ye may ken:
The Lord he open'd the ass's mou'
   The minister open'd 's ain.
      He's a' wrang &c.

The puir precentor cudna sing,
   He gruntit like a swine;
The verra elders cudna pass
   The ladles till his min'.
And for the rulin' elder's grace,
   It wasna worth a horn;
He didna half uncurse the meat,
   Nor pray for mair the morn.
      He's a' wrang, &c.

And aye he gied his nose a thraw,
 And aye he crookit his mou';
And aye he cockit up his ee,
 And said, "Tak' tent the noo."
We leuch ahint our loof, man,
 And never said him nay:
And aye he spak'—jist lat him speik!
 And aye he said his say:
   Ye're a' wrang, &c.

Quo' oor guidman: "The crater's daft;
 But wow! he has the claik;
Lat's see gin he can turn a han'
 Or only luik and craik.
It's true we maunna lippen till him—
 He's fairly crack wi' pride;
But he maun live, we canna kill him—
 Gin he can work, he s' bide."
   He was a' wrang, &c.

It's true it's but a laddie's turn,
 But we'll begin wi' a sma' thing;
There's a' thae weyds to gather an' burn—
 An' he's the man for a' thing."
We gaed oor wa's, and loot him be,
 To do jist as he micht;
We think to hear nae mair o' him,
 Till we come hame at nicht;
   But we're a' wrang, &c.

For, losh! or it was denner-time,
 The lift was in a low;
The reek rase up, as it had been
 Frae Sodom-flames, I vow.
We ran like mad; but corn and byre
 War blazin'—wae's the fell!
As gin the deil had broucht the fire,
 To mak' anither hell.
   'Twas a' wrang, &c.

And by the blaze the carl stud,
  Wi's han's aneath his tails;
And aye he said—"I tauld ye sae,
  An' ye're to blame yersels.
It's a' your wite, for ye're a' wrang—
  Ye'll maybe own't at last:
What gart ye burn thae deevilich weyds,
  Whan the win' blew frae the wast?
      Ye're a' wrang, and a' wrang,
      And a'thegither a' wrang;
      There's no a man in a' the warl'
      But's a'thegither a' wrang."

ENGLISH

There came a man to our town-end,
  Saying "All the world's awry!"
With a great snub-nose, and a crooked mouth,
  And a cock in his left eye.
And ever he spied, and ever he spoke;
  But the burden of his song
Was still the same, and over again:
  There's none of you all but's wrong.
      You're all wrong, and all wrong,
      And altogether all wrong;
      There's not a man about the town,
      But's altogether all wrong.

That's not the way to bake the bread,
  Nor yet to brew the beer;
That's not the way to hold the plough,
  Nor yet the mill to steer.
That's not the way to milk the cow,
  Nor yet to wean the calf;
Nor yet to fill the meal-chest up—
  You don't know your work by half.
      You're all wrong, &c.

The minister wasn't fit to pray,
  And let alone to preach;
He neither had the gift of grace,
  Nor yet the gift of speech.
He made him think of Balaam's ass,
  With a difference often known:
The Lord he opened the ass's mouth
  The minister opened his own.
      He's all wrong, &c.

The poor precentor couldn't sing,
  He grunted like a swine;
The very elders couldn't pass
  The ladles to his mind.
And for the ruling elder's grace,
  It filled his soul with sorrow;
He didn't half uncurse the meat,
  Nor pray more for the morrow.
      He's all wrong, &c.

And still he gave his nose a twist,
  And down turned his mouth and brow;
And still he raised a scornful eye,
  And said, "Be careful, now!"
We laughed behind our hands, man,
  And never said him nay:
And still he spoke—just let him speak!
  And still he said his say:
      You're all wrong, &c.

Said our Goodman: "The fellow's daft;
  But wow! for talk he's fine;
Let's see if he can turn a hand
  Or only look and whine.
It's true we'll put no faith in him—
  He's fairly cracked with pride;
But yet, we can't do scathe to him—
  If he can work, he can bide.
      He was all wrong, &c.

It's true it's but a laddie's turn,
    But we'll begin with a small thing;
There's all those weeds to gather and burn—
    And he's the man for all things."
We went our ways, and let him be,
    To do just as he might;
We think to hear no more of him,
    Till we come home at night;
        But we're all wrong, &c.

For, Lord! ere it was dinner-time,
    The sky was all afire;
The smoke rose up, as it had been
    From Sodom's ancient pyre.
We ran like mad, but corn and byre
    Were blazing—woe befell!
As if the devil had brought the fire,
    To make another hell.
        'Twas all wrong, &c.

And by the blaze the fellow stood,
    With his hands beneath his tails;
And still he said—"I told you so,
    For nothing you do avails.
It's all your fault, for you're all wrong—
    Perhaps now you'll confess:
What made you burn those devilish weeds,
    When the wind blew from the west?
        You're all wrong, and all wrong,
        And altogether all wrong,
        There's not a man in all the world
        But's altogether all wrong."

Before the recitation was over, which was performed with considerable spirit and truth, Annie and Dowie were listening attentively, along with Alec, who had returned to take Annie back, and who now joined loudly in the applause which followed the conclusion of the verses.

"Faith, that was a man to avoid," said Alec to Rory. "And you said the song well. You should learn to sing it though."

"Maybe I will, some day; if I could but get a wee grain of salt to put upon the tail of the bird that knows its tune. What do they call you, now?"

"Alec Forbes," answered the owner of the name.

"Ay," interposed Annie, addressing herself to Dowie, who still held her in his arms; "this is Alec, that I told you about. He's right good to me. Alec, here's Dooie, that I like better than anyone else in the world."

And she turned and kissed the bronzed face, which was a clean face, notwithstanding the contrary appearance given to it by a beard of three days' growth, which Annie's kiss was too full of love to mind.

Annie would have been yet more ready to tell Dowie and Alec each who the other was, had she not been occupied in her own mind with a discovery she had made. For had not those verses given evident delight to the company—Alec among the rest? Had he not applauded loudest of all?—Was there not here something she could do, and so contribute to the delight of the workmen, Alec and Willie, and thus have her part in the boat growing beneath their hands? She would then be no longer a tolerated beholder, indebted to their charity for permission to enjoy their society, but a contributing member of the working community—if not working herself, yet upholding those that wrought. The germ of all this found itself in her mind that moment, and she resolved before next night to be able to emulate Rory.

Dowie carried her home in his arms, and on the way she told him all about the kindness of Alec and his mother. He asked her many questions about the Bruces; but her patient nature, and the instinctive feeling that it would make Dowie unhappy, withheld her from representing the discomforts of her position in strong colours. Dowie, however, had his own thoughts on the matter.

"How are you tonight, Mr Dow?" said Robert, who treated him with oily respect, because he was not only acquainted with all Annie's affairs, but was a kind of natural, if not legal, guardian of her and her property. "And where did you fall in with this stray lamb of ours?"

"She's been with me this long time," answered Dow, declining, with Scotch instinct, to give an answer, before he understood all the drift of the question. A Scotchman would always like the last question first.

"She's a bad lass for running out," said Bruce, with soft words addressed to Dow, and a cutting look flung at Annie, "without asking leave, and we don't know where she goes; and that's not right for young girls."

"Never you mind her, Mr Bruce," replied Dow. "I know her better than you, not meaning any offence, seeing she was in my arms before she was a week old. Let her go where she likes, and if she does what she shouldn't do, I'll take all the blame of it."

Now there was no great anxiety about Annie's welfare in the mind of Mr or Mrs Bruce. The shop and their own children, chiefly the former occupied their thoughts, and the less trouble they had from the presence of Annie, the better pleased they were—always provided they could escape the censure of neglect. Hence it came that Annie's absences were but little inquired into. All the attention they did show her, seemed to them to be of free grace and to the credit of their charity.

But Bruce did not like the influence that James Dow had with her; and before they retired for the night, he had another lecture ready for Annie.

"Annie," he said, "it's not becoming for one in your station to be so familiar. You'll be a young lady some day, and it's not right to take up with servants. There's James Dow, just a labouring man, and beneath your station altogether, and he takes you up in his arms, as if you were a child of his own. It's not proper."

"I like Jamie Doo better than anybody in the whole world," said Annie, "except—"

Here she stopped short. She would not expose her heart to the gaze of that man.

"Except who?" urged Bruce.

"I'm not going to say," returned Annie firmly.

"You're an obstinate lassie," said Bruce, pushing her away with a forceful acidity in the combination of tone and push.

She walked off to bed, caring nothing for his rebuke. For since Alec's kindness had opened to her a well of the water of life, she had almost ceased to suffer from the ungeniality of her guardians. She forgot them as soon as she was out of their sight. And certainly they were nicer to forget than to remember.

CHAPTER XXII

As soon as she was alone in her room she drew from her pocket a parcel containing something which Dowie had bought for her on their way home. When undone it revealed two or three tallow candles, a precious present in view of her hopes. But how should she get a light—for this was long before lucifer matches had risen even upon the horizon of Glamerton? There was but one way.

She waited, sitting on the edge of her bed, in the cold and darkness, until every sound in the house had ceased. Then she stepped cautiously down the old stair, which would crack now and then, use what care and gentleness she might.

It was the custom in all the houses of Glamerton to *rest* the fire; that is, to keep it gently alive all night by the help of a *truff*, or sod cut from the top of a peat-moss—a coarse peat in fact, more loose and porous than the peat proper—which they laid close down upon the fire, destroying almost all remaining draught by means of coal-dust. To this sealed fountain of light the little maiden was creeping through the dark house, with one of her *dips* in her hand—the pitcher with which she was about to draw from the fountain.

And a pretty study she would have made for any child-loving artist, when, with her face close to the grate, her mouth puckered up to do duty as the nozzle of a pair of bellows, one hand holding a twisted piece of paper between the bars, and the other buttressing the whole position from the floor, she blew at the live but reluctant fire, a glow spreading at each breath over her face, and then fading as the breath ceased, till at last the paper caught, and lighting it up from without with flame, and from within with the shine of success, made the lovely child-countenance like the face of one that has found the truth after the search of weary days.

Thus she lighted her candle, and again with careful steps she made her way to her own room. Setting the candle in a hole in the floor, left by the departure of a resinous knot, she opened her box, in which lay the few books her aunt had thrown into it when she left her old home. She had not yet learned to care much about books; but one of these had now become precious in her eyes, because she knew it contained poems that her father had been fond of reading. She soon found it—a volume by some Scotch poet of little fame, whose inward commotions had generated their own alleviation in the harmonies of ordered words in which they embodied themselves. In it Annie searched for something to learn before the following night, and found a ballad the look of which she liked, and which she very soon remembered as one she had heard her father read. It was very cold work to learn it at midnight, in winter, and in a garret too; but so intent was she, that before she went to bed, she had learned four or five verses so thoroughly that she could repeat them without thinking of what came next, and these she kept saying over and over again even in her dreams.

As soon as she woke in the dark morning she put her hand under her pillow to feel the precious volume, which she hoped would be the bond to bind her yet more closely to the boat and its builders. She took it to school in her pocket, learning the whole way as she went, and taking a roundabout road that her cousins might not interrupt her. She kept repeating and peeping every possible moment during school hours, and then all the way home again. So that by the time she had had her dinner, and the gauzy twilight had thickened to the "blanket of the dark," she felt quite ready to carry her offering of "the song that lightens toil," to George Macwha's workshop.

How clever they must be, she thought, as she went along, to make such a beautiful thing as the boat was now growing to! And she felt in her heart a kind of love for the look of living grace that the little craft already wore. Indeed before it was finished she had learned to regard it with a feeling of mingled awe, affection, and admiration, and the little boat had made for itself a place in her brain.

When she entered, she found the two boys already in busy talk; and without interrupting them by a word, she took her place on the heap of shavings which had remained undisturbed since last night. After the immediate consultation was over, and the young carpenters had settled to their work—not knowing what introduction to give to her offering, she produced it without any at all. The boys did not know what to make of it at first, hearing something come all at once from Annie's lips which was neither question nor remark, and broke upon the silence like an alien sound. But they said nothing—only gave a glance at each other and at her, and settled down to listen and to work. Nor did they speak one word until she had finished the ballad.

"THE LAST WOOING,"

said Annie, all at once, and went on:

"O lat me in, my bonnie lass!
 It's a lang road ower the hill;
And the flauchterin' snaw began to fa',
 As I cam by the mill."

"This is nae change-hoose, John Munro,
 And ye needna come nae mair:
Ye crookit yer mou', and lichtlied me,
 Last Wednesday, at the fair."

"I lichtlied ye!" "Aboon the glass."
 "Foul-fa' the ill-faured mouth
That made the leein' word to pass,
 By rowin' 't in the truth.

The fac' was this: I dochtna bide
 To hear yer bonnie name,
Whaur muckle mous war opened wide
 Wi' lawless mirth and shame.

And a' I said was: 'Hoot! Lat sit;
 She's but a bairn, the lass.'
It turned the spait o' words a bit,
 And loot yer fair name pass."

"Thank ye for naething, John Munro!
 My name can gang or bide;
It's no a sough o' drucken words
 Wad turn my heid aside."

"O Elsie, lassie o' my ain!
 The drift is cauld and strang;
O tak me in ae hour, and syne
 I'll gather me and gang."

"Ye're guid at fleechin', Jock Munro.
 For ye heedna fause and true:
Gang in to Katie at the Mill,
 She lo'es sic like as you."

He turned his fit; he spak nae mair.
   The lift was like to fa';
And Elsie's heart grew grit and sair,
   At sicht o' the drivin' snaw.

She laid her doun, but no to sleep,
   For her verra heart was cauld;
And the sheets war like a frozen heap
   O' snaw aboot her faul'd.

She rase fu' ear'. And a' theroot
   Was ae braid windin' sheet;
At the door-sill, or winnock-lug,
   Was never a mark o' feet.

She crap a' day aboot the hoose,
   Slow-fittit and hert-sair,
Aye keekin' oot like a frichtit moose,—
   But Johnnie cam nae mair!

When saft the thow begud to melt
   Awa' the ghaistly snaw,
Her hert was safter nor the thow,
   Her pride had ta'en a fa'.

And she oot ower the hill wad gang,
   Whaur the sun was blinkin' bonnie,
To see his auld Minnie in her cot,
   And speir aboot her Johnnie.

But as alang the hill she gaed,
   Through snaw and slush and weet,
She stoppit wi' a chokin' cry—
   'Twas Johnnie at her feet.

His heid was smoored aneath the snaw,
   But his breist was maistly bare;
And 'twixt his breist and his richt han',
   He claisp't a lock o' hair.

'Twas gowden hair: she kent it weel.
   Alack, the sobs and sighs!
The warm win' blew, the laverock flew,
   But Johnnie wadna rise.

The spring cam ower the wastlin hill,
   And the frost it fled awa';
And the green grass luikit smilin' up,
   Nane the waur for a' the snaw.

And saft it grew on Johnnie's grave,
   Whaur deep the sunshine lay;
But, lang or that, on Elsie's heid
   The gowden hair was gray.

ENGLISH

"O let me in, my bonnie lass!
   It's a long road over the hill;
And the fluttering snow began to fall,
   As I came by the mill."

"This is no change-house, John Munro,
   Stay away for what I care:
You twisted your lip, and slighted me,
   Last Wednesday, at the fair."

"I slighted you!" "Above the glass."
   "A curse on the hateful mouth
That made the lying word to pass,
   By wrapping it in the truth.

The fact was this: I couldn't bear
   To hear your bonnie name,
Where yawning mouths were opened wide
   With lawless mirth and shame.

And all I said was: 'Let it sit;
   She's but a child, the lass.'
It turned the spate of words a bit,
   And let your fair name pass."

"Thank you for nothing, John Munro!
   My name can go or stay;
It's not a breath of drunken words
   Would turn my head that way."

"O Elsie, lassie of my own!
   The drift is cold and strong;
O take me in one hour, and then
   Farewell, for the road is long."

"You're good at begging, Jock Munro.
   For you heed not false and true:
Go in to Katie at the Mill,
   She loves such like as you."

He turned his foot; he spoke no more.
   The signs in the sky said "go";
And Elsie's heart grew great and sore,
   At sight of the driving snow.

She laid her down, but not to sleep,
   For her very heart was cold
And the sheets were like a frozen heap
   Wrapped round her, fold on fold.

Early she rose, and all outside
   Was one broad winding sheet;
But at the doorstep, or window-sill,
   Was never a mark of feet.

She crept all day about the house,
   Slow-footed and heart-sore,
Still peeping out like a frightened mouse,—
   But Johnnie came no more!

When soft the thaw began to melt
   Away the ghostly pall,
Her heart was softer than the thaw,
   Her pride had taken a fall.

And she across the hill would go,
   Where the sun was blinking bonnie,
To see his old mother in her cot,
   And ask about her Johnnie.

But as along the hill she went,
   Through snow and slush and sleet,
She started with a choking cry—
   'Twas Johnnie at her feet.

His head was smothered 'neath the snow,
   But his breast was mostly bare;
And 'twixt his breast and his right hand,
   He clasped a lock of hair.

'Twas golden hair: she knew it well.
   Alack, the sobs and sighs!
The warm wind blew, the gay lark flew,
   But Johnnie wouldn't rise.

The spring came o'er the westward hill,
   And the frost it fled away;
And the green grass it looked smiling up,
   No worse for the snow that day.

And soft it grew on Johnnie's grave,
   Where deep the sunshine lay;
But, long ere that, on Elsie's head
   The golden hair was gray.

* * *

George Macwha, who was at work in the other end of the shop when she began, had drawn near, chisel in hand, and joined the listeners.

"Weel dune, Annie!" exclaimed he, as soon as she had finished—feeling very shy and awkward, now that her experiment had been made. But she had not long to wait for the result.

"Say't ower again, Annie," said Alec, after a moment's pause.

Could she have wished for more?

She did say it over again.

"Eh, Annie! that's rale bonnie. Whaur did ye get it?" he asked.

"In an auld buikie o' my father's," answered she.

"Is there ony mair in't like it?"

"Ay, lots."

"Jist learn anither, will ye, afore the morn's nicht?"

"I'll do that, Alec."

"Dinna ye like it, Curly?" asked Alec, for Curly had said nothing.

"Ay, fegs!" was Curly's emphatic and uncritical reply.

Annie therefore learned and repeated a few more, which, if not received with equal satisfaction, yet gave sufficient pleasure to the listeners. They often, however, returned to the first, demanding it over and over again, till at length they knew it as well as she.

But a check was given for a while to these forenight meetings.

But a check was given for a while to these forenight meetings.

CHAPTER XXIII

A rapid thaw set in, and up through the vanishing whiteness dawned the dark colours of the wintry landscape. For a day or two the soft wet snow lay mixed with water over all the road. After that came mire and dirt. But it was still so far off spring, that nobody cared to be reminded of it yet. So when, after the snow had vanished, a hard black frost set in, it was welcomed by the schoolboys at least, whatever the old people and the poor people, and especially those who were both old and poor, may have thought of the change. Under the binding power of this frost, the surface of the slow-flowing Glamour and of the swifter Wan-Water, were once more chilled and stiffened to ice, which every day grew thicker and stronger. And now, there being no coverlet of snow upon it, the boys came out in troops, in their iron-shod shoes and their clumsy skates, to skim along those floors of delight that the winter had laid for them. To the fishes the ice was a warm blanket cast over them to keep them from the frost. But they must have been dismayed at the dim rush of so many huge forms above them, as if another river with other and awful fishes had buried theirs. Alec and Willie left their boat—almost for a time forgot it—repaired their skates, joined their school-fellows, and shot along the solid water with the banks flying past them. It was strange to see the banks thus from the middle surface of the water. All was strange about them; and the delight of the strangeness increased the delight of the motion, and sent the blood through their veins swift as their flight along the frozen rivers.

For many afternoons and into the early nights, Alec and Curly held on the joyful sport, and Annie was for the time left lonely. But she was neither disconsolate nor idle. The boat was a sure pledge for them. To the boat and her they must return. She went to the shop still, now and then, to see George Macwha, who, of an age beyond the seduction of ice and skates, kept on steadily at his work. To him she would repeat a ballad or two, at his request, and then go home to increase her stock. This was now a work of some difficulty, for her provision of candles was exhausted, and she had no money with which to buy more. The last candle had come to a tragical end. For, hearing steps approaching her room one morning, before she had put it away in its usual safety in her box, she hastily poked it into one of the holes in the floor and forgot it. When she sought it at night, it was gone. Her first dread was that she had been found out; but hearing nothing of it, she concluded at last that her enemies the *rottans* had carried it off and devoured it.

"Devil choke them upon the wick of it!" exclaimed Curly, when she told him the next day, seeking a partner in her grief.

But a greater difficulty had to be encountered. It was not long before she had exhausted her book, from which she had chosen the right poems by insight, wonderfully avoiding by instinct the unsuitable, without knowing why, and repelled by the mere tone.

She thought day and night where additional *pabulum* might be procured, and at last came to the resolution of applying to Mr Cowie the clergyman. Without consulting any one, she knocked on an afternoon at Mr Cowie's door.

"Could I see the minister?" she said to the maid.

"I don't know. What do you want?" was the maid's reply.

But Annie was Scotch too, and perhaps perceived that she would have but a small chance of being admitted into the minister's presence if she communicated the object of her request to the servant. So she only replied,

"I want to see himself, if you please."

"Well, come in, and I'll tell him. What's your name?"

"Annie Anderson."

"Where do you live?"

"At Mr Bruce's, in the West Wynd."

The maid went, and presently returning with the message that she was to "gang (go) up the stair," conducted her to the study where the minister sat—a room, to Annie's amazement, filled with from the top to the bottom of every wall. Mr Cowie held out his hand to her, and said,

"Well, my little maiden, what do you want?"

"Please, sir, wad ye len' me a sang-buik?"

"A psalm-book?" said the minister, hesitatingly, supposing he had not heard aright, and yet doubting if this could be the correction of his auricular blunder.

"Na, sir; I hae a psalm-buik at hame. It's a sang-buik that I want the len' o'."

Now the minister was one of an old school—a very worthy kind-hearted man, with nothing of what has been called *religious experience*. But he knew what some of his Lord's words meant, and amongst them certain words about little children. He had a feeling likewise, of more instinctive origin, that to be kind to little children was an important branch of his office. So he drew Annie close to him, as he sat in his easy-chair, laid his plump cheek against her thin white one, and said in the gentlest way:

"And what do you want a song-book for, dawtie?"

"To learn bonnie sangs oot o', sir. Dinna ye think they're the bonniest things in a' the warl',—sangs, sir?"

For Annie had by this time learned to love ballad-verse above everything but Alec and Dowie.

books from the top to the bottom of every wall. Mr Cowie held out his hand to her, and said,

"Well, my little maiden, what do you want?"

"Please, sir, would you lend me a song-book?"

"A psalm-book?" said the minister, hesitatingly, supposing he had not heard aright, and yet doubting if this could be the correction of his auricular blunder.

"Na, sir; I have a psalm-book at home. It's a song-book I'd like to borrow."

Now the minister was one of an old school—a very worthy kind-hearted man, with nothing of what has been called *religious experience*. But he knew what some of his Lord's words meant, and amongst them certain words about little children. He had a feeling likewise, of more instinctive origin, that to be kind to little children was an important branch of his office. So he drew Annie close to him, as he sat in his easy-chair, laid his plump cheek against her thin white one, and said in the gentlest way:

"And what do you want a song-book for, my dear?"

"To learn bonnie songs out of, sir. Don't you think they're the bonniest things in all the world,—songs, sir?"

For Annie had by this time learned to love ballad-verse above everything but Alec and Dowie.

"And what kind of songs do you like?" the clergyman asked, instead of replying.

"I like them best that make you cry, sir."

At every answer, she looked up in his face with her open clear blue eyes. And the minister began to love her not merely because she was a child, but because she was this child.

"Do you sing them?" he asked, after a little pause of pleased gazing into the face of the child.

"Na, na; I only say them. I don't know the tunes of them."

"And do you say them to Mr Bruce?"

"Mr Bruce, sir! Mr Bruce would say I was daft. I wouldn't say a song to him, sir, for—for—for all the sweeties in the shop."

"Well, who do you say them to?"

"To Alec Forbes and Willie Macwha. They're building a boat, sir; and they like to have me by them, as they build, to say songs to them. And I love to do it."

"It'll be a lucky boat, surely," said the minister, "to rise to the sound of rhyme, like some old Norse war-ship."

"I don't know, sir," said Annie, who certainly did not know what he meant.

Now the minister's acquaintance with any but the classic poets was very small indeed; so that, when he got up and stood before his bookshelves, with the design of trying what he could do for her, he could think of nobody but Milton.

So he brought the *Paradise Lost* from its place, where it had not been disturbed for years, and placing it before her on the table, for it was a quarto copy, asked her if that would do. She opened it slowly and gently, with a reverential circumspection, and for the space of about five minutes, remained silent over it, turning leaves, and tasting, and turning, and tasting again. At length, with one hand resting on the book, she turned to Mr Cowie, who was watching with much interest and a little anxiety the result of the experiment, and said gently and sorrowfully:

"I dinna think this is the richt buik for me, sir. There's nae sang in't that I can fin' out. It gangs a' straucht on, and never turns or halts a bit. Noo ye see, sir, a sang aye turns roun', and begins again, and afore lang it comes fairly to an en', jist like a day, sir, whan we gang to oor beds an' fa' asleep. But this hauds on and on, and there's no end till't ava. It's jist like the sun that 'never tires nor stops to rest.'"

"I don't think this is the right book for me, sir. There's no song in it that I can find out. It goes all straight on, and never turns or halts a bit. Now you see, sir, a song always turns round, and begins again, and before long it comes fairly to an end, just like a day, sir, when we go to our beds and fall asleep. But this keeps on and on, and there's no end to it at all. It's just like the sun that 'never tires nor stops to rest.'"

"'But round the world he shines,'" said the clergyman, completing the quotation, right good-humouredly, though he was somewhat bewildered; for he had begun to fall a-marvelling at the little dingy maiden, with the untidy hair and dirty frock, who had thoughts of her own, and would not concede the faculty of song to the greatest of epic poets.

Doubtless if he had tried her with some of the short poems at the end of the *Paradise Regained*, which I doubt if he had ever even read, she would at least have allowed that they were not devoid of song. But it was better perhaps that she should be left free to follow her own instincts. The true teacher is the one who is able to guide those instincts, strengthen them with authority, and illuminate them with revelation of their own fundamental truth. The best this good minister could do was not to interfere with them. He was so anxious to help her, however, that, partly to gain some minutes for reflection, partly to get the assistance of his daughters, he took her by the hand, and led her to the dining-room, where tea was laid for himself and his two grown-up girls. She went without a thought of question or a feeling of doubt; for however capable she was of ordering her own way, nothing delighted her more than blind submission, wherever she felt justified in yielding it. It was a profound pleasure to her not to know what was coming next, provided some one whom she loved did. So she sat down to tea with the perfect composure of submission to a superior will. It never occurred to her that she had no right to be there; for had not the minister himself led her there? And his daughters were very kind and friendly. In the course of the meal, Mr Cowie having told them the difficulty he was in, they said that perhaps they might be able to find what she wanted, or something that might take the place of it; and after tea, one of them brought two volumes of ballads of all sorts, some old, some new, some Scotch, some English, and put them into Annie's hands, asking her if that book would do. The child eagerly opened one of the volumes, and glanced at a page: It sparkled with the right ore of ballad-words. The Red, the colour always of delight, grew in her face. She closed the book as if she could not trust herself to look at it while others were looking at her, and said with a sigh:

"Eh, mem! Ye wonna lippen them *baith* to me?"

"Eh, ma'am! You won't trust them *both* to me?"

"Yes, I will," said Miss Cowie. "I am sure you will take care of them."

"Yes, I will," said Miss Cowie. "I am sure you will take care of them."

"*That—I—will*," returned Annie, with an honesty and determination of purpose that made a great impression upon Mr Cowie especially. And she ran home with a feeling of richness of possession such as she had never before experienced.

Her first business was to scamper up to her room, and hide the precious treasures in her *kist*,[1] there to wait all night, like the buried dead, for the coming morning.

When she confessed to Mr Bruce that she had had tea with the minister, he held up his hands in the manner which commonly expresses amazement; but what the peculiar character or ground of the amazement might be remained entirely unrevealed, for he said not a word to elucidate the gesture.

The next time Annie went to see the minister it was on a very different quest from the loan of a song-book.

---

1   KIST (Scots): chest/trunk

CHAPTER XXIV

One afternoon, as Alec went home to dinner, he was considerably surprised to find Mr Malison leaning on one of the rails of the foot-bridge over the Glamour, looking down upon its frozen surface. There was nothing supernatural or alarming in this, seeing that, after school was over, Alec had run up the town to the saddler's, to get a new strap for one of his skates. What made the fact surprising was, that the scholars so seldom encountered the master anywhere except in school. Alec thought to pass, but the moment his foot was on the bridge the master lifted himself up, and faced round.

"Well, Alec," he said, "where have *you* been?"

"To get a new strap for my skatcher[1]," answered Alec.

"You're fond of skating—are you, Alec?"

"Yes, sir."

"I used to be when I was a boy. Have you had your dinner?"

"No, sir."

"Then I suppose your mother has not dined, either?"

"She never does till I go home, sir."

"Then I won't intrude upon her. I did mean to call this afternoon."

"She will be very glad to see you, sir. Come and take a share of what there is."

"I think I had better not, Alec."

"Do, sir. I am sure she will make you welcome."

Mr Malison hesitated. Alec pressed him. He yielded; and they went along the road together.

I shall not have to show much more than half of Mr Malison's life—the school half, which, both inwardly and outwardly, was very different from the other. The moment he was out of the school, the moment, that is, that he ceased for the day to be responsible for the moral and intellectual condition of his turbulent subjects, the whole character—certainly the whole deportment—of the man changed. He was now as meek and gentle in speech and behaviour as any mother could have desired.

Nor was the change a hypocritical one. The master never interfered,

---

[1] SKATCHER (Scots): skate

or only upon the rarest occasions when pressure from without was brought to bear upon him, as in the case of Juno, with what the boys did out of school. He was glad enough to accept utter irresponsibility for that portion of his time; so that between the two parts of the day, as they passed through the life of the master, there was almost as little connection as between the waking and sleeping hours of a somnambulist.

But, as he leaned over the rail of the bridge, whither a rare impulse to movement had driven him, his thoughts had turned upon Alec Forbes and his antagonism. Out of school, he could not help feeling that the boy had not been very far wrong, however subversive of authority his behaviour had been; but it was not therefore the less mortifying to think how signally he had been discomfited by him. And he was compelled moreover to acknowledge to himself that it was a mercy that Alec was not the boy to follow up his advantage by heading—not a party against the master, but the whole school, which would have been ready enough to follow such a victorious leader. So there was but one way of setting matters right, as Mr Malison had generosity enough left in him to perceive; and that was, to make a friend of his adversary. Indeed there is that in the depths of every human breast which makes a reconciliation the only victory that can give true satisfaction. Nor was the master the only gainer by the resolve which thus arose in his mind the very moment before he felt Alec's tread upon the bridge.

They walked together to Howglen, talking kindly the whole way; to which talk, and most likely to which kindness between them, a little incident had contributed as well. Alec had that day rendered a passage of Virgil with a remarkable accuracy, greatly pleasing to the master, who, however, had no idea to what this isolated success was attributable. I forget the passage; but it had reference to the setting of sails, and Alec could not rest till he had satisfied himself about its meaning; for when we are once interested in anything, we want to see it nearer as often as it looms in sight. So he had with some difficulty cleared away the mists that clung about the words, till at length he beheld and understood the fact embodied in them.

Alec had never had praise from Mr Malison before—at least none that had made any impression on him—and he found it very sweet. And through the pleasure dawned the notion that perhaps he might be a scholar after all if he gave his mind to it. In this he was so far right: a fair scholar he might be, though a learned man he never could be, without developing an amount of will, and effecting a degree of self-conquest, sufficient for a Jesuit,—losing at the same time not only what he was especially made for knowing, but, in a great measure, what he was especially made for being. Few, however, are in danger of going so grievously against the intellectual impulses of their nature: far more are in danger of following them without earnestness, or if earnestly, then with the absorption of an eagerness only worldly.

Mrs Forbes, seeing the pleasure expressed on Alec's countenance, received Mr Malison with more than the usual cordiality, forgetting when he was present before her eyes what she had never failed to think of with bitterness when he was only present to her mind.

As soon as dinner was over Alec rushed off to the river, leaving his mother and the master together. Mrs Forbes brought out the whisky-bottle, and Mr Malison, mixing a tumbler of toddy, filled a wine-glass for his hostess.

"We'll make a man of Alec some day yet," said he, giving an ill-considered form to his thoughts.

"'Deed!" returned Mrs Forbes, irritated at the suggestion of any difficulty in the way of Alec's ultimate manhood, and perhaps glad of the opportunity of speaking her mind—"'Deed! Mr Malison, ye made a bonnie munsie o' him a month ago. It wad set ye weel to try yer hand at makin' a man o' him noo."

"Indeed!" returned Mrs Forbes, irritated at the suggestion of any difficulty in the way of Alec's ultimate manhood, and perhaps glad of the opportunity of speaking her mind—"Indeed! Mr Malison, you made a bonnie munsie (*a fine mess*) of him a month ago. It would well beseem you to try and make a man of him now."

Had Alec been within hearing, he would never have let his mother forget this speech. For had not she, the immaculate, the reprover, fallen herself into the slough of the vernacular? The fact is, it is easier to speak the truth in a *patois*, for it lies nearer to the simple realities than a more conventional speech.

I do not however allow that the Scotch is a *patois* in the ordinary sense of the word. For had not Scotland a living literature, and that a high one, when England could produce none, or next to none—I mean in the fifteenth century? But old age, and the introduction of a more polished form of utterance, have given to the Scotch all the other advantages of a *patois*, in addition to its own directness and simplicity.

For a moment the dominie was taken aback, and sat reddening over his toddy, which, not daring even to taste it, he went on stirring with his toddy-ladle. For one of the disadvantages of a broken life is, that what a person may do with a kind of conscience in the one part, he feels compelled to blush for in the other. The despotism exercised in the school, even though exercised with a certain sense of justice and right, made the autocrat, out of school, cower before the parents of his helpless subjects. And this quailing of heart arose not merely from the operation of selfish feelings, but from a deliquium that fell upon his principles, in consequence of their sudden exposure to a more open atmosphere. But with a sudden perception that his only chance was to throw himself on the generosity of a woman, he said:

"Well, ma'am, if you had to keep seventy boys and girls quiet, and hear them their lessons at the same time, perhaps you would find yourself in danger of doing in haste what you might repent at leisure."

"Weel, weel, Mr Malison, we'll say nae mair aboot it. My laddie's nane the waur for't noo; and I hope ye will mak a man o' him some day, as ye say."	"Well, well, Mr Malison, we'll say no more about it. My laddie's none the worse for it now; and I hope you will make a man of him some day, as you say."
"He translated a passage of Virgil to-day in a manner that surprised me."	"He translated a passage of Virgil to-day in a manner that surprised me."

"Did he though? He's not a dunce, I know; and if it weren't for that stupid boat he and William Macwha are building, he might be made a scholar of, I shouldn't wonder. George should have more sense than encourage such a waste of time and money. He's always wanting something or other for the boat, and I confess I can't find in my heart to refuse him, for, whatever he may be at school, he's a good boy at home, Mr Malison."

But the schoolmaster did not reply at once, for a light had dawned upon him: this then was the secret of Alec's translation—a secret in good sooth worth his finding out. One can hardly believe that it should have been to the schoolmaster the first revelation of the fact that a practical interest is the strongest incitement to a theoretical acquaintance. But such was the case. He answered after a moment's pause—

"I suspect, ma'am, on the contrary, that the boat, of which I had heard nothing till now, was Alec's private tutor in the passage of Virgil to which I have referred."

"I don't understand you, Mr Malison."

"I mean, ma'am, that his interest in his boat made him take an interest in those lines about ships and their rigging. So the boat taught him to translate them."

"I see, I see."

"And that makes me doubt, ma'am, whether we shall be able to make him learn anything to good purpose that he does not take an interest in."

"Well, what *do* you think he is fit for, Mr Malison? I should like him to be able to be something else than a farmer, whatever he may settle down to at last."

Mrs Forbes thought, whether wisely or not, that as long as she was able to manage the farm, Alec might as well be otherwise employed. And she had ambition for her son as well. But the master was able to make no definite suggestion. Alec seemed to have no special qualification for any profession; for the mechanical and constructive faculties had alone reached a notable development in him as yet. So after a long talk, his mother and the schoolmaster had come no nearer than before to a determination of what he was fit for. The interview, however, restored a good understanding between them.

CHAPTER XXV

It was upon a Friday night that the frost finally broke up. A day of wintry rain followed, dreary and depressing. But the two boys, Alec Forbes and Willie Macwha, had a refuge from the *ennui* commonly attendant on such weather, in the prosecution of their boat-building. Hence it came to pass that in the early evening of the following Saturday, they found themselves in close consultation in George Macwha's shop, upon a doubtful point involved in the resumption of their labour. But they could not settle the matter without reference to the master of the mystery, George himself, and were, in the mean time, busy getting their tools in order—when he entered, in conversation with Thomas Crann the mason, who, his bodily labours being quite interrupted by the rain, had the more leisure apparently to bring his mental powers to bear upon the condition of his neighbours.

"It's a sod pity, George," he was saying as he entered, "that a man like you wadna, ance for a', tak thoucht a bit, and consider the en' o' a' thing that the sun shines upo'."

"Hoo do ye ken, Thamas, that I dinna tak thoucht?"

"Will ye say 'at ye *div* tak thoucht, George?"

"I'm a bit o' a Protestant, though I'm nae missionar; an' I'm no inclined to confess, Thamas—meanin' no ill-will to *you* for a' that, ye ken," added George, in a conciliatory tone.

"Weel, weel. I can only say that I hae seen no signs o' a savin' seriousness aboot ye, George. Ye're sair ta'en up wi' the warl'."

"Hoo mak' ye that oot? Ye big

"It's a great pity, George," he was saying as he entered, "that a man like you wouldn't, once and for all, take thought a bit, and consider the end of everything that the sun shines upon."

"How do you know, Thomas, that I don't take thought?"

"Will you say that you *do* take thought, George?"

"I'm a bit of a Protestant, though I'm no missonar; and I'm not inclined to confess, Thomas—meaning no ill-will to *you* for all that, you know," added George, in a conciliatory tone.

"Well, well. I can only say that I have seen no signs of a saving seriousness about you, George. You're very worldly-minded."

"Why do you think that? You

hooses, an' I mak' doors to them. And they'll baith stan' efter you an' me's laid i' the mouls.—It's weel kent forbye that ye hae a bit siller i' the bank, and I hae none."

"Not a bawbee hae I, George. I can pray for my daily breid wi' an honest hert; for gin the Lord dinna sen' 't, I hae nae bank to fa' back upo'."

"I'm sorry to hear 't, Thamas," said George.—"But Guid guide 's!" he exclaimed, "there's the twa laddies, hearkenin' to ilka word 'at we say!"

He hoped thus, but hoped in vain, to turn the current of the conversation.

"A' the better for that!" persisted Thomas. "They need to be remin't as well as you and me, that the fashion o' this warld passeth away. Alec, man, Willie, my lad, can ye big a boat to tak' ye ower the river o' Deith?—Na, ye'll no can do that. Ye maun gae through that watshod, I doobt! But there's an ark o' the Covenant that'll carry ye safe ower that and a waur flood to boot—and that's the flood o' God's wrath against evil-doers.—'Upon the wicked he shall rain fire and brimstone—a furious tempest.'—We had a gran' sermon upo' the ark o' the Covenant frae young Mr Mirky last Sabbath nicht. What for will na ye come and hear the Gospel for ance and

build houses, and I make doors for them. And they'll both stand after the pair of us are laid in the ground.—It's well known besides that you have some money in the bank, and I have none."

"Not a penny have I, George. I can pray for my daily bread with an honest heart; for if the Lord doesn't send it, I have no bank to fall back upon."

"I'm sorry to hear it, Thomas," said George.—"But my goodness!" he exclaimed, "there's the two laddies, listening to every word we say!"

He hoped thus, but hoped in vain, to turn the current of the conversation.

"So much the better then!" persisted Thomas. "They need to be reminded as well as you and me, that the fashion of this world passeth away. Alec, man, Willie, my lad, can you build a boat to take you over the river of Death?—Na, you can't do that. You must wet your feet in crossing that, I think! But there's an ark of the Covenant that'll carry you safe over that and a worse flood to boot—and that's the flood of God's wrath against evil-doers.—'Upon the wicked he shall rain fire and brimstone—a furious tempest.'—We had a grand sermon on the ark of the Covenant from young Mr Mirky last Sabbath night. Why won't you come and hear the gospel for once in a way at least, George Macwha? You can sit in my seat."

"I'm obliged to you," answered George; "but the parish church does well enough for me. And you know I'm precentor, now, besides."

"The parish church!" repeated Thomas, in a tone of contempt. "What do you get there but the dry bones of morality, upon which the wind of the word has never blown to put life into the poor worn-out skeleton. Come to our church, and you'll get a rousing, I can tell you, man. Eh! man, if you were once converted, you would know how to sing. It's no great singing that *you* guide."

Before the conversation had reached this point another listener had arrived: the blue eyes of Annie Anderson were fixed upon the speaker from over the half-door of the workshop. The drip from the thatch-eaves was dropping upon her shabby little shawl as she stood, but she was utterly heedless of it in the absorption of hearkening to Thomas Crann, who talked with authority, and a kind of hard eloquence of persuasion.

I ought to explain here that the *muckle kirk* meant the parish church; and that the religious community to which Thomas Crann belonged was one of the first results of the propagation of English Independency in Scotland. These Independents went commonly by the name of *Missionars* in all that district; a name arising apparently from the fact that they were the first in the neighbourhood to advocate the sending of missionaries to the heathen. The epithet was, however, always used with a considerable admixture of contempt.

"Aren't you going to get a minister of your own, Thomas?" resumed George, after a pause, still wishing to turn the cart-wheels of the conversation out of the deep ruts in which the stiff-necked Thomas seemed determined to keep them moving.

"Na; we'll wait a bit, and try the spirits. We're not like you—forced to drink any jabble[1] of lukewarm water that's been standing in the sun from year's end to year's end, just because the pâtron[2] pleases to stick a pump into it and call it a well of salvation. We'll know where the water comes from. We'll taste them all, and choose accordingly."

"Well, I wouldn't like the trouble nor yet the responsibility."

"I daresay not."

"Na. Nor yet the shame of pretending to judge my betters," added George, now a little nettled, as was generally the result at last of Thomas's sarcastic tone.

"George," said Thomas solemnly, "none but them that have the spirit can know the spirit."

With these words, he turned and strode slowly and gloomily out of the shop—no doubt from dissatisfaction with the result of his attempt.

Who does not see that Thomas had a hold of something to which George was altogether a stranger? Surely it is something more to stand with Moses upon Mount Sinai, and see the back of God through ever so many folds of cloudy darkness, than be sitting down to eat and drink, or rising up to play about the golden calf, at the foot of the mountain. And that Thomas was possessed of some divine secret, the heart of child Annie was perfectly convinced; the tone of his utterance having a greater share in producing this conviction than anything he had said. As he passed out, she looked up reverently at him, as one to whom deep things lay open. Thomas had a kind of gruff gentleness towards children which they found very attractive; and this meek maiden he

---

1   JABBLE (Scots): A weak/watery liquid
2   PÂTRON/PAATRON (SCOTS): The individual responsible for presenting a new minister to the local parish church.

could not threaten with the vials of wrath. He laid his hard heavy hand kindly on her head, saying:

"You'll be one of the Lord's lambs, won't you? You'll go into the fold after him, won't you?"

"Ay, I will," answered Annie, "if He'll let in Alec and Curly too."

"You mustn't make bargains with him; but if they'll go in, he won't keep them out."

And away, somewhat comforted, the honest stonemason strode, through the darkness and the rain, to his own rather cheerless home, where he had neither wife nor child to welcome him. An elderly woman took care of his house, whose habitual attitude towards him was one half of awe and half of resistance. The moment he entered, she left the room where she had been sitting, without a word of welcome, and betook herself to the kitchen, where she prepared his plate of porridge or bowl of brose. With this in one hand, and a jug of milk in the other, she soon returned, placing them like a peace-offering on the table before him. Having completed the arrangement by the addition of a horn spoon from a cupboard in the wall, she again retired in silence. The moment she vanished Thomas's blue bonnet was thrown into a corner, and with folded hands and bent head he prayed a silent prayer over his homely meal.

By this time Alec and Curly, having received sufficient instruction from George Macwha, were in full swing with their boat-building. But the moment Thomas went, Alec had taken Annie to the forge to get her well-dried, before he would allow her to occupy her old place in the heap of spales.

"Who's preaching at the missionar-church tomorrow, Willie?" asked the boy's father. For Willie knew everything that took place in Glamerton.

"Mr Brown," answered Curly.

"He's a good man that, anyway," returned his father. "There's not many like him. I think I'll turn missionar myself, for once in a way, and go and hear him tomorrow night."

At the same instant Annie entered the shop, her face glowing with the heat of the forge and the pleasure of rejoining her friends. Her appearance turned the current, and no more was said about the missionar-kirk.—Many minutes did not pass before she had begun to repeat to the eager listeners one of the two new poems which she had got ready for them from the book Miss Cowie had lent her.

CHAPTER XXVI

Whatever effect the remonstrances of Thomas might or might not have upon the rest, Annie had heard enough to make her want to go to the missionar-kirk. For was it not plain that Thomas Crann knew something that she did not know? and where could he have learned it but at the said kirk? There must be something going on there worth looking into. Perhaps there she might learn just what she needed to know; for, happy as she was, she would have been much happier had it not been for a something—she could neither describe nor understand it—which always rose between her and the happiness. She did not lay the blame on circumstances, though they might well, in her case, have borne a part of it. Whatever was, to her was right; and she never dreamed of rebelling against her position. For she was one of those simple creatures who perceive at once that if they are to set anything right for themselves or other people, they must begin with their own selves, their inward being and life. So without knowing that George Macwha intended to be there, with no expectation of seeing Alec or Curly, and without having consulted any of the Bruce family, she found herself, a few minutes after the service had commenced, timidly peering through the inner door of the chapel, and starting back, with mingled shyness and awe, from the wide solemnity of the place. Every eye seemed to have darted upon her the moment she made a chink of light between the door and its post. How spiritually does every child-nature feel the solemnity of the place where people, of whatever belief or whatever intellectual rank, meet to worship God! The air of the temple belongs to the poorest meeting-room as much as to the grandest cathedral. And what added to the effect on Annie was, that the reputation of Mr Brown having drawn a great congregation to hear him preach that evening, she, peeping through the door, saw nothing but live faces; whereas Mr Cowie's church, to which she was in the habit of going, though much larger, was only so much the more empty. She withdrew in dismay to go up into the gallery, where, entering from behind, she would see fewer faces, and might creep unperceived into the shelter of a pew; for she felt "little better than one of the wicked" in having arrived late. So she stole up the awful stair and into the wide gallery, as a chidden dog might steal across the room to creep under the master's table. Not daring to look up, she went with noiseless difficulty down a steep step or two, and perched herself timidly on the edge of a seat, beside an old lady, who had kindly made room for her. When she ventured to lift her eyes, she found herself in the middle of a sea of heads. But she saw in the same glance that no one was taking any notice of her, which discovery acted wonderfully as a restorative. The minister was reading, in a solemn voice, a terrible chapter of denunciation out of the prophet Isaiah, and Annie was soon seized with a deep listening awe. The severity of the chapter was, however, considerably mollified by the gentleness of the old lady, who put into her hand a Bible, smelling sweetly of dried starry leaves and southernwood, in which Annie followed the reading word for word, feeling sadly condemned if she happened to allow her eyes to wander for a single moment from the book. After the long prayer, during which they all stood—a posture certainly more reverential than the sitting which so commonly passes for kneeling—and the long psalm, during which they all sat, the sermon began; and again for a moment Annie ventured to look up, feeling protected from behind by the back of the pew, which reached high above her head. Before her she saw no face but that of the minister, between which and her, beyond the front of the gallery, lay a gulfy space, where, down in the bottom, sat other listening souls, with upturned faces and eyes, unseen of Annie, all their regards converging upon the countenance of the minister. He was a thin-faced cadaverous man, with a self-severe saintly look, one to whom religion was clearly a reality, though not so clearly a gladness, one whose opinions—vague half-monstrous embodiments of truth—helped to give him a consciousness of the life which sprung from a source far deeper than his consciousness could reach. I wonder if one will ever be able to understand the worship of his childhood—that revering upward look which must have been founded on a reality, however much after experience may have shown the supposed grounds of reverence to be untenable. The moment Annie looked in the face of Mr Brown, she submitted absolutely; she enshrined him and worshipped him with an awful reverence. Nor to the end of her days did she lose this feeling towards him. True, she came to see that he was a man of ordinary stature, and that some of the religious views which he held in common with his brethren were dishonouring of God, and therefore could not be elevating to the creature. But when she saw these and other like facts, they gave her no shock—they left the reflex of the man in her mind still unspotted, unimpaired. How could this be? Simply because they left unaltered the conviction that this man believed in God, and that the desire of his own heart brought him into some real, however undefinable, relation to him who was yet nearer to him than that desire itself, and whose presence had caused its birth.

He chose for his text these words of the Psalmist: "The wicked shall be turned into hell, and all the nations that forget God." His sermon was less ponderous in construction and multitudinous in division than usual; for it consisted simply of answers to the two questions: "Who are the wicked?" and "What is their fate?" The answer to the former question was, "The wicked are those that forget God;" the answer to the latter, "The torments of everlasting fire." Upon Annie the sermon produced the immediate conviction that she was one of the wicked, and that she was in danger of hell-fire. The distress generated by the earlier part of the sermon, however, like that occasioned by the chapter of prophecy, was considerably mitigated by the kindness of an unknown hand, which, appearing occasionally over her shoulder from behind, kept up a counteractive ministration of peppermint lozenges. But the representations grew so much in horror as the sermon approached its end, that, when at last it was over, and Annie drew one long breath of exhaustion, hardly of relief, she became aware that the peppermint lozenge which had been given her a quarter of an hour before, was lying still undissolved in her mouth.

What had added considerably to the effect of the preacher's words, was that, in the middle of the sermon, she had, all at once, caught sight of the face of George Macwha diagonally opposite to her, his eyes looking like ears with the intensity of his listening. Nor did the rather comical episode of the snuffing of the candles in the least interfere with the solemnity of the tragic whole. The gallery was lighted by three *coronae* of tallow candles, which, persisting in growing long-nosed and dim-sighted, had, at varying periods, according as the necessity revealed itself to a certain half-witted individual of the congregation, to be *snodded* laboriously. Without losing a word that the preacher uttered, Annie watched the process intently. What made it ludicrous was, that the man, having taken up his weapon with the air of a pious executioner, and having tipped the chandelier towards him, began, from the operation of some occult sympathy, to open the snuffers and his own mouth simultaneously; and by the time the black devouring jaws of the snuffers had reached their full stretch, his own jaws had become something dragonlike and hideous to behold—when both shut with a convulsive snap. Add to this that he was long-sighted and often missed a candle several times before he succeeded in snuffing it, whereupon the whole of the opening and shutting process had to be repeated, sometimes with no other result than that of snuffing the candle out, which had then to be pulled from its socket and applied to the next for re-illumination. But nothing could be farther from Annie's mood than a laugh or even a smile, though she gazed as if she were fascinated by the snuffers, which were dreadfully like one of the demons in a wood-cut of the Valley of the Shadow of Death in the *Pilgrim's Progress* without boards, which had belonged to her father.

When all had ceased—when the prayer, the singing, and the final benediction were over, Annie crept out into the dark street as if into the Outer Darkness. She felt the rain falling upon something hot, but she hardly knew that it was her own cheeks that were being wetted by the heavy drops. Her first impulse was to run to Alec and Curly, put her arms about their necks, and entreat them to flee from the wrath to come. But she could not find them to-night. She must go home. For herself she was not much afraid; for there was a place where prayer was heard as certainly as at the mercy-seat of old—a little garret room namely, with holes in the floor, out of which came rats; but with a door as well, in at which came the prayed-for cat.

But alas for poor Annie and her chapel-going! As she was creeping slowly up from step to step in the dark, the feeling came over her that it was no longer against rats, nor yet against evil things dwelling in the holes and corners of a neglected human world, that she had to pray. A spiritual terror was seated on the throne of the universe, and was called God—and to whom should she pray against it? Amidst the darkness, a deeper darkness fell.

She knelt by her bedside, but she could not lift up her heart; for was she not one of them that forget God? and was she not therefore wicked? and was not God angry with her every day? Was not the fact that she could not pray a certain proof that she was out of God's favour, and counted unworthy of his notice?

But there was Jesus Christ: she would cry to him. But did she believe in him? She tried hard to convince herself that she did; but at last she laid her weary head on the bed, and groaned in her young despair. At the moment a rustling in the darkness broke the sad silence with a throb of terror. She started to her feet. She was exposed to all the rats in the universe now, for God was angry with her, and she could not pray. With a stifled scream she darted to the door, and half tumbled down the stair in an agony of fear.

"Why must you make such a din in the house on the Sabbath night?" screamed Mrs Bruce.

But little did Annie feel the reproof. And as little did she know that the dreaded rats had this time been the messengers of God to drive her from a path in which lies madness.

She was forced at length to go to bed, where God made her sleep and forget him, and the rats did not come near her again that night.

Curly and Alec had been in the chapel too, but they were not of a temperament to be disturbed by Mr Brown's discourse.

CHAPTER XXVII

Little as Murdoch Malison knew of the worlds of thought and feeling—Annie's among the rest—which lay within those young faces and forms assembled the next day as usual, he knew almost as little of the mysteries that lay within himself.

Annie was haunted all day with the thought of the wrath of God. When she forgot it for a moment, it would return again with a sting of actual physical pain, which seemed to pierce her heart. Before school was over she had made up her mind what to do.

And before school was over Malison's own deed had opened his own eyes, had broken through the crust that lay between him and the vision of his own character.

There is not to be found a more thorough impersonation of his own theology than a Scotch schoolmaster of the rough old-fashioned type. His pleasure was law, irrespective of right or wrong, and the reward of submission to law was immunity from punishment. He had his favourites in various degrees, whom he chose according to inexplicable directions of feeling ratified by "the freedom of his own will." These found it easy to please him, while those with whom he was not primarily pleased, found it impossible to please him.

Now there had come to the school, about a fortnight before, two unhappy-looking little twin orphans, with white thin faces, and bones in their clothes instead of legs and arms, committed to the mercies of Mr Malison by their grandfather. Bent into all the angles of a grasshopper, and lean with ancient poverty, the old man tottered away with his stick in one hand, stretched far out to support his stooping frame, and carried in the other the caps of the two forsaken urchins, saying, as he went, in a quavering, croaking voice,

"I'll jist tak them wi' me, or they'll no be fit for the Sawbath aboon a fortnicht. They're terrible laddies to blaud their claes!"

Turning with difficulty when he had reached the door, he added:

"Noo ye jist gie them their

"I'll just take them with me, or they won't be fit for the Sabbath above a fortnight. They're terrible laddies for spoiling their clothes!"

Turning with difficulty when he had reached the door, he added:

"Now you just drub them well,

whups weel, Maister Mailison, for ye ken that he that spareth the rod blaudeth the bairn."	Mister Malison, for you know that he that spareth the rod spoileth the child."

Thus authorized, Malison certainly did "gie them their whups weel." Before the day was over they had both lain shrieking on the floor under the torture of the lash. And such poor half-clothed, half-fed creatures they were, and looked so pitiful and cowed, that one cannot help thinking it must have been for his own glory rather than their good that he treated them thus.

But, in justice to Malison, another fact must be mentioned, which, although inconsistent with the one just recorded, was in perfect consistency with the theological subsoil whence both sprang. After about a week, during which they had been whipt almost every day, the orphans came to school with a cold and a terrible cough. Then his observant pupils saw the man who was both cruel judge and cruel executioner, feeding his victims with liquorice till their faces were stained with its exuberance.

The old habits of severity, which had been in some measure intermitted, had returned upon him with gathered strength, and this day Annie was to be one of the victims. For although he would not dare to whip her, he was about to incur the shame of making this day, pervaded as it was, through all its spaces of time and light, with the fumes of the sermon she had heard the night before, the most wretched day that Annie's sad life had yet seen. Indeed, although she afterwards passed many more sorrowful days, she never had to pass one so utterly miserable. The spirits of the pit seemed to have broken loose and filled Murdoch Malison's school-room with the stench of their fire and brimstone.

As she sat longing for school to be over, that she might follow a plan which had a glimmer of hope in it, stupified with her labouring thoughts, and overcome with wretchedness, she fell fast asleep. She was roused by a smart blow from the taws, flung with unerring aim at the back of her bare bended neck. She sprang up with a cry, and, tottering between sleep and terror, proceeded at once to take the leather snake back to the master. But she would have fallen in getting over the form had not Alec caught her in his arms. He re-seated her, and taking the taws from her trembling hand, carried it himself to the tyrant. Upon him Malison's fury, breaking loose, expended itself in a dozen blows on the right hand, which Alec held up without flinching. As he walked to his seat, burning with pain, the voice of the master sounded behind him; but with the decree it uttered, Alec did not feel himself at liberty to interfere.

"Ann Anderson," he bawled, "stand up on the seat."

With trembling limbs, Annie obeyed. She could scarcely stand at first, and the form shook beneath her. For some time her colour kept alternating between crimson and white, but at last settled into a deadly pallor. Indeed, it was to her a terrible punishment to be exposed to the looks of all the boys and girls in the school. The elder Bruce tried hard to make her see one of his vile grimaces, but, feeling as if every nerve in her body were being stung with eyes, she never dared to look away from the book which she held upside down before her own sightless eyes.—This pillory was the punishment due to falling asleep, as hell was the punishment for forgetting God; and there she had to stand for a whole hour.

"*What a shame! Damn that Malison!*" and various other subdued exclamations were murmured about the room; for Annie was a favourite with most of the boys, and yet more because she was the General's sweetheart, as they said; but these ebullitions of popular feeling were too faint to reach her ears and comfort her isolation and exposure. Worst of all, she had soon to behold, with every advantage of position, an outbreak of the master's temper, far more painful than she had yet seen, both from its cruelty and its consequences.

A small class of mere children, amongst whom were the orphan Truffeys, had been committed to the care of one of the bigger boys, while the master was engaged with another class. Every boy in the latter had already had his share of *pandies*, when a noise in the children's class attracting the master's attention, he saw one of the Truffeys hit another boy in the face. He strode upon him at once, and putting no question as to provocation, took him by the neck, fixed it between his knees, and began to lash him with hissing blows. In his agony, the little fellow contrived to twist his head about and get a mouthful of the master's leg, inserting his teeth in a most canine and praiseworthy manner. The master caught him up, and dashed him on the floor. There the child lay motionless. Alarmed, and consequently cooled, Malison proceeded to lift him. He was apparently lifeless; but he had only fainted with pain. When he came to himself a little, it was found that his leg was hurt. It appeared afterwards that the knee-cap was greatly injured. Moaning with pain, he was sent home on the back of a big parish scholar.

At all this Annie stared from her pillory with horror. The feeling that God was angry with her grew upon her; and Murdoch Malison became for a time inseparably associated with her idea of God, frightfully bewildering all her aspirations.

The master still looked uneasy, threw the *tag* into his desk, and beat no one more that day. Indeed, only half an hour of school-time was left. As soon as that was over, he set off at a swinging pace for the old grandfather's cottage.

What passed there was never known. The other Truffey came to school the next day as usual, and told the boys that his brother was in bed. In that bed he lay for many weeks, and many were the visits the master paid him. This did much with the townsfolk to wipe away his reproach. They spoke of the affair as an unfortunate accident, and pitied the schoolmaster even more than the sufferer.

When at length the poor boy was able to leave his bed, it became apparent that, either through unskilful treatment, or as the unavoidable result of the injury, he would be a cripple for life.

The master's general behaviour was certainly modified by this consequence of his fury; but it was some time before the full reaction arrived.

CHAPTER XXVIII

When Annie descended from her hateful eminence, just before the final prayer, it was with a deeper sense of degradation than any violence of the tawse on her poor little hands could have produced. Nor could the attentions of Alec, anxiously offered as soon as they were out of school, reach half so far to console her as they might once have reached; for such was her sense of condemnation, that she dared not take pleasure in anything. Nothing else was worth minding till something was done about that. The thought of having God against her took the heart out of everything.—As soon as Alec left her, she walked with hanging head, pale face, and mournful eyes, straight to Mr Cowie's door.

She was admitted at once, and shown into the library, where the clergyman sat in the red dusky glow of the firelight, sipping a glass of wine, and looking very much like an ox-animal chewing the cud; for the meditation in which the good man indulged over his wine was seldom worthy of being characterized otherwise than as mental rumination.

"Well, Annie, my dear, come away," said he, "I am glad to see you. How does the boat get on?"	"Welcome, Annie, my dear," said he, "I am glad to see you. How does the boat get on?"
Deeply touched by a kindness which fell like dew upon the parching misery of the day, Annie burst into tears. Mr Cowie was greatly distressed. He drew her between his knees, laid his cheek against hers, as was his way with children, and said with soothing tenderness:	Deeply touched by a kindness which fell like dew upon the parching misery of the day, Annie burst into tears. Mr Cowie was greatly distressed. He drew her between his knees, laid his cheek against hers, as was his way with children, and said with soothing tenderness:
"Walawa! What's the matter with my dawtie?"	"Welladay! what's the matter with my darling?"
After some vain attempts at speech, Annie succeeded in giving the following account of the matter, much interrupted with sobs and fresh outbursts of weeping.	After some vain attempts at speech, Annie succeeded in giving the following account of the matter, much interrupted with sobs and fresh outbursts of weeping.

"You see, sir, I went last night to the missionar church to hear Mr Brown. And he preached a grand sermon, sir. But I haven't been able to bear myself since. For I think I'm one of the wicked that God hates, and I'll never get to heaven at all, for I can't help forgetting him sometimes. And the wicked will be turned into hell, and all the nations that forget God. That was his text, sir. And I can't bear it."

In the bosom of the good man rose a gentle indignation against the schismatics who had thus terrified and bewildered that sacred being, a maid-child. But what could he say? He thought for a moment, and betook himself, in his perplexity, to his common sense.

"You haven't forgotten your father, have you, Annie?" said he.

"I think about him almost every day," answered Annie.

"But there comes a day now and then when you don't think much about him, does there not?"

"Yes, sir."

"Do you think he would be angry with his child because she was so much taken up with her books or her play—"

"I never play at anything, sir."

"Well—with learning songs to say to Alec Forbes and Willie Macwha—do you think he would be angry that you didn't think about him that day, especially when you can't see him?"

"No indeed, sir. He wouldn't be so hard upon me as that."

"What would he say, do you think?"

"If Mr Bruce were to cast it up to me, he would say: 'Let the lassie be. She'll think about me tomorrow—time enough.'"

"Well, don't you think your Father in heaven would say the same?"

"Perhaps he might, sir. But you see my father was my own father, and would make the best of me."

"And is not God kinder than your father?"

"He can hardly be that, sir. And there's the Scripture!"

"But he sent his only Son to die for us."

"Ay—for the elect, sir," returned the little theologian.

Now this was more than Mr Cowie was well prepared to meet, for certainly this terrible doctrine was perfectly developed in the creed of the Scotch Church; the assembly of divines having sat upon the Scripture egg till they had hatched it in their own likeness. Poor Mr Cowie! There were the girl-eyes, blue, and hazy with tearful question, looking up at him hungrily.—O starving little brothers and sisters! God does love you, and all shall be, and therefore is, well.—But the minister could not say this, gladly as he would have said it if he could; and the only result of his efforts to find a suitable reply was that he lost his temper—not with Annie, but with the doctrine of election.

"Go home, Annie, my bairn," said he, talking Scotch now, "and don't trouble yer head about election, and all that. It's not a canny doctrine. No mortal man could ever win at the bottom o' it. I'm thinkin' we haven't much to do with it. Go home, dawtie (*darling*) and say your prayers to be preserved from the wiles o' Satan. There's a sixpence for ye."

His kind heart was sorely grieved that all it could give was money. She had asked for bread, and he had but a stone, as he thought, to give her. So he gave it her with shame. He might however have reversed the words of St Peter, saying, "Spiritual aid I have none, but such as I have give I thee;" and so offered her the sixpence. But, for my part, I think the sixpence had more of bread in it than any theology he might have been expected to have at hand; for, so given, it was the symbol and the sign of love, which is the heart of the divine theology.

Annie, however, had a certain Scotchness in her which made her draw back from the offer.

"Na, thank you, sir," she said; "I don't want it."

"Won't you take it to please an old man, bairn?"

"Indeed I will, sir. I would do much more than that to please you."

And again the tears filled her

blue eyes as she held out her hand—receiving in it a shilling which Mr Cowie, for more relief to his own burdened heart, had substituted for the sixpence.

"It's a shilling, sir!" she said, looking up at him with the coin lying on her open palm.

"Well, why not? Isn't a shilling a sixpence?"

"Ay, sir. It's two."

"Well, Annie," said the old man, suddenly elevated into prophecy for the child's need—for he had premeditated nothing of the sort—"maybe when God offers us a sixpence, it may turn out to be two. Good night, my bairn."

But Mr Cowie was sorely dissatisfied with himself. For not only did he perceive that the heart of the child could not be thus satisfied, but he began to feel something new stirring in his own bosom. The fact was that Annie was further on than Mr Cowie. She was a child looking about to find the face of her Father in heaven: he was but one of God's babies, who had been lying on his knees, receiving contentedly and happily the good things he gave him, but never looking up to find the eyes of him from whom the good gifts came. And now the heart of the old man, touched by the motion of the child's heart—yearning after her Father in heaven, and yet scarcely believing that he could be so good as her father on earth—began to stir uneasily within him. And he went down on his knees and hid his face in his hands.

But Annie, though not satisfied, went away comforted. After such a day of agony and humiliation, Mr Cowie's kiss came gracious with restoration and blessing. It had something in it which was not in Mr Brown's sermon. And yet if she had gone to Mr Brown, she would have found him kind too—very kind; but solemnly kind—severely kind; his long saintly face beaming with religious tenderness—not human cordiality; and his heart full of interest in her spiritual condition, not sympathy with the unhappiness which his own teaching had produced; nay, rather inclined to gloat over this unhappiness as the sign of grace bestowed and an awakening conscience.

But notwithstanding the comfort Mr Cowie had given her—the best he had, poor man!—Annie's distress soon awoke again. To know that she could not be near God in peace and love without fulfilling certain mental conditions—that he would not have her just as she was now, filled her with an undefined but terribly real misery, only the more distressing that it was vague with the vagueness of the dismal negation from which it sprung.

It was not however the strength of her love to God that made her unhappy in being thus barred out from him. It was rather the check thus given to the whole upward tendency of her being, with its multitude of undefined hopes and longings now drawing nigh to the birth. It was in her ideal self rather than her conscious self that her misery arose. And now, dearly as she loved Mr Cowie, she began to doubt whether he knew much about the matter. He had put her off without answering her questions, either because he thought she had no business with such things, or because he had no answer to give. This latter possibly added not a little to her unhappiness, for it gave birth to a fearful doubt as to the final safety of kind Mr Cowie himself.

But there was one man who knew more about such secret things, she fully believed, than any man alive; and that man was Thomas Crann. Thomas was a rather dreadful man, with his cold eyes, high shoulders, and wheezing breath; and Annie was afraid of him. But she would have encountered the terrors of the Valley of the Shadow of Death, as surely as the Pilgrim, to get rid of the demon nightmare that lay upon her bosom, crushing the life out of her heart. So she plucked up courage, like Christian of old, and resolved to set out for the house of the Interpreter. Judging, however, that he could not yet be home from his work, she thought it better to go home herself first.

After eating a bit of oat cake, with a mug of blue milk for *kitchie* (*Latin "obsonium"*), she retired to her garret and waited drearily, but did not try to pray.

CHAPTER XXIX

It was very dark by the time she left the house, for the night was drizzly; but she knew the windings of Glamerton almost as well as the way up her garret-stair. Thomas's door was half open, and a light was shining from the kitchen. She knocked timidly. At the same moment she heard the voice of Thomas from the other end of the house, which consisted only of a *but and a ben*. In the ben-end (*the inner* originally, hence *better room*) there was no light: Thomas often sat in the dark.

"Jean, come ben to worship," he cried roughly.	"Jean, come through to worship," he cried roughly.
"Comin', Thamas," answered Jean.	"Coming, Thomas," answered Jean.
Again Annie knocked, but again without result. Her knock was too gentle. After a moment's pause, dreading that the intended prayers might interfere with her project, she knocked yet again; but a second time her knock was overwhelmed in the gruff call of Thomas, sounding yet more peremptory than before.	Again Annie knocked, but again without result. Her knock was too gentle. After a moment's pause, dreading that the intended prayers might interfere with her project, she knocked yet again; but a second time her knock was overwhelmed in the gruff call of Thomas, sounding yet more peremptory than before.
"Jean, come ben to worship."	"Jean, come through to worship."
"Hoot, Thamas, hae patience, man. I canna come."	"Heavens, Thomas, have patience, man. I can't come."
"Jean, come ben to worship direckly."	"Jean, come through to worship at once."
"I'm i' the mids' o' cleanin' the shune. I hae dooble wark o' Mononday, ye ken."	"I'm in the middle of cleaning the shoes. I have double work on Mondays, you know."
"The shune can bide."	"The shoes can wait."
"Worship can bide."	"Worship can wait."
"Haud yer tongue. The shune can bide."	"Hold your tongue. The shoes can wait."
"Na, na; they canna bide."	"Na, na; they can't wait."

"Gin ye dinna come ben this minute, I'll hae worship my lane."

Vanquished by the awful threat, Jean dropped the shoe she held, and turned her apron; but having to pass the door on her way to the ben-end, she saw Annie standing on the threshold, and stopped with a start, ejaculating:

"The Lord preserve's, lassie!"

"Jean, what are ye sweerin' at?" cried Thomas, angrily.

"At Annie Anderson," answered Jean simply.

"What for are ye sweerin' at *her*? I'm sure she's a douce lassie. What does the bairn want?"

"What do ye want, Annie?"

"I want to see Thomas, gin ye please," answered Annie.

"She wants to see you, Thomas," screamed Jean; remarking in a lower voice, "He's as deef's a door-nail, Annie Anderson."

"Lat her come in, than," bawled Thomas.

"He's tellin' ye to come in, Annie," said Jean, as if she had been interpreting his words. But she detained her nevertheless to ask several unimportant questions. At length the voice of Thomas rousing her once more, she hastened to introduce her.

"Gang in there, Annie," she said, throwing open the door of the dark room. The child entered and stood just within it, not knowing even where Thomas sat. But a voice came to her out of the gloom:

"You're not afraid of the dark, are you, Annie? Come in."

"I don't know where I'm going."

"Never mind that. Come straight forward. I'm watching you."

For Thomas had been sitting in the dark till he could see in it (which, however, is not an invariable result), while out of the little light Annie had come into none at all. But she obeyed the voice, and went straight forward into the dark, evidently much to the satisfaction of Thomas, who seizing her arm with one hand, laid the other, horny and heavy, on her head, saying:

"Now, my lass, you'll know what faith means. When God tells you to go into the dark, go!"

"But I don't like the dark," said Annie.

"No human soul *can*," responded Thomas. "Jean, bring a candle directly."

Now Thomas was an enemy to everything that could be, justly or unjustly, called *superstition;* and this therefore was not the answer that might have been expected of him. But he had begun with the symbolic and mystical in his reception of Annie, and perhaps there was something in the lovely childishness of her unconscious faith (while she all the time thought herself a dreadful unbeliever) that kept Thomas to the simplicities of the mystical part of his nature. Besides, Thomas's mind was a rendezvous for all extremes. In him they met, and showed that they met by fighting all day long. If you knocked at his inner door, you never could tell what would open it to you—all depending on what happened to be *uppermost* in the wrestle.

The candle was brought and set on the table, showing two or three geranium plants in the window. Why her eyes should have fixed upon these, Annie tried to discover afterwards, when she was more used to

"You're not afraid of the dark, are you, Annie? Come in."

thinking. But she could not tell, except it were that they were so scraggy and wretched, half drowned in the darkness, and half blanched by the miserable light, and therefore must have been very like her own feelings, as she stood before the ungentle but not unkind stone-mason.

"Weel, lassie," said he, when Jean had retired, "what do ye want wi' me?"

Annie burst into tears again.

"Jean, gae butt the hoose direckly," cried Thomas, on the mere chance of his attendant having lingered at the door. And the sound of her retreating footsteps, though managed with all possible care, immediately justified his suspicion. This interruption turned Annie's tears aside, and when Thomas spoke next, she was able to reply.

"Noo, my bairn," he said, "what's the maitter?"

"I was at the missionar kirk last nicht," faltered Annie.

"Ay! And the sermon took a grip o' ye?—Nae doot, nae doot. Ay. Ay."

"I canna help forgettin' *him*, Thomas."

"But ye maun try and no forget him, lassie."

"Sae I do. But it's dour wark, and 'maist impossible."

"Sae it maun aye be; to the auld Aidam impossible; to the young Christian a weary watch."

Hope began to dawn upon Annie.

"A body micht hae a chance," she asked with meditative suggestion, "allooin' 'at she did forget him whiles?"

"Well, lassie," said he, when Jean had retired, "what do you want with me?"

Annie burst into tears again.

"Jean, go to the kitchen at once," cried Thomas, on the mere chance of his attendant having lingered at the door. And the sound of her retreating footsteps, though managed with all possible care, immediately justified his suspicion. This interruption turned Annie's tears aside, and when Thomas spoke next, she was able to reply.

"Now, my child," he said, "what's the matter?"

"I was at the missionar church last night," faltered Annie.

"Ay! And the sermon took a grip of you?—No doubt, no doubt. Ay. Ay."

"I can't help forgetting *him*, Thomas."

"But you must try not to forget him, lassie."

"So I do. But it's dour work, and almost impossible."

"So it must always be; to the old Adam impossible; to the young Christian a weary watch."

Hope began to dawn upon Annie.

"A body might have a chance," she asked with meditative suggestion, "even if she did forget him sometimes?"

"No doubt, lassie. The nations that forget God are those that don't care, that never bother their heads, or their hearts either, about him—those that were never called, never chosen."

Annie's trouble returned like a sea-wave that had only retired to gather strength.

"But how's a body to know whether she *be* one of the elect?" she said, quaking.

"That's a hard matter. You don't need to know it beforehand. Just let that alone for now."

"But I can't let it alone. It's not altogether for myself either. Could *you* let it alone, Thomas?"

This home-thrust prevented any questioning about the second clause of her answer. And Thomas dearly loved plain dealing.

"You have me there, lassie. Na, I couldn't let it alone. And I never did let it alone. I plagued the Lord night and day till he let me know."

"I tried hard last night," said Annie, "but the rats were too many for me."

"Satan has many wiles," said the mason reflectively.

"Do you think they weren't rats?" asked Annie.

"Oh! no doubt. I daresay."

"Because, if I thought they were only devils, I wouldn't care a straw[1] for them."

"It's much the same what you call them, if they drive you from the throne of grace, lassie."

---

1   The literal English translation of *buckie* is *periwinkle*

"What am I to do then, Thomas?"

"You must keep at it, lassie, just as the poor widow did with the unjust judge. And if the Lord hears you, you'll know you're one of the elect, for it's only his own elect that the Lord does hear. Eh! lassie, it's little you know about praying and not fainting."

Alas for the parable if Thomas's theories were to be carried out in its exposition! For they would lead to the conclusion that the Lord and the unjust judge were one and the same person. But it is our divine aspirations and not our intellectual theories that need to be carried out. The latter may, nay must in some measure, perish; the former will be found in perfect harmony with the divine Will; yea, true though faint echoes of that Will—echoes from the unknown caves of our deepest humanity, where lies, yet swathed in darkness, the divine image.

To Thomas's words Annie's only reply was a fixed gaze, which he answered thus, resuming his last words:

"Aye, lassie, little you know about watching and praying. When it pleased the Lord to call me, I was standing alone in the midst of a peat-moss, looking west, where the sun had left a red light behind him, as if he had just burned out of the sky, and hadn't gone down at all. And it reminded me of the day

jeedgment. An' there I steid and luikit, till the licht itsel' deid oot, an' naething was left but a gray sky an' a feow starns intil't. An' the cloods gethered, an' the lift grew black an' mirk; an' the haill countryside vainished, till I kent no more aboot it than what my twa feet could answer for. An' I daurna muv for the fear o' the pits o' water an' the walleen on ilka han'. The lee-lang nicht I stood, or lay, or kneeled upo' my k-nees, cryin' to the Lord for grace. I forgot a' aboot election, an' cried jist as gin I could gar him hear me by haudin' at him. An' i' the mornin', whan the licht cam', I faund that my face was to the risin' sun. And I crap oot o' the bog, an' hame to my ain hoose. An' ilka body 'at I met o' the road took the tither side o' 't, and glowert at me as gin I had been a ghaist or a warlock. An' the bairns playin' aboot the doors ran in like rabbits whan they got sicht o' me. An' I begud to think 'at something fearsome had signed me for a reprobate; an' I jist closed my door, and gaed to my bed, and loot my wark stan', for wha cud wark wi' damnation hingin' ower his heid? An' three days gaed ower me, that nothing passed my lips but a drap o' milk an' water. An' o' the fourth day, i' the efternoon, I gaed to my wark wi' my heid swimmin' and my hert like	of judgement. And there I stood and looked, till the light itself died out, and nothing was left but a gray sky with a few stars in it. And the clouds gathered, and the sky grew black and dark; and the whole countryside vanished, till I knew no more about it than what my two feet could answer for. And I didn't dare move for fear of the pits of water and the walleen (*well-eyes—quagmire-springs*) on every hand. The lee-long night I stood, or lay, or kneeled upon my knees, crying to the Lord for grace. I forgot all about election, and cried just as if I could make him hear me by keeping at him. And in the morning, when the light came, I found that my face was to the rising sun. And I crept out of the bog, and home to my own house. And everyone I met on the road took the other side of it, and glowered at me as if I had been a ghost or a warlock. And the children playing about the doors ran in like rabbits when they saw me. And I began to think that something fearsome had signed me for a reprobate; and I just closed my door, and went to my bed, and let my work stand, for who could work with damnation hanging over his head? And three days went by, that nothing passed my lips but a drop of milk and water. And on the fourth day, in the afternoon, I went to my work with my head swimming and

to brak for verra glaidness. I *was* ane o' the chosen."

"But hoo did ye fin' that oot, Thomas?" asked Annie, trembling.

"Weel, lassie," answered Thomas, with solemn conviction in every tone, "it's my firm belief that, say what they like, there is, and there can be, but *one* way o' comin' to the knowledge o' that secret."

"And what's that?" entreated Annie, whose life seemed to hang upon his lips.

"Jist this. Get a sicht o' the face o' God.—It's my belief, an' a' the minnisters in creation'll no gar me alter my min', that no man can get a glimp' o' the face o' God but ane o' the chosen. I'm no sayin' 'at a man's no ane o' the elec' that hasna had that favour vouchsaufed to *him*; but this I *do* say, that he canna ken his election wi'oot that. Try ye to get a sicht o' the face o' God, lassie: syne ye'll ken and be at peace. Even Moses himsel' cudna be saitisfeed wi'oot that."

"What is't like, Thomas?" said Annie, with an eagerness which awe made very still.

"No words can tell that. It's all in the speerit. Whan ye see't ye'll ken't. There's no fear o' mistakin' *that*."

Teacher and scholar were silent. Annie was the first to speak. She had gained her quest.

"Am I to gang hame noo, Thomas?"

my heart like to break for very gladness. I *was* one of the chosen."

"But how did you find that out, Thomas?" asked Annie, trembling.

"Well, lassie," answered Thomas, with solemn conviction in every tone, "it's my firm belief that, say what they like, there is, and there can be, but *one* way of coming to the knowledge of that secret."

"And what's that?" entreated Annie, whose life seemed to hang upon his lips.

"Just this. Get a sight of the face of God.—It's my belief, and all the ministers in creation won't make me alter my mind, that no man can get a glimpse of the face of God but one of the chosen. I'm not saying that a man's not one of the elect that hasn't had that favour vouchsafed to *him*; but I *do* say, that he can't know his election without that. You try and get a sight of God's face, lassie: then you'll know and be at peace. Even Moses himself couldn't be satisfied without that."

"What's it like, Thomas?" said Annie, with an eagerness which awe made very still.

"No words can tell that. It's all in the spirit. When you see it you'll know it. There's no fear of mistaking *that*."

Teacher and scholar were silent. Annie was the first to speak. She had gained her quest.

"Am I to go home now, Thomas?"

"Ay, gang hame, lassie, to yer prayers. But I doobt it's dark. I'll gang wi' ye.—Jean, my shune!"

"Na, na; I could gang hame blinlins," remonstrated Annie.

"Haud yer tongue. I'm gaein hame wi' ye, bairn.—Jean, my shune!"

"Hoot, Thamas! I've jist cleaned them," screeched Jean from the kitchen at the second call.

"Fess them here direckly. It's a jeedgment on ye for sayin' worship cud bide better nor the shune."

"Ay, go home, lassie, to your prayers. But I expect it's dark. I'll go with you.—Jean, my shoes!"

"Na, na; I could go home with my eyes shut," remonstrated Annie.

"Hold your tongue. I'm going home with you, child. —Jean, my shoes!"

"Heavens, Thomas! I've just cleaned them," screeched Jean from the kitchen at the second call.

"Bring them at once. It's a judgement on you for saying worship could wait better than the shoes."

Janet brought them and put them down sulkily. In another minute the great shoes, full of nails half an inch broad, were replaced on the tired feet, and with her soft little hand clasped in the great horny hand of the stonemason, Annie trotted home by his side. With Scotch caution, Thomas, as soon as they entered the shop, instead of taking leave of Annie, went up to the counter, and asked for an "unce o' tobawco," as if his appearance along with Annie were merely accidental; while Annie, with perfect appreciation of the reticence, ran through the gap in the counter.

She was so far comforted and so much tired, that she fell asleep at her prayers by the bedside. Presently she awoke in terror. It was Pussy however that had waked her, as she knew by the green eyes lamping in a corner. But she closed her prayers rather abruptly, clambered into bed, and was soon fast asleep.

And in her sleep she dreamed that she stood in the darkness of the same peat-moss which had held Thomas and his prayers all the night long. She thought she was *kept in* there, till she should pray enough to get herself out of it. And she tried hard to pray, but she could not. And she fell down in despair, beset with the terrors of those frightful holes full of black water which she had seen on her way to Glamerton. But a hand came out of the darkness, laid hold of hers, and lifting her up, led her through the bog. And she dimly saw the form that led her, and it was that of a man who walked looking upon the earth. And she tried to see his face, but she could not, for he walked ever a little before her.

And he led her home to the old farm. And her father came to the door to meet them. And he looked just the same as in the old happy days, only that his face was strangely bright. And with the joy of seeing her father she awoke to a gentle sorrow that she had not seen also the face of her deliverer.

The next evening she wandered down to George Macwha's, and found the two boys at work. She had no poetry to give them, no stories to tell them, no answer to their questions as to where she had been the night before. She could only stand in silence and watch them. The skeleton of the boat grew beneath their hands, but it was on the workers and not on their work that her gaze was fixed. For her heart was burning within her, and she could hardly restrain herself from throwing her arms about their necks and imploring them to seek the face of God. Oh! if she only knew that Alec and Curly were of the elect! But they only could find that out. There was no way for her to peer into that mystery. All she could do was to watch their wants, to have the tool they needed next ready to their hand, to clear away the spales from before the busy plane, and to lie in wait for any chance of putting to her little strength to help. Perhaps they were not of the elect! She would minister to them therefore—oh, how much the more tenderly!

"What's come ower (*over*) Annie?" said the one to the other when she had gone.

But there was no answer to be found to the question. Could they have understood her if she had told them what had come over her?

CHAPTER XXX

And so the time went on, slow-paced, with its silent destinies. Annie said her prayers, read her Bible, and tried not to forget God. Ah! could she only have known that God never forgot her, whether she forgot him or not, giving her sleep in her dreary garret, gladness even in Murdoch Malison's school-room, and the light of life everywhere! He was now leading on the blessed season of spring, when the earth would be almost heaven enough to those who had passed through the fierceness of the winter. Even now, the winter, old and weary, was halting away before the sweet approaches of the spring—a symbol of that eternal spring before whose slow footsteps Death itself, "the winter of our discontent," shall vanish. Death alone can die everlastingly.

I have been diffuse in my account of Annie's first winter at school, because what impressed her should impress those who read her history. It is her reflex of circumstance, in a great measure, which makes that history. In regard to this portion of her life, I have little more to say than that by degrees the school became less irksome to her; that she grew more interested in her work; that some of the reading-books contained extracts which she could enjoy; and that a taste for reading began to wake in her. If ever she came to school with her lesson unprepared, it was because some book of travel or history had had attractions too strong for her. And all that day she would go about like a guilty thing, oppressed by a sense of downfall and neglected duty.

With Alec it was very different. He would often find himself in a similar case; but the neglect would make no impression on his conscience; or if it did, he would struggle hard to keep down the sense of dissatisfaction which strove to rise within him, and enjoy himself in spite of it.

Annie, again, accepted such as her doom, and went about gently unhappy, till neglect was forgotten in performance. There is nothing that can wipe out wrong but right.

And still she haunted George Macwha's workshop, where the boat soon began to reveal the full grace of its lovely outlines. Of all the works of man's hands, except those that belong to Art, a boat is the loveliest, and, in the old sense of the word, the *liveliest*. Why is this? Is it that it is born between Wind and Water?—Wind the father, ever casting himself into multitudinous shapes of invisible tides, taking beauteous form in the sweep of a "lazy-paced cloud," or embodying a transient informing freak in the waterspout, which he draws into his life from the bosom of his mate;—Water, the mother, visible she, sweeping and swaying, ever making and ever unmade, the very essence of her being—beauty, yet having no form of her own, and yet again manifesting herself in the ceaseless generation of passing forms? If the boat be the daughter of these, the stable child of visible and invisible subtlety, made to live in both, and shape its steady course between their varying and conflicting forces—if her Ideal was modelled between the flap of airy pinions and the long ranging flow of the serpent water, how could the lines of her form fail of grace?

Nor in this case were the magic influences of verse wanting to mould and model a boat which from prow to stern should be lovely and fortunate. As Pandemonium

> "Rose like an exhalation, with the sound
> Of dulcet symphonies and voices sweet,"

so the little boat grew to the sound of Annie's voice uttering not Runic Rhymes, but old Scotch ballads, or such few sweet English poems, of the new revelation, as floated across her way, and folded their butterfly wings in her memory.

I have already said that reading became a great delight to her. Mr Cowie threw his library, with very little restriction, open to her; and books old and new were all new to her. She carried every fresh one home with a sense of riches and a feeling of *upliftedness* which I can ill describe. She gloated over the thought of it, as she held it tight in her hand, with feelings resembling, and yet how unlike, those of Johnny Bruce when he crept into his rabbits' barrel to devour the pennyworth of *plunky* (a preparation of treacle and flour) which his brother would else have compelled him to share. Now that the days were longer, she had plenty of time to read; for although her so-called guardians made cutting remarks upon her idleness, they had not yet compelled her to nursing or needlework. If she had shown the least inclination to either, her liberty would have been gone from that moment; but, with the fear of James Dow before their eyes, they let her alone. As to her doing anything in the shop, she was far too much of an alien to be allowed to minister in the lowliest office of that sacred temple of Mammon. So she read everything she could lay her hands upon; and as often as she found anything peculiarly interesting, she would take the book to the boat, where the boys were always ready to listen to whatever she brought them. And this habit made her more discerning and choice.

Before I leave the school, however, I must give one more scene out of its history.

One mid-day in spring, just as the last of a hail-shower was passing away, and a sickly sunbeam was struggling out, the schoolroom-door opened, and in came Andrew Truffey, with a smile on his worn face, which shone in touching harmony with the watery gleam of the sun between the two hail-storms—for another was close at hand. He swung himself in on the new pivot of his humanity, namely his crutch, which every one who saw him believed at once he was never more to go without, till he sank wearied on the road to the grave, and had to be carried the rest of the way. He looked very long and deathly, for he had grown much while lying in bed.

The master rose hurriedly from his desk, and advanced to meet him. A deep stillness fell upon the scholars. They dropped all their work, and gazed at the meeting. The master held out his hand. With awkwardness and difficulty Andrew presented the hand which had been holding the crutch; and, not yet thoroughly used to the management of it, staggered in consequence and would have fallen. But the master caught him in his arms and carried him to his old seat beside his brother.

"Thank ye, sir," said the boy with another gleamy smile, through which his thin features and pale, prominent eyes told yet more plainly of sad suffering—all the master's fault, as the master knew.

"Leuk at the dominie," said Curly to Alec. "He's greitin'."

For Mr Malison had returned to his seat and had laid his head down on the desk, evidently to hide his emotion.

"Haud yer tongue, Curly. Dinna leuk at him," returned Alec. "He's sorry for poor Truffey."

"Thank you, sir," said the boy with another gleamy smile, through which his thin features and pale, prominent eyes told yet more plainly of sad suffering—all the master's fault, as the master knew.

"Look at the dominie," said Curly to Alec. "He's crying."

For Mr Malison had returned to his seat and had laid his head down on the desk, evidently to hide his emotion.

"Hold your tongue, Curly. Don't look at him," returned Alec. "He's sorry for poor Truffey."

Every one behaved to the master that day with marked respect. And from that day forward Truffey was in universal favour.

Let me once more assert that Mr Malison was not a bad man. The misfortune was, that his notion of right fell in with his natural fierceness; and that, in aggravation of the too common feeling with which he had commenced his relations with his pupils, namely, that they were not only the natural enemies of the master, but therefore of all law, theology had come in and taught him that they were in their own nature bad—with a badness for which the only set-off he knew or could introduce was blows. Independently of any remedial quality that might be in them, these blows were an embodiment of justice; for "every sin," as the catechism teaches, "deserveth God's wrath and curse both in this life and that which is to come." The master therefore was only a co-worker with God in every pandy he inflicted on his pupils.

I do not mean that he reasoned thus, but that such-like were the principles he had to act upon. And I must add that, with all his brutality, he was never guilty of such cruelty as one reads of occasionally as perpetrated by English schoolmasters of the present day. Nor were the boys ever guilty of such cruelty to their fellows as is not only permitted but excused in the public schools of England. The taws, likewise, is a far less cruel instrument of torture than the cane, which was then unknown in that region.

And now the moderation which had at once followed upon the accident was confirmed. Punishment became less frequent still, and where it was yet inflicted for certain kinds and degrees of offence, its administration was considerably less severe than formerly; till at length the boys said that the master never put on black stockings now, except when he was "oot o' white anes."[1] Nor did the discipline of the school suffer in consequence. If one wants to make a hard-mouthed horse more responsive to the rein, he must relax the pressure and friction of the bit, and make the horse feel that he has got to hold up his own head. If the rider supports himself by the reins, the horse will pull.

But the marvel was to see how Andrew Truffey haunted and dogged the master. He was as it were a conscious shadow to him. There was no hour of a holiday in which Truffey could not tell precisely where the master was. If one caught sight of Andrew, *hirpling* down a passage, or leaning against a corner, he might be sure the master would pass within a few minutes. And the haunting of little Truffey worked so on his con-

---

[1] "out of white ones"

science, that, if the better nature of him had not asserted itself in love to the child, he would have been compelled to leave the place. For think of having a visible sin of your own, in the shape of a lame-legged boy, peeping at you round every other corner!

But he did learn to love the boy; and therein appeared the divine vengeance—ah! how different from human vengeance!—that the outbreak of unrighteous wrath reacted on the wrong-doer in shame, repentance, and love.

CHAPTER XXXI

At length the boat was calked, tarred, and painted.

One evening as Annie entered the workshop, she heard Curly cry,

"Here she is, Alec!"

and Alec answer,

"Let her come. I'm just done."

Alec stood at the stern of the boat, with a pot in one hand, and a paint-brush in the other; and, when Annie came near, she discovered to her surprise, and not a little to her delight, that he was just finishing off the last E of "THE BONNIE ANNIE."

"There," said he, "that's her name. Hoo (*how*) de ye like it, Annie?"

Annie was too much pleased to reply. She looked at it for a while with a flush on her face: and then turning away, sought her usual seat on the heap of spales.

How much that one winter, with its dragons and its heroes, its boat-building and its rhymes, its discomforts at home and its consolations abroad, its threats of future loss, and comforts of present hope, had done to make the wild country child into a thoughtful little woman!

Now who should come into the shop at the moment but Thomas Crann!—the very man of all men not to be desired on the occasion; for the boys had contemplated a certain ceremony of christening, which they dared not carry out in the presence of the stone-mason; without which, however, George Macwha was very doubtful whether the little craft would prove a lucky one.—By common understanding they made no allusion to the matter, thus postponing it for the present.

"Ay! ay! Alec," said Thomas; "so your boat's built at last!"

He stood contemplating it for a moment, not without some hardly perceptible signs of admiration, and then said:

"If you had her out upon a great sea, do you think you would jump out over her side, if the Saviour told you, Alec Forbes?"

"Ay wad I, gin I war richt sure he wantit me."

"Ye wad stan' an' parley wi' him, nae doot?"

"I bude to be richt sure it was his ain sel', ye ken, an' that he did call me."

"Ow ay, laddie! That's a' richt. Weel, I houp ye wad. I aye had guid houps o' ye, Alec, my man. But there may be sic a thing as loupin' into the sea o' life oot o' the ark o' salvation; an' gin ye loup in whan he doesna call ye, or gin ye getna a grip o' his han', whan he does, ye're sure to droon, as sure's ane o' the swine that ran heedlong in and perished i' the water."

"Ay I would, if I were certain he wanted me."

"You would stand and parley with him, no doubt?"

"I'd have to be right sure it was his own self, you know, and that he did call me."

"Oh ay, laddie! That's all right. Well, I hope you would. I always had good hopes of you, Alec, my man. But there may be such a thing as jumping into the sea of life out of the ark of salvation; and if you jump in when he doesn't call you, or if you don't get a grip of his hand, when he does, you're sure to drown, as sure as one of the swine that ran headlong in and perished in the water."

Alec had only a dim sense of his meaning, but he had faith that it was good, and so listened in respectful silence. Surely enough of sacred as well as lovely sound had been uttered over the boat to make her faithful and fortunate!

The hour arrived at length when *The Bonnie Annie* was to be launched. It was one of a bright Saturday afternoon, in the month of May, full of a kind of tearful light, which seemed to say: "Here I am, but I go to-morrow!" Yet though there might be plenty of cold weather to come, though the hail might fall in cart-loads, and the snow might lie thick for a day or two, there would be no more frozen waters, and the boughs would be bare and desolate no more. A few late primroses were peeping from the hollows damp with moss and shadow along the banks, and the trees by the stream were in small young leaf. There was a light wind full of memories of past summers and promises for the new one at hand, one of those gentle winds that blow the eyes of the flowers open, that the earth may look at the heaven. In the midst of this baby-waking of the world, the boat must glide into her new life.

Alec got one of the men on the farm to *yoke a horse* to bring the boat to the river. With the help of George she was soon placed in the cart, and Alec and Curly got in beside her. The little creature looked very much like a dead fish, as she lay jolting in the hot sun, with a motion irksome to her delicate sides, her prow sticking awkwardly over the horse's back, and her stern projecting as far beyond the cart behind. Thus often is the human boat borne painfully to the stream on which thereafter it shall glide contentedly through and out of the world.

When they had got about halfway, Alec said to Curly:

"I wonder what's become of Annie, Curly? It would be a shame to launch the boat without her."

"Indeed it would. I'll just run and look after her, and you can look after the boat."

So saying, Curly was out of the cart with a bound. Away he ran over a field of potatoes, straight as the crow flies, while the cart went slowly on towards the Glamour.

"Where's Annie Anderson?" he cried, as he burst into Robert Bruce's shop.

"What's *your* business?" asked the Bruce—a question which evidently looked for no answer.

"Alec wants her."

"Well, he will want her," retorted Robert, shutting his jaws with a snap, and grinning a smileless grin from ear to ear, like the steel clasp of a purse. By such petty behaviour he had long ago put himself on an equality with the young rascals generally, and he was no match for them on their own level.

Curly left the shop at once, and went round by the close into the garden, where he found Annie loitering up and down with the baby in her arms, and looking very weary. This was in fact the first time she had had to carry the baby, and it fatigued her dreadfully. Till now Mrs Bruce had had the assistance of a ragged child, whose father owed them money for groceries: he could not pay it, and they had taken his daughter instead.

Long ago, however, she had slaved it out, and had at length gone back to school. The sun was hot, the baby was heavy, and Annie felt all arms and back—they were aching so with the unaccustomed drudgery. She was all but crying when Curly darted to the gate, his face glowing with his run, and his eyes sparkling with excitement.

"Come, Annie," cried he; "we're going to launch the boat."

"I can't, Curly; I have the baby to mind."

"Take the baby to its mother."

"I daren't."

"Lay it down on the table, and run."

"Na, na, Curly; I couldn't do that. Poor little thing!"

"Is the beastie heavy?" asked Curly, with deceitful interest.

"Very."

"Let's try."

"You'll let her fall."

"No fear. I'm not so feeble. Give me a hold of her."

Annie yielded her charge; but no sooner had Curly possession of the baby, than he bounded away with her out of the garden into the back yard adjoining the house. Now in this yard, just opposite the kitchen-window, there was a huge sugar-cask, which, having been converted into a reservoir, stood under a spout, and was at this moment half full of rain-water. Curly, having first satisfied himself that Mrs Bruce was at work in the kitchen, and therefore sure to see him, mounted a big stone that lay beside the barrel, and pretended to lower the baby into the water, as if trying how much she would endure with equanimity. In a moment, he received such a box on the ear that, had he not been prepared for it, he would in reality have dropped the child into the barrel. The same moment the baby was in its mother's arms, and Curly sitting at the foot of the barrel, nursing his head, and pretending to suppress a violent attack of weeping. The angry mother sped into the house with her rescued child.

No sooner had she disappeared than Curly was on his feet scudding back to Annie, who had been staring over the garden-gate in utter bewilderment at his behaviour. She could no longer resist his entreaties: off she ran with him to the banks of the Glamour, where they soon came upon Alec and the man in the act of putting the boat on the slip, which, in the present instance, was a groove hollowed out of a low part of the bank, so that she might glide in more gradually.

"Hurrah! There's Annie!" cried Alec.—"Welcome, Annie. Here's a glass of whisky I got from my mother to christen the boat. Fling it at the name of her."

Annie did as she was desired, to the perfect satisfaction of all present, particularly of the long, spare, sinewy farm-servant, who had contrived, when Alec's back was turned, to swallow the whisky and substitute Glamour water, which no doubt did equally well for the purposes of the ceremony. Then with a gentle push from all, the *Bonnie Annie* slid into the Glamour, where she lay afloat in contented grace, as unlike herself in the cart as a swan waddling wearily to the water is unlike the true swan-self when her legs have no longer to support her weight, but to oar her along through the friendly upholding element.

"Isn't she bonnie?" cried Annie in delight.

And indeed she was bonnie, in her green and white paint, lying like a great water-beetle ready to scamper over the smooth surface. Alec sprang on board, nearly upsetting the tiny craft. Then he held it by a bush on the bank while Curly handed in Annie, who sat down in the stern. Curly then got in himself, and Alec and he seized each an oar.

But what with their inexperience and the nature of the channel, they found it hard to get along. The river was full of great stones, making narrow passages, so that, in some parts, it was not possible to row. They knew nothing about the management of a boat, and were no more at ease than if they had been afloat in a tub. Alec being stronger in the arms than Curly, they went round and round for some time, as if in a whirlpool, with a timeless and grotesque spluttering and sprawling. At last they gave it up in weariness, and allowed the *Bonnie Annie* to float along the stream, taking care only to keep her off the rocks. Past them went the banks—here steep and stony, but green with moss where little trickling streams found their way into the channel; there spreading into low alluvial shores, covered with lovely grass, starred with daisies and buttercups, from which here and there rose a willow, whose low boughs swept the water. A little while ago, they had skated down its frozen surface, and had seen a snowy land shooting past them; now with an unfelt gliding, they floated down, and the green meadows dreamed away as if they would dream past them for ever.—Suddenly, as they rounded the corner of a rock, a great roar of falling water burst on their ears, and they started in dismay,

"The sluice is up!" cried Alec. "Tak' (*take*) to yer oar, Curly."

Along this part of the bank, some twenty feet above them, ran a mill-race, which a few yards lower down communicated by means of a sluice with the river. This sluice was now open, for, from the late rains, there was too much water; and the surplus rushed from the race into the Glamour in a foaming cataract. Annie seeing that the boys were uneasy, got very frightened, and, closing her eyes, sat motionless. Louder and louder grew the tumult of the waters, till their sound seemed to fall in a solid thunder on her brain. The boys tried hard to row against the stream, but without avail. Slowly and surely it carried them down into the very heart of the boiling fall; for on this side alone was the channel deep enough for the boat, and the banks were too steep and bare to afford any hold. At last, the boat drifting stern foremost, a torrent of water struck Annie, and tumbled into the boat as if it would beat out the bottom of it. Annie was tossed about in fierce waters, and ceased to know anything. When she came to herself, she was in an unknown bed, with the face of Mrs Forbes bending anxiously over her. She would have risen, but Mrs Forbes told her to lie still, which indeed Annie found much more pleasant.

As soon as they got under the fall the boat had filled and foundered. Alec and Curly could swim like otters, and were out of the pool at once. As they went down, Alec had made a plunge to lay hold of Annie, but had missed her. The moment he got his breath, he swam again into the boiling pool, dived, and got hold of her; but he was so stupefied by the force of the water falling upon him and beating him down, that he could not get out of the raging depth—for here the water was many feet deep—and as he would not leave his hold of Annie, was in danger of being drowned. Meantime Curly had scrambled on shore and climbed up to the mill-race, where he shut down the sluice hard. In a moment the tumult had ceased, and Alec and Annie were in still water. In a moment more he had her on the bank, apparently lifeless, whence he carried her home to his mother in terror. She immediately resorted to one or two of the usual restoratives, and was presently successful.

As soon as she had opened her eyes, Alec and Curly hurried off to get out their boat. They met the miller in an awful rage; for the sudden onset of twice the quantity of water on his overshot wheel, had set his machinery off as if it had been bewitched, and one old stone, which had lost its iron girdle, had flown in pieces, to the frightful danger of the miller and his men.

"Ye ill-designed villains!" cried he at a venture, "what gart ye close the sluice? I s' learn ye to min' what ye're aboot. Deil tak' ye for rascals!"

And he seized one in each brawny hand.

"Annie Anderson was droonin' aneath the waste-water," answered Curly promptly.

"The Lord preserve 's!" said the miller, relaxing his hold. "Hoo was that? Did she fa' in?"

"You ill-natured villains!" cried he at a venture, "what made you close the sluice? I'll teach you to mind what you're about. Devil take you for rascals!"

And he seized one in each brawny hand.

"Annie Anderson was drowning beneath the waste-water," answered Curly promptly.

"The Lord preserve us!" said the miller, relaxing his hold. "How was that? Did she fall in?"

The boys told him the whole story. In a few minutes more the backfall was again turned off, and the miller was helping them to get their boat out. The *Bonnie Annie* was found uninjured. Only the oars and stretchers had floated down the stream, and were never heard of again.

Alec had a terrible scolding from his mother for getting Annie into such mischief. Indeed Mrs Forbes did not like the girl's being so much with her son; but she comforted herself with the probability that by and by Alec would go to college, and forget her. Meantime, she was very kind to Annie, and took her home herself, in order to excuse her absence, the blame of which she laid entirely on Alec, not knowing that thereby she greatly aggravated any offence of which Annie might have been guilty. Mrs Bruce solemnly declared her conviction that a judgment had fallen upon her for Willie Macwha's treatment of her baby.

"Gin I hadna jist gotten a glimp   "If I hadn't just caught a glimpse

o' him in time, he wad hae drooned the bonny infant afore my verra een. It's weel waured on them!"	of him in time, he would have drowned the bonny infant before my very eyes. They well deserve it!"

It did not occur to her that a wet skin was so very moderate a punishment for child-murder, that possibly there had been no connection between them.

This first voyage of the *Bonnie Annie* may seem a bad beginning; but I am not sure that most good ends have not had such a bad beginning. Perhaps the world itself may be received as a case in point. Alec and Curly went about for a few days with a rather subdued expression. But as soon as the boat was refitted, they got George Macwha to go with them for cockswain; and under his instructions, they made rapid progress in rowing and sculling. Then Annie was again their companion, and, the boat being by this time fitted with a rudder, had several lessons in steering, in which she soon became proficient. Many a moonlight row they had on the Glamour; and many a night after Curly and Annie had gone home, would Alec again unmoor the boat, and drop down the water alone, letting the banks go dreaming past him—not always sure that he was not dreaming himself, and would not suddenly awake and find himself in his bed, and not afloat between heaven and earth, with the moon above and the moon below him. I think it was in these seasons that he began first to become aware of a certain stillness pervading the universe like a law; a stillness ever being broken by the cries of eager men, yet ever closing and returning with gentleness not to be repelled, seeking to infold and penetrate with its own healing the minds of the noisy children of the earth. But he paid little heed to the discovery then, for he was made for activity, and in activity he found his repose.

CHAPTER XXXII

My story must have shown already that, although several years younger than Alec, Annie had much more character and personality than he. Alec had not yet begun to look realities in the face. The very nobility and fearlessness of his nature had preserved him from many such actions as give occasion for looking within and asking oneself whereto things are tending. Full of life and restless impulses to activity, all that could properly be required of him as yet was that the action into which he rushed should be innocent, and if conventionally mischievous, yet actually harmless. Annie, comfortless at home, gazing all about her to see if there was a rest anywhere for her, had been driven by the outward desolation away from the window of the world to that other window that opens on the regions of silent being where God is, and into which when his creatures enter, or even look, the fountain of their life springs aloft with tenfold vigour and beauty. Alec, whose home was happy, knew nothing of that sense of discomfort which is sometimes the herald of a greater need. But he was soon to take a new start in his intellectual relations; nor in those alone, seeing the change was the result of a dim sense of duty. The fact of his not being a scholar to the mind of Murdoch Malison, arose from no deficiency of intellectual *power*, but only of intellectual *capacity*—for the indefinite enlargement of which a fitting excitement from without is alone requisite.

The season went on, and the world, like a great flower afloat in space, kept opening its thousandfold blossom. Hail and sleet were things lost in the distance of the year—storming away in some far-off region of the north, unknown to the summer generation. The butterflies, with wings looking as if all the flower-painters of fairyland had wiped their brushes upon them in freakful yet artistic sport, came forth in the freedom of their wills and the faithful ignorance of their minds. The birds, the poets of the animal creation—what though they never get beyond the lyrical!—awoke to utter their own joy, and awake like joy in others of God's children. The birds grew silent, because their history laid hold upon them, compelling them to turn their words into deeds, and keep eggs warm, and hunt for worms. The butterflies died of old age and delight. The green life of the earth rushed up in corn to be ready for the time of need. The corn grew ripe, and therefore weary, hung its head, died, and was laid aside for a life beyond its own. The keen sharp old mornings and nights of autumn came back as they had come so many thousand times before, and made human limbs strong and human hearts sad and longing. Winter would soon be near enough to stretch out a long forefinger once more, and touch with the first frosty shiver some little child that loved summer, and shrunk from the cold.

One evening in early autumn, when the sun, almost on the edge of the horizon, was shining right in at the end of one of the principal streets, filling its whole width with its glory of molten roses, all the shopkeepers were standing in their doors. Little groups of country people, bearing a curious relation to their own legs, were going in various directions across the square. Loud laughter, very much like animal noises, now and then invaded the ear; but the sound only rippled the wide lake of the silence. The air was perfumed with the scent of peat fires and the burning of weeds and potato-tops. There was no fountain to complete the harmony, but the intermittent gushes from the spout of the great pump in the centre of the square were no bad substitute. At all events, they supplied the sound of water, without which Nature's orchestra is not full.

Wattie Sim, the watchmaker, long and lank, with grey bushy eyebrows meeting over his nose, wandered, with the gait of a heedless pair of compasses, across from his own shop to Redford the bookseller's, at whose door a small group was already gathered.

"Well, Wattie," said Captain Clashmach, "how goes the world with you?"

"Muckle the same's wi' yersel', Captain, and the doctor there," answered Wattie with a grin. "Whan the time's guid for ither fowk, it's but sae sae for you and me. I haena had a watch come in for a haill ook."

"Hoo de ye accoont for that, Mr Sim?" asked a shoemaker who stood near without belonging to the group.

"It's the ile, man, the ile. Half the mischeef o' watches is the ile."

"Well, Wattie," said Captain Clashmach, "how goes the world with you?"

"Much the same as with you, Captain, and the doctor there," answered Wattie with a grin. "When the time's good for other folk, it's but so so for you and me. I haven't had a watch come in for a whole week."

"How do you account for that, Mr Sim?" asked a shoemaker who stood near without belonging to the group.

"It's the oil, man, the oil. Half the mischief of watches is the oil."

"But I don't see," said the doctor, "how that can be, Sim."

"Well, you see, sir," answered Wattie—and the words seemed somehow to have come tumbling silently down over the ridge of his nose, before he caught them in his mouth and articulated them—"you see, sir, watches are delicate things. They're not to be treated like folk's insides with anything that comes first. If I could just get the middle half-pint out of the heart of a hogshead of sperm oil, I know I should keep all your watches going like the very universe. But it would be a bad thing for me, you know. So maybe all's for the best after all.—Now, you see, in this hot weather, the oil keeps fine and soft, and doesn't clog the works.—But Lord preserve us all! What's that?"

Staring up the street towards the sunset, which coloured all their faces a red bronze, stood a group of townsfolk, momently increasing, from which, before Wattie's party could reach it, burst a general explosion of laughter. It was some moments, however, before they understood what was the matter, for the great mild sun shone full in their eyes. At length they saw, as if issuing from the huge heavy orb, a long dark line, like a sea-serpent of a hundred joints, coming down the street towards them, and soon discovered that it was a slow procession of animals. First came Mistress Stephen, Stumpin Steenie the policeman's cow, with her tail at full stretch behind her. To the end of her tail was tied the nose of Jeames Joss the cadger's horse—a gaunt sepulchral animal, which age and ill-treatment had taught to move as if knees and hocks were useless refinements in locomotion. He had just enough of a tail left to tie the nose of another cow to; and so, by the accretion of living joints, the strange monster lengthened out into the dim fiery distance.

When Mrs Stephen reached the square, she turned to lead her train diagonally across it, for in that direction lay her home. Moved by the same desire, the cadger's horse wanted to go in exactly the opposite direction. The cow pulled the one way, and the horse pulled the other; but the cow, having her head free, had this advantage over the horse, which was fast at both ends. So he gave in, and followed his less noble leader. Cow after horse, and horse after cow, with a majority of cows, followed, to the number of twenty or so; after which the joints began to diminish in size. Two calves were at the tail of the last cow, a little Highland one, with a sheep between them. Then came a goat belonging to Charles Chapman the wool-carder, the only goat in the place, which as often as the strain on his own tail slackened, made a butt at that of the calf in front of him. Next came a diminishing string of disreputable dogs, to the tail of the last of which was fastened the only cat the inventors of this novel pastime had been able to catch. At her tail followed—alas!—Andrew Truffey's white rabbit, whose pink eyes, now fixed and glazed, would no more delight the imagination of the poor cripple; and whose long furry hind legs would never more bang the ground in sovereign contempt, as he dared pursuit; for the dull little beast, having, with the stiffneckedness of fear, persisted in pulling against the string that tied him to the tail of Widow Wattles's great tom-cat, was now trailed ignominiously upon his side, with soiled fur and outstretched neck—the last joint, and only dead one, of this bodiless tail.

Before Mistress Stephen had reached her home, and just as the last link of the chain had appeared on the square, the mirth was raised to a yet higher pitch by the sudden rush of several women to the rescue, who had already heard the news of the ignominious abduction of their honoured *kye*, and their shameful exposure to public ridicule. Each made for her own four-footed property.

"Guid preserve's, Hawkie! are ye come to this?" cried Lucky Lapp, as she limped, still and ever lame with rheumatism, towards the third member of the procession. "Gin I had the loon that did it," she went on, fumbling, with a haste that defeated itself, at the knot that bound Hawkie's nose to the tail of the cadger's horse—"gin I had the loon 'at did it, I wad ding the sowl oot o' his wame, the villain!"

"Good heavens, Hawkie! Are you come to this?" cried Lucky Lapp, as she limped, still and ever lame with rheumatism, towards the third member of the procession. "If I had the boy that did it," she went on, fumbling, with a haste that defeated itself, at the knot that bound Hawkie's nose to the tail of the cadger's horse—"if I had the boy that did it, I would strike the soul from his body, the villain!"

"Losh! it's my ain cat, as weel's my ain coo," screamed Lucky Wattles in twofold indignation. "Gin I cud but redd the scoonrel's heid wi' your cleuks, Baudrons!" she added, as she fondled the cat passionately, "he wadna be in sic a doom's hurry to han'le ye again, Is' wad."

By this time Stumpin' Steenie, having undone his cow's tail, was leading her home amid shouts of laughter.

"Pit her i' the lock-up, Steenie. She's been takin' up wi' ill loons," screeched an urchin.

"Haud yer ill tongue, or I s' tak' you up, ye rascal," bawled Steenie.

"Ye'll hae to saiddle Mistress Stephen afore ye can catch me, Stumpin' Steenie!"

Steenie, inflamed with sudden wrath, forsook the cow, and made an elephantine rush at the offender, who vanished in the crowd, and thus betrayed the constable to another shout of laughter.

While the laugh was yet ringing, the burly figure of the stonemason appeared, making his way by the momentum of great bulk and slow motion to the front of the crowd. Without a word to any one, he drew a knife from his pocket, and proceeded to cut every cord that bound the helpless animals, the people staring silent all the while.

It was a sight to see how the dogs scampered off in the delight of their recovered freedom. But the rabbit lay where the cat had left him. Thomas took it with some sign of tenderness, and holding it up in his huge hand, put the question to the crowd in general.

"Wha's aucht this?"

"It's cripple Truffey's!" piped a shrill little voice.

"Tell him 'at I'll account for't," rejoined Thomas, and putting the animal in his pocket, departed.

He took the nearest way to George Macwha's workshop, where he found Alec and Curly, as he had expected, busy or appearing to be busy about something belonging to their boat. They looked considerably hotter, however, than could be accounted for by their work. This confirmed Thomas's suspicions.

"A fine joke that for a young gentleman, Alec!" said he.

"What joke, Thomas?" asked Alec, with attempted innocence.

"You know well enough what joke I mean, man."

"Well, supposing I do—there's not that much harm done, to make a fuss about, surely, Thomas."

"Call you that no harm?" rejoined Thomas, pulling the dead rabbit out of his pocket, and holding it up by the ears. "Call you that no harm?" he repeated.

Alec stared in dismay. Thomas well knew his regard for animals, and had calculated upon it.

"Look at the poor thing with its bonny red eyes closed for ever! It's a mercy to think that there's no blazing and burning future in store for it, poor bunny!"

"Heavens, Thomas, man! Isn't that being righteous overmuch, as our minister would say?"

The question came in the husky voice of Peter Whaup, the blacksmith, who was now discovered leaning in over the half-door of the shop.

"And who's *your* minister,

"Mr Cowie, as you well know, Thomas."

"I thought as much. The doctrine savours of the man, Peter. There's no fear of him or any of his followers being righteous over-much."

"Well, you know, that's nothing but a rabbit in your hand. It would have been worried some day. How did it come by its death?"

"I didn't mean to kill it. It was all for fun, you know," said Alec, addressing Thomas.

"There's a heap of fun," answered Thomas with solemnity, "that carries death in the tail of it. Here's the poor cripple laddie's rabbit as dead as a herring, and him at home crying his eyes out, I daresay."

Alec caught up his cap and made for the door.

"I'll go and see him. Curly, who has any rabbits to sell?"

"Doddles's gave birth about a month ago."

"Where does Doddles live?"

"I'll show you."

The boys were hurrying together from the shop, when Thomas caught Alec by the arm.

"You can't restore the rabbit, Alec."

"Heavens! Thomas, one rabbit's as good as another," interposed the smith, in a tone indicating disapprobation, mingled with a desire to mollify.

"Ay—to them that care for neither. But there's such a thing as a human election, as well as a divine one; and one's not the same as another, once it's a chosen one."

"Well, I pity them that the Lord has no pity upon," sighed the smith, with a passing thought of his own fits of drinking.

"Go and try him. He may have pity upon you—who knows?" said Thomas, as he followed Alec, whom he had already released, out of the shop.

"You see, Alec," he resumed in a low voice, when they were in the open air—Curly going on before them, "it's time that you were growing a man, and putting away childish things. Your mother will be depending upon you, soon, to keep things going; and you know if you miss your chance at school, your time won't come over again. Man, you should try to do something for conscience-sake. Have you learned your lessons for tomorrow, now?"

"No, Thomas. But I will. I'm just going to buy a pair of rabbits for Truffey; and then I'll go home."

"There's a good lad. You'll be a comfort to your mother some day yet."

With these words, Thomas turned and left them.

There had been a growing, though it was still a vague sense, in Alec's mind, that he was not doing well; and this rebuke of Thomas Crann brought it full into the light of his own consciousness. From that day he worked better. Mr Malison saw the change, and acknowledged it. This reacted on Alec's feeling for the master; and during the following winter he made three times the progress he had made in any winter preceding.

For the sea of summer ebbed away, and the rocky channels of the winter appeared, with its cold winds, its ghost-like mists, and the damps and shiverings that cling about the sepulchre in which Nature lies sleeping. The boat was carefully laid up, across the rafters of the barn, well wrapped in a shroud of tarpaulin. It was buried up in the air; and the Glamour on which it had floated so gaily, would soon be buried under the ice. Summer alone could bring them together again—the one from the dry gloom of the barn, the other from the cold seclusion of its wintry hebetude.

Meantime Mrs Forbes was somewhat troubled in her mind as to what should be done with Alec; and she often talked with the schoolmaster about him. Herself of higher birth, socially considered, than her husband, she had the ambition that her son should be educated for some profession. Now in Scotland education is more easily got than almost anything else; and whether there might be room for the exercise of the profession afterwards, was a matter of less moment to Mrs Forbes, seeing she was not at all willing that the farm which had been in her husband's family for hundreds of years, should pass into the hands of strangers, and Alec himself had the strongest attachment to the ancestral soil; for to be loved it is not necessary that land should be freehold. At length his increased diligence, which had not escaped her observation, and was testified to by Mr Malison, confirmed her determination that he should at least go to college. He would be no worse a farmer for having an *A.M.* after his name; while the curriculum was common to all the professions. So it was resolved that, in the following winter, he should *compete for a bursary*.

The communication that his fate lay in that direction roused Alec still more. Now that an ulterior object rendered them attractive, he turned his attention to the classics with genuine earnestness; and, on a cloudy day in the end of October, found himself on the box-seat of the Royal Mail, with his trunk on the roof behind him, bound for a certain city whose advantages are not confined to the possession of a university.

CHAPTER XXXIII

After driving through long streets, brilliant with shops of endless marvel, the coachman pulled up for the last time. It was a dull drizzly evening, with sudden windy gusts, and, in itself, dark as pitch. But Alec descended, cold and wet, in a brilliant light which flowed from the door of the hotel as if it had been the very essence of its structure. A porter took charge of his box, hoisted it on his back, and led the way to the address he gave him.

Notwithstanding the drizzle, and the angry rushes of the wind round the street-corners, the foot-pavements were filled with men and women, moving in different directions, like a double row of busy ants. Through queer short cuts that terribly bewildered the way, the porter led him to the house, and pushing the door open, went up two flights of stone stairs and knocked at a door on the landing. Alec was shown into a room where a good fire was blazing away with a continuous welcome; and when seated by it drinking his tea, he saw the whole world golden through the stained windows of his imagination.

But his satisfaction gradually passed into a vague longing after something else. Would human nature be more perfect were it capable of being satisfied with cakes and ale? Alec felt as if he had got to the borders of fairy-land, and *something* was going to happen. A door would open and admit him into the secret of the world. But the door was so long in opening, that he took to unpacking his box; when, as he jumped up to thank his mother for some peculiar remembrance of his likings, the whole affair suddenly changed to a rehearsal of death; and his longings for the remainder of the night were towards the past.

He rose in the morning with the feeling revived, that something intense was going on all around. But the door into life generally opens behind us, and a hand is put forth which draws us in backwards. The sole wisdom for man or boy who is haunted with the hovering of unseen wings, with the scent of unseen roses, and the subtle enticements of "melodies unheard," is *work*. If he follow any of those, they will vanish. But if he work, they will come unsought, and, while they come, he will believe that there is a fairy-land, where poets find their dreams, and prophets are laid hold of by their visions. The idle beat their heads against its walls, or mistake the entrance, and go down into the dark places of the earth.

Alec stood at the window, and peered down into the narrow street, through which, as in a channel between rocks burrowed into dwellings, ran the ceaseless torrent of traffic. He felt at first as if life at least had opened its gates, and he had been transported into the midst of its drama. But in a moment the show changed, turning first into a meaningless procession; then into a chaos of conflicting atoms; re-forming itself at last into an endlessly unfolding coil, no break in the continuity of which would ever reveal the hidden mechanism. For to no mere onlooker will Life any more than Fairy-land open its secret. A man must become an actor before he can be a true spectator.

Weary of standing at the window, he went and wandered about the streets. To his country-bred eyes they were full of marvels—which would soon be as common to those eyes as one of the furrowed fields on his father's farm. The youth who thinks the world his oyster, and opens it forthwith, finds no pearl therein.

What is this *nimbus* about the new? Is the marvel a mockery? Is the shine that of demon-gold? No. It is a winged glory that alights beside the youth; and, having gathered his eyes to itself, flits away to a further perch; there alights, there shines, thither entices. With outstretched hands the child of earth follows, to fall weeping at the foot of the gray disenchanted thing. But beyond, and again beyond, shines the lapwing of heaven—not, as a faithless generation thinks, to delude like them, but to lead the seeker home to the nest of the glory.

Last of all, Alec was forced to take refuge in his books.

The competition fell on the next day, and he gained a small bursary.

CHAPTER XXXIV

As it happened, no one but Alec had come up from Glamerton that year. He did not know one of his fellow-students. There were very few in the first class indeed who had had any previous acquaintance with each other. But before three days were over like had begun to draw to like, and opposites to their natural opposites. These mutual attractions, however, were considerably influenced by the social sphere, as indicated by style of dress, speech, and manners, in which each had been accustomed to move. Some of the youths were of the lowliest origin—the sons of ploughmen and small country shopkeepers; shock-headed lads, with much of the looks and manners of year-old bullocks, mostly with freckled faces and a certain general irresponsiveness of feature, soon to vanish as the mental and nervous motions became more frequent and rapid, working the stiff clay of their faces into a readier obedience to the indwelling plasticity. Some, on the other hand, showed themselves at once the aristocracy of the class, by their carriage and social qualifications or assumptions. These were not generally the best scholars; but they set the fashion in the cut of their coats, and especially in the style of their neckerchiefs. Most of them were of Highland families; some of them jolly, hearty fellows; others affected and presumptuous, evidently considering it beneath them to associate with the multitude.

Alec belonged to a middle class. Well-dressed, he yet knew that his clothes had a country air, and that beside some of the men he cut a poor figure in more than in this particular. For a certain superiority of manner distinguished them, indicating that they had been accustomed to more of the outward refinements of life than he. Now let Alec once feel that a man was wiser and better than himself, and he was straightway incapable of envying him any additional superiority possible—would, in a word, be perfectly willing that he should both wear a better coat and be a better scholar than himself. But to any one who did not possess the higher kind of superiority, he foolishly and enviously grudged the lower kinds of pre-eminence. To understand this it must be remembered, that as yet he had deduced for himself no principles of action or feeling: he was only a boy well-made, with little goodness that he had in any way verified for himself.

On the second day after the commencement of lectures, it was made known to the first class that the Magistrand (*fourth-class*) Debating Society would meet that evening. The meetings of this society, although under the control of the magistrands, were open, upon equal terms in most other respects, to the members of the inferior classes. They were held in the Natural Philosophy class-room, at seven o'clock in the evening; and to the first meeting of the session Alec went with no little curiosity and expectation.

It was already dark when he set out from his lodgings in the new town, for the gateway beneath the tower with that crown of stone which is the glory of the ancient borough gathered beneath it. Through narrow crooked streets, with many dark courts on each side, he came to the open road which connected the two towns. It was a starry night, dusky rather than dark, and full of the long sound of the distant sea-waves falling on the shore beyond the *links*. He was striding along whistling, and thinking about as nearly nothing as might be, when the figure of a man, whose footsteps he had heard coming through the gloom, suddenly darkened before him and stopped. It was a little spare, slouching figure, but what the face was like, he could not see.

"Whustlin'?" said the man, interrogatively.

"Ay; what for no?" answered Alec cheerily.

"Haud yer een aff o' rainbows, or ye'll brak' yer shins upo' gravestanes," said the man, and went on, with a shuffling gait, his eyes flashing on Alec, from under projecting brows, as he passed.

"Whistling?" said the man, interrogatively.

"Ay; why not?" answered Alec cheerily.

"Keep your eyes off rainbows, or you'll break your shins upon gravestones," said the man, and went on, with a shuffling gait, his eyes flashing on Alec, from under projecting brows, as he passed.

Alec concluded him drunk, although drink would not altogether account for the strangeness of the address, and soon forgot him. The arch echoed to his feet as he entered the dark quadrangle, across which a glimmer in the opposite tower guided him to the stairs leading up to the place of meeting. He found the large room lighted by a chandelier, and one of the students seated as president in the professor's chair, while the benches were occupied by about two hundred students, most of the freshmen or *bejans* in their red gowns.

Various preliminary matters were discussed with an energy of utterance, and a fitness of speech, which would have put to shame the general elocution of both the pulpit and the bar. At length, however, a certain *semi* (second-classman, or more popularly *sheep*) stood up to give his opinion on some subject in dispute, and attempting to speak too soon after his dinner, for he was one of the more fashionable order, hemmed and stammered till the weariness of the assembly burst upon him in a perfect torrent of hisses and other animal exclamations. Among the loudest in this inarticulate protestation, were some of the red-gowned bejans, and the speaker kindled with wrath at the presumption of the yellow-beaks (*becs jaunes: bejans*), till, indignation bursting open the barriers of utterance, he poured forth a torrent of sarcastic contempt on the young clod-hoppers, who, having just come from herding their fathers' cows, could express their feelings in no more suitable language than that of the bovine animals which had been their principal and fit associates. As he sat down, his eyes rested with withering scorn upon Alec Forbes, who instantly started to his feet amidst a confusion of plaudits and hisses, but, finding it absolutely impossible to speak so as to be heard, contented himself with uttering a sonorous *ba-a-a-a*, and instant dropped into his seat, all the other outcries dissolving in shouts of laughter. In a moment he received a candle full in the face; its companions went flying in all directions, and the room was in utter darkness. A scramble for the door followed; and amidst struggling, shouting, and swearing, the whole company rolled down the stair into the quadrangle, most of them without their caps, and some with their new gowns torn from bottom to top. The night was hideous with the uproar. In the descent, Alec received a blow on the head which half stunned him; but he did not imagine that its severity was other than an accident of the crush. He made the best of his way home, and went to bed.

After this he was popular; and after this, as often as Patrick Beauchamp and he passed each other in walking up and down the arcade, Beauchamp's high curved upper lip would curve yet higher, and Alec would feel with annoyance that he could not sustain the glance of his gray eyes.

Beauchamp was no great favourite even in his own set; for there is one kind of religion in which the more devoted a man is, the fewer proselytes he makes: the worship of himself.

CHAPTER XXXV

One morning, about two months from the beginning of the session, after the students had been reading for some time in the Greek class, the professor was seen, not unexpectedly to part of the assembly, to look up at the ceiling with sudden discomposure. There had been a heavy fall of snow in the night, and one of the students, whose organ of humour had gained at the expense of that of veneration, had, before the arrival of the professor, gathered a ball of the snow, and thrown it against the ceiling with such forceful precision, that it stuck right over the centre of the chair. This was perhaps the first time that such a trick had been dared in the first class, belonging more properly to the advanced depravity of the second or third. When the air began to get warm, the snow began to drop upon the head of the old professor; and this was the cause of his troubled glance at the ceiling. But the moment he looked up, Alec, seeing what was the matter, and feeling all his natural loyalty roused, sprang from his seat, and rushing out of the class-room, returned with a long broom which the sacrist had been using to clear foot-paths across the quadrangle. The professor left his chair, and Alec springing on the desk, swept the snow from the ceiling. He then wiped the seat with his handkerchief and returned to his place. The gratitude of the old man shone in his eyes. True, he would only have had to send for the sacrist to rescue him; but here was an atonement for the insult, offered by one of the students themselves.

"Thank you, Mr Forbes," he stammered; "I am ek—ek—ek—exceedingly obliged to you."

The professor was a curious, kindly little man—lame, with a brown wig, a wrinkled face, and a long mouth, of which he only made use of the half on the right side to stammer out humorous and often witty sayings—at least so they appeared to those who had grace enough to respect his position and his age. As often as reference is made in my hearing to Charles Lamb and his stutter, up comes the face of dear old Professor Fraser, and I hear him once more stammering out some joke, the very fun of which had its source in kindliness. Somehow the stutter never interfered with the point of the joke: that always came with a rush. He seemed, while hesitating on some unimportant syllable, to be arranging what was to follow and strike the blow.

"Gentlemen," he continued upon this occasion, "the Scripture says you're to heap c-c-c-coals of fire on your enemy's head. When you are to heap drops of water on your friend's w-w-wig, the Scripture doesn't say."

The same evening Alec received a note from him asking him to breakfast with him the following morning, which was Saturday, and consequently a holiday. It was usual with the professors to invite a dozen or so of the students to breakfast on Saturdays, but on this occasion Alec was the sole guest.

As soon as he entered the room, Mr Fraser hobbled to meet him, with outstretched hand of welcome, and a kindly grin on his face.

"Mr Forbes," he said, "I h-h-hope well of you; for you can respect an old man. I'm very glad to see you. I hope you've brought an appetite with you. Sit down. Always respect old age, Mr Forbes. You'll be old yourself some day—and you won't like it any more than I do. I've had my young days, though, and I mustn't grumble."

And here he smiled; but it was a sad smile, and a tear gathered in the corner of one of his old eyes. He caught up a globular silver tea-pot, and began to fill the tea-cups. Apparently the reflection of his own face in the tea-pot was too comical to resist, for the old man presently broke into what was half a laugh and half a grin, and, without in any way accounting for it, went on talking quite merrily for the rest of the meal.

"My mother told me," said Alec at length, "in a letter I had from her yesterday, that your brother, sir, had married a cousin of hers."

"What! what! Are you a son of Mr Forbes of Howglen?"

"Yes, sir."

"You young rascal! Why didn't your mother send you to me?"

"She didn't like to trouble you, I suppose, sir."

"People like me, that haven't any relations, must make the most of the relations they have. I am in no danger of being troubled that way. You've heard of my poor brother's death?"

"No, sir."

"He died last year. He was a clergyman, you know. When you come up next session, I hope to show you his daughter—your cousin, you know. She is coming to live with me. People that don't marry don't deserve to have children. But I'm going to have one after all. She's at school now. What do you think of turning to, Mr Forbes?"

"I haven't thought much about it yet, sir."

"Ah! I daresay not. If I were you, I would be a doctor. If you're honest, you're sure to do some good. I think you're just the man for a doctor now—you respect your fellow-men. You don't laugh at old age, Mr Forbes."

And so the kind garrulous old man went on, talking about everything except Greek. For that he had no enthusiasm. Indeed, he did not know enough to have, by possibility, any feeling about it. What he did know, however, he taught well, and very conscientiously.

This was the first time that Alec's thoughts had been turned towards a profession. The more he thought about it the better he liked the idea of being a doctor; till at length, after one or two talks about it with Mr Fraser, he resolved, notwithstanding that the session was considerably advanced, to attend the anatomical course for the rest of it. The Greek and Latin were tolerably easy to him, and it would be so much time gained if he entered the first medical class at once. He need not stand the examination except he liked, and the fee was not by any means large. His mother was more than satisfied with the proposal, and, although what seemed a trifle to Alec was of some consequence to her, she sent him at once the necessary supplies. Mr Fraser smoothed the way for him with the professor, and he was soon busy making up his distance by a close study of the class-books.

CHAPTER XXXVI

The first day of his attendance in the dissecting-room was a memorable one, and had memorable consequences. He had considerable misgivings about the new experience he had to meet, and sought, by the concentration of his will, to prepare himself to encounter the inevitable with calmness, and, if possible, with seeming indifference. But he was not prepared after all for the disadvantage of entering a company already hardened to those peculiarities of the position for which a certain induration is as desirable as unavoidable.

When he entered the room, he found a group already gathered. He drew timidly towards the table on the other side, not daring to glance at something which lay upon it—"white with the whiteness of what is dead;" and, feeling as if all the men were looking at him, as indeed most of them were, kept staring, or trying to stare, at other things in the room. But all at once, from an irresistible impulse, he faced round, and looked at the table.

There lay the body of a woman, with a young sad face, beautiful in spite of a terrible scar on the forehead, which indicated too plainly with what brutal companions she had consorted. Alec's lip quivered, and his throat swelled with a painful sensation of choking. He turned away, and bit his lip hard to keep down his emotion.

The best quality he possessed was an entire and profound reverence for women. Indignation even was almost quelled in the shock he received, when one of the students, for the pleasure of sneering at his discomposure, and making a boast of his own superiority to such weakness, uttered a brutal jest. In vain the upturned face made its white appeal to the universe: a laugh billowed the silence about its head.

But no rudeness could hurt that motionless heart—no insult bring a blush on that pale face. The closed eyes, the abandoned hands seemed only to pray:

"Let me into the dark—out of the eyes of those men!"

Alec gave one sob in the vain effort to master the conflicting emotions of indignation and pity. It reverberated in the laugh which burst from the students of the healing art. Almost quenched in the laugh he heard one word however, in the same voice which had made the jest—a voice he knew well enough—that of Patrick Beauchamp. His face blazed up; his eyes flashed; and he had made one step forward, when he was arrested by the still face of the dead woman, which, ghostly as the morning moon, returned no glow in the red sunlight of his wrath; and in reverence he restrained his anger. In another moment, the professor arrived.

During the lecture and accompanying demonstrations, Alec was deaf and blind from burning rage; in the midst of which, however, he almost forgot his own wrong in regarding that done to the dead. He became, in his own eyes, the champion of one whom nature and death had united to render defenceless. From the verge of a gulf more terrible than the grave, her cry had reached him, and he would rise to avenge her.

As soon as they came out, he walked up to Beauchamp.

"You called me a spoony," he said through his set teeth.

"I did," answered Beauchamp, with an admirable drawl of indifference.

Alec replied with a blow; whereupon Beauchamp knocked him down. But he was up in a moment; and, although his antagonist was both older and bigger, the elasticity of his perfect health soon began to tell. There was little science between them, and what there was lay on Beauchamp's side; yet he defended himself more and more feebly, for his wind had soon given way. At length, after receiving a terrible blow on the mouth, Beauchamp dropped his arms and turned his back; and Alec, after some hesitation, let him go without the parting kick which he was tempted to give him, and which he had so well deserved.

The men dispersed without remark, ashamed of themselves, and admiring the bumpkin—most of them were gentlemen enough for that; while each of the combatants retired unaccompanied to his own lodging—Alec with a black eye, which soon passed through yellow back to its own natural hue, and Beauchamp with a cut, the scar of which deepened the sneer on his upper lip, and was long his evil counsellor from the confessional of the mirror.

CHAPTER XXXVII

The encounter fortunately took place upon a Friday, so that the combatants had both Saturday and Sunday, with the deodand of a slight fine for being absent from chapel, to recover appearances. Alec kept to the house both days, and read hard at his medical and anatomical books. His landlady took charge of his eye, and ministered to it with assiduity and discretion, asking no questions, and courting no confidences, only looking at him comically now and then out of gray motherly eyes, that might have been trusted with the universe. She knew the ways of students. In the course of one of the dressings, she said:

"You'll be growing weary, Mr Forbes, of having to stay home with that blackamoor eye of yours. Why don't you go upstairs to Mr Cupples, and have a laugh with him?"

"I didn't know you had anybody upstairs. Who's Mr Cupples?"

"Well, he knows that best himself! But he's a strange one, alright. He's a terrible scholar though, folk say—grand at the Greek, and real bonny on the mathematics. Only you mustn't be frightened at him."

"I scare easily," said Alec, with a laugh. "But I would like to see him."

"Go up, then, and knock at the garret door on the left."

"But what reason am I to give for disturbing him?" asked Alec.

"Oh none at all. Just take a mouthful of Greek with you to ask the right meaning of, if you must have a reason."

"That will do just first-rate," said Alec; "for here I have been puzzling over a sentence for the last half hour with nobody but this dim-sighted ghost of a Schrevelius to help me out with it. I'll go directly. But I look such a blackguard with this game eye!"

The landlady laughed.

"You'll sune forget that whan ye see Mr Cupples."

To the dismay of his nurse, Alec pulled the bandage off his eye, and amidst her expostulations caught up his book, and rushing away, bounded up the garret stairs, which ascended outside the door of the *flat*. At the top, he found himself under the bare roof, with only boards and slates between him and the clouds. The landing was lighted by a skylight, across which diligent and undisturbed spiders had woven their webs for years. He stood for a moment or two, puzzled as to which door he ought to assail, for all the doors about looked like closet-doors, leading into dingy recesses. At last, with the aid of his nose, he made up his mind, and knocked.

"Come in," cried a voice of peculiar tone. It reminded Alec of something he could not at all identify, which was not wonderful, seeing it was of itself, heard once before, that it reminded him. It was the same voice which, as he walked to the debate, the first night, had warned him not to look at rainbows.

He opened the door and entered.

"What do you want?" said the voice, its source almost invisible in the thick fumes of genuine pigtail, through which it sent cross odours of as genuine Glenlivat.

"I want you to help me with a bit of Homer, if you please, Mr Cupples—I'm not up to Homer yet."

"Do ye think I hae naething ither to do than to grin' the grandur o' an auld haythen into spunemate for a young sinner like you?"

"Ye dinna ken what I'm like, Mr Cupples," returned Alec, remembering his landlady's injunction not to be afraid of him.

| "Come athort the reek, and lat's luik at ye." | "Come across the smoke, and let's look at you." |

Alec obeyed, and found the speaker seated by the side of a little fire, in an old easy-chair covered with horsehair; and while undergoing his scrutiny, took his revenge in kind. Mr Cupples was a man who might have been of almost any age from five-and-twenty to fifty—at least, Alec's experience was insufficient for the task of determining to what decade of human years he belonged. He was a little man, in a long black tail-coat much too large, and dirty gray trousers. He had no shirt-collar visible, although a loose rusty stock revealed the whole of his brown neck. His hair, long, thin, fair, and yet a good deal mingled with grey, straggled about over an uncommonly high forehead, which had somehow the neglected and ruinous look of an old bare tower no ivy had beautified. His ears stood far out from his great head. His nose refuses to be described. His lips were plentiful and loose; his chin was not worth mentioning; his eyes were rather large, beautifully formed, bright, and blue. His hand, small, delicately shaped, and dirty, grasped, all the time he was examining Alec, a tumbler of steaming toddy; while his feet, in list slippers of different colours, balanced themselves upon the fender.

"You've been fighting, you young rascal!" said Mr Cupples, in a tone of authority, the moment he had satisfied himself about Alec's countenance. "That won't do. It's not respectable."

And he gave the queerest unintelligible grin.

Alec found himself strangely attracted to him, and impelled—a feeling not unfrequent with him—to tell the truth, the whole truth, and nothing but the truth.

"The world itself isn't the most respectable planet in the system, Mr Cupples," said he; "and no honest inhabitant of it can be always respectable either."

Mr Cupples chuckled and laughed groggily, muttering somewhere in his chest—

"You young dog! There's stuff in you!" Then composing himself a little, he said aloud: "Tell me all about it directly."

Alec obeyed, and, not without emotion, gave Mr Cupples the whole history of the affair.

"Damn you!" remarked Mr Cupples in a husky voice, as he held out a trembling hand to Alec, "you're one of the right sort. I'll do anything for you I can. Where's your Homer?"

So saying, he rose with care and went towards a cupboard in the corner. His pipe had been so far interrupted during their conversation, that Alec was now able, by the light of the tallow candle, to see the little garret room, with its ceiling on one side sloping nearly to the floor, its walls begrimed with smoke, and the bare plaster covered with grotesque pencil-drawings—caricatures of Homeric heroes in the guise of schoolboys, polemic clergymen of the city in the garb of fish-wives militant, and such like. A bed and a small chest of drawers stood under the slope of the roof, and the rest of the room was occupied by a painted table covered with papers, and a chair or two. An old broadsword leaned against the wall in a corner. A half-open cupboard revealed bottles, glasses, and a dry-looking cheese. To the corresponding cupboard, on the other side of the fire, which had lost a corner by the descent of the roof, Mr Cupples now dragged his slippers, feeling in his waistcoat pocket, as he went, for the key.—There was another door still, partly sunk in the slope of the ceiling.

When he opened the cupboard, a dusky glimmer of splendid bindings filling the whole recess, shone out upon the dingy room. From a shelf he took a volume of Homer, bound in vellum, with red edges—a copy of far greater value than Alec had knowledge of books to understand—and closing the door again, resumed his seat in the easy-chair. Having found the passage, he read it through aloud in a manner which made Homer for the first time sound like poetry in Alec's ears, and almost revealed the hidden significance. Then pouncing at once upon the shadowy word which was the key to the whole, he laid open the construction and meaning in one sentence of explanation.

"Thank you! thank you!" exclaimed Alec. "I see it all now as plain as English."

"Stop, stop, my young bantam!" said Mr Cupples. "Don't think you're going to break into my privacy and get off with the booty so cheaply. Just you construe the whole sentence to me."

Alec did so tolerably well; for the passage was only an easy extract, the class not having reached Homer yet. Mr Cupples put several questions to him, which gave him more insight into Greek than a week's work in the class would have done, and ended with a small lecture suggested by the passage, drinking away at his toddy all the time. The lecture and the toddy ended together. Turning his head aside, where it lay back in the horse-hair chair, he said sleepily:

"Go away—I don't know your name.—Come and see me to-morrow night. I'm drunk now."

Alec rose, made some attempt at thanks, received no syllable of reply, and went out, closing the door behind him, and leaving Mr Cupples to his dreams.

His countenance had not made much approximation to respectability before the Monday. He therefore kept it as well as he could out of Mr Fraser's sight, to whom he did not wish to give explanations to the prejudice of any of his fellow-students. Mr Fraser, however, saw his black eye well enough, but was too discreet to ask questions, and appeared quite unaware of the transitory blemish.

CHAPTER XXXVIII

Meantime, at Glamerton the winter passed very much like former winters to all but three—Mrs Forbes, Annie Anderson, and Willie Macwha. To these the loss of Alec was dreary. So they were in a manner compelled to draw closer together. At school, Curly assumed the protectorship of Annie which had naturally devolved upon him, although there was now comparatively little occasion for its exercise; and Mrs Forbes, finding herself lonely in her parlour during the long *forenights*, got into the habit of sending Mary at least three times a week to fetch her. This was not agreeable to the Bruce, but the kingly inheritor abode his hour; and Mrs Forbes had no notion of the amount of offence she gave by doing so.

That parlour at Howglen was to Annie a little heaven hollowed out of the winter. The warm curtains drawn, and the fire blazing defiantly,—the angel with the flaming sword to protect their Paradise from the frost, it was indeed a contrast to the sordid shop, and the rat-haunted garret.

After tea they took it in turns to work and to read. Mrs Forbes had never sought to satisfy the religious public as to the state of her mind, and so had never been led astray into making frantic efforts to rouse her own feelings; which is, in fact, to apply to them the hottest searing iron of all, next to that of sin. Hence her emotional touch remained delicate, and what she could understand she could feel. The good books she liked best were stories of the Scotch Covenanters and Worthies, whose example, however much of stiff-neckedness may have mingled with their devotion, was yet the best that Annie could have, inasmuch as they were simply martyrs—men who would not say *yes* when they ought to say *no*. Nor was Mrs Forbes too religious to enjoy the representation given of these Covenanters in *Old Mortality*. Her feelings found nothing repulsive in the book, although she never discovered the reason in the fact that Sir Walter's feelings were the same as her own, whatever his opinions might be, and had given the chief colour and tone to the representation of his characters. There were more books in the house than was usual even in that of a *gentleman farmer*; and several of Sir Walter's novels, besides some travels, and a little Scotch history, were read between them that winter. In poetry, Annie had to forage for herself. Mrs Forbes could lend her no guiding hand in that direction.

The bond between them grew stronger every day. Annie was to Mrs Forbes an outlet for her maternity, which could never have outlet enough without a girl as well as a boy to love; and Annie, in consequence, was surrounded by numberless holy influences, which, operating in a time when she was growing fast, had their full effect upon mind and body both. In a condition of rapid change, the mass is more yielding and responsive. One result in her was, that a certain sober grace, like that of the lovely dull-feathered hen-birds, began to manifest itself in her carriage and her ways. And this leads me to remark that her outward and visible feathers would have been dull enough had not Mrs Forbes come to her aid with dresses of her own, which they remade between them; for it will easily be believed that no avoidable outlay remained unavoided by the Bruces. Indeed, but for the feeling that she must be decent on Sundays, they would have let her go yet shabbier than she was when Mrs Forbes thus partially adopted her. Now that she was warmly and neatly dressed, she began to feel and look more like the lady-child she really was. No doubt the contrast was very painful when she returned from Mrs Forbes's warm parlour to sleep in her own garret, with the snow on the roof, scanty clothing on the bed, and the rats in the floor. But there are two sides to a contrast; and it is wonderful also how one gets through what one cannot get out of.

A certain change in the Bruce-habits, leading to important results for Annie, must now be recorded.

Robert Bruce was making money, but not so fast as he wished. For his returns came only in small sums, although the profits were great. His customers were chiefly of the poorer classes of the town and the neighbourhood, who preferred his unpretending shop to the more showy establishments of some of his rivals. A sort of *couthy, pauky,* confidentially flattering way that he had with them, pleased them, and contributed greatly to keep them true to his counter. And as he knew how to buy as well as how to sell, the poor people, if they had not the worth of their money, had at least what was good of its sort. But, as I have said, although he was making haste to be rich, he was not succeeding fast enough. So he bethought him that the Missionar Kirk was getting "verra throng."[1]

A month or two before this time, the Missionars had made choice of a very able man for their pastor—a man of genuine and strong religious feeling, who did not allow his theology to interfere with the teaching

---

[1] VERRA THRONG (Scots): Very thronged/crowded

given him by God's Spirit more than he could help, and who, if he had been capable of making a party at all, would have made it with the poor against the rich. This man had gathered about him a large congregation of the lower classes of Glamerton; and Bruce had learned with some uneasiness that a considerable portion of his customers was to be found in the Missionar Kirk on Sundays, especially in the evenings. For there was a grocer amongst the Missionars, who, he feared, might draw some of his subjects away from their allegiance, seeing he must have a certain religious influence of which Robert was void, to bring to bear upon them. What therefore remained but that he too should join the congregation? For then he would not only retain the old, but have a chance of gaining new customers as well. So he took a week to think about it, a Sunday to hear Mr Turnbull in order that the change might not seem too abrupt, and a pew under the gallery before the next Sunday arrived; in which, five minutes before the hour, he and his family were seated, adding greatly to the consequence both of the place and of himself in the eyes of his Missionar customers.

This change was a source of much pleasure to Annie. For although she found the service more wearisome than good Mr Cowie's, lasting as it did about three quarters of an hour longer and the sermon was not invariably of a kind in which she could feel much interest, yet, occasionally, when Mr Turnbull was in his better moods, and testified of that which he had himself seen and known, the honest heart of the maiden recognized the truth, and listened absorbed. The young Bruces, for their parts, would gladly have gone to sleep, which would perhaps have been the most profitable use to which they could put the time; but they were kept upright and in a measure awake, by the constant application, "spikewise," of the paternal elbow, and the judicious administration, on the part of the mother, of the unfailing peppermint lozenges, to which in the process of ages a certain sabbatical character has attached itself. To Annie, however, no such ministration extended, for it would have been downright waste, seeing she could keep awake without it.

One bright frosty morning, the sermon happening to have no relation to the light around or within them, but only to the covenant made with Abraham—such a legal document constituting the only reliable protection against the character, inclinations, and duties of the Almighty, whose uncovenanted mercies are of a very doubtful nature—Annie, neither able to enter into the subject, nor to keep from shivering with the cold, tried to amuse herself with gazing at one brilliant sun-streak on the wall, which she had discovered to be gradually shortening itself, and retreating towards the window by which it had entered. Wondering how far it would have moved before the sermon was over, and whether it would have shone so very bright if God had made no covenant with Abraham, she was earnestly watching it pass from spot to spot, and from cobweb to cobweb, as if already it fled before the coming darkness of the long winter night, when she caught a glimpse of a very peculiar countenance turned in the same direction—that is, not towards the minister, but towards this travelling light. She thought the woman was watching it as well as she, and wondered whether she too was hoping for a plate of hot broth as soon as the sunbeam had gone a certain distance—broth being the Sunday fare with the Bruces—and, I presume, with most families in Scotland. The countenance was very plain, seamed and scarred as if the woman had fallen into the fire when a child; and Annie had not looked at her two seconds, before she saw that she was perfectly blind. Indeed she thought at first that she had no eyes at all; but as she kept gazing, fascinated with the strangeness and ugliness of the face, she discovered that the eyelids, though incapable of separating, were in constant motion, and that a shrunken eye-ball underneath each kept rolling and turning ever, as if searching for something it could not find. She saw too that there was a light on the face, a light which came neither from the sun in the sky, nor the sunbeam on the wall, towards which it was unconsciously turned. I think it must have been the heavenly bow itself, shining upon all human clouds—a bow that had shone for thousands of ages before ever there was an Abraham, or a Noah, or any other of our faithless generation, which will not trust its God unless he swear that he will not destroy them. It was the ugliest face. But over it, as over the rugged channel of a sea, flowed the transparent waves of a heavenly delight.

When the service was over, almost before the words of the benediction had left the minister's lips, the people, according to Scotch habit, hurried out of the chapel, as if they could not possibly endure one word more. But Annie, who was always put up to the top of the pew, because there, by reason of an intruding pillar, it required a painful twist of the neck to see the minister, stood staring at the blind woman as she felt her way out of the chapel. There was no fear of putting her out by staring at her. When, at length, she followed her into the open air, she found her standing by the door, turning her sightless face on all sides, as if looking for some one and trying hard to open her eyes that she might see better. Annie watched her, till, seeing her lips move, she knew, half by instinct, that she was murmuring, "The bairn's forgotten me!" Thereupon she glided up to her and said gently:

"If you tell me where you live, I'll take you home."

"What do they call *you*, child?" returned the blind woman, in a gruff, almost manlike voice, hardly less unpleasant to hear than her face was to look at.

"Annie Anderson," answered Annie.

"Oh, ay! I thought as much. I know all about you. Give me a hold of your hand. I live in that wee house down at the bridge, between the dam and the Glamour, you know. You'll keep me off the stones?"

"Ay, I will." answered Annie confidently.

"I could go alone, but I'm growing quite old now, and I'm just rather scared of falling."

"What made you think it was me—I never spoke to you before?" asked Annie, as they walked on together.

"Well, it's just half guessing, and half a kind of judgement—putting things together, you know, my child. You see, I knew all the bairns that come to our church well enough already. I know the word and almost the step of them. And I heard tell that Mister Bruce was come to our church. So when a lassie spoke to me that I never saw before, I just sort of knew that it had to be yourself."

All this was spoken in the same harsh voice, full of jars, as if ever driving against corners, and ready to break into a hoarse whisper. But the woman held Annie's hand kindly, and yielded like a child to her guidance which was as careful as that of the angel that led Peter.

It was a new delight to Annie to have some one to whom she a child could be a kind of mother, towards whom she could fulfil a woman's highest calling—that of *ministering unto;* and it was with something of a sacred pride that she led her safe home, through the snowy streets, and down the steep path that led from the level of the bridge, with its three high stone arches, to the little meadow where her cottage stood. Before they reached it, the blind woman, whose name was Tibbie (*Isobel*) Dyster, had put many questions to her, and without asking one indiscreet, had yet, by her gift for fitting and fusing things in the retort of her own brain, come to a tolerably correct knowledge of her character, circumstances, and history.

As soon as they entered the cottage, Tibbie was entirely at her ease. The first thing she did was to lift the kettle from the fire, and feel the fire with her hands in order to find out in what condition it was. She would not allow Annie to touch it: she could not trust the creature that had nothing but eyes to guide her, with such a delicate affair. Her very hands looked blind and trying to see, as, with fine up-curved tips, they went wandering over the tops of the live peats. She re-arranged them, put on some fresh pieces, blew a little at them all astray and to no purpose, was satisfied, coughed, and sank upon a chair, to put her bonnet off. Most women of her station wore only a *mutch* or close cap, but Tibbie wore a bonnet with a brilliantly gay ribbon, so fond was she of bright colours, although she had nothing but the testimony of others, vague enough ere it succeeded in crossing the dark distances of her brain, as to the effect of those even with which she adorned her own person. Her room was very bare, but as clean as it was possible for room to be. Her bed was in the wall which divided it from the rest of the house, and this one room was her whole habitation. The other half of the cottage was occupied by an old cripple, nearly bedridden, to whose many necessities Tibbie used to minister. The eyes of the one and the legs of the other worked in tolerable harmony; and if they had a quarrel now and then, it was no greater than gave a zest to their intercourse. These particulars, however, Annie did not learn till afterwards.

She looked all about the room, and seeing no sign of any dinner for Tibbie, was reminded thereby that her own chance had considerably diminished.

"I maun awa hame," she said with a sigh.	"I must be getting home," she said with a sigh.

"Ay, lassie; they'll be bidin' their denner for ye."	"Ay, lassie; they'll be waiting on you for dinner."
"Na, nae fear o' that," answered Annie, adding with another little sigh, "I doot there winna be muckle o' the broth to the fore or I win hame."	"Na, no fear of that," answered Annie, adding with another little sigh, "I expect there'll be little of the broth left by the time I get home."
"Weel jist bide, bairn, an' tak' a cup o' tay wi' me. It's a' 'at I hae to offer ye. Will ye bide?"	"Well, just stay, bairn, and take a cup of tea with me. It's all that I have to offer you. Will you stay?"
"Maybe I wad be i' yer gait," objected Annie feebly.	"Maybe I would be in your way," objected Annie feebly.
"Na, na; nae fear o' that. Ye'll read a bit to me efterhin."	"Na, na; no fear of that. You'll read a bit to me afterwards."
"Ay will I."	"Ay, I will."

And Annie stayed all the afternoon with Tibbie, and went home with the Bruces after the evening service. This was the beginning of her acquaintance with Tibbie Dyster.

It soon grew into a custom for Annie to take Tibbie home from the chapel—a custom which the Bruces could hardly have objected to, had they been so inclined. But they were not so inclined, for it saved the broth—that is, each of them got a little more in consequence, and Annie's absence was therefore a Sabbath blessing.

Much as she was neglected at home, however, Annie was steadily gaining a good reputation in the town. Old men said she was a gude bairn, and old women said she was a douce lassie; while those who enjoyed finding fault more than giving praise, turned their silent approbation of Annie into expressions of disapproval of the Bruces—"lattin' her gang like a beggar, as gin she was no kith or kin o' theirs, whan it's weel kent whase heifer Rob Bruce is plooin' wi'."[1]

But Robert nevertheless grew and prospered all day, and dreamed at night that he was the king, digging the pits for the English cavalry, and covering them again with the treacherous turf. Somehow the dream never went further. The field and the kingship would vanish and he only remain, the same Robert Bruce, the general dealer, plotting still, but in his own shop.

---

[1] "letting her go like a beggar, as if she was no kith or kin of theirs, when it's well known whose heifer Rob Bruce is ploughing with."

CHAPTER XXXIX

Responsive to Mr Cupples's last words uttered from the brink of the pit into which his spirit was sinking, and probably forgotten straightway, Alec knocked at his door upon the Sunday evening, and entered. The strange creature was sitting in the same position as before, looking as if he had not risen since he spoke those words. But there was an alteration in the place, a certain Sunday look about the room, which Alec could not account for. The same caricatures jested from the walls; the same tumbler of toddy was steaming on the table amidst the same litter of books and papers covered with the same dust and marked with the same circles from the bottoms of wet tumblers and glasses. The same cutty-clay, of enviable blackness, reposed between the teeth of Mr Cupples.

After he had been seated for a few moments, however, Alec all at once discovered the source of the reformation-look of the place: Mr Cupples had on a shirt-collar—clean and of imposing proportions. To this no doubt was attached a shirt, but as there was no further sign of its presence, it could not have affected the aspect of things. Although, however, this shirt-collar was no doubt the chief cause of the change of expression in the room, Alec, in the course of the evening, discovered further signs of improvement in the local morals; one, that the hearth had been cleared of a great heap of ashes, and now looked modest and moderate as if belonging to an old maid's cottage, instead of an old bachelor's garret; and another, that, upon the untidy table, lay an open book of divinity, a volume of Gurnall's *Christian Armour* namely, which I fear Mr Cupples had chosen more for its wit than its devotion. While making these discoveries, Alec chanced to observe—he was quick-eyed—that some of the dusty papers on the table were scrawled over with the first amorphous appearance of metrical composition. These moved his curiosity; for what kind of poetry could the most unpoetic-looking Mr Cupples produce from that great head of his with the lanky colourless hair?—But meantime we must return to the commencement of the interview.

"Ony mair[1] Greek, laddie?" asked Mr Cupples.

---

[1] ONY MAIR (Scots): Any more

"No, thank you, sir," answered Alec. "I only came to see you. You told me to come again to-night."

"Did I? Well, it may stand. But I protest against being made accountable for anything that fellow Cupples may choose to say when I'm not at home."

Here he emptied his glass of toddy, and filled it again from the tumbler.

"Shall I go away?" asked Alec, half bewildered.

"No, no; sit still. You're a good sort of innocent, I think. I won't give you any toddy though. You needn't look so greedy at it."

"I don't want any toddy, sir. I never drank a tumbler in my life."

"For God's sake," exclaimed Mr Cupples, with sudden energy, leaning forward in his chair, his blue eyes flashing on Alec—"for God's sake, never drink a drop.—Rainbows. Rainbows."

These last two words were spoken after a pause, and in a tone of sadness. Alec thought he was drunk again, and half rose to go.

"Don't go yet," said Mr Cupples, authoritatively. "You come at your own will: you must go at mine.—If I could but get a kick at that fellow Cupples! But I declare I can't help it. If I were God, I would cure him of drink. It's the very first thing I would do."

Alec could not help being shocked at the irreverence of the words. But the solemnity of Mr Cupples's face speedily dissipated the feeling. Suddenly changing his tone, he went on:

"What's your name?"

"Alec Forbes."

"Alec Forbes. I'll try to remember it. I seldom remember anybody's name, though. I sometimes forget my own. What was the fellow's name you thrashed the other day?"

"Patrick Beauchamp. I did not mention it before."

"The devil it was!" exclaimed Mr Cupples, half-starting from his seat. "Did you give him a *good* thrashing?"

"I think he had the worst of it. He gave in, any way."

"He comes of a bad lot! *I* know all about them. They're from Strathspey, where my father came from—at least his father was. If the young fellow turns out well, it'll be a wonder. I'll tell you all about them."

Mr Cupples here launched into a somewhat discursive account of Patrick Beauchamp's antecedents, indicating by its minuteness that there must have been personal relations of some kind between them or their families. Perhaps he glanced at something of the sort when he said that old Beauchamp was a hard man even for a lawyer. I will condense the story from the more diffuse conversational narrative, interrupted by question and remark on the part of Alec, and give it the shape of formal history.

Beauchamp's mother was the daughter of a Highland chief, whose pedigree went back to an Irish king of date so remote that his existence was doubtful to every one not personally interested in the extraction. Mrs Beauchamp had all the fierceness without much of the grace belonging to the Celtic nature. Her pride of family, even, had not prevented her from revenging herself upon her father, who had offended her, by running away with a handsome W.S., who, taken with her good looks, and flattered by the notion of overcoming her pride, had found a conjunction of circumstances favourable to the conquest. It was not long, however, before both repented of the step. That her father should disown her was not of much consequence in any point of view, but that nobody in Edinburgh would admit her claims to distinction—which arose from the fact that they were so unpleasantly asserted that no one could endure herself—did disgust her considerably; and her annoyance found vent in abuse of her husband for having failed to place her in the sphere to which she had a just claim. The consequence was, that he neglected her; and she sat at home brooding over her wrongs, despising and at length hating her husband, and meditating plans of revenge as soon as her child should be born. At length, within three months after the birth of Patrick, she found that he was unfaithful to her, and immediately demanded a separate maintenance. To this her husband made no further objection than policy required. But when she proceeded to impose an oath upon him that he would never take her child from her, the heart of the father demurred. Whereupon she swore that, if ever he made the attempt, she would poison the child rather than that he should succeed. He turned pale as death, and she saw that she had gained her point. And, indeed, the woman was capable of anything to which she had made up her mind—a power over one's self and friends not desirable except in view of such an object as that of *Lady Macbeth*. But Mrs Beauchamp, like her, considered it only a becoming strength of spirit, and would have despised herself if she had broken one resolution for another indubitably better. So her husband bade her farewell, and made no lamentation except over the probable result of such training as the child must receive at the hands of such a mother. She withdrew to a country town not far from the Moray Frith, where she might live comfortably on her small income, be a person of some consideration, and reap all the advantages of the peculiar facilities which the place afforded for the education of her boy, whom she would mould and model after her own heart.

"So you see, Mr—I forget yer name—Forbes? yes, Forbes, if the rascal takes after his mother, you have made a dangerous enemy," said Mr Cupples, in conclusion.

Alec laughed.

"I advise you," resumed Mr Cupples, "to keep a gleg ee in yer heid, though—seriously. A body may lauch ower aften. It winna do to gang glowerin' at rainbows. They're bonnie things, but they're nae brig-backs. Gin ye lippen to them, ye'll be i' the water in a cat-loup."

Alec was beginning to enter into the humour of the man.

"I see something like poetry lying about the table, Mr Cupples," said he, with a sly allusion to the rainbows. "Would you let me look at it?"

Mr Cupples glanced at him sharply; but replied immediately:

"Broken bits of them! And the rainbows fade badly, once you take the key-stone out of them. Let them sit up there, bridges over nothing, with no road upon the top of them, like the stone bridge of Drumdochart after the flood. Keep your hands and your eyes off them, as I told you before.—Ay, ay, you can look at those screeds if you like. Only don't say a word to me about any of them. And take warning by them yourself, never to write one word of poetry, to keep you from going to pieces."

"Small fear of that!" returned Alec, laughing.

"Well, I hope so.—You can make a church and a mill of them, if you like. They have lain there long enough. Now, hold your tongue. I'm going to fill my pipe again, before I burn out the dottle. I won't drink more tonight, cause it's the Sabbath, and I'm going to read my book."

So saying, he proceeded to get the *dottle* out of his pipe, by knocking it on the hob; while Alec took up the paper that lay nearest. He found it contained a fragment of a poem in the Scotch language; and, searching amongst the rest of the scattered sheets, he soon got the whole of it together.

Now, although Alec had but little acquaintance with verse, he was able, thanks to Annie Anderson, to enjoy a ballad very heartily; and there was something in this one which, associating itself in his mind with the strange being before him, moved him more than he could account for. It was called:

TIME AND TIDE.

As I was walkin' on the strand,
   I spied an auld man sit
On ane auld rock; and aye the waves
   Cam washin' to its fit.
And aye his lips gaed mutterin',
   And his ee was dull and blae.
As I cam near, he luik'd at me,
   But this was a' his say:
"Robbie and Jeannie war twa bonnie bairns,
   And they played thegither upo' the shore:
Up cam the tide 'tween the mune and the sterns,
   And pairtit the twa wi' an eerie roar."

What can the auld man mean, quo' I,
   Sittin' upo' the auld rock?
The tide creeps up wi' moan and cry,
   And a hiss 'maist like a mock.
The words he mutters maun be the en'
   O' a weary dreary sang—
   A deid thing floatin' in his brain,
   That the tide will no lat gang.
"Robbie and Jeannie war twa bonnie bairns,
   And they played thegither upo' the shore:
Up cam the tide 'tween the mune and the sterns,
   And pairtit the twa wi' an eerie roar."

What pairtit them, auld man? I said;
   Did the tide come up ower strang?
'Twas a braw deith for them that gaed,
   Their troubles warna lang.
Or was ane ta'en, and the ither left—
   Ane to sing, ane to greet?
It's sair, richt sair, to be bereft,
   But the tide is at yer feet.
"Robbie and Jeannie war twa bonnie bairns,
   And they played thegither upo' the shore:
Up cam the tide 'tween the mune and the sterns,
   And pairtit the twa wi' an eerie roar."

    Maybe, quo' I, 'twas Time's gray sea,
        Whase droonin' 's waur to bide;
But Death's a diver, seekin' ye
    Aneath its chokin' tide.
And ye'll luik in ane anither's ee
    Triumphin' ower gray Time.
But never a word he answered me,
    But ower wi' his dreary chime—
"Robbie and Jeannie war twa bonnie bairns,
    And they played thegither upo' the shore:
Up cam the tide 'tween the mune and the sterns,
    And pairtit the twa wi' an eerie roar."

    Maybe, auld man, said I, 'twas Change
        That crap atween the twa?
Hech! that's a droonin' awfu' strange,
    Ane waur than ane and a'.
He spak nae mair. I luik't and saw
    That the auld lips cudna gang.
The tide unseen took him awa—
    Left me to end his sang:
"Robbie and Jeannie war twa bonnie bairns,
    And they played thegither upo' the shore:
Up cam the tide 'tween the mune and the sterns,
    And tuik them whaur pairtin' shall be no more."

ENGLISH

    As I was walking on the strand,
        I saw an old man take root
On one old rock; and still the waves
    Came washing to its foot.
And still his lips went muttering,
    And his eye had a dull blue ray.
As I came near, he looked at me,
    But this was all his say:
"Robbie and Jeannie were two bonnie bairns,
    And they played together upon the shore:
Up came the tide 'tween the moon and the stars,
    And parted the two with an eerie roar."

What can the old man mean, said I,
   Sitting upon the old rock?
The tide creeps up with moan and cry,
   And a hiss that's almost a mock.
The words he mutters must be the end
   Of a weary dreary song—
A dead thing swirling in his brain,
   That the tide won't float along.
"Robbie and Jeannie were two bonnie bairns,
   And they played together upon the shore:
Up came the tide 'tween the moon and the stars,
   And parted the two with an eerie roar."

What parted them, old man? I said;
   Did the tide come up too strong?
'Twas a fine death for them that went,
   Their troubles weren't over long.
Or was one taken, the other left—
   One made whole, one incomplete?
It's sore, right sore, to be bereft,
   But the tide is at your feet.
"Robbie and Jeannie were two bonnie bairns,
   And they played together upon the shore:
Up came the tide 'tween the moon and the stars,
   And parted the two with an eerie roar."

Maybe, said I, 'twas Time's gray sea,
   Whose drowning's worse to bide;
But Death's a diver, as all will see
   Beneath its choking tide.
And you'll look in each other's eyes with glee
   Triumphing over gray Time.
But never a word he answered me,
   But on with his dreary chime—
"Robbie and Jeannie were two bonnie bairns,
   And they played together upon the shore:
Up came the tide 'tween the moon and the stars,
   And parted the two with an eerie roar."

> Maybe, old man, said I, 'twas Change
>   That crept between to appal?
> Faith! that's a drowning awful strange,
>   One worse than one and all.
> He spoke no more. To my dismay
>   The old man was borne along
> By a tide unseen that took him away—
>   I was left to end his song:
> "Robbie and Jeannie were two bonnie bairns,
>   And they played together upon the shore:
> Up came the tide 'tween the moon and the stars,
>   And took them where parting shall be no more."

Before he had finished reading, the refrain had become so familiar to Alec, that he unconsciously murmured the last, changed as it was from the preceding form, aloud. Mr Cupples looked up from Gurnall uneasily, fidgeted in his chair, and said testily:

"A' nonsense! Moonshine and rainbows! Haud yer tongue! The last line's a' wrang."

"All nonsense! Moonshine and rainbows! Hold your tongue! The last line's all wrong."

He then returned with a determined air to the consideration of his *Christian Armour*, while Alec, in whom the minor tone of the poem had greatly deepened the interest he felt in the writer, gazed at him in a bewilderment like that one feels when his eyes refuse to take their proper relation to the perspective before them. He could not get those verses and Mr Cupples into harmony. Not daring to make any observation, however, he sat with the last leaf still in his hand, and a reverential stare upon his face, which at length produced a remarkable effect upon the object of it. Suddenly lifting his eyes—

"What are ye glowerin' at me for?" he exclaimed, flinging his book from him, which, missing the table, fell on the floor on the further side of it. "I'm neither ghaist nor warlock. Damn ye! gang oot, gin ye be gaun to stick me throu and throu wi' yer een, that gait."

"What are you glowering at me for?" he exclaimed, flinging his book from him, which, missing the table, fell on the floor on the further side of it. "I'm neither ghost nor warlock. Damn you! go out, if you're going to stick me through and through with your eyes, like that."

"I beg your pardon, Mr Cupples. I didn't mean to be rude," said Alec humbly.

"Well, cut your stick, I've had enough of you for one night. I can't stand glowering eyes, especially in the heads of idiots of innocents like you."

I am sorry to have to record what Alec learned from the landlady afterwards, that Mr Cupples went to bed that night, notwithstanding it was the Sabbath, more drunk than she had ever known him. Indeed he could not properly be said to have gone to bed at all, for he had tumbled on the counter-pane in his clothes and clean shirt-collar; where she had found him fast asleep the next morning, with Gurnall's *Christian Armour* terribly crumpled under him.

"But," said Alec, "what *is* Mr Cupples?"

"He could hardly answer you that himself," was the reply. "He does a heap of things; writes for the lawyers sometimes; buys and sells queer books; gives lessons in Greek and Hebrew—but he doesn't like that—he can't bear opposition, and laddies are very contrary; helps anybody that wants help in the way of figures—when their books go wrong you know, for figures are awful for getting jumbled. He's a kind of librarian at your own college just now, Mr Forbes. The old man's dead, and Mr Cupples is just doing the work. They won't give him the place—'cause he has an ill name for drink—but they'll get as much work out of him as if they did, and for half the money. The man keeps at anything well enough all day, but the minute he comes home, out comes the tappit hen (*store-bottle*), and he just sits down and drinks till he turns the world upon the top of him."

The next day, about noon, Alec went into the library, where he found Mr Cupples busy re-arranging the books and the catalogue, both of which had been neglected for years. This was the first of many visits to the library, or rather to the librarian.

There was a certain mazy sobriety of demeanour about Mr Cupples all day long, as if in the presence of such serious things as books he was bound to be upon his good behaviour, and confine his dissipation to taking snuff in prodigious quantities. He was full of information about books, and had, besides, opinions concerning them, which were always ready to assume quaint and decided expression. For instance: one afternoon, Alec having taken up *Tristram Shandy* and asked him what kind of a book it was, the pro-librarian snatched it from his hands and put it on the shelf again, answering:

"A palace of dirt and impudence and spiritual stink. The clever devil had his entrails in his breast and his heart in his belly, and regarded neither God nor his own mother. His laughter's not like the crackling of thorns under a pot, but like the sniggering of a devil behind the wainscot. Let him sit and rot there!"

Asking him another day what sort of poet Shelley was, Alec received the answer:

"A bonny creature, with more thoughts than there was room for in his head. Consequently he

gaed staiggerin' aboot as gin he had been tied to the tail o' an inveesible balloon. Unco licht heidit, but no muckle hairm in him by natur'."	went staggering about as if he had been tied to the tail of an invisible balloon. Very light headed, but not much harm in him by nature."

He never would remain in the library after the day began to ebb. The moment he became aware that the first filmy shadow had fallen from the coming twilight, he caught up his hat, locked the door, gave the key to the sacrist, and hurried away.

The friendly relation between the two struck its roots deeper and deeper during the session, and Alec bade him good-bye with regret.

Mr Cupples was a baffled poet trying to be a humourist—baffled—not by the booksellers or the public—for such baffling one need not have a profound sympathy—but baffled by his own weakness, his incapacity for assimilating sorrow, his inability to find or invent a theory of the universe which should show it still beautiful despite of passing pain, of checked aspiration, of the ruthless storms that lay waste the Edens of men, and dissolve the high triumph of their rainbows. He had yet to learn that through "the heartache and the thousand natural shocks that flesh is heir to," man becomes capable of the blessedness to which all the legends of a golden age point. Not finding, when he most needed it, such a theory even in the New Testament—for he had been diligently taught to read it awry—Mr Cupples took to jesting and toddy; but, haunting the doors of Humour, never got further than the lobby.

With regard to Patrick Beauchamp, as far as Alec could see, his dignity had succeeded in consoling itself for the humiliation it had undergone, by an absolute and eternal renunciation of all knowledge of Alec Forbes's existence.

CHAPTER XL

Winter had begun to withdraw his ghostly troops, and Glamerton began to grow warmer. Not half so many cold feet dangled from the cold legs of little children in the torturing churches; not half so many coughs tore the chests of the poor old men and women as they stooped over their little fires, with the blasts from door and window-sill in their ankles and the backs of their necks. Annie, who had been very happy all the time, began to be aware of something more at hand. A flutter scarcely recognizable, as of the wings of awaking delight, would stir her little heart with a sensation of physical presence and motion; she would find herself giving an involuntary skip as she walked along, and now and then humming a bit of a psalm tune. A hidden well was throbbing in the child's bosom. Its waters had been frozen by the winter; and the spring, which sets all things springing, had made it flow and swell afresh, soon to break bubbling forth. But her joy was gentle, for even when she was merriest, it was in a sober, *douce*, and maidenly fashion, testifying that she had already walked with Sorrow, and was not afraid of her.

Robert Bruce's last strategical move against the community had been tolerably successful, even in his own eyes; and he was consequently so far satisfied with himself, that he could afford to be in good humour with other people. Annie came in for a share of this humour; and although she knew him too well to have any regard for him, it was yet a comfort to her to be on such terms with him as not to have to dread a bitter word every time she chanced to meet him. This comfort, however, stood on a sandy foundation; for the fact that an expected customer had not called upon the Saturday might be enough to set the acetous fermentation at work all the Sunday in the bosom of Robert Bruce.

At length, one bright day in the end of March, Alec came home, not the worse to friendly eyes for having been at college. He seemed the same cheery, active youth as before. The chief differences apparent were, that he had grown considerably, and that he wore a coat. The hat, at that time a necessary portion of the college costume, he had discarded, wearing his old cap in preference. There was likewise a certain indescribable alteration in tone and manner, a certain general crystallization and polish, which the same friends regarded as an indubitable improvement.

The day after his arrival, crossing the square of Glamerton, he spied, in a group of men talking together, his old friend, Thomas Crann. He went up and shook hands with him, and with Andrew Constable, the clothier.

"Hasn't he grown a long man?" said Andrew to Thomas, regarding Alec kindly.

"Humph!" returned Thomas, "he'll just need the longer coffin."

Alec laughed; but Andrew said, "Heavens, man!"

Thomas and Alec walked away together. But scarcely a sentence had been exchanged before the stonemason, with a delicacy of perception of which his rough manner and horny hands gave no indication, felt that a film of separation had come between the youth and himself. Anxious to break through it, he said abruptly,

"How's your immortal part, Alec? Remember, there's a knowledge that worketh death."

Alec laughed—not scornfully—but he laughed.

"You may laugh, but it's a sore truth," said the mason.

Alec held out his hand, for here their way diverged. Thomas shook it kindly, but walked away gloomy. Arrived at home, he shut to his door, and went down on his knees by his bedside. When Jean came with his supper she found the door fast.

In order to prepare for the mathematical studies of the following year, Alec went to the school again in the morning of most days, Mr Malison being well able to render him all the assistance he required. The first time he made his appearance at the door, a silence as of death was the sign of his welcome; but a tumult presently arose, and discipline was for a time suspended. I am afraid he had a slight feeling of condescension, as he returned the kind greeting of his old companions.—Raise a housemaid to be cook, and she will condescend to the new housemaid.

Annie sat still, staring at her book, and turning red and pale alternately. But he took no notice of her, and she tried to be glad of it.

When school was over, however, he came up to her in the lane, and addressed her kindly.

But the delicate little maiden felt, as the rough stonemason had felt, that a change had passed over the old companion and friend. True, the change was only a breath—a mere shadow. Yet it was a measureless gulf between them. Annie went to her garret that night with a sense of sad privation.

But her pain sprung from a source hardly so deep as that of the stonemason. For the change she found in Alec was chiefly of an external kind, and if she had a vague feeling of a deeper change, it had scarcely yet come up into her consciousness. When she saw the *young gentleman* her heart sank within her. Her friend was lost; and a shape was going about, as he did, looking awfully like the old Alec, who had carried her in his arms through the invading torrent. Nor was there wanting, to complete the bewilderment of her feeling, a certain additional reverence for the apparition, which she must after all regard as a further development of the same person.

Mrs Forbes never asked her to the house now, and it was well for her that her friendship with Tibbie Dyster had begun. But as she saw Alec day after day at school, the old colours began to revive out of the faded picture—for to her it was a faded picture, although new varnished. And when the spring had advanced a little, the boat was got out, and then Alec could not go rowing in the *Bonnie Annie* without thinking of its godmother, and inviting her to join them. Indeed Curly would not have let him forget her if he had been so inclined; for he felt that she was a bond between him and Alec, and he loved Alec the more devotedly that the rift between their social positions had begun to show itself. The devotion of the schoolboy to his superior in schoolboy arts had begun to change into something like the devotion of the clansman to his chief—not the worst folly the world has known—in fact not a folly at all, except it stop there: many enthusiasms are follies only because they are not greater enthusiasms. And not unfrequently would an odd laugh of consciousness between Annie and Curly, unexpectedly meeting, reveal the fact that they were both watching for a peep or a word of Alec.

In due time the harvest came; and Annie could no more keep from haunting the harvest than the crane could keep from flying south when the summer is over. She watched all the fields around Glamerton; she knew what response each made to the sun, and which would first be ripe for the reaping; and the very day that the sickle was put in, there was Annie to see and share in the joy. How mysterious she thought those long colonnades of slender pillars, each supporting its own waving comet-head of barley! Or when the sun was high, she would lie down on the ground, and look far into the little forest of yellow polished oat-stems, stretching away and away into the unseen—alas, so soon to fall, and leave a naked commonplace behind! If she were only small enough to go wandering about in it, what wonders might she not discover!—But I forget that I am telling a story, and not writing a fairy-tale.—Unquestioned as uninvited, she was, as she had often been before, one of the company of reapers, gatherers, binders, and stookers, assembled to collect the living gold of the earth from the early fields of the farm of Howglen. Sadly her thoughts went back to the old days when Dowie was master of the field, and she was Dowie's little mistress. Not that she met with anything but kindness—only it was not the kindness she had had from Dowie. But the pleasure of being once more near Alec almost made up for every loss. And he was quite friendly, although, she must confess, not quite so familiar as of old. But that did not matter, she assured herself.

The labourers all knew her, and themselves took care that she should have the portion of their food which her assistance had well earned, and which was all her wages. She never refused anything that was offered her, except money. That she had taken only once in her life—from Mr Cowie, whom she continued to love the more dearly for it, although she no longer attended his church.

But again the harvest was safely lodged, and the sad old age of the year sank through rains and frosts to his grave.

The winter came and Alec went.

He had not been gone a week when Mrs Forbes's invitations re-commenced; and, as if to make up for the neglect of the summer, they were more frequent than before. No time was so happy for Annie as the time she spent with her. She never dreamed of accusing her of fickleness or unevenness, but received whatever kindness she offered with gratitude. And, this winter, she began to make some return in the way of household assistance.

One day, while searching in the lumber-room for something for Mrs Forbes, she came upon a little book lying behind a box. It was damp and swollen and mouldy, and the binding was decayed and broken. The inside was dingy and spotted with brown spots, and had too many *f*'s in it, as she thought. Yet the first glance fascinated her. It had opened in the middle of *L'Allegro*. Mrs Forbes found her standing spell-bound, reading the rhymed poems of the man whose blank-verse, two years before, she had declined as not what poetry ought to be. I have often seen a child refuse his food, and, after being compelled to eat one mouthful, gladly devour the whole. In like manner Annie, having once tasted Milton's poetry, did not let it go till she had devoured even the *Paradise Lost*, of which when she could not make sense, she at least made music—the chords of old John Milton's organ sounding through his son's poetry in the brain of a little Scotch lassie who never heard an organ in her life.

CHAPTER XLI

"Hillo, bantam!" exclaimed Mr Cupples, to Alec, entering his garret within an hour of his arrival in his old quarters, and finding the soul of the librarian still hovering in the steam of his tumbler, like one of Swedenborg's damned over the odour of his peculiar hell. As he spoke he emptied the glass, the custom of drinking from which, instead of from the tumbler itself—rendering it impossible to get drunk all at once—is one of the atonements offered by the Scotch to their tutelar god—Propriety.—"Come in. What are you standing there for, as if you weren't at home," he added, seeing that Alec lingered on the threshold. "Sit down. I'm not altogether sorry to see you."

"Have you been to the country, Mr Cupples?" asked Alec, as he took a chair.

"The country! Na, I haven't been in the country. I'm a town-snail. The country's for calves and geese. It's too green for me. I like the gray stones—well built, to keep out the cold. I just reverse the opinion of the old duke in Shakespeare;—for this my life

'Find trees in tongues, its running brooks in books,
    Stones in sermons,—'

and I can't go on any farther with it. The last's true anyway. I won't give you any toddy though."

"I don't want any."

"That's right. Keep to that negation as an anchor of the soul, sure and steadfast. There's no bottom to the sea you'll go down in if you cut the cable that holds you to that anchor. Here's to you!"

And again Mr Cupples emptied his glass.

"How are you prepared for your mathematics?" he resumed.

"Just middling," answered Alec.

"That's as I thought. Small preparation does well enough for Professor Fraser's Greek; but you'll find it's another story with the mathematics. You'll just have to come to me with them as you did with the Greek."

"Thank you, Mr Cupples," said Alec heartily. "I don't know how to repay you."

"Repay me! I want no repayment. Only ask me no questions, and go away when I'm drunk."

After all his summer preparation, Alec was still behind in mathematics; for while, with a distinct object in view, he was capable of much—without one, reading was a weariness to him. His medical studies, combining, as they did, in their anatomical branch, much to be learned by the eye and the hand with what was to be learned from books, interested him more and more.

One afternoon, intent upon a certain course of investigation, he remained in the dissecting room after the other students had gone, and worked away till it grew dark. He then lighted a candle, and worked on. The truth was unfolding itself gently and willingly. At last, feeling tired, he laid down his scalpel, dropped upon a wooden chair, and, cold as it was, fell fast asleep. When he awoke, the candle was *bobbing* in its socket, alternately lighting and shadowing the dead man on the table. Strange glooms were gathering about the bottles on the shelves, and especially about one corner of the room, where—but I must not particularize too much. It must be remembered that he had awaked suddenly, in a strange place, and with a fitful light. He confessed to Mr Cupples that he had felt a little uncomfortable—not frightened, but *eerie*. He was just going to rise and go home, when, as he stretched out his hand for his scalpel, the candle sunk in darkness, and he lost the guiding glitter of the knife. At the same moment, he caught a doubtful gleam of two eyes looking in at him from one of the windows. That moment the place became insupportable with horror. The vague sense of an undefined presence turned the school of science into a charnel-house. He started up, hurried from the room, feeling as if his feet took no hold of the floor and his back was fearfully exposed, locked the door, threw the key upon the porter's table, and fled. He did not recover his equanimity till he found himself in the long narrow street that led to his lodgings, lighted from many little shop-windows in stone gable and front.

By the time he had had his tea, and learned a new proposition of Euclid, the fright seemed to lie far behind him. It was not so far as he thought, however, for he started to his feet when a sudden gust of wind shook his windows. But then it was a still frosty night, and such a gust was not to be expected. He looked out. Far above shone the stars.

"How they sparkle in the frost!" he said, as if the frost reached them. But they did look like the essential life that makes snow-flakes and icy spangles everywhere—they were so like them, only they were of fire. Even snow itself must have fire at the heart of it.—All was still enough up there.

Then he looked down into the street, full of the comings and goings of people, some sauntering and staring, others hastening along. Beauchamp was looking in at the window of a second-hand book-shop opposite.

Not being able to compose himself again to his studies, he resolved, as he had not called on Mr Fraser for some time, and the professor had not been at the class that day, to go and inquire after him now.

Mr Fraser lived in the quadrangle of the college; but in the mood Alec was in, nothing would do him so much good as a walk in the frost. He was sure of a welcome from the old man; for although Alec gave but little attention to Greek now, Mr Fraser was not at all dissatisfied with him, knowing that he was doing his best to make himself a good doctor.

His friendliness towards him had increased; for he thought he saw in him noble qualities; and now that he was an old man, he delighted to have a youth near him with whose youthfulness he could come into harmonious contact. It is because the young cannot recognize the youth of the aged, and the old will not acknowledge the experience of the young, that they repel each other.

Alec was shown into the professor's drawing-room. This was unusual. The professor was seated in an easy-chair, with one leg outstretched before him.

"Excuse me, Mr Forbes," he said, holding out his left hand without rising. "I am laid up with the gout—I don't know why. The port wine my grandfather drunk, I suppose. *I* never drink it. I'm afraid it's old age. And yon's my nurse.—Mr Forbes, your cousin, Kate, my dear."

Alec started. There, at the other side of the fire, sat a girl, half smiling and half blushing as she looked up from her work. The candles between them had hid her from him. He advanced, and she rose and held out her hand. He was confused; she was perfectly collected, although the colour rose a little more in her cheek. She might have been a year older than Alec.

"So you are a cousin of mine, Mr Forbes!" she said, when they were all seated by the blazing fire—she with a piece of plain work in her hands, he with a very awkward nothing in his, and the professor contemplating his swathed leg on the chair before him.

"So your uncle says," he answered, "and I am very happy to believe him. I hope we shall be good friends."

Alec was recovering himself.

"I hope we shall," she responded, with a quick, shy, asking glance from her fine eyes.

Those eyes were worth looking into, if only as a study of colour. They were of many hues marvellously blended. I think grey and blue and brown and green were all to be found in them. Their glance rather discomposed Alec. He had not learned before that ladies' eyes are sometimes very discomposing. Yet he could not keep his from wandering towards them; and the consequence was that he soon lost the greater part of his senses. After sitting speechless for some moments, and feeling as if he had been dumb for as many minutes, he was seized by a horrible conviction that if he remained silent an instant longer, he would be driven to do or say something absurd. So he did the latter at once by bursting out with the stupid question,

"What are you working at?"

"A duster," she answered instantly—this time without looking up.

Now the said duster was of the finest cambric; so that Alec could not help seeing that she was making game of him. This banished his shyness, and put him on his mettle.

"I see," he said, "when I ask questions, you—"

"Tell lies," she interposed, without giving him time even to hesitate; adding,

"Does your mother answer all your questions, Mr Forbes?"

"I believe she does—one way or other."

"Then it is sometimes the other way? Is she nice?"

"Who?" returned Alec, surprised into doubt.

"Your mother."

"She's the best woman in the world," he answered with vehemence, almost shocked at having to answer such a question.

"Oh! I beg your pardon," returned Kate, laughing; and the laugh curled her lip, revealing very pretty teeth, with a semi-transparent pearly-blue shadow in them.

"I am glad she is nice," she went on. "I should like to know her. Mothers are not *always* nice. I knew a girl at school whose mother wasn't nice at all."

She did not laugh after this childish speech, but let her face settle into perfect stillness—sadness indeed, for a shadow came over the stillness. Mr Fraser sat watching the two with his amused old face, one side of it twitching in the effort to suppress the smile which sought to break from the useful half of his mouth. His gout could not have been very bad just then.

"I see, Katie, what that long chin of yours is thinking," he said.

"What is my chin thinking, uncle?" she asked.

"That uncles are not always nice either. They snub little girls, sometimes, don't they?"

"I know one who *is* nice, all except one naughty leg."

She rose, as she said this, and going round to the back of his chair, leaned over it, and kissed his forehead. The old man looked up to her gratefully.

"Ah, Katie!" he said, "you may make game of an old man like me. But don't try your tricks on Mr Forbes there. He won't stand them."

Alec blushed. Kate went back to her seat, and took up her duster again.

Alec was a little short-sighted, though he had never discovered it till now. When Kate leaned over her uncle's chair, near which he was sitting, he saw that she was still prettier than he had thought her before.—There are few girls who to a short-sighted person look prettier when they come closer; the fact being that the general intent of the face, which the generalizing effect of the shortness of the sight reveals, has ordinarily more of beauty in it than has yet been carried out in detail; so that, as the girl approaches, one face seems to melt away, and another, less beautiful, to dawn up through it.

But, as I have said, this was not Alec's experience with Kate; for, whatever it might indicate, she looked prettier when she came nearer. He found too that her great mass of hair, instead of being, as he had thought, dull, was in reality full of glints and golden hints, as if she had twisted up a handful of sunbeams with it in the morning, which, before night, had faded a little, catching something of the duskiness and shadowiness of their prison. One thing more he saw—that her hand—she rested it on the back of the dark chair, and so it had caught his eye—was small and white; and those were all the qualities Alec was as yet capable of appreciating in a hand. Before she got back to her seat, he was very nearly in love with her. I suspect that those generally who fall in love at first sight have been in love before. At least such was Romeo's case. And certainly it was not Alec's. Yet I must confess, if he had talked stupidly before, he talked worse now; and at length went home with the conviction that he had made a great donkey of himself.

As he walked the lonely road, and the street now fast closing its windows and going to sleep, he was haunted by a very different vision from that which had accompanied him a few hours ago. Then it was the dead face of a man, into which his busy fancy had reset the living eyes that he had seen looking in at the window of the dissecting room; now it was the lovely face of his new-found cousin, possessing him so that he could fear nothing. Life had cast out death. Love had cast out fear.

But love had cast out more. For he found, when he got home, that he could neither read nor think. If Kate could have been *conscious* of its persistent intrusion upon Alec's thoughts, and its constant interruption of his attempts at study, she would have been ashamed of that pretty face of hers, and ready to disown it for its forwardness. At last, he threw his book to the other end of the room, and went to bed, where he found it not half so difficult to go to sleep as it had been to study.

The next day things went better; for he was not yet so lost that a night's rest could do him no good. But it was fortunate that there was no Greek class, and that he was not called up to read Latin that day. For the anatomy, he was in earnest about that; and love itself, so long as its current is not troubled by opposing rocks, will not disturb the studies of a real student—much.

As he left the dissecting-room, he said to himself that he would just look in and see how Mr Fraser was. He was shown into the professor's study.

Mr Fraser smiled as he entered with a certain grim comicality which Alec's conscience interpreted into: "This won't do, my young man."

"I hope your gout is better to-day, sir," he said, sending his glance wide astray of his words.

"Yes, I thank you, Mr Forbes," answered Mr Fraser, "it is better. Won't you sit down?"

Warned by that smile, Alec was astute enough to decline, and presently took his leave. As he shut the study door, however, he thought he would just peep into the dining-room, the door of which stood open opposite. There she was, sitting at the table, writing.

"Who can that letter be to?" thought Alec. But it was early days to be jealous.

"How do you do, Mr Forbes?" said Kate, holding out her hand.

Could it be that he had seen her only yesterday? Or was his visual memory so fickle that he had forgotten what she was like? She was so different from what he had been fancying her!

The fact was merely this—that she had been writing to an old friend, and her manner for the time, as well as her expression, was affected by her mental proximity to that friend;—so plastic—so fluent even—was her whole nature. Indeed Alec was not long in finding out that one of her witcheries was, that she was never the same. But on this the first occasion, the alteration in her bewildered him.

"I am glad to find your uncle better," he said.

"Yes.—You have seen him, then?"

"Yes. I was very busy in the dissecting-room, till—"

He stopped; for he saw her shudder.

"I beg your pardon," he hastened to substitute.—"We are so used to those things, that—"

"Don't say a word more about it, please," she said hastily. Then, in a vague kind of way—"Won't you sit down?"

"No, thank you. I must go home," answered Alec, feeling that she did not want him. "Good night," he added, advancing a step.

"Good night, Mr Forbes," she returned in the same vague manner, and without extending her hand.

Alec checked himself, bowed, and went with a feeling of mortification, and the resolution not to repeat his visit too soon.

She interfered with his studies notwithstanding, and sent him wandering in the streets, when he ought to have been reading at home. One bright moonlight night he found himself on the quay, and spying a boat at the foot of one of the stairs, asked the man in it if he was ready for a row. The man agreed. Alec got in, and they rowed out of the river, and along the coast to a fishing village where the man lived, and whence Alec walked home. This was the beginning of many such boating excursions made by Alec in the close of this session. They greatly improved his boatmanship, and strengthened his growing muscles. The end of the winter was mild, and there were not many days unfit for the exercise.

CHAPTER XLII

The next Saturday but one Alec received a note from Mr Fraser, hoping that his new cousin had not driven him away, and inviting him to dine that same afternoon.

He went. After dinner the old man fell asleep in his chair.

"Where were you born?" Alec asked Kate.

She was more like his first impression of her.

"Don't you know?" she replied. "In the north of Sutherlandshire—near the foot of a great mountain, from the top of which, on the longest day, you can see the sun, or a bit of him at least, all night long."

"How glorious!" said Alec.

"I don't know. *I* never saw him. And the winters are so long and terrible! Nothing but snowy hills about you, and great clouds always coming down with fresh loads of snow to scatter over them."

"Then you don't want to go back?"

"No. There is nothing to make me wish to go back. There is no one there to love me now."

She looked very sad for a few moments.

"Yes," said Alec, thoughtfully; "a winter without love must be dreadful. But I like the winter; and we have plenty of it in our quarter too."

"Where is your home?"

"Not many miles north of this."

"Is it a nice place?"

"Of course I think so."

"Ah! you have a mother. I wish I knew her."

"I wish you did.—True: the whole place is like her to me. But I don't think everybody would admire it. There are plenty of bare snowy hills there too in winter. But I think the summers and the harvests are as delightful as anything can be, except—"

"Except what?"

"Don't make me say what will make you angry with me."

"Now you must, else I shall fancy something that will make me *more* angry."

"Except your face, then," said Alec, frightened at his own boldness, but glancing at her shyly.

She flushed a little, but did not look angry.

"I don't like that," she said. "It makes one feel awkward."

"At least," rejoined Alec, emboldened, "you must allow it is your own fault."

"I can't help my face," she said, laughing.

"Oh! you know what I mean. You made me say it."

"Yes, after you had half-said it already. Don't do it again."

And there followed more of such foolish talk, uninteresting to my readers.

"Where were you at school?" asked Alec, after a pause. "Your uncle told me you were at school."

"Near London," she answered.

"Ah! that accounts for your beautiful speech."

"There again. I declare I will wake my uncle if you go on in that way."

"I beg your pardon," protested Alec; "I forgot."

"But," she went on, "in Sutherlandshire we don't talk so horribly as they do here."

"I daresay not," returned Alec, humbly.

"I don't mean you. I wonder how it is that you speak so much better than all the people here."

"I suppose because my mother speaks well. She never lets me speak broad Scotch to her."

"Your mother again! She's everything to you."

Alec did not reply.

"I *should* like to see her," pursued Kate.

"You must come and see her, then."

"See whom?" asked Mr Fraser, rousing himself from his nap.

"My mother, sir," answered Alec.

"Oh! I thought you had been speaking of Katie's friend," said the professor, and fell asleep again.

"Uncle means Bessie Warner, who is coming by the steamer from London on Monday. Isn't it kind of uncle to ask her to come and see me here?"

"He is kind always. Was Miss Warner a schoolfellow of yours?"

"Yes—no—not exactly. She was one of the governesses. I *must* go and meet her at the steamer. Will you go with me?"

"I shall be delighted. Do you know when she arrives?"

"They say about six. I daresay it is not very punctual."

"Oh! yes, she is—when the weather is decent. I will make inquiries, and come and fetch you."

"Thank you.—I suppose I may, uncle?"

"What, my dear?" said the professor, rousing himself again.

"Have my cousin to take care of me when I go to meet Bessie?"

"Yes, certainly. I shall be much obliged to you, Mr Forbes. I am not quite so agile as I was at your age, though my gouty leg *is* better."

This conversation would not have been worth recording were it not that it led to the walk and the waiting on Monday.—They found, when they reached the region of steamers, that she had not yet been signalled, but her people were expecting the signal every minute. So Alec and Kate walked out along the pier, to pass the time. This pier runs down the side of the river, and a long way into the sea. It had begun to grow dark, and Alec had to take great care of Kate amongst the tramways, coils of rope, and cables that crossed their way. At length they got clear of these, and found themselves upon the pier, built of great rough stones—lonely and desert, tapering away into the dark, its end invisible, but indicated by the red light far in front.

"It is a rough season of the year for a lady to come by sea," said Alec.

"Bessie is very fond of the sea," answered Kate. "I hope you will like her, Mr Forbes."

"Do you want me to like her better than you?" rejoined Alec. "Because if you do—"

"Look how beautiful that red light is on the other side of the river," interrupted Kate. "And there is another further out."

"When the man at the helm gets those two lights in a line," said Alec, "he may steer straight in, in the darkest night—that is, if the tide serves for the bar."

"Look how much more glorious the red shine is on the water below!" said Kate.

"It looks so wet!" returned Alec,—"just like blood."

He almost cursed himself as he said so, for he felt Kate's hand stir as if she would withdraw it from his arm. But after fluttering like a bird for a moment, it settled again upon its perch, and there rested.

The day had been quite calm, but now a sudden gust of wind from the north-east swept across the pier and made Kate shiver. Alec drew her shawl closer about her, and her arm further within his. They were now close to the sea. On the other side of the wall which rose on their left, they could hear the first of the sea-waves. It was a dreary place—no sound even indicating the neighbourhood of life. On one side, the river below them went flowing out to the sea in the dark, giving a cold sluggish gleam now and then, as if it were a huge snake heaving up a bend of its wet back, as it hurried away to join its fellows; on the other side rose a great wall of stone, beyond which was the sound of long waves following in troops out of the dark, and falling upon a low moaning coast. Clouds hung above the sea; and above the clouds two or three disconsolate stars.

"Here is a stair," said Alec. "Let us go up on the top of the sea-wall, and then we shall catch the first glimpse of the light at her funnel."

They climbed the steep rugged steps, and stood on the broad wall, hearing the sea-pulses lazily fall at its foot. The wave crept away after it fell, and returned to fall again like a weary hound. There was hardly any life in the sea. How mournful it was to lie out there, the wintry night, beneath an all but starless heaven, with the wind vexing it when it wanted to sleep!

Alec feeling Kate draw a deep breath like the sigh of the sea, looked round in her face. There was still light enough to show it frowning and dark and sorrowful and hopeless. It was in fact a spiritual mirror, which reflected in human forms the look of that weary waste of waters. She gave a little start, gathered herself together, and murmured something about the cold.

"Let us go down again," said Alec.—"The wind has risen considerably, and the wall will shelter us down below."

"No, no," she answered; "I like it. We can walk here just as well. I don't mind the wind."

"I thought you were afraid of falling off."

"No, not in the dark. I should be, I daresay, if I could see how far we are from the bottom."

So they walked on. The waves no longer fell at the foot of the wall, but leaned their breasts against it, gleaming as they rose on its front, and darkening as they sank low towards its deep base.

The wind kept coming in gusts, tearing a white gleam now and then on the dark surface of the sea. Behind them shone the dim lights of the city; before them all was dark as eternity, except for the one light at the end of the pier. At length Alec spied another out at sea.

"I believe that is the steamer," he said. "But she is a good way off. We shall have plenty of time to walk to the end—that is, if you would like to go."

"Certainly; let us go on. I want to stand on the very point," answered Kate.

They soon came to the lighthouse on the wall, and there descended to the lower part of the pier, the end of which now plunged with a steep descent into the sea. It was constructed of great stones clamped with iron, and built into a natural foundation of rock. Up the slope the waves rushed, and down the slope they sank again, with that seemingly aimless and resultless rise and fall, which makes the sea so dreary and sad to those men and women who are not satisfied without some goal in view, some outcome of their labours; for it goes on and on, answering ever to the call of sun and moon, and the fierce trumpet of the winds, yet working nothing but the hopeless wear of the bosom in which it lies bound for ever.

They stood looking out into the great dark before them, dark air, dark sea, dark sky, watching the one light which grew brighter as they gazed. Neither of them saw that a dusky figure was watching them from behind a great cylindrical stone that stood on the end of the pier, close to the wall.

A wave rushed up almost to their feet.

"Let us go," said Kate, with a shiver. "I can't bear it longer. The water is calling me and threatening me. There! How that wave rushed up as if it wanted me at once!"

Alec again drew her closer to him, and turning, they walked slowly back. He was silent with the delight of having that lovely creature all to himself, leaning on his arm, in the infolding and protecting darkness, and Kate was likewise silent.

By the time they reached the quay at the other end of the pier, the steamer had crossed the bar, and they could hear the *thud* of her paddles treading the water beneath them, as if eagerly because she was near her rest. After a few struggles, she lay quiet in her place, and they went on board.

Alec saw Kate embrace a girl perhaps a little older than herself, helped her to find her luggage, put them into a chaise, took his leave, and went home.

He did not know that all the way back along the pier they had been followed by Patrick Beauchamp.

CHAPTER XLIII

Excited, and unable to settle to his work, Alec ran upstairs to Mr Cupples, whom he had not seen for some days. He found him not more than half-way towards his diurnal goal.

"What's become of *you*, bantam, this many a day?" said Mr Cupples.

"I saw you last Saturday," said Alec.

"Last Saturday week, you mean," rejoined the librarian. "How's the mathematics coming on?"

"To tell the truth, I'm rather behind with them," answered Alec.

"I was thinking as much. Rainbows! Those rainbows! And the anatomy?"

"Not just standing still completely."

"That's well. You haven't been falling asleep again over the prodded carcass of an old pauper—have you?"

Alec stared. He had never told any one of his adventure in the dissecting-room.

"I saw you, my man. But I wasn't the only one that saw you. You might have had a worse fright if I hadn't come up, for Mr Beauchamp was taking your bearings through the window, and when I slippit awa' like a wraith. There ye lay, wi' yer heid back, and yer mou' open, as gin you and the deid man had been tryin' whilk wad sleep the soun'est. But ye hae ta'en to ither studies sin' syne. Ye hae a fresh subject—a bonnie young ane. The Lord hae mercy upo' ye! The goddess o' the rainbow hersel's gotten a haud o' ye, and ye'll be seein' naething but rainbows for years to come.—Iris bigs bonnie brigs, but they hae nowther pier, nor buttress, nor key-stane, nor parapet. And no fit can gang ower them but her ain, and whan she steps aff, it's upo' men's herts, and yours can ill bide her fit, licht as it may be."

"What are ye propheseein' at, Mr Cupples?" said Alec, who did not more than half understand him.

"Verra weel. I'm no drunk yet," rejoined Mr Cupples, oracularly. "But that chield Beauchamp's no rainbow—that lat me tell ye. He'll do you a mischeef yet, gin ye dinna luik a' the shairper. I ken the breed o' him. He was luikin' at ye throu the window like a hungry deevil. And jist min' what ye're aboot wi' the lassie—she's rael bonnie—or ye may chance to get her into trouble, withoot ony wyte o' yer ain. Min' I'm tellin' ye. Gin ye'll tak my advice, ye'll tak a dose o' mathematics direckly. It's a fine

went up, he slipped away like a wraith. There you lay, with your head back, and your mouth open, as if you and the dead man had been trying which would sleep the soundest. But you've taken to other studies since then. You have a fresh subject—a bonnie young one. The Lord have mercy upon you! The goddess of the rainbow herself has a hold of you, and you'll be seeing nothing but rainbows for years to come.—Iris builds bonnie bridges, but they have neither pier, nor buttress, nor key-stone, nor parapet. And no foot can go over them but her own, and when she steps off, it's upon men's hearts, and yours can ill stand her foot, light as it may be."

"What are you prophesying at, Mr Cupples?" said Alec, who did not more than half understand him.

"Very well. I'm not drunk yet," rejoined Mr Cupples, oracularly. "But that man Beauchamp's no rainbow—that let me tell you. He'll do you a mischief yet, if you don't look all the sharper. I know the breed of him. He was looking at you through the window like a hungry devil. And just mind what you're about with the lassie—she's real bonnie—or you may chance to get her into trouble, through no fault of your own. Mind, I'm telling you. If you'll take my advice, you'll take a dose of mathematics directly. It's a fine alterative as alterative as weel as antidote, though maybe whusky's....the verra broo o' the deevil's ain pot," he concluded, altering his tone entirely, and swallowing the rest of his glass at a gulp.

"What do ye want me to do?" asked Alec.

"To tak tent o' Beauchamp. And meantime to rin doon for yer Euclid and yer Hutton, and lat's see whaur ye are."

well as antidote, though maybe whisky's....the very brew of the devil's own pot," he concluded, altering his tone entirely, and swallowing the rest of his glass at a gulp.

"What do you want me to do?" asked Alec.

"To beware of Beauchamp. And meantime to run down for your Euclid and your Hutton, and let's see where you are."

There was more ground for Mr Cupples's warning than Alec had the smallest idea of. He had concluded long ago that all possible relations, even those of enmity—practical enmity at least—were over between them, and that Mr Beauchamp considered the bejan sufficiently punished for thrashing him, by being deprived of his condescending notice for the rest of the ages. But so far was this from being the true state of the case, that, although Alec never suspected it, Beauchamp had in fact been dogging and haunting him from the very commencement of the session, and Mr Cupples had caught him in only one of many acts of the kind. In the anatomical class, where they continued to meet, he still attempted to keep up the old look of disdain, as if the lesson he had received had in no way altered their relative position. Had Alec known with what difficulty, and under what a load of galling recollection, he kept it up, he would have been heartily sorry for him. Beauchamp's whole consciousness was poisoned by the memory of that day. Incapable of regarding any one except in comparative relation to himself, the effort of his life had been to maintain that feeling of superiority with which he started every new acquaintance; for occasionally a flash of foreign individuality would break through the husk of satisfaction in which he had inclosed himself, compelling him to feel that another man might have claims. And hitherto he had been very successful in patching up and keeping entire his eggshell of conceit. But that affair with Alec was a very bad business. Had Beauchamp been a coward, he would have suffered less from it. But he was no coward, though not quite so courageous as Hector, who yet turned and fled before Achilles. Without the upholding sense of duty, no man can be sure of his own behaviour, simply because he cannot be sure of his own nerves. Duty kept the red-cross knight "forlorne and left to losse," "haplesse and eke hopelesse,"

> "Disarmd, disgraste, and inwardly dismayde,
>   And eke so faint in every joynt and vayne,"

from turning his back on the giant Orgoglio, and sent him pacing towards him with feeble steps instead. But although he was not wanting in mere animal courage, Beauchamp's pride always prevented him from engaging in any contest in which he was not sure of success, the thought of failure being to him unendurable. When he found that he had miscalculated the probabilities, he was instantly dismayed; and the blow he received on his mouth reminding his vanity of the danger his handsome face was in, he dropped his arms and declined further contest, comforting himself with the fancy of postponing his vengeance to a better opportunity.

But within an hour he knew that he had lost his chance, as certainly as he who omits the flood-tide of his fortune. He not only saw that he was disgraced, but felt in himself that he had been cowardly; and, more mortifying still, felt that, with respect to the clodhopper, he was cowardly now. He was afraid of him. Nor could he take refuge in the old satisfaction of despising him; for that he found no longer possible. He was on the contrary compelled to despise himself, an experience altogether new; so that his contempt for Alec changed into a fierce, slow-burning hate.

Now hate keeps its object present even more than the opposite passion. Love makes everything lovely; hate concentrates itself on the one thing hated. The very sound of Alec's voice became to the ears of Beauchamp what a filthy potion would have been to his palate. Every line of his countenance became to his eyes what a disgusting odour would have been to his nostrils. And yet the fascination of his hate, and his desire of revenge, kept Beauchamp's ears, eyes, and thoughts hovering about Forbes.

No way of gratifying his hatred, however, although he had been brooding over it all the previous summer, had presented itself till now. Now he saw the possibility of working a dear revenge. But even now, to work surely, he must delay long. Still the present consolation was great.

Nor is it wonderful that his pride should not protect him from the deeper disgrace of walking in underground ways. For there is nothing in the worship of self to teach a man to be noble. Honour even will one day fail him who has learned no higher principle. And although revenge be "a kind of wild justice," it loses the justice, and retains only the wildness, when it corrupts into hatred. Every feeling that Beauchamp had was swallowed up in the gulf eaten away by that worst of all canker-worms.

Notwithstanding the humiliation he had experienced, he retained as yet an unlimited confidence in some gifts which he supposed himself to possess by nature, and to be capable of using with unequalled art. And true hate, as well as true love, knows how to wait.

CHAPTER XLIV

In the course of her study of Milton, Annie had come upon Samson's lamentation over his blindness; and had found, soon after, the passage in which Milton, in his own person, bewails the loss of light. The thought that she would read them to Tibbie Dyster was a natural one. She borrowed the volumes from Mrs Forbes; and, the next evening, made her way to Tibbie's cottage, where she was welcomed as usual by her gruff voice of gratefulness.

"You're a good bairn to come all this way through the snow to see an old blind body like me. It's pelting down—isn't it, bairn?"

"Ay, it is. How do you know, Tibbie?"

"I don't know how I know. I wasn't sure. The snow makes very little noise, you see. It comes down like the spirit himself upon quiet hearts."

"Did you ever see, Tibbie?" asked Annie, after a pause.

"Na; not that I remember. I was but two years old, my mother used to tell folk, when I had the pock, and it just closed up my eyes for ever—in this world, you know. I'll see some day as well as any of you, lass."

"Do you know what light is, Tibbie?" said Annie, whom Milton had set meditating on Tibbie's physical in relation to her mental condition.

"Ay, well enough," answered Tibbie, with a touch of indignation at the imputed ignorance. "Why not? What makes you ask?"

"Oh! I just wanted to know."

"How could I not know? Doesn't the Saviour say: 'I am the light of the world?'—He that walketh in Him must know what light is, lassie. Then you have the light in yourself—in your own heart; and you must know what it is. You can't mistake it."

Annie was neither able nor willing to enter into an argument on the matter, although she was not satisfied. She would rather think than dispute about it. So she changed the subject in a measure.

"Did you ever hear of John Milton, Tibbie?" she asked.

"Oh! ay. He was blind like myself, wasn't he?"

"Ay, he was. I have been reading a lot of his poetry."

"Eh! I'd be delighted to hear some of it."

"Well, here's a bit that he made as if Samson was saying it to himself, like, after they had put out his eyes—the Philistines, you know."

"Ay, I know well enough. Read it."

Annie read the well-known passage. Tibbie listened to the end, without word of remark or question, her face turned towards the reader, and her sightless balls rolling under their closed lids. When Annie's voice ceased, she said, after a little reflection:

"Ay! ay! It's bonnie, an' verra true. And, puir man! it was waur for him nor for me and Milton; for it was a' his ain wyte; and it was no to be expecket he cud be sae quaiet as anither. But he had no richt to queston the ways o' the Maker. But it's bonnie, rael bonnie."

"Noo, I'll jist read to ye what Milton says aboot his ain blin'ness. But it's some ill to unnerstan'."

"Maybe I'll unnerstan' 't better nor you, bairn. Read awa'."

So admonished, Annie read. Tibbie fidgeted about on her seat. It was impossible either should understand it. And the proper names were a great puzzle to them.

"Tammy Riss!" said Tibbie; "I ken naething aboot *him*."

"Na, neither do I," said Annie; and beginning the line again, she blundered over *"blind Maeonides."*

"Ye're readin' 't wrang, bairn. It sud be '*nae ony days*,' for there's nae days or nichts either to the blin'. They dinna ken the differ, ye see."

"I'm readin' 't as I hae't," answered Annie. "It's a muckle M."

"I ken naething aboot yer muckle or yer little Ms," retorted

without word of remark or question, her face turned towards the reader, and her sightless balls rolling under their closed lids. When Annie's voice ceased, she said, after a little reflection:

"Ay! ay! It's bonnie, and very true. And, poor man! it was worse for him than for me and Milton; for it was all his own fault; and it wasn't to be expected he could be so quiet as another. But he had no right to question the ways of the Maker. But it's bonnie, real bonnie."

"Now, I'll just read to you what Milton says about his own blindness. But it's quite hard to understand."

"Maybe I'll understand it better than you, child. Read away."

So admonished, Annie read. Tibbie fidgeted about on her seat. It was impossible either should understand it. And the proper names were a great puzzle to them.

"Tammy Riss!" said Tibbie; "I know nothing about *him*."

"Na, neither do I," said Annie; and beginning the line again, she blundered over *"blind Maeonides."*

"You're reading it wrong, bairn. It should be '*nae ony days*,' for there's no days or nights either to the blind. They don't know the difference, you see."

"I'm reading it as I have it," answered Annie. "It's a big M."

"I know nothing about your big or your little Ms," retorted

Tibbie, with indignation. "If that isn't what it means, it's beyond me. Read away. Maybe we'll come to something better."

"Ay we will!" said Annie, and resumed.

With the words, *"Thus with the year seasons return,"* Tibbie's attention grew fixed; and when the reader came to the passage,

"So much the rather thou, Celestial Light,
 Shine inward,"

her attention rose into rapture.

"Ay, ay, lassie! That man knew all about it! He would never have asked if a blind creature like me knew what the light was. He knew what it was well. Ay, he did!"

"But, you see, he was a very old man before he lost his eyesight," Annie ventured to interpose.

"So much the better! He knew both kinds. And he knew that the sight without the eyes is better than the sight of the eyes. Folk no doubt have both; but I sometimes think that the Lord gives a wee grain more of the inside light to make up for the loss of the outside; and indeed it doesn't want much to do that."

"But you don't know what it is," objected Annie, with unnecessary persistency in the truth.

"Do you tell me that again?" returned Tibbie, harshly. "You'll anger me, child. If you knew how I lie awake at night, unable to sleep for thinkin' 'at the day *will* come whan I'll see—wi' my ain open een—the verra face o' him that bore oor griefs an' carried oor sorrows, till I jist lie and greit, for verra wissin', ye wadna say 'at I dinna ken what the sicht o' a body's een is. Sae nae mair o' that! I beg o' ye, or I'll jist need to gang to my prayers to haud me ohn been angry wi' ane o' the Lord's bairns; for that ye *are*, I do believe, Annie Anderson. Ye canna ken what blin'ness is; but I doobt ye ken what the licht is, lassie; and, for the lave, jist ye lippen to John Milton and me."

Annie dared not say another word. She sat silent—perhaps rebuked. But Tibbie resumed:

"Ye maunna think, hooever, 'cause sic longin' thouchts come ower me, that I gang aboot the hoose girnin' and compleenin' that I canna open the door and win oot. Na, na. I could jist despise the licht, whiles, that ye mak' sic a wark aboot, and sing and shout, as the Psalmist says; for I'm jist that glaid, that I dinna ken hoo to haud it in. For the Lord's my frien'. I can jist tell him a' that comes into my puir blin' heid. Ye see there's ither ways for things to come intil a body's heid. There's mair doors nor the een. There's back doors, whiles, that lat ye oot to the bonnie gairden, and that's better nor the road-side. And the smell o' the braw flooers comes

sleep for thinking that the day *will* come when I'll see—with my own open eyes—the very face of him that bore our griefs and carried our sorrows, till I just lie and weep, for very wishing, you wouldn't say that I don't know what the sight of a person's eyes is. So no more of that! I beg of you, or I'll just need to go to my prayers to keep me from being angry with one of the Lord's bairns; for that you *are*, I do believe, Annie Anderson. You can't know what blindness is; but I expect you know what the light is, lassie; and, for the rest, just you trust to John Milton and me."

Annie dared not say another word. She sat silent—perhaps rebuked. But Tibbie resumed:

"You mustn't think, however, because such longing thoughts come over me, that I go about the house grumbling and complaining that I can't open the door and get out. Na, na. I could just despise the light, sometimes, that you make such a work about, and sing and shout, as the Psalmist says; for I'm just that glad, that I don't know how to hold it in. For the Lord's my friend. I can just tell him all that comes into my poor blind head. You see there's other ways for things to come into your head. There's more doors than the eyes. There's back doors, sometimes, that let you out to the bonnie garden, and that's better than the road-side. And the smell of the lovely flowers comes in at the back windows, you know.—Which of the bonnie flowers do you think likest *Him*, Annie Anderson?"

"Eh! I don't know, Tibbie. I'm thinking they must be all like him."

"Ay, ay, no doubt. But some of them may be liker him than others."

"Well, which do *you* think likest him, Tibbie?"

"I think it must be the mignonette—so clean and so fine and so well content."

"Ay, you're speaking by the smell, Tibbie. But if you saw the rose—"

"Heavens! I've seen the rose many a time. No doubt it's bonnier to look at—" and here her fingers went moving about as if they were feeling the full-blown sphere of a rose—"but I think, for my part, that the mignonette's likest Him."

"May be," was all Annie's reply, and Tibbie went on.

"There must be faces liker him than others. Come here, Annie, and let me feel whether you be like him or not."

"How can you know that?—you never saw him."

"Never saw him! I have seen him over and over again. I see him when I like. Come here, I say."

Annie went and knelt down beside her, and the blind woman passed her questioning fingers in solemn silence over and over the features of the child. At length, with her hands still resting upon Annie's head, she uttered her judgment.

"Ay. Quite like him, no doubt. But she'll be a heap liker him when she sees him as he is."

When a Christian proceeds to determine the rightness of his neighbour by his approximation to his fluctuating ideal, it were well if the judgment were tempered by such love as guided the hands of blind Tibbie over the face of Annie in their attempt to discover whether or not she was like the Christ of her visions.

"Do you think *you're* like him, Tibbie?" said Annie with a smile, which Tibbie at once detected in the tone.

"Heavens, bairn! I had the pox dreadful, you know."

"Well, maybe we've all had something or other that keeps us from being so bonny as we might have been. For one thing, there's the guilt of Adam's first sin, you know."

"Quite right, bairn. No doubt that's spoiled many a face—'the want of original righteousness, and the corruption of our whole nature.' The wonder is that we're like Him at all. But we must be like Him, for He was a man born of a woman. Think of that, lass!"

At this moment the latch of the door was lifted, and in walked

Robert Bruce. He gave a stare when he saw Annie, for he had thought her out of the way at Howglen, and said in a tone of asperity,

"You're everywhere at once, Annie Anderson. A downright vagabond!"

"Let the child be, Mister Bruce," said Tibbie. "She's doing the Lord's will, whether you may think it or not. She's visiting them that's in the prison-house of the dark, She's ministering to them that have many privileges no doubt, but have room for more."

"I'm not saying anything," said Bruce.

"You are saying. You're offending one of his little ones. Beware of the millstone."

"Pooh pooh! Tibbie. I was only wishing that she would keep a small part of her ministrations for her own home and her own folk that have the ministering to her. There's the mistress and me just martyrs to that shop! And there's the wee baby in want of some *ministration* now and then, if that be what you call it."

A grim compression of the mouth was all Tibbie's reply. She did not choose to tell Robert Bruce that although she was blind—and probably *because* she was blind—she heard rather more gossip than anybody else in Glamerton, and that consequently his appeal to her sympathy had no effect upon her. Finding she made no other answer, Bruce turned to Annie.

"Now, Annie," said he, "you're not wanted here any longer. I have a word or two to say to Tibbie. Go home and learn your lessons for tomorrow."

"It's Saturday night," answered Annie.

"But you have your lessons to learn for the Monday."

"Oh ay! But I have a book or two to take home to Mistress Forbes. And I daresay I'll stay, and come to the church with her in the morning."

Now, although all that Bruce wanted was to get rid of her, he went on to oppose her; for common-minded people always feel that they give the enemy an advantage if they show themselves content.

"It's not safe to run about in the dark. It's pelting down besides. You'll be all wet, and maybe fall into the dam. You couldn't see your hand before your face—once out of the town."

"I know the way to Mistress Forbes's as well as the way up your garret-stairs, Mr Bruce."

"Oh no doubt!" he answered, with a sneering acerbity peculiar to him, in which his voice seemed sharpened and concentrated to a point by the contraction of his lips. "And there's tykes about," he added, remembering Annie's fear of dogs.

But by this time Annie, gentle as she was, had got a little angry.

"The Lord'll tak care o' me frae the dark and the tykes, and the lave o' ye, Mr Bruce," she said.

And bidding Tibbie goodnight, she took up her books, and departed, to wade through the dark and the snow, trembling lest some unseen *tyke* should lay hold of her as she went.

As soon as she was gone, Bruce proceeded to make himself agreeable to Tibbie by retailing all the bits of gossip he could think of. While thus engaged, he kept peering earnestly about the room from door to chimney, turning his head on every side, and surveying as he turned it. Even Tibbie perceived, from the changes in the sound of his voice, that he was thus occupied.

"Sae your auld landlord's deid, Tibbie!" he said at last.

"Ay, honest man! He had aye a kin' word for a poor body."

"Ay, ay, nae doobt. But what wad ye say gin I tell't ye that I had boucht the bit hoosie, and was yer new landlord, Tibbie?"

"I wad say that the door-sill wants men'in', to haud the snaw oot; an' the bit hoosie's sair in want o' new thack. The verra cupples'll be rottit awa' or lang."

"Weel that's verra rizzonable, nae doobt, gin a' be as ye say."

"Be as I say, Robert Bruce?"

"Ay, ay; ye see ye're nae a'thegither like ither fowk. I dinna mean

But by this time Annie, gentle as she was, had got a little angry.

"The Lord'll take care of me from the dark and the tykes, and the rest of you, Mr Bruce," she said.

And bidding Tibbie goodnight, she took up her books, and departed, to wade through the dark and the snow, trembling lest some unseen *tyke* should lay hold of her as she went.

As soon as she was gone, Bruce proceeded to make himself agreeable to Tibbie by retailing all the bits of gossip he could think of. While thus engaged, he kept peering earnestly about the room from door to chimney, turning his head on every side, and surveying as he turned it. Even Tibbie perceived, from the changes in the sound of his voice, that he was thus occupied.

"So your old landlord's dead, Tibbie!" he said at last.

"Ay, honest man! He always had a kind word for a poor body."

"Ay, ay, no doubt. But what would you say if I told you that I had bought the house, and was your new landlord, Tibbie?"

"I would say that the door-sill wants mending, to keep the snow out; and the house is in great need of new thatch. The very rafters will be rotted away before long."

"Well, that's very reasonable, no doubt, if all be as you say."

"Be as I say, Robert Bruce?"

"Ay, ay; you see you're not altogether like other folk. I don't mean any offence, you know, Tibbie; but you haven't the sight of your eyes."

"Maybe I haven't the feeling of my old bones, either, Mister Bruce! Maybe I'm too blind to have the rheumatics; or to smell the old wet thatch when there's been a scattering of snow or a drop of rain on the roof!"

"I didn't want to anger you, Tibbie. All that you say deserves attention. It would be a shame to let an old body like you—"

"Not that old, Mister Bruce, if you knew the truth!"

"Well, you're not too young to need to be taken good care of—are you, Tibbie?"

Tibbie grunted.

"Well, to come to the point. There's no doubt the house wants a deal of attention."

"Indeed it does," interposed Tibbie. "It'll want a new door. For besides the door being almost as wide as two normal doors, it was once in two halves like a shop-door. And they're ill joined together, and the wind comes through like a knife, and nearly cuts you in two. You see the house was once the dyer's drying house, before he went further down the water."

"No doubt you're right, Tibbie. But seeing that I must lay out so much, I'll be compelled to put another thruppence on to the rent."

"Another thruppence, Robert Bruce! That's three thruppences in the week instead of two. That's unco rise! Ye canna mean what ye say! It's a' that I'm able to do to pay my saxpence. An auld blin' body like me disna fa' in wi' saxpences whan she gangs luikin aboot wi' her lang fingers for a pirn or a prin that she's looten fa'."

"But ye do a heap o' spinnin', Tibbie, wi' thae lang fingers. There's naebody in Glamerton spins like ye."

"Maybe ay and maybe no. It's no muckle that that comes till. I wadna spin sae weel gin it warna that the Almichty pat some sicht into the pints o' my fingers, 'cause there was nane left i' my een. An' gin ye mak ither thrippence a week oot o' that, ye'll be turnin' the wather that He sent to ca my mill into your dam; an' I doot it'll play ill water wi' your wheels."

"Hoot, hoot! Tibbie, woman! It gangs sair against me to appear to be hard-hertit."

"I hae nae doobt. Ye dinna want to *appear* sae. But do ye ken that I mak sae little by the spinnin' ye mak sae muckle o', that the kirk alloos me a shillin' i' the week to mak up wi'? And gin it warna for kin' frien's, it's ill livin' I wad hae in dour weather like this. Dinna ye imaigine, Mr Bruce, that I hae a pose o' my ain. I hae naething ava, excep' sevenpence in a stockin'-fit. And it wad hae to come aff o' my tay or something ither 'at I wad ill miss."

some rise! You can't mean what you say! It's all that I'm able to do to pay my sixpence. An old blind body like me doesn't fall in with sixpences when she goes looking about with her long fingers for a pirn (*bobbin*) or a pin she's let fall."

"But you do a heap of spinning, Tibbie, with those long fingers. There's nobody in Glamerton spins like you."

"Maybe aye and maybe no. It's not much that that comes to. I wouldn't spin so well if it weren't that the Almighty put some sight into the points of my fingers, 'cause there was none left in my eyes. And if you make another thruppence a week out of that, you'll be turning the water that He sent to drive my mill into your dam; and I expect it'll play ill water with your wheels."

"Heavens! Tibbie, woman! It goes sore against me to appear to be hard-hearted."

"I'm sure. You don't want to *appear* so. But do you know that I make so little by the spinning you make so much of, that the church allows me a shilling in the week to make up with? And if it weren't for kind friends, it's hard living I would have in dour weather like this. Don't you imagine, Mr Bruce, that I have a hoard of my own. I have nothing at all, except sevenpence in a stocking-foot. And it would have to come off my tea or something else that I would badly miss."

"Well, that may be all very true," rejoined Bruce; "but a body must have their own for all that. Wouldn't the church give you the other thruppence?"

"Do you think I would take from the church to put into your till?"

"Well, say sevenpence, then, and we'll be quits."

"I tell you what, Robert Bruce: rather than pay you one penny more than the sixpence, I'll turn out in the snow, and let the Lord look after me."

Robert Bruce went away, and did not purchase the cottage, which was in the market at a low price, He had intended Tibbie to believe, as she did, that he had already bought it; and if she had agreed to pay even the sevenpence, he would have gone from her to secure it.

On her way to Howglen, Annie pondered on the delight of Tibbie—Tibbie Dyster who had never seen the "human face divine"—when she should see the face of Jesus Christ, most likely the first face she would see. Then she turned to what Tibbie had said about knowing light from knowing the Saviour. There must be some connection between what Tibbie said and what Thomas had said about the face of God. There was a text that said "God is light, and in him is no darkness at all." So she was sure that the light that was in a Christian, whatever it meant, must come from the face of God. And so what Thomas said and what Tibbie said might be only different ways of saying the same thing.

Thus she was in a measure saved from the perplexity which comes of any *one* definition of the holy secret, compelling a man to walk in a way between walls, instead of in a path across open fields.

There was no day yet in which Annie did not think of her old champion with the same feeling of devotion which his championship had first aroused, although all her necessities, hopes, and fears were now beyond any assistance he could render. She was far on in a new path: he was loitering behind, out of hearing. He would not have dared to call her solicitude nonsense; but he would have set down all such matters as belonging to women, rather than youths beginning the world. The lessons of Thomas Crann were not despised, for he never thought about them. He began to look down upon all his past, and, in it, upon his old companions. Since knowing Kate, who had more delicate habits and ways than he had ever seen, he had begun to refine his own modes concerning outside things; and in his anxiety to be like her, while he became more polished, he became less genial and wide-hearted.

But none of his old friends forgot him. I believe not a day passed in which Thomas did not pray for him in secret, naming him by his name, and lingering over it mournfully—"Alexander Forbes—the young man that I thought would have been plucked from the burning before now. But thy time's the best, O Lord. It's all thy work; and there's no good thing in us. And thou canst turn the heart of man as the rivers of water. And maybe thou hast given him grace to repent already, though I know nothing about it."

CHAPTER XLV

This had been a sore winter for Thomas, and he had had plenty of leisure for prayer. For, having gone up on a scaffold one day to see that the wall he was building was properly protected from the rain, he slipped his foot on a wet pole, and fell to the ground, whence, being a heavy man, he was lifted terribly shaken, besides having one of his legs broken. Not a moan escaped him—a murmur was out of the question. They carried him home, and the surgeon did his best for him. Nor, although few people liked him much, was he left unvisited in his sickness. The members of his own religious community recognized their obligation to minister to him; and they would have done more, had they guessed how poor he was. Nobody knew how much he gave away in other directions; but they judged of his means by the amount he was in the habit of putting into the plate at the chapel-door every Sunday. There was never much of the silvery shine to be seen in the heap of copper, but one of the gleaming sixpences was almost sure to have dropped from the hand of Thomas Crann. Not that this generosity sprung altogether from disinterested motives; for the fact was, that he had a morbid fear of avarice; a fear I believe not altogether groundless; for he was independent in his feelings almost to fierceness—certainly to ungraciousness; and this strengthened a natural tendency to saving and hoarding. The consciousness of this tendency drove him to the other extreme. Jean, having overheard him once cry out in an agony, "Lord, hae mercy upo' me, and deliver me frae this love o' money, which is the root of all evil,"[1] watched him in the lobby of the chapel the next Sunday—"and as sure's deith," said Jean—an expression which it was well for her that Thomas did not hear—"he pat a siller shillin' into the plate that day, mornin' *an*' nicht."[2]

---

1 "Lord, have mercy upon me, and deliver me from this love of money, which is the root of all evil"
2 "and as sure as death,"…"he put a silver shilling into the plate that day, morning and night."

"Tak' care hoo ye affront him, whan ye tak' it," said Andrew Constable to his wife, who was setting out to carry him some dish of her own cooking—for Andrew's wife belonged to the missionars—"for weel ye ken Thamas likes to be unner obligation to nane but the Lord himsel'."

"Lea' ye that to me, Anerew, my man. You 'at's rouch men disna ken hoo to do a thing o' that sort. I s' manage Thamas weel eneuch. I ken the nater o' him."

And sure enough he ate it up at once, that she might take the dish back with her.

Annie went every day to ask after him, and every day had a kind reception from Jean, who bore her no grudge for the ignominious treatment of Thomas on that evening memorable to Annie. At length, one day, after many weeks, Jean asked her if she would not like to see him.

"Ay wad I; richt weel," answered she.

Jean led her at once into Thomas's room, where he lay in a bed in the wall. He held out his hand. Annie could hardly be said to take it, but she put hers into it, saying timidly,

"Is yer leg verra sair, Thamas?"

"Ow na, dawtie; nae noo. The Lord's been verra mercifu'—jist like himsel'. It was ill to bide for a while whan I cudna sleep. But I jist sleep noo like ane o' the beloved."

"Take care how you affront him, when you take it," said Andrew Constable to his wife, who was setting out to carry him some dish of her own cooking—for Andrew's wife belonged to the missionars—"for well you know Thomas likes to be under obligation to none but the Lord himself."

"Leave that to me, Andrew, my man. You rough men don't know how to do a thing of that sort. I'll manage Thomas well enough. I know the nature of him."

And sure enough he ate it up at once, that she might take the dish back with her.

Annie went every day to ask after him, and every day had a kind reception from Jean, who bore her no grudge for the ignominious treatment of Thomas on that evening memorable to Annie. At length, one day, after many weeks, Jean asked her if she would not like to see him.

"Ay, I would; very much," answered she.

Jean led her at once into Thomas's room, where he lay in a bed in the wall. He held out his hand. Annie could hardly be said to take it, but she put hers into it, saying timidly,

"Is your leg very sore, Thomas?"

"Oh na, pet; not now. The Lord's been very merciful—just like himself. It was hard to bear for a while when I couldn't sleep. But I just sleep now like one of the beloved."

"I was right sorry for you, Thomas."

"Ay, you've a kind heart, lassie. And I can't help thinking—they may say what they like—but I can't help thinking that the Lord was sorry for me himself. It came into my head as I lay here one night, and couldn't sleep a wink, and couldn't rest, and yet dared not move for my broken shin. And as soon as that came into my head I was so uplifted, that I forgot all about my leg, and began, before I knew it, to sing the hundred and seventh psalm. And then when the pain came back with a terrible stound, I just almost laughed; and I thought that if he would break me all to bits, I would never cry *hold*, nor turn my finger to make him stop. Now, you're one of the Lord's bairns—"

"Eh! I don't know," cried Annie, half-terrified at such an assurance from Thomas, and the responsibility devolved on her thereby, and yet delighted beyond expression.

"Ay, you are," continued Thomas confidently; "and I want to know what you think about it. Do you think it was a wrong thought to come into my head?"

"How could that be, Thomas, when it set you singing—and such a psalm—'O that men would praise the Lord for his goodness?'"

"The Lord be praised once more!" exclaimed Thomas. "'Out of the mouth of babes and sucklings!

no that ye're jist that, Annie, but ye're no muckle mair. Sit ye doon aside me, and rax ower to the Bible, and jist read that hunner and saivent psalm. Eh, lassie! but the Lord is guid. Oh! that men wad praise him! An' to care for the praises o' sic worms as me! What richt hae I to praise him?"

"Ye hae the best richt, Thomas, for hasna he been good to ye?"

"Ye're richt, lassie, ye're richt. It's wonnerfu' the common sense o' bairns. Gin ye wad jist lat the Lord instruck them! I doobt we mak ower little o' them. Nae doobt they're born in sin, and brocht farth in iniquity; but gin they repent ear', they win far aheid o' the auld fowk."

—not that you're exactly that, Annie, but you're not much more. Sit down beside me, and reach over to the Bible, and just read that hundred and seventh psalm. Eh, lassie! but the Lord is good. Oh! that men would praise him! And to care for the praises of such worms as me! What right have I to praise him?"

"You have the best right, Thomas, for hasn't he been good to you?"

"You're right, lassie, you're right. It's wonderful the common sense of bairns. If you would just let the Lord instruct them! I suspect we make too little of them. No doubt they're born in sin, and brought forth in iniquity; but if they repent early, they win far ahead of the old folk."

Thomas's sufferings had made him more gentle—and more sure of Annie's election. He was one on whom affliction was not thrown away.—Annie saw him often after this, and he never let her go without reading a chapter to him, his remarks upon which were always of some use to her, notwithstanding the limited capacity and formal shape of the doctrinal moulds in which they were cast; for wherever there is genuine religious feeling and *experience*, it will now and then crack the prisoning pitcher, and let some brilliant ray of the indwelling glory out, to discomfit the beleaguering hosts of troublous thoughts.

Although the framework of Thomas was roughly hewn, he had always been subject to such fluctuations of feeling as are more commonly found amongst religious women. Sometimes, notwithstanding the visions of the face of God "vouchsafed to him from the mercy-seat," as he would say, he would fall into fits of doubting whether he was indeed one of the elect; for how then could he be so hard-hearted, and so barren of good thoughts and feelings as he found himself? At such times he was subject to an irritation of temper, alternately the cause and effect of his misery, upon which, with all his efforts, he was only capable yet of putting a very partial check. Woe to the person who should then dare to interrupt his devotions! If Jean, who had no foresight or anticipation of consequences, should, urged by some supposed necessity of the case, call to him through the door bolted against Time and its concerns, the saint who had been kneeling before God in utter abasement, self-contempt, and wretchedness, would suddenly wrench it open, a wrathful, indignant man, boiling brimful of angry words and unkind objurgations, through all which would be manifest, notwithstanding, a certain unhappy restraint. Having driven the enemy away in confusion, he would bolt his door again, and return to his prayers in two-fold misery, conscious of guilt increased by unrighteous anger, and so of yet another wall of separation raised between him and his God.

Now this weakness all but disappeared during the worst of his illness, to return for a season with increased force when his recovery had advanced so far as to admit of his getting out of bed. Children are almost always cross when recovering from an illness, however patient they may have been during its severest moments; and the phenomenon is not by any means confined to children.

A deacon of the church, a worthy little weaver, had been half-officially appointed to visit Thomas, and find out, which was not an easy task, if he was in want of anything. When he arrived, Jean was out. He lifted the latch, entered, and tapped gently at Thomas's door—too gently, for he received no answer. With hasty yet hesitating imprudence, he opened the door and peeped in. Thomas was upon his knees by the fireside, with his plaid over his head. Startled by the weaver's entrance, he raised his head, and his rugged leonine face, red with wrath, glared out of the thicket of his plaid upon the intruder. He did not rise, for that would have been a task requiring time and caution. But he cried aloud in a hoarse voice, with his two hands leaning on the chair, like the paws of some fierce rampant animal:

"Jeames, ye're takin' the pairt o' Sawton upo' ye, drivin' a man frae his prayers!"	"James, you're taking the part of Satan upon you, driving a man from his prayers!"
"Hoot, Thamas! I beg yer pardon," answered the weaver, rather flurried; "I thoucht ye micht hae been asleep."	"Heavens, Thomas! I beg your pardon," answered the weaver, rather flurried; "I thought you might have been asleep."
"Ye had no business to think for yersel' in sic a maitter. What do ye want?"	"You had no business to think for yourself in such a matter. What do you want?"

"I just came to see whether *you* were in want of anything, Thomas."

"I'm in want of nothing. Good night to you."

"But, really, Thomas," expostulated the weaver, emboldened by his own kindness—"you'll excuse me, but you have no business to go down on your knees with your leg in such a weak condition."

"I won't excuse you, James. What do you know about my leg? And what's the use of knees, but to go down upon? Go home, and go down upon your own, James; and don't disturb other folk that know what theirs were made for."

Thus admonished, the weaver dared not linger. As he turned to shut the door, he wished the mason good night, but received no answer. Thomas had sunk forward upon the chair, and had already drawn his plaid over his head.

But the secret place of the Most High will not be entered after this fashion; and Thomas felt that he was shut out. It is not by driving away our brother that we can be alone with God. Thomas's plaid could not isolate him with his Maker, for communion with God is never isolation. In such a mood, the chamber with the shut door shuts out God too, and one is left alone with himself, which is the outer darkness. The love of the brethren opens the door into God's chamber, which is within ours. So Thomas—who was far enough from hating his brother, who would have struggled to his feet and limped to do him a service, though he would not have held out his hand to receive one, for he was only good, not gracious—Thomas, I say, felt worse than ever, and more as if God had forgotten him, than he had felt for many a day. He knelt still and sighed sore.

At length another knock came, which although very gentle, he heard and knew well enough.

"Who's there?" he asked, notwithstanding, with a fresh access of indignant feeling.

"Annie Anderson," was the answer through the door, in a tone which at once soothed the ruffled waters of Thomas's spirit.

"Come in," he said.

She entered, quiet as a ghost.

"Come awa', Annie. I'm glaid to see ye. Jist come and kneel doon aside me, and we'll pray thegither, for I'm sair troubled wi' an ill-temper."

Without a word of reply, Annie kneeled by the side of his chair. Thomas drew the plaid over her head, took her hand, which was swallowed up in his, and after a solemn pause, spoke thus:

"O Lord, wha dwellest in the licht inaccessible, whom mortal eye hath not seen nor can see, but who dwellest with him that is humble and contrite of heart, and liftest the licht o' thy coontenance upo' them that seek it, O Lord,"—here the solemnity of the appeal gave way before the out-bursting agony of Thomas's heart—"O Lord, dinna lat's cry in vain, this thy lammie, and me, thine auld sinner, but, for the sake o' him wha did no sin, forgive my sins and my vile temper, and help me to love my neighbour as mysel'. Lat Christ dwell in me and syne I shall be meek and lowly of heart like him. Put thy speerit in me, and syne I shall do richt—no frae mysel', for I hae no good thing in me, but frae thy speerit that dwelleth in us."

After this prayer, Thomas felt refreshed and hopeful. With slow labour he rose from his knees at last, and sinking into his chair,

"Come in," he said.

She entered, quiet as a ghost.

"Welcome, Annie. I'm glad to see you. Just come and kneel down beside me, and we'll pray together, for I'm much troubled with a bad temper."

Without a word of reply, Annie kneeled by the side of his chair. Thomas drew the plaid over her head, took her hand, which was swallowed up in his, and after a solemn pause, spoke thus:

"O Lord, who dwellest in the light inaccessible, whom mortal eye hath not seen nor can see, but who dwellest with him that is humble and contrite of heart, and liftest the light of thy countenance upon them that seek it, O Lord,"—here the solemnity of the appeal gave way before the out-bursting agony of Thomas's heart—"O Lord, don't let us cry in vain, this thy lamb, and me, thine old sinner, but, for the sake of him who did no sin, forgive my sins and my vile temper, and help me to love my neighbour as myself. Let Christ dwell in me and then I shall be meek and lowly of heart like him. Put thy spirit in me, and then I shall do right—not from myself, for I have no good thing in me, but from thy spirit that dwelleth in us."

After this prayer, Thomas felt refreshed and hopeful. With slow labour he rose from his knees at last, and sinking into his chair, drew Annie towards him, and kissed her. Then he said,

"Will you run a wee errand for me, Annie?"

"That I will, Thomas. I would run myself off my legs for you."

"Na, na. I don't want so much running tonight. But I'd be much obliged to you if you would just run down to James Johnstone, the weaver, and tell him, with my compliments, you know, that I'm very sorry I spoke to him as I did tonight; and I would take it right kindly of him if he would come and take a cup of tea with me tomorrow night, and we could have a crack together, and then we could have worship together. And tell him he must think no more of the way I spoke to him, for I was troubled in my mind, and I'm an ill-natured man."

"I'll tell him all that you say," answered Annie, "as well as I can recall it; and I bet I won't forget much of it. Would you like me to come back tonight and tell you what he says?"

"Na, na, lassie. It'll be nearly time for you to go to your bed. And it's a cold night. I know that by my leg. And you see James Johnstone's not a bad-tempered man like me. He's a kindly man, and he's sure to be well-pleased and come to his tea. Na, na; you needn't come back. Good night to you, my pet. The Lord bless you for coming to pray with a bad-tempered man."

Annie sped upon her mission of love through the murky streets and lanes of Glamerton, as certainly a divine messenger as any seraph crossing the blue empyrean upon level wing. And if any one should take exception to this, on the ground that she sought her own service and neglected home duties, I would, although my object has not been to set her forth as an exemplar, take the opportunity of asking whether to sleep in a certain house and be at liberty to take one's meals there, be sufficient to make it home, and the source of home-obligations—to indicate the will of God as to *the* region of one's labour, other regions lying open at the same time. Ought Annie to have given her aid as a child where there was no parental recognition of the relationship—an aid whose value in the eyes of the Bruces would have consisted in the leisure it gave to Mrs Bruce for ministering more devotedly in the temple of Mammon? I put the question, not quite sure what the answer ought to be.

CHAPTER XLVI

Now that Kate had got a companion, Alec never saw her alone. But he had so much the better opportunity of knowing her. Miss Warner was a nice, open-eyed, fair-faced English girl, with pleasant manners, and plenty of speech; and although more shy than Kate—English girls being generally more shy than Scotch girls—was yet ready enough to take her share in conversation. Between the two, Alec soon learned how ignorant he was in the things that most interest girls. Classics and mathematics were not *very* interesting to himself, and anatomy was not available. He soon perceived that they were both fond of poetry; but if it was not the best poetry, he was incapable of telling them so, although the few lessons he had had were from a better mistress than either of them, and with some better examples than they had learned to rejoice in.

The two girls had got hold of some volumes of Byron, and had read them together at school, chiefly after retiring to the chamber they shared together. The consequences were an unbounded admiration and a facility of reference, with the use of emotional adjectives. Alec did not know a single poem of that writer, except the one about the Assyrian coming down like a wolf on the fold.

Determined, however, not to remain incapable of sympathizing with them, he got copies of the various poems from the library of the college, and for days studied Byron and anatomy—nothing else. Like all other young men, he was absorbed, entranced, with the poems. Childe Harold he could not read, but the tales were one fairy region after another. Their power over young people is remarkable, but not more remarkable than the fact that they almost invariably lose this power over the individual, while they have as yet retained it over the race; for of all the multitude which does homage at the shrine of the poet few linger long, and fewer still, after the turmoil of life has yielded room for thought, renew their homage. Most of those who make the attempt are surprised—some of them troubled—at the discovery that the shrine can work miracles no more. The Byron-fever is in fact a disease belonging to youth, as the hooping-cough to childhood,—working some occult good no doubt in the end. It has its origin, perhaps, in the fact that the poet makes no demand either on the intellect or the conscience, but confines himself to friendly intercourse with those passions whose birth long precedes that of choice in their objects—whence a wealth of emotion is squandered. It is long before we discover that far richer feeling is the result of a regard bent on the profound and the pure.

Hence the chief harm the poems did Alec, consisted in the rousing of his strongest feelings towards imaginary objects of inferior excellence, with the necessary result of a tendency to measure the worth of the passions themselves by their strength alone, and not by their character—by their degree, and not by their kind. That they were the forge-bellows, supplying the blast of the imagination to the fire of love in which his life had begun to be remodelled, is not to be counted among their injurious influences.

He had never hitherto meddled with his own thoughts or feelings—had lived an external life to the most of his ability. Now, through falling in love, and reading Byron, he began to know the existence of a world of feeling, if not of thought; while his attempts at conversation with the girls had a condensing if not crystallizing influence upon the merely vaporous sensations which the poetry produced. All that was wanted to give full force to the other influences in adding its own, was the presence of the sultry evenings of summer, with the thunder gathering in the dusky air. The cold days and nights of winter were now swathing that brain, through whose aerial regions the clouds of passion, driven on many shifting and opposing winds, were hurrying along to meet in human thunder and human rain.

I will not weary my readers with the talk of three young people enamoured of Byron. Of course the feelings the girls had about him differed materially from those of Alec; so that a great many of the replies and utterances met like unskilful tilters, whose staves passed wide. In neither was the admiration much more than an uneasy delight in the vivid though indistinct images of pleasure raised by the magic of that "physical force of words" in which Byron excels all other English poets, and in virtue of which, I presume, the French persist in regarding Byron as our greatest poet, and in supposing that we agree with them.

Alec gained considerably with Kate from becoming able to talk about her favourite author, while she appeared to him more beautiful than ever—the changes in the conversation constantly bringing out new phases on her changeful countenance. He began to discover now what I have already ventured to call the *fluidity* of her expression; for he was almost startled every time he saw her, by finding her different from what he had expected to find her. Jean Paul somewhere makes a lamentation over the fact that girls will never meet you in the morning with the same friendliness with which they parted from you the night before. But this was not the kind of change Alec found. She behaved with perfect evenness to him, but always *looked* different, so that he felt as if he could never know her quite—which was a just conclusion, and might have been arrived at upon less remarkable though more important grounds. Occasionally he would read something of Byron's; and it was a delight to him such as he had never known before, to see Kate's strangely beautiful eyes flash with actual visible fire as he read, or cloud over with mist and fill slowly with the dew of feeling. No doubt he took more of the credit than belonged to him—which was greedy, seeing poor Byron had none of the pleasure.

Had it not been for the help Mr Cupples gave him towards the end of the session, he would have made a poor figure both in Greek and mathematics. But he was so filled with the phantasm of Kate Fraser, that, although not insensible of his obligation to Mr Cupples, he regarded it lightly; and, ready to give his life for a smile from Kate, took all his kindness, along with his drunken wisdom, as a matter of course.

And when he next saw Annie and Curly, he did not speak to them quite so heartily as on his former return.

CHAPTER XLVII

In one or two of his letters, which were never very long, Alec had just mentioned Kate; and now Mrs Forbes had many inquiries to make about her. Old feelings and thoughts awoke in her mind, and made her wish to see the daughter of her old companion. The absence of Annie, banished once more at the suggestion of worldly prudence, but for whose quiet lunar smile not even Alec's sunny presence could quite make up, contributed no doubt to this longing after the new maiden. She wrote to Mr Fraser, asking him to allow his niece to pay her a visit of a few weeks; but she said nothing about it to Alec. The arrangement happened to be convenient to Mr Fraser, who wished to accept an invitation himself. It was now the end of April; and he proposed that the time should be fixed for the beginning of June.

When this favourable response arrived, Mrs Forbes gave Alec the letter to read, and saw the flush of delight that rose to his face as he gathered the welcome news. Nor was this observation unpleasant to her; for that Alec should at length marry one of his own people was a grateful idea.

Alec sped away into the fields. To think that all these old familiar places would one day be glorified by her presence! that the daisies would bend beneath the foot of the goddess! and the everlasting hills put on a veil of tenderness from the reflex radiance of her regard! A flush of summer mantled over the face of nature, the flush of a deeper summer than that of the year—of the joy that lies at the heart of all summers. For a whole week of hail, sleet, and "watery sunbeams" followed, and yet in the eyes of Alec the face of nature still glowed.

When, after long expectation, the day arrived, Alec could not rest. He wandered about all day, haunting his mother as she prepared his room for Kate, hurrying away with a sudden sense of the propriety of indifference, and hurrying back on some cunning pretext, while his mother smiled to herself at his eagerness and the transparency of his artifice. At length, as the hour drew near, he could restrain himself no longer. He rushed to the stable, saddled his pony, which was in nearly as high spirits as himself, and galloped off to meet the mail. The sun was nearing the west; a slight shower had just fallen; the thanks of the thirsty earth were ascending in odour; and the wind was too gentle to shake the drops from the leaves. To Alec, the wind of his own speed was the river that bore her towards him; the odours were wafted from her approach; and the sunset sleepiness around was the exhaustion of the region that longed for her Cytheraean presence.

At last, as he turned a corner of the road, there was the coach; and he had just time to wheel his pony about before it was up with him. A little gloved hand greeted him; the window was let down; and the face he had been longing for shone out lovelier than ever. There was no inside passenger but herself; and, leaning with one hand on the coach-door, he rode alongside till they drew near the place where the gig was waiting for them, when he dashed on, gave his pony to the man, was ready to help her as soon as the coach stopped, and so drove her home in triumph to his mother.

Where the coach stopped, on the opposite side of the way, a grassy field, which fell like a mantle from the shoulders of a hill crowned with firs, sloped down to the edge of the road. From the coach, the sun was hidden behind a thick clump of trees, but his rays, now red with rich age, flowed in a wide stream over the grass, and shone on an old Scotch fir which stood a yard or two from the highway, making its red bark glow like the pools which the prophet saw in the desert. At the foot of this tree sat Tibbie Dyster; and from her red cloak the level sun-tide was thrown back in gorgeous glory; so that the eyeless woman, who only felt the warmth of the great orb, seemed, in her effulgence of luminous red, to be the light-fountain whence that torrent of rubescence burst. From her it streamed up to the stem and along the branches of the glowing fir; from her it streamed over the radiant grass of the up-sloping field away towards the western sun. But the only one who saw the splendour was a shoemaker, who rubbed his rosiny hands together, and felt happy without knowing why.

Alec would have found it difficult to say whether or not he had seen the red cloak. But from the shadowy side of it there were eyes shining upon him, with a deeper and truer, if with a calmer, or, say, colder devotion, than that with which he regarded Kate. The most powerful rays that fall from the sun are neither those of colour nor those of heat.—Annie sat by Tibbie's side—the side away from the sun. If the East and the West might take human shape—come forth in their Oreads from their hill-tops, and meet half-way between—there they were seated side by side: Tibbie, old, scarred, blind Tibbie, was of the west and the sunset, the centre of a blood-red splendour; cold, gentle Annie, with her dark hair, blue eyes, and the sad wisdom of her pale face, was of the sun-deserted east, between whose gray clouds, faintly smiling back the rosiness of the sun's triumphal death, two or three cold stars were waiting to glimmer.

Tibbie had come out to bask a little, and, in the dark warmth of the material sun, to worship that Sun whose light she saw in the hidden world of her heart, and who is the Sun of all the worlds; to breathe the air, which, through her prison-bars, spoke of freedom; to give herself room to long for the hour when the loving Father would take her out of the husk which infolded her, and say to her: "*See, my child.*" With the rest of the travailing creation, she was groaning in hopeful pain—not in the pain of the mother, but in the pain of the child, soon to be forgotten in the following rest.

If my younger readers want to follow Kate and Alec home, they will take it for a symptom of the chill approach of "unlovely age," that I say to them: 'We will go home with Tibbie and Annie, and hear what they say. I like better to tell you about ugly blind old Tibbie than about beautiful young Kate.—But you shall have your turn. Do not think that we old people do not care for what you care for. We want more than you want—a something without which what you like best cannot last.'

"What did the coach stop for, Annie, lass?" asked Tibbie, as soon as the mail had driven on.

"It's a lady going to Mistress Forbes's at Howglen."

"How do you know that?"

"'Cause Alec Forbes rode out to meet her, and then took her home in the gig."

"Ay! ay! I thought I heard more than the usual number of horse-feet as the coach came up. He's a fine lad, that Alec Forbes—isn't he?"

"Ay, he is," answered Annie, sadly; not from jealousy, for her admiration of Alec was from afar; but as looking up from purgatorial exclusion to the paradise of Howglen, where the beautiful lady would have all Mrs Forbes, and Alec too, to herself.

The old woman caught the tone, but misinterpreted it.

"I expect," she said, "he won't get any good at that college."

"Why not?" returned Annie. "I was at the school with him, and never saw anything to find fault with."

"Oh na, lassie. You had no business to find fault with him. His father was a respectable man, and maybe a God-fearing man, though he made but small profession. I think we're too hard at times upon some of them that promise little, and maybe do the more. You remember what you read to me before we came out together, about the lad that said to his father, *I go not;* but afterwards he repented and went?"

"Ay."

"Well, I think we'll go home now."

They rose, and went, hand in hand, over the bridge, and round the end of its parapet, and down the steep descent to the cottage at its foot, Tibbie's cloak shining all the way, but, now that the sun was down, with a chastened radiance. When she had laid it aside, and was seated on her low wooden chair within reach of her spinning-wheel,

"Now," said Tibbie, "you'll just read a chapter to me, lassie, before you go home, and then I'll go to my bed. Blindness is a great saving of candles."

She forgot that it was summer, when, in those northern regions, the night has no time to gather before the sun is flashing again in the east.

The chapter Annie chose was the ninth of St John's Gospel, about Jesus curing the man blind from his birth. When she had finished, Annie said,

"Mightn't he cure you, Tibbie, if you asked him?"

"Ay he might, and ay he will," answered Tibbie. "I'm only just biding his time. But I'm thinking he'll cure me better yet than he cured that blind man. He'll just take the body off me altogether, and then I'll see, not with eyes like yours, but with my whole spiritual body. You remember that verse in the prophecies of Ezekiel: I know it well by heart. It says: 'And their whole body, and their backs, and their hands, and their wings, and the wheels, were full of eyes round about, even the wheels that they four had.' Isn't that a grand text? I wish Mr Turnbull would take it into his head to preach from that text sometime before it comes, which won't be that long, I'm thinking. The wheels'll be stopping at my door soon."

"What makes you think that, Tibbie? There's no sign of death about you, I'm sure," said Annie.

"Well, you see, I can hardly say. Blind folk somehow know more than other folk about things that the sight of the eyes has very little to do with. But never mind. I'm bide i' the dark as lang as He likes. It's eneuch for ony bairn to ken that its father's stan'in' i' the licht, and seein' a' aboot him, and sae weel able to guide hit, though it kensna whaur to set doon its fit neist. And I wat He's i' the licht. Ye min' that bit aboot the Lord pittin' Moses intil a clift o' the rock, and syne coverin' him wi' his han' till he was by him?"

"Ay, fine that," answered Annie.

"Weel, I canna help thinkin' whiles, that the dark aboot me's jist the how o' the Lord's han'; and I'm like Moses, only wi' this differ, that whan the Lord tak's his han' aff o' me, it'll be to lat me luik i' the face o' him, and no to lat me see only his back pairts, which was a' that he had the sicht o'; for ye see Moses was i' the body, and cudna bide the sicht o' the face o' God. I daursay it wad hae blin' 't him. I hae heard that ower muckle licht'll ca fowk blin' whiles. What think ye, lassie?"

"Ay; the lichtnin' blin's fowk whiles. And gin I luik straucht at the sun, I can see nothing efter't for a whilie."

"I tell ye sae!" exclaimed Tibbie triumphantly. "And do ye min' the veesion that the apostle John saw in Pawtmos? I reckon he micht hae thocht lang there, a' him lane, gin it hadna been for the bonnie things, and the gran' things, and

willing to stay in the dark as long as He likes. It's enough for any child to know that its father's standing in the light, and seeing all about him, and so well able to guide it, though it doesn't know where to set down its foot next. And I know He's in the light. You remember that bit about the Lord putting Moses into a cleft of the rock, and then covering him with his hand till he was by him?"

"Ay, perfectly," answered Annie.

"Well, I can't help thinking sometimes, that the dark about me's just the hollow of the Lord's hand; and I'm like Moses, only with this difference, that when the Lord takes his hand off me, it'll be to let me look in his face, and not to let me see only his back parts, which was all that he had the sight of; for you see Moses was in the body, and couldn't bear the sight of the face of God. I daresay it would have blinded him. I have heard that too much light will drive folk blind sometimes. What think you, lassie?"

"Ay; the lightning blinds folk sometimes. And if I look straight at the sun, I can see nothing after it for a while."

"I tell you so!" exclaimed Tibbie triumphantly. "And do you remember the vision that the apostle John saw in Patmos? I reckon he might have grown weary there, all alone, if it hadn't been for the bonnie things, and the grand things, and the terrible things 'at the Lord loot him see. They *war* gran' sichts! It was the veesion o' the Saviour himsel'—Christ himsel'; and he says that his coontenance was as the sun shineth in his strength. What think ye o' that, lass!"

the terrible things that the Lord let him see. They *were* grand sights! It was the vision of the Saviour himself—Christ himself; and he says that his countenance was as the sun shineth in his strength. What do you think of that, lass!"

This was not a question, but an exulting exclamation. The vision in Patmos proved that although Moses must not see the face of God because of its brightness, a more favoured prophet might have the vision. And Tibbie, who had a share in the privileges of the new covenant, who was not under the law like Moses, but under grace like John, would one day see the veil of her blindness shrivel away from before her deeper eyes, burnt up by the glory of that face of God, which is a consuming fire.—I suppose that Tibbie was right in the main. But was it not another kind of brightness, a brightness without effulgence, a brightness grander and more glorious, shining in love and patience, and tenderness and forgiveness and excuse, that Moses was unfit to see, because he was not well able to understand it, until, ages after, he descended from heaven upon the Mount of Transfiguration, and the humble son of God went up from the lower earth to meet him there, and talk with him face to face as a man with his friend?

Annie went home to her garret. It was a singular experience the child had in the changes that came to her with the seasons. The winter with its frost and bitter winds brought her a home at Howglen; the summer, whose airs were molten kisses, took it away, and gave her the face of nature instead of the face of a human mother. For the snug little chamber in which she heard with a quiet exultation the fierce rush of the hail-scattering tempest against the window, or the fluffy fall of the snow-flakes, like hands of fairy babies patting the glass, and fancied herself out in the careering storm, hovering on the wings of the wind over the house in which she lay soft and warm—she had now the garret room, in which the curtainless bed, with its bare poles, looked like a vessel in distress at sea, and through the roof of which the winds found easy way. But the winds were warm now, and through the skylight the sunbeams illuminated the floor, showing all the rat-holes and wretchedness of decay.

There was comfort out of doors in the daytime—in the sky and the fields and all the "goings-on of life." And this night, after this talk with Tibbie, Annie did not much mind going back to the garret. Nor did she lie awake to think about the beautiful lady Alec had taken home with him.

And she dreamed again that she saw the Son of Man. There was a veil over his face like the veil that Moses wore, but the face was so bright that it almost melted the veil away, and she saw what made her love that face more than the presence of Alec, more than the kindness of Mrs Forbes or Dowie, more than the memory of her father.

CHAPTER XLVIII

Alec did not fall asleep so soon. The thought that Kate was in the house—asleep in the next room, kept him awake. Yet he woke the next morning earlier than usual. There were bands of golden light upon the wall, though Kate would not be awake for hours yet.

He sprung out of bed, and ran to the banks of the Glamour. Upon the cold morning stream the sun-rays fell slanting and gentle. He plunged in, and washed the dreams from his eyes with a dive, and a swim under water. Then he rose to the surface and swam slowly about under the overhanging willows, and earthy banks hollowed by the river's flow into cold damp caves, up into the brown shadows of which the water cast a flickering shimmer. Then he dressed himself, and lay down on the meadow grass, each blade of which shadowed its neighbour in the slant sunlight. Cool as it still was with the coldness of the vanished twilight, it yet felt warm to his bare feet, fresh from the waters that had crept down through the night from the high moorlands. He fell fast asleep, and the sheep came and fed about him, as if he had been one of themselves. When he woke, the sun was high; and when he reached the house, he found his mother and Kate already seated at breakfast—Kate in the prettiest of cotton dresses, looking as fresh and country-like as the morning itself. The window was open, and through the encircling ivy, as through a filter of shadows, the air came fresh and cool. Beyond the shadow of the house lay the sunshine, a warm sea of brooding glory, of still power; not the power of flashing into storms of splendour beneath strange winds, but of waking up and cherishing to beauty the shy life that lay hidden in all remotest corners of the teeming earth.

"What are you going to do with Kate to-day, Alec?" said his mother.

"Whatever Kate likes," answered Alec.

"I have no choice," returned Kate. "I don't know yet what I have to choose between. I am in your hands, Alec."

It was the first time she had called him by his name, and a spear of sunshine seemed to quiver in his heart. He was restless as a hyena till she was ready. He then led her to the banks of the river, here low and grassy, with plenty of wild flowers, and a low babblement everywhere.

"This is delightful," said Kate. "I will come here as often as you like, and you shall read to me."

"What shall I read? Would you like one of Sir Walter's novels?"

"Just the thing."

Alec started at full speed for the house.

"Stop," cried Kate. "You are not going to leave me alone beside this—talking water?"

"I thought you liked the water," said Alec.

"Yes. But I don't want to be left alone beside it. I will go with you, and get some work."

She turned away from the stream with a strange backward look, and they walked home.

But as Kate showed some disinclination to return to the river-side, Alec put a seat for her near the house, in the shadow of a silver birch, and threw himself on the grass at her feet. There he began to read the *Antiquary*, only half understanding it, in the enchantment of knowing that he was lying at her feet, and had only to look up to see her eyes. At noon, Mrs Forbes sent them a dish of curds, and a great jug of cream, with oatcakes, and butter soft from the churn; and the rippling shadow of the birch played over the white curds and the golden butter as they ate.

Am I not now fairly afloat upon the gentle stream of an idyl? Shall I watch the banks as they glide past, and record each fairy-headed flower that looks at its image in the wave? Or shall I mow them down and sweep them together in a sentence?

I will gather a few of the flowers, and leave the rest. But first I will make a remark or two upon the young people.

Those amongst my readers who have had the happiness to lead innocent boy-lives, will know what a marvellous delight it was to Alec to have this girl near him in his own home and his own haunts. He never speculated on her character or nature, any more than Hamlet did about those of Ophelia before he was compelled to doubt womankind. His own principles were existent only in a latent condition, undeveloped from good impulses and kind sentiments. For instance: he would help any one whose necessity happened to make an impression upon him, but he never took pains to enter into the feelings of others—to understand them from their own point of view: he never had said to himself, "That is another me."

Correspondent to this condition were some of Kate's theories of life and its duties.

The question came up, whether a certain lady in fiction had done right in running away with her lover. Mrs Forbes made a rather decided remark on the subject. Kate said nothing, but her face glowed.

"Tell us what you think about it, Katie," said Mrs Forbes.

Katie was silent for a moment. Then with the air of a martyr, from whom the rack can only extort a fuller confession of his faith—though I fear she had no deeper gospel at the root of it than Byron had brought her—she answered:

"I think a woman must give up everything for love."

She was then precisely of the same opinion as Jean Paul's Linda in *Titan*.

"That is very true, I daresay," said Mrs Forbes; "but I fear you mean only one kind of love. Does a woman owe no love to her father or mother because she has a lover?"

To this plain question Kate made no reply, but her look changed to one of obstinacy.

Her mother died when she was a child, and her father had kept himself shut up in his study, leaving her chiefly to the care of a Shetland nurse, who told her Scandinavian stories from morning to night, with invention ever ready to supply any blank in the tablets of her memory.

Alec thought his mother's opinion the more to be approved, and Kate's the more to be admired; showing the lack of entireness in his nature, by thus dissociating the good and the admirable. That which is best cannot be less admirable than that which is not best.

CHAPTER XLIX

The next day saw Alec walking by the side of Kate mounted on his pony, up a steep path to the top of one of the highest hills surrounding the valley. It was a wild hill, with hardly anything growing on it but heather, which would make it regal with purple in the autumn: no tree could stand the blasts that blew over that hill in winter. Having climbed to the topmost point, they stood and gazed. The country lay outstretched beneath in the glow of the June day, while around them flitted the cool airs of heaven. Above them rose the soaring blue of the June sky, with a white cloud or two floating in it, and a blue peak or two leaning its colour against it. Through the green grass and the green corn below crept two silvery threads, meeting far away and flowing in one—the two rivers which watered the valley of Strathglamour. Between the rivers lay the gray stone town, with its roofs of thatch and slate. One of its main streets stopped suddenly at the bridge with the three arches above Tibbie's cottage; and at the other end of the bridge lay the green fields.

The landscape was not one of the most beautiful, but it had a beauty of its own, which is all a country or a woman needs; and Kate sat gazing about her in evident delight. She had taken off her hat to feel the wind, and her hair fell in golden heaps upon her shoulders, and the wind and the sunbeams played at hide-and-seek in it.

In a moment the pleasure vanished from her face. It clouded over, while the country lay full in the sun. Her eyes no longer looked wide abroad, but expressed defeat and retirement. Listlessly she began to gather her hair together.

"Do you ever feel as if you could not get room enough, Alec?" she said, wearily.

"No, I don't," he answered, honestly and stupidly. "I have always as much as I want. I should have thought you would—up here."

"I did feel satisfied for a moment; but it was only a moment. It is all gone now. I shall never have room enough."

Alec had nothing to say in reply. He never had anything to give Kate but love; and now he gave her more love. It was all he was rich in. But she did not care for his riches. And so, after gazing a while, she turned towards the descent. Alec picked up her hat, and took his place at the pony's head. He was not so happy as he thought he should be. Somehow she was of another order, and he could not understand her—he could only worship her.

The whole of the hot afternoon they spent on the grass, whose mottling of white clover filled the wandering airs with the odours of the honey of Hymettus. And after tea Kate sang, and Alec drank every tone as if his soul lived by hearing.

In this region the sun works long after hours in the summer, and they went out to see him go down weary. They leaned together over the gate and looked at the level glory, which now burned red and dim. Lamp of life, it burns all night long in the eternal night of the universe, to chase the primeval darkness from the great entrance hall of the "human mortals."

"What a long shadow everything throws!" said Kate. "When the shadows gather all together, and melt into one, then it is night. Look how the light creeps about the roots of the grass on the ridge, as if it were looking for something between the shadows. They are both going to die. Now they begin."

The sun diminished to a star—a spark of crimson fire, and vanished. As if he had sunk in a pool of air, and made it overflow, a gentle ripple of wind blew from the sunset over the grass. They could see the grass bending and swaying and bathing in its coolness before it came to them. It blew on their faces at length, and whispered something they could not understand, making Kate think of her mother, and Alec of Kate.

Now that same breeze blew upon Tibbie and Annie, as they sat in the patch of meadow by the cottage, between the river and the *litster's dam*. It made Tibbie think of death, the opener of sleeping eyes, the uplifter of hanging hands. For Tibbie's darkness was the shadow of her grave, on the further border of which the light was breaking in music. Death and resurrection were the same thing to blind old Tibbie.

When the gentle, washing wind blew upon Annie, she thought of the wind that bloweth were it listeth; and that, if ever the Spirit of God blew upon her, she would feel it just like that wind of summer sunset—so cool, so blessed, so gentle, so living! And was it not God that breathed that wind upon her? Was he not even then breathing his Spirit into the soul of that woman-child?

It blew upon Andrew Constable, as he stood in his shop-door, the easy labour of his day all but over. And he said to his little weasel-faced, *douce*, old-fashioned child who stood leaning against the other door-cheek:

"That's a fine fresh blast, Isie! Don't you like to feel it blowing upon your hot cheeks, pet?"

And she answered,

"Ay, I like it well, daddie; but it reminds me a bit of the winter."

And Andrew looked anxiously at the pale face of his child, who, at six years old, in the month of June, had no business to know that there was any winter. But she was the child of elderly parents, and had not been born in time; so that she was now in reality about twenty.

It blew upon Robert Bruce, who had just run out into the *yard*, to see how his potatoes and cabbages were coming on. He said:

"That's quite a nip," and ran in again to put on his hat.

Alec and Kate, I have said, stood looking into the darkening field. A great flock of rooks which filled the air with their rooky gossip, was flying straight home to an old gray ruin just visible amongst some ancient trees. They had been gathering worms and grubs all day, and now it was bed time. They felt, through all their black feathers, the coolness of that evening breeze which came from the cloudy mausoleum already built over the grave of the down-gone sun.

Kate hearing them rejoicing far overhead, searched for them in the darkening sky, found them, and watched their flight, till the black specks were dissolved in the distance. They are not the most poetic of birds, but in a darkening country twilight, over silent fields, they blend into the general tone, till even their noisy caw suggests repose. But it was room Kate wanted, not rest. She would know one day, however, that room and rest are the same, and that the longings for both spring from the same need.

"What place is that in the trees?" she asked.

"The old Castle of Glamerton," answered Alec. "Would you like to go and see it?"

"Yes; very much."

"We'll go to-morrow, then."

"The dew is beginning to fall, Kate," said Mrs Forbes, who now joined them. "You had better come in."

Alec lingered behind. An unknown emotion drew his heart towards the earth. He would see her go to sleep in the twilight, which was now beginning to brood over her, as with the brown wings of a lovely dull-hued hen-bird. The daisies were all asleep, spotting the green grass with stars of carmine; for their closed red tips, like the finger-points of two fairy hands, tenderly joined together, pointed up in little cones to keep the yellow stars warm within, that they might shine bright when the great star of day came to look for them. The light of the down-gone sun, the garment of Aurora, which, so short would be her rest, she had not drawn close around her on her couch, floated up on the horizon, and swept slowly northwards, lightly upborne on that pale sea of delicate green and gold, to flicker all night around the northern coast of the sky, and, streaming up in the heavens, melt at last in the glory of the uprisen Titan. The trees stood still and shadowy as clouds, but breathing out mysterious odours. The stars overhead, half-molten away in the ghostly light that would not go, were yet busy at their night-work, ministering to the dark sides of the other worlds. There was no moon. A wide stillness and peace, as of a heart at rest, filled space, and lying upon the human souls with a persistent quietness that might be felt, made them know what *might* be theirs. Now and then a bird sprang out with a sudden tremor of leaves, suddenly stilled. But the bats came and went in silence, like feelings yet unembodied in thoughts, vanishing before the sight had time to be startled at their appearing. All was marvel. And the marvel of all was there—where the light glimmered faintly through the foliage. He approached the house with an awe akin to that with which an old poetic Egyptian drew near to the chamber of the goddess Isis.

He entered, and his Isis was laughing merrily.

In the morning, great sun-crested clouds with dark sides hung overhead; and while they sat at breakfast, one of those glorious showers, each of whose great drops carries a sun-spark in its heart, fell on the walks with a tumult of gentle noises, and on the grass almost as silently as if it had been another mossy cloud. The leaves of the ivy hanging over the windows quivered and shook, each for itself, beneath the drops; and between the drops, one of which would have beaten him to the earth, wound and darted in safety a great humble bee.

Kate and Alec went to the open window and looked out on the rainy world, breathing the odours released from the grass and the ground. Alec turned from the window to Kate's face, and saw upon it a keen, yet solemn delight. But as he gazed, he saw a cloud come over it. The arched upper lip dropped sadly upon the other, and she looked troubled and cold. Instinctively he glanced out again for the cause. The rain had become thick and small, and a light opposing wind disordered its descent with broken and crossing lines.

This change from a summer to a winter rain had altered Kate's mood, and her face was now, as always, a reflex of the face of nature.

"Shut the window, please Alec," she said, with a shiver.

"We'll have a fire directly," said Alec.

"No, no," returned Kate, trying to smile. "Just fetch me a shawl from the closet in my room."

Alec had not been in his own room since Kate came. He entered it with a kind of gentle awe, and stood just within the door, gazing as if rebuked.

From a pair of tiny shoes under the dressing-table, radiated a whole roomful of femininity. He was almost afraid to go further, and would not have dared to look in the mirror. In three days her mere presence had made the room marvellous.

Recovering himself, he hastened to the closet, got the shawl, and went down the stair three steps at a time.

"Couldn't you find it, Alec?" said Kate.

"Oh! yes; I found it at once," answered Alec, blushing to the eyes.

I wonder whether Kate guessed what made the boy blush. But it does not matter much now. She did look curiously at him for a moment.

"Just help me with my shawl," she said.

CHAPTER L

During all this time, Annie had seen scarcely anything of her aunt Margaret Anderson. Ever since Bruce had offended her, on the occasion of her first visit, she had taken her custom elsewhere, and had never even called to see her niece. Annie had met her several times in the street, and that was all. Hence, on one of the fine afternoons of that unusually fine summer, and partly, perhaps, from missing the kindness of Mrs Forbes, Annie took a longing to see her old aunt, and set out for Clippenstrae to visit her. It was a walk of two miles, chiefly along the high road, bordered in part by accessible plantation. Through this she loitered along, enjoying the few wild flowers and the many lights and shadows, so that it was almost evening before she reached her destination.

"Preserve us all! Annie Anderson, what brings you here this time of night?" exclaimed her aunt.

"It's a long time since I saw you, auntie, and I wanted to see you."

"Well, come to the kitchen. You're growing a great big girl," said her aunt, inclined to a favourable consideration of her by her growth.

Margaret "didn't like bairns—ill-bred creatures—always wanting other folk to do for them!" But growth was a kind of regenerating process in her eyes, and when a girl began to look like a woman, she regarded it as an outward sign of conversion, or something equally valuable.—So she conducted her into the presence of her uncle, a little old man, worn and bent, with gray locks peeping locks peeping out from under a Highland bonnet.

"This is my brither Jeames's bairn," she said.

The old man received her kindly, called her his dawtie, and made her sit down by him on a three-legged *creepie*, talking to her as if she had been quite a child, while she, capable of high converse as she was, replied in corresponding terms. Her great-aunt was confined to her bed with rheumatism. Supper was preparing, and Annie was not sorry to have a share, for indeed, during the summer, her meals were often scanty enough. While they ate, the old man kept helping her to the best, talking to her all the time.

"Will ye no come and bide wi' me, dawtie?" he said, meaning little by the question.

"Na, na," answered Margaret for her. "She's at the schule, ye ken, uncle, and we maunna interfere wi' her schoolin.'—Hoo does that leein' ted, Robert Bruce, carry himsel' to ye, bairn?"

"Ow! I jist never min' him," answered Annie.

"Weel, it's a' he deserves at your han'. But gin I war you, I wad let him ken that gin he saws your corn ye hae a richt to raither mair nor his gleanins."

"I dinna ken what ye mean," answered Annie.

"Ow! na; I daursay no. But ye may jist as weel ken noo, that

out from under a Highland bonnet.

"This is my brother Jeames's child," she said.

The old man received her kindly, called her his dawtie [*pet*], and made her sit down by him on a three-legged *creepie*, talking to her as if she had been quite a child, while she, capable of high converse as she was, replied in corresponding terms. Her great-aunt was confined to her bed with rheumatism. Supper was preparing, and Annie was not sorry to have a share, for indeed, during the summer, her meals were often scanty enough. While they ate, the old man kept helping her to the best, talking to her all the time.

"Won't you come and stay with me, pet?" he said, meaning little by the question.

"Na, na," answered Margaret for her. "She's at the school, you know, uncle, and we mustn't interfere with her schooling.—How does that lying toad, Robert Bruce, carry himself to you, bairn?"

"Oh! I just never heed him," answered Annie.

"Well, it's all he deserves at your hand. But if I were you, I would let him know that if he sows your corn you have a right to rather more than his gleanings."

"I don't know what you mean," answered Annie.

"Oh! na; I daresay not. But you may just as well know now, that

that toad, Robert Bruce, has two hundred pounds odd of your own, lassie; and if he doesn't use you well, you can just tell him that I told you so."

This piece of news had not the overpowering effect upon Annie which, perhaps, her aunt had expected. No doubt the money seemed in her eyes a limitless fortune; but then Bruce had it. She might as soon think of robbing a bear of her whelps as getting her own from Bruce. Besides, what could she do with it if she had it? And she had not yet acquired the faculty of loving money for its own sake. When she rose to take her leave, she felt little richer than when she entered, save for the kind words of John Peterson.

"It's too late for you to go home alone, pet," said the old man.

"I'm not that frightened," answered Annie.

"Well, if you walk with Him, the dark'll be light about you," said he, taking off his Highland bonnet, and looking up with a silent recognition of the care of *Him*. "Be a good lass," he resumed, replacing his bonnet, "and run home as fast as you can. Good night to you, pet."

Rejoicing as if she had found her long-lost home, Annie went out into the deep gloaming feeling it impossible she should be frightened at anything. But when she came to the part of the road bordered with trees, she could not help fancying she saw a figure flitting along from tree to tree just within the deeper dusk of the wood, and as she hurried on, fancy grew to fear. Presently she heard awful sounds, like the subdued growling of wild beasts. She would have taken to her heels in terror, but she reflected that thereby she would only insure pursuit, whereas she might slip away unperceived. As she reached a stile leading into the wood, however, a dusky figure came bounding over it, and advanced towards her. To her relief it went on two legs; and when it came nearer she thought she recognized some traits of old acquaintance about it. When it was within a couple of yards of her, as she still pursued her way towards Glamerton, she stopped and cried out joyfully:

"Curly!"—for it was her old vice-champion.

"Annie!" was the equally joyful response.

"I thought you were a wild beast!" said Annie.

"I was only growling for fun to myself," answered Curly, who would have done it all the more if he had known there was any one on the road. "I didn't know that I was scaring anyone. And how are you, Annie? And how's Blister Bruce?"

For Curly was dreadfully prolific in nicknames.

Annie had not seen him for six months. He had continued to show himself so full of mischief, though of a comparatively innocent sort, that his father thought it better at last to send him to a town at some distance to learn the trade of a saddler, for which he had shown a preference.

This was his first visit to his home. Hitherto his father had received no complaints of his behaviour, and had now begged a holiday.

"Ye're grown sair, Annie," he said.

"Sae are ye, Curly," answered Annie.

"An' hoo's Alec?"

"He's verra weel."

Whereupon much talk followed, which need not be recorded. At length Curly said:

"And hoo's the rottans?"

"Ower weel and thrivin'."

"Jist pit yer han' i' my coat-pooch, and see what I hae broucht ye."

Knowing Curly's propensities, Annie refused.

"It's a wild beast," said Curly. "I'll lat it oot upo' ye. It was it 'at made a' that roarin' i' the plantin'."

So saying, he pulled out of his pocket the most delicate tortoise-shell kitten, not half the beauty of which could be perceived in the gloaming, which is all the northern summer night. He threw it at Annie, but she had seen enough not to be afraid to catch it in her hands.

"Did ye fess this a' the road frae Spinnie to me, Curly?"

"Ay did I, Annie. Ye see I dinna like rottans. But ye maun haud it oot o' their gait for a feow weeks, or they'll rive't a' to bits. It'll sune be a match for them though, I s' warran'. She comes o' a killin' breed."

Annie took the kitten home, and it shared her bed that night.

"What's that meowlin?" asked Bruce the next morning, the

"You're fairly grown, Annie!" he said.

"So are you, Curly," answered Annie.

"And how's Alec?"

"He's very well."

Whereupon much talk followed, which need not be recorded. At length Curly said:

"And how's the rats?"

"Too well and thriving."

"Just put your hand in my coat-pocket, and see what I've brought you."

Knowing Curly's propensities, Annie refused.

"It's a wild beast," said Curly. "I'll let it out upon you. It was it that made all that roaring in the wood."

So saying, he pulled out of his pocket the most delicate tortoise-shell kitten, not half the beauty of which could be perceived in the gloaming, which is all the northern summer night. He threw it at Annie, but she had seen enough not to be afraid to catch it in her hands.

"Did you bring this all the way from Spinnie to me, Curly?"

"Ay, I did, Annie. You see I don't like rats. But you must keep it out of their way for a few weeks, or they'll tear it all to bits. It'll soon be a match for them though, I bet. She comes of a killing breed."

Annie took the kitten home, and it shared her bed that night.

"What's that meowling?" asked Bruce the next morning,

moment he rose from the genuflexion of morning prayers.

"It's my kittlin'," answered Annie. "I'll lat ye see't."

"We hae ower mony mou's i' the hoose already," said Bruce, as she returned with the little peering baby-animal in her arms. "We hae nae room for mair. Here, Rob, tak the cratur, an' pit a tow aboot its neck, an' a stane to the tow, an' fling't into the Glamour."

Annie, not waiting to parley, darted from the house with the kitten.

"Rin efter her, Rob," said Bruce, "an' tak' it frae her, and droon't. We canna hae the hoose swarmin'."

Rob bolted after her, delighted with his commission. But instead of finding her at the door, as he had expected, he saw her already a long way up the street, flying like the wind. He started in keen pursuit. He was now a great lumbering boy, and although Annie's wind was not equal to his, she was more fleet. She took the direct road to Howglen, and Rob kept floundering after her. Before she reached the footbridge she was nearly breathless, and he was gaining fast upon her. Just as she turned the corner of the road, leading up on the other side of the water, she met Alec and Kate. Unable to speak, she passed without appeal. But there was no need to ask the cause of her pale agonized face, for there was young Bruce at her heels. Alec collared him instantly.

"What are you up to?" he asked.

"Naething," answered the panting pursuer.

"Gin ye be efter naething, ye'll fin' that nearer hame," retorted Alec, twisting him round in that direction, and giving him a kick to expedite his return. "Lat me

the moment he rose from the genuflexion of morning prayers.

"It's my kitten," answered Annie. "I'll let you see it."

"We have too many mouths in the house already," said Bruce, as she returned with the little peering baby-animal in her arms. "We haven't room for more. Here, Rob, take the creature, and put a rope about its neck, and a stone to the rope, and fling it into the Glamour."

Annie, not waiting to parley, darted from the house with the kitten.

"Run after her, Rob," said Bruce, "and take it from her, and drown it. We can't have the house swarming."

"What are you up to?" he asked.

"Nothing," answered the panting pursuer.

"If it's nothing you're after, you'll find it nearer home," retorted Alec, twisting him round in that direction, and giving him a kick to expedite his return. "Let me hear of you troubling Annie Anderson, and I'll make you jump out of your skin the next time I lay hands upon you. Go home."

Rob obeyed like a frightened dog, while Annie pursued her course to Howglen, as if her enemy had been still on her track. Rushing into the parlour, she fell on the floor before Mrs Forbes, unable to utter a word. The kitten sprung mewing out of her arms, and took refuge under the sofa.

"Ma'am, ma'am," she gasped at length, "take care of my kitten. They want to drown it. It's my own. Curly gave it to me."

Mrs Forbes comforted her, and readily undertook the tutelage. Annie was very late for school, for Mrs Forbes made her have another breakfast before she went. But Mr Malison was in a good humour that day, and said nothing. Rob Bruce looked devils at her. What he had told his father I do not know; but whatever it was, it was all written down in Bruce's mental books to the debit of Alexander Forbes of Howglen.

Mrs Forbes's heart smote her when she found to what persecution her little friend was exposed during those times when her favour was practically although not really withdrawn; but she did not see how she could well remedy it. She was herself in the power of Bruce, and expostulation from her would be worth little; while to have Annie to the house as before would involve consequences unpleasant to all concerned. She resolved to make up for it by being kinder to her than ever as soon as Alec should have followed Kate to the precincts of the university; while for the present she comforted both herself and Annie by telling her to be sure to come to her when she found herself in any trouble.

But Annie was not one to apply to her friends except she was in great need of their help. The present case had been one of life and death. She found no further occasion to visit Mrs Forbes before Kate and Alec were both gone.

CHAPTER LI

On a sleepy summer afternoon, just when the sunshine begins to turn yellow, Annie was sitting with Tibbie on the grass in front of her little cottage, whose door looked up the river. The cottage stood on a small rocky eminence at the foot of the bridge. Underneath the approach to it from the bridge, the dyer's mill-race ran by a passage cut in the rock, leading to the third arch of the bridge built over the Glamour. Towards the river, the rock went down steep to the little meadow. It was a triangular piece of smooth grass growing on the old bed of the river, which for many years had been leaving this side, and wearing away the opposite bank. It lay between the river, the dyer's race, and the bridge, one of the stone piers of which rose from it. The grass which grew upon it was short, thick, and delicate. On the opposite side of the river lay a field for bleaching the linen, which was the chief manufacture of that country. Hence it enjoyed the privilege of immunity from the ploughshare. None of its daisies ever met the fate of Burn's

"Wee, modest, crimson-tippit flower."

But indeed so constantly was the grass mown to keep it short, that there was scarcely a daisy to be seen in it, the long broad lines of white linen usurping their place, and in their stead keeping up the contrast of white and green. Around Tibbie and Annie however the daisies were shining back to the sun, confidently, with their hearts of gold and their rays of silver. And the butter-cups were all of gold; and the queen-of-the-meadow, which grew tall at the water-side, perfumed the whole region with her crown of silvery blossom. Tibbie's blind face was turned towards the sun; and her hands were busy as ants with her knitting needles, for she was making a pair of worsted stockings for Annie against the winter. No one could fit stockings so well as Tibbie.

"Wha's that comin', lassie?" she asked.

Annie, who had heard no one, glanced round, and, rising, said, "It's Thomas Crann."

"That's not Thomas Crann," rejoined Tibbie. "I don't hear his cough."

Thomas came up, pale and limping a little.

"That's not Thomas Crann?" repeated Tibbie, before he had time to address her.

"Why not, Tibbie?" returned Thomas.

"'Cause I can't hear your breath, Thomas."

"That's a sign that I have the more of it, Tibbie. I'm so much better of that asthma, that I think sometimes the Lord must have blown into my nostrils another breath of that life that he breathed first into Adam and Eve."

"I'm right glad to hear it, Thomas. Breath must come from him one way or another."

"No doubt, Tibbie."

"Will you sit down beside us, Thomas? It's long since I've seen you."

Tibbie always spoke of *seeing* people.

"Ay, I will, Tibbie. I haven't much upon my hands today. You see I haven't got properly back into my work yet."

"Annie and me, we've just been having a crack together about this thing and that thing, Thomas," said Tibbie, dropping her knitting on her knees, and folding her palms together. "Maybe *you* could tell me whether there be any likeness between the licht that I canna see and that soun' o' the water rinnin', aye rinnin', that I like sae weel to hear."

For it did not need the gentle warm wind, floating rather than blowing down the river that afternoon, to bring to their ears the sound of the *entick*, or dam built across the river, to send the water to the dyer's wheel; for that sound was in Tibbie's cottage day and night, mingled with the nearer, gentler, and stronger gurgling of the swift, deep, *deedie* water in the race, that hurried, aware of its work, with small noise and much soft-sliding force towards the wheel.

"Weel, ye see, Tibbie," answered Thomas, "it's nearhan' as ill for the like o' us to unnerstan' your blin'ness as it may be for you to unnerstan' oor sicht."

"Deed maybe neyther o' 's kens muckle aboot oor ain gift either o' sicht or blin'ness.—Say onything ye like, gin ye dinna tell me, as the bairn here ance did, that I cudna ken what the licht was. I kenna what yer sicht may be, and I'm thinkin' I care as little. But weel ken I what the licht is."

"Tibbie, dinna be ill-nater'd, like me. Ye hae no call to that same. I'm tryin' to answer your queston. And gin ye interrup' me again, I'll rise an' gang hame."

"Say awa', Thamas. Never heed me. I'm some cankert whiles. I ken that weel eneuch."

the light that I can't see and that sound of the water running, always running, that I like so well to hear."

For it did not need the gentle warm wind, floating rather than blowing down the river that afternoon, to bring to their ears the sound of the *entick*, or dam built across the river, to send the water to the dyer's wheel; for that sound was in Tibbie's cottage day and night, mingled with the nearer, gentler, and stronger gurgling of the swift, deep, *deedie* (industrious) water in the race, that hurried, aware of its work, with small noise and much soft-sliding force towards the wheel.

"Well, you see, Tibbie," answered Thomas, "it's almost as hard for the likes of us to understand your blindness as it may be for you to understand our sight."

"Indeed maybe neither of us knows much about our own gift either of sight or blindness.—Say anything you like, if you don't tell me, as the bairn here once did, that I couldn't know what the light was. I don't know what your sight may be, and I think I care as little. But I know well what the light is."

"Tibbie, don't be bad-tempered, like me. You have no reason for it. I'm trying to answer your question. And if you interrupt me again, I'll rise and go home."

"Say on, Thomas. Never heed me. I'm a bit cross sometimes. I know that well enough."

"Ye hae nae business to be cankert, Tibbie."

"Nae mair nor ither fowk."

"Less, Tibbie; less, woman."

"Hoo mak' ye that oot?" asked Tibbie, defensively.

"Ye dinna see the things to anger ye that ither fowk sees.—As I cam' doon the street this minute, I cam' upo' twa laddies—ye ken them—they're twins—ane o' them cripple—"

"Ay, that was Murdoch Malison's wark!" interposed Tibbie, with indignant reminiscence.

"The man's been sorry for't this mony a day," said Thomas; "sae we maunna come ower't again, Tibbie."

"Verra weel, Thamas; I s' haud my tongue. What about the laddies?"

"They war fechtin' i' the verra street; ruggin' ane anither's heids, an' peggin' at ane anither's noses, an' doin' their verra endeevour to destroy the image o' the Almichty—it wasna muckle o' 't that was left to blaud. I teuk and throosh them baith."

"An' what cam' o' the image o' the Almichty?" asked Tibbie, with a grotesque contortion of her mouth, and a roll of her veiled eyeballs. "I doobt, Thamas," she continued, "ye angert yersel' mair nor ye quaietit them wi' the thrashin'. The wrath o' man, ye ken, Thamas, worketh not the richtyisness o' God."

"You have no business to be cross, Tibbie."

"No more than other folk."

"Less, Tibbie; less, woman."

"How do you make that out?" asked Tibbie, defensively.

"You don't see the things to anger you that other folk see.—As I came down the street this minute, I came upon two laddies—you know them—they're twins—one of them cripple—"

"Ay, that was Murdoch Malison's work!" interposed Tibbie, with indignant reminiscence.

"The man's been sorry for it this many a day," said Thomas; "so we mustn't mention it again, Tibbie."

"Very well, Thomas; I'll hold my tongue. What about the laddies?"

"They were fighting in the very street; tugging one another's heads, and whacking at one another's noses, and trying their very hardest to destroy the image of the Almighty—it wasn't much of it that was left to spoil. I took and thrashed them both."

"And what came of the image of the Almighty?" asked Tibbie, with a grotesque contortion of her mouth, and a roll of her veiled eyeballs. "I expect, Thomas," she continued, "you angered yourself more than you quieted them with the thrashing. The wrath of man, you know, Thomas, worketh not the righteousness of God."

There was not a person in Glamerton who would have dared to speak thus to Thomas Crann but Tibbie Dyster, perhaps because there was not one who had such a respect for him. Possibly the darkness about her made her bolder; but I think it was her truth, which is another word for *love*, however unlike love the outcome may look, that made her able to speak in this fashion.

Thomas was silent for a long minute. Then he said:

"Maybe you're right, Tibbie. You always anger me; but I would rather have someone anger me with telling me the truth, than I would have all the fair words in the dictionary. It's a strange thing, woman, but whenever a man's trying most to walk upright he's sure to catch a dreadful fall. There I've been fighting my ill-temper more than ever I did in my life before; and I never in my days licked two laddies for licking one another till just this very day. And I prayed against myself before I came out. I can't understand it."

"There's worse things than a bad temper, Thomas. Not that it's bonnie at all. And it's nothing like Him that was meek and lowly of heart. But, as I say, there's worse faults than a bad temper. It would be no gain to you, Thomas, and no glory to Him whose will's your sanctification, if you were to overcome yersel' that ye had done't. Maybe that's what for yer no allooed to be victorious in yer endeevours."

"'Deed, maybe, Tibbie," said Thomas solemnly. "And I'm some doobtfu' forbye, whether I mayna be tryin' to ripe oot the stockin' frae the wrang en' o' 't. I doobt the fau't's nae sae muckle i' my temper as i' my hert. It's mair love that I want, Tibbie. Gin I lo'ed my neebor as mysel', I cudna be sae ill-natert till him; though 'deed, whiles, I'm angry eneuch at mysel'—a hantle waur nor at him."

"Verra true, Thamas," answered Tibbie. "Perfect love casteth oot fear, 'cause there's nae room for the twa o' them; and I daursay it wad be the same wi' the temper."

"But I'm no gaein' to gie in to bein' ill-natert for a' that," said Thomas, as if alarmed at the possible consequences of the conclusion.

"Na na. Resist ye the deevil, Thamas. Haud at him, man. He's sure to rin at the lang last. But I'm feared ye'll gang awa' ohn tellt me aboot the licht and the water. Whan I'm sittin' here o' the girse, hearkenin' to the water, as it comes murrin', and soufflin', and gurglin', on to me, and syne by me and awa', as gin it war spinnin' and twistin' a lot o' bonnie wee sounies a' intil ae muckle

your temper, and then think a heap of yourself that you had done it. Maybe that's why your efforts haven't been crowned with victory."

"Maybe so, Tibbie," said Thomas solemnly. "And I'm doubtful, besides, whether I mightn't be trying to rip out the stocking from the wrong end. I suspect the fault's not so much in my temper as in my heart. It's more love that I want, Tibbie. If I loved my neighbour as myself, I couldn't be so bad-tempered to him; though indeed, at times, I'm angry enough at myself—a deal worse than at him."

"Very true, Thomas," answered Tibbie. "Perfect love casteth out fear, 'cause there's no room for the two of them; and I daresay it would be the same with the temper."

"But I'm not going to give in to being bad-tempered for all that," said Thomas, as if alarmed at the possible consequences of the conclusion.

"Na na. Resist the devil, Thomas. Keep at him, man. He's sure to run at the long last. But I'm afraid you'll go away without telling me about the light and the water. When I'm sitting here on the grass, listening to the water, as it comes murmuring, and singing, and gurgling, on to me, and then by me and away, as if it were spinning and twisting a lot of bonnie wee sounds all into one big grand sound, it reminds me of that text that says, 'His voice was as the sound of many waters.' Now his face is light—you know that, don't you?—and if his voice be like the water, there must be a likeness between the light and the water, you know. That's what made me ask you, Thomas."

"Well, I don't rightly know how to answer you, Tibbie; but at this moment the light's playing bonny upon the dam—shimmering and breaking upon the water, as it breaks upon the stones before it falls. And what falls, it looks as if it took the light with it in its hollow, like. Eh! it's bonnie, woman; and I wish you had the sight of your eyes to see it with; though you do pretend to think little of it."

"Well, well! my time's coming, Thomas; and I have just to wait till it comes. You can't help me, I see that. If I could only open my eyes for one minute, I would know all about it, and be able to answer myself.—I think we'll go into the house, for I can't stand it longer."

All the time they were talking Annie was watching Alec's boat, which had dropped down the river, and was floating in the sunshine above the dam. Thomas must have seen it too, for it was in the very heart of the radiance reflected to them from the watery mirror. But Alec was a painful subject with Thomas, for when they chanced to meet now, nothing more than the passing salute of ordinary acquaintance was exchanged. And Thomas was not able to be indulgent to young people. Certain facts in his nature, as well as certain articles in his creed, rendered him unable. So, being one of those who never speak of what is painful to them if they can avoid it—thinking all the more, he talked about the light, and said nothing about the boat that was in the middle of it. Had Alec been rowing, Tibbie would have heard the oars; but he only paddled enough to keep the boat from drifting on to the dam. Kate sat in the stern looking at the water with half-closed eyes, and Alec sat looking at Kate, as if his eyes were made only for her. And Annie sat in the meadow, and she too looked at Kate; and she thought how pretty she was, and how she must like being rowed about in the old boat. It seemed quite an old boat now. An age had passed since her name was painted on it. She wondered if *The Bonnie Annie* was worn off the stern yet; or if Alec had painted it out, and put the name of the pretty lady instead. When Tibbie and Thomas walked away into the house, Annie lingered behind on the grass.

The sun sank slanting and slow, yet he did sink, lower and lower; till at length Alec leaned back with a stronger pull on the oars, and the boat crept away up the stream, lessening as it crept, and, turning a curve in the river, was lost. Still she sat on, with one hand lying listlessly in her lap, and the other plucking blades of grass and making a little heap of them beside her, till she had pulled a spot quite bare, and the brown earth peeped through between the roots. Then she rose, went up to the door of the cottage, called a good night to Tibbie, and took her way home.

CHAPTER LII

My story has not to do with city-life, in which occur frequent shocks, changes, and recombinations, but with the life of a country region; and is, therefore, "to a lingering motion bound," like the day, like the ripening of the harvest, like the growth of all good things. But clouds and rainbows will come in the quietest skies; adventures and coincidences in the quietest village.

As Kate and Alec walked along the street, on their way to the castle, one of the coaches from the county-town drove up with its four thorough-breds.

"What a handsome fellow the driver is!" said Kate.

Alec looked up at the box. There sat Beauchamp, with the ribbons in his grasp, handling his horses with composure and skill. Beside him sat the owner of the coach, a *laird* of the neighbourhood.

Certainly Beauchamp was a handsome fellow. But a sting went through Alec's heart. It was the first time that he thought of his own person in comparison with another. That she should admire Beauchamp, though he was handsome!

The memory even of that moment made him writhe on his bed years after; for a mental and bodily wound are alike in this, that after there is but the scar of either left, bad weather will revive the torture. His face fell. Kate saw it, and did him some injustice. They walked on in silence, in the shadow of a high wall. Kate looked up at the top of the wall and stopped. Alec looked at her. Her face was as full of light as a diamond in the sun. He forgot all his jealousy. The fresh tide of his love swept it away, or at least covered it. On the top of the wall, in the sun, grew one wild scarlet poppy, a delicate transparent glory, through which the sunlight shone, staining itself red, and almost dissolving the poppy.

The red light melted away the mist between them, and they walked in it up to the ruined walls. Long grass grew about them, close to the very door, which was locked, that if old Time could not be kept out, younger destroyers might. Other walls stood around, vitrified by fire—the remnants of an older castle still, about which Jamblichus might have spied the lingering phantoms of many a terrible deed.

They entered by the door in the great tower, under the spiky remnants of the spiral stair projecting from the huge circular wall. To the right, a steep descent, once a stair, led down to the cellars and the dungeon; a terrible place, the visible negations of which are horrid, and need no popular legends such as Alec had been telling Kate, of a walled-up door and a lost room, to add to their influence. It was no wonder that when he held out his hand to lead her down into the darkness and through winding ways to the mouth of the far-off beehive dungeon—it was no wonder, I say, that she should shrink and draw back. A few rays came through the decayed planks of the door which Alec had pushed to behind them, and fell upon the rubbish of centuries sloping in the brown light and damp air down into the abyss. One larger ray from the keyhole fell upon Kate's face, and showed it blanched with fear, and her eyes distended with the effort to see through the gloom.

At that moment, a sweet, low voice came from somewhere, out of the darkness, saying:

"Don't be afraid, ma'am, to go where Alec wants you to go. You can trust to *him*."

Staring in the direction of the sound, Kate saw the pale face of a slender—half child, half maiden, glimmering across the gulf that led to the dungeon. She stood in the midst of a sepulchral light, whose faintness differed from mere obscuration, inasmuch as it told how bright it was out of doors in the sun. Annie, I say, stood in this dimness—a dusky and yet radiant creature, seeming to throw off from her a faint brown light—a lovely, earth-stained ghost.

"Oh! Annie, is that you?" said Alec.

"Ay, it is, Alec," Annie answered.

"This is an old schoolfellow of mine," he said, turning to Kate, who was looking haughtily at the girl.

"Oh! is it?" said Kate, condescending.

Between the two, each looking ghostly to the other, lay a dark cavern-mouth that seemed to go down to Hades.

"Won't you go down, ma'am?" said Annie.

"No, thank you," answered Kate, decisively.

"Alec'll take good care of you, ma'am."

"Oh! yes, I daresay; but I had rather not."

Alec said nothing. Kate would not trust him then! He would not have thought much of it, however, but for what had passed before. Would she have gone with Beauchamp if he had asked her? Ah! if he had asked Annie, she too would have turned pale, but she would have laid her hand in his, and gone with him.

"If you want to go up, then," she said, "I'll let you see the easiest road. It's round this way."

And she pointed to a narrow ledge between the descent and the circular wall, by which they could cross to where she stood. But Alec, who had no desire for Annie's company, declined her guidance, and took Kate up a nearer though more difficult ascent to the higher level. Here all the floors of the castle lay in dust beneath their feet, mingled with fragments of chimney-piece and battlement. The whole central space lay open to the sky.

Annie remained standing on the edge of the dungeon-slope.

She had been on her way to see Tibbie, when she caught a glimpse of Kate and Alec as they passed. Since watching them in the boat the evening before, she had been longing to speak to Alec, longing to see

Kate nearer: perhaps the beautiful lady would let her love her. She guessed where they were going, and across the fields she bounded like a fawn, straight as the crows flew home to the precincts of that "ancient rest," and reached it before them. She did not need to fetch the key, for she knew a hole on the level of the grass, wide enough to let her creep through the two yards of wall. So she crept in and took her place near the door.

After they had rambled over the lower part of the building, Alec took Kate up a small winding stair, past a succession of empty doorways like eyeless sockets, leading nowhither because the floors had fallen. Kate was so frightened by coming suddenly upon one after another of these defenceless openings, that by the time she reached the broad platform, which ran, all bare of parapet or battlement, around the top of the tower, she felt faint; and when Alec scampered off like a goat to reach the bartizan at the other side, she sank in an agony of fear upon the landing of the stair.

Looking down upon her from the top of the little turret, Alec saw that she was ill, and returning instantly in great dismay, comforted her as well as he could, and got her by degrees to the bottom. There was a spot of grass inside the walls, on which he made her rest; and as the sun shone upon her through one of the ruined windows, he stood so that his shadow should fall across her eyes. While he stood thus a strange fancy seized him. The sun became in his eyes a fiery dragon, which having devoured half of the building, having eaten the inside out of it, having torn and gnawed it everywhere, and having at length reached its kernel, the sleeping beauty, whose bed had, in the long years, mouldered away, and been replaced by the living grass, would swallow her up anon, if he were not there to stand between and defend her. When he looked at her next, she had indeed become the sleeping beauty he had fancied her; and sleep had already restored the colour to her cheeks.

Turning his eyes up to the tower from which they had just descended, he saw, looking down upon them from one of the isolated doorways, the pale face of Patrick Beauchamp. Alec bounded to the stair, rushed to the top and round the platform, but found nobody. Beginning to doubt his eyes, his next glance showed him Beauchamp standing over the sleeping girl. He darted down the screw of the stair, but when he reached the bottom Beauchamp had again disappeared.

The same moment Kate began to wake. Her first movement brought Alec to his senses: why should he follow Beauchamp? He returned to her side, and they left the place, locked the door behind them, took the key to the lodge, and went home.

After tea, Alec, believing he had locked Beauchamp into the castle, returned and searched the building from top to bottom, even got a candle and a ladder, and went down into the dungeon, found no one, and went home bewildered.

While Alec was searching the vacant ruin, Beauchamp was comfortably seated on the box of the Spitfire, tooling it halfway home—namely, as far as the house of its owner, the laird above mentioned, who was a relative of his mother, and whom he was then visiting. He had seen Kate and Alec take the way to the castle, and had followed them, and found the door unlocked. Watching them about the place, he ascended the stair from another approach. The moment Alec looked up at him, he ran down again, and had just dropped into a sort of well-like place which the stair had used to fill on its way to a lower level, when he heard Alec's feet thundering up over his head. Determined then to see what the lady was like, for he had never seen her close, or without her bonnet, which now lay beside her on the grass, he scrambled out, and, approaching her cautiously, had a few moments to contemplate her before he saw—for he kept a watch on the tower—that Alec had again caught sight of him, when he immediately fled to his former refuge, which communicated with a low-pitched story lying between the open level and the vaults.

The sound of the ponderous and rusty bolt reached him across the cavernous space. He had not expected their immediate departure, and was rather alarmed. His first impulse was to try whether he could not shoot the bolt from the inside. This he soon found to be impossible. He next turned to the windows in the front, but there the ground fell away so suddenly that he was many feet from it—an altogether dangerous leap. He was beginning to feel seriously concerned, when he heard a voice:

"Do ye want to win oot, sir? They hae lockit the door."[1]

He turned but could see no one. Approaching the door again, he spied Annie, in the dark twilight, standing on the edge of the descent to the vaults. He had passed the spot not a minute before, and she was certainly not there then. She looked as if she had just glided up that slope from a region so dark that a spectre might haunt it all day long. But Beauchamp was not of a fanciful disposition, and instead of taking her for a spectre, he accosted her with easy insolence!

---

1   "Do you want to get out, sir? They have locked the door."

"Tell me how to get out, my pretty girl, and I'll give you a kiss."

Seized with a terror she did not understand, Annie darted into the cavern between them, and sped down its steep into the darkness which lay there like a lurking beast. A few yards down, however, she turned aside, through a low doorway, into a vault. Beauchamp rushed after her, passed her, and fell over a great stone lying in the middle of the way. Annie heard him fall, sprung forth again, and, flying to the upper light, found her way out, and left the discourteous knight a safe captive, fallen upon that horrible stair.—A horrible stair it was: up and down those steps, then steep and worn, now massed into an incline of beaten earth, had swarmed, for months together, a multitude of naked children, orphaned and captive by the sword, to and from the troughs at which they fed like pigs, amidst the laughter of the lord of the castle and his guests; while he who passed down them to the dungeon beyond, had little chance of ever retracing his steps upward to the light.

Annie told the keeper that there was a gentleman shut into the castle, and then ran a mile and a half to Tibbie's cottage, without stopping. But she did not say a word to Tibbie about her adventure.

CHAPTER LIII

A spirit of prophecy, whether from the Lord or not, was abroad this summer among the clergy of Glamerton, of all persuasions. Nor was its influences confined to Glamerton or the clergy. The neighbourhood and the laity had their share. Those who read their Bibles, of whom there were many in that region, took to reading the prophecies, all the prophecies, and scarcely anything but the prophecies. Upon these every man, either for himself or following in the track of his spiritual instructor, exercised his individual powers of interpretation, whose fecundity did not altogether depend upon the amount of historical knowledge. But whatever was known, whether about ancient Assyria or modern Tahiti, found its theoretic place. Of course the Church of Rome had her due share of the application from all parties; but neither the Church of England, the Church of Scotland, nor either of the dissenting sects, went without its portion freely dealt, each of the last finding something that applied to all the rest. There were some, however, who cared less for such modes, and, themselves given to a daily fight with antichrist in their own hearts, sought—for they too read the prophecies—to fix their reference on certain sins, and certain persons classed according to these their sins. With a burning desire for the safety of their neighbours, they took upon them the strongest words of rebuke and condemnation, so that one might have thought they were revelling in the idea of the vengeance at hand, instead of striving for the rescue of their neighbours from the wrath to come. Among these were Thomas Crann and his minister, Mr Turnbull. To them Glamerton was the centre of creation, providence, and revelation. Every warning finger in The Book pointed to it; every burst of indignation from the labouring bosom of holy prophet was addressed to its sinners. And what the ministers spoke to classes from the pulpit, Thomas, whose mode of teaching was in so far Socratic that he singled out his man, applied to the individual—in language occasionally too much to the point to admit of repetition in the delicate ears of the readers of the nineteenth century, some of whom are on such friendly terms with the vices themselves, that they are shocked at the vulgarity and rudeness of the *names* given them by their forefathers.

"You know well enough you're a drunken wretch, Peter Peterson. And you know well enough that you're no better, besides, than you should be. Nobody ever accused you of stealing; but if you keep on as you're doing, that'll come next. But I expect the wrath of the Almighty'll be down upon us like a spate, as it was in the days of Noah, before you have time to learn to steal, Peter Peterson. You'll have *your* share in bringing destruction upon this town, and all its belongings. The very church-yard won't hide you that day from the wrath of Him that sitteth upon the throne. Be warned, and repent, Peter; or it'll be the worse for you."

The object of this terrible denunciation of the wrath of the Almighty was a wretched little object indeed, just like a white rabbit—with pink eyes, a grey face and head, poor thin legs, a long tail-coat that came nearly to his heels, an awfully ragged pair of trowsers, and a liver charred with whisky. He had kept a whisky-shop till he had drunk all his own whisky; and as no distiller would let him have any on trust, he now hung about the inn-yard, and got a penny from one, and twopence from another, for running errands.—Had they been sovereigns they would all have gone the same way—namely, for whisky.

He listened to Thomas with a kind of dazed meekness, his eyes wandering everywhere except in the direction of Thomas's. One who did not know Thomas would have thought it cowardly in him to attack such a poor creature. But Thomas was just as ready to fly at the greatest man in Glamerton. All the evildoers of the place feared him—the rich manufacturer and the strong horse-doctor included. They called him a wheezing, canting hypocrite, and would go streets out of their way to avoid him.

But on the present occasion he went too far with Peter.

"And it's weel kent your dochter Bauby's no better nor she sud be; for—"

Peter's face flushed crimson, though where the blood could have come from was an anatomical mystery; he held up his hands with the fingers crooked like the claws of an animal, for the poor creature had no notion of striking; and, dancing backwards and forwards from one foot to the other, and grinning with set teeth in an agony of impotent rage, cried out:

"Tam Crann, gin ye daur to say anither word against my Bauby wi' that foul mou' o' yours, I'll—I'll—I'll—worry ye like a mad dog—ye ill-tongued scoonrel!"

His Bawby had already had two children—one to the rich manufacturer, the other to the strong horse-doctor.

Thomas turned in silence and went away rebuked and ashamed. Next day he sent Peter a pair of old corduroy trowsers, into either leg of which he might have been buttoned like one of Paddy's twins.

In the midst of this commotion of mind and speech, good Mr Cowie died. He had taken no particular interest in what was going on, nor even in the prophecies themselves. Ever since Annie's petition for counsel, he had been thinking, as he had never thought before, about his own relation to God; and had found this enough without the prophecies. Now he had carried his thoughts into another world. While Thomas Crann was bending his spiritual artillery upon the poor crazy tub in which floated the earthly presence of Peter Peterson, Mr Cowie's bark was lying stranded upon that shore whither the tide of time is slowly drifting each of us.

He was gently regretted by all—even by Thomas.

"Ay! ay!" he said, with slow emphasis, 'long drawn out'; "he's gane, is he, honest man? Weel, maybe he had the root o' the maitter in him, although it made unco little show aboon the yird. There was sma' flower and less fruit. But jeedgment disna belang to us, ye see, Jean, lass."

Thomas would judge the living from morning to night; but the dead—he would leave them alone in the better hands.

"I'm thinkin'," he added, "he's been taen awa' frae the evil to come—frae seein' the terrible consequences o' sic a saft way o' dealin' wi' eternal trowth and wi' perishin' men—taen awa' like Eli, whan he brak his neck at the ill news. For the fire and brimstane that overthrew Sodom and Gomorrha, is, I doobt, hingin' ower this toon, ready to fa' and smore us a'."

"Hoot! hoot! dinna speyk sic awfu' words, Thamas, Ye're nae the prophet Jonah, ye ken."

"Are ye the whaul than, to swallow me and my words thegither, Jean? I tell ye the wrath o' God *maun* be roused against this toon, for it's been growin' waur and waur for mony a year; till the verra lasses are no to be lippent oot them-lanes."

"What ken ye aboot the lasses, Thamas? Haud ye to the men. The lasses are nae waur nor in ither pairts. I wat I can come and gang

"Ay! ay!" he said, with slow emphasis, 'long drawn out'; "he's gone, is he, honest man? Well, maybe he had the root of the matter in him, although it made very little show above ground. There was small flower and less fruit. But judgement doesn't belong to us, you see, Jean, lass."

Thomas would judge the living from morning to night; but the dead—he would leave them alone in the better hands.

"I'm thinking," he added, "he's been taken away from the evil to come—from seeing the terrible consequences of such a soft way of dealing with eternal truth and with perishing men—taken away like Eli, when he broke his neck at the ill news. For the fire and brimstone that overthrew Sodom and Gomorrha, is, I suspect, hanging over this town, ready to fall and smother us all."

"Heavens! don't speak such awful words, Thomas. You're not the prophet Jonah, you know."

"Are you the whale then, to swallow me and my words together, Jean? I tell you the wrath of God *must* be roused against this town, for it's been growing worse and worse for many a year; till the very lasses aren't to be trusted out alone."

"What do you know about the lasses, Thomas? You stick to the men. The lasses are no worse than in other parts. I know I can whan and whaur I like. Never a body says a word to me."

This was true but hardly significant; seeing Jean had one shoulder and one eye twice the size of the others, to say nothing of various obliquities and their compensations. But, rude as Thomas was, he was gentleman enough to confine his reply to a snort and a silence. For had he not chosen his housekeeper upon the strength of those personal recommendations of the defensive importance of which she was herself unaware?

Except his own daughters there was no one who mourned so deeply for the loss of Mr Cowie as Annie Anderson. She had left his church and gone to the missionars, and there found more spiritual nourishment than Mr Cowie's sermons could supply, but she could not forget his kisses, or his gentle words, or his shilling, for by their means, although she did not know it, Mr Cowie's self had given her a more confiding notion of God, a better feeling of his tenderness, than she could have had from all Mr Turnbull's sermons together. What equal gift could a man give? Was it not worth bookfuls of sound doctrine? Yet the good man, not knowing this, had often looked back to that interview, and reproached himself bitterly that he, so long a clergyman of that parish, had no help to give the only child who ever came to him to ask such help. So, when he lay on his death-bed, he sent for Annie, the only soul, out of all his parish, over which he felt that he had any pastoral cure.

When, with pale, tearful face, she entered his chamber, she found him supported with pillows in his bed. He stretched out his arms to her feebly, but held her close to his bosom, and wept.

"I'm going to die, Annie," he said.

"And go to heaven, sir, to the face o' God," said Annie, not sobbing, but with the tears streaming silently down her face.

"I don't know, Annie. I've been of no use; and I'm afraid God does not care much for me."

"If God loves you half as much as I do, sir, ye'll be well off in heaven. And I'm thinkin' he maun love ye mair nor me. For, ye see, sir, God's love itsel'."

"I'm going to die, Annie," he said.

"And go to heaven, sir, to the face of God," said Annie, not sobbing, but with the tears streaming silently down her face.

"I don't know, Annie. I've been of no use; and I'm afraid God does not care much for me."

"If God loves you half as much as I do, sir, you'll be well off in heaven. And I'm thinking he must love you more than me. For, you see, sir, God's love itself."

"I don't know, Annie. But if I ever get there, which'll be more than I deserve, I'll tell him about you, and ask him to give you the help that I couldn't give you."

Love and Death make us all children.—Can Old Age be an evil thing, which does the same?

The old clergyman had thought himself a good Protestant at least, but even his Protestantism was in danger now. Happily Protestantism was nothing to him now. Nothing but God would do now.

Annie had no answer but what lay in her tears. He called his daughter, who stood weeping in the room. She came near.

"Bring my study Bible," he said to her feebly.

She went and brought it—a large quarto Bible.

"Here, Annie," said the dying man, "here's my Bible that I've made but too little use of myself. Promise me, if ever you have a house of your own, that you'll read out of that book every day at worship. I want you not to forget me, as, if all's well, I shall never forget you."

"That *will* I, sir," responded Annie earnestly.

"And you'll find a new five-pound note between the leaves. Take it, for my sake."

Money! Ah, well! Love can turn gold into grace.

"Yes, sir," answered Annie, feeling this was no time for objecting to anything.

"And good-bye, Annie. I can't speak more."

He drew her to him again, and kissed her for the last time. Then he turned his face to the wall, and Annie went home weeping, with the great Bible in her arms.

In the inadvertence of grief, she ran into the shop.

"What have you got there, lassie?" said Bruce, as sharply as if she might have stolen it.

"Mr Cowie gave me his Bible, 'cause he's dying himself, and doesn't want it any longer," answered Annie.

"Let's look at it."

Annie gave it up with reluctance.

"It's a fine book, and bonnie boards—though gold and purple matter little to the Bible. We'll just lay it upon the room-table, and we'll have worship out of it when anybody's with us, you know."

"I want it myself," objected Annie, in dismay, for although she did not think of the money at the moment, she had better reasons for not liking to part with the book.

"You can have it when you want it. That's enough, surely."

Annie could hardly think his saying so enough, however, seeing the door of *the room* was kept locked, and Mrs Bruce, patient woman as she was, would have boxed any one's ears whom she met coming from within the sacred precincts.

CHAPTER LIV

Before the next Sunday Mr Cowie was dead; and, through some mistake or mismanagement, there was no one to preach. So the congregation did each as seemed right in his own eyes; and Mrs Forbes went to the missionar kirk in the evening to hear Mr Turnbull. Kate and Alec accompanied her.

By this time Robert Bruce had become a great man in the community—after his own judgment at least; for although, with a few exceptions, the missionars yielded him the influence he sought, nobody respected him; they only respected his money. He had managed to secure one of the most fashionable pews in the chapel; and now when Mrs Forbes's party entered, and a little commotion arose in consequence, they being more of gentlefolk than the place was accustomed to entertain, Bruce was the first to walk from his seat, and request them to occupy his pew. Alec would have passed on, for he disliked the man, but Mrs Forbes having reasons for being complaisant, accepted his offer. Colds kept the rest of the Bruces at home, and Annie was the only other occupant of the pew. She crept up to the top of it, like a little shy mouse, to be as far out of the way as possible.

"Come oot, Annie," said Bruce, in a loud whisper.

Annie came out, with a warm flush over her pale face, and Mrs Forbes entered, then Kate, and last of all, Alec, much against his will. Then Annie re-entered, and Bruce resumed his place as Cerberus of the pew-door. So Annie was seated next to Alec, as she had never been, in church or chapel, or even in school, before, except on that memorable day when they were both *kept in* for the Shorter Catechism. But Annie had no feeling of delight and awe like that with which Alec sat close to his beautiful cousin. She had a feeling of pleasure, no doubt, but the essence of the pleasure was faith. She trusted him and believed in him as much as she had ever done. In the end, those who trust most will find they are nearest the truth. But Annie had no philosophy, either worldly or divine. She had only common sense, gentleness, and faithfulness. She was very glad, though, that Alec had come to hear Mr Turnbull, who knew the right way better than anybody else, and could show it quite as well as Evangelist in the *Pilgrim's Progress*.

Nor was she far wrong in her judgment of the height of Mr Turnbull's star, calculated from the horizon of Glamerton. He was a good man who ventured to think for himself—as far as that may be possible for one upon whose spirit have converged, even before he was born, the influences of a thousand theological ancestors.

After reading the curses on Mount Ebal, he preached an eloquent sermon from the text:

"Thou art wearied in the greatness of thy way; yet saidst thou not 'there is no hope.'"

He showed his hearers that they had all been seeking satisfaction in their own pursuits, in the pride of their own way; that they had been disappointed, even to weariness; and that yet, such was their perversity, they would not acknowledge the hopelessness of the pursuit, and turn to that God who was ready to pardon, and in whose courts a day would give them more delight than a thousand in the tents of wickedness. And opening his peroration by presumptuously appropriating the words of the Saviour, "Verily, verily, I say unto you, it shall be more tolerable for Sodom and Gomorrha, in that day, than for you," the preacher concluded with a terrible denunciation of wrath upon the sinners who had been called and would not come. "Woe unto you, for ye would not be warned! Woe unto you, for ye knew your Lord's will, and yet committed things worthy of stripes! Therefore your whip shall be one of scorpions! Woe unto you! I say; for, when the bridegroom cometh, ye shall knock in vain at the closed door; ye shall stand without, and listen for a brief moment to the music and dancing within—listen with longing hearts, till the rush of coming wings overpowers the blissful sounds, and the angels of vengeance sweep upon you, and bearing you afar through waste regions, cast you into outer darkness, where shall be weeping and wailing and gnashing of teeth, to the endless ages of a divine eternity."

With these words the preacher burst into impassioned prayer for the souls which he saw exposed to a hell of which he himself knew not the horrors, else he dared not have preached it; a hell the smoke of whose torments would arise and choke the elect themselves about the throne of God—the hell of Exhausted Mercy.

As long as the stream of eloquence flowed the eyes of the congregation were fixed upon the preacher in breathless silence. When it ceased they sank, and a sigh of exhaustion and relief arose. In that ugly building, amidst that weary praying and inharmonious singing, with that blatant tone, and, worse than all, that merciless doctrine, there was yet *preaching*—that rare speech of a man to his fellow-men whereby in their inmost hearts they know that he in his inmost heart believes. There was hardly an indifferent countenance in all that wide space beneath, in all those far-sloping galleries above. Every conscience hung out the red or pale flag.

When Alec ventured to look up, as he sat down after the prayer, he saw the eyes of Thomas Crann, far away in the crowd, fixed on him. And he felt their force, though not in the way Thomas intended. Thomas never meant to dart *personal* reproaches across the house of God; but Alec's conscience told him nevertheless, stung by that glance, that he had behaved ill to his old friend. Nor did this lessen the general feeling which the sermon had awakened in his mind, un-self-conscious as it was, that something ought to be done; that something was wrong in him somewhere; that it ought to be set right somehow—a feeling which every one in the pew shared, except one. His heart was so moth-eaten and rusty, with the moths and the rust which Mammon brings with him when he comes in to abide with a man, that there was not enough of it left to make the terrible discovery that the rest of it was gone. Its owner did not know that there was anything amiss with it. What power can empty, sweep, and garnish such a heart? Or what seven devils entering in, can make the last state of that man worse than the first?

A special prayer-meeting having been appointed, to be held after the sermon, Robert Bruce remained, to join in the intercession for the wicked town and its wicked neighbourhood. He even "engaged in prayer," for the first time in public, and astonished some of the older members by his gift in devotion. He had been received into the church only a week or two before, upon profession of faith in the merits of Christ, not in Christ himself—that would not have been definite enough for them. But it would have been all the same to Robert Bruce, for he was ready to believe that he believed anything advantageous.

There had been one or two murmurs against his reception, and he had been several times visited and talked with, before the Church was satisfied as to his conversion. But nothing was known against him beyond the fact that "he luikit at baith sides o' a bawbee;"[1] and having learned many of their idioms, he had succeeded in persuading his examiners, and had possibly persuaded himself at the same time, that he had passed through all the phases of conversion, including conviction, repentance, and final acceptance of offered mercy on the terms proposed, and was now undergoing the slow and troublesome process of sanctification; in corroboration of which he went on to produce

---

1   He looked at both sides of a penny

talk, and coppers at the chapel-door. Good people as many of those were who thus admitted him to their communion, in the full belief that none but conscious Christians should enjoy that privilege, his reputation for wealth had yet something to do with it. Probably they thought that if the gospel proved mighty in this new disciple, more of his money might be accessible by and by for good purposes: amongst the rest, for sending missionaries to the heathen, teaching them to divorce their wives and wear trowsers. And now he had been asked to pray, and had prayed with much propriety and considerable unction. To be sure Tibbie Dyster did sniff a good deal during the performance; but then that was a way she had of relieving her feelings, next best to that of speaking her mind.

When the meeting was over, Robert Bruce, Thomas Crann, and James Johnstone, who was one of the deacons, walked away together. Very little conversation took place between them, for no subject but a religious one was admissible; and the religious feelings of those who had any were pretty nearly exhausted. Bruce's, however, were not in the least exhausted. On the contrary, he was so pleased to find that he could pray as well as any of them, and the excitement of doing so before judges had been so new and pleasant to him, that he thought he should like to try it again. He thought, too, of the grand Bible lying up there on the room-table.

"Come in, sirs," he said, as they approached his door, "and tak' a pairt in our faimily worship; and sae the day'll gang oot wi' prayer, as it cam in wi' prayer. And the Lord'll maybe hae mercy upo' 's, and no destroy the place, shops an' a', for the sins o' the inhaibitants—them 'at sees, for them 'at 's blin'."

"Come in, sirs," he said, as they approached his door, "and take a part in our family worship; and so the day'll go out with prayer, as it came in with prayer. And the Lord'll maybe have mercy upon us, and not destroy the place, shops and all, for the sins of the inhabitants—those that see, for those that are blind."

Neither of his companions felt much inclined to accede to his request: they both yielded notwithstanding. He conducted them up-stairs, unlocked the musty room, pulled up the blinds, and admitted enough of lingering light for the concluding devotions of the day. He then proceeded to gather his family together, calling them one by one.

"Mother!" he cried, from the top of the stair, meaning his wife.

"Yes, father," answered Mrs Bruce.

"Come to worship.—Robert!"

"Ay, father."

"Come to worship.—Johnnie!"

And so he went through the family roll-call, as if it were a part of some strange liturgy. When all had entered and seated themselves, the head of the house went slowly to the side-table, took from it reverentially the late minister's study Bible, sat down by the window, laid the book on his knees, and solemnly opened it.

Now a five-pound note is not thick enough to make a big Bible open between the pages where it is laid; but the note might very well have been laid in at a place where the Bible was in the habit of opening. Without an instant's hesitation, Robert slipped it away, and crumpling it up in his hand, gave out the twenty-third psalm, over which it had lain, and read it through. Finding it too short, however, for the respectability of worship, he went on with the twenty-fourth, turning the leaf with thumb and forefinger, while the rest of the fingers clasped the note tight in his palm, and reading as he turned,

"He that hath clean hands and a pure heart—"

As soon as he had finished this psalm, he closed the book with a snap; feeling which to have been improper, he put an additional compensating solemnity into the tone in which he said:

"Thomas Crann, will you engage in prayer?"

"Pray yersel'," answered Thomas gruffly.

Whereupon Robert rose, and, kneeling down, did pray himself.

But Thomas, instead of leaning forward on his chair when he knelt, glanced sharply round at Bruce. He had seen him take something from the Bible, and crumple it up in his hand, but would not have felt any inclination to speculate about it, had it not been for the peculiarly keen expression of eager surprise and happy greed which came over his face in the act. Having seen that, and being always more or less suspicious of Bruce, he wanted to know more; and was thus led into an action of which he would not have believed it possible he should ever be guilty.

He saw Bruce take advantage of the posture of devotion which he had assumed, to put something into his pocket unseen of his guests, as he believed.

When worship was over, Bruce did not ask them to stay to supper. Prayers did not involve expense; supper did. But Thomas at least could not have stayed longer.

He left his friends and went home pondering. The devotions of the day were not to be concluded

"Without an instant's hesitation, Robert slipped away the five-pound note..."

for him with any social act of worship. He had many anxious prayers yet to offer before his heart would be quiet in sleep. Especially there was Alec to be prayed for, and his dawtie, Annie; and in truth the whole town of Glamerton, and the surrounding parishes—and Scotland, and the world. Indeed sometimes Thomas went further, and although it is not reported of him that he ever prayed for the devil, as that worthiest of Scotch clergymen prayed, he yet did something very like it once or twice, when he prayed for "the whole universe of God, and all the beings in it, up and down, that we know precious little about."

CHAPTER LV

The next morning Kate and Alec rose early, to walk before breakfast to the top of one of the hills, through a young larch-wood which covered it from head to foot. The morning was cool, and the sun exultant as a good child. The dew-diamonds were flashing everywhere, none the less lovely that they were fresh-made that morning. The lark's song was a cantata with the sun and the wind and the larch-odours, in short, the whole morning for the words. How the larks did sing that morning! The only clouds were long pale delicate streaks of lovely gradations in gray; here mottled, there swept into curves. It was just the morning to rouse a wild longing for motion, for the sea and its shore, for endless travel through an endless region of grace and favour, the sun rising no higher, the dew lingering on every blade, and the lark never wearying for his nest. Kate longed for some infinite of change without vicissitude—ceaseless progress towards a goal endlessly removed! She did not know that the door into that life might have been easier to find in that ugly chapel than even here in the vestibule of heaven.

"My nurse used to call the lark 'Our Lady's hen,'" said Kate.

"How pretty!" answered Alec, and had no more to say.

"Are the people of Glamerton very wicked, Alec?" asked Kate, making another attempt to rouse a conversation.

"I'm sure I don't know," answered Alec. "I suppose they're no worse than other people."

"I thought from Mr Turnbull's sermon that they must be a great deal worse."

"Oh! they all preach like that—except good Mr Cowie, and he's dead."

"Do you think he knew better than the rest of them?"

"I don't know that. But the missionars do know something that other people don't know. And that Mr Turnbull always speaks as if he were in earnest."

"Yes, he does."

"But there's that fellow Bruce!"

"Do you mean the man that put us into his seat?"

"Yes. I *can't* think what makes my mother so civil to him."

"Why shouldn't she be?"

"Well, you see—I can't bear him. And I can't understand my mother. It's not like her."

In a moment more they were in a gentle twilight of green, flashed with streaks of gold. A forest of delicate young larches crowded them in, their rich brown cones hanging like the knops that looped up their dark garments fringed with paler green.

And the scent! What a thing to *invent*—the smell of a larch wood! It is the essence of the earth-odour, distilled in the thousand-fold alembics of those feathery trees. And the light winds that awoke blew murmurous music, so sharply and sweetly did that keen foliage divide the air.

Having gazed their fill on the morning around them, they returned to breakfast, and after breakfast they went down to the river. They stood on the bank, over one of the deepest pools, in the bottom of which the pebbles glimmered brown. Kate gazed into it abstracted, fascinated, swinging her neckerchief in her hand. Something fell into the water.

"Oh!" she cried, "what shall I do? It was my mother's."

The words were scarcely out of her mouth when Alec was in the water. Bubbles rose and broke as he vanished. Kate did not scream, but stood, pale, with parted lips, staring into the pool. With a boiling and heaving of the water, he rose triumphant, holding up the brooch. Kate gave a cry and threw herself on the grass. When Alec reached her, she lay sobbing, and would not lift her head.

"You are very unkind, Alec," she said at last, looking up. "What will your mother say?"

And she hid her face and began to sob afresh.

"It was your mother's brooch," answered Alec.

"Yes, yes; but we could have got it out somehow."

"No other how.—I would have done that for any girl. You don't know what I would do for *you*, Kate."

"You shouldn't have frightened me. I had been thinking how greedy the pool looked," said Kate, rising now, as if she dared not remain longer beside it.

"I didn't mean to frighten you, Kate. I never thought of it. I am almost a water-rat."

"And now you'll get your death of cold. Come along."

Alec laughed. He was in no hurry to go home. But she seized his hand and half-dragged him all the way. He had never been so happy in his life.

Kate had cried because he had jumped into the water!

That night they had a walk in the moonlight. It was all moon—the air with the mooncore in it; the trees confused into each other by the sleep of her light; the bits of water, so many moons over again; the flowers, all pale phantoms of flowers: the whole earth, transfused with reflex light, was changed into a moon-ghost of its former self. They were walking in the moon-world.

The silence and the dimness sank into Alec's soul, and it became silent and dim too. The only sound was the noise of the river, quenched in that light to the sleepy hush of moon-haunted streams.

Kate felt that she had more room now. And yet the scope of her vision was less, for the dusk had closed in around her.

She had ampler room because the Material had retired as behind a veil, leaving the Immaterial less burdened, and the imagination more free to work its will. The Spiritual is ever putting on material garments; but in the moonlight, the Material puts on spiritual garments.

Kate sat down at the foot of an old tree which stood alone in one of the fields. Alec threw himself on the grass, and looked up in her face, which was the spirit-moon shining into his world, and drowning it in dreams.—The Arabs always call their beautiful women *moons*.—Kate sat as silent as the moon in heaven, which rained down silence. And Alec lay gazing at Kate, till silence gave birth to speech:

"Oh Kate! How I love you!" he said.

Kate started. She was frightened. Her mind had been full of gentle thoughts. Yet she laid her hand on his arm and accepted the love.—But how?

"You dear boy!" she said.

Perhaps Kate's answer was the best she could have given. But it stung Alec to the heart, and they went home in a changed silence.—The resolution she came to upon the way was not so good as her answer.

She did not love Alec so. He could not understand her; she could not look up to him. But he was only a boy, and therefore would not suffer much. He would forget her as soon as she was out of his sight. So as he was a very dear boy, she would be as kind to him as ever she could, for she was going away soon.

She did not see that Alec would either take what she gave for more than she gave, or else turn from it as no gift at all.

When they reached the house, Alec, recovering himself a little, requested her to sing. She complied at once, and was foolish enough to sing the following

BALLAD.

It is May, and the moon leans down all night
   Over a blossomy land.

By her window sits the lady white,
   With her chin upon her hand.

"O sing to me, dear nightingale,
   The song of a year ago;
I have had enough of longing and wail,
   Enough of heart-break and woe.

O glimmer on me, my apple-tree,
   Like living flakes of snow;
Let odour and moonlight and melody,
   In the old rich harmony flow.

The dull odours stream; the cold blossoms gleam,
   And the bird will not be glad.
The dead never speak when the living dream—
   They are too weak and sad.

She listened and sate till night grew late,
   Bound by a weary spell;
Then a face came in at the garden-gate
   And a wondrous thing befell:

Up rose the joy as well as the love,
   In the song, in the scent, in the show!
The moon grew glad in the sky above,
   The blossom grew rosy below.

The blossom and moon, the scent and the tune
   In ecstasy rise and fall;
But they had no thanks for the granted boon:
   For the lady forgot them all.

There was no light in the room except that of the shining air. Alec sat listening, as if Kate were making and meaning the song. But notwithstanding the enchantment of the night, all rosy in the red glow of Alec's heart; notwithstanding that scent of gilly-flowers and sweet-peas stealing like love through every open door and window; notwithstanding the radiance of her own beauty, Kate was only singing a song. It is sad to have all the love and all the mystery to oneself—the other being the centre of the glory, and yet far beyond its outmost ring, sitting on a music-stool at a common piano old-fashioned and jingling, not in fairyland at all in fact, or even believing in its presence.

But that night the moon was in a very genial humour, and gave her light plentiful and golden. She would even dazzle a little, if one looked at her too hard. She could not dazzle Tibbie though, who was seated with Annie on the pale green grass, with the moon about them in the air and beneath them in the water.

"Ye say it's a fine munelicht nicht, Annie."

"Ay, 'deed is't. As bonnie a nicht as ever I saw."

"Weel, it jist passes my comprehension—hoo ye can see, whan the air's like this. I' the winter ye canna see, for it's aye cauld whan the sun's awa; and though it's no cauld the nicht, I fin' that there's no licht i' the air—there's a differ; it's deid-like. But the soun' o' the water's a' the same, and the smell o' some o' the flowers is bonnier i' the nicht nor i' the day. That's a' verra weel. But hoo ye can see whan the sun's awa, I say again, jist passes my comprehension."

"It's the mune, ye ken, Tibbie."

"Weel, what's the mune? I dinna fin' 't. It mak's no impress upo' me.—Ye *canna* see sae weel's ye say, lass!" exclaimed Tibbie, at length, in a triumph of incredulity and self assertion.

"Weel, gin ye winna believe me o' yer ain free will, Tibbie, I maun jist gar ye," said Annie. And she rose, and running into the cottage, fetched from it a small pocket Bible.

"You say it's a fine moonlight night, Annie."

"Ay, indeed it is. As bonnie a night as ever I saw."

"Well, it just passes my comprehension—how you can see, when the air's like this. In the winter you can't see, for it's always cold when the sun's away; and though it's not cold tonight, I feel that there's no light in the air—there's a difference; it's dead-like. But the sound of the water's all the same, and the smell of some of the flowers is bonnier in the night than in the day. That's all very well. But how you can see when the sun's away, I say again, just passes my comprehension."

"It's the moon, you know, Tibbie."

"Well, what's the moon? I don't feel it. It makes no impress upon me.—You *can't* see as well as you say, lass!" exclaimed Tibbie, at length, in a triumph of incredulity and self assertion.

"Well, if you won't believe me of your own free will, Tibbie, I must just make you," said Annie. And she rose, and running into the cottage, fetched from it a small pocket Bible.

"Now, just you listen, Tibbie," she said, as she returned. And, opening the Bible, she read one of Tibbie's favourite chapters, rather slowly no doubt, but with perfect correctness.

"Well, lassie, I can't make head or tail of it."

"I'll tell you, Tibbie, what the moon always reminds me of. The face of God's like the sun, as you've told me; for no man could see him and live."

"That's not saying, you know," interposed Tibbie, "that we can't see him after we're dead."

"But the moon," continued Annie, disregarding Tibbie's interruption, "must be like the face of Christ, for it gives light and you can look at it notwithstanding. The moon's just like the sun with the too-much taken out of it. Or like Moses with the veil over his face, you know. The folk couldn't look at him till he put the veil on."

"Na, na, lass; that won't do; for you know his countenance was as the sun shineth in his strength."

"Ay, but that was after the resurrection, you know. I'm thinking there had been a kind of a veil over his face all the time he was upon the earth; and then when he went where there were only heavenly eyes to look at him, eyes that could bear it, he took it off."

"Well, I wouldn't wonder. Maybe you're right. And if you *be* right, that accounts for the Transfiguration. He just lifted the

'm a wee, and the glory aneath it lap oot wi' a leme like the lichtnin'. But that munelicht! I can mak naething o' 't."

"Weel, Tibbie, I canna mak you oot ony mair nor ye can the munelicht. Whiles ye appear to ken a' thing aboot the licht, an' ither whiles ye're clean i' the dark."

"Never ye min' me, lass. I s' be i' the licht some day. Noo we'll gang in to the hoose."

veil off himself a bit, and the glory beneath it leapt out with a blaze like the lightning. But that moonlight! I can make nothing of it."

"Well, Tibbie, I can't make you out any more than you can the moonlight. Sometimes you appear to know everything about the light, and other times you're clean in the dark."

"Never you mind me, lass. I'll be in the light some day. Now we'll go in to the house."

CHAPTER LVI

Murdoch Malison, the schoolmaster, was appointed to preach in the parish church the following Sunday. He had never preached there, for he had been no favourite with Mr Cowie. Now, however, that the good man was out of the way, they gave him a chance, and he caught at it, though not without some misgivings. In the school-desk, "he was like a maister or a pope;" but the pulpit—how would he fill that? Two resolutions he came to; the first that he would not read his sermon, but *commit* it and deliver it as like the extempore utterance of which he was incapable as might be—a piece of falsehood entirely understood, and justified by Scotch custom; the second, to take rather more than a hint from the fashion of preaching now so much in favour amongst the seceders and missionars: he would be a *Jupiter tonans*, wielding the forked lightnings of the law against the sins of Glamerton.

So, on the appointed day, having put on a new suit of black, and the gown over it, he ascended the pulpit stairs, and, conscious of a strange timidity, gave out the psalm. He cast one furtive glance around, as he took his seat for the singing, and saw a number of former as well as present pupils gathered to hear him, amongst whom were the two Truffeys, with their grandfather seated between them. He got through the prayer very well, for he was accustomed to that kind of thing in the school. But when he came to the sermon, he found that to hear boys repeat their lessons and punish them for failure, did not necessarily stimulate the master's own memory.

He gave out his text: The Book of the Prophet Joel, first chapter, fourth verse. Joel, first and fourth. "That which the palmer-worm hath left, hath the locust eaten; and that which the locust hath left, hath the canker-worm eaten; and that which the canker-worm hath left, hath the caterpillar eaten."

Now, if he could have read his sermon, it would have shown itself a most creditable invention. It had a general introduction upon the temporal punishment of sin; one head entitled, "The completeness of the infliction;" and another, "The punishment of which this is the type;" the latter showing that those little creeping things were not to be compared to the great creeping thing, namely, the worm that never dies. These two heads had a number of horns called *particulars*; and a tail called an *application*, in which the sins of his hearers were duly chastised, with vague and awful threats of some vengeance not confined to the life to come, but ready to take present form in such a judgment as that described in the text.

But he had resolved not to read his sermon. So he began to repeat it, with sweeps of the hands, pointings of the fingers, and other such tricks of second-rate actors, to aid the self-delusion of his hearers that it was a genuine present outburst from the soul of Murdoch Malison. For they all knew as well as he did, that his sermon was only "cauld kail het again."[1] But some family dishes—Irish stew, for example, or Scotch broth—may be better the second day than the first; and where was the harm? All concerned would have been perfectly content, if he had only gone on as he began. But, as he approached the second head, the fear suddenly flashed through his own that he would not be able to recall it; and that moment all the future of his sermon was a blank. He stammered, stared, did nothing, thought nothing—only felt himself in hell. Roused by the sight of the faces of his hearers growing suddenly expectant at the very moment when he had nothing more to give them, he gathered his seven fragmentary wits, and as a last resort, to which he had had a vague regard in putting his manuscript in his pocket, resolved to read the remainder. But in order to give the change of mode an appearance of the natural and suitable, he managed with a struggle to bring out the words:

"But, my brethren, let us betake ourselves to the written testimony."

Every one concluded he was going to quote from Scripture; but instead of turning over the leaves of the Bible, he plunged his hand into the abysses of his coat. Horror of horrors for the poor autocrat!—the pocket was as empty as his own memory; in fact it was a mere typical pocket, typical of the brains of its owner. The cold dew of agony broke over him; he turned deadly pale; his knees smote one another; but he made yet, for he was a man of strong will, a final frantic effort to bring his discourse down the inclined plane of a conclusion.

"In fine," he stammered, "my beloved brethren, if you do not repent and be converted and return to the Lord, you will—you will—you will have a very bad harvest."

Having uttered this solemn prediction, of the import of which he, like some other prophets, knew nothing before he uttered it, Murdoch Malison sat down, a *stickit minister* (failed minister). His brain was a

---

1 Cold kale hot again

vacuum; and the thought of standing up again to pray was intolerable. No more could he sit there; for if he sat, the people would sit too. Something must be done, and there was nobody to do anything. He must get out and then the people would go home. But how could he escape? He durst not go down that pulpit stair in the sight of the congregation.— He cared no more for his vanished reputation. His only thought was how to get out.

Meantime the congregation was variously affected. Some held down their heads and laughed immoderately. These were mostly of Mr Malison's scholars, the fine edge of whose nature, if it ever had any, had vanished under the rasp of his tortures. Even Alec, who, with others of the assembly, held down his head from sympathetic shame, could not help remembering how the master had made Annie Anderson stand upon the form, and believing for the time in a general retribution in kind.

Andrew Truffey was crying bitterly. His sobs were heard through the church, and some took them for the sobs of Murdoch Malison, who had shrunk into the pulpit like a snail into its shell, so that not an atom of his form was to be seen except from the side-galleries. The maiden daughter of the late schoolmaster gave a shriek, and went into a small fit; after which an awful, quite sepulchral silence reigned for a few moments, broken only by those quivering sobs from Truffey, whom his grandfather was feebly and ineffectually shaking.

At length the precentor, George Macwha, who had for some time been turning over the leaves of his psalm-book, came to the rescue. He rose in the lectern and gave out *The hundred and fifty-first psalm*. The congregation could only find a hundred and fifty, and took the last of the psalms for the one meant. But George, either from old spite against the tormentor of boys and girls, or from mere coincidence—he never revealed which—had chosen in reality a part of the *fifty-first* psalm.

"The hunner an' fifty-first psalm," repeated George, "from the fifteent verse. An' syne we'll gang hame.

"The hundred and fifty-first psalm," repeated George, "from the fifteenth verse. And then we'll go home.

  My closed lips, O Lord, by thee,
  Let them be opened."

As soon as the singing was over, George left the desk, and the congregation following his example, went straggling out of the church, and home, to wait with doubtful patience for the broth which as yet could taste only of onions and the stone that scoured the pot.

As soon as the sounds of retiring footsteps were heard no more in the great echoing church, uprose, like one of Dante's damned out of a torture-tomb, the form of Murdoch Malison, above the edge of the pulpit. With face livid as that of a corpse, he gave a scared look around, and not seeing little Truffey concealed behind one of the pillars, concluded the place empty, and half crawled, half tumbled down the stair to the vestry, where the sexton was waiting him. It did not restore his lost composure to discover, in searching for his handkerchief, that the encumbrance of the gown had made him put his hand ten times into the same pocket, instead of five times into each, and that in the other his manuscript lay as safe as it had been useless.

But he took his gown off very quietly, put on his coat and forgot the bands, bade the old sexton a gentle *good day*, and stole away home through the streets. He had wanted to get out, and now he wanted to get in; for he felt very much as Lady Godiva would have felt if her hair or her heroism had proved unworthy of confidence.

Poor Murdoch had no mother and no wife; he could not go home and be comforted. Nor was he a youth, to whom a first failure might be of small consequence. He was five and forty, and his head was sprinkled with grey; he was schoolmaster, and everybody knew him; he had boys under him. As he walked along the deserted streets, he felt that he was running the gauntlet of scorn; but every one who saw him coming along with his head sunk on his bosom, drew back from the window till he had gone by. Returning to the window to look after him, they saw, about twenty yards behind him, a solitary little figure, with the tears running down its face, stumping slowly step by step, and keeping the same distance, after the dejected master.

When Mr Malison went into the vestry, Truffey had gone into the porch, and there staid till he passed on his way home. Then with stealthily set crutch, putting it down as the wild beast sets down his miching paw, out sprang Truffey and after the master. But however silently Truffey might use his third leg, the master heard the *stump-stump* behind him, and felt that he was followed home every foot of the way by the boy whom he had crippled. He felt, too, in some dim degree which yet had practical results, that the boy was taking divine vengeance upon him, heaping on his head the coals of that consuming fire which is love, which is our God. And when the first shame was over, the thought of Truffey came back with healing on his lonely heart.

When he reached his own door, he darted in and closed it behind, as if to shut out the whole world through which he had passed with that burden of contempt upon his degraded shoulders. He was more ashamed of his failure than he had been sorry for laming Truffey. But the shame would pass; the sorrow would endure.

Meantime two of his congregation, sisters, poor old *mutched wifies*, were going home together. They were distantly related to the schoolmaster, whom they regarded as the honour of the family, as their bond of relation with the world above them in general and with the priesthood in particular. So when Elspeth addressed Meg with reference to the sermon in a manner which showed her determination to acknowledge no failure, Meg took her cue directly.

"Eh! woman; it's a sair ootluik for puir fowk like us, gin things be gaein that gait!"	"Eh! woman; it's a harsh outlook for poor folk like us, if things be going that way!"
"And 'deed it's that, lass! Gin the hairst be gaein to the moles and the bats, it's time we war awa hame; for it'll be a cauld winter."	"Indeed, it is that, lass! If the harvest be going to the moles and the bats, it's time we were away home; for it'll be a cold winter."
"Ay, that it will! The minister was sair owercome at the prospec', honest man. It was a' he cud do, to win at the en' o' his discoorse ohn grutten ootricht."	"Ay, that it will! The minister was touched to the heart at the prospect, honest man. It was all he could do, to finish his discourse without crying outright."
"He sees into the will o' the Almichty. He's far ben wi' Him—that's verra clear."	"He sees into the will of the Almighty. He's deep in His counsels—that's very clear."
"Ay, lass, ay."	"Ay, lass, ay."

And hence, by slow degrees, in the middle of the vague prophecies of vengeance gathered a more definite kernel of prediction, believed by some, disbelieved, yet feared, by others—that the harvest would be so eaten of worms and blasted with smut, that bread would be up to famine prices, and the poor would die of starvation.

But still the flowers came out and looked men in the face and went in again; and still the sun shone on the evil and on the good, and still the rain fell on the just and on the unjust.

And still the denunciations from the pulpits went on; but the human souls thus exposed to the fires seemed only to harden under their influences.

CHAPTER LVII

Before the period of Kate's visit arrived, a letter from Professor Fraser, to the purport that if Mrs Forbes did not mind keeping Kate a little longer he would be greatly indebted to her, came to Alec like a reprieve from execution. And the *little longer* lengthened into the late harvest of that country.

The summer shone on, and the corn grew, green and bonnie. And Alec's love grew with the corn; and Kate liked him better and better, but was not a whit more inclined to fall in love with him.

One night, after the house was quiet, Alec, finding he could not sleep, rose and went out to play the ghost a while. It was a sultry night. Great piles of cloud were heaped up in the heavens. The moon gleamed and vanished by fits, looking old and troubled when she sighed herself out of a cloud.

"There's a storm coming," said Alec to himself; and watched and waited. There was no wind below. The leaves of the black poplar, so ready to tremble, hung motionless; and not a bat came startling on its unheard skinny wing. But ere long a writhing began in the clouds overhead, and they were twisted and torn about the moon. Then came a blinding flash, and a roar of thunder, followed by a bellowing, as if the air were a great drum, on which Titanic hands were beating and rolling. Then the rain poured down, and the scent of the earth rose into the air. Alec ran to look up at Kate's window. His heart bounded when he saw a white figure looking out into the stormy dark.

"Kate! Kate!" he cried, in a loud whisper, "come out—do come out. It's so splendid!"

She started and drew back. Presently she reappeared, and opening the window, said,

"Alec! do come in."

"No, no. You come out, Kate. You don't know what it's like. You have only to get into bed again."

Kate hesitated. But in a moment more she withdrew. Alec saw she meant to come, and flew round to the door. In a few minutes she glided silently out, and fronted the black sky. The same moment another flash, in which her spirit seemed to her to be universal, flung the darkness aside. She could have counted the houses of Glamerton. The hills rose up within her very soul. The Glamour shone in silver. The harvest gleamed in green. The larch-forest hung like a cloud on the horizon. Then the blank dark folded again its scared wings over the world; and the trees rustled their leaves with one wavy sweep, and were still. And again the rain came down in a tumult—warm, genial summer rain, full of the life of lightning. Alec stood staring through the dull dark, as if he would see Kate by the force of his will alone. The tempest in the heavens had awaked a like tempest in his bosom: would the bosom beside his receive his lightning and calm his pent-up storm by giving it space to rave? His hand took hers beseechingly. Another flash came, and he saw her face. The whole glory of the night gloomed and flashed and flowed in that face. But alas! its response was to the stormy heaven alone, not to the stormy human soul. As the earth answers the heaven with lightning of her own, so Kate, herself a woman-storm, responded to the elemental cry.

Her shawl had fallen back, and he saw a white arm uplifted, bare to the shoulder, gleaming through the night, and an eye flashing through the flood that filled it. He could not mistake her passion. He knew that it was not for him; that she was a harp played upon by the elements; yet, passioned still more with her passion, he cried aloud,

"Oh, Kate! if you do not love me I shall die."

Kate started, and sought to take her hand from his, but she could not.

"Let me go, Alec," she said, pleadingly.

His fingers relaxed, and she sped into the house like a bird, leaving him standing in the night.

There was no more lightning. The rain fell heavy and persistent. The wind rose. And when the dawn came, the clouds were drifting over the sky; and the day was a wet gray fringy mass of wind and rain and cloud, tossing trees, and corn hard bested.

He rose and dragged himself away. He had thrown himself upon the grass, and had burned there till his exhausted feelings lay like smouldering fire under the pale ashes of the dawn.

When Kate made her appearance at breakfast she looked bright and cold. She had told his mother about last night, though how much he could only guess. When he asked her whether he might not read to her, she only said,

"If you like."

Whereupon he did not like.

It was a dreary day. He crept about the house like a child in disgrace, and the darkness seemed an age in coming. When the candles were brought, he went to bed; and when his mother went up, she found him asleep, but feverish. When he woke he was delirious.

For a week there was nothing but wet and windy weather. Alec was in bed. Kate was unhappy. Mrs Forbes was anxious.

The corn was badly lodged. Patches lay prone, tangled, spiky, and rough; and it was evident that if sunshine, strong, healthy sunshine, did not soon break out, the wretched mooncalf-prediction of Murdoch Malison would come true, for the corn, instead of ripening, would start a fresh growth, and the harvest would be a very bad one indeed, whether the people of Glamerton repented or not.

But after a grievous week, that blessed sunshine did come. The corn rose up from its low estate, looked at the sun, gathered heart, and began to ripen diligently.

But Alec was very ill, and did not see Kate for weeks.

Through his wanderings—so strangely does the thousand times o'erwritten palimpsest of the brain befool the mind and even the passions by the redawning of old traces—he talked on about Annie and their schooldays with Mr Malison, and never mentioned Kate.

Annie went often to inquire after him, and Mrs Forbes behaved to her with her old kindness—just a little diluted by anxiety and the possession of Kate.

When Annie thought with herself what she could do for him, she could never think of anything except saying *sangs* to him. But the time for that was long gone by. So, like many other devotions, hers found no outlet but in asking how he was.

At length, one day, he was brought down to the dining-room and laid upon the sofa. Then for the first time since his illness he saw Kate. He looked in her face pitifully and kissed her hand. She put her face down to his. The blood surged up into his cheek, and the light into his eyes, and he murmured:

"That is worth being ill for, Kate. I would be ill again for that."

She could only say *hush*, and then kiss him again, lest he should be hurt, thinking with a soundless sigh:

"I shall be forced to marry him some day."

And he was neither her own virgin-born ideal; nor had his presence the power to beget another and truer ideal in her brain.

From that day he made rapid progress. Kate would read to him for hours; and when for love and weakness—an ill-matched pair—he could not look in her face any more, he would yet lie and listen, till her voice filled him with repose, and he slept in music.

CHAPTER LVIII

On the Monday morning after his terrible failure, Mr Malison felt almost too ill to go to the school. But he knew that if he gave in he must leave the place. And he had a good deal of that courage which enables a man to front the inevitable, and reap, against his liking, the benefits that spring from every fate steadfastly encountered. So he went, keeping a calm exterior over the shame and mortification that burned and writhed within him. He prayed the morning prayer, falteringly but fluently; called up the Bible-class; corrected their blunders with an effort over himself which imparted its sternness to the tone of the correction and made him seem oblivious of his own, though in truth the hardest task he had ever had was to find fault that Monday; in short, did everything as usual, except bring out the *tag*. How could he punish failure who had himself so shamefully failed in the sight of them all? And, to the praise of Glamerton be it recorded, never had there been a quieter day, one of less defiance of law, than that day of the master's humiliation. In the afternoon Andrew Truffey laid a splendid bunch of cottage-flowers on his desk, and the next morning it was so crowded with offerings of the same sort that he had quite a screen behind which to conceal his emotion.

Wonderful, let me say once more, is the divine revenge! The children would wipe away the humiliation of their tyrant. His desk, the symbol of merciless law, the ark containing no pot of manna, only the rod that never budded, became an altar heaped with offerings, behind which the shamed divinity bowed his head and acknowledged a power greater than that of stripes—overcome by his boys, who hated spelling and figures, hated yet more the Shorter Catechism, could hardly be brought to read the book of Leviticus with decency, and hated to make bricks without straw; and yet, forgetting it all, loved the man beneath whose lashes they had writhed in torture. In his heart the master vowed, with a new love which loosed the millstone of many offences against the little ones, that had for years been hanging about his neck—vowed that, be the shame what it might, he would never leave them, but spend his days in making up for the hardness of his heart and hand; vowed that he would himself be good, and so make them good; that he would henceforth be their friend, and let them know it. Blessed failure ending in such a victory! Blessed purgatorial pulpit! into which he entered full of self and self-ends; and from which he came down disgusted with that paltry self as well as its deserved defeat. The gates of its evil fortress were now undefended, for Pride had left them open in scorn; and Love, in the form of flower-bearing children, rushed into the citadel. The heart of the master was forced to yield, and the last state of that man was better than the first.

"Swift Summer into the Autumn flowed," and yet there was no sign of the coming vengeance of heaven. The green corn turned pale at last before the gaze of the sun. The life within had done its best and now shrunk back to the earth, leaving the isolated life of its children to the ripening of the heavens. Anxious farmers watched their fields, and joyfully noted every shade of progress. All day the sun shone strong; and all night the moon leaned down from heaven to see how things were going on, and keep the work gently moving, till the sun should return to take it up again. Before he came, a shadowy frost would just breathe on the earth, which, although there was only death in its chill, yet furthered the goings on of life in repelling the now useless sap, and so helping the sun to dry the ripening ears. At length the new revelation of ancient life was complete, and the corn stood in living gold, and men began to put in the sickle, because the time of the harvest was come.

And with it came the *hairst-play*, the event of school-life both to master and scholars. But the feelings with which the master watched and longed for it were sadly different from those of the boys. It was delight itself to the latter to think of having nothing to do on those glorious hot days but gather blaeberries, or lie on the grass, or bathe in the Glamour and dry themselves in the sun ten times a day. For the master, he only hoped to get away from the six thousand eyes of Glamerton. Not one allusion had been made in his hearing to his dismal degradation, but he knew that that was only because it was too dreadful to be alluded to. Every time he passed a woman with a baby in her arms at a cottage door, the blind eyes in the back of his head saw her cuddling her child, and the ears that are always hearing what never was said, heard her hope that *he* would never bring such disgrace upon himself and upon her. The tone of additional kindness and consideraton with which many addressed him, only made him think of what lay behind, and refuse every invitation given him. But if he were once "in secret shadow far from all men's sight," his oppressed heart would begin to revive, and he might gather strength enough to face with calmness what he would continue to face somehow, in the performance of his arrears of duty to the boys and girls of Glamerton.

Can one ever bring up arrears of duty? Can one ever make up for wrong done? Will not heaven be an endless repentance?

It would need a book to answer the first two of these questions. To the last of them I answer, "Yes—but a glad repentance."

At length the slow hour arrived. Longing thoughts had almost obliterated the figures upon Time's dial, and made it look a hopeless undivided circle of eternity. But at length twelve o'clock on Saturday came; and the delight would have been almost unendurable to some, had it not been calmed by the dreary proximity of the Sabbath lying between them and freedom. To add to their joy, there was no catechism that day. The prayer, although a little longer than usual, was yet over within a minute after the hour. And almost as soon as the *Amen* was out of the master's mouth, the first boys were shouting jubilantly in the open air. Truffey, who was always the last, was crutching it out after the rest, when he heard the master's voice calling him back. He obeyed it with misgiving—so much had fear become a habit.

"Ask your grandfather, Andrew, if he will allow you to go down to the seaside with me for a fortnight or three weeks," said the master.

"Yes, sir," Truffey meant to say, but the attempt produced in reality an unearthly screech of delight, with which he went off on a series of bounds worthy of a kangaroo, lasting all the way to his grandfather's, and taking him there in half the usual time.

And the master and Truffey did go down to the sea together. The master borrowed a gig and hired a horse and driver; and they sat all three in the space meant for two, and their boxes went by the carrier. To happy Truffey a lame leg or two was not to be compared with the exultant glory of that day. Was he not the master's friend henceforth? And was he not riding in a gig—bliss supreme? And was not the harvest around them, the blue tent of the sun over their heads, and the sea somewhere before them? Truffey was prouder than Mr Malison could have been if, instead of the result of that disastrous Sunday, he had been judged to surpass Mr Turnbull in pulpit gifts, as he did in scholastic acquirements. And if there be as much joy in the universe, what matter how it be divided!—whether the master be raised from the desk to the pulpit, or Truffey have a ride in a gig!

About this time Tibbie, sitting too late one evening upon the grass, caught a bad cold and cough, and was for a fortnight confined to bed.

Within two days Annie became her constant companion—that is, from the moment *the play* commenced.

"I told you I would have the light before long," she said the first time Annie came to her.

"Heavens, Tibbie! It's only a bad cold and a cough," said Annie, who from being so much with her and Thomas had caught the modes of an elderly woman. "You mustn't be downhearted."

"Downhearted! The lassie's babbling! Who dared to say I was downhearted within sight of the New Jerusalem? Order your words better, lassie, or else hold your tongue."

"I beg your pardon, Tibbie. It was thoughtless. But you see however willing you may be to go, we're none so willing to lose our grip of you."

"You'll be much better without me, lass. Oh, my head! And the cough's just like to tear me in bits, as the prophets tore their clothes when the folk defied them beyond endurance. Well! this body's nothing but some clothes for my soul; and not very well made either, for the holes for my eyes were forgotten in the making.—I'm but joking, lassie; for it was the Lord's hand that made and mismade my clothes; and I'm well willing to wear them as long as he likes. Just make me a drop of gruel. Maybe it'll oil my throat a bit. I won't be long behind Eppie Shawn."

That was the woman who had occupied the other end of the cottage and had died in the spring.

So Annie waited on Tibbie day and night. And that year, for the first time since she came to Glamerton, the harvest began without her. But when Tibbie got a little better, she used to run out now and then to see what progress the reapers were making.

One bright forenoon Tibbie, feeling better, said to her,

"Now, bairn, I'm much better today, and you must just run out and play yourself. You're but a child, though you have the wit of a woman. You'll be laid up yourself if you don't get a stomachful of the fresh air now and then. So just run away, and don't let me see you before dinner-time."

At Howglen, there happened, this year, to be a field of oats not far from the house, the reaping of which was to begin that day. It was very warm, and glorious with sunshine. So, after a few stooks had been set up, Alec crawled out with the help of his mother and Kate, and lay down on some sheaves, sheltered from the sun by a stook, and watched. The men and women and corn leaned all one way. The oats hung their curved heads of little pendulous bells, and gave out a low murmuring sibilation—its only lament that its day was over, and sun and wind no more for it. Through the high stalks gleamed now and then the lowly corn flower, and he watched for the next blue star that would shine out as they cut the golden cloud away. But the sun rose till the stook could shelter him no more. First came a flickering of the shadows of the longest heads athwart his face, and then the sun shone full upon him. His mother and Kate had left him for a while, and, too weak or too lazy to move, he lay with closed eyes, wishing that some one would come to his help. Nor had he to wait long. A sudden shadow came over him. When he looked up to find the source of the grateful relief, he could see nothing but an apron held up in two little hands behind the stook—hiding both the sun and the face of the helper.

"Who's there?" he asked.

"It's me—Annie Anderson," came from behind the un-moving apron.

Now why would not Alec accept this attention from Annie?

"Dinna stan' there, Annie," he said. "I dinna want it. My mother will be here in a minute. I see her comin'."[1]

Annie dropped her arms, and turned away in silence. If Alec could have seen her face, he would have been sorry that he had refused her service. She vanished in a moment, so that Mrs Forbes and Kate never saw her. They sat down beside him so as to shelter him, and he fell fast asleep. When he woke, he found his head in Kate's lap, and her parasol casting a cool green shadow over him. His mother had gone again. Having made these discoveries, he closed his eyes, and pretending to be still asleep, lay in a waking dream. But dreams themselves must come to an end. Kate soon saw that his face was awake, although his eyes were closed.

"I think it is time we went into the house, Alec," she said. "You have been asleep nearly an hour."

"Happy so long, and not know it?" returned he, looking up at her from where he lay.

Kate blushed a little. I think she began to feel that he was not quite a boy. But he obeyed her like a child, and they went in together.

When Annie vanished among the stooks after the rejection of her offered shadow, a throbbing pain at her heart kept her from returning to the reapers. She wandered away up the field towards a little old cottage, in which some of the farm servants resided. She knew that Thomas Crann was at work there, and found him busy rough-casting the outside of it.

"Ye're busy harlin', Thomas," said Annie, for the sake of saying something.

"Ay, jist helpin' to mak' a heepocreet," answered Thomas, with a nod and a grim smile, as he threw a trowelful of mortar mixed with small pebbles against the wall.

"You're busy harling, Thomas," said Annie, for the sake of saying something.

"Ay, just helping to make a hypocrite," answered Thomas, with a nod and a grim smile, as he threw a trowelful of mortar mixed with small pebbles against the wall.

---

[1] "Don't stand there, Annie," he said. "I don't want it. My mother will be here in a minute. I see her coming."

"What mean ye by that?" rejoined Annie.

"Gin ye kent this auld bothie as weel as I do, ye wadna need to spier that question. It sud hae been pu'ed doon fra the riggin to the fundation a century afore noo. And here we're pittin a clean face upo' 't, garrin' 't luik as gin it micht stan' anither century, and nobody had a richt to luik asclent at it."

"It *luiks* weel eneuch."

"I tell't ye that I was makin' a heepocreet. There's no a sowl wants this hoose to stan' but the mistress doon there, that doesna want to waur the siller, and the rottans inside the wa's o' 't, that doesna want to fa' into the cluiks o' Bawdrins and Colley—wha lie in wait for sic like jist as the deevil does for the sowl o' the heepocreet.—Come oot o' the sun, lassie. This auld hoose is no a'thegither a heepocreet: it can haud the sun aff o' ye yet."

Thomas had seen Annie holding her hand to her head, an action occasioned partly by the heat and partly by the rebuff Alec had given her. She stepped into the shadow beside him.

"Isna the warl' fu' o' bonnie things cheap?" Thomas went on. "The sun's fine and het the day. And syne whan he's mair nor we can bide, there's lots o' shaidows lyin' aboot upo' the face o' the warl'; though they say there's some

"What do you mean by that?" rejoined Annie.

"If you knew this old bothie as well as I do, you wouldn't need to ask that question. It should have been pulled down from the roof to the foundation a century ago. And here we are putting a clean face upon it, making it look as if it might stand another century, and no one had a right to look askance at it."

"It *looks* well enough."

"I told you that I was making a hypocrite. There's not a soul wants this house to stand but the mistress down there, that doesn't want to spend the money, and the rats inside its walls, that don't want to fall into the claws of Puss and Colley—who lie in wait for them just as the devil does for the soul of the hypocrite.—Come out of the sun, lassie. This old house isn't altogether a hypocrite: it can keep the sun off you yet."

Thomas had seen Annie holding her hand to her head, an action occasioned partly by the heat and partly by the rebuff Alec had given her. She stepped into the shadow beside him.

"Isn't the world full of bonnie things cheap?" Thomas went on. "The sun's fine and hot today. And then when he's more than we can bear, there's lots of shadows lying about upon the face of the world; though they say there's some countries where they're scarce, and the shadow of a great rock's thought something of in a weary land! But we shouldn't think less of a thing because there's plenty of it. We have a heap of the gospel, but we don't think the less of it for that. Because you see it's not whether shadows be dear (*expensive*) or not that we think much or little of them, but whether we be right hot and tired when we reach one of them. That's what makes the difference."

Sorrow herself will reveal one day that she was only the beneficent shadow of Joy.

Will Evil ever show herself the beneficent shadow of Good?

"Where did Robert Bruce get that grand Bible, Annie, do you know?" resumed Thomas, after whitening his hypocrite in silence for a few moments.

"That's my Bible, Thomas. Old Mr Cowie gave it to me when he was lying at death's door."

"Hm! hm! ay! ay! And why didn't you take it and put it in your own chest?"

"Mister Bruce took it and laid it in the room as soon as I brought it home."

"Did Mister Cowie say anything to you about anything that was in it?"

"Ay, he did. He spoke of a five-pound note that he had put in it. But when I looked for it, I couldn't find it."

"Ay! ay! Whan did ye luik for't?"

"I forgot it for twa or three days—maybe a week."

"Do ye min' that Sunday nicht that twa or three o' 's cam hame wi' Bruce, and had worship wi' him an' you?"

"Ay, weel eneuch. It was the first time he read oot o' my Bible."

"Was't afore or efter that 'at ye luikit for the nott?"

"It was the neist day; for the sicht o' the Bible pat it i' my min'. I oughtna to hae thocht aboot it o' the Sawbath; but it cam' o' 'tsel'; and I didna luik till the Mononday mornin', afore they war up. I reckon Mr Cowie forgot to pit it in efter a'."

"Hm! hm! Ay! ay!—Weel, ye see, riches taks to themsels wings and flees awa'; and sae we maunna set oor herts upo' them, for it's no manner o' use. We get nothing by 't. The warst bank that a man can lay up his siller in is his ain hert. And I'll tell ye hoo that is. Ye ken whan meal's laid up ower lang it breeds worms, and they eat the meal. But they do little hairm forbye, for they're saft craters, and their teeth canna do muckle ill to the girnell. But there's a kin' o' roost that gathers and a kin' o' moth that breeds i' the gowd and siller whan they're laid up i' the hert; and the roost's an awfu' thing for eatin' awa', and the moth-craters hae teeth as

"Ay! ay! When did you look for it?"

"I forgot it for two or three days—maybe a week."

"Do you remember that Sunday night that two or three of us came home with Bruce, and had worship with him and you?"

"Ay, well enough. It was the first time he read out of my Bible."

"Was it before or after that that you looked for the note?"

"It was the next day; for the sight of the Bible put it in my mind. I shouldn't have thought about it on the Sabbath; but it came of itself; and I didn't look till the Monday morning, before they were up. I reckon Mr Cowie forgot to put it in after all."

"Hm! hm! Ay! ay!—Well, you see, riches take wings to themselves and fly away; and so we mustn't set our hearts upon them, for it's no manner of use. We get nothing by it. The worst bank that a man can lay up his money in is his own heart. And I'll tell you how that is. You know when meal's laid up too long it breeds worms, and they eat the meal. But they do little harm besides, for they're soft creatures, and their teeth can't injure the barrel. But there's a kind of rust that gathers and a kind of moth that breeds in the gold and silver when they're laid up in the heart; and the rust's an awful thing for eating away, and the moths have teeth as hard

hard's the siller that breeds them; and instead o' eatin' the siller, like the meal-worms, they fa' upo' the girnel itsel'—that's the heart; and afore lang the hert itsel's roostit awa' wi' the roost, and riddlet through and through wi' the moths, till it's a naisty fushionless thing, o' no use to God or man, not even to mak' muck o'. Sic a crater's hardly worth damnin'."

as the money that breeds them; and instead of eating the money, like the meal-worms, they fall upon the barrel itself—that's the heart; and before long the heart itself's rusted away with the rust, and riddled through and through with the moths, till it's a nasty spiritless thing, of no use to God or man, not even to make muck of. Such a creature's hardly worth damning."

And Thomas threw trowelful after trowelful of rough-cast upon the wall, making his hypocrite in all the composure of holy thoughts. And Annie forgot her trouble in his presence. For Thomas was one of those whom the prophet foresaw when he said: "And a man shall be as an hiding-place from the wind, and a covert from the tempest; as rivers of water in a dry place, as a shadow of a great rock in a weary land." I do not mean that Thomas was felt to be such by all whom he encountered; for his ambition was to rouse men from the sleep of sin; to set them face to face with the terrors of Mount Sinai; to "shak' them ower the mou' (*mouth*) o' the pit," till they were all but choked with the fumes of the brimstone. But he was a shelter to Annie—and to Tibbie also, although she and he were too much of a sort to appear to the best advantage in their intercourse.

"Hoo's Tibbie the day?" said Thomas.

"She's a wee bit better the day," answered Annie.

"It's a great preevileege, lassie, and ane that ye'll hae to answer for, to be sae muckle wi' ane o' the Lord's elec' as ye are wi' Tibbie Dyster. She's some thrawn whiles, but she's a good honest woman, wha has the glory o' God sair at her hert. And she's tellt me my duty and my sins in a mainner worthy o' Debohrah the prophetess; and I aye set mysel' to

"How's Tibbie today?" said Thomas.

"She's a wee bit better today," answered Annie.

"It's a great privilege, lassie, and one that you'll have to answer for, to be so much with one of the Lord's elect as you are with Tibbie Dyster. She's quite peevish sometimes, but she's a good honest woman, who has her heart set on the glory of God. And she's told me my duty and my sins in a manner worthy of Deborah the prophetess; and I always set myself

owercome them as gin they had been the airmy o' Sisera, wham Jael, the wife o' Heber, the Kenite, killed efter a weel-deserved but some cooardly faushion."	to overcome them as if they had been the army of Sisera, whom Jael, the wife of Heber, the Kenite, killed after a well-deserved but pretty cowardly fashion."

Annie did not return to the harvest-field that day. She did not want to go near Alec again. So, after lingering a while with Thomas, she wandered slowly across some fields of barley-stubble through which the fresh young clover was already spreading its soft green. She then went over the Glamour by the bridge with the three arches, down the path at the other end, over the single great stone that crossed the dyer's dam, and so into Tibbie's cottage.

Had Annie been Robert Bruce's own, she would have had to mind the baby, to do part of the house work, and, being a wise child, to attend in the shop during meals, and so expedite the feeding-process which followed the grace. But Robert Bruce was ignorant of how little Annie knew about the investment of her property. He took her freedom of action for the result of the knowledge that she paid her way, whereas Annie followed her own impulse, and never thought about the matter. Indeed, with the reticence of Scotch people, none of her friends had given her any information about her little fortune. Had Bruce known this, there would have been no work too constant for her, and no liberty too small.

Thomas did not doubt that Robert Bruce had stolen the note. But he did not see yet what he ought to do about it. The thing would be hard to prove, and the man who would steal would lie. But he bitterly regretted that such a man should have found his way into their communion.

CHAPTER LIX

At length the corn was gathered in, all over the valley of the two rivers. The wool of the sheep grows again after they are shorn, to keep them warm in the winter: when the dry stubble sticks up short and bristly over the fields, to keep them warm "He scattereth his snows like wool."

The master returned from the sea-coast, bringing Truffey with him, radiant with life. Nothing could lengthen that shrunken limb, but in the other and the crutch together he had more than the function of two.

And the master was his idol.

And the master was a happier man. The scene of his late failure had begun to fade a little from his brain. The expanse of the church and the waiting people was no longer a vision certain to arise in the darkness that surrounds sleep. He had been loving and helping; and love and help had turned into a great joy, whose tide washed from out his heart the bitterness of his remembered sin. When we love truly, all oppression of past sin will be swept away. Love is the final atonement, of which and for which the sacrifice of the atonement was made. And till this atonement is made in every man, sin holds its own, and God is not all in all.

So the earth and all that was therein did the master good. And he came back able to look people in the face—humble still, but no longer humiliated. And when the children gathered once more on a Monday morning, with the sad feeling that the holidays were over, the master's prayer was different from what it used to be, and the work was less irksome than before, and school was not so very hateful after all. Even the Shorter Catechism was not the instrument of torture which it had been wont to be. The cords of the rack were not strained so tight as heretofore.

But the cool bright mornings, and the frosty evenings, with the pale green sky after sundown, spoke to the heart of Alec of a coming loss. Not that Kate had ever shown that she loved him, so that he even felt a restless trouble in her presence which had not been favourable to his recovery. Yet as he lay in the gloaming, and watched those crows flying home, they seemed to be bearing something away with them on their black wings; and as the light sank and paled on the horizon, and the stars began to condense themselves into sparks amid the sea of green, like those that fleet phosphorescent when the prow of the vessel troubles the summer sea, and then the falling stars of September shot across the darkening sky, he felt that a change was near, that for him winter was coming before its time. And the trees saw from their high watch-tower the white robe of winter already drifting up above the far horizon on the wind that followed his footsteps, and knew what that wind would be when it howled tormenting over those naked fields. So their leaves turned yellow and gray, and the frosty red of age was fixed upon them, and they fell, and lay.

On one of those bright mornings, which make the head feel so clear, the limbs so strong, and the heart so sad, the doom fell in the expected form, that of a letter from the Professor. He was at home at last, and wanted his niece to mix his toddy, and scold his servants for him, from both of which enjoyments he said he desired to wean himself in time. Alec's heart sank within him.

"Don't go yet, Kate," he said. But he felt that she must go.

An early day was fixed for her return; and his summer would go with her.

The day before her departure they were walking together along one of the rough parish-roads leading to the hills.

"Oh, Kate!" exclaimed Alec, all at once, in an outburst of despair, "what *shall* I do when you are gone? Everything will look so hateful!"

"Oh, Alec!" rejoined Kate, in a tone of expostulation.

"They will all look the same as if you had not gone away!—so heartless, so selfish!"

"But I shall see you in November again."

"Oh, yes. You will see me. But shall I see *you*?—this very *you*? Oh, Kate! Kate! I feel that you will be different then. You will not look at me as you do now. You are kind to me because I have been ill. You pity me for my white face. It is very good of you. But *won't* you love me, Kate? I don't deserve it. But I've read so often of beautiful women loving men who did not deserve it. Perhaps I may be worthy of it some day. And by that time you will have loved somebody else!"

He turned involuntarily, and walked towards home. He recovered himself instantly, however, and returning put his hand on Kate's arm, who was frightened and anxious. Like a child praying to his mother, he repeated:

"*Won't* you love me, Kate?—Just a little?—How can I go into that room after you are gone—and all your things out of it? I am not good enough ever to sleep there again. *Won't* you love me, Kate? A little?"

"I do love you dearly. You know that, Alec. Why do you always press me to say more?"

"Because I do not like the way you say it."

"You want me to speak your way, not my own, and be a hypocrite?"

"Kate! Kate! I understand you too well."

They walked home in silence.

Now, although this was sad enough for Alec, yet there was room for hope. But she was going away, and he would not know what she was doing or thinking. It was as if she were going to die. Nor was that all;—for—to misuse the quotation—

"For, in that sleep of death, what dreams may come!"

She might dream of some one, love some one—yes, marry some one, and so drive him mad.

When the last night arrived, he followed her up-stairs, and knocked at her room door, to see her once again, and make one more appeal. Now an appeal has only to do with justice or pity. With love it is of no use. With love it is as unavailing as wisdom or gold or beauty. But no lover believes this.

There was no answer to the first, the inarticulate appeal. He lost his courage, and dared not knock again; and while Kate was standing with her head on one side, and her dress half off, wondering if any one had knocked, he crept away to his bed ashamed. There was only a partition of lath and plaster between the two, neither of whom could sleep, but neither of whom could have given the other any comfort. Not even another thunder-storm could have brought them together again that night.

At length the pitiless dawn, which *will* come, awoke Alec, and he saw the last few aged stars wither away as the great young star came up the hill, the despot who, crowned with day, drives men up and abroad, be the weather, inside or out, what it may. It was the dreariest dawn Alec had ever known.

Kate appeared at breakfast with indescribable signs of preparation about her. The breakfast was dull and cheerless. The autumn sun was brilliant. The inevitable gig appeared at the door. Alec was not even to drive it. He could only help her into it, kiss her gloved hand on the rail, and see her vanish behind the shrubbery.

He then turned in stern endurance, rushed up into the very room he had thought it impossible ever to enter again, caught up a handkerchief she had left behind her, pressed it to his face, threw himself on her bed, and—well, he fell fast asleep.

He woke not so miserable as he had expected. Of this he was so much ashamed that he tried hard to make himself more miserable, by going over all the miseries in store for him. But his thoughts would not obey him. They would take their own way, fly where they pleased, and alight where they would. And the meeting in November was the most attractive object in sight.—So easily is Hope born, when the time of her birth is come!

But he soon found that Grief is like some maidens: she will not come when she is called; but if you leave her alone, she will come of herself. Before the day was over he had sacrificed griefs enough upon the altar of Love. All at once the whole vacant region rushed in upon him with a ghostly sense of emptiness and desolation. He wandered about the dreary house like a phantom about a cenotaph. The flowers having nothing to say, because they had ceased to mean anything, looked ashamed of themselves. The sunshine was hastening to have done with it, and let the winter come as soon as he liked, for there was no more use in shining like this. And Alec being in love, could feel all this, although he had not much imagination. For the poetic element has its share in the most common pug-faced man in creation; and when he is in love, what of that sort there is in him, as well as what there is of any sort of good thing, will come to the surface, as the trout do in the balmy summer evenings. Therefore let every gentle maiden be warned how she takes such a manifestation of what is in the man for the man himself. It is the deepest, it is the best in him, but it may not be in the least his own yet. It is one thing to have a mine of gold in one's ground, know it, and work it; and another to have the mine still but regard the story as a fable, throw the aureal hints that find their way to the surface as playthings to the woman who herself is but a plaything in the owner's eyes, and mock her when she takes them for precious. In a word, every man in love shows better than he is, though, thank God, not better than he is meant to become.

After Kate's departure, Alec's health improved much more rapidly. Hope, supplied by his own heart, was the sunlight in which he revived. He had one advantage over some lovers—that he was no metaphysician. He did not torture himself with vain attempts to hold his brain as a mirror to his heart, that he might read his heart there. The heart is deaf and dumb and blind, but it has more in it—more life and blessedness, more torture and death—than any poor knowledge-machine of a brain can understand, or even delude itself into the fancy of understanding.

From the first, Kate's presence had not been favourable to his recovery, irrespectively of the excitement and restlessness which it occasioned; for she was an absorbent rather than a diffuser of life. Her own unsatisfied nature, her excitableness, her openness to all influences from the external world, and her incapacity for supplying her needs in any approximate degree from inward resources; her consequent changeableness, moodiness, and dependency—were all unfavourable influences upon an invalid who loved her.

The first thing he did was to superintend the painting and laying up of his boat for the winter. It was placed across the rafters of the barn, wrapt in tarpaulin.

The light grew shorter and shorter. A few rough rainy days stripped the trees of their foliage; and although the sun shone out again and made lovely weather,

> Saint Martin's summer, halcyon days,

it was plain to all the senses that the autumn was drawing to a close.

CHAPTER LX

All the prophetic rumours of a bad harvest had proved themselves false. Never a better harvest had been gathered in the strath, nor had one ever been carried home in superior condition. But the passion for prophecy had not abated in Glamerton. It was a spiritual epidemic over the whole district.

Now a certain wily pedler had turned the matter over and resolved to make something of it.

One day there appeared in the streets of Glamerton a man carrying in his hand a bundle of papers as a sample of what he had in the pack upon his shoulders. He bore a burden of wrath. They were all hymns and ballads of a minacious description, now one and now another of which he kept repeating in lugubrious recitative. Amongst them some of Watts's, quite unknown to Glamerton worshippers, carried the palm of horror. But there were others which equalled them in absurdity, although their most ludicrous portions affected the populace only as a powerful realization of the vague and awful. One of these had the following stanzas:

> "The dragon's tail shall be the whip
>   Of scorpions foretold,
> With which to lash them thigh and hip
>   That wander from the fold.
> And when their wool is burnt away—
>   Their garments gay, I mean—
> Then this same whip they'll feel, I say,
>   Upon their naked skin.

The probability seems to be that, besides collecting from all sources known to him, the pedler had hired an able artist for the production of original poems of commination. His scheme succeeded; for great was the sale of these hymns and ballads at a halfpenny a piece in the streets of Glamerton. Even those who bought to laugh, could not help feeling an occasional anticipatory sting of which, being sermon-seared, they were never conscious under pulpit denunciation.

The pedler having emptied his wallet—not like that of Chaucer's Pardoner,

"Bretful of pardon brought from Rome all hot,"

but crammed with damnation brought all hot from a different place—vanished; and another wonder appeared in the streets of Glamerton—a man who cried with a loud voice, borrowing the cry of the ill-tempered prophet: "Yet forty days, and Glamerton shall be destroyed."

This cry he repeated at awful intervals of about a minute, walking slowly through every street, lane, and close of the town. The children followed him in staring silence; the women gazed from their doors in awe as he passed. The insanity which gleamed in his eyes, and his pale long-drawn countenance, heightened the effect of the terrible prediction. His belief took theirs by storm.

The men smiled to each other, but could not keep it up in the presence of their wives and sisters. They said truly that he was only a madman. But as prophets have always been taken for madmen, so madmen often pass for prophets; and even Stumpin' Steenie, the town-constable, had too much respect either to his prophetic claims, or his lunacy, perhaps both, to take him into custody. So through the streets of Glamerton he went on his bare feet, with tattered garments, proclaiming aloud the coming destruction. He walked in the middle of the street, and turned aside for nothing. The coachman of the Royal Mail had to pull up his four greys on their haunches to keep them off the defiant prophet, and leave him to pursue the straight line of his mission. The ministers warned the people on the following Sunday against false prophets, but did not say that man was a false prophet, while with their own denunciations they went on all the same. The chief effects of it all were excitement and fear. There was little sign of repentance. But the spiritual physicians did not therefore doubt their exhibition. They only increased the dose. The prophet appeared one day. He had vanished the next.

But within a few days, a still more awful prediction rose, cloud-like, on the spiritual sky. A placard was found affixed to the doors of every place of worship in the town, setting forth in large letters that, according to certain irrefragable calculations from "the number of a man" and other such of the more definite utterances of Daniel and St John, the day of judgment must without fail fall upon the next Sunday week. Whence this announcement came no one knew. But the truth is, every one was willing it should remain shrouded in the mystery congenial to such things. On the door of the parish-church, it found an especially suitable place; for that, not having been painted for many years, still retained the mourning into which it had been put on occasion of the death of the great man of the neighbourhood, the owner of all Glamerton, and miles around it—this mourning consisting of a ground of dingy black, over which at small regular distances had been painted a multitude of white spots with tails, rather more like commas than tadpoles, intended to represent the falling tears of lamenting tenants and humble servants generally. Curly's grandfather had been the artist of the occasion. In the middle of this door stood the awful prophecy, surrounded on every side by the fall of the faded tears; and for anything anybody knew, it might have been a supernatural exudation from the damp old church, full of decay for many a dreary winter. Dreadful places, those churches, hollow and echoing all the week! I wonder if the souls of idle parsons are condemned to haunt them, and that is what gives them that musty odour and that exhausting air.

Glamerton was variously affected by this condensation of the vapour of prophecy into a definite prediction.

"What think ye o' 't, Thomas Crann?" said Andrew Constable. "The calcleation seems to be a' correck. Yet somehoo I canna believe in't."

"Dinna fash yer heid aboot it, Anerew. There's a heep o' judgments atween this an' the hinner en'. The Lord'll come whan naebody's luikin' for him. And sae we maun be aye ready. Ilka year's an anno dominy. But I dinna think the man that made that calcleation as ye ca' 't 's jist a'thegeether infallible. An' for ae thing, he's forgotten to mak' allooance for the laip years."

"The day's by, than!" exclaimed Andrew, in a tone contrasting pretty strongly with his previous expressions of unbelief.

"Or else it's nae comin' sae

"What do you think of it, Thomas Crann?" said Andrew Constable. "The calculation seems to be all correct. Yet somehow I can't believe in it."

"Don't bother your head about it, Andrew. There's a heap of judgements between this and the last day. The Lord'll come when nobody's looking for him. And so we must always be ready. Every year's an anno domini. But I don't think the man that made that calculation as you call it is just altogether infallible. And for one thing, he's forgotten to make allowance for the leap years."

"The day's by, then!" exclaimed Andrew, in a tone contrasting pretty strongly with his previous expressions of unbelief.

"Or else it's not coming so

soon as the prophet thought. I'm not clear about it at this moment. But it's a small matter that."

Andrew's face fell, and he looked thoughtful.

"How do you make that out?" said he.

"Heavens man!" answered Thomas; "don't you see that if the man was capable of making such a mistake as that, in the midst of his perfect confidence in his own knowledge and judgement, he could hardly have been intended by Providence for an interpreter of dark sayings of old?"

Andrew burst into a laugh.

"Who could have thought, Thomas, that you could have picked such gumption out of stones!"

And so they parted, Andrew laughing, and Thomas with a curious smile.

CHAPTER LXI

Towards the middle of the following week the sky grew gloomy, and a thick small incessant rain brought the dreariest weather in the world. There was no wind, and miles of mist were gathered in the air. After a day or two the heavens grew lighter, but the rain fell as steadily as before, and in heavier drops. Still there was little rise in either the Glamour or the Wan Water, and the weather could not be said to be anything but seasonable.

On the Saturday afternoon, weary of some poor attempts at Greek and Latin, weary of the wretched rain, and weary with wishing to be with Kate, Alec could stay in the house no longer, and went out for a walk. Along the bank of the river he wandered, through the rain above and the wet grass below, to the high road, stood for a moment on the bridge gazing at the muddy Glamour, which came down bank-full,—Annie saw him from Tibbie's window as he stood,—and then turned and followed its course below the bridge through a wild, and now dismal country, to where the waters met. It was getting dusk when he reached the place. With what a roar the Wan Water came down its rocks, rushing from its steeper course into the slow incline of the Glamour! A terrible country they came from—those two ocean-bound rivers—up among the hill-tops. There on the desolate peat-mosses, spongy, black, and cold, the rain was pouring into the awful holes whence generations had dug their fuel, and into the natural chasms of the earth, soaking the soil, and sending torrents, like the flaxen hair of a Titanic Naiad, rolling into the bosom of the rising river-god below. The mist hung there, darkening everything with its whiteness, ever sinking in slow fall upon the slippery peat and the heather and the gray old stones. By and by the pools would be filled, and the hidden caves; their sides would give way; the waters would rush from the one into the other, and from all down the hill-sides, and the earth-sponge would be drained off.

"Gin this hauds, we'll hae a spate,"[1] said Alec to himself, when he saw how the waters met, flooding the *invers*, and beginning to invade the trees upon the steep banks below. The scene was in harmony with

---

1   "If this holds, we'll have a spate"

his feelings. The delight of the sweeping waters entered his soul, and filled him with joy and strength. As he took his way back through the stunted trees, each swathed in its own mist, and dripping as if it were a separate rain-cloud; and through the bushes that wetted him like pools; and through the streams that poured down the steep bank into the Glamour; he thought how different it was when he walked there with Kate, when the sun was bright, and the trees were covered with green, and the heather was in patches of blossom, and the river went clear-hearted and singing over its stony channel below. But he would rather have it thus, now that Kate was gone.

The floods then were slower in rising, and rose to a much greater height than now. In the present day, the numerous drains provide a rapid and steady escape, so that there is no accumulation of waters, and no bursting of the walls of natural or accidental reservoirs. And I presume that from slow changes produced in the climate by cultivation, there may be a less fall of water now than there used to be; for in some parts of that country the rivers have, within the memory of middle-aged men, considerably decreased in volume.

That evening, in the schoolmaster's lodgings, Truffey sat at the tea-table triumphant. The master had been so pleased with an exercise which he had written for him—written in verse too—that he had taken the boy home to tea with him, dried him well at his fire, and given him as much buttered toast as he could eat. Truffey had often had a like privilege, but never for an ovation, as now. How he loved the master!

"Truffey," said Mr Malison, after a long pause, during which he had been staring into the fire, "how's your leg?"

"Quite weel, thank ye, sir," answered Truffey, unconsciously putting out the foot of the wrong leg on the fender. "There wasna onything the maitter wi' 't."

"I mean the other leg, Truffey—the one that I—that I—hurt."

"Perfectly weel, sir. It's no worth speirin' efter. I wonner that ye tak sic pains wi' me, sir, whan I was sic a nickum."

The master could not reply. But he was more grateful for Truffey's generous forgiveness than he would have been for the richest living in Scotland. Such forgiveness is just giving us back ourselves—clean and happy. And for what gift can we be more grateful? He vowed over again to do all he could for Truffey. Perhaps a stickit minister might have a hand in making a minister that would not stick.

Then the master read Truffey's queer composition aloud, and notwithstanding all his conscientious criticism, Truffey was delighted with his own work when removed to an objective distance by the master's reading. At length Mr Malison said:

"It's time to go home, Andrew Truffey. Put on my cloak—there. And keep out of the puddles as much as you can."

"I'll pit the sma' fit in," said Truffey, holding up the end of his crutch, as he stretched it forward to make one bound out of the door. For he delighted in showing off his agility to the master.

CHAPTER LXII

When Alec looked out of his window the next morning, he saw a broad yellow expanse below. The Glamour was rolling, a mighty river, through the land. A wild waste foamy water, looking cold and torn and troubled, it swept along the fields where late the corn had bowed to the autumn winds. But he had often seen it as high. And all the corn was safe in the yard.

Neither he nor his mother regretted much that they could not go to church. Mrs Forbes sat by the fire and read Hannah More's *Christian Morals*, and Alec sat by the window reading James Montgomery's *World before the Flood*, and watching the river, and the splashing of the rain in the pluvial lake, for the water was nearly a foot deep around the house, although it stood upon a knoll of gravel.

All night Tibbie Dyster had lain awake in her lonely cottage, listening to the quiet heavy *go* of the water from which all the sweet babbling sounds and delicate music-tones had departed. The articulation of the river-god was choked in the weight and hurry of its course to the expectant sea. Tibbie was still far from well, had had many relapses, and was more than ever convinced that the Lord was going to let her see his face.

Annie would have staid with her that Saturday night, as she not unfrequently did, had she not known that Mrs Bruce would make it a pretext for giving her no change of linen for another week.

The moment Bruce entered the chapel—for no weather deprived him of his Sabbath privileges—Annie, who had been his companion so far, darted off to see Tibbie. When Bruce found that she had not followed him, he hurried to the door, but only to see her halfway down the street. He returned in anger to his pew, which he was ashamed of showing thus empty to the eyes of his brethren. But there were many pews in like condition that morning.

The rain having moderated a little in the afternoon, the chapel was crowded in the evening. Mrs Bruce was the only one of the Bruce-family absent. The faces of the congregation wore an expectant look, for they knew Mr Turnbull would *improve the occasion:* he always sought collateral aid to the influences of the truth, and sometimes attempted to suborn Nature herself to give effect to his persuasions. The text he had chosen was: "But as the days of Noe were, so shall also the coming of the Son of Man be." He made no allusion to the paper which the rain was busy washing off the door of the chapel; nor did he wish to remind the people that this was the very day foreseen by the bill-sticking prophet, as appointed for the advent of judgment. But when, in the middle of the sermon, a flash of lightning seemed to extinguish the array of candles, and was followed by an instant explosion of thunder, and a burst of rain, as if a waterspout had broken over their heads, coming down on the roof like the trampling of horses and the noise of chariot-wheels, the general start and pallor of the congregation showed that they had not forgotten the prediction. This then was the way in which judgment was going to be executed: a second flood was about to sweep them from the earth. So, although all stared at the minister as if they drank in every word of his representation of Noah's flood, with its despairing cries, floating carcases, and lingering deaths on the mountain-tops as the water crept slowly up from peak to peak, yet they were much too frightened at the little flood in the valley of two rivers, to care for the terrors of the great deluge of the world, in which, according to Mr Turnbull, eighty thousand millions of the sons and daughters of men perished, or to heed the practical application which he made of his subject. For once the contingent of nature was too powerful for the ends of the preacher.

When the service was over, they rushed out of the chapel.

Robert Bruce was the first to step from the threshold up to the ankles in water. The rain was falling—not in drops, but in little streams.

"The Lord preserve 's!" he exclaimed. "It's risen a fit upo' Glamerton a'ready. And there's that sugar i' the cellar! Bairns, rin hame yer lanes. I canna bide for ye."

And he was starting off at the top of his speed.

"Hoots! man," cried Thomas Crann, who came behind him, "ye're sae sair ta'en up wi' the warl, 'at ye hae nae room for ordinar' common sense. Ye're only stannin' up to the mou's o' yer shune i' the hole 'at ye unnertook

"The Lord preserve us!" he exclaimed. "It's risen a foot upon Glamerton already. And there's that sugar in the cellar! Bairns, run home yourselves. I can't wait for you."

And he was starting off at the top of his speed.

"Heavens! man," cried Thomas Crann, who came behind him, "you're so taken up with the world, that you've no room for ordinary common sense. You're only standing up to the mouths of your shoes in the hole you were yersel' to fill up wi' the lime 'at was ower efter ye had turned yer dry stane dyke intil a byre-wa'."

Robert stepped out of the hole and held his tongue. At that moment, Annie was slipping past him to run back to Tibbie. He made a pounce upon her and grabbed her by the shoulder.

"Nae mair o' this, Annie!" he said. "Come hame for cowmon dacency, and dinna gang stravaguin' in a nicht like this, naebody kens whaur."

"A' body kens whaur," returned Annie. "I'm only gaun to sleep wi' Tibbie Dyster, puir blin' body!"

"Lat the blin' sleep wi' the blin', an' come ye hame wi' me," said Robert oracularly, abusing several texts of Scripture in a breath, and pulling Annie away with him. "Ye'll be drooned afore the mornin' in some hole or ither, ye fashous rintheroot! And syne wha'll hae the wyte o' 't?"

going to fill yourself with the lime that was left after you'd turned your dry stone wall into a byre-wall."

Robert stepped out of the hole and held his tongue. At that moment, Annie was slipping past him to run back to Tibbie. He made a pounce upon her and grabbed her by the shoulder.

"No more of this, Annie!" he said. "Come home for common decency, and don't go gadding about in a night like this, nobody knows where."

"Everyone knows where," returned Annie. "I'm only going to sleep with Tibbie Dyster, poor, blind body!"

"Let the blind sleep with the blind, and come home with me," said Robert oracularly, abusing several texts of Scripture in a breath, and pulling Annie away with him. "You'll be drowned before the morning in some hole or other, you bothersome vagrant! And then who'll bear the blame of it?"

Heartily vexed and disappointed, Annie made no resistance, for she felt it would be uncomely. And how the rain did pour as they went home! They were all wet to the skin in a moment except Mr Bruce, who had a big umbrella, and reasoned with himself that his Sabbath clothes were more expensive than those of the children.

The best way certainly was to send the wet ones to bed as soon as they got home. But how could Annie go to bed when Tibbie was lying awake listening for her footsteps, and hearing only the sounds of the rising water? She made up her mind what to do. Instead of going into her room, she kept listening on the landing for the cessation of footsteps. The rain poured down on the roof with such a noise, and rushed so fiercely along the spouts, that she found it difficult to be sure. There was no use in changing her clothes only to get them wet again, and it was well for her that the evening was warm. But at length she was satisfied that her gaolers were at supper, whereupon she stole out of the house as quietly as a kitten, and was out of sight of it as quickly. Not a creature was to be seen. The gutters were all choked and the streets had become river-beds, already torn with the rush of the ephemeral torrents. But through it all she dashed fearlessly, bounding on to Tibbie's cottage.

"Eh, preserve's! sic a nicht, Peter Whaup!" said Peter's wife to Peter as he sat by the fire with his cutty in his teeth. "It'll be an awfu' spate."

"Ay will't," rejoined Peter. "There's mair water nor whusky already. Jist rax doon the bottle, gudewife. It tak's a hantle to quawlifee sic weet's this. Tak' a drappy yersel', 'oman, to haud it oot."

"Ye hae had plenty, Peter. I dinna want nane. Ye're a true smith, man: ye hae aye a spark i' yer throat."

"Toots! There never was sic a storm o' water sin' the ark o' the covenant—"

"Ye mean Noah's ark, Peter, man."

"Weel, weel! onything ye like. It's a' the same, ye ken. I was only jist remarkin' that we haena sic a fa' o' rain ilka day, an' we sud jist haud the day in min', pay 't respec' like, keep it wi' a tumler, ye ken—cummummerate it, as they ca' 't. Rax doon the bottle, lass, and I'll jist gie a luik oot an' see whether the water's likely to come in

"Eh, preserve us! such a night, Peter Whaup!" said Peter's wife to Peter as he sat by the fire with his cutty in his teeth. "It'll be an awful spate!"

"Ay, it will," rejoined Peter. "There's more water than whisky already. Just hand down the bottle, goodwife. It takes a lot to take the edge off wetness like this. Have a drop yourself, woman, to keep it out."

"You've had plenty, Peter. I don't want any. You're a true smith, man: you have always a spark in your throat."

"Tut! There never was such a storm of water since the ark of the covenant—"

"You mean Noah's ark, Peter, man."

"Well, well! anything you like. It's all the same, you know. I was only just remarking that we haven't seen such a fall of rain every day, and we should just keep the day in mind, pay it respect, like, keep it with a tumbler, you know—commemorate it, as they call it. Hand down the bottle, lass, and I'll just give a look out and see whether the water's likely ower the door-sill; for gin it ance crosses the thrashol', I doot there wonno be whusky eneuch i' the hoose, and bein' the Sawbath nicht, we canna weel win at ony mair."

Thus entreated, Mistress Whaup got the bottle down. She knew her husband must have whisky, and, like a wise woman, got him to take as large a proportion of the immitigable quantity as possible at home. Peter went to the door to reconnoitre.

"Guid guide 's!" he cried; "there's a lassie run by like a maukin, wi' a splash at ilka fit like a wauk-mill. An' I do believe it was Annie Anderson. Will she be rinnin' for the howdie to Mistress Bruce? The cratur'll be droont. I'll jist rin efter her."

"An' be droont yersel, Peter Whaup! She's a wise lass, an' can tak care o' hersel. Lat ye her rin."

But Peter hesitated.

"The water's bilin'," cried Mrs Whaup.

And Peter hesitated no longer.

Nor indeed could he have overtaken Annie if he had tried. Before Peter's tumbler was mixed she was standing on the stone across the dyer's *dam*, looking down into the water which had risen far up the perpendicular sides of its rocky conduit. Across the stone the water from the street above was pouring into the Glamour.

to come in over the door-sill; for if it once crosses the threshold, I expect there won't be enough whisky in the house, and being the Sabbath night, we can't well get at any more."

Thus entreated, Mistress Whaup got the bottle down. She knew her husband must have whisky, and, like a wise woman, got him to take as large a proportion of the immitigable quantity as possible at home. Peter went to the door to reconnoitre.

"Goodness!" he cried; "there's a lassie run by like a hare, with a splash at every foot like a fulling-mill. And I do believe it was Annie Anderson. Will she be running for the midwife for Mistress Bruce? The girl will be drowned. I'll just run after her."

"And be drowned yourself, Peter Whaup! She's a wise lass, and can take care of herself. Let her run."

But Peter hesitated.

"The water's boiling," cried Mrs Whaup.

And Peter hesitated no longer.

Nor indeed could he have overtaken Annie if he had tried. Before Peter's tumbler was mixed she was standing on the stone across the dyer's *dam*, looking down into the water which had risen far up the perpendicular sides of its rocky conduit. Across the stone the water from the street above was pouring into the Glamour.

"Tibbie," she said, as she entered the cottage, "I think there's going to be a terrible flood."

"Let it come," cried Tibbie. "The house is founded on a rock, and the rains may fall, and the winds may blow, and the floods may drive at the house, but it won't fall, it can't fall, for it's founded on a rock."

Perhaps Tibbie's mind was wandering a little, for when Annie entered, she found her face flushed, and her hands moving restlessly. But what with this assurance of her confidence, and the pleasure of being with her again, Annie thought no more about the waters of the Glamour.

"What kept you so long, lassie?" said Tibbie wearily after a moment's silence, during which Annie had been redisposing the peats to get some light from the fire.

She told her the whole story.

"And have you had no supper?"

"Na. But I don't want any."

"Put off your wet clothes, then, and come to your bed."

Annie crept into the bed beside her—not dry even then, for she was forced to retain her last garment. Tibbie was restless, and kept moaning, so that neither of them could sleep. And the water kept sweeping on faster, and rising higher up the rocky mound on which the cottage stood. The old woman and the young girl lay within and listened fearless.

CHAPTER LXIII

Alec too lay awake and listened to the untiring rain. Weary of the house, he had made use of the missionar kirk to get out of it, and had been one of Mr Turnbull's congregation that night. Partly because his mind was unoccupied by any fear from without, for he only laughed at the prophecy, something in that sermon touched him deeper than any one else in the place perhaps, awoke some old feelings of responsibility that had been slumbering for a long time, and made him reflect upon an unquestioned article of his creed—the eternal loss and misery and torture of the soul that did not repent and believe. At the same time, what repentance and belief really meant—what he had to do first—he did not know. All he seemed to know was that he was at that moment in imminent danger of eternal damnation. And he lay thinking about this while the rain kept pouring upon the roof out of the thick night overhead, and the Glamour kept sweeping by through the darkness to the sea. He grew troubled, and when at last he fell asleep, he dreamed frightfully.

When he woke, it was a dull morning, full of mist and rain. His dreams had fled even from his memory, but had left a sense of grievous discomfort. He rose and looked out of the window. The Glamour spread out and rushed on like the torrent of a sea forsaking its old bed. Down its course swept many dark objects, which he was too far off to distinguish. He dressed himself, and went down to its edge—not its bank: that lay far within and far beneath its torrent. The water, outspread where it ought not to be, seemed to separate him from the opposite country by an impassable gulf of space, a visible infinitude—a vague marvel of waters. Past him swept trees torn up by the roots. Down below, where he could not see, stones were rolling along the channel. On the surface, sheaves and trees went floating by. Then a cart with a drowned horse between the shafts, heaved past in the central roll of the water. Next came something he could not understand at first. It was a great water-wheel. This made him think of the mill, and he hurried off to see what the miller was doing.

Truffey went stumping through the rain and the streams to the morning school. Gladly would he have waited on the bridge, which he had to cross on his way, to look at the water instead. But the master would be there, and Truffey would not be absent. When Mr Malison came, Truffey was standing in the rain waiting for him. Not another boy was there. He sent him home. And Truffey went back to the bridge over the Glamour, and there stood watching the awful river.

Mr Malison sped away westward towards the Wan Water. On his way he found many groups of the inhabitants going in the same direction. The bed of the Wan Water was here considerably higher than that of the Glamour, although by a rapid descent it reached the same level a couple of miles below the town. But its waters had never, to the knowledge of any of the inhabitants, risen so high as to surmount the ridge on the other slope of which the town was built. Consequently they had never invaded the streets. But now people said the Wan Water would be down upon them in the course of an hour or two, when Glamerton would be in the heart of a torrent, for the two rivers would be one. So instead of going to school, all the boys had gone to look, and the master followed them. Nor was the fear without foundation; for the stream was still rising, and a foot more would overtop the ground between it and the Glamour.

But while the excited crowd of his townsmen stood in the middle of a stubble-field, watching the progress of the enemy at their feet, Robert Bruce was busy in his cellar preparing for its reception. He could not move his cask of sugar without help, and there was none of that to be had. Therefore he was now, in his shirt-sleeves, carrying the sugar up the cellar-stairs in the coal-scuttle, while Mrs Bruce, in a condition very unfit for such efforts, went toiling behind him with the *meal-bossie* filled far beyond the brim. As soon as he had finished his task, he hurried off to join the watchers of the water.

James Johnstone's workshop was not far from the Glamour. When he went into it that morning, he found the treadles under water, and thought he had better give himself *the play*.

"I'll jist tak a daun'er doon to the brig to see the spate gang by," he said to himself, and, putting on his grandfather's hat, went out into the rain.

"I'll just take a stroll down to the bridge to see the spate go by," he said to himself, and, putting on his grandfather's hat, went out into the rain.

As he came near the bridge, he saw cripple Truffey leaning over the parapet with horror-stricken looks. The next moment he bounded to his one foot and his crutch, and *spanged* (leapt) over the bridge as if he had been gifted with six legs.

When James reached the parapet, he could see nothing to account for the terror and eagerness in Truffey's pale face, nor for his precipitate flight. But being short-sighted and inquisitive, he set off after Truffey as fast as the dignity proper to an elderly weaver and a deacon of the missionars would permit.

As Alec came near the mill he saw two men standing together on the verge of the brown torrent which separated them from it. They were the miller—the same whose millstone Curly had broken by shutting down the sluice—and Thomas Crann, the latest architect employed about the building. Thomas had been up all night, wandering hither and thither along the shore of the Wan Water, sorely troubled about Glamerton and its careless people. Towards morning he had found himself in the town again, and, crossing the Glamour, had wandered up the side of the water, and so come upon the sleepless miller contemplating his mill in the embrace of the torrent.

"Ye maun alloo it's *hard*, Thamas," said the miller.

"Hard!" retorted Thomas with indignation. "Hoo daur ye say sic a thing! Here hae ye been stickin' yer bit water-wheel i' the mids o' ane o' the Lord's burns, and the Lord has ca'd it roon and roon for you and yer forbears aboon a hunner yer, and ye've grun' yer breid oot o' 't, and the breid o' yer bairns, and noo whan it's i' the Lord's gait, and he maun hae mair room to sen' doon the waters frae his hills, ye grummle an' compleen at the spate that's been foreordeen't frae the verra black mirk o' eternity. What wad ye think o' a bairn gaein' compleenin' o' you 'cause your backwater had ta'en awa' his wheelie o' rashes, whaur it was whurlin' bonnie afore ye liftit the sluice?"

"You must allow it's *hard*, Thomas," said the miller.

"Hard!" retorted Thomas with indignation. "How dare you say such a thing! Here have you been sticking your water-wheel in the midst of one of the Lord's burns, and the Lord has driven it round and round for you and your forbears above a hundred years, and you've ground your bread out of it, and the bread of your bairns, and now when it's in the Lord's way, and he must have more room to send down the waters from his hills, you grumble and complain at the spate that's been foreordained from the very black darkness of eternity. What would you think of a bairn going complaining of you 'cause your backwater had taken away his wheel of rashes, where it was whirling bonny before you lifted the sluice?"

Thomas's zeal had exposed him to the discomfiture of those who, if they do not actually tell lies for God, yet use very bad arguments for him. The miller rejoined:

"You or me, Thomas, would see bairn and wheel alike safe, before we lifted the sluice. The Lord *might* have managed without taking away my mill."

"Your mill's not down the water yet, Simon. It's in some extremity, I confess; but whether it's to be life or death, none knows but one. Go home, man, and go down upon your knees, and pray."

"Pray to God about an old meal-mill?" said Simon with indignation. "Indeed, I won't be so ill-bred."

And so saying, he turned and went home, leaving Thomas muttering—

"If a man would pray about anything, they might, maybe, take a liking to it. A prayer may do a man good when it's not just of the kind to be altogether acceptable to the mind of the Almighty. But I expect he has a sharp ear for any prayer that goes up to him."

The last two sentences were spoken aloud as he shook hands with Alec, of whose presence he had been aware from the first, although he had taken no notice of his arrival.

Before another word was uttered, their attention was attracted by a large mass floating down the river.

"What's that, Thomas?" said Alec. "I houp it winna tak' awa' the brig."

He meant the wooden bridge a few hundred yards below them, which, inaccessible from either side, was now very little above the level of the water.

"It's jist the riggin' o' some cottar's bit hoosie," answered Thomas. "What's come o' them that was aneath it, the Lord only kens. The water's jist liftit the roof bodily. There it gangs—throu' aneath the brig.—The brig's doon. It's no doon.—It's stan'in' yet.—But the puir fowk, Alec!—Eh, gin they warna preparet! Think o' that, Alec."

"I houp they wan oot," answered Alec.

"Houps are feckless things, Alec," returned Thomas, censoriously.

Before another word was uttered, their attention was attracted by a large mass floating down the river.

"What's that, Thomas?" said Alec. "I hope it won't take away the bridge."

He meant the wooden bridge a few hundred yards below them, which, inaccessible from either side, was now very little above the level of the water.

"It's just the roof of some cottar's wee house," answered Thomas. "What's become of them that were under it, the Lord only knows. The water's just lifted the roof bodily. There it goes—through beneath the bridge.—The bridge is down. It's not down.—It's standing yet.—But the poor folk, Alec!—Eh, if they weren't prepared! Think of that, Alec."

"I hope they made it out," answered Alec.

"Hopes are feckless things, Alec," returned Thomas, censoriously.

But the talk was turned into another channel by the appearance—a few ridges off—for they were standing in a field—of Truffey, who, with frantic efforts to get on, made but little speed, so deep did his crutch sink in the soaked earth. He had to pull it out at every step, and seemed mad in his foiled anxiety to reach them. He tried to shout, but nothing was heard beyond a crow like that of a hoarse chicken. Alec started off to meet him, but just as he reached him his crutch broke in the earth, and he fell and lay unable to speak a word. With slow and ponderous arrival, Thomas Crann came up.

"Annie Anderson!" panted out Truffey at length.

"What aboot *her*?" said both in alarm.

"Annie Anderson!" panted out Truffey at length.

"What about *her*?" said both in alarm.

"Tibbie Dyster!" sobbed Truffey in reply.

"Here's James Johnstone!" said Thomas; "he'll tell us all about it."

He surmised the facts, but waited in painful expectation of assurance from the deacon, who came slipping and sliding along the wet ridges.

"What's this?" he cried fiercely, as James came within hearing.

"What is it?" returned the weaver eagerly.

If Thomas had been a swearing man, what a terrible oath he would have sworn in the wrath which this response of the weaver roused in his apprehensive soul! But Truffey was again trying to speak, and with a

"Be ashamed of yourself, James Johnstone," the mason bent his ear to listen.

"They'll be drowned. They'll be taken away. They can't get out."

Thomas and Alec turned and stared at each other.

"The boat!" gasped Thomas.

Alec made no reply. That was a terrible water to look at. And the boat was small.

"Can you guide it, Alec?" said Thomas, his voice trembling, and the muscles of his face working.

The terrors of the night had returned upon Alec. Would the boat live? Was there more than a chance? And if she went down, was he not damned for ever? He made no reply. He was afraid.

"Alec!" shouted Thomas, in a voice that might have been heard across the roar of the Glamour, "Will you let the women drown?"

"Thomas," answered Alec, meekly, trembling from head to foot, "if I go to the bottom, I go to hell."

"Better be damned, doing the will of God, than saved doing nothing!" said Thomas.

The blood shot into Alec's face. He turned and ran.

"Thomas," said James Johnstone, with shy interposition, laying his forefinger upon the stonemason's broad chest, "have you considered what you're driving the young man to?"

"Ay, well enough, James Johnstone. You're one of those mealy-mouthed friends that like a man so well they would rather have him go with his back to the plough, than drive it in the face of a cold wind. I would rather see my friend hanged than see him deserve hanging. Keep away with you. If he doesn't go, I'll go myself, and I never was in a boat in my life."

"Come on, Thomas," cried Alec, already across three or four ridges; "I can't carry her alone."

Thomas followed as fast as he could, but before he reached the barn, he met Alec and one of the farm-servants, with the boat on their shoulders.

It was a short way to the water. They had her afloat in a

few minutes, below the footbridge. At the edge the water was as still as a pond.

Alec seized the oars, and the men shoved him off.

"Pray, Alec," shouted Thomas.

"I haven't time. Pray yourself," shouted Alec in reply, and gave a stroke that shot him far towards the current. Before he reached it, he shifted his seat, and sat facing the bows. There was little need for pulling, nor was there much fear of being overtaken by any floating mass, while there was great necessity for looking out ahead. The moment Thomas saw the boat laid hold of by the current, he turned his back to the Glamour, fell upon his knees in the grass, and cried in an agony:

"Lord, let not the curse of the widow and the childless be upon me, Thomas Crann."

Thereafter he was silent.

Johnstone and the farm-lad ran down the river-side. Truffey had started for the bridge again, having tied up his crutch with a string. Thomas remained kneeling, with his arms stretched out as stiff as the poles of a scaffold, and the joints of his clasped fingers buried in the roots of the grass. The stone piers of the wooden bridge fell into the water with a rush, but he never heard it. The bridge floated past him bodily, but his back was towards it. Like a wretch in sanctuary, he dared not leave "the footstool of grace," or expose himself to the inroads of the visible world around him, by opening his eyes.

Alec did not find it so hard as he had expected to keep his boat from capsizing. But the rapidity with which the banks swept past him was frightful. The cottage lay on the other side of the Glamour, lower down, and all that he had to do for a while, was to keep the bows of his boat down the stream. When he approached the cottage, he drew a little out of the centre of the current, which, confined within rising ground, was here fiercer than anywhere above. But out of the current he could not go; for the cottage lay between the channel of the river and the mill-race. Except for its relation, however, to the bridge behind it, which he saw crowded with anxious spectators, he would not have known where it ought to be—so much was the aspect of everything altered. He could see that the water was more than half way up the door, right at which he had resolved to send his boat. He was doubtful whether the doorway was wide enough to let it through, but he saw no other way of doing. He hoped his momentum would be sufficient to force the door open, or, better still, to carry away the posts, and give him more room. If he failed no doubt the boat would be in danger, but he would not make any further resolutions, till action, becoming absolute, should reveal the nature of its own necessity. As he drew near his mark, therefore, he resumed the seat of a rower, kept taking good aim at the door, gave a few vigorous pulls, and unshipping his oars, bent his head forward from the shock. Bang went the *Bonnie Annie;* away went door and posts; and the lintel came down on Alec's shoulders.

But I will now tell how the night had passed with Tibbie and Annie.

CHAPTER LXIV

Tibbie's moaning grew gentler and less frequent, and both fell into a troubled slumber. From this Annie awoke at the sound of Tibbie's voice. She was talking in her dream.

"Don't wake him," she said; "don't wake him; he's fell (Ger. *viel*) tired and sleepy. Let the wind blow, lads. Do you think He can't see when his eyes are shut? If the water meddle with you, he'll soon let it know it's in the wrong. You'll see it cowering at his feet like a colley-dog. I'll just wipe the wet off my Lord's face.—Well, wake him if you will. *I would rather go to the bottom myself.*"

A pause followed. It was clear that she was in a dream-boat, with Jesus in the hinder part asleep upon a pillow. The sounds of the water outside had stolen through her ears and made a picture in her brain. Suddenly she cried out:

"I told you so! I told you so! Look at it! The waves go down as if they were so many whelpies!"

She woke with the cry—weeping.

"I thought *I* had the sight of my eyes," she said sobbing, "and the Lord was blind with sleep."

"Do you hear the water?" said Annie.

"Who cares for *that* water!" she answered, in a tone of contempt. "Do you think He can't manage *it*!"

But there was a *jabble* in the room beside them, and Annie heard it. The water was yelping at the foot of the bed.

"The water's in the house!" cried she, in terror, and proceeded to rise.

"Lie still, child," said Tibbie, authoritatively. "If the water be in the house, there's no way out. It'll be down before the morning. Lie still."

Annie lay down again, and Tibbie resumed:

"If we be in the water, the water's in the hollow of his hand. If we go to the bottom, he has only to open his fingers, and there we are, lying in the palm of his hand, dry and warm. Lie still."

And Annie lay so still, that in a few minutes more she was asleep again. Tibbie slept too.

But Annie woke from a terrible dream—that a dead man was pursuing her, and had laid a cold hand upon her. The dream was gone, but the cold hand remained.

"Tibbie!" she cried, "the water's in the bed."

"What's that, lassie?" returned Tibbie, waking up.

"The water's in the bed."

"Well, lie still. We can't sweep it out."

The water was in the bed. And it was pitch dark. Annie, who lay at the front, stretched her arm over the side. It sunk to the elbow. In a moment more the bed beneath her was like a full sponge. She lay in silent terror, longing for the dawn.

"I'm terribly cold," said Tibbie.

Annie tried to answer her, but the words would not leave her throat. The water rose. They were lying half-covered with it. Tibbie broke out singing. Annie had never heard her sing, and it was not very musical.

> "Saviour, through the desert lead us.
> Without thee, we cannot go."

"Are you waking, lassie?"

"Ay," answered Annie.

"I'm terribly cold, and the water's up to my throat. I can't move, I'm so cold. I didn't think the water had been so cold."

"I'll help you to sit up a bit. You'll have dreadful rheumatics after this, Tibbie," said Annie, as she got up on her knees, and proceeded to lift Tibbie's head and shoulders, and draw her up in the bed.

But the task was beyond her strength. She could not move the helpless weight, and, in her despair, she let Tibbie's head fall back with a dull plash upon the bolster.

Seeing that all she could do was to sit and support her, she got out of bed and waded across the floor to the fireside to find her clothes. But they were gone. Chair and all had been floated away, and although she groped till she found the floating chair, she could not find the clothes. She returned to the bed, and getting behind Tibbie, lifted her head on her knees, and so sat.

An awful dreary time followed. The water crept up and up. Tibbie moaned a little, and then lay silent for a long time, drawing slow and feeble breaths. Annie was almost dead with cold.

Suddenly in the midst of the darkness Tibbie cried out,

"I see light! I see light!"

A strange sound in her throat followed, after which she was quite still. Annie's mind began to wander. Something struck her gently on the arm, and kept bobbing against her. She put out her hand to feel what it was. It was round and soft. She said to herself:

"It's only somebody's head that the water's torn off," and put her hand under Tibbie again.

In the morning she found it was a drowned hen.

At length she saw motion rather than light. The first of the awful dawn was on the yellow flood that filled the floor. There it lay throbbing and swirling. The light grew. She strained her eyes to see Tibbie's face. At last she saw that the water was over her mouth, and that her face was like the face of her father in his coffin. Child as she was, she knew that Tibbie was dead. She tried notwithstanding to lift her head out of the water, but she could not. So she crept from under her, with painful effort, and stood up in the bed. The water almost reached her knees. The table was floating near the bed. She got hold of it, and scrambling on to it, sat with her legs in the water. For another long space, half dead and half asleep, she went floating about, dreaming that she was having a row in the *Bonnie Annie* with Alec and Curly. In the motions of the water, she had passed close to the window looking down the river, and Truffey had seen her.

Wide awake she started from her stupor at the terrible bang with which the door burst open. She thought the cottage was falling, and that her hour was come to follow Tibbie down the dark water.

But in shot the sharp prow of the *Bonnie Annie*, and in glided after it the stooping form of Alec Forbes. She gave one wailing cry, and forgot everything.

"...in shot the sharp prow of the Bonnie Annie, and after it the stooping form of Alec Forbes."

That cry however had not ceased before she was in Alec's arms. In another moment, wrapt in his coat and waistcoat, she was lying in the bottom of the boat.

Alec was now as cool as any hero should be, for he was doing his duty, and had told the devil to wait a bit with his damnation. He looked all about for Tibbie, and at length spied her drowned in her bed.

"So much the more chance for Annie and me!" he said. "But I wish I had been in time."

What was to be done next? Down the river he must go, and they would be upon the bridge in two moments after leaving the cottage.—He must shoot the middle arch, for that was the highest. But if he escaped being dashed against the bridge before he reached the arch, and even had time to get in a straight line for it, the risk was a terrible one, with the water within a few feet of the keystone.

But when he shot the *Bonnie Annie* again through the door of the cottage, neither arch nor bridge was to be seen, and the boat went down the open river like an arrow.

CHAPTER LXV

Alec, looking down the river on his way to the cottage, had not seen the wooden bridge floating after him. As he turned to row into the cottage, it went past him.

The stone bridge was full of spectators, eagerly watching the boat, for Truffey had spread the rumour of the attempt; while the report of the situation of Tibbie and Annie having reached even the Wan Water, those who had been watching it were now hurrying across to the bridge of the Glamour.

The moment Alec disappeared in the cottage, some of the spectators caught sight of the wooden bridge coming down full tilt upon them. Already fears for the safety of the stone bridge had been openly expressed, for the weight of water rushing against it was tremendous; and now that they saw this ram coming down the stream, a panic, with cries and shouts of terror, arose, and a general rush left the bridge empty just at the moment when the floating mass struck one of the principal piers. Had the spectators remained upon it, the bridge might have stood.

But one of the crowd was too much absorbed in watching the cottage to heed the sudden commotion around him. This was Truffey, who, leaning wearily on the parapet with his broken crutch looking over it also at his side, sent his soul through his eyes to the cottage window. Even when the bridge struck the pier, and he must have felt the mass on which he stood tremble, he still kept staring at the cottage. Not till he felt the bridge begin to sway, I presume, had he a notion of his danger. Then he sprang up, and made for the street. The half of the bridge crumbled away behind him, and vanished in the seething yellow abyss.

At this moment, the first of the crowd from the Wan Water reached the bridge-foot. Amongst them came the schoolmaster. Truffey was making desperate efforts to reach the bank. His mended crutch had given way, and he was hopping wildly along. Murdoch Malison saw him, and rushed upon the falling bridge. He reached the cripple, caught him up in his strong arms, turned and was half way to the street, when with a swing and a sweep and a great plash, the remaining half of the bridge reeled into the current and vanished. Murdoch Malison and Andrew Truffey left the world each in the other's arms.

Their bodies were never found.

A moment after the fall of the bridge, Robert Bruce, gazing with the rest at the triumphant torrent, saw the *Bonnie Annie* go darting past. Alec was in his shirt-sleeves, facing down the river, with his oars level and ready to dip. But Bruce did not see Annie in the bottom of the boat.

"I wonder how old Margaret is," he said to his wife the moment he reached home.

But his wife could not tell him. Then he turned to his two younger children.

"Bairns," he said, "Annie Anderson's drowned. Ay, she's drowned," he continued, as they stared at him with frightened faces. "The Almighty's taken vengeance upon her for her disobedience, and for breaking the Sabbath. See what you'll come to, bairns, if you take up with bad boys, and don't heed what's said to you. *She's* come to a bad end!"

Mrs Bruce cried a little. Robert would have set out at once to see Margaret Anderson, but there was no possibility of crossing the Wan Water.

Fortunately for Thomas Crann, James Johnstone, who had reached the bridge just before the alarm arose, sped to the nearest side, which was that away from Glamerton. So, having seen the boat go past, with Alec still safe in it, he was able to set off with the good news for Thomas. After searching for him at the miller's and at Howglen, he found him where he had left him, still on his knees, with his hands in the grass.

"Alec's a' (*all*) safe, man," he cried.

Thomas fell on his face, and he thought he was dead. But he was only giving lowlier thanks.

James took hold of him after a moment's pause. Thomas rose from the earth, put his great horny hand, as a child might, into that of the little weaver, and allowed him to lead him whither he would. He was utterly exhausted, and it was hours before he spoke.

There was no getting to Glamerton. So James took him to the miller's for shelter and help, but said nothing about how he had found him. The miller made Thomas drink a glass of whisky and get into his bed.

"I saw you, Thomas, upon your knees," said he; "but I didn't dare come near you. Put in a word for me, next time, man."

Thomas made him no reply.

Down the Glamour and down the Wan-Water, for the united streams went by the latter name, the terrible current bore them. Nowhere could Alec find a fit place to land, till they came to a village, fortunately on the same side as Howglen, into the street of which the water flowed. He bent to his oars, got out of the current, and rowed up to the door of a public-house, whose fat kind-hearted landlady had certainly expected no guests that day. In a few minutes Annie was in a hot bath, and before an hour had passed, was asleep, breathing tranquilly. Alec got his boat into the coach-house, and hiring a horse from the landlord, rode home to his mother. She had heard only a confused story, and was getting terribly anxious about him, when he made his appearance. As soon as she learned that he had rescued Annie, and where he had left her, she had Dobbin put to the gig, and drove off to see after her neglected favourite.

From the moment the bridge fell, the flood began to subside. Tibbie's cottage did not fall, and those who entered, the next day, found her body lying in the wet bed, its face still shining with the reflex of the light which broke upon her spirit as the windows were opened for it to pass.

"She sees now," said Thomas Crann to James Johnstone, as they walked together at her funeral. "The Lord sent that spate to wash the scales from her eyes."

Mrs Forbes brought Annie home to Howglen as soon as she was fit to be moved.

Alec went to town again, starting a week before the commencement of the session.

CHAPTER LXVI

It was on a bright frosty evening in the end of October, that Alec entered once more the streets of the great city. The stars were brilliant over-head, the gems in Orion's baldric shining oriently, and the Plough glittering with frost in the cold blue fields of the northern sky. Below, the streets shone with their own dim stars; and men and women wove the web of their life amongst them as they had done for old centuries, forgetting those who had gone before, and careless of those who were to come after.

The moment he had succeeded in satisfying his landlady's inquisition, he rushed up to Mr Cupples's room. Mr Cupples was out. What was Alec to do? He could not call on Mr Fraser that night; and all space between him and Kate growing more immeasurable the nearer he came to her, he could not rest for the feeling of distance. So he wandered out, and along the sea-shore till under the wall of the pier. The tide was low, and the wall high over his head. He followed it to the edge of the water, and gazed out over the dim lead-coloured sea. While he stood thus, he thought he heard voices in the air, and looking up, saw, far over him, on the top of the wall, two heads standing out against the clear sky, one in a bonnet, the other in a Glengarry. Why should he feel a pang in his heart? Surely there were many girls who took starlight walks on that refuge in the sea. And a Glengarry was no uncommon wear for the youths of the city. He laughed at his own weak fancies, turned his back on the pier, and walked along the shore towards the mouth of the other river which flowed into the same bay. As he went, he glanced back towards the top of the wall, and saw the outline of the man. He was in full Highland dress. The woman he could not see, for she was on the further side of her companion. By the time he was halfway to the college, he had almost forgotten them.

It was a desolate shore along which he walked. Two miles of sand lay by the lip of the sea on his right. On his left rose irregular and changeful mounds of dry sand, upon which grew coarse grass and a few unpleasant-looking plants. From the level of the tops of these mounds stretched away a broad expanse of flat uncultivated ground, covered with thin grass. This space had been devoted, from time immemorial, to the sports of the city, but at this season, and especially at this hour, it was void as the Sahara. After sauntering along for half an hour, now listening to the wind that blew over the sand-hills, and now watching the spiky sparkle of the wintry stars in the sea, he reached a point whence he could descry the windows of Mr Fraser's part of the college. There was no light in Kate's window. She must be in the dining-room with her uncle—or—or—on the pier—with whom? He flung himself on the sand. All the old despair of the night of thunder, of the moonlight ramble, of the last walk together, revived. He dug with his fingers into the sand; and just so the horrible pain was digging, like a live creature with claws, into his heart. But Kate was indeed sitting quietly with her uncle, while he lay there on the sea-shore.

Time passes quickly in any torment—merciful provision. Suddenly something cold seemed to grasp him by the feet. He started and rose. Like a wild beast in the night, the tide had crept up upon him. A horror seized him, as if the ocean were indeed a slimy monster that sought to devour him where he lay alone and wretched. He sprang up the sand before him, and, sliding back at every step, gained the top with difficulty, and ran across the *links* towards the city. The exercise pumped the blood more rapidly through his brain, and before he reached home hope had begun to dawn. He ascended the garret-stairs, and again knocked at Mr Cupples's door.

"Come in," reached his ear in a strange dull tone. Mr Cupples had shouted into his empty tumbler while just going to swallow the last few drops without the usual intervention of the wine-glass. Alec hesitated, but the voice came again with its usual ring, tinged with irritation, and he entered.

"Hillo, bantam!" exclaimed Mr Cupples, holding out a grimy hand, that many a lady might have been pleased to possess and keep clean and white: "Hoo's the soo? And hoo's a' the cocks and hens?"

"Brawly," returned Alec. "Hoo's the *tappit hen?*"—a large bottle, holding six quarts, in which Mr Cupples kept his whisky.

Mr Cupples opened his eyes wide, and stared at Alec, who saw that he had made a blunder.

"I'll hae nae jaw frae you, younker," said he slowly. "Gin ye be sae ill at ease 'at ye maun tak' leeberties for the sake o' bein' facetious, ye can jist gang doon the stair wi' a quaiet sough."

"I beg your pardon, Mr Cupples," said Alec earnestly, for he was vexed with himself. "But ye're quite richt; I am some ill at ease."

"I thocht as muckle. Is the rainbow beginnin' to cast a wee? Has the fit o' Iris ca'd a hole i' the airch o' c't? Eh, man! man! Tak' to the mathemawtics and the anawtomy, and fling the conic sections an' the banes i' the face o' the bonny jaud—Iris, I mean, man, no ither, lass or leddy."

For Mr Cupples had feared, from the expression of Alec's face, that he had given him offence in return. A silence of a few seconds followed, which Alec gladly broke.

"Are you still acting as librarian, Mr Cupples?" he said.

"Ay. I'm actin' *as* librarian," returned Cupples dryly. "And I'm thinkin'," he added, "that the buiks are beginnin' to ken by this time what they're aboot; for sic a throuither disjaskit midden o' lere, I never saw. Ye micht hae taicklet it wi' a graip" (*a three-pronged fork*, a sort of agricultural trident). "Are ye gaun to tak' the cheemistry alang wi' the naiteral philoasophy?"

"I'll have no jaw from you, younker," said he slowly. "If you're so ill at ease that you must take liberties for the sake of being facetious, you can just go downstairs and be quiet."

"I beg your pardon, Mr Cupples," said Alec earnestly, for he was vexed with himself. "But you're quite right; I am a bit ill at ease."

"I thought as much. Is the rainbow beginning to fade a bit? Has the foot of Iris knocked a hole in its arch? Eh, man! Take to the mathematics and the anatomy, and fling the conic sections and the bones in the face of the bonny jade—Iris, I mean, man, no other, lass or lady."

For Mr Cupples had feared, from the expression of Alec's face, that he had given him offence in return. A silence of a few seconds followed, which Alec gladly broke.

"Are you still acting as librarian, Mr Cupples?" he said.

"Ay. I'm acting *as* librarian," returned Cupples dryly. "And I'm thinking," he added, "that the books are beginning to know by this time what they're about; for such a disordered dejected midden of lore, I never saw. You might have tackled it with a graip" (*a three-pronged fork*, a sort of agricultural trident). "Are you going to take the chemistry along with the natural philosophy?"

"Ay."

"Weel, ye jist come to me, as ye hae done afore. I'm no sae gude at thae things as I am at the Greek; but I ken mair already nor ye'll ken when ye ken a' 'at ye will ken. And that's nae flattery either to you or me, man."

"Ay."

"Well, you just come to me, as you have done before. I'm not so good at those things as I am at the Greek; but I know more already than you'll know when you know all that you will know. And that's no flattery either to you or me, man."

With beating heart, Alec knocked the next day at Mr Fraser's door, and was shown into the drawing-room, where sat Kate alone. The moment he saw her, he knew that there was a gulf between them as wide as the Glamour in a spate. She received him kindly, nor was there anything in her manner or speech by which he could define an alteration; and yet, with that marvellous power of self-defence, that instinctive knowledge of spirituo-military engineering with which maidens are gifted, she had set up such a palisade between them, dug such a fosse, and raised such a rampart, that without knowing how the effect was produced, he felt that he could not approach her. It is strange how women can put out an invisible arm and push one off to an infinite removal.

With a miserable sense of cold exhaustion and aching disappointment, he left her. She shook hands with him warmly, was very sorry her uncle was out, and asked him whether he would not call again to-morrow, when he would certainly be at home? He thanked her in a voice that seemed to him not his own, while her voice appeared to him to come out of some far-off cave of the past. The cold frosty air received him as he stepped from the door, and its breath was friendly. If the winter would only freeze him to one of its icicles, and still that heart of his which would go on throbbing although there was no reason for it to throb any more! Yet had he not often found her different from what he had expected? And might not this be only one of her many changeful moods? Perhaps.

So feeling that he had nothing to do and only one thing to think about, he wandered further through the old burgh, past the lingering fragment of its once mighty cathedral, and down to the bridge which, with its one Gothic arch as old as the youth of Chaucer, spanned the channel, here deep and narrow, of the long-drawn Highland river. Beyond it lay wintry woods, clear-lined against the pale blue sky. Into these he wandered, and was going on, seeing nothing, thinking nothing, almost feeling nothing, when he heard a voice behind him.

"Hillo, bantam!" it cried; and Alec did not need to turn to know who called.

"I saw ye come oot o' Professor Fraser's," said Cupples, "and I thocht a bit dauner i' the caller air wad do me no ill; sae I jist cam' efter ye."

Then changing his tone, he added,

"Alec, man, haud a grip o' yersel'. Dinna tyne that. Lowse onything afore ye lowse haud o' yersel'."

"What do you mean, Mr Cupples?" asked Alec, not altogether willing to understand him.

"Ye ken weel eneuch what I mean. There's a trouble upo' ye. I'm no speirin' ony questons. But jist haud a grip o' yersel'. Rainbows! Rainbows!—We'll jist hae a walk thegither, an' I'll instruck ye i' the first prenciples o' naiteral philosophy.—First, ye see, there's the attraction o' graivitation, and syne there's the attraction o' cohesion, and syne there's the attraction o' adhesion; though I'm thinkin', i' the lang run, they'll be a' fun' to be ane and the same. And syne there's the attraction o' affeenity, whilk differs mair nor a tae's length frae the lave. In hit, ye see, ae thing taks till anither for a whilie, and hauds gey and sicker till 't, till anither comes 'at it likes better, whaurupon there's a proceedin' i' the Chancery o'

Nature—only it doesn't always last long, and there's no lawyers' fees—and the one's straightway divorced from the other."

And so he went on, giving a kind of humorous travesty of a lecture on physics, which, Alec could not help perceiving, glanced every now and then at his mental condition, especially when it came to treat of the mechanical powers. It was evident that the strange being had some perception of the real condition of Alec's feelings. After walking a couple of miles into the open country, they retraced their footsteps. As they approached the college, Mr Cupples said:

"Now, Alec, you must go home to your dinner. I'll be home before night. And if you like, you can come with me to the library tomorrow, and I'll give you something to do."

Glad of anything to occupy his thoughts, Alec went to the library the next day; and as Mr Cupples was making a catalogue, and at the same time a thorough change in the arrangement of the books—both to be after his own heart—he found plenty for him to do.

Alec soon found his part in the catalogue-work becoming agreeable. But although there was much to be done as well in mending old covers, mounting worn title-pages, and such like, in this department Mr Cupples would accept no assistance. Indeed if Alec ventured to take up a book destined for repair, he would dart at him an anxious, almost angry glance, and keep watching him at uneasy intervals till he had laid it down again. Books were Mr Cupples's gold and jewels and furniture and fine clothes, in fact his whole *gloria mundi*.

But the opening day was at hand, after which Alec would have less time. Still he resolved, as some small return for the kindness of Mr Cupples, that he would continue to give him what help he could; for he had discovered that the pro-librarian lived in continual dread lest the office should be permanently filled before he had completed his labour of re-organization.

During the few days passed in the library, he called once upon Mr Fraser, and met with a warm reception from him. Kate gave him a kind one as before; but he had neither the satisfaction nor the pain of being alone with her.

At the opening, appeared amongst the rest Patrick Beauchamp—claiming now the name and dignity of The Mac Chattachan, for his grandfather was dead, and he was heir to the property. He was, if possible, more haughty than before; but students are not, as a class, ready to respond to claims of superiority upon such grounds as he possessed, and, except by a few who were naturally obsequious, he continued to be called Beauchamp, and by that name I shall call him too.

It soon came out that when lecture-hours were over, he put off his lowland dress, and went everywhere in Highland costume. Indeed on the first day Alec met him in the gloaming thus attired; and the flash of his cairngorms as he passed seemed to scorch his eyes, for he thought of the two on the pier, and the miserable hour that followed. Beauchamp no longer attended the anatomical lectures; and when Alec observed his absence, he recalled the fact that Kate could never bear even a distant reference to that branch of study. Whether he would have gone in for it with any heartiness himself this session, had it not been for the good influence of Mr Cupples, is more than doubtful. But he gave him constant aid, consisting in part of a liberal use of any kind of mental goad that came to his hand—sometimes praise, sometimes rebuke, sometimes humorous execration.

Fortunately for the designs of Beauchamp, Mr Fraser had been visiting in his mother's neighbourhood; and nothing was easier for one who, like most Celts, possessed more than the ordinary power of ingratiating, than to make himself agreeable to the old man. When he took his leave to return to the college, Mr Fraser declared himself sorry that he had made no better acquaintance with him before, and begged that he would call upon him when he came up.

CHAPTER LXVII

Soon after the commencement of the session, a panic seized the townspeople in consequence of certain reports connected with the school of anatomy, which stood by itself in a low neighbourhood. They were to the effect that great indignities were practised upon the remains of the subjects, that they were huddled into holes about the place, and so heedlessly, that dogs might be seen tearing portions from the earth. What truth there may have been at the root of these reports, I cannot tell; but it is probable they arose from some culpable carelessness of the servants. At all events, they were believed in the neighbourhood, occupied by those inhabitants of the city readiest to receive and dwell upon anything revolting. But what pushed the indignation beyond the extreme of popular endurance, was a second rumour, in the consternation occasioned by which the whole city shared: the resurrectionists were at their foul work, and the graveyard, the place of repose, was itself no longer a sanctuary! Whether the authorities of the medical school had not been guilty of indifference, contenting themselves with asking no questions about the source whence the means of prosecuting their art was derived, may be a question. But fear altogether outstripped investigation, and those even who professed unbelief, took precautions; whence the lights of the watchers of the dead might be seen twinkling, far into the morning, in the solemn places around the city churches; while many a poor creature who would have sold his wife's body for five pounds, was ready to tear a medical student to pieces on the mere chance that his scalpel had touched a human form stolen from the sacred enclosure.

Now whether Beauchamp, who had watched Alec in the same situation before, had anything to do with what follows I cannot tell; but his conduct then lays him open to suspicion now.

Alec, who found some escape if not relief from painful thought in the prosecution of his favourite study, was thus occupied one evening, no very unfrequent occurrence, by candlelight. He had almost reached a final understanding of the point in pursuit, when he was roused from his absorption by a yell outside. He had for some time previous heard a sound of gathering commotion, but had paid no attention to it. He started up from his stooping posture, and having blown out his candle, perceived by the lamps outside, that a crowd of faces, pale in the darkness, was staring through the high iron palisade which surrounded the school. They had seen his light, and were now watching for his coming out. He knew that upon the smallest additional excitement the locked gates and palisade would not keep them off more than half a minute; so he instantly barred the shutters, and betook himself to the porter's room. As he crossed the small open corner between the two doors, he heard the sough of their angry speech swelling and falling like a wind in the upper regions of the night; but they did not see him. Fortunately, there was a side door in the railing, seldom used, of which the key hung in the porter's room. By this door Alec let himself out, and relocked it. But the moment he turned to go home, he heard an urchin, who had peeped round a corner, screech to the crowd across the enclosure:

"He's oot at the back yet! He's oot at the back yett and awa'!"[1]

Another yell arose, and the sounds of trampling feet.

Alec knew that his only chance lay in his heels, and took to them faithfully. Behind him came the crowd in hot pursuit. The narrow streets rang with their shouts of execration. Such curses could hardly be heard elsewhere in Europe. Alec, knowing most of the courts and passages, doubled on his pursuers in the hope of eluding them. But discovering that he had his instrument still in his hand, he stopped to put it down the bars of a grating, for a cut from it would have been most perilous, as he had been using it a day too soon; and before he had gained another turning, his pursuers were on his track and had caught sight of him. But Alec's wind and muscles were both good; and in five minutes more he was at the back entrance to his own lodging, having left the mob far behind him. He darted up to Mr Cupples, and as soon as he found breath enough, told him his adventure, saying with a laugh, as he concluded,

"It's a mercy there's as muckle o' me to the fore as can tell the tale!"

"Jist tak' ye tent, bantam," returned Mr Cupples, who had suddenly assumed a listening attitude, with his head on one side, "or ye mayna tell the neist. Hark!"

"It's a mercy there's as much of me left as can tell the tale!"

"Just be careful, bantam," returned Mr Cupples, who had suddenly assumed a listening attitude, with his head on one side, "or you mightn't tell the next. Hark!"

---

[1] "He's out at the back gate! He's out at the back gate and away!"

From far below arose the dull sound of many feet on the stone-stairs. Mr Cupples listened for a moment as if fascinated, then turning quietly in his chair, put the poker in the fire. Alec rose.

"Sit down, you fool!" cried Cupples; and Alec obeyed.

By this time the mob was thundering at the door of the flat below. And the fact that they knew where Alec lived adds to my suspicion of Beauchamp. The landlady wisely let them in, and for a few minutes they were busy searching the rooms. Then the noise of their feet was heard on the wooden stair leading up to the garret, whereupon Mr Cupples turned the poker in the fire, and said to Alec,

"Run into that hole there, at once."

He pointed with the red-hot poker to the door already mentioned as partly sunk in the slope of the ceiling, and then stuck the poker in the fire again. Alec pulled the door open, and entering closed it behind him. The next moment, guided by the light from under it, the foremost footsteps reached the door, and the same instant Mr Cupples appeared in it with his glowing weapon in his hand. Faces with flashing eyes filled the dark garret outside.

"What do you want?" asked Mr Cupples.

"We want a resurrectioner that lives in this house—a foul bone-picking doctor," answered a huge, black-faced smith.

"What do ye want with him?"

"What are you standing jawing there for? Keep out of the way. If he isn't in your box, what's the odds of our looking in it?"

"Hold your tongue, my man," answered Cupples, raising the point of the worn old weapon, the fervency of whose whiteness had already dimmed to a dull scaly red, "or I'll let you know that I'm in my own house. My word! but this'll go through you as if you were so many kegs of salt butter!"

And he gave a flourish with his rapier—the crowd yielding a step before it—as he asked once more—

"What do you want with him?"

"To drive the soul from the belly of him, the devil's imp!" said a limping ostler.

"I'll cram his mouth with the hip of a corpse," cried a pale-faced painter, who seemed himself to belong to the injured fraternity of corpses.

A volley of answers too horrible for record, both in themselves and in the strange devilry of their garnish of oaths, followed. Mr Cupples did not flinch a step from his post. But, alas! his fiery sword had by this time darkened into an iron poker, and the might of its enchantment vanished as the blackness usurped its glow. He was just going to throw it away, and was stretching out his other hand for his grandfather's broadsword, which he had put in the corner by the door ready to replace it, when a long arm, with a fist at the end of it, darted from between the heads in front of him, hurled him across the room, and laid him bleeding and senseless on his own hearth. The poker flew from his hand as he fell. The crowd rushed in after him, upset his table, broke open the door that protected his precious books, and with one vigorous kick from the blacksmith's apprentice, sent in the door of Alec's retreat. But at that moment Alec was contemplating the crowd below from a regal seat between two red chimney-pots.

For as soon as he had drawn-to the door of the closet, instead of finding darkness, he became aware of moonshine, coming through a door that led out upon the roof. This he managed to open, and found himself free of the first floor of the habitable earth, the cat-walk of the world. As steady in foot and brain as any sailor, he scrambled up the roof, seated himself as I have said, and gave himself up to the situation. A sort of stubby underwood of chimney-pots grew all about him out of red and blue ridges. Above him the stars shone dim in the light of the moon, which cast opal tints all around her on the white clouds; and beneath him was a terrible dark abyss, full of raging men, dimly lighted with lamps. Cavernous clefts yawned in all directions, in the sides of which lived men and women and children. What a seething of human emotions was down there! Would they ever be sublimed out of that torture-pit into the pure air of the still heaven, in which the moon rode like the very throne of peace?

Alec had gone through enough of trouble already to be able to feel some such passing sympathy for the dwellers in the city below. But the sounds of search in the closet recalled him to a sense of his position. If his pursuers looked out at the door, they would see him at once. He was creeping round to the other side of the chimney to cower in its shadow, when a sudden bellow from the street apprized him that the movement had discovered him to the crowd. Presently stones came flying about the chimneys, and a busy little demon bounded into the house to tell the ringleaders that he was on the roof. He therefore slid down the slope away from the street, and passed on to the roof of the next house, and thence to the third.

Arriving at a dingy dormer window, he found that it opened with ease, admitting him into a little room crowded with dusty books and cobwebs. He knew then that he was in the territorial outskirts of a certain second-hand bookseller, with whom he had occasional dealings. He closed the window, and sat down upon a pile of neglected volumes. The moon shining through the clouded window revealed rows of books all about him, of which he could not read even the names. But he was in no want of the interest they might have afforded him. His thoughts turned to Kate. She always behaved to him so that he felt both hurt and repelled, and found it impossible to go to her so often as he would. Yet now when seated in the solitude of this refuge, his thoughts went back to her tenderly; for to her they always returned like birds to their tree, from all the regions whither the energetic dispersion of Mr Cupples might have scattered them for their pickings of intellectual crumbs. Now, however, it was but as to a leafless wintry tree, instead of a nest bowered in green leaves. Yet he was surprised to find that he was not ten times more miserable; the fact being that, as he had no reason to fear that she preferred any one else, there was plenty of moorland space left for Hope to grow upon. And Alec's was one of those natures that sow Hope everywhere. All that such need is room to sow. Take that away and they are desperate. Alec did not know what advantage Beauchamp had been taking of the Professor's invitation to visit him.

After a time the tumult in the street gradually died away, and Alec thought he might venture to return to Mr Cupples. Clambering back over the roofs, he entered, and found the inner door of the closet broken from its hinges. As he moved it aside, a cry of startled fear discovered that his landlady was in the room.

"Lord preserve us, Mr Forbes!" she cried; "where have you come from, and what have you been about, to raise the whole town upon you? I trust you have no legs or arms of a cold corpse about you. The folk in the back streets can't stand that. And I won't allow it in my house. Just look at poor Mr Cupples here."

Mr Cupples lay on the bed, with his head bound in a bloody bandage. He had fallen upon the fender, and a bad cut had been the consequence. He held out his hand to Alec, and said feebly,

"Bantam, I thought you had your neck wrung by now. How the great devil did you escape their clutches?"

"By playing the cat a bit," answered Alec.

"It's the first time," remarked Mr Cupples, "I ever knew I had a door to the sky. But faith! my soul was nearly going out at this new one in my own roof. If it hadn't been for the goodwife here, that came up, after the rabble had taken themselves off, and found me fand me lying upo' the hearthstane, I wad hae been deid or noo. Was my heid aneath the grate, guidwife?"

"Na, nae freely that, Mr Cupples; but the blude o' 't was. And ye maun jist haud yer tongue, and lie still. Mr Forbes, ye maun jist come doon wi' me; for he winna haud's tongue's lang's ye're there. I'll jist mak' a cup o' tay till him."

"Tay, guidwife! Deil slocken himsel' wi yer tay! Gie me a sook o' the tappit hen."

"'Deed, Mr Cupples, ye s' hae neither sook nor sipple o' that spring."

"Ye rigwiddie carlin!" grinned the patient.

"Gin ye dinna haud yer tongue, I'll gang for the doctor."

"I'll fling him doon the stair.—Here's doctor eneuch!" he added, looking at Alec. "Gie me half a glaiss, nate."

"Never a glaiss nor glaiss sall ye hae frae my han', Mr Cupples. It wad be the deid o' ye. And forbye, thae ill-faured gutter-partans toomed the pig afore they gaed. And guid faith! it was the only wise-like thing they did. Fess the twa halves o' 't, Mr Forbes, an' lat him see 't wi' the een o' misbelief."

"Gang oot o' my chaumer wi' yer havers," cried Mr Cupples, "and lea' me wi' Alec Forbes. He winna deave me wi' his clash."

lying upon the hearthstone, I would have been dead by now. Was my head beneath the grate, goodwife?"

"Na, not quite that, Mr Cupples; but the blood of it was. And you'll just hold your tongue and lie still. Mr Forbes, you must just come down with me; for he won't hold his tongue as long as you're there. I'll just make a cup of tea for him."

"Tea, goodwife! Devil quench himself with your tea! Give me a suck of the tappit hen."

"Indeed, Mr Cupples, you'll have neither suck nor sipple of that spring."

"You rascally crone!" grinned the patient.

"If you don't hold your tongue, I'll go for the doctor."

"I'll fling him down the stairs.—Here's doctor enough!" he added, looking at Alec. "Give me half a glass, neat."

"Never a glass nor gill shall you have from my hand, Mr Cupples. It would be the death of you. And besides, those impudent gutter-crabs emptied the pig before they left. And good faith! it was the only wise-like thing they did. Bring the two halves of it, Mr Forbes, and let him see it with the eyes of misbelief."

"Go out of my room with your nonsense," cried Mr Cupples, "and leave me with Alec Forbes. He won't bother me with his prattle."

"'Deed, I'll no lea' twa sic fules thegither. Come doon the stair direckly, Mr Forbes."

Alec saw that it was better to obey. He went up on the sly in the course of the evening, however, but peeping in and seeing that he slept, came down again. He insisted upon sitting up with him though, to which, after repeated vows of prudence and caution, their landlady consented.

He was restless and feverish during the night. Alec gave him some water. He drank it eagerly. A flash of his humour broke through the cloud of his suffering as he returned the tumbler.

"Eh, man! that's gran' tipple," he said. "Hoo do ye ca' 't?"

In the morning he was better; but quite unable to rise. The poor fellow had very little blood for ordinary organic purposes, and the loss of any was a serious matter to him.

"I canna lift my heid, Alec," he said. "Gin that thrawn wife wad hae but gien me a drappy o' whusky, I wad hae been a' richt."

"Jist lie ye still, Mr Cupples," said Alec. "I winna gang to the class the day. I'll bide wi' you."

"Ye'll do nae sic thing. What's to come o' the buiks forbye, wantin' you or me to luik efter them? An' the senawtus'll be sayin' that I got my heid clured wi' fa'in' agen the curbstane."

"I'll tell them a' aboot it, ane efter anither o' them."

"Indeed, I won't leave two such fools together. Come downstairs directly, Mr Forbes."

Alec saw that it was better to obey. He went up on the sly in the course of the evening, however, but peeping in and seeing that he slept, came down again. He insisted upon sitting up with him though, to which, after repeated vows of prudence and caution, their landlady consented.

He was restless and feverish during the night. Alec gave him some water. He drank it eagerly. A flash of his humour broke through the cloud of his suffering as he returned the tumbler.

"Eh, man! that's grand tipple," he said. "What do you call it?"

In the morning he was better; but quite unable to rise. The poor fellow had very little blood for ordinary organic purposes, and the loss of any was a serious matter to him.

"I can't lift my head, Alec," he said. "If that stubborn woman would have but given me a drop of whisky, I would have been alright."

"Just lie still, Mr Cupples," said Alec. "I won't go to the class today. I'll stay with you."

"You'll do no such thing. What's to become of the books besides, without you or me to look after them? And the senatus'll be saying that I got my head battered with falling against the curbstone."

"I'll tell them all about it, one after another of them."

"Ay; jist do sae. Tell them a' aboot it. It wad brak my hert to pairt wi' the buiks afore I got them pitten in dacent order. Faith! I wadna lie still i' my coffin. I wad be thrawin' and turnin', and curfufflin' a' my win'in' sheet, sae that I wadna be respectable when I bude to get up again. Sae ye maunna lat them think that I'm ower drucken for the buiks to keep company wi', ye ken."

"Ay; just do so. Tell them all about it. It would break my heart to part with the books before I got them put into decent order. Faith! I wouldn't lie still in my coffin. I would be twisting and turning, and creasing all my winding sheet, so that I wouldn't be respectable when I had to get up again. So you mustn't let them think that I'm too drunk for the books to keep company with, you know."

Alec promised to do all he could to keep such a false conclusion from entering the minds of the senatus, and, satisfied that he would best serve the interests of Mr Cupples by doing so at once, set off for college, to call on the professors before lectures.

The moment he was out of the room, Mr Cupples got out of bed, and crawled to the cupboard. To his mortification, however, he found that what his landlady had said was in the main true; for the rascals had not left a spoonful either in the bottle which he used as a decanter, or in the store-bottle called the *tappit* (crested) *hen* by way of pre-eminence. He drained the few drops which had gathered from the sides of the latter, for it was not in two halves as she had represented, and crawled back to bed. A fresh access of fever was the consequence of the exertion. It was many days before he was able to rise.

After the morning-classes were over, Alec went to tell Mr Fraser, the only professor whom he had not already seen, about his adventure, and the consequences of the librarian's generous interference.

"I was uneasy about you, Mr Forbes," said the professor, "for I heard from your friend Beauchamp that you had got into a row with the blackguards, but he did not know how you had come off."

His friend Beauchamp! How did he know about it? And when could he have told Mr Fraser?—But Kate entered, and Alec forgot Beauchamp. She hesitated, but advanced and held out her hand. Alec took it, but felt it tremble in his with a backward motion as of reluctance, and he knew that another thickness of the parting veil had fallen between her and him.

"Will you stay and take tea with us?" asked the professor. "You never come to see us now."

Alec stammered out an unintelligible excuse.

"Your friend Beauchamp will be here," continued Mr Fraser.

"I fear Mr Beauchamp is no friend of mine," said Alec.

"Why do you think that? He speaks very kindly of you—always."

Alec made no reply. Ugly things were vaguely showing themselves through a fog.

Kate left the room.

"You had better stay," said the old man kindly.

"I was up all night with Mr Cupples," answered Alec, longing to be alone that he might think things out, "and I am anxious about him. I should be quite uneasy if I did stay—thank you, Mr Fraser."

"Ah! well; your excuse is a good one," answered the old man. And they parted.

Alec went home with such a raging jealousy in his heart, that he almost forgot Mr Cupples, and scarcely cared how he might find him. For this was the first time he had heard of any acquaintance between the professor and Beauchamp. And why should Kate hesitate to shake hands with him? He recalled how her hand had trembled and fluttered on his arm when he spoke of the red stain on the water; and how she had declined to shake hands with him when he told her that he had come from the dissecting-room. And the conviction seized him that Beauchamp had been working on her morbid sensitiveness to his disadvantage—taking his revenge on him, by making the girl whom he worshipped shrink from him with irrepressible loathing.

And in the lulls of his rage and jealousy, he had some glimpses into Kate's character. Not that he was capable of thinking about it; but flashes of reality came once and again across the vapours of passion. He saw too that her nerves came, as it were, nearer the surface than those of other people, and that thence she was exposed to those sudden changes of feeling which had so often bewildered him. And now that delicate creature was in the hands of Beauchamp—a selfish and vulgar-minded fellow! That he whom he had heard insult a dead woman, and whom he had chastised for it, should dare to touch Kate! His very touch was defilement. But what could he do? Alas! he could only hate. And what was that, if Kate should love! But she could not love him already. He would tell her what kind of a person he was. But she would not believe him, and would set it down to jealousy. And it would be mean to tell her. Was Kate then to be left to such a fate without a word of warning? He *would* tell her, and let her despise him.—And so the storm raged all the way home. His only comfort lay in saying over and over again that Kate could not be in love with him yet.

But if he had seen Kate, that same evening, looking up into Beauchamp's face with a beauty in her own such as he had never beheld there, a beauty more than her face could hold, and overflowing in light from her eyes, he would have found this poor reed of comfort break in his hand and pierce his heart. Nor could all his hatred have blinded him to the fact that Beauchamp looked splendid—his pale face, with its fine, regular, clear-cut features, reflecting the glow of hers, and his Highland dress setting off to full advantage his breadth of shoulders and commanding height. Kate had at last found one to whom she could look up, in whom she could trust!

He had taken her by storm, and yet not without well-laid schemes. For instance, having discovered her admiration of Byron, instead of setting himself, like Alec, to make himself acquainted with that poet, by which he could have gained no advantage over her, he made himself her pupil, and listened to everything she had to say about Byron as to a new revelation. But, at the same time, he began to study Shelley; and, in a few days, was able to introduce, with sufficient application, one or two passages gathered from his pages. Now, to a mind like that of Kate, with a strong leaning to the fantastic and strange, there was that in Shelley which quite overcrowed Byron. She listened with breathless wonder and the feeling that now at last she had found a poet just to her mind, who could raise visions of a wilder beauty than had ever crossed the horizon of her imagination. And the fountain whence she drank the charmed water of this delight was the lips of that grand youth, all nobleness and devotion. And how wide his reading must be, seeing he knew a writer so well, of whom she had scarcely heard!

Shelley enabled Beauchamp to make the same discovery, with regard to Kate's peculiar constitution, on the verge of which Alec had lingered so long. For upon one occasion, when he quoted a few lines from the Sensitive Plant—if ever there was a Sensitive Plant in the human garden, it was Kate—she turned "white with the whiteness of what is dead," shuddered, and breathed as if in the sensible presence of something disgusting. And the cunning Celt perceived in this emotion not merely an indication of what he must avoid, but a means as well of injuring him whose rival he had become for the sake of injury. Both to uncle and niece he had always spoken of Alec in familiar and friendly manner; and now, he would occasionally drop a word or two with reference to him and break off with a laugh.

"What *do* you mean, Mr Beauchamp?" said Kate on one of these occasions.

"I was only thinking how Forbes would enjoy some lines I found in Shelley yesterday."

"What are they?"

"Ah, I must not repeat them to you. You would turn pale again, and it would kill me to see your white face."

Whereupon Kate pressed the question no further, and an additional feeling of discomfort associated itself with the name of Alec Forbes.

CHAPTER LXVIII

I have said that Mrs Forbes brought Annie home with her. For several months she lay in her own little room at Howglen. Mrs Forbes was dreadfully anxious about her, often fearing much that her son's heroism had only prolonged the process—that she was dying notwithstanding from the effects of that awful night. At length on a morning in February, the first wave of the feebly returning flow of the life-tide visited her heart, and she opened her eyes, seekingly. Through her little window, at which in summer she knew that the honeysuckle leaned in as if peeping and hearkening, she saw the country wrapt in a winding-sheet of snow, through which patches of bright green had begun to dawn, just as her life had begun to show its returning bloom above the wan waves of death.—Sickness is just a fight between life and death.—A thrill of gladness, too pleasant to be borne without tears, made her close her eyes. They throbbed and ached beneath their lids, and the hot tears ran down her cheeks. It was not gladness for this reason or for that, but the essential gladness of being that made her weep: there lay the world, white and green; and here lay she, faint and alive. And nothing was wanting to the gladness and kindness of Mrs Forbes but the indescribable aroma of motherhood, which she was not divine-woman enough to generate, save towards the offspring of her own body; and that Annie did not miss much, because all knowledge she had of such "heavenly health" was associated with the memory of her father.

As the spring advanced, her strength increased, till she became able to move about the house again. Nothing was said of her return to the Bruces, who were not more desirous of having her than Mrs Forbes was of parting with her. But if there had ever been any danger of Alec's falling in love with Annie, there was much more now. For as her health returned, it became evident that a change had passed upon her. She had always been a womanly child; now she was a childlike woman. Her eyes had grown deeper, and the outlines of her form more graceful; and a flush as of sunrise dawned oftener over the white roses of her cheeks. She had ripened under the snow of her sickness. She had not grown much, and was rather under than over the ordinary height; but her shape produced the impression of tallness, and suggested no probability of further growth. When first Thomas Crann saw her after her illness, he held her at arm's length, and gazed at her.

"Eh, lassie!" he said, "you're grown a woman! You'll have the bigger heart to love the Lord with. I thought he would have taken you away a child, before ever we had seen what you would turn out; and sorely I'd have missed you, bairn! And all the sorer that I've lost old Tibbie. A man can't do well without some woman or other to tell him the truth. I *do* wish I hadn't been so cross with her, sometimes."

"I never heard her say that you were ever cross, Thomas."

"No, I daresay not. She wouldn't say it. She wouldn't say it. She was a kind-hearted old body."

"But she didn't like to be called old," interposed Annie, with a smile half in sad reminiscence of her friend's peculiarities, half in gentle humour, seeking to turn the conversation, and so divert Thomas from further self-accusation.

"Well, she's not that old now!" he answered with a responsive smile. "Eh, lassie! it must be a fine thing to have the wisdom of age along with the light heart and the strong bones of youth. I'm growing quite old myself. I was once proud of that arm"—and it was a brawny right arm he stretched out—"and there was no man within ten miles of Glamerton that could lift what I could lift when I was five-and-twenty.

luiks gey auld to you, no?—But ony lad i' the mason-trade micht ding me at liftin' noo; for I'm stiff i' the back, and my airm's jist reid-het whiles wi' the rheumateeze; and gin I lift onything by ordinar', it gars me host like a cat wi' the backbane o' a herrin' in her thrapple.—Ye'll be gaun back to Robert Bruce or lang, I'm thinkin'."

"I dinna ken. The mistress has said naething aboot it yet. And I'm in nae hurry, I can tell ye, Thomas."

"Weel, I daursay no. Ye maun tak a heap o' care, lass, that the plenty and content ye're livin' in doesna spring up and choke the word."

"Ay, Thomas," answered Annie with a smile; "it's a fine thing to hae reamy milk to yer parritch, in place o' sky-blue to meal and water."

What could ail the lassie? She had never spoken lightly about anything before. Was she too, like his old friend Alec, forgetting the splendour of her high calling?

Such was the thought that passed through Thomas's mind; but the truth was that, under the genial influences of home tenderness and early womanhood, a little spring of gentle humour had begun to flow softly through the quiet fields of her childlike nature.

The mason gazed at her I daresay that looks very old to you, no?—But any lad in the mason-trade might beat me at lifting now; for I'm stiff in the back, and my arm's just red-hot sometimes with the rheumatics; and if I lift anything too heavy, it makes me cough like a cat with the backbone of a herring in her throat.—You'll be going back to Robert Bruce soon, I'm thinking."

"I don't know. The mistress has said nothing about it yet. And I'm in no hurry, I can tell you, Thomas."

"Well, I daresay not. You must take a heap of care, lass, that the plenty and content you're living in doesn't spring up and choke the word."

"Ay, Thomas," answered Annie with a smile; "it's a fine thing to have creamy milk to your porridge, in place of sky-blue to meal and water."

What could ail the lassie? She had never spoken lightly about anything before. Was she too, like his old friend Alec, forgetting the splendour of her high calling?

Such was the thought that passed through Thomas's mind; but the truth was that, under the genial influences of home tenderness and early womanhood, a little spring of gentle humour had begun to flow softly through the quiet fields of her childlike nature.

The mason gazed at her

doubtfully, and was troubled. Annie saw his discomposure, and taking his great hand in her two little ones, looked full into his cold grey eyes, and said, still smiling,

"Eh, Thomas! wadna ye hae a body mak' a grainy fun whiles whan it comes o' itsel' like?"

But Thomas, anxious about the state of mind that produced the change, did not show himself satisfied.

"We dinna hear 'at the Saviour himsel' ever sae muckle as smiled," said he.

"Weel, that wad hae been little wonner, wi' what he had upo' 'm. But I'm nae sure that he didna, for a' that. Fowk disna aye tell whan a body lauchs. I'm thinkin' gin ane o' the bairnies that he took upo' 's knee,—an' he was ill-pleased wi' them 'at wad hae sheued them awa',—gin ane o' them had hauden up his wee timmer horsie, wi' a broken leg, and had prayed him to work a miracle an' men' the leg, he wadna hae wrocht a miracle maybe, I daursay, but he wad hae smilet, or maybe lauchen a wee, and he wad hae men't the leg some gait or ither to please the bairnie. And gin 't had been me, I wad raither hae had the men'in' o' 's ain twa han's, wi' a knife to help them maybe, nor twenty miracles upo' 't."

Thomas gazed at her for a

doubtfully, and was troubled. Annie saw his discomposure, and taking his great hand in her two little ones, looked full into his cold grey eyes, and said, still smiling,

"Eh, Thomas! wouldn't you have a person make a grain of fun sometimes when it comes of itself, like?"

But Thomas, anxious about the state of mind that produced the change, did not show himself satisfied.

"We don't hear that the Saviour himself ever so much as smiled," said he.

"Well, that would have been little wonder, with what he had upon him. But I'm not sure that he didn't, for all that. Folk don't always tell when a person laughs. I'm thinking if one of the bairns he took upon his knee,—and he was ill-pleased with them that would have shooed them away,—if one of them had held up his wee wooden horse, with a broken leg, and had prayed him to work a miracle and mend the leg, he mightn't have wrought a miracle, I daresay, but he would have smiled, or maybe laughed a bit, and he would have mended the leg some way or other to please the bairn. And if it had been me, I would rather have had the mending of his own two hands, with a knife to help them maybe, than twenty miracles upon it."

Thomas gazed at her for a

moment in silence. Then with a slow shake of the head, and a full-blown smile on his rugged face, he said:

"You're a curious creature, Annie. I don't rightly know what to make of you at times. You're like a suckling babe and a grandmother both in one. But I'm thinking, between the two, you're mostly in the right. And you've set me right before now.—So you're not going home to the Bruces again?"

"I didn't say that," answered Annie; "I only said I had heard nothing about it yet."

"Why don't you join the church, now?" said Thomas abruptly, after having tried in vain to find a gradual introduction to the question. "Don't you think it's a duty to keep in mind what the great Shepherd did for his own chosen flock?"

"No doubt of that, Thomas. But I never thought of such a thing. I don't even know that I am one of the elect."

"You don't know yet?"

"No," answered Annie, sorrowfully.

"I wonder at that," returned Thomas.

"And, besides," resumed Annie, "if I were, I'm not good enough yet. And besides that—"

But here she stopped and remained silent.

"What were you going to say?" asked Thomas, encouragingly.

But Annie did not reply. She looked perplexed. With the intuition of sympathy springing from like thoughts, Thomas guessed what was moving in her mind.

"I know what you're thinking, lassie," he said. "You can't help thinking that there's some in our midst who may as well be nameless, since they're no credit to us, neither would be to any body of which they were joined members. Isn't that your trouble, child?"

"Indeed it is, in part, Thomas. But it's more the state of my own feelings with regard to one in particular, than the fact that he's a member of the church. If I could be sure that Mr Bruce would always be at the other end of the seat, I might think of it. It's not that I wouldn't let him take it. I daren't meddle with that. But if I had to take it from his hand, I just couldn't regard it as the sacred thing that it has to be considered."

Thomas remained silent, with downcast thoughtful look.

It may be necessary to state, in explanation of Annie's feelings, that the Scotch, at the celebration of the Eucharist, sit in long rows, and pass the bread, each breaking off a portion for himself, and the wine, from the one to the other.

The compressed lips and motionless countenance of Thomas showed that he was thinking more than he was prepared to clothe in words. After standing thus for a few moments, he lifted his head, and returning no answer to Annie's exposition of her feelings, bade her *good-by*, and walked away.

The drift of Thomas's reflections I shall now help my reader to see.

Their appetite for prophecy having assuaged with the assuaging flood, the people of Glamerton had no capacity for excitement left.

The consequence was that the congregations, especially the evening congregations, began at once to diminish. Having once ceased to feel anxiety about some vague impending vengeance, comparatively few chose to be rated any longer about their sins; while some seeing how in the *spate* the righteous were taken and the wicked left, felt themselves aggrieved, and staid at home on the Sunday nights. Nor was the deterioration confined to the congregations. Not only had the novelty of Mr Turnbull's style worn off, but he felt himself that he could not preach with the same fervour as before; the fact being that he had exhausted the electric region of the spiritual brain, and without repose it could never fulminate again. A second and worse consequence was that, in his dissatisfaction with himself, he attempted to *get up* his former excitement by preaching as if he were still under its influences. Upon this his conscience sternly accused him of hypocrisy and pretence, which reacted in paralysis; and the whole business became wretched. Even his greatest admirers were compelled to acknowledge that Mr Turnbull had lost much of his unction, and that except the Spirit were poured down upon them from on high, their prospects were very disheartening. For even the best men in *the Church*, as, following apostolic example without regard to circumstance, they called each separate community of the initiate, were worldly enough to judge of the degree of heavenly favour shown them, not by the love they bore to the truth and to each other, not by the purity of their collective acts and the prevalence of a high standard of morality in the individual—poor as even these divine favours would have been as a measure of the divine favour—but, in a great degree, by the success which attended the preaching of their pastor, in adding to their esoteric communion, and, still worse, by the numbers which repaired to their court of the Gentiles—their exoteric congregation. Nor, it must be confessed, was even Thomas Crann, in many things so wise and good, and in all things so aspiring, an exception. Pondering over the signs of disfavour and decay, he arrived at the conclusion that there must be an Achan in the camp. And indeed if there were an Achan, he had known well enough, for a long time, who would turn out to represent that typical person. Of course, it could be no other than the money-loving, the mammon-worshipping Robert Bruce. When, therefore, he found that such a pearl of price as Annie Anderson was excluded from their "little heaven below," by the presence of this possible anti-typical Achan, he could not help feeling his original conviction abundantly strengthened. But he did not see what could be done.

Meantime, on the loving, long-remembering Annie dawned a great pleasure. James Dow came to see her, and had a long interview with Mrs Forbes, the result of which she learned after his departure. One of the farm-servants who had been at Howglen for some years was going to leave at the next term, and Mrs Forbes had asked Dow whether he knew of one to take his place. Whereupon he had offered himself, and they had arranged everything for his taking the position of grieve or foreman, which post he had occupied with James Anderson, and was at present occupying some ten or twelve miles up the hill-country. Few things could have pleased Mrs Forbes more; for James Dow was recognized throughout the country as the very pattern of what a foreman ought to be; his character for saving his employers all possible expense, having more than its just proportion in generating this reputation; for this is a capacity which, in a poor country where it is next to impossible to be enterprising, will naturally receive at least its full share of commendation. Of late, Mrs Forbes had found it more difficult to meet her current expenses; for Alec's requirements at college were heavier this year than they had been before; so that, much to her annoyance, she had been compelled to delay the last half-yearly payment of Bruce's interest. Nor could she easily bear to recall the expression upon his keen ferret-like face when she informed him that it would be more convenient to pay the money a month hence. That month had passed, and another, before she had been able to do so. For although the home-expenses upon a farm in Scotland are very small, yet in the midst of plenty, money is often scarce enough. Now, however, she hoped that, with James Dow's management, things would go better, and she would be able to hold her mental head a little higher in her own presence. So she was happy, knowing nothing of the cloud that was gathering over the far-off university, soon to sweep northward, and envelop Howglen in its dusky folds.

CHAPTER LXIX

A state of something like emotional stupefaction succeeded to the mental tumult of that evening when first Alec saw that his worst and wildest forebodings might be even already on the point of realization. The poor glimmer of hope that remained was only enough to show how terrible was the darkness around it. It was well for him that gratitude required of him some ministrations beyond those which he took out of his landlady's hands the moment he came in from college. His custom was to carry his books to the sick man's room, and wearily pretend, without even seeming, to be occupied with them. While thus unemployed he did not know how anxiously he was watched by the big blue eyes of his friend, shining like two fallen stars from the cavern of his bed. But, as I have said, he had more to do for him than merely to supply his few wants when he came home. For the patient's uneasiness about the books and the catalogue led him to offer not only to minister to the wants of the students in the middle of the day, but to spend an hour or two every evening in carrying on the catalogue. This engagement was a great relief to the pro-librarian, and he improved more rapidly thenceforth. Whether Alec's labour was lightened or not by the fact that he had a chance of seeing Kate pass the windows, I cannot tell, but I think any kind of emotion lightens labour. And I think the labour lightened his pain; and I know he was not so absorbed in his unhappiness, though at times the flashes of a keen agony broke from the dull cloud of his misery, as to perform the duties he had undertaken in a perfunctory manner. The catalogue made slow but steady progress. And so did the librarian.

"Mr Forbes," said Mr Fraser, looking at him kindly, one morning after the lecture, "you are a great stranger now. Won't you come and spend to-morrow evening with us? We are going to have a little party. It is my birthday, though I'm sure I don't know why an old man like me should have any birthdays. But it's not my doing. Kate found it out, and she would have a merry-making. I think myself after a man's forty, he should go back to thirty-nine, thirty-eight, and so on, indicating his progress towards none at all. That gives him a good sweep before he comes to two, one, nought. At which rate I shall be thirteen to-morrow."

The old man had rattled on as if he saw the cloud on Alec's face and would dispel it by kindness. I believe he was uneasy about him. Whether he divined the real cause of his gloom, or feared that he was getting into bad ways, I cannot tell.

He did not succeed, however, in dispelling the cloud; for the thought at this moment passing through Alec's mind was, that Kate had wanted the merry-making in order to have Beauchamp there. But with a feeling like that which makes one irritate a smarting wound, or urge on an aching tooth, he resolved to go and have his pain in earnest.

He was the first to arrive.

Kate was in the drawing-room at the piano, radiant in white—lovelier than ever. She rose and met him with some embarrassment, which she tried to cover under more than usual kindness. She had not wished Alec to be one of the company, knowing it would make him unhappy and her uncomfortable.

"Oh Kate!" said Alec, overpowered with her loveliness.

Kate took it for a reproach, and making no reply, withdrew her hand and turned away. Alec saw as she turned that all the light had gone out of her face. But that instant Beauchamp entered, and as she turned once more to greet him, the light flashed from her face and her eyes, as if her heart had been a fountain of rosy flame. Beauchamp was magnificent, the rather quiet tartan of his clan being lighted up with all the silver and jewels of which the dress admits. In the hilt of his dirk, in his brooch, and for buttons, he wore a set of old family topazes, instead of the commoner cairngorm, so that as he entered he flashed golden light from the dark green cloud of his tartan. Not observing Alec, he advanced to Kate with the confidence of an accepted lover; but some motion of her hand or glance from her eyes warned him in time. He looked round, started a little, and greeted him with a slight bow, of which Alec took no notice. He then turned to Kate and began to talk in a low tone, to which she listened with her head hanging like the topmost bell of a wild hyacinth. As he looked, the last sickly glimmer of Alec's hope died out in darkness. But he bore up in bitterness, and a demon awoke in him laughing. He saw the smooth handsome face, the veil of so much that was mean and wretched, bending over the loveliness he loved, yet the demon in him only laughed.

It may appear strange that they should behave so like lovers in the presence of any third person, much more in the presence of Alec. But Beauchamp had now made progress enough to secure his revenge of mortification; and for that, with the power which he had acquired over

Kate's sensitive nature, he drew her into the sphere of his flaunted triumph, and made her wound Alec to the root of his vulnerable being. Had Alec then seen his own face, he would have seen upon it the sneer that he hated so upon that of Beauchamp. For all wickedness tends to destroy individuality, and declining natures assimilate as they sink.

Other visitors arrived, and Alec found a strange delight in behaving as if he knew of no hidden wound, and his mind were in a state of absolute *negligé*. But how would he meet the cold wind blowing over the desolate links?

Some music, and a good deal of provincial talk—not always less human and elevating than the metropolitan—followed. Beauchamp moderated his attentions to Kate; but Alec saw that it was in compliance with his desire that, though reluctant, she went a second time to the piano. The song she had just sung was insignificant enough; but the second was one of the ballads of her old Thulian nurse, and had the merit of an antique northern foundation at least, although it had evidently passed through the hands of a lowland poet before it had, in its present form, found its way northwards again to the Shetland Isles. The first tone of the ghostly music startled Alec, and would have arrested him even if the voice had not been Kate's.

> "Sweep up the flure, Janet;
>   Put on anither peat.
> It's a lown and starry nicht, Janet,
>   And neither cauld nor weet.
>
> And it's open hoose we keep the nicht
>   For ony that may be oot.
> It's the nicht atween the Sancts and Souls,
>   Whan the bodiless gang aboot.
>
> Set the chairs back to the wa', Janet;
>   Mak ready for quaiet fowk.
> Hae a'thing as clean as a win'in' sheet:
>   They comena ilka ook.
>
> There's a spale upo' the flure, Janet;
>   And there's a rowan-berry:
> Sweep them intil the fire, Janet,—
>   They'll be welcomer than merry.

Syne set open the door, Janet—
    Wide open for wha kens wha;
As ye come ben to your bed, Janet,
    Set it open to the wa'."

She set the chairs back to the wa',
    But ane made o' the birk;
She sweepit the flure,—left that ae spale—
    A lang spale o' the aik.

The nicht was lowne, and the stars sat still
    Aglintin' doon the sky;
And the souls crap oot o' their mooly graves,
    A' dank wi' lyin' by.

She had set the door wide to the wa',
    And blawn the peats rosy reid;
They war shoonless feet gaed oot and in,
    Nor clampit as they gaed.

When midnicht cam', the mither rase—
    She wad gae see and hear.
Back she cam' wi' a glowerin' face
    And sloomin' wi' verra fear.

"There's ane o' them sittin' afore the fire!
    Janet, gang na to see:
Ye left a chair afore the fire,
    Whaur I tauld ye nae chair sud be."

Janet she smiled in her mother's face:
    She had brunt the roddin reid,
And she left aneath the birkin chair
    The spale frae a coffin lid.

She rase and she gaed butt the hoose,
    Aye steekin' door and door.
Three hours gaed by or her mother heard
    Her fit upo' the floor.

But whan the gray cock crew, she heard
    The sound o' shoeless feet;
When the red cock crew, she heard the door,
    And a sough o' wind and weet.

And Janet cam back wi' a wan face,
    But never a word said she;
No man ever heard her voice lood oot,
    It cam' like frae ower the sea.

And no man ever heard her lauch,
    Nor yet say alas or wae;
But a smile aye glimmert on her wan face,
    Like the moonlicht on the sea.

And ilka nicht 'tween the Sancts and the Souls,
    Wide open she set the door;
And she mendit the fire, and she left ae chair,
    And that spale upo' the floor.

And at midnicht she gaed butt the hoose,
    Aye steekin' door and door.
Whan the reid cock crew, she cam benn the hoose
    Aye wanner than afore—

Wanner her face, and sweeter her smile;
    Till the seventh All Souls' eve.
Her mother she heard the shoeless feet,
    Said "she's comin' I believe."

But she camna benn, and her mother lay;
    For fear she cudna stan'.
But up she rase and butt she gaed,
    When the gowden cock had crawn.

And Janet sat upo' the chair,
    White as the day did daw;
Her smile was a sunlight left on the sea,
    Whan the sun has gane awa'.

ENGLISH

"Sweep up the floor, Janet;
    Put on another peat.
It's a calm and starry night, Janet,
    With neither cold nor sleet.

And it's open house we keep tonight
    For any that may be out.
It's the night between the Saints and Souls,
    When the bodiless go about.

Set the chairs back to the wall, Janet;
    Make ready for quiet wights.
Have all as clean as a winding sheet:
    They're not a common sight.

There's a spale upon the floor, Janet;
    And there's a rowan-berry:
Sweep them into the fire, Janet,—
    They'll be welcomer than merry.

Then set open the door, Janet—
    Wide open for who knows who;
As you come in to your bed, Janet,
    Set it open, to let them through."

She set the chairs back to the wall,
    But one made of the birch;
She swept the floor,—left that one spale—
    Of oak wood, unbesmirched.

The night was calm, and the stars sat still
    Aglinting down the sky;
And the souls crept out of their earthy graves,
    All dank with lying by.

She had set the door wide to the wall,
    And blown the peats rosy red;

They were shoeless feet went out and in,
   Nor clumped where'er they sped.

When midnight came, the mother rose—
   She would go see and hear.
Back she came with a glowering face
   And wilting with very fear.

"There's one of them sitting before the fire!
   Janet, don't go to see:
You left a chair before the fire,
   Where I told you no chair should be."

Janet she smiled in her mother's face:
   She had burnt the rowan red,
And she left beneath the birchwood chair
   The spale from a coffin lid.

She rose and to the kitchen went,
   Always shutting door and door.
Three hours went by ere her mother heard
   Her foot upon the floor.

But when the gray cock crew, she heard
   The sound of shoeless feet;
When the red cock crew, she heard the door,
   And a rush of wind and sleet.

And Janet came back with a wan face,
   But never a word said she;
No man ever heard her voice loud out,
   It came like from over the sea.

And no man ever heard her laugh,
   Nor yet say alas or woe's me;
But a smile ever glimmered on her wan face,
   Like the moonlight on the sea.

And every night 'tween the Saints and the Souls,
   Wide open she set the door;

> And she mended the fire, and she left one chair,
>   And that spale upon the floor.
>
> And at midnight to the kitchen she went,
>   Always shutting door and door.
> When the red cock crew, she came back through
>   Always wanner than before—
>
> Wanner her face, and sweeter her smile;
>   Till the seventh All Souls' eve.
> Her mother she heard the shoeless feet,
>   Said "she's coming I believe."
>
> But she came not through, and her mother lay;
>   She knew not what her fears might bode.
> But up she rose and through she went,
>   When the golden cock had crowed.
>
> And Janet sat upon the chair,
>   White as the day did dawn;
> Her smile was a sunlight left on the sea,
>   When the sun himself has flown.

    Alec had never till now heard her sing really. Wild music and eerie ballad together filled and absorbed him. He was still gazing at her lovely head, when the last wailing sounds of the accompaniment ceased, and her face turned round, white as Janet's. She gave one glance of unutterable feeling up into Beauchamp's face, and hiding her own in her handkerchief, sobbed out, "You would make me sing it!" and left the room.

    Alec's heart swelled with indignant sympathy. But what could he do? The room became insupportable the moment she had quitted it, and he made his way to the door. As he opened it, he could not help glancing at Beauchamp. Instead of the dismay he expected, he saw triumph on his pale countenance, and in the curl of his scarred lip.—He flew frantic from the house. The sky was crowded with the watchings of starry eyes. To his fancy, they were like Beauchamp's, and he hated them. Seeking refuge from their gaze, he rushed to the library, and threw himself on a heap of foreign books, which he had that morning arranged for binding. A ghostly glimmer from the snow, and the stars overhead, made the darkness thinner about the windows; but there was no other light in the place; and there he lay, feeling darker within than the night around him. Kate was weeping in her room; that contemptible ape had wounded her; and instead of being sorry for it, was rejoicing in his power. And he could not go to her; she would receive no comfort from him.

It was a bitter hour. Eternity must be very rich to make up for some such hours.

He had lain a long time with his face down upon the books, when he suddenly started and listened. He heard the sound of an opening door, but not of the door in ordinary use. Thinking it proceeded from some thievish intent, he kept still. There was another door, in a corner, covered with books, but it was never opened at all. It communicated with a part of the buildings of the quadrangle which had been used for the abode of the students under a former economy. It had been abandoned now for many years, as none slept any longer within the walls of the college. Alec knew all this, but he did not know that there was also a communication between this empty region and Mr Fraser's house; or that the library had been used before as a *tryst* by Beauchamp and Kate.

The door closed, and the light of a lantern flashed to the ceiling. Wondering that such a place should excite the cupidity of housebreakers, yet convinced that such the intruders were, Alec moved gently into the embrasure of one of the windows, against the corner of which abutted a screen of book-shelves. A certain light rustling, however, startled him into doubt, and the doubt soon passed into painful conviction.

"Why were you so unkind, Patrick?" said the voice of Kate. "You know it kills me to sing that ballad. I cannot bear it."

"Why should you mind singing an old song your nurse taught you?"

"My nurse learned it from my mother. Oh Patrick! what *would* my mother say if she knew that I met you this way? You shouldn't ask me. You know I can refuse you nothing; and you should be generous."

Alec could not hear his answer, and he knew why. That scar on his lip! Kate's lips there!

Of course Alec ought not to have listened. But the fact was, that, for the time, all consciousness of free will and capability of action had vanished from his mind. His soul was but a black gulf into which poured the Phlegethontic cataract of their conversation.

"Ah, yes, Patrick! Kisses are easy. But you hurt me terribly sometimes. And I know why. You hate my cousin, poor boy!—and you want me to hate him too. I wonder if you love me as much as he does!—or did; for surely I have been unkind enough to cure him of loving me. Surely you are not jealous of him?"

"Jealous of *him!*—I should think not!"

Human expression could have thrown no more scorn into the word.

"But you hate him."

"I don't hate him. He's not worth hating—the awkward steer!—although I confess I have cause to dislike him, and have some gratification in mortifying him. But he's not a pleasant subject to me."

"His mother has been very kind to me. I wish you would make it up with him for my sake, Patrick. He may be uncouth and awkward—I don't know—but that's no reason for hating him. I love you so that I could love anybody that loved you. You don't know how I love you, Patrick—though you are unkind sometimes. The world used to look so cold, and narrow, and grey; but now there is a flush like sunset over everything, and I am so happy! Patrick, don't make me do things before my cousin that will hurt him."

Alec knew that she pressed closer to Beauchamp, and offered him her face.

"Listen, my Kate," said Beauchamp. "I know there are things you cannot bear to hear; but you must hear this."

"No, no, not now!" answered Kate, shuddering.

Alec knew how she looked—saw her with the eyes of his memory as she had looked once or twice—and listened unconscious of any existence but that of hearing.

"You must, Kate, and you shall," said Beauchamp. "You asked me only yesterday how I came by that scar on my lip. I will tell you. I rebuked that cousin of yours for unmanly behaviour in the dissecting-room, the very first time he entered it. He made no reply; but when we came out, he struck me."

The icy mood passed away, and such a glow of red anger rushed through Alec's veins, that he felt as if the hot blast from molten metal were playing upon his face. That Kate should marry such a man! The same moment he stood in the light of the lantern, with one word on his lips:

"Liar!"

Beauchamp's hand sprang to the hilt of his dirk. Alec laughed with bitter contempt.

"Pooh!" he said; "even you will not say I am a coward. Do if you dare!"

After her first startled cry, Kate had stood staring and trembling. Beauchamp's presence of mind returned. He thrust his half-drawn dirk into its sheath, and with a curl of the scarred lip, said coldly—

"Eaves-dropping."

"Lying," retorted Alec.

"Well, I must say," returned Beauchamp, assuming his most polished tone, "that this kind of conversation is at least unusual in the presence of a lady."

Without making him any reply, Alec turned to Kate.

"Kate," he said, "I swear to you that I struck him only after fair warning, after insult to myself, and insult to the dead. He did not know that I was able to give him the chastisement he deserved."

I doubt if Kate heard any of this speech. She had been leaning against a book-case, and from it she now slipped sideways to the floor.

"You brute!" said Beauchamp. "You will answer to me for this."

"When you please," returned Alec. "Meantime you will leave this room, or I will make you."

"Go to the devil!" said Beauchamp, again laying his hand on his dirk.

"You can claim fair play no more than a wolf," said Alec, keeping his eye on his enemy's hand. "You had better go. I have only to ring this bell and the sacrist will be here."

"That is your regard for your cousin! You would expose her to the servants!"

"I will expose her to anything rather than to you. I have held my tongue too long."

"And you will leave her lying here?"

"*You* will leave her lying here."

"That is your revenge, is it?"

"I want no revenge even on you, Beauchamp. Go."

"I will neither forestall nor forget mine," said Beauchamp, as he turned and went out into the quadrangle.

When Alec came to think about it, he could not understand the ease of his victory. He did not know what a power their first encounter had given him over the inferior nature of Beauchamp, in whom the animal, unsupported by the moral, was cowed before the animal in Forbes, backed by the sense of right.

And above all things Beauchamp hated to find himself in an awkward position, which certainly would have been his case if Alec had rung for the sacrist. Nor was he capable of acting well on the spur of any moment. He must have plans: those he would carry out remorselessly.—So he went away to excogitate further revenge. But he was in love with Kate just enough to be uneasy as to the result of Alec's interview with her.

Returning to Kate, Alec found her moaning. He supported her head as she had done for him in that old harvest field, and chafed her chilly hands. Before her senses had quite returned, she began to talk, and, after several inarticulate attempts, her murmured words became plain.

"Never mind, dear," she said; "the boy is wild. He doesn't know what he says. Oh, Patrick, my heart is aching with love to you. It is good love, I know; and you must be kind to me, and not make me do what I don't like to do. And you must forgive my poor cousin, for he did not mean to tell lies. He fancies you bad, because I love you so much more than him. But you know I can't help it, and I daresay he can't either."

Alec felt as if a green flame were consuming his brain. And the blood surged so into his head and eyes, that he saw flashes of fire between him and Kate. He could not remain in such a false position, with Kate taking him for her lover. But what an awful shock it would be to her when she discovered the truth! How was it to be avoided? He must get her home before she recovered quite. For this there was but one chance, and that lay in a bold venture. Mr Fraser's door was just across a corner of the quadrangle. He would carry her to her own room. The guests must be gone, and it was a small household, so that the chance of effecting it undiscovered was a good one. He did effect it; in three minutes more he had laid her on her own bed, had rung her bell, and had sped out of the house as fast and as quietly as he could.

His gratification at having succeeded in escaping Kate's recognition, bore him up for a little, but before he reached home his heart felt like a burnt-out volcano.

Meantime Mr Cupples had been fretting over his absence, for he had come to depend very much upon Alec. At last he had rung the bell, knowing that Mrs Leslie was out, and that it would be answered by a dirty girl in nailed shoes turned down at the heel; she would be open to a bribe. Nor did she need much persuasion besides. Off she ran with his empty bottle, to get it filled at the grocer's over the way.

When Alec came home, he found his friend fast asleep in bed, the room smelling strongly of toddy, and the bottle standing on the table beside the empty tumbler. Faint in body, mind, and spirit, as if from the sudden temptation of an unholy power, he caught up the bottle. The *elixir mortis* flowed gurgling from the narrow neck into the tumbler which Mr Cupples had lately emptied. Heedless and reckless, he nearly filled it, and was just lifting it to his lips, when a cry half-moulded into a curse rang from the bed, and the same instant the tumbler was struck from his hand. It flew in fragments against the grate, and the spirit rushed in a roaring flame of demoniacal wrath up the chimney.

"Damn you!" half-shrieked, half-panted Mr Cupples in his night-shirt, at Alec's elbow, still under the influence of the same spirit he had banned on its way to Alec Forbes's empty house—"damn you, bantam! ye've broken my father's tumler. De'il tak' ye for a vaigabon'! I've a guid min' to thraw the neck o' ye!"

Seeing Mr Cupples was only two-thirds of Alec's height, and one-half of his thickness, the threat, as he then stood, was rather ludicrous. Miserable as he was, Alec could not help laughing.

"Ye may lauch, bantam! but I want no companion in hell to cast his damnation in my teeth. Gin ye touch that bottle again, faith, I'll brain ye, and sen' ye into the ither warl' withoot that handle at least for Sawtan to catch a grip o' ye by. And there *may* be a handle somewhaur o' the richt side o' ye for some saft-hertit angel to lay han' upo' and gie ye a lift whaur ye ill deserve to gang, ye thrawn buckie! Efter a' that I hae said to ye!—Damn ye!"

Alec burst into a loud roar of laughter. For there was the little man standing in his shirt, shaking

"Damn you!" half-shrieked, half-panted Mr Cupples in his night-shirt, at Alec's elbow, still under the influence of the same spirit he had banned on its way to Alec Forbes's empty house—"damn you, bantam! you've broken my father's tumbler. Devil take you for a vagabond! I've a good mind to wring your neck!"

Seeing Mr Cupples was only two-thirds of Alec's height, and one-half of his thickness, the threat, as he then stood, was rather ludicrous. Miserable as he was, Alec could not help laughing.

"You may laugh, bantam! but I want no companion in hell to cast his damnation in my teeth. If you touch that bottle again, faith, I'll brain you, and send you into the other world without that handle at least for Satan to catch a grip of you by. And there *may* be a handle somewhere on the right side of you for some soft-hearted angel to lay hand upon and give you a lift where you ill deserve to go, you obstinate boy! After all that I have said to you!—Damn you!"

Alec burst into a loud roar of laughter. For there was the little man standing in his shirt, shaking a trembling fist at him, stammering with eagerness, and half-choked with excitement.

"Go to your bed, Mr Cupples, or you'll take your death of cold. Look here."

And Alec seized the bottle once more. Mr Cupples flew at him, and would have knocked the bottle after the glass, had not Alec held it high above his reach, exclaiming,

"Tut, man! I'm going to put it into its own nook. Go to your bed, and trust to me."

"You give me your word, you won't put it to your mouth?"

"I do," answered Alec.

The same moment Mr Cupples was floundering on the bed in a perplexed attempt to get under the bed-clothes. A violent fit of coughing was the consequence of the exertion.

"You're like to empty your own chest before you brain my pan, Mr Cupples," said Alec.

"Hold your tongue, and let me cough in peace," panted Mr Cupples.

When the fit was over, he lay still, and stared at Alec. Alec had sat down in Mr Cupples's easy-chair, and was staring at the fire.

"I see," muttered Mr Cupples. "This'll do no longer. The laddie's going to the dogs for want of being looked after. I must be up tomorrow. It's those women! those women! Poor things! they can't always help it; but, devil take them for bonnie owls! Many's the fine laddie they drive into old Horney's (*Satan's*) clutches. Mightn't some grand discovery be made in Physiology, to enable the world to go on without them? But, Lord preserve me! I would have nothing left worth crying about!"

He hid his face in the bed-clothes.

Alec hearing part of this muttered discourse, had grown attentive, but there was nothing more forthcoming. He sat for a little, staring helplessly into the fire. The world was very blank and dismal.

Then he rose to go to bed; for Mr Cupples did not require him now. Finding him fast asleep under the bed-clothes, he made him as comfortable as he could. Then he locked the closet where the whisky was, and took the key with him.

Their mutual care in this respect was comical.

CHAPTER LXX

The next morning, Alec saw Mr Cupples in bed before he left. His surprise therefore was great when, entering the library after morning lectures, he found him seated in his usual place, hard at work on his catalogue. Except that he was yet thinner and paler than before, the only difference in his appearance was that his eyes were brighter and his complexion was clearer.

"You here, Mr Cupples!" he exclaimed.

"What made you lock the cupboard last night, you devil?" returned the librarian, paying no attention to Alec's expression of surprise. "But I say, bantam," he continued, not waiting for a reply, which indeed was unnecessary, "you have done your work well—very near as well as I could have done it myself."

"I'm sure, Mr Cupples, it was the least thing I could do."

"You impudent cock! It was the very best you could do, or you wouldn't have come within sight of me. I may not be much at thrashing attorneys, or cutting up dead corpses, but I defy you to come up to me at anything connected with books."

"Faith! Mr Cupples, you may go farther than that. After what you've done for me, if I were a general, you should lead the Forlorn Hope."

"Ay, ay. It's a forlorn hope, all that I'm fit for, Alec Forbes," returned Cupples sadly.

This struck Alec so near his own grief that he could not reply with even seeming cheerfulness. He said nothing. Mr Cupples resumed.

"I have a few words to say to you, Alec Forbes. Can you believe in a man as well as you can in a woman?"

"I can believe in you, Mr Cupples. That I'll swear to."

"Well, just sit down there, and carry on from where you let sit. Then after the three o'clock lecture—who is it you're attending this session?—we'll go down to Luckie Cumstie's, and have a mouthful of dinner—she'll do her best for me—and I'll have just a tumbler of toddy—but devil a drop shall you have, bantam—and devil a word will I say to you there. But we'll come back here, and in the gloaming, I'll give you an episode in my life.—Episode did I call it? Faith it's my life itself, and not worth much, either. You'll be the first man that ever I told it to. And you may judge of my regard for you from that fact."

Alec worked away at his catalogue, and then attended the afternoon lecture. The dinner at Luckie Cumstie's followed— of the plainest, but good. Alec's trouble had not yet affected the region in which Paley seats the organ of happiness. And while an appetite exists, a dinner will be interesting. Just as the gloaming was fading into night, they went back to the library.

"Will I run over to the sacrist's for a light?"

"Na, na; let be. The dark's merciful, sometimes."

"I can't understand you, Mr Cupples. Since ever I knew you in this library, I never knew you stay till night. As soon as the gloaming began to fall, you always flew to your hat, and out at the door as if there had been a ghost getting its bones together out of the dark to come at you."

"Maybe so there was, bantam. So none of your joking."

"I didn't mean to anger you, Mr Cupples."

"Where nothing's meant, nothing's done. I'm not angry. And that you'll soon see. Sit you down there, and take your plaid about you, or you'll be cold."

"You have no plaid yourself. You're more likely to be cold than I am."

"I wear my plaid on my inside. You haven't had any toddy. Devil's brew! It may well keep a body warm. It comes from a hot quarter."

The open oak ceiling overhead was getting very dark by this time; and the room, divided and crowded with books in all directions, left little free course to the light that struggled through the dusty windows. The friends seated themselves on the lower steps of an open circular oak staircase which wound up to a gallery running round the walls.

"Efter I had taen my degree," began Mr Cupples, "frae the han' o' this same couthy auld mither, I heard o' a grit leebrary i' the north—I winna say whaur—that wantit the han' o' a man that kenned what he was aboot, to pit in dacent order, sae that a body cud lay his han's upon a buik whan he wantit it, and no be i' the condition o' Tantalus, wi' watter at the mou, but nane for the hause. Dinna imaigin' it was a public library. Na, na. It belonged to a grit an' gran' hoose—the Lord hae respec till't, for it's no joke o' a hoose that—as I weel kent afore a' was ower! Weel, I wrought awa', likin' the wark weel, for a buik's the bonniest thing i' the warl' but ane, and there's no dirl in't whan ye lay han's upo' 't, as there is, guid kens, in the ither. Man, ye had better lay han's upon a torpedo, or a galvanic battery, nor upon a woman—I mean a woman that ye hae ony attraction till—for she'll gar ye dirl till ye dinna ken yer thoomb frae yer muckle tae. But I was speikin' aboot buiks an' no aboot women, only somehoo whatever a man begins wi', he'll aye en' aff wi' the same thing. The Lord hae a care o' them, for they're awfu' craters! They're no like ither fowk a'thegither. Weel, ye see, I had a room till mysel', forby the library an' my bedroom—an' a gran' place that was! I didna see onything o'

"After I had taken my degree," began Mr Cupples, "from the hand of this same friendly old mother, I heard of a great library in the north—I won't say where—that wanted the hand of a man that knew what he was about, to put in decent order, so that a man could lay his hands upon a book when he wanted it, and not be in the condition of Tantalus, with water at the mouth but none for the throat. Don't imagine it was a public library. Na, na. It belonged to a great and grand house—the Lord have respect to it, for it's no joke of a house that—as I well knew before all was over! Well, I toiled away, liking the work well, for a book's the bonniest thing in the world but one, and there's no thrill in it when you lay your hands upon it, as there is, Lord knows, in the other. Man, you had better lay your hands upon a torpedo, or a galvanic battery, than upon a woman—I mean a woman that you have any attraction to—for she'll thrill you till you don't know your thumb from your big toe. But I was speaking about books and not about women, only somehow whatever a man begins with, he'll always end off with the same thing. The Lord have a care of them, for they're awful creatures! They're not like other folk altogether. Well, you see, I had a room to myself, besides the library and my bed-the family, for I had my denner and my wine and a' thing human stammack cud desire served up till me i' my ain room. But ae day my denner was made up o' ae mess efter anither, vera fine nae doot, but unco queer and ootlandish, and I had nae appeteet, and I cudna eat it. Sae I rase, afore my ordinar' time, and gaed back to my wark. I had taen twa or three glasses o' a dooms fine tipple they ca' Madeira, an' a moufu' o' cheese—that was a'. Weel, I sat doon to my catalogue there, as it micht be here; but I hadna sat copyin' the teetles o' the buiks laid out upo' the muckle table afore me, for mair nor twa minutes, whan I heard a kin' o' a reestlin', an' I thocht it was mice, to whilk I'm a deidly enemy ever sin they ate half o' a first edition o' the *Fairy Queen*, conteenin' only the first three buiks, ye ken, o' whilk they consumed an' nae doot assimilated ae haill buik and full a half o' anither. But whan I luikit up, what sud I see but a wee leddy, in a goon the colour o' a clood that's takin' nae pairt i' the sunset, but jist lookin' on like, stan'in afore the buik-shelves i' the further en' o' the room. Noo I'm terrible lang-sichtit, and I had pitten the buiks i' that pairt a' richt already wi' my ain han'—and I saw her put her han' upon

room—and a grand place that was! I didn't see anything of the family, for I had my dinner and my wine and all that human stomach could desire served up to me in my own room. But one day my dinner was made up of one mess after another, very fine no doubt, but very queer and outlandish, and I had no appetite, and I couldn't eat it. So I rose, before my usual time, and went back to my work. I had taken two or three glasses of a mighty fine tipple they call Madeira, and a mouthful of cheese—that was all. Well, I sat down to my catalogue there, as it might be here; but I hadn't sat copying the titles of the books laid out upon the great table before me, for more than two minutes, when I heard a kind of a rustling, and I thought it was mice, to which I'm a deadly enemy ever since they ate half of a first edition of the *Fairy Queen*, containing only the first three books, you know, of which they consumed, and no doubt assimilated one whole book and a full half of another. But when I looked up, what should I see but a wee lady, in a gown the colour of a cloud that's taking no part in the sunset, but just looking on like, standing before the book-shelves in the further end of the room. Now I'm terribly long-sighted, and I had put the books in that part all right already with my own hand—and I saw her put her hand a buik that was no fit for her. I winna say what it was. Some hermaphrodeet cratur had written't that had no respec for man or woman, an' whase neck sud hae been thrawn by the midwife, for that buik cam o' sparin' o' 'm!

"'Dinna touch that buik, my bonny leddy,' I cried. 'It's awfu' fu' o' dist and stoor. It'll smore ye to open the twa brods o' 't. Yer rosy goon'll be clean blaudit wi' the stew o' 't.'

"She startit and luikit roon some frichtit like, and I rase an' gaed across the flure till her. And her face grew bonnier as I cam nearer till her. Her nose an' her twa eebrees jist min'd ye upo' the picturs o' the Holy Ghost comin' doon like a doo; and oot aneath ilka wing there luikit a hert o' licht—that was her twa een, that gaed throu and throu me as gin I had been a warp and they twa shuttles; and faith! they made o' my life and o' me what it is and I am. They wove the wab o' me.

"Ay. They gaed oot and in, and throu and throu, and back and fore, and roon and aboot, till there wasna a nerve or a fibre o' my bein', but they had twisted it up jist as a spither does a flee afore he sooks the life oot o' 't. But that's a prolepsis."

"'Are you the librarian?' said she, saft and sma', like hersel.

upon a book that wasn't fit for her. I won't say what it was. Some hermaphrodite creature had written it that had no respect for man or woman, and whose neck should have been wrung by the midwife, for that book came of sparing him.

"'Don't touch that book, my bonny lady,' I cried. 'It's nothing but a dust-heap. It'll choke you to open the two boards of it. Your rosy gown'll be ruined with its dust.'

"She started and looked round quite frightened like, and I rose and went across the floor to her. And her face grew bonnier as I came nearer to her. Her nose and her two eyebrows just recalled to you the pictures of the Holy Ghost coming down like a dove; and out beneath each wing there looked a heart of light—that was her two eyes, that went through and through me as if I had been a warp and they two shuttles; and faith! they made of my life and of me what it is and I am. They wove the web of me.

"Ay. They went out and in, and through and through, and back and fore, and round and about, till there wasn't a nerve or a fibre of my being, but they had twisted it up just as a spider does a fly before he sucks the life out of it. But that's a prolepsis."

"'Are you the librarian?' said she, soft and small, like herself.

"'That I am, ma'am,' said I. 'My name's Cupples—at your service, ma'am.'

"'I was looking, Mr Cupples,' said she, 'for some book to help me to learn Gaelic. I want very much to read Gaelic.'

"'Well, ma'am,' said I, 'if it had been any of the Romance languages, or any one of the Teutonic breed, I might have given you a lift. But I expect you'll have to wait till you go to Edinburgh, or Aberdeen, where you'll easily meet some long-legged bejan that'll be proud to instruct you, and count himself overpaid with the sight of your bonny face.'

"She turned quite red at that, and I was afraid that I'd angered her. But she gave a small laugh, and out at the door she went, with her 'rosy fleece of fire' glowing and glimmering about her, just like one of the seraphim that old Crashaw sings about. Only she was very small for a seraph, though they're not too big. Well, you see, that was the first time I saw her. And I didn't think too much more about her. But in a day or two there she was again. And she had a deal to ask me about; and it took all the knowledge I had of books in general to answer her questions. In fact I was sometimes compelled to confess my ignorance, which isn't pleasant when a man wants to stand well with a bonny creature

questons. Whan she gaed, I gaed efter her, followin' aboot at her—i' my thochts, I mean—like a hen efter her ae chucken. She was bonnier this time than the last. She had tired o' the rosy clood, and she had on a bonny goon o' black silk, sae modest and sae rich, wi' diamond buttons up the front o' the briest o' 't. Weel, to mak a lang story short, and the shorter the better, for it's nae a pleasant ane to me, she cam aftener and aftener. And she had sae muckle to say and speir aboot, that at last we had to tak doon buiks, and I had to clear a neuk o' the table. At lenth I cam to luik for her as reglar as gin she had been a ghaist, and the time that chappit upo' the auld clock had belongt to the midnicht instead o' the mornin'. Ye'll be wonnerin' what like she was. As I tell't ye, she was a wee body, wi' muckle black een, that lay quaiet in her face and never cam oot till they war wantit, an' a body gimp and sma', but roon' and weel proportioned throohoot. Her hand and her fit war jist past expression bonny. And she had a' her features conformin'—a' sma' but nane o' them ower sma' in relation to ane anither. And she had a licht way wi' her, that was jist dazin'. She seemed to touch ilka thing wi' the verra tips o' her fingers, and syne ken a'thing aboot it, as gin she had a universal

that asks questions. When she went, I went after her, following her about—in my thoughts, I mean—like a hen after her one chicken. She was bonnier this time than the last. She had tired of the rosy cloud, and she had on a bonny gown of black silk, so modest and so rich, with diamond buttons up the front of its breast. Well, to make a long story short, and the shorter the better, for it's not a pleasant one to me, she came oftener and oftener. And she had so much to say and ask about, that at last we had to take down books, and I had to clear a corner of the table. At length I came to look for her as regular as if she had been a ghost, and the time that struck upon the old clock had belonged to the midnight instead of the morning. You'll be wondering what she was like. As I told you, she was a wee body, with great black eyes, that lay quiet in her face and never came out till they were wanted, and a body slender and small, but round and well proportioned throughout. Her hand and her foot were just bonny past expression. And she had all her features conforming—all small but none of them too small in relation to one another. And she had a light way with her, that just dazed you. She seemed to touch everything with the very tips of her fingers, and then know all

insicht; or raither, I wad say, her natur, notwithstandin' its variety, was sae homogeneous, that whan ae nerve o' her spiritual being cam in contack wi' onything, the haill sowl o' her cam in contack wi' 't at the same time and thereby; and ilka pairt read the report efter its ain fashion, translatin' 't accordin' to 'ts ain experience: as the different provinces and languages o' the Chinese Empire read the universal written tongue. A heap o' pains I took that I micht never hae to say *I dinna ken* to sic a gleg-ee'd cratur as that. And ilka day she cam to read wi' me, and we jist got on like a mail-coach—at least I did—only the wrang road. An' she cam aye i' the efternoon and bade till the gloamin' cam doon an' it grew ower mirk to ken the words frae ane anither. And syne she wad gang and dress hersel' for denner, as she said.

"Ye may say I was a muckle gowk. And ye may lauch at a bairn for greitin' efter the mune; but I doot that same avarice o' the wee man comes frae a something in him that he wad be ill aff wi'oot. Better greit for the mune than no be cawpable o' greetin' for the mune. And weel I wat, I grat for the mune, or a' was dune, and didna get it, ony mair than the lave o' my greedy wee brithers."

about it, as if she had a universal insight; or rather, I would say, her nature, notwithstanding its variety, was so homogenous, that when one nerve of her spiritual being came in contact with anything, her whole soul came in contact with it at the same time and thereby; and every part read the report after its own fashion, translating it according to its own experience: as the different provinces and languages of the Chinese Empire read the universal written tongue. A heap of pains I took that I might never have to say *I don't know* to such a sharp-eyed creature as that. And every day she came to read with me, and we just got on like a mail-coach—at least I did—only the wrong way. And she always came in the afternoon and stayed till the gloaming came down and it grew too dark to know the words from one another. And then she would go and dress herself for dinner, as she said.

"You may say I was a great fool. And you may laugh at a child for crying after the moon; but I suspect that same avarice of the wee man comes from a something in him that he would be ill off without. Better cry for the moon than not be capable of crying for the moon. And indeed, I cried for the moon, before all was done, and didn't get it any more than the rest of my greedy wee brothers."

The night had gathered thick about them. And for a few moments out of the darkness came no sound. At length Mr Cupples resumed:

"I maun jist confess, cauf that I was—and yet I wad hae been a greater cauf gin it hadna been sae—I cud hae lickit the verra dist aff o' the flure whaur her fit had been. Man, I never saw onything like her. The hypostasis o' her was jist perfection itsel'. Weel, ae nicht—for I wrocht full late, my een war suddenly dazed wi' the glimmer o' something white. I thocht the first minute that I had seen a ghost, and the neist that I was a ghost mysel'. For there she was in a fluffy cloud o' whiteness, wi' her bonny bare shouthers and airms, and jist ae white rose in her black hair, and deil a diamond or ruby aboot her!

"'It's so hot,' said she, 'in the drawing-room! And they're talking such nonsense there! There's nobody speaks sense to me but you, Mr Cupples.'

"'Deed, mem,' says I, 'I dinna ken whaur it's to come frae the nicht. For I hae nae sense left but ane, and that's nearhan' 'wi' excess o' brightness blind.' Auld Spenser says something like that, doesna he, mem?' I added, seein' that she luikit some grave. But what she micht hae said or dune, I dinna ken; for I sweir to ye, bantam, I

The night had gathered thick about them. And for a few moments out of the darkness came no sound. At length Mr Cupples resumed:

"I must just confess, calf that I was—and yet I would have been a greater calf if it hadn't been so—I could have licked the very dust off the floor where her foot had been. Man, I never saw anything like her. The hypostasis of her was just perfection itself. Well, one night—for I worked rather late, my eyes were suddenly dazed with the glimmer of something white. I thought the first minute that I had seen a ghost, and the next that I was a ghost myself. For there she was in a fluffy cloud of whiteness, with her bonny bare shoulders and arms, and just one white rose in her black hair, and never a diamond or ruby about her!

"'It's so hot,' said she, 'in the drawing-room! And they're talking such nonsense there! There's nobody speaks sense to me but you, Mr Cupples.'

"'Indeed, ma'am,' says I, 'I don't know where it's to come from tonight. For I have no sense left but one, and that's nearly 'with excess of brightness blind.' Old Spenser says something like that, doesn't he, ma'am?' I added, seeing that she looked quite grave. But what she might have said or done, I don't know; for I swear to know nothing that happent efter, till I cam' to mysel' at the soun' o' a lauch frae outside the door. I kenned it weel eneuch, though it was a licht flutterin' lauch. Maybe I heard it the better frae the conductin' pooer o' timmer, for my broo was doon o' the buirds o' the flure. I sprang to my feet, but the place reeled roon', and I fell. It was the lauch that killed me. What for sud she lauch?—And sic a ane as her that was no licht-heidit lassie, but cud read and unnerstan', wi the best? I suppose I had gane upo' my knees till her, and syne like the lave o' the celestials she tuik to her feathers and flew. But I ken nae mair than this: that for endless ages I gaed followin' her through the heavenly halls, aye kennin as sure's gospel that she was ahint the neist door, and aye openin' that door upon an empty glory, to be equally certain that she was ahint the neist. And sae on I gaed till, ahint ane o' the thoosan' doors, I saw the reek-enamelled couples o' my auld mither's bit hoosie upo' the mairgin o' the bog, and she was hingin' ower me, sayin' her prayers as gin she wad gang efter them like a balloon wi' verra fervour. And whan she saw my een open, she drappit upo' her knees and gaed on prayin'. And I wonner that thae prayers warna hearkent till. I never cud unnerstan' that."

you, bantam, I know nothing that happened after, till I came to myself at the sound of a laugh from outside the door. I knew it well enough, though it was a light fluttering laugh. Maybe I heard it the better from the conducting power of wood, for my brow was down on the floorboards. I sprang to my feet, but the place reeled round, and I fell. It was the laugh that killed me. Why should she laugh?—And such a one as her that was no light-headed lassie, but could read and understand, with the best? I suppose I had gone upon my knees to her, and then like the rest of the celestials she took to her feathers and flew. But I know no more than this: that for endless ages I went following her through the heavenly halls, always knowing as sure as gospel that she was behind the next door, and always opening that door upon an empty glory, to be equally certain that she was behind the next. And so on I went till, behind one of the thousand doors, I saw the smoke-enamelled couples of my old mother's house upon the margin of the bog, and she was hanging over me, saying her prayers as if she would go after them like a balloon with very fervour. And when she saw my eyes open, she dropped upon her knees and went on praying. And I wonder that those prayers weren't listened to. I never could understand that."

"Hoo ken ye that they warna hearkent till?" asked Alec.

"Luik at me! Do ye ca' that hearkenin' till a prayer? Luik what she got me back for. Ca' ye that an answer to prayers like my auld mither's? Faith! I'll be forced to repent some day for her sake, though there sudna be anither woman atween Venus and Mars but wad rive wi' lauchin at a word frae Cosmo Cupples. But, man! I wad hae repentit lang syne gin I cud hae gotten ae glimp o' a possible justice in pittin a hert as grit's mine into sic a misgreein', scrimpit, contemptible body as this. The verra sowl o' me has to draw up the legs o' 't to haud them inside this coffin o' a corpus, and haud them ohn shot oot into the everlastin' cauld. Man, the first thing I did, whan I cam' to mysel', was to justify her afore God for lauchin at me. Hoo could onybody help lauchin at me? It wasna her wyte. And eh! man, ye dinna ken hoo quaiet and comfortable I was in my ain min', as sune's I had gotten her justified to mysel' and had laid it doon that I was ane fit to be lauchen at.—I winna lat you lauch at me, though, bantam. I tell ye that."

"Mr Cupples! Laugh at you! I would rather be a doormat to the devil," exclaimed Alec.

"Thank you, bantam.—Weel, ye see, ance I had made up my min' aboot that, I jist began followin'

"How do you know they weren't listened to?" asked Alec.

"Look at me! Do you call that listening to a prayer? Look what she got me back for. Call you that an answer to prayers like my old mother's? Faith! I'll be forced to repent some day for her sake, though there shouldn't be another woman between Venus and Mars but would burst with laughing at a word from Cosmo Cupples. But, man! I would have repented long ago if I could have gotten one glimpse of a possible justice in putting a heart as great as mine into such an unfit, scrimped, contemptible body as this. My very soul has to draw up its legs to keep them inside this coffin of a corpse, and keep them from shooting out into the everlasting cold. Man, the first thing I did, when I came to myself, was to justify her before God for laughing at me. How could anybody help laughing at me? It wasn't her fault. And eh! man, you don't know how quiet and comfortable I was in my own mind, as soon as I had gotten her justified to myself and had laid it down that I was one fit to be laughed at.—I won't let you laugh at me, though, bantam. I tell you that."

"Mr Cupples! Laugh at you! I would rather be a doormat to the devil," exclaimed Alec.

"Thank you, bantam.—Well, you see, once I had made up my mind about that, I just began folat her again like a hungry tyke that stops the minute ye liuk roon efter him—I mean i' my thochts, ye ken—jist as I had been followin' her, a' the time o' my fiver, throu the halls o' heaven, as I thoucht them, whan they war only the sma' crinkle-crankle convolutions o' my cerebral dome—a puir heaven for a man to bide in! I hae learnt that waur and better than maist men, as I'm gaein to tell ye; for it was for the sake o' that that I begud this dismal story.—Whan I grew some better, and wan up—wad ye believe 't?—the kin'ness o' the auld, warpit, broon, wrinklet woman that brocht me furth, me Cosmo Cupples, wi' the muckle hert and the sma' body, began to console me a wee for the lauch o' that queen o' white-skinned leddies. It was but a wee, ye ken; still it was consolation. My mither thocht a heap o' me. Fowk thinks mair o' fowk, the mair they are themsels. But I wat it was sma' honour I brocht her hame, wi' my een brunt oot wi' greetin' for the mune.—I'll tell ye the lave o' 't efter we win hame. I canna bide to be here i' the dark. It's the quaiet beuks a' roon' me that I canna bide. It was i' the mids o' beuks, i' the dark, that I heard that lauch. It jist blastit me and the beuks and a' thing. They aye luik as

lowing her again like a hungry dog that stops the minute you look round after him—I mean in my thoughts, you know—just as I had been following her, all the time of my fever, through the halls of heaven, as I thought them, when they were only the small crinkle-crankle convolutions of my cerebral dome—a poor heaven for a man to live in! I have learned that worse and better than most men, as I'm going to tell you; for it was for the sake of that that I began this dismal story.—When I grew a bit better, and back on my feet—would you believe it?—the kindness of the old, warped, brown, wrinkled woman that brought me forth, me Cosmo Cupples, with the great heart and the small body, began to console me a little for the laugh of that queen of white-skinned ladies. It was but a little, you know; still it was consolation. My mother thought a heap of me. Folk think more of folk, the more they are themselves. But I know it was small honour I brought her home, with my eyes burned out with crying for the moon.—I'll tell you the rest of it when we get home. I can't bear to be here in the dark. It's the quiet books all round me that I can't stand. It was in the midst of books, in the dark, that I heard that laugh. It just blasted me and the books and everything. They always look as if they were hear-

gin they war hearin' 't. For the first time I loot the gloamin come doon upo' me i' this same leebrary, a' at ance I heard the sma' nicher o' a woman's lauch frae somewhaur in or oot o' the warl'. I grew as het's hell, and was oot at the door in a cat-loup. And as sure's death I'll hear't again, gin I bide ae minute langer. Come oot wi' ye."

There was light in Mr Fraser's drawing-room, and a shadow flitted across the blind. The frosty night, and the keenness of the stars, made Mr Cupples shiver. Alec was in a feverous glow. When they reached home, Mr Cupples went straight to the cupboard, swallowed a glass of the *merum*, put coals on the fire, drew his chair close to it, and said:

"It's dooms cauld! Sit doon there, bantam. Pit on the kettle first. It's an ac' o' the purest disinteresstitness, for deil a drap sall ye drink! But I'll sing ye a sang, by way o' upmak'."

"I never heard ye sing, Mr Cupples. Ye can do a' thing, I think."

"I cudna gar a bonnie, high-born, white-handit leddy fa' in love wi' a puir futteret o' a crater—a shargar like Cosmo Cupples, bantam. But I can do twa or three things; an' ane o' them is, I can mak' a sang; and anither is, I can mak' a tune till't; and a third is, I can sing the tane to the tither, that is whan I haena had either

ing it. For the first time I let the gloaming come down upon me in this same library, all at once I heard the small snicker of a woman's laugh from somewhere in or out of the world. I grew as hot as hell, and was out at the door in a cat-leap. And as sure as death I'll hear it again, if I stay one minute longer. Come out with you."

There was light in Mr Fraser's drawing-room, and a shadow flitted across the blind. The frosty night, and the keenness of the stars, made Mr Cupples shiver. Alec was in a feverous glow. When they reached home, Mr Cupples went straight to the cupboard, swallowed a glass of the *merum*, put coals on the fire, drew his chair close to it, and said:

"It's mighty cold! Sit down there, bantam. Put on the kettle first. It's an act of the purest disinterestedness, for devil a drop shall you drink! But I'll sing you a song, to make it up to you."

"I never heard you sing, Mr Cupples. You can do everything, I think."

"I couldn't make a bonnie, high-born, white-handed lady fall in love with a poor weasel of a thing—a scrag like Cosmo Cupples, bantam. But I can do two or three things; and one of them is, I can make a song; and another is, I can make a tune to it; and a third is, I can sing the one to the other, that is when I haven't had either

ower muckle or ower little o' the tappit hen. Noo, heark ye. This ane's a' my ain:	too much or too little of the tappit hen. Now, listen. This one's all my own:

GAEIN' AND COMIN'.

Whan Andrew frae Strathbogie gaed,
    The lift was lowerin' dreary;
The sun he wadna lift his heid;
    The win' blew laich and eerie.
In's pooch he had a plack or twa,
    I vow he hadna mony,
Yet Andrew like a linty sang,
    For Lizzie was sae bonny!

    O Lizzie, Lizzie, bonny lassie!
    Bonnie, saucy hizzy!
    What richt had ye to luik at me,
    And drive me daft and dizzy?

Whan Andrew to Strathbogie cam',
    The sun was shinin' rarely;
He rade a horse that pranced and sprang—
    I vow he sat him fairly.
And he had gowd to spend and spare,
    And a heart as true as ony;
But's luik was doon, and his sigh was sair,
    For Lizzie was sae bonny!

    O Lizzie, Lizzie, bonny hizzy!
    Ye've turned the daylicht dreary.
    Ye're straucht and rare, ye're fause and fair!—
    Hech! auld John Armstrong's deary!"

ENGLISH

When Andrew from Strathbogie went,
    The sky was lowering dreary;
The sun in the sky was almost spent;
    The wind blew low and eerie.

> In his pocket he'd a coin or two,
>   I vow he hadn't many,
> Yet Andrew like a linnet sang,
>   For Lizzie was so bonny!
>
>   O Lizzie, Lizzie, bonny lassie!
>   Bonnie, saucy missie!
>   What right had you to look at me,
>   And drive me daft and dizzy?
>
> When Andrew to Strathbogie came,
>   The sun was shining rarely;
> He rode a horse that pranced and sprang—
>   I vow he sat him fairly.
> And he had gold to spend and spare,
>   And a heart as true as any;
> But his look was down, he was full of care,
>   For Lizzie was so bonny!
>
>   O Lizzie, Lizzie, bonny missie!
>   You've turned the daylight dreary.
>   You're straight and rare, you're false and fair!—
>   Hech! old John Armstrong's deary!"

His voice was mellow, and ought to have been even. His expression was perfect.

The kettle was boiling. Mr Cupples made his toddy, and resumed his story.

"As sune's I was able, I left my mither greitin'—God bless her!—and cam to this toon, for I wasna gaein' to be eaten up with idleset as weel's wi' idolatry. The first thing I tuik till was teachin'. Noo that's a braw thing, whan the laddies and lassies want to learn, and hae questons o' their ain to speir. But whan they dinna care, it's the verra deevil. Or lang, a'thing grew

"As soon as I was able, I left my mother weeping—God bless her!—and came to this town, for I wasn't going to be eaten up with idleness as well as idolatry. The first thing I took to was teaching. Now that's a fine thing, when the lads and lassies want to learn, and have questions of their own to ask. But when they don't care, it's the very devil. Soon enough, all grew grey. I cared for naething and naebody. My verra dreams gaed frae me, or cam only to torment me, wi' the reid hert o' them changed to yallow and grey.

"Weel, ae nicht I had come hame worn oot wi' warstlin' to gar bairns eat that had no hunger. I spied upo' the table a bottle o' whusky. A frien' o' mine—a grocer he was—had sent it across the street to me, for it was hard upo' Hogmanay. I rang the bell incontinent. Up comes the lass, and says I, 'Bell, lat's hae a kettlefu' o' het water.' And to mak' a lang story short, I could never want het water sin syne. For I hadna drunken aboon a twa glaiss, afore the past began to revive as gin ye had come ower't wi' a weet sponge. A' the colours cam' oot upo' 't again, as gin they had never turned wan and grey; and I said to mysel' wi' pride: 'My leddy canna, wi' a' her breedin' and her bonnie skin, haud Cosmo Cupples frae lo'ein' her.' And I followed aboot at her again throu a' the oots and ins o' the story, and the past was restored to me.—That's hoo it appeared to me that nicht.—Was't ony wonner that the first thing I did when I cam' hame the neist nicht was to ring for the het water? I wantit naething frae Providence or Natur' but jist that the colour michtna be a' ta'en oot o' my life. The muckle deevil was in't, that I cudna stan' up to my

grey. I cared for nothing and nobody. My very dreams left me, or came only to torment me, with their red heart changed to yellow and grey.

"Well, one night I had come home worn out with striving to make children eat that had no hunger. I spied on the table a bottle of whisky. A friend of mine—a grocer he was—had sent it across the street to me, for it was nearly Hogmanay. I rang the bell incontinent. Up comes the lass, and says I, 'Bell, let's have a kettleful of hot water.' And to make a long story short, I could never go wanting hot water since. For I hadn't drunk more than two glasses, before the past began to revive as if you had wiped it with a wet sponge. All the colours came out upon it again, as if they had never turned wan and gray; and I said to myself with pride: 'My lady can't, with all her breeding and her bonnie skin, keep Cosmo Cupples from loving her.' And I followed her about again through all the outs and ins of the story, and the past was restored to me.—That's how it appeared to me that night.—Was it any wonder that the first thing I did when I came home the next night was to ring for the hot water? I wanted nothing from Providence or Nature but just that the colour might not be all taken out of my life. The great devil was in it, that I couldn't fate like a man, and, gin my life was to cast the colour, jist tak my auld cloak aboot me, and gang on content. But I cudna. I bude to see things bonnie, or my strength gaed frae me. But ye canna slink in at back doors that gait. I was pitten oot, and oot I maun bide. It wasna that lang afore I began to discover that it was a' a delusion and a snare. Whan I fell asleep, I wad dream whiles that, openin' the door into ane o' thae halls o' licht, there she was stan'in' lauchin' at me. And she micht hae gane on lauchin' to a' eternity—for onything I cared. And—ten times waur—I wad whiles come upon her greitin' and repentin', and haudin' oot her han' to me, and me carin' no more for her than for the beard o' a barley-stalk. And for makin' a sang—I jist steikit my lugs whan I heard a puir misguidit canary singin' i' the sunshine. And I begud to hear a laich lauch far awa', and it cam' nearer and nearer ilka week, till it was ringin' i' my verra lug. But a' that was naething compairateevely. I' the mids o' a quaiet contemplation, suddenly, wi' an awfu' stoon, a ghaistly doobt pat it's heid up i' my breist, and cried: 'It's a' fause. The grey luik o' life's the true ane, and the only aspec' ye hae a richt to see.' And efter that, a' the whusky in Glenlivat cudna console me.—Luik at me noo. Ye see what I am. I can whiles sing

stand up to my fate like a man, and, if my life was to lose its colour, just take my old cloak about me, and go on content. But I couldn't. I had to see things bonnie, or my strength went from me. But you can't slink in at back doors that way. I was put out, and out I must stay. It wasn't that long before I began to discover that it was all a delusion and a snare. When I fell asleep, I would dream sometimes that, opening the door into one of those halls of light, there she was standing laughing at me. And she might have gone on laughing to all eternity—for anything I cared. And—ten times worse—I would sometimes come upon her weeping and repenting, and holding out her hand to me, and me caring no more for her than for the beard of a barley-stalk. And for making a song—I just stopped my ears when I heard a poor neglected canary singing in the sunshine. And I began to hear a low laugh far away, and it came nearer and nearer every week, till it was ringing in my very ear. But all that was nothing comparatively. In the midst of a quiet contemplation, suddenly, with an awful stound, a ghostly doubt popped up in my breast, and cried: 'It's all false. The gray look of life's the true one, and the only aspect you have a right to see.' And after that, all the whisky in Glenlivat couldn't console me.—Look at me now. You see what I am.

an auld sang—but mak' a new ane!—Lord, man! I can hardly believe 'at ever I made a sang i' my life. Luik at my han' hoo it trimles. Luik at my hert. It's brunt oot. There's no a leevin' crater but yersel' that I hae ony regaird for, sin my auld mither deid. Gin it warna for buiks, I wad amaist cut my throat. And the senawtus disna think me bye and aboon half a proper companion for buiks even; as gin Cupples micht corrup' Milton himsel, although he was ten feet ower his heid bottled in a buik. And whan I saw ye poor oot the whusky in that mad-like mainner, as gin 't had been some sma' tipple o' penny ale, it jist drave me mad wi' anger."

"Weel, Mr Cupples," Alec ventured to say, "what for dinna ye sen' the bottle to the devil?"

"What, my ain auld tappit hen!" exclaimed Mr Cupples, with a sudden reaction from the seriousness of his late mood; "Na, na, she shanna gang to the deil till we gang thegither. Eh! but we'll baith hae dry insides or we win frae him again, I doobt. That drouth's an awfu' thing to contemplate. But speyk o' giein' ower the drink! The verra attemp'—an' dinna ye think that I haena made it—aich! What for sud I gang to hell afore my time? The deils themselves compleen o' that. Na, na. Ance ye hae learned to drink, ye *canna* do

I can sometimes sing an old song—but make a new one!—Lord, man! I can hardly believe that ever I made a song in my life. Look at my hand how it trembles. Look at my heart. It's burnt out. There's not a living creature but yourself that I have any regard for, since my old mother died. If it weren't for books, I would almost cut my throat. And the senatus doesn't think me more than half a fit companion for books even; as if Cupples might corrupt Milton himself, although he was ten feet over his head bottled in a book. And when I saw you pour out the whisky in that mad-like manner, as if it had been some small tipple of penny ale, it just drove me mad with anger."

"Well, Mr Cupples," Alec ventured to say, "why don't you send the bottle to the devil?"

"What, my own old tappit hen!" exclaimed Mr Cupples, with a sudden reaction from the seriousness of his late mood; "Na, na, she shan't go to the devil till we go together. Eh! but we'll both have dry insides by the time we're free of him, I expect. That thirst's an awful thing to contemplate. But speak of giving up the drink! The very attempt—and don't you think that I haven't made it—aich! Why should I go to hell before my time? The devils themselves complain of that. Na, na. Once you have learned to drink, you *can't* do wantin' 't. Man, dinna touch 't. For God's sake, for yer mither's sake, for *ony* sake, dinna lat a drap o' the hell-broth gang ower yer thrapple—or ye're damned like me for ever and ever. It's as guid's signin' awa' yer sowl wi' yer ain han' and yer ain blude."

Mr Cupples lifted his glass, emptied it, and, setting it down on the table with a gesture of hatred, proceeded to fill it yet again.

without it. Man, don't touch it. For God's sake, for your mother's sake, for *any* sake, don't let a drop of the hell-broth down your throat—or you're damned like me for ever and ever. It's as good as signing away your soul with your own hand and your own blood."

Mr Cupples lifted his glass, emptied it, and, setting it down on the table with a gesture of hatred, proceeded to fill it yet again.

CHAPTER LXXI

"I say, Forbes, you keep yourself all to yourself and old Cupples, away there in the new town. Come and take some supper with me to-night. It's my birthday, old boy."

"I don't do much in that way, you know, Gibby."

"Oh yes, I know. You're never jolly but amongst the shell-fish. At least that's what the Venall thinks of you. But for once in a way you might come."

"Well, I don't mind," said Alec, really not caring what came to him or of him, and glad of anything to occupy him with no-thinking. "When shall I come?"

"At seven. We'll have a night of it. To-morrow's Saturday."

It was hardly worth while to go home. He would not dine to-day. He would go and renew his grief by the ever-grieving sea. For his was a young love, and his sorrow was interesting to him: he embalmed his pangs in the amber of his consciousness. So he crossed the links to the desolate sandy shore; there let the sound of the waves enter the portals of his brain and fill all its hollow caves with their moaning; and then wandering back to the old city, stood at length over the keystone of the bridge, and looked down into the dark water below the Gothic arch.

He heard a footstep behind him on the bridge. Looking round he saw Beauchamp. Without reason or object, he walked up to him and barred his way. Beauchamp started, and drew back.

"Beauchamp," said Alec, "you are my devil."

"Granted," said Beauchamp, coolly, but on his guard.

"What are you about with my cousin?"

"What is that to you?"

"She is my cousin."

"I don't care. She's not mine."

"If you play her false, as you have played me—by heavens!—"

"Oh! I'll be very kind to her. You needn't be afraid. I only wanted to take down your damned impudence. You may go to her when you like."

Alec's answer was a blow, which Beauchamp was prepared for and avoided. Alec pursued the attack with a burning desire to give him the punishment he deserved. But he turned suddenly sick, and, although he afterwards recalled a wrestle, knee to knee, the first thing he was aware of was the cold waters of the river closing over him. The shock restored him. When he rose to the surface he swam down the stream, for the banks were precipitous in the neighbourhood of the bridge. At length he succeeded in landing, and set out for home. He had not gone far, however, before he grew very faint, and had to sit down on a doorstep. Then he discovered that his arm was bleeding, and knew that Beauchamp had stabbed him. He contrived to tie it up after a fashion, and reached home without much more difficulty. Mr Cupples had not come in. So he got his landlady to tie up his arm for him, and then changed his clothes. Fortunately the wound, although long and deep, ran lengthways between the shoulder and elbow, on the outside of the arm, and so was not of a serious character. After he was dressed, feeling quite well, he set off to keep his engagement with Gilbert Gordon.

Now how could such a thing have taken place in the third decade of the nineteenth century?—The parapet was low and the struggle was fierce. I do not think that Beauchamp intended murder, for the consequences of murder must be a serious consideration to every gentleman. He came of a wild race, with whom a word and a steel blow had been linked for ages. And habits transmitted become instincts. He was of a cold temperament, and such a nature, once roused, is often less under control than one used to excitement: a saint will sometimes break through the bonds of the very virtue which has gained him all his repute. If we combine these considerations with the known hatred of Beauchamp, the story Alec told Cupples the next day may become in itself credible. Whether Beauchamp tried to throw him from the bridge may remain doubtful, for when the bodies of two men are locked in the wrestle of hate, their own souls do not know what they intend. Beauchamp must have sped home with the conscience of a murderer; and yet when Alec made his appearance in the class, most probably a revival of hatred was his first mental experience. But I have had no opportunity of studying the morbid anatomy of Beauchamp, and I do not care about him, save as he influences the current of this history. When he vanishes, I shall be glad to forget him.

Soon after Alec had left the house, Cupples came home with a hurried inquiry whether the landlady had seen anything of him. She told him as much as she knew, whereupon he went up-stairs to his Æschylus, &c.

Alec said nothing about his adventure to any of his friends, for, like other Scotchmen young and old, he liked to keep things in his own hands till he knew what to do with them. At first, notwithstanding his loss of blood, he felt better than he had felt for some time; but in the course of the evening he grew so tired, and his brain grew so muddy and brown, that he was glad when he heard the order given for the boiling water. He had before now, although Mr Cupples had never become aware of the fact, partaken of the usual source of Scotch exhilaration, and had felt nothing the worse; and now heedless of Mr Cupples's elaborate warning—how could he be expected to mind it?—he mixed himself a tumbler eagerly. But although the earth brightened up under its influences, and a wider horizon opened about him than he had enjoyed for months before, yet half-frightened at the power of the beverage over his weakened frame, he had conscience enough to refuse a second tumbler, and rose early and went home.

The moment he entered the garret, Mr Cupples, who had already consumed his nightly portion, saw that he had been drinking. He looked at him with blue eyes, wide-opened, dismay and toddy combining to render them of uncertain vision.

"Eh, bantam! bantam!" he said, and sank back in his chair; "ye hae been at it in spite o' me."

And Mr Cupples burst into silent tears—no unusual phenomenon in men under the combined influences of emotion and drink. Notwithstanding his own elevated condition, Alec was shocked.

"Mr Cupples," he said, "I want to tell you all about it."

Mr Cupples took no notice. Alec began his story notwithstanding, and as he went on, his friend became attentive, inserting here and there an expletive to the disadvantage of Beauchamp, whose behaviour with regard to Kate he now learned for the first time. When Alec had finished, Cupples said solemnly:

"I warned ye against him, Alec. But a waur enemy nor Beau-

Beauchamp has got a firmer hold of you, I think. Do what he liked, Beauchamp's dirk (dagger) couldn't hurt you as much as your own hand, when you lifted the first glass to your own mouth tonight. You have despised all my warnings. And sorrow and shame will come of it. And I'll have to bear all the blame of it. Your mother'll just hate me like the very black toad that no woman can stand. Go away to your bed. I can't stand the sight of you."

Alec went to bed, rebuked and distressed. But not having taken enough to hurt him much, he was unfortunately able, the next morning, to regard Mr Cupples's lecture from a ludicrous point of view. And what danger was he in more than the rest of the fellows, few of whom would refuse a tumbler of toddy, and fewer of whom were likely to get drunk?—Had not Alec been unhappy, he would have been in less danger than most of them; but he was unhappy.

And although the whisky had done him no great immediate injury, yet its reaction, combined with the loss of blood, made him restless all that day. So that, when the afternoon came, instead of going to Mr Cupples in the library, he joined some of the same set he had been with the evening before. And when he came home, instead of going up-stairs to Mr Cupples, he went straight to bed.

The next morning, while he was at breakfast, Mr Cupples made his appearance in his room.

"What became of you last night, bantam?" he asked kindly, but with evident uneasiness.

"I came home pretty tired, and went straight to my bed."

"But you weren't home very early."

"I wasn't that late."

"You have been drinking again. I know by the look of your eyes."

Alec had a very even temper.

But a headache and a sore conscience together were enough to upset it. To be out of temper with oneself is to be out of temper with the universe.

"Did my mother commission you to look after me, Mr Cupples?" he asked, and could have dashed his head against the wall the next moment. But the look of pitying and yet deprecating concern in Mr Cupples's face fixed him so that he could say nothing.

Mr Cupples turned and walked slowly away, with only the words:

"Eh! bantam! bantam! The Lord hae pity upo' ye—and me too!"

He went out at the door bowed like an old man.

"Preserve's, Mr Cupples! What ails ye?" exclaimed his landlady meeting him in the passage.

"The whusky's disagreed wi' me," he said. "It's verra ill-faured o' 't. I'm sure I pay't ilka proper attention."

Then he went down the stairs, murmuring—

"Rainbows! Rainbows! Naething for me but rainbows! God help the laddie!"

CHAPTER LXXII

It may appear strange to some of my renders that Alec should fall into this pit immediately upon the solemn warning of his friend. He had listened to the story alone; he had never felt the warning: he had never felt the danger. Had he not himself in his own hands? He was not fond of whisky. He could take it or leave it. And so he took it; and finding that there was some comfort in it, took it again and again, seeking the society in which it was the vivifying element.—Need I depict the fine gradations by which he sank—gradations though fine yet so numerous that, in a space of time almost too brief for credit, the bleared eye, the soiled garments, and the disordered hair, would reveal how the night had been spent, and the clear-browed boy looked a sullen, troubled, dissatisfied youth? The vice had laid hold of him like a fast-wreathing, many-folded serpent. He had never had any conscious religion. His life had never looked up to its source. All that was good in him was good of itself, not of him. So it was easy to go down, with grief staring at him over the edge of the pit. All return to the unific rectitude of a manly life must be in the face of a scorching past and a dank future—and those he could not face.

And as his life thus ebbed away from him, his feelings towards Beauchamp grew more and more bitter, approximating in character to those of Beauchamp towards him. And he soon became resolved to have his revenge on him, though it was long before he could make up his mind as to what the revenge should be.

Beauchamp avoided him constantly.

And Mr Cupples was haunting him unseen. The strong-minded, wise-headed, weak-willed little poet, wrapped in a coat of darkness, dogged the footsteps of a great handsome, good-natured, ordinary-gifted wretch, who *could* never make him any return but affection, and had now withdrawn all interchange of common friendship in order that he might go the downward road unchecked. Cupples was driven almost distracted. He drank harder than ever, but with less satisfaction than ever, for he only grew the more miserable. He thought of writing to Alec's mother, but, with the indecision of a drunkard, he could not make up his mind, and pondered over every side of the question, till he was lost in a maze of incapacity.

Bad went to worse. Vice grew upon vice.

There are facts in human life which human artists cannot touch. The great Artist can weave them into the grand whole of his Picture, but to the human eye they look too ugly and too painful. Even the man who can do the deeds dares not represent them. Mothers have to know such facts of their sons, and such facts of women like themselves.

Alec had fallen amongst a set of men who would not be satisfied till he should be as low as they—till there should be nothing left in him to remind them that they had once been better. The circle in which he began to drink had gradually contracted about him. The better sort had fallen away, and the worse had remained—chiefly older men than he, men who had come near to the enjoyment of vileness for its own sake, if that be possible, and who certainly enjoyed making others like themselves. Encouraged by their laughter and approbation, Alec began to emulate them, and would soon have had very little to learn if things had not *taken a turn*. A great hand is sometimes laid even on the fly-wheel of life's engine.

CHAPTER LXXIII

Andrew Constable, with his wife and old-fashioned child Isie, was seated at tea in the little parlour opening from the shop, when he was called out by a customer. He remained longer than was likely to be accounted for by the transaction of business at that time of the day. And when he returned his honest face looked troubled.

"Who was that?" asked his wife.

"Oh! it was nobody but James Johnston, wanting a bit of flannel for his wife's petticoat."

"And what had he to say that kept you till your tea's not fit to drink?"

"Oh! my tea'll do well enough. It's not especially cold."

"But what said he?"

"Well! hm! hm!—He said it was fine frosty weather."

"Ay, no doubt! He knew that by the way the shuttle flew. Was that all?"

"Na, not quite. But cogues (*wooden milking vessels*) have ears, and bairns have big eyes."

For Isie sat on her stool staring at her father and mother alternately, and watching for the result of her mother's attempt at picking the lock of her father's reticence. But the moment she heard the word *ears*, she knew that she had no chance, and her eyes grew less and their pupils grew larger. Fearing he had hurt her, Andrew said,

"Won't you have a spot of jam, Isie? It's gooseberry-jam."

"Na, thank you, daddy. Maybe it would give me a sore tummy," answered the solemn old-faced Scotchwoman of seven.

A child who refuses jam lest it should serve her as the little book did the Apostle John, might be considered prudent enough to be intrusted with a secret. But not a word more was said on the subject, till Isie was in bed, and supposed to be fast asleep, in a little room that opened off the parlour. But she was not asleep. And the door was always left open, that she might fall asleep in the presence of her parents. Their words therefore flowed freely into her ears, although the meaning only played on her mind with a dull glimmer like that which played on her wall from the fire in the room where they sat talking.

"Ay, woman," began Andrew, "it'll be sore news, this, to the lady over the water."

"You don't mean Mistress Forbes, Andrew?"

"That's just who I do mean."

"Is it her son? Has he met with any mischief? What's happened to him? Is he drowned, or killed? The Lord preserve us! She'll die of it."

"Na, lass. It's much worse than all that."

The woodcuts in *Fox's Book of Martyrs*, of which three folio volumes in black letter lay in the room whence the conversation flowed to Isie's ears, rose in all their hideousuess before the mental vision of the child. In no other way than as torture could she conceive of worse than being killed.

"You give me chills," said Mrs Constable, with a shudder.

"Ay, woman, you know little of the wickedness of great towns—how they lie in wait at every corner, with their gins and their snares and their pits that they dig to catch the unwary youth," said Andrew, in something of the pride of superior knowledge.

"Andrew, don't you try to speak like a chapter of the Proverbs of Solomon, the son of David. Say straight out that those wicked jades that hang about in the gloaming have got a grip of the bonnie lad. Eh! but he'll fare ill; and the Lord have mercy upon him—and none upon them!"

"Tut! tut! lass; don't speak with such a venom. You know who says *Vengeance is mine?*"

"Ay, ay, well enough. And I hope He'll take His own upon such brazen hussies. You men-folk think you know a lot of things that you would keep us from knowing. But none know the wiles of a woman, least of all them that fall into them, but another woman."

"It's no saving lore," said Andrew, a little troubled that his wife should assert a familiar acquaintance with such things. But she went on.

"Women are just dreadful. When once they go the bad road, they're neither to hold nor bind. And to think of them laying hands upon such a bonnie well-behaved laddie as that Alec Forbes, a civil, hearty lad, with a kind word and a joke even for the beggar that he gave a penny to! Well, he'll come out of their clutches, maybe not that much the worse after all, as many a man from King David downwards before him."

"Now, woman!" said Andrew, in a tone of authority blended with rising indignation; "you're sliding off your own stool, and you'll be on the ground before you reach mine. Right or wrong about the women, I must know more about the men than you do; and I dare affirm and uphold that never man came out of the grip of those poor deluded creatures—"

Mrs Constable interposed with one single emphatic epithet, not admittable to the ears of this generation; but Andrew resumed, and went on.

"—poor deluded creatures, without losing a great part of what was left in him of the image of God after the fall. Woman, he loses a heap!"

"How should you know anything about that, Andrew?" returned his wife sharply.

"The same way that you know so well about the she side of the question, lass. We may just enlighten one another a bit about some things, perhaps."

Meantime the ears of the little pitcher in bed had been growing longer and longer with curious horror. The something in itself awfully vague about Alec's fate was wrapt in yet deeper clouds of terror and mystery by the discord of opinion with regard to it on the part of her father and mother, whom she had rarely heard differ. She pictured to herself the image of his Maker being scratched off Alec by the claws of furies; and hot pincers tearing nail after nail from the hand which had once given her a penny. And her astonishment was therefore paralyzing when she heard her father say:

"But you must keep a quiet tongue in your head, goodwife; for well as you like the laddie, you may blast his character if you say a word about it."

"I bet it's been all over Glamerton before it came to your ears, Andrew," returned her mother. "They're not that sharp after such news. But I'd dearly like to know who sent home the word of it."

"I'm thinking it's been young Bruce."

"The Lord be praised for a lie!" exclaimed Mrs Constable. "Haven't I told you before now, so that it's no invention to pick the lock of the occasion, Andrew, that Rob Bruce has a spite at that family for taking so much notice of Annie Anderson. And I wouldn't wonder if he had set his heart upon having her marry his own Rob, and so keeping her money in the family. If that be so, he might weel gie Alec Forbes a back-handit cloot."

"'Deed! maybe, gudewife. He's a burnin' and a shinin' licht amo' you missioners, though; and ye maunna say ill o' 'm, for fear he has ye up afore the kirk."

"Ay, deed is he! He's a burnin' shame, and a stinkin' lamp; for the grace o' God wasna hauden to the nib o' 'm lang eneuch to set him in a low, but only lang eneuch to gar the ile o' 'm reek fit to scomfish a haill Sodom."

"Hoot, lass! Ye're ower sair even upo' him. But it's verra true that gin the story cam' frae that en' o' the toon, there's room for rizzonable doobts. Sae we'll awa' to our beds, and houp things mayna be sae far gane as the soun' o' them. Only I drede there's aye some water whaur the stirkie droons."

"well give Alec Forbes a back-handed blow."

"Indeed! maybe, goodwife. He's a burning and a shining light among you missionars, though; and you mustn't say ill of him, for fear he has you up before the church."

"Ay, so he is! He's a burning shame, and a stinking lamp; for the grace of God wasn't held to his nose long enough to set him in a flame, but only long enough to make his oil smell so it would choke a whole Sodom."

"Heavens, lass! You're too hard even upon him. But it's very true that if the story came from that end of the town, there's room for reasonable doubts. So we'll go to bed, and hope things mightn't be so far gone as the sound of them. Only I fear there's always some water where the bullock drowns."

It was long before little Isie got to sleep, what with attempting to realize the actual condition of Alec Forbes, and trying to excogitate the best means for his deliverance. Why should not all Glamerton set out in a body with flails and pitchforks? And if she must not meddle for that, seeing her father had said the matter must not be mentioned, yet his prohibition could not include Alec's mother, whom it would be wicked to keep in ignorance. For what would Isie think if she was taken prisoner by a cruel woman and they would not tell her mother? So she fell asleep, to wake in the morning with the sense of a mission upon her important little mind.

What rendered it probable that the rumour came from "that end of the town" was, that Bruce the younger was this year a bejan at Alec's college, and besides was the only other scion of Glamerton there grafted, so that any news about Alec other than he would care to send himself, must in all likelihood have come through him.—For Bruce the elder had determined that in his son he would restore the fallen fortunes of the family, giving him such an education as would entitle him to hold up his head with the best, and especially with that proud upstart, Alec Forbes.

The news had reached Thomas Crann, and filled him with concern. He had, as was his custom in trouble, betaken himself straightway to "the throne of grace," and "wrestled in prayer" with God that he would restore the prodigal to his mother. What would Thomas have thought if he had been told that his anxiety, genuine as it was, that his love, true as it was, did not come near the love and anxiety of another man who spent his evenings in drinking whisky and reading heathen poets, and who, although he knew not a little of his Bible, never opened it from one end of the year to the other? If he had been told that Cosmo Cupples had more than once, after the first tumbler of toddy and before the second, betaken himself to his prayers for his poor Alec Forbes, and entreated God Almighty to do for him what he could not do, though he would die for him—to rescue him from the fearful pit and the miry clay of moral pollution—if he had heard this, he would have said that it was a sad pity, but such prayers could not be answered, seeing he that prayed was himself in the gall of bitterness and the bond of iniquity.

There was much shaking of the head amongst the old women. Many an ejaculation and many a meditative *eh me!* were uttered over Alec's fall; and many a word of tender pity for his poor mother floated forth on the frosty air of Glamerton; but no one ventured to go and tell the dreary tidings. The men left it to the women; and the women knew too well how the bearer of such ill news would appear in her eyes, to venture upon the ungracious task. So they said to themselves she must know it just as well as they did; or if she did not know, poor woman! she would know time enough for all the good it would do her. And that came of sending sons to colleges! &c., &c.

But there was just one not so easily satisfied about the extent of her duties: that was little Isie Constable.

CHAPTER LXXIV

The tertians gave a supper at Luckie Cumstie's, and invited the magistrands. On such an occasion Beauchamp, with his high sense of his own social qualities, would not willingly be absent. When the hour arrived, he took his place near the head of the table.

After all the solid and a part of the liquid entertainment was over, Alec rose in the space between two toasts, and said:

"Mr Chairman and gentlemen, I propose, at my own proper cost, to provide something for your amusement."

Beauchamp and all stared at the speaker.

"It is to be regretted," Alec went on, "that students have no court of honour to which to appeal. This is the first opportunity I have had of throwing myself on the generosity of my equals, and asking them to listen to my story."

The interest of the company was already roused. All the heads about the long table leaned towards the speaker, and cries of *hear, hear*, arose in all directions. Alec then gave a brief statement of the facts of the encounter upon the bridge. This was the only part of his relations with Beauchamp which he chose to bring before the public; for the greater wrong of lying defamation involved his cousin's name. He told how Beauchamp had sought the encounter by deliberate insult, had used a weapon against an unarmed enemy, and then thrown him from the bridge.

"Now," he concluded, "all I ask of you, gentlemen, is to allow me the fair arena of your presence while I give this sneaking chieftain the personal chastisement which he has so richly merited at my hands."

Beauchamp had soon recovered his self-possession after the first surprise of the attack. He sat drinking his toddy all the time Alec spoke, and in the middle of his speech he mixed himself another tumbler. When Alec sat down, he rose, glanced round the assembly, bent his lip into its most scornful curves, and, in a clear, unwavering voice, said:

"Mr Chairman and gentlemen, I repel the accusation."

Alec started to his feet in wrath.

"Mr Forbes, sit down," bawled the chairman; and Alec obeyed, though with evident reluctance.

"I say the accusation is false," repeated Beauchamp. "I do not say that Mr Forbes consciously invented the calumny in order to take away my character: such an assertion would preclude its own credence. Nor do I venture to affirm that he never was stabbed, or thrown into the river. But I ask any gentleman who happens to be aware of Mr Forbes's devotions at the shrine of Father Lyaeus, which is the more likely—that a fellow-student should stab and throw him into the water, or that, as he was reeling home at midnight, the treacherous divinity of the bowl should have handed him over to the embrace of his brother deity of the river. Why then should even his imagination fix upon me as the source of the injury? Gentlemen, a foolish attachment to the customs of a long line of ancestors has led me into what I find for the first time to be a dangerous habit—that of wearing arms;—dangerous, I mean, to myself; for now I am wounded with my own weapon. But the real secret of the affair is—I am ashamed to say—jealousy. Mr Forbes knows what I say to be true—that a lady whom he loves prefers me to him."

"Don't bring her name in, you brute!" roared Alec, starting again to his feet, "or I'll tear your tongue out."

"You hear, gentlemen," said Beauchamp, and sat down.

A murmur arose. Heads gathered into groups. No one stood up. Alec felt with the deepest mortification that his adversary's coolness and his own violence had turned the scale against him. This conviction, conjoined with the embarrassment of not knowing how to say a word in his own defence without taking some notice of the close of his adversary's speech, fixed him to his seat. For he had not yet fallen so low as to be capable of even alluding to the woman he loved in such an assembly. He would rather abandon the field to his adversary.

Probably not many seconds had passed, but his situation was becoming intolerable, when a well-known voice rose clear above the confused murmur; and glancing to the lower end of the room, he saw Cosmo Cupples standing at the end of the table.

"I ken weel eneuch, gentlemen," he said, "that I hae no richt to be here. Ye a' ken me by the sicht o' the een. I'm a graduate o' this university, and at present your humble servant the librarian. I intrude for the sake o' justice, and I cast mysel' upo' your clemency for a fair hearin'."

"I know well enough, gentlemen," he said, "that I have no right to be here. You all know me by the sight of the eyes. I'm a graduate of this university, and at present your humble servant the librarian. I intrude for the sake of justice, and I cast myself upon your clemency for a fair hearing."

This being accorded by general acclamation,

"Gentlemen," he resumed, "I stan' afore ye wi' a sair hert. I hae occupied the position o' tutor to Mr Forbes; for, as Sir Pheelip Sidney says in a letter to his brither Rob, wha was efterwards Yerl o' Leicester upo' the demise o' Robert Dudley, 'Ye may get wiser men nor yersel' to converse wi' ye and instruck ye, in ane o' twa ways—by muckle ootlay or muckle humility.' Noo, that laddie was ane o' the finest naturs I ever cam' across, and his humility jist made it a pleesur to tak' chairge o' 'm baith mentally and morally. That I had a sair doon come whan he took to the drink, I am forced to confess. But I aye thocht he was strauchtforet, notwithstandin' the whusky. I wasna prepared for sic a doonfa' as this.—I maun jist confess, Mr Cheerman, that I heard him throu' the crack o' the door-cheek. And he broucht sic deevilich accusations—"

"Mr Cupples!" cried Alec.

"Haud yer tongue, Alec Forbes, and lat this company hear me. Ye appealed to the company yersel' first o' a'.—I say hoo cud he bring sic deevilich accusations against a gentleman o' sic birth and breedin' and accomplishments as the Laird o' Chattachan!—Maybe the Laird wad jist condescend to say

This being accorded by general acclamation,

"Gentlemen," he resumed, "I stand before you with a sore heart. I have occupied the position of tutor to Mr Forbes; for, as Sir Philip Sidney says in a letter to his brother Rob, who was afterwards Earl of Leicester upon the demise of Robert Dudley, 'You may get wiser men than yourself to converse with you and instruct you, in one of two ways—by much outlay or much humility.' Now, that laddie was one of the finest natures I ever came across, and his humility just made it a pleasure to take charge of him both mentally and morally. That I had a great blow when he took to the drink, I am forced to confess. But I always thought he was honest, despite the whisky. I wasn't prepared for such a downfall as this.—I must just confess, Mr Chairman, that I heard him through the crack of the door-cheek. And he brought such devilish accusations—"

"Mr Cupples!" cried Alec.

"Hold your tongue, Alec Forbes, and let this company hear me. You appealed to the company yourself first of all. —I say how could he bring such devilish accusations against a gentleman of such birth and breeding and accomplishments as the Laird of Chattachan!— Maybe the Laird would just condescend to say where he was upon the night in question; for if we could get the rampaging misguided laddie once fairly into the yard, with the gates shut, he would see that lying wouldn't serve his turn."

Alec was in chaotic confusion. Notwithstanding the hard words Mr Cupples had used, he could ill believe that he had turned his enemy. He had behaved very badly to Mr Cupples, but was Mr Cupples one to revenge himself?

Mr Cupples had paused with his eyes resting on Beauchamp. He, without rising, replied carelessly:

"Really, sir, I do not keep a register of my goings and comings. I might have done so had I known its importance. I have not even been informed when the occurrence is said to have taken place."

"I can prod your memory upon the dates, sir. For I know well the night when Alec Forbes came home with a long and a deep cut upon the outside of his left arm between the shoulder and the elbow. I may well remember it to my grief; for though he came home as sober as he was dripping wet—I have our goodwife's testimony to that—he went out again, and when he came home once more, he was the worse for drink for the first time since ever I knew him. Now, sir, it all took the same day that ye cam' to the leebrary, and tuik awa' wi' ye a novell ca'd *Aiken Drum*. I tauld ye it wad ill repay ye, for it was but a fule thing. And I remember 't the better that I was expeckin' Alec Forbes in ilka minute, and I was feared for a collieshangie atween ye."

"I remember all about that night perfectly, now you call it to my recollection. I went straight home, and did not go out again—I was so taken up with *Aiken Drum*."

"I tell't ye sae!" cried Cupples, triumphantly. "Wha wadna tak' the word o' The MacChattachan? There's sma' profit in addin' my testimony to the weight o' that; but I wad jist like to tell this company, Mr Cheerman and gentlemen, hoo I cam' to ken mair aboot the affair nor my frien' Alec Forbes is awar' o'. That same efternoon, I expeckit him i' the leebrary as I hae said, and whan he didna come, I took my hat—that was about a half-hoor efter the laird left me—and gaed oot to luik for him. I gaed ower the links; for my man had the profitless habit at that time, whilk he's gien up for a mair profitless still, o' stravaguin' aboot upo' the seashore, wi' 's han's in 's pooches, and his chin reposin' upo' the third button o' 's waistcoat—all which bears hard upo' what the laird says

place the same day that you came to the library, and borrowed a novel called *Aiken Drum*. I told you it would ill repay you, for it was but a foolish thing. And I remember it the better that I was expecting Alec Forbes in every minute, and I feared an outbreak between you."

"I remember all about that night perfectly, now you call it to my recollection. I went straight home, and did not go out again—I was so taken up with *Aiken Drum*."

"I told you so!" cried Cupples, triumphantly. "Who wouldn't take the word of The MacChattachan? There's small profit in adding my testimony to the weight of that; but I would just like to tell this company, Mr Chairman and gentlemen, how I came to know more about the affair than my friend Alec Forbes is aware of. That same afternoon, I expected him in the library as I've said, and when he didn't come, I took my hat—that was about a half-hour after the laird left me—and went out to look for him. I went over the links; for my man had the profitless habit at that time, which he's given up for a more profitless still, of roaming about the seashore, with his hands in his pockets, and his chin resting on the third button of his waistcoat—all which bears hard upon what the laird says about

aboot's jealousy. The mune was jist risin' by the time I wan to the shore, but I saw no sign o' man or woman alang that dreary coast. I was jist turnin' to come hame again, whan I cam' upo' tracks i' the weet san'. And I kent the prent o' the fit, and I followed it on to the links again, and sae I gaed back at my leisure. And it was sic a bonny nicht, though the mune wasna that far up, drivin' lang shaidows afore her, that I thocht I wad jist gang ance ower the brig and back again, and syne maybe turn into Luckie Cumstie's here. But afore I wan to the brig, whan I was i' the shaidow o' Baillie Bapp's hoose, I heard sic a scushlin' and a shochlin' upo' the brig! and I saw something gang reelin' aboot; and afore I cud gaither my wits and rin foret, I heard an awfu' splash i' the water; and by gangs somebody wi' lang quaiet strides, and never saw me. He had on the kilts and the lave o' the fandangles. And he turned into the quadrangle, and throu't he gaed and oot at the corner o' 't. I was close ahint him—that is, I was into the quadrangle afore he was oot o' 't. And I saw the sacrist come oot at the door o' the astronomical tooer jist afore the Hielanman turned the neuk o' 't. And I said to Thomson, says I, 'Wha was that gaed by ye, and oot the back gait?' And says he,

his jealousy. The moon was just rising by the time I reached the shore, but I saw no sign of man or woman along that dreary coast. I was just turning to come home again, when I came upon tracks in the wet sand. And I knew the print of the foot, and I followed it on to the links again, and so I went back at my leisure. And it was such a bonny night, though the moon wasn't that far up, driving long shadows before her, that I thought I would just go once over the bridge and back again, and then maybe turn into Luckie Cumstie's here. But before I reached the bridge, when I was in the shadow of Ballie Bapp's house, I heard such a shuffling and a shambling upon the bridge! and I saw something go reeling about; and before I could gather my wits and run forward, I heard an awful splash in the water; and by goes somebody with long quiet strides, and never saw me. He had on the kilts and the rest of the fandangles. And he turned into the quadrangle, and through it he went and out at the corner of it. I was close behind him—that is, I was into the quadrangle before he was out of it. And I saw the sacrist come out at the door of the astronomical tower just before the Highlandman turned the corner of it. And I said to Thomson, says I, 'Who was that went by you, and out the back way?' And says he, 'It was Mister Beauchamp.' "Are you sure of that?' says I. 'As sure as death,' says he. You know William's phrase, gentlemen."

Beauchamp's nonchalance had disappeared for some time. When his own name came out, his cheeks grew deathly pale, and thin from the falling of his jaw. Cupples, watching him, went on.

"As soon as I was sure of my man, I saw what a damned idiot I was to run after him. And back I flew to the bridge. I knew full well who the other man had to be. It could be none but my own Alec Forbes; for I swear to you, gentlemen, I have watched The Mac-Chattachan watching Alec Forbes more than two or three times since Alec thrashed him for being foul-mouthed in the face of the dead."

By this time Beauchamp, having swallowed the rest of his tumbler at a gulp, had recovered a little. He rose with defiance on his face.

"Don't let him go, gentlemen," cried Cupples, "till I tell you one other God's truth. —I ran back to the bridge, as hard as my legs could carry me, consoling myself with the reflection that if Alec hadn't been badly hurt in the scuffle, there was no fear of him. For I heard him fall clean into the water, and I knew you might as soon drown a herring as Alec Forbes. I ran right to the middle of the bridge and there was his black head bobbing away down the water in the heart of the moonlight. I'm terribly long-sighted, gentlemen. I can't swear that I saw his face, seeing the back of his head was to me; but that it was Alec Forbes, I have no more doubt than of my own existence. I was just turning, almost in tears, for I loved the laddie well, when I saw something glinting bonnie upon the parapet of the bridge. And now I beg to restore it to its rightful owner. Would you pass it up the table, gentlemen. Some of you will recognise it as one of the laird's bonnie cairngorm-buttons."

Handing the button to the man nearest him, Mr Cupples withdrew into a corner, and leaned his back against the wall. The button made many a zigzag from side to side of the table, but Beauchamp saw the yellow gleam of it coming nearer and nearer. It seemed to fascinate him. At last bursting the bonds of dismay, the blood rushed into his pale face, and he again moved to go:

"A conspiracy, gentlemen!" he cried. "You are all against me. I will not trouble you longer with my presence. I will bide my time."

"Stop a moment, Mr Beauchamp," said the chairman—the pale-faced son of a burly ploughman—rising. "Your departure will scarcely satisfy us now. Gentlemen, form yourselves in a double row, and grace the exit of a disgrace. I leave it to yourselves to kick him or not as you may think proper. But I think myself the way is to be merciful to the confounded. Better leave him to his own conscience."

Beauchamp's hand, following its foolish habit, fell upon the hilt of his dirk.

"Draw that dirk one inch," said the chairman hastily, clenching his fist, "and I'll have you thrown on Luckie Cumstie's midden."

Beauchamp's hand dropped. The men formed as directed.

"Now," said the chairman sternly.

And Beauchamp without a word marched down the long avenue white as a ghost, and looking at nobody. Each made him a low bow as he passed, except the wag of the tertians, who turned his back on him and bowed to the universe in general. Mr Cupples was next the door, and bowed him out. Alec alone stood erect. He could not insult him.

Beauchamp's feelings I do not care to analyze. As he passes from that room, he passes from my history.—I do not think a man with such an unfavourable start, could arrive at the goal of repentance in this life.

"Mr Cupples," cried the chairman, "will you oblige us by spending the rest of the evening with us?"

"You do me mair honour nor I deserve, sir," replied Mr Cupples; "but that villain Alec Forbes has cost me sae muckle in drink to haud my hert up, that I winna drink in his company. I micht tak' ower muckle and disgrace mysel' forbye. Good nicht to ye a', gentlemen, and my best thanks."

So saying, Mr Cupples left the room before Alec could get near him with a word or a sign of gratitude. But sorry and ashamed as he was, his spirits soon returned. Congratulation restored him to his worse self; and ere long he felt that he had deserved well of the community. The hostess turned him out with the last few at midnight, for one of the professors was provost; and he went homewards with another student, who also lived in the new town.

The two, however, not having had enough of revelry yet, turned aside into a lane, and thence up a court leading to a low public-house, which had a second and worse reputation. Into this Alec's companion went. Alec followed. But he was suddenly seized in the dark, and ejected with violence. Recovering himself from his backward stagger into the court, he raised his arm to strike. Before him stood a little man, who had apparently followed him out of the public-house. His hands were in the pockets of his trowsers, and the wind was blowing about the tails of his old dress-coat.

Nor was Alec too far gone to recognize him.

"You, Mr Cupples!" he exclaimed. "I didna expect to see you here."

"I never was across the door-sill o' sic a place afore," said Mr Cupples, "nor, please God, will either you or me ever cross sic a door-sill again."

"Hooly, hooly, Mr Cupples! Speak for ane at a time. I'm gaein in this minute. Luckie Cumstie turned on the caller air ower sune for me."

"Man!" said Cupples, laying hold of Alec's coat, "think that ye hae a mither. Ilka word that ye hear frae a worthless woman is an affront to yer mither."

"Dinna stan' preachin' to me. I'm past that."

"Alec, ye'll wiss to God ye hadna, whan ye come to marry a bonnie wife."

It was a true but ill-timed argument. Alec flared up wildly.

"Wife!" he cried, "there's no wife for me. Haud oot o' my gait. Dinna ye see I hae been drinkin'? And I winna be contred."

"Drinkin'!" exclaimed Mr Cupples. "Little ye ken aboot drinkin'. I hae drunken three times as muckle as you. And gin that be ony argument for me haudin' oot o' your gait, it's mair argument yet for you to haud oot o' mine. I sweir to God I winna stan' this ony langer. Ye're to come hame wi' me frae this mou' o' hell and ugsome deith. It gangs straucht to the everlastin' burnin's. Eh, man! to think nae mair o' women nor *that!*"

And the brave little man placed

sill of such a place before," said Mr Cupples, "nor, please God, will either you or me ever cross such a door-sill again."

"Easy now, Mr Cupples! Speak for one at a time. I'm going in this minute. Luckie Cumstie turned on the cool air too soon for me."

"Man!" said Cupples, laying hold of Alec's coat, "think that you have a mother. Every word that you hear from a worthless woman is an affront to your mother."

"Don't stand preaching to me. I'm past that."

"Alec, you'll wish to God you hadn't, when you come to marry a bonnie wife."

It was a true but ill-timed argument. Alec flared up wildly.

"Wife!" he cried, "there's no wife for me. Keep out of my way. Don't you see I've been drinking? And I won't be resisted."

"Drinking!" exclaimed Mr Cupples. "Little you know about drinking. I've drunk three times as much as you. And if that be any argument for me keeping out of your way, it's more argument yet for you to keep out of mine. I swear to God I won't stand this any longer. You're to come home with me from this mouth of hell and frightful death. It goes straight to the everlasting burnings. Eh, man! to think no more of women than *that!*"

And the brave little man placed

himself right between Alec and the door, which now opened halfway, showing several peering and laughing faces.

But the opposition of Mr Cupples had increased the action of the alcohol upon Alec's brain, and he blazed up in a fury at the notion of being made a laughter to the women. He took one step towards Mr Cupples, who had restored his hands to his pockets and backed a few paces towards the door of the house, to guard against Alec's passing him.

"Keep out of my way, or I'll make you," he said fiercely.

"I will not," answered Mr Cupples, and lay senseless on the stones of the court.

Alec strode into the house, and the door closed behind him.

By slow degrees Mr Cupples came to himself. He was half dead with cold, and his head was aching frightfully. A pool of blood lay on the stones already frozen. He crawled on his hands and knees, till he reached a wall, by which he raised and steadied himself. Feeling along this wall, he got into the street; but he was so confused and benumbed that if a watchman had not come up, he would have died on some doorstep. The man knew him and got him home. He allowed both him and his landlady to suppose that his condition was the consequence of drink; and so was helped up to his garret and put to bed.

CHAPTER LXXV

All the night during which Isie Constable lay dreaming of racks, pincers, screws, and Alec Forbes, the snow was busy falling outside, shrouding the world once more; so that next day the child could not get out upon any pretence. Had she succeeded in escaping from the house, she might have been lost in the snow, or drowned in the Glamour, over which there was as yet only a rude temporary bridge to supply the place of that which had been swept away. But although very uneasy at the obstruction of her projects, she took good care to keep her own counsel.—The snow was very obstinate to go. At length, after many days, she was allowed to go out with stockings over her shoes, and play in the garden. No sooner was she alone, than she darted out of the garden by the back-gate, and before her mother missed her, was crossing the Glamour. She had never been so far alone, and felt frightened; but she pushed bravely forward.

Mrs Forbes and Annie Anderson were sitting together when Mary put her head in at the door and told her mistress that the daughter of Mr Constable, the clothier, wanted to see her.

"Why, she's a mere infant, Mary!" exclaimed Mrs Forbes.

"'Deed is she, mem; but she's nane the less doon the stair i' the kitchie. Ye wad hae seen her come yersel' but she's ower wee. Ye cudna get a glimp o' her ower the edge o' the snaw i' the cuttin' doon to the yett. Hoo her fowk cud lat her oot! She's a puir wee white-faced elf o' a crater, but she's byous auld-farrand and wise-like, and naething will do but she maun see yersel', mem."

"Bring her up, Mary. Poor little thing! What can she want?"

Presently Isie entered the room, looking timidly about her.

"Well, my dear, what do you want?"

"It's aboot Alec, mem," said Isie, glancing towards Annie.

"Well, what about him?" asked Mrs Forbes, considerably bewildered, but not fearing bad news from the mouth of such a messenger.

"Hae ye heard naething aboot him, mem?"

"Nothing particular. I haven't heard from him for a fortnight."

"That's easy accoontit for, mem."

"What do you mean, my dear? Speak out."

"Weel, mem, the way I heard it was raither particlar, and I wadna like a'body to ken."

Here she glanced again at Annie.

"You needn't be afraid of Annie Anderson," said Mrs Forbes smiling. "What is it?"

"Weel, mem, I didna richtly ken. But they hae ta'en him intil a dreidfu' place, and whether they hae left a haill inch o' skin upon's body, is mair nor I can tell; but they hae rackit him, and pu'd o' 's nails aff, maybe them a', and—"

"Good heavens!" exclaimed Mrs Forbes, with a most unusual inclination to hysterics, seeing something terrible peep from behind the grotesque report of Isie, "what *do* you mean, child?"

Presently Isie entered the room, looking timidly about her.

"Well, my dear, what do you want?"

"It's about Alec, ma'am," said Isie, glancing towards Annie.

"Well, what about him?" asked Mrs Forbes, considerably bewildered, but not fearing bad news from the mouth of such a messenger.

"Have you heard nothing about him, ma'am?"

"Nothing particular. I haven't heard from him for a fortnight."

"That's easily explained, ma'am."

"What do you mean, my dear? Speak out."

"Well, ma'am, the way I heard it was rather particular, and I wouldn't like everyone to know."

Here she glanced again at Annie.

"You needn't be afraid of Annie Anderson," said Mrs Forbes smiling. "What is it?"

"Well, ma'am, I didn't rightly know. But they've taken him into a dreadful place, and whether they have left a whole inch of skin upon his body, is more than I can tell; but they have racked him, and pulled some of his nails off, maybe all of them, and—"

"Good heavens!" exclaimed Mrs Forbes, with a most unusual inclination to hysterics, seeing something terrible peep from behind the grotesque report of Isie, "what *do* you mean, child?"

"I'm telling you it as I heard it, ma'am. I hope they haven't burnt him yet. You must go and take him out of their hands."

"Whose hands, child? Who's doing all this to him?"

"They stand about the corners of the streets, ma'am, in great towns, and they catch a hold of young lads, and they trail them away with them, and they just torment the life out of them. They say they're women; but I don't believe that. It's not possible. They must be men dressed up in women's clothes."

Was it a great relief to the mother's heart to find that the childish understanding of Isie had misinterpreted and misrepresented? She rose and left the room, and her troubled step went to and fro overhead. And the spirit of Annie was troubled likewise. How much she understood, I cannot determine; but I believe that a sense of vague horror and pity overwhelmed her heart. Yet the strength of her kindness forced her to pay some attention to the innocent little messenger of evil.

"Where heard you all that, Isie, dear?"

"I heard my father and my mother going on lamenting over him after I was in my bed, and they thought I was asleep. But if Mistress Forbes won't take him away, I'll go and tell all the ministers in Glamerton, and see whether they won't raise the town."

Annie stared in amazement at the wee blue-eyed wizened creature before her speaking with the decision of a minor prophet.

"Is the child here still?" said Mrs Forbes with some asperity as she re-entered the room. "I must go by the mail this afternoon, Annie."

"That's right, ma'am," said Isie. "The sooner the better, I'm sure. He may not be dead yet."

"What a very odd child!" said Mrs Forbes.

"Wouldn't it be better to write first, ma'am?" suggested Annie.

Before Mrs Forbes could reply, the white mutch of Mrs Constable appeared over the top of the snow that walled the path. She was in hot pursuit of her child, whose footsteps she had traced. When shown into the dining-room, she rushed up to her, and caught her to her bosom, crying,

"You mischievous wee rogue! What have you been about, running away like this? I wonder you weren't drowned in the Glamour."

"I don't see what better you could expect of your own child, Mrs Constable, if you go spreading reports against other people's children," said Mrs Forbes bitterly.

"It's a lie whoever said so," retorted Mrs Constable fiercely. "Who told you that?"

"Where else could your child have heard such reports, then?"

"Isie! Isie! My poor wee bairn! What have you been about to take away your mother's good name?"

And she hugged the child closer yet.

Isie hung down her head, and began to have dim perceptions that she might have been doing mischief with the best possible intentions.

"I only told Mistress Forbes how bad they were to Alec."

After a moment's reflection, Mrs Constable turned with a subdued manner to Mrs Forbes.

"Isie's a curious child, ma'am," she said. "And she's overheard her father and me speaking together as if it had been only one person thinking. For if ever two were one, that two and that one are Andrew Constable and myself."

"But what right had you to talk about my son?"

"Well, ma'am, that's quite a far-reaching question. What's already proclaimed from the house-tops may surely be spoken in the ear in closets—for our back-room is but a closet. If you think that folk'll hold their tongues about your child more than anyone else's you're mistaken, ma'am. But nobody heard it from me, and I can take my bodily oath for my man, for he's just a wonder for holding his tongue. I could hardly worm it out of him myself."

Mrs Forbes saw that she had been too hasty.

"What does it all mean, Mrs Constable?" she said, "for I am quite ignorant."

"You may well be that, ma'am. And maybe there's not a word of truth in the story, for I'm thinking the wind that brought it blew from a bad quarter."

"I really don't understand you, Mrs Constable. What do they say about him?"

"Oh, just that he's keeping the worst of bad company, ma'am. But as I said to Andrew, maybe he'll come out of their clutches not that much the worse, after all."

Mrs Forbes sank on the sofa, and hid her face in her hands. Annie turned white as death, and left the room. When Mrs Forbes lifted her head, Mrs Constable and her strange child had vanished.

Mrs Forbes and Annie wept together bitterly, in the shadow of death which the loved one cast upon them across the white plains and hills. Then the mother sat down and wrote, begging him to deny the terrible charge; after which they both felt easier. But when the return of post had brought no reply, and the next day was likewise barren of tidings, Mrs Forbes resolved to go to the hateful city at once.

CHAPTER LXXVI

When Alec woke in the morning, it rushed upon his mind that he had had a terrible dream; and he reproached himself that even in a dream he should be capable of striking to the earth the friend who had just saved him from disgrace, and wanted to save him from more. But as his headache began to yield to cold water, discomposing doubts rose upon his clearing mental horizon. They were absurd, but still they were unpleasant. It *could* be only a dream that he had felled the man twice his age, and half his size, who had once shed his blood for him. But why did it look so like fact, if it was only a dream? Horrible thought! Could it?—It could—It must be—It was a fact!

Haggard with horror as well as revelry, he rushed towards the stair, but was met by Mrs Leslie, who stopped him and said:

"Mr Forbes, if you and Mr Cupples go on at this rate, I'll be forced to give you both warning to leave. I ought to have written to your mother before now. You'll break her heart in the end. Eh! it's a sad thing when young lads take to drink, and turn reprobates in a jiffy."

"I don't go to your church, and you needn't preach to me. What's the matter with Mr Cupples? He hasn't taken to drink in a jiffy, has he?"

"You scorner! He came home last night bleeding at the head, and in the hands of the watchman. Poor man! he could hardly get up the stair. I can't think how he came to fall so badly; for they say there's a special Providence watches over drunk men and children. He was an awful sight, honest man! A terrible mixture of red and white."

"What said he about it?" asked Alec, trembling.

"Oh, nothing. He had nothing to say. You mustn't go near him; for I left him fast asleep. Go away through to your own room, and I'll be in with your breakfast in ten minutes. Eh! but you would be a fine lad if you would only give up the drink and the bad company."

Alec obeyed, ashamed and full of remorse. The only thing he could do was to attend to Mr Cupples's business in the library, where he worked at the catalogue till the afternoon lecture was over.

Nobody had seen Beauchamp, and the blinds of Kate's windows were drawn down.

All day his heart was full of Mr Cupples; and as he went home he recalled everything with perfect distinctness, and felt that his conduct had been as vile as it was possible for conduct to be. Because a girl could not love him, he had ceased to love his mother, had given himself up to Satan, and had returned the devotion of his friend with a murderous blow. Because he could not have a bed of roses, he had thrown himself down in the pig-stye. He rushed into a public-house, and swallowed two glasses of whisky. That done, he went straight home, and ran up to Mr Cupples's room.

Mr Cupples was sitting before the fire, with his hands on his knees and his head bound in white, bloodstained. He turned a ghastly face, and tried to smile. Alec's heart gave way utterly. He knelt at Mr Cupples's feet, laid his head on his knee, and burst into very unsaxon but most gracious tears. Mr Cupples laid a small trembling hand on the boy's head, saying,

"Eh! bantam, bantam!" and could say no more.

"Mr Cupples," sobbed Alec, "forgive me. I'll cut my throat, if you like."

"You would do better to cut the devil's throat."

"Hoo could I do that? Tell me, and I'll do 't."

"Wi' the broken whisky-bottle, man. That's at the root o' a' the mischeef. It's no you. It's the drink. And eh! Alec, we micht be richt happy thegither efter that. I wad mak a scholar o' ye."

"Weel, Mr Cupples, ye hae a richt to demand o' me what ye like; for henceforth ye hae the pooer o' life or deith ower me. But gin I try to brak throu the drinkin', I maun haud oot ower frae the smell o' 't; an' I doobt," added Alec slyly, "ye wadna hae the chance o' makin' muckle o' a scholar o' me in that case."

And now the dark roots of thought and feeling blossomed into the fair flower of resolution.

"Bantam," said Mr Cupples solemnly, "I sweir to God, gin ye'll gie ower the drink and the lave o' yer ill gaits, I'll gie ower the drink as weel. I hae naething ither to gie ower. But that winna be easy," he added with a sigh, stretching his hand towards his glass.

From a sudden influx of energy, Alec stretched his hand likewise towards the same glass, and laying hold on it as Mr Cupples was raising it to his lips, cried:

"I sweir to God likewise— And noo," he added, leaving his hold of the glass, "ye daurna drink it."

Mr Cupples threw glass and all into the fire.

"How could I do that? Tell me, and I'll do it."

"With the broken whisky-bottle, man. That's at the root of all the mischief. It's not you. It's the drink. And eh! Alec, we might be right happy together after that. I would make a scholar of you."

"Well, Mr Cupples, you have a right to demand of me what you like; for henceforth you have the power of life or death over me. But if I try to break through the drinking, I must avoid the smell of it; and I suspect," added Alec slyly, "you wouldn't have the chance of making much of a scholar of me in that case."

And now the dark roots of thought and feeling blossomed into the fair flower of resolution.

"Bantam," said Mr Cupples solemnly, "I swear to God, if you'll give up the drink and the rest of your bad ways, I'll give up the drink as well. I have nothing else to give up. But that won't be easy," he added with a sigh, stretching his hand towards his glass.

From a sudden influx of energy, Alec stretched his hand likewise towards the same glass, and laying hold on it as Mr Cupples was raising it to his lips, cried:

"I swear to God likewise— And now," he added, leaving his hold of the glass, "you daren't drink it."

Mr Cupples threw glass and all into the fire.

"That's my farewell libation to the infernal Bacchus," he said. "Let it go to swell the fire of Phlegethon. But eh! it's a terrible undertaking. It's more than Hercules himself could have made anything of. Bantam! I have sacrificed myself to you. Keep to your part, or I can't keep to mine."

It was indeed a terrible undertaking. I doubt whether either of them would have had courage for it, had he not been under those same exciting influences—which, undermining all power of manly action, yet give for the moment a certain amount of energy to expend. But the limits are narrow within which, by wasting his capital, a man secures a supply of pocket-money. And for them the tug of war was to come.

They sat on opposite sides of the table and stared at each other. As the spirituous tide ebbed from the brain, more and more painful visions of the near future steamed up. Yet even already conscience began to sustain them. Her wine was strong, and they were so little used to it that it even excited them.

With Alec the struggle would soon be over. His nervous system would speedily recover its healthy operations. But Cupples—from whose veins alcohol had expelled the blood, whose skull was a Circean cup of hurtful spells—would not delirium follow for him?

Suddenly Alec laid his hand on the bottle. Mr Cupples trembled. Was he going to break his vow already?

"Wouldn't it be better to fling this into the next yard, Mr Cupples?" said Alec. "We daren't fling it in the fire. It would set the chimney in a flame."

"Na, na. Let it sit," returned Mr Cupples. I'd be ashamed of myself if I couldn't see and forbear. You may just put it into the cupboard though. A body needn't lay burdens grievous to be borne upon himself more than on other folk. Now, let's have a game of cribbage, to keep our minds off it."

They played two or three games. It was pathetic to see how Mr Cupples's right hand, while he looked at the cards in his left, would go blindly flitting about the spot where his glass had always used to stand; and how, when he looked up unable to find it, his face shadowed over with disappointment. After those two or three games, he threw down the cards, saying,

"It won't do, bantam. I don't like the cards tonight. Without anything to wet them, they're mighty dry. What say you to a chorus of Æschylus?"

Alec's habits of study had been quite broken up of late. Even the medical lectures and the hospital classes had been neglected. So Æschylus could not be much of a consolatory amusement in the blank which follows all exorcism. But Cupples felt that if no good spirit came into the empty house, sweeping and garnishing would only entice the seven to take the place of the one. So he tried to interest his pupil once again in his old studies; and by frequent changes did ere long succeed in holding tedium at bay.

But all his efforts would have resulted in nothing but that vain sweeping and garnishing, had not both their hearts been already tenanted by one good and strong spirit—essential life and humanity. That spirit was Love, which at the long last will expel whatsoever opposeth itself. While Alec felt that he must do everything to please Mr Cupples, he, on his part, felt that all the future of the youth lay in his hands. He forgot the pangs of alcoholic desire in his fear lest Alec should not be able to endure the tedium of abstinence; and Alec's gratitude and remorse made him humble as a slave to the little big-hearted man whom he had injured so cruelly.

"I'm tired and must go to bed, for I've a headache," said Mr Cupples, that first night.

"That's my doing!" said Alec, sorrowfully.

"If this new repentance of yours and mine turns out to have anything in it, we'll both have reason to be thankful that you dinted my skull, Alec. But eh me! I'm afraid I won't sleep much tonight."

"Would you like me to sit up with you?" asked Alec. "I could sleep in your chair well enough."

"Na, na. We have both need to say our prayers, and we couldn't do that well together. Go away to your bed, and remember your vow to God and me. And don't forget your prayers, Alec."

Neither of them forgot his prayers. Alec slept soundly—Mr Cupples not at all.

"I think," he said, when Alec appeared in the morning, "I won't take such a hardship upon me another night. Just open the cat's door and fling the bottle into somebody's yard. I hope it won't cut anyone's feet."

Alec flew to the cupboard, and dragged out the demon.

"Now," said Mr Cupples, "open the two doors wide, and fling it with a birr, that I may hear its last speech and dying declaration."

Alec did as he was desired, and the bottle fell on the stones of a little court. The clash rose to the ears of Mr Cupples.

"Thank God!" he said with a sigh.—"Alec, no man that hasn't

gane throu the same, can tell what I hae gane throu this past nicht, wi' that deevil i' the press there cryin' 'Come pree me! come pree me!' But I heard and hearkened not. And yet whiles i' the nicht, although I'm sure I didna sleep a wink, I thocht I was fumblin' awa' at the lock o' the press an' cudna get it opened. And the press was a coffin set up upo' its en', an' I kent that there was a corp inside it, and yet I tried sair to open't. An' syne again, I thocht it was the gate o' Paradees afore which stud the angel wi' the flamin' sword that turned ilka gait, and wadna lat me in. But I'm some better sin the licht cam, and I wad fain hae a drappy o' that fine caller tipple they ca' watter."

Alec ran down and brought it cold from the pump, saying, as Mr Cupples returned the tumbler with a look of thanks,

"But there's the tappit hen. I doot gin we lea' her i' the press, she'll be wantin' to lay."

"Na, na, nae fear o' that. She's as toom's a cock. Gang and luik. The last drap in her wame flaw oot at the window i' that bottle. Eh! Alec, but I'll hae a sair day, and ye maun be true to me. Gie me my Homer, or I'll never win throu't. An ye may lay John Milton within my rax; for I winna pit my leg oot o' the blankets till ye come hame. Sae ye maunna be langer nor ye can help."

gone through the same, can tell what I have gone through this past night, with that devil in the cupboard there crying 'Come taste me! come taste me!' But I heard and hearkened not. And yet sometimes in the night, although I'm sure I didn't sleep a wink, I thought I was fumbling away at the lock of the cupboard and couldn't get it opened. And the cupboard was a coffin set up upon its end, and I knew there was a body in it, and yet I tried hard to open it. And then again, I thought it was the gate of Paradise before which stood the angel with the flaming sword that turned every way, and wouldn't let me in. But I'm a bit better since the light came, and I'd love a drop of that fine fresh tipple they call water."

Alec ran down and brought it cold from the pump, saying, as Mr Cupples returned the tumbler with a look of thanks,

"But there's the tappit hen. I'm afraid if we leave her in the cupboard, she'll be wanting to lay."

"Na, na, no fear of that. She's as empty as a cock. Go and look. The last drop in her belly flew out at the window in that bottle. Eh! Alec, but I'll have a trying day, and you must be true to me. Give me my Homer, or I'll never get through it. And you may lay John Milton within my reach; for I won't put my leg out of the blankets till you come home. So you mustn't be longer than you can help."

Alec promised, and set off with a light heart.

Beauchamp was at none of the classes. And the blinds of Kate's windows were still drawn down.

For a whole week he came home as early as possible and spent the rest of the day with Mr Cupples. But many dreary hours passed over them both. The suffering of Mr Cupples and the struggle which he had to sustain with the constant craving of his whole being, are perhaps indescribable; but true to his vow and to his friend, he endured manfully. Still it was with a rueful-comical look and a sigh, sometimes, that he would sit down to his tea, remarking,

"Eh, man! this is miserable stuff—awful weak tipple—a pagan invention altogether."

But the tea comforted the poor half-scorched, half-sodden nerves notwithstanding, and by slow degrees they began to gather tone and strength; his appetite improved; and at the end of the week he resumed his duties in the library. And thenceforth, as soon as his classes were over, Alec would go to the library to Mr Cupples, or on other days Mr Cupples would linger near the medical school or hospital, till Alec came out, and then they would go home together. Once home, both found enough to do in getting one of them up to the mark of the approaching examinations.—Two pale-faced creatures they sat there, in Mr Cupples's garret, looking wretched and subdued enough, although occasionally they broke out laughing, as the sparks of life revived and flickered into merriment.

Inquiring after Miss Fraser, Alec learned that she was ill. The maid inquired in return if he knew anything about Mr Beauchamp.

CHAPTER LXXVII

Mr Cupples and Alec were hard at work—the table covered with books and papers; when a knock came to the door—the rarest occurrence in that skyey region—and the landlady ushered in Mrs Forbes.

The two men sprang to their feet, and Mrs Forbes stared with gratified amazement. The place was crowded with signs of intellectual labour, and not even a pack of cards was visible.

"Why didn't you answer my last letter, Alec?" she said.

It had dropped behind some books, and he had never seen it.

"What is the meaning, then, of such reports about you?" she resumed, venturing to put the question in the presence of Mr Cupples in the hope of a corroborated refutation.

Alec looked confused, grew red, and was silent. Mr Cupples took up the reply.

"Ye see, mem, it's a pairt o' the edication o' the human individual, frae the time o' Adam and Eve doonwith, to learn to refuse the evil and chowse the guid. This doesna aye come o' eatin' butter and honey, but whiles o' eatin' aise and dirt. Noo, my pupil, here, mem, your son, has eaten that dirt and made that chice. And I'll be caution for him that he'll never mair return to wallow i' that mire. It's three weeks, mem, sin ae drop o' whusky has passed his mou."

"Whisky!" exclaimed the mother. "Alec! Is it possible?"

"Mem, mem! It wad become ye better to fa' doon upo' yer knees and thank the God that's brocht him oot o' a fearfu' pit and oot o' the miry clay and set his feet upon a rock. But the rock's some sma' i' the fit-haud, and ae word micht jist caw him aff o' 't again. Gin ye fa' to upbraidin' o' 'm, ye may gar him clean forget's washin'."

But Mrs Forbes was proud, and did not like interference between her and her son. Had she found things as bad as she had expected, she would have been humble. Now that her fears had abated, her natural pride had returned.

"Take me to your own room, Alec," she said.

"Ay, ay, mem. Tak' him wi' ye. But caw cannie, ye ken, or ye'll gie me a deevil o' a job wi' 'm."

With a smile to Cupples, Alec led the way.

He would have told his mother almost everything if she had been genial. As she was, he contented himself with a general confession that he had been behaving very badly, and would have grown ten times worse but for Mr Cupples, who was the best friend that he had on earth.

"Better than your mother, Alec?" she asked, jealously.

"I was no kith or kin of his, and yet he loved me," said Alec.

"He ought to have behaved more like a gentleman to me."

"Mother, you don't understand Mr Cupples. He's a strange creature. He takes a pride in speaking the broadest Scotch, when he could talk to you in more languages than you ever heard of, if he liked."

"I don't think he's fit company for you anyhow. We'll change the subject, if you please."

So Alec was yet more annoyed, and the intercourse between mother and son was forced and uncomfortable. As soon as she retired to rest, Alec bounded up stairs again.

"Never mind my mother," he cried. "She's a good woman, but she's vexed with me, and lets it out on you."

"Mind her!" answered Mr Cupples; "she's a verra fine woman; and she may say what she likes to me. She'll be a' richt the morn's mornin'. A woman wi' ae son's like a coo wi' ae horn, some kittle, ye ken. I cud see in her een haill coal-pits o' affection. She wad dee for ye, afore ye cud say—'Dinna, mither.'"

"Mind her!" answered Mr Cupples; "she's a very fine woman; and she may say what she likes to me. She'll be alright tomorrow moning. A woman with one son's like a cow with one horn, quite ticklish, you know. I could see in her eyes whole coal-pits of affection. She would die for you, before you could say—'Don't, mother.'"

Next day they went to call on Professor Fraser. He received them kindly, and thanked Mrs Forbes for her attentions to his niece. But he seemed oppressed and troubled. His niece was far from well, he said—had not left her room for some weeks, and could see no one.

Mrs Forbes associated Alec's conduct with Kate's illness, but said nothing about her suspicions. After one day more, she returned home, reassured by but not satisfied with her visit. She felt that Alec had outgrown his former relation to her, and had a dim perception that her pride had prevented them from entering upon a yet closer relation. It is their own fault when mothers lose by the *growth* of their children.

CHAPTER LXXVIII

Meantime, Annie was passing through a strange experience. It gave her a dreadful shock to know that such things were reported of her hero, her champion. They could not be true, else Chaos was come again. But when no exultant denial of them arrived from the pen of his mother, although she wrote as she had promised, then she understood by degrees that the youth had erred from the path, and had denied the Lord that bought him. She brooded and fancied and recoiled till the thought of him became so painful that she turned from it, rather than from him, with discomfort amounting almost to disgust. He had been to her the centre of all that was noble and true. And he revelled in company of which she knew nothing except from far-off hints of unapproachable pollution! Her idol all of silver hue was blackened with the breath of sulphur, and the world was overspread with the darkness which radiated from it.

In this mood she went to the week-evening service at Mr Turnbull's chapel. There she sat listless, looking for no help, and caring for none of the hymns or prayers. At length Mr Turnbull began to read the story of the Prodigal Son. And during the reading her distress vanished like snow in the sunshine. For she took for her own the character of the elder brother, prayed for forgiveness, and came away loving Alec Forbes more than ever she had loved him before. If God could love the Prodigal, might she not, ought she not to love him too?—The deepest source of her misery, though she did not know that it was, had been the fading of her love to him.

And as she walked home through the dark, the story grew into other comfort. A prodigal might see the face of God, then! He was no grand monarch, but a homely father. He would receive her one day, and let her look in his face.

Nor did the trouble return any more. From that one moment, no feeling of repugnance ever mingled with her thought of Alec. For such a one as he could not help repenting, she said. He would be sure to rise and go back to his Father. She would not have found it hard to believe even, that, come early, or linger late, no swine-keeping son of the Father will be able to help repenting at last; that no God-born soul will be able to go on trying to satisfy himself with the husks that the swine eat, or to refrain from thinking of his Father's house, and wishing himself within its walls even in the meanest place; or that such a wish is prelude to the best robe and the ring and the fatted calf, when the Father would spend himself in joyous obliteration of his son's past and its misery—having got him back his very own, and better than when he went, because more humble and more loving.

When Mrs Forbes came home, she entered into no detail, and was disinclined to talk about the matter at all, probably as much from dissatisfaction with herself as with her son, But Annie's heart blossomed into a quiet delight when she learned that the facts were not so bad as the reports, and that there was no doubt he would yet live them all down.

The evil time was drawing nigh, ushered by gentler gales and snowdrops, when she must be turned out for the spring and summer. She would feel it more than ever, but less than if her aunt had not explained to her that she had a right to the shelter afforded her by the Bruces.

Meantime arrived a letter from Mr Cupples.

"DEAR MADAM,—After all the efforts of Mr Alec, aided by my best endeavours, but counteracted by the grief of knowing that his cousin, Miss Fraser, entertained a devoted regard for a worthless class-fellow of his—after all our united efforts, Mr Alec has not been able to pass more than two of his examinations. I am certain he would have done better but for the unhappiness to which I have referred, combined with the illness of Miss Fraser. In the course of a day or two, he will return to you, when, if you can succeed, as none but mothers can, in restoring him to some composure of mind, he will be perfectly able during the vacation to make up for lost time.

I am, dear madam, your obedient servant,
"COSMO CUPPLES."

Angry with Kate, annoyed with her son, vexed with herself, and indignant at the mediation of "that dirty vulgar little man," Mrs Forbes forgot her usual restraint, and throwing the letter across the table with the words "Bad news, Annie," left the room. But the effect produced upon Annie by the contents of the letter was very different.

Hitherto she had looked up to Alec as a great strong creature. Her faith in him had been unquestioning and unbounded. Even his wrong-doings had not impressed her with any sense of his weakness. But now, rejected and disgraced, his mother dissatisfied, his friend disappointed, and himself foiled in the battle of life, he had fallen upon evil days, and all the woman in Annie rose for his defence. In a moment they had changed places in the world of her moral imagination. The strong youth was weak and defenceless: the gentle girl opened the heart almost of motherhood, to receive and shelter the worn outraged man. A new tenderness, a new pity took possession of her. Indignant with Kate, angry with the professors, ready to kiss the hands of Mr Cupples, all the tenderness of her tender nature gathered about her fallen hero, and she was more like his wife defending him from *her* mother. Now she could be something if not to him yet for him. He had been a "bright particular star" "beyond her sphere," but now the star lay in the grass, shorn of its beams, and she took it to her bosom.

Two days passed. On the third evening in walked Alec, pale and trembling, evidently ill, too ill to be questioned. His breathing was short and checked by pain.

"If I hadn't come at once, mother," he said, "I should have been laid up there. It's pleurisy, Mr Cupples says."

"My poor boy!"

"Oh! I don't care."

"You've been working too hard, dear."

Alec laughed bitterly.

"I did work, mother; but it doesn't matter. She's dead."

"Who's dead?" exclaimed his mother.

"Kate's dead. And I couldn't help it. I tried hard. And it's all my fault too. Cupples says she's better dead. But I might have saved her."

He started from the sofa, and went pacing about the room, his face flushed and his breath coming faster and shorter. His mother got him to lie down again, and asked no more questions. The doctor came and bled him at the arm, and sent him to bed.

When Annie saw him worn and ill, her heart swelled till she could hardly bear the aching of it. She would have been his slave, and she could do nothing. She must leave him instead. She went to her room, put on her bonnet and cloak, and was leaving the house when Mrs Forbes caught sight of her.

"Annie! what *do* you mean, child? You're not going to leave me?"

"I thought you wouldn't want me any more, ma'am."

"You silly child!"

Annie ran back to her room, thus compromising with a strong inclination to dance back to it.

When Mr Cupples and Alec had begun to place confidence in each other's self-denial, they cared less to dog each other.—Alec finding at the Natural Philosophy examination that he had no chance, gathered his papers, and leaving the room, wandered away to his former refuge when miserable, that long desolate stretch of barren sand between the mouths of the two rivers. Here he wandered till long after the dusk had deepened into night.—A sound as of one singing came across the links, and drew nearer and nearer. He turned in the direction of it, for something in the tones reminded him of Kate; and he almost believed the song was her nurse's ghostly ballad. But it ceased; and after walking some distance inland, he turned again towards the sea. The song rose once more, but now between him and the sea. He ran towards it, falling repeatedly on the broken ground. By the time he reached the shore, the singing had again ceased, but presently a wild cry came from seawards, where the waves far out were still ebbing from the shore. He dashed along the glimmering sands, thinking he caught glimpses of something white, but there was no moon to give any certainty. As he advanced he became surer, but the sea was between. He rushed in. Deeper and deeper grew the water. He swam. But before he could reach the spot, for he had taken to the water too soon, with another cry the figure vanished, probably in one of those deep pits which abound along that shore. Still he held on, diving many times, but in vain. His vigour was not now what it had once been, and at length he was so exhausted, that when he came to himself, lying on his back in the dry sands, he had quite forgotten how he came there. He would have rushed again into the water, but he could scarcely move his limbs. He actually crawled part of the way across the links to the college. There he inquired if Miss Fraser was in the house. The maid assured him that she was in her own room, whereupon he went home. But he had scarcely gone before they discovered that her room was deserted, and she nowhere to be found. The shock of this news rendered it impossible for him to throw off the effects of his exposure. But he lingered on till Mr Cupples compelled him to go home. Not even then, however, had her body been recovered. Alec was convinced that she had got into one of the quicksands; but it was cast ashore a few days after his departure, and it was well that he did not see it. He did not learn the fact till many years after.

It soon transpired that she had been out of her mind for some time.

Indeed rumours of the sort had been afloat before. The proximate cause of her insanity was not certainly known. Some suspicion of the worthlessness of her lover, some enlightenment as to his perfidy, or his unaccountable disappearance alone, may have occasioned its manifestation. But there is great reason to believe that she had a natural predisposition to it. And having never been taught to provide for her own mental sustenance, and so nourish a necessary independence, she had been too ready to squander the wealth of a rich and lovely nature upon an unworthy person, and the reaction had been madness and death. But anything was better than marrying Beauchamp.

One strange fact in the case was her inexplicable aversion to water —either a crude prevision of her coming fate, or, in the mysterious operations of delirious reasoning, the actual cause of it. The sea, visible from her window over the dreary flat of the links, may have fascinated her, and drawn her to her death. Such cases are not unknown.

During the worst period of Alec's illness, he was ever wandering along that shore, or swimming in those deadly waters. Sometimes he had laid hold of the drowning girl and was struggling with her to the surface. Sometimes he was drawing her in an agony from the swallowing gullet of a quicksand, which held her fast, and swallowed at her all the time that he fought to rescue her from its jawless throat.

Annie took her turn in the sick chamber, watching beside the half-unconscious lad, and listening anxiously to the murmurs that broke through the veil of his dreams. The feeling with which she had received the prodigal home into her heart, spread its roots deeper and wider, and bore at length a flower of a pale-rosy flush—Annie's love revealed to herself—strong although pale, delicate although strong. It seemed to the girl she had loved him so always, only she had not thought about it. He had fought for her and endured for her at school; he had saved her life from the greedy waters of the Glamour at the risk of his own: she would be the most ungrateful of girls if she did not love him.—And she did love him with a quiet intensity peculiar to her nature.

Never had she happier hours than those in which it seemed that only the stars and the angels were awake besides herself. And if while watching him thus at night she grew sleepy, she would kneel down and pray God to keep her awake, lest any harm should befall Alec. Then she would wonder if even the angels could do without sleep always, and fancy them lying about the warm fields of heaven between their own shadowy wings. She would wonder next if it would be safe for God to close his eyes for one minute—safe for the world, she meant; and hope that, if ever he did close his eyes, that might not be the one moment when she should see his face. Then she would nod, and wake up with a start, flutter silently to her feet, and go and peep at the slumberer. Never was woman happier than Annie was during those blessed midnights and cold grey dawns. Sometimes, in those terrible hours after midnight that belong neither to the night nor the day, but almost to the primeval darkness, the terrors of the darkness would seize upon her, and she would sit "inhabiting trembling." But the lightest movement of the sleeper would rouse her, and a glance at the place where he lay would dispel her fears.

CHAPTER LXXIX

One night she heard a rustling amongst the bushes in the garden; and the next moment a subdued voice began to sing:

> I waited for the Lord my God and patiently did bear;
> At length to me he did incline, my voice and cry to hear.
> He took me from a fearful pit, and from the miry clay,
> And on a rock he set my feet, establishing my way.

The tune was that wildest of trustful wailings—*Martyrs'*.

"I didna ken that ye cared aboot psalm-tunes, Mr Cupples," murmured Alec.

The singing went on and he grew restless.

It was an *eerie* thing to go out, but she must stop the singing. If it was Mr Cupples, she could have nothing to fear. Besides, a bad man would not sing that song.— As she opened the door, a soft spring wind blew upon her full of genial strength, as if it came straight from those dark blue clefts between the heavy clouds of the east. Away in the clear west, the half-moon was going down in dreaming stillness. The dark figure of a little man stood leaning against the house, singing gently.

"Are you Mr Cupples?" she said.

The man started, and answered,
"Yes, my lass. And wha are ye?"

"I'm Annie Anderson. Alec's quite disturbed with your singing. You'll wake him up, and he'll be much the worse for it."

"I won't sing another stave. It was lonesome standing upon the outside here, as if I were one of the foolish virgins."

"Eh! wouldn't that be dreadful?" responded Annie simply. Her words awoke an echo in Mr Cupples's conscience, but he returned no reply.

"How's Alec?" he asked.

"A little better. He's recovering, though it's a slow process."

"And do they trust you to look after him?"

"Ay. Why not? His mother would be worn to death if she sat up every night. He can't bear anybody but her or me."

"Well, you're a young one to have such a charge. —I wrote to Mrs Forbes two or three times, but I got but one scrimped answer. So as soon as I could get away, I came to ask after him myself."

"When did you come, Mr Cupples?"

"This night. Or I reckon it's last night now. But by the time I got here, you were all in your beds, and I dared not disturb you. So I sat down in a summer-seat that I came upon, and smoked my pipe and looked at the stars and the clouds. And I tried to sing a song, but nothing but psalms would come, for the night's so awfully solemn, when you get right into the heart of it! It just distresses me that there's nobody up to worship God all night in a night like this."

"No doubt there's many praising him that we can't see."

"Oh, ay; no doubt. But beneath this sky, and breathing the hopeful air of this divine darkness."

Annie did not quite understand him.

"I must go back to Alec," she said. "You'll come over tomorrow, Mr Cupples, and hear all about him?"

"I will do that, my bairn. What do they call you—for I'm always forgetting names?"

"Annie Anderson."

"Ay, ay; Annie Anderson—I've surely heard that name before.—Well, I won't forget *you*, whether I forget your name or not."

"But have you a bed?" said the thoughtful girl, to whom the comfort of every one who came near her was an instinctive anxiety.

"Oh, ay. I have a bed at the house of a small, jabbering, dirty fellow they call King Robert the Bruce."

Annie knew that he must be occupying her room; and was on the point of expressing a hope that he "wouldn't be disturbed by the rats," when she saw that it would lead to new explanations and delays.

"Good night, Mr Cupples," she said, holding out her hand.

Mr Cupples took it kindly, saying:

"Are you a niece, or a grand-daughter of the house, or a hired servant, or what are you?—for you're a wise-spoken lass and a bonnie."

"I'm a servant of the house," said Annie. Then after a moment's hesitation, she added, "but not a hired one."

"You're worth hiring anyway, honey; and they're well of that have you in the house in any capacity. An old man like me may say that to your face. So I'll be off to my bed, and sing the rest of my psalm as I go."

Mr Cupples had a proclivity to garrets. He could not be comfortable if any person was over his head. He could breathe, he said, when he got next to the stars. For the rats he cared nothing, and slept as if the garret were a cellar in heaven.

It had been a sore trial of his manhood to keep his vow after he knew that Alec was safe in the haven of a sick-bed. He knew that for him, if he were once happy again, there was little danger of a relapse; for his physical nature had not been greatly corrupted: there had not been time for that. He would rise from his sickness newborn. Hence it was the harder for Mr Cupples, in his loneliness, to do battle with his deep-rooted desires. He would never drink as he had done, but might he not have just one tumbler?—That one tumbler he did not take. And—rich reward!—after two months the well of song within him began to gurgle and heave as if its waters would break forth once more in the desert; the roseate hue returned to the sunsets; and the spring came in with a very childhood of greenness.—The obfuscations of self-indulgence will soon vanish where they have not been sealed by crime and systematic selfishness.

Another though inferior reward was, that he had money in his pocket: with this money he would go and see Alec Forbes. The amount being small, however, he would save it by walking. Hence it came that he arrived late and weary. Entering the first shop he came to, he inquired after a cheap lodging. For he said to himself that the humblest inn was beyond his means; though probably his reason for avoiding such a shelter was the same as made him ask Alec to throw the bottle out of the garret. Robert Bruce heard his question, and, regarding him keenly from under his eyebrows, debated with himself whether the applicant was respectable—that is, whether he could pay, and would bring upon the house no discredit by the harbourage. The signs of such a man as Cupples were inscrutable to Bruce; therefore his answer hung fire.

"Are you deaf, man? said Cupples; "or are you scared to lose a chance by giving a fair answer to a fair question?"

The arrow went too near the mark not to irritate Bruce.

"Clear off," said he. "We don't want tramps in this town."

"Well, I am a tramp, no doubt," returned Cupples; "for I've come every bit of the way on foot; but I have read in history of two or three tramps that were respectable folk for all that. You won't *give* anything in this shop, I expect—not even information.—Will you *sell* me an ounce of pigtail?"

"Oh, ay. I'll sell it if you'll buy it."

"There's the pennies," said Cupples, laying the orthodox pence on the counter. "And now will you tell me where I can get a respectable, decent place to lie down in? I'll want it for a week, at any rate."

Before he had finished the question, the door behind the counter had opened, and young Bruce had entered. Mr Cupples knew him well enough by sight as a last year's bejan.

"How are you?" he said. "I know you, though I don't know your name."

"My name's Robert Bruce, Mr Cupples."

"A fine name—Robert Bruce," he replied.

The youth turned to his father, and said—

"This gentleman is the librarian of our college, father."

Bruce took his hat off his head, and set it on the counter.

"I beg your pardon, sir," he said. "I'm terribly short-sighted in candle-light."

"I'm used to being mistaken," answered Cupples simply, perceiving that he had got hold of a character. "Make no apologies, I beg you, but answer my question."

"Well, sir, to tell the truth, seeing you're a gentleman, we have a room ourselves. But it's a garret-room, and maybe—"

"Then I'll have it, whatever it be, if you don't want too much for it."

"Well, you see, sir, your college is a great expense to humble folk like ourselves, and we have to make it up the best way that we can."

"No doubt. How much do you want?"

"Would you think five shillings too much?"

"Indeed I would."

"Weel, we'll say three than—to *you*, sir."

"I winna gie ye mair nor half-a-croon."

"Hoot, sir! It's ower little."

"Well, I'll look further," said Mr Cupples, putting on English, and moving to the door.

"Na, sir; ye'll do nae sic thing. Do ye think I wad lat the leebrarian o' my son's college gang oot at my door this time o' nicht, to luik for a bed till himsel'? Ye s' jist hae't at yer ain price, and welcome. Ye'll hae yer tay and sugar and bitties o' cheese frae me, ye ken?"

"Of course—of course. And if you could get me some tea at once, I should be obliged to you."

"Mother," cried Bruce through the house-door, and held a momentary whispering with the partner of his throne.

"So your name's Bruce, is it?" resumed Cupples, as the other returned to the counter.

"Robert Bruce, sir, at your service."

"It's a gran' *name*," said Cupples with emphasis.

"'Deed is't, and I hae a richt to beir 't."

"Ye'll be a descendant, nae doot, o' the Yerl o' Carrick?" said Cupples, guessing at his weakness.

"O' the king, sir. Fowk may think little o' me; but I come o' him that freed Scotland. Gin it

"Well, we'll say three then—to *you*, sir."

"I won't give you more than half-a-crown."

"Heavens, sir! It's too little."

"Well, I'll look further," said Mr Cupples, putting on English, and moving to the door.

"Na, sir; you'll do no such thing. Do you think I would let the librarian of my son's college go out at my door this time of night, to look for a bed for himself? You'll just have it at your own price, and welcome. You'll have your tea and sugar and bits of cheese from me, you know?"

"Of course—of course. And if you could get me some tea at once, I should be obliged to you."

"Mother," cried Bruce through the house-door, and held a momentary whispering with the partner of his throne.

"So your name's Bruce, is it?" resumed Cupples, as the other returned to the counter.

"Robert Bruce, sir, at your service."

"It's a grand *name*," said Cupples with emphasis.

"Indeed it is, and I have a right to bear it."

"You'll be a descendant, no doubt, of the Earl of Carrick?" said Cupples, guessing at his weakness.

"Of the king, sir. Folk may think little of me; but I come of him that freed Scotland. If it hadn't hadna been for Bannockburn, sir, whaur wad Scotland hae been the day?"

"Nearhan' civileezed unner the fine influences o' the English, wi' their cultivation and their mainners, and, aboon a', their gran' Edwards and Hairries."

"I dinna richtly unnerstan' ye, sir," said Bruce. "Ye hae heard hoo the king clave the skull o' Sir Henry dee Bohunn—haena ye, sir?"

"Ow, aye. But it was a pity it wasna the ither gait. Lat me see the way to my room, for I want to wash my han's and face. They're jist barkit wi' stour."

Bruce hesitated whether to show Mr Cupples out or in. His blue blood boiled at this insult to his great progenitor. But a half-crown would cover a greater wrong than that even, and he obeyed. Cupples followed him up-stairs, murmuring to himself:

"Shades o' Wallace and Bruce! forgie me. But to see sma' craters cock their noses and their tails as gin they had inherited the michty deeds as weel as the names o' their forbears, jist scunners me, and turns my blude into the gall o' bitterness—and that's scripter for't."

After further consultation, Mr and Mrs Bruce came to the conclusion that it might be politic, for Robert's sake, to treat the librarian with consideration.

been for Bannockburn, sir, where would Scotland have been today?"

"Nearly civilized under the fine influences of the English, with their cultivation and their manners, and, above all, their grand Edwards and Harries."

"I don't rightly understand you, sir," said Bruce. "You have heard how the king clave the skull of Sir Henry de Bohun—haven't you, sir?"

"Oh, aye. But it was a pity it wasn't the other way. Let me see the way to my room, for I want to wash my hands and face. They're just filthy with dust."

Bruce hesitated whether to show Mr Cupples out or in. His blue blood boiled at this insult to his great progenitor. But a half-crown would cover a greater wrong than that even, and he obeyed. Cupples followed him up-stairs, murmuring to himself:

"Shades of Wallace and Bruce! forgive me. But to see small creatures cock their noses and their tails as if they had inherited the mighty deeds as well as the names of their forbears, just sickens me, and turns my blood into the gall of bitterness—and that's scripture for it."

After further consultation, Mr and Mrs Bruce came to the conclusion that it might be politic, for Robert's sake, to treat the librarian with consideration.

Consequently Mrs Bruce invited him to go down to his tea in *the room*. Descending before it was quite ready, he looked about him. The only thing that attracted his attention was a handsomely bound Bible. This he took up, thinking to get some amusement from the births of the illustrious Bruces; but the only inscription he could find, besides the name of *John Cowie*, was the following in pencil:

"*Super Davidis Psalmum tertium vicesimum, syngrapham pecuniariam centum solidos valentem, quæ, me mortuo, a Annie Anderson, mihi dilecta, sit, posui.*"

Then came some figures, and then the date, with the initials *J. C.*

Hence it was that Mr Cupples thought he had heard the name of Annie Anderson before.

"It's a grand Bible this, goodwife," he said as Mrs Bruce entered.

"Aye it is. It belonged to our parish minister."

Nothing more passed, for Mr Cupples was hungry.

After a long sleep in the morning, he called upon Mrs Forbes, and was kindly received; but it was a great disappointment to him to find that he could not see Alec. As he was in the country, however, he resolved to make the best of it, and enjoy himself for a week. For his asserted dislike to the country, though genuine at the time, was anything but natural to him. So every day he climbed to the top of one or other of the hills which inclosed the valley, and was rewarded with fresh vigour and renewed joy. He had not learned to read Wordsworth; yet not a wind blew through a broom-bush, but it blew a joy from it into his heart. He too was a prodigal returned at least into the *vestibule* of his Father's house. And the Father sent the servants out there to minister to him; and Nature, the housekeeper, put the robe of health upon him, and gave him new shoes of strength, and a ring, though not the Father's white stone. The delights of those spring days were endless to him whose own nature was budding with new life. Familiar with all the cottage ways, he would drop into any *hoosie* he came near about his dinnertime, and asking for a *piece* (of oat-cake) and a *coguie o' milk*, would make his dinner off those content, and leave a trifle behind him in acknowledgment. But he would always contrive that as the gloamin began to fall, he should be near Howglen, that he might inquire after his friend. And Mrs Forbes began to understand him better.—Before the week was over, there was not a man or woman about Howglen whom he did not know even by name; for to his surprise, even his forgetfulness was fast vanishing in the menstruum of the earth-spirit, the world's breath blown over the corn. In particular he had made the acquaintance of James Dow, with whose knowing simplicity he was greatly taken.

On the last day but one of his intended stay, as he went to make his daily inquiry, he dropped in to see James Dow in the "harled hypocrite." James had come in from his work, and was sitting alone on a bench by the table, in a corner of the earth-floored kitchen. The great pot, lidless, and full of magnificent potatoes, was hanging above the fire, that its contents might be quite dry for supper. Through the little window, a foot and a half square, Cupples could see the remains of a hawthorn hedge, a hundred years old—a hedge no longer, but a row of knobby, gnarled trees, full of knees and elbows; and through the trees the remains of an orange-coloured sunset.—It was not a beautiful country, as I have said before; but the spring was beautiful, and the heavens were always beautiful; and, like the plainest woman's face, the country itself, in its best moods, had no end of beauty.

"Hoo are ye, Jeames Doo?"

"Fine, I thank ye, sir," said James rising.

"I wad raither sit doon mysel', nor gar you stan' up efter yer day's work, Jeames."

"Ow! I dinna warstle mysel' to the deith a'thegither."

But James, who was not a healthy man, was often in the wet

"How are you, James Dow?"

"Fine, I thank you, sir," said James rising.

"I would rather sit down myself, than make you stand up after your day's work, James."

"Oh! I don't work myself to death altogether."

But James, who was not a healthy man, was often in the wet

field when another would have been in bed, and righteously in bed. He had a strong feeling of the worthlessness of man's life in comparison with the work he has to do, even if that work be only the spreading of a fother of dung. His mistress could not keep him from his work.

Mr Cupples sat down, and James resumed his seat.

"You're awful muddy about the feet, Mr Cupples. Just give me off your shoes, and I'll give them a scrape and a lick with the blacking-brush," said James, again rising.

"Devil take me if I do any such thing!" exclaimed Mr Cupples. "My shoes will do well enough."

"Where did you get all that mud, sir? The roads are middling today."

"I don't always stick to the roads, James. I got into a bog first, and then into some ploughed land that was all lumps of clay shining green in the sun. So it's no wonder if I've got myself covered in it. Will you give me a potato, James, instead of the blacking-brush?"

"Ay, twenty. But won't you wait till Mysie comes in, and have a drop of milk with them? They're fine potatoes this year."

"Na, na, I haven't time."

"Well, just dip into the pot, and help yourself, sir; and I'll look for a grain of salt."

"How's your mistress, Jeames? A fine woman that!"

"Nae that ill, but some forfochten wi' norsin' Mr Alec. Eh! sir, that's a fine lad, gin he wad only haud steady."

"I'm thinkin' he winna gang far wrang again. He's gotten the arles and he winna want the wages.—That's a fine lassie that's bidin' wi' them—Annie Anderson they ca' her."

"'Deed is she, sir. I kent her father afore her day, and I hae kent her sin ever she had a day. She's ane o' the finest bairns ever was seen."

"Is she ony relation to the mistress?"

"Ow, na. Nae mair relation nor 'at a' gude fowk's sib."

And Dow told Cupples the girl's story, including the arrangement made with Bruce in which he had had a principal part.

"*Annie Anderson*—I canna mak' oot whaur I hae heard her name afore."

"Ye're bidin' at Bruce's, arena ye, Mr Cupples?"

"Ay. That is, I'm sleepin' there, and payin' for't."

"Weel, I hae little doobt ye hae heard it there."

"I dinna think it. But maybe.—What kin o' chiel' 's Bruce?"

"He's terrible greedy."

"A moudiwarp wi' ae ee wad see that afore he had winkit twice."

"'Deed micht he."

"Is he honest?"

"That's hard to answer. But I s' gar him be honest wi' regaird to her, gin I can."

"Not that bad, but pretty worn out with nursing Mr Alec. Eh! sir, that's a fine lad, if only he would hold steady."

"I'm thinking he won't go far wrong again. He's had the earnest and he won't want the wages.—That's a fine lassie that's living with them—Annie Anderson they call her."

"Indeed she is, sir. I knew her father before her day, and I've known her since ever she had a day. She's one of the finest bairns ever was seen."

"Is she any relation to the mistress?"

"Oh, na. No more relation than that all good folk are kin."

And Dow told Cupples the girl's story, including the arrangement made with Bruce in which he had had a principal part.

"*Annie Anderson*—I can't make out where I've heard her name before."

"You're staying at Bruce's, aren't you, Mr Cupples?"

"Ay. That is, I'm sleeping there, and paying for it."

"Well, I have little doubt you've heard it there."

"I don't think so. But maybe.—What kind of man is Bruce?"

"He's terribly greedy."

"A mole with one eye would see that before he'd winked twice."

"Indeed he might."

"Is he honest?"

"That's hard to answer. But I'll make him be honest with regard to her, if I can."

"Would he cheat?"

"Ay. Na. He wouldn't cheat *much*. I wouldn't turn my back to him, though, without peeking over my shoulder to make sure of him. He wouldn't mind doing ill that good might come."

"Ay, ay; I know him.—And the *ill* would be whatever hurt another man, and the *good* whatever furthered himself?" said Mr Cupples as he dipped the last morsel of his third potato in the salt which he held in the palm of his left hand.

"You've said it, Mr Cupples."

And therewith, Mr Cupples bade James good-night, and went to *the hoose*.

There he heard the happy news that Alec insisted on seeing him. Against her will, Mrs Forbes had given in, as the better alternative to vexing him. The result of the interview was, that Cupples sat up with him that night, and Mrs Forbes and Annie both slept. In the morning he found a bed ready for him, to which he reluctantly betook himself and slept for a couple of hours. The end of it was, that he did not go back to Mr Bruce's except to pay his bill. Nor did he leave Howglen for many weeks.

At length, one lovely morning, when the green corn lay soaking in the yellow sunlight, and the sky rose above the earth deep and pure and tender like the thought of God about it, Alec became suddenly aware that life was good, and the world beautiful. He tried to raise himself, but failed. Cupples was by his side in a moment. Alec held out his hand with his old smile so long disused. Cupples propped him up with pillows, and opened the window that the warm waves of the air might break into the cave where he had lain so long deaf to its noises and insensible to its influences. The tide flowed into his chamber like Pactolus, all golden with sunbeams. He lay with his hands before him and his eyes closed, looking so happy that Cupples gazed with reverent delight, for he thought he was praying. But he was only blessed. So easily can God make a man happy! The past had dropped from him like a wild but weary and sordid dream. He was reborn, a new child, in a new bright world, with a glowing summer to revel in. One of God's lyric prophets, the larks, was within earshot, pouring down a vocal summer of jubilant melody. The lark thought nobody was listening but his wife; but God heard in heaven, and the young prodigal heard on the earth. He would be a good child henceforth, for one bunch of sunrays was enough to be happy upon. His mother entered. She saw the beauty upon her boy's worn countenance; she saw the noble watching love on that of his friend; her own filled with light, and she stood transfixed and silent. Annie entered, gazed for a moment, fled to her own room, and burst into adoring tears.—For she had seen the face of God, and that face was Love—love like the human, only deeper, deeper—tenderer, lovelier, stronger. She could not recall what she had seen, or how she had known it; but the conviction remained that she had seen his face, and that it was infinitely beautiful.

"He has been wi' me a' the time, my God! He gied me my father, and sent Broonie to tak' care o' me, and Dooie, and Thomas Crann, and Mrs Forbes, and Alec. And he sent the cat whan I gaed till him aboot the rottans. An' he's been wi' me I kenna hoo lang, and he's wi' me noo. And I hae seen his face, and I'll see his face again. And I'll try sair to be a gude bairn. Eh me! It's jist wonnerfu! And God's jist....naething but God Himsel'."

"He has been with me all the time, my God! He gave me my father, and sent Broonie to take care of me, and Dooie, and Thomas Crann, and Mrs Forbes, and Alec. And he sent the cat when I went to him about the rats. And he's been with me I don't know how long, and he's with me now. And I have seen his face, and I'll see his face again. And I'll try my hardest to be a good child. Eh me! It's just wonderful! And God's just....nothing but God Himself."

CHAPTER LXXX

Although Mr Cupples had been educated for the Church, and was indeed at this present time a licentiate, he had given up all thought of pursuing what had been his mother's ambition rather than his own choice. But his thoughts had not ceased to run in some of the old grooves, although a certain scepticism would sometimes set him examining those grooves to find out whether they had been made by the wheels of the gospel-chariot, or by those of Juggernaut in the disguise of a Hebrew high priest, drawn by a shouting Christian people. Indeed, as soon as he ceased to go to church, which was soon after ceasing to regard the priesthood as his future profession, he began to look at many things from points of view not exclusively ecclesiastical. So that, although he did go to church at Glamerton for several Sundays, the day arriving when he could not face it again, he did not scruple to set off for the hills. Coming home with a great grand purple foxglove in his hand, he met some of the missionars returning from their chapel, and amongst the rest Robert Bruce, who stopped and spoke.

"I'm surprised to see ye carryin' that thing o' the Lord's day, Mr Cupples. Fowk'll think ill o' ye."

"Weel, ye see, Mr Bruce, it angert me sae to see the ill-faured thing positeevely growin' there upo' the Lord's day, that I pu'd it up 'maist by the reet. To think o' a weyd like that prankin' itsel' oot in its purple and its spots upo' the Sawbath day! It canna ken what it's aboot. I'm only feared I left eneuch o' 't to be up again afore lang."

"I doobt, Mr Cupples, ye haena come unner the pooer o' grace yet."

"I'm surprised to see you carrying that thing on the Lord's day, Mr Cupples. Folk'll think ill of you."

"Well, you see, Mr Bruce, it angered me so to see the impudent thing positively growing there upon the Lord's day, that I pulled it up almost by the root. To think of a weed like that decking itself out in its purple and its spots upon the Sabbath day! It can't know what it's about. I'm only afraid I left enough of it to be up again before long."

"I suspect, Mr Cupples, you haven't come under the power of grace yet."

"A pour o' creysh! Na, thank ye. I dinna want to come unner a pour o' creysh. It wad blaud me a'thegither. Is that the gait ye baptize i' your conventicle?"

"There's nane sae deif's them 'at winna hear, Mr Cupples," said Bruce. "I mean—ye're no convertit yet."

"Na. I'm no convertit. 'Deed no. I wadna like to be convertit. What wad ye convert me till? A swine? Or a sma' peddlin' crater that tak's a bawbee mair for rowin' up the pigtail in a foul paper? Ca' ye that conversion? I'll bide as I am."

"It's waste o' precious time speikin' to you, Mr Cupples," returned Bruce, moving off with a red face.

"'Deed is't," retorted Cupples; "and I houp ye winna forget the fac'? It's o' consequens to me."

But he had quite another word on the same subject for Annie Anderson, whom he overtook on her way to Howglen—she likewise returning from the missionar kirk.

"Isna that a bonnie ring o' *deid man's bells*, Annie?" said he, holding out the foxglove, and calling it by its name in that part of the country.

"Ay is't. But that was ower muckle a flooer to tak' to the kirk wi' ye. Ye wad gar the fowk lauch."

"A pour of grease! Na, thank you. I don't want to come under a pour of grease. It would spoil me altogether. Is that the way you baptize in your conventicle?"

"There's none so deaf as those that won't hear, Mr Cupples," said Bruce. "I mean—you're not converted yet."

"Na. I'm not converted. No indeed. I wouldn't like to be converted. What would you convert me to? A swine? Or a small peddling creature that takes a penny more for wrapping up the pigtail in a foul paper? Call you that conversion? I'll stay as I am."

"It's waste of precious time speaking to you, Mr Cupples," returned Bruce, moving off with a red face.

"Indeed it is," retorted Cupples; "and I hope you won't forget the fact? It's of consequence to me."

But he had quite another word on the same subject for Annie Anderson, whom he overtook on her way to Howglen—she likewise returning from the missionar kirk.

"Isn't that a bonnie ring of *dead man's bells*, Annie?" said he, holding out the foxglove, and calling it by its name in that part of the country.

"Ay it is. But that was too big a flower to take to the church with you. You would make the folk laugh."

"What's the richt flooer to tak' to the kirk, Annie?"

"Ow! sober floories that smell o' the yird, like."

"Ay! ay! Sic like's what?" asked Cupples, for he had found in Annie a poetic nature that delighted him.

"Ow! sic like's thyme and southren-wood, and maybe a bittie o' mignonette."

"Ay! ay! And sae the cowmon custom abuses you, young, bonnie lammies o' the flock. Wadna ye tak' the rose o' Sharon itsel', nor the fire-reid lilies that made the text for the Saviour's sermon? Ow! na. Ye maun be sober, wi' flooers bonnie eneuch, but smellin' o' the kirkyard raither nor the blue lift, which same's the sapphire throne o' Him that sat thereon."

"Weel, but allooin' that, ye sudna gar fowk lauch, wi' a bonnie flooer, but ridickleous for the size o' 't, 'cep' ye gie 't room. A kirk's ower little for't."

"Ye're richt there, my dawtie. And I haena been to the kirk ava'. I hae been to the hills."

"And what got ye there?"

"I got this upo' the road hame."

"But what got ye there?"

"Weel, I got the blue lift."

"And what was that to ye?"

"It *said* to me that I was a foolish man to care aboot the claiks and the strifes o' the warl'; for a' was quaiet aboon, whatever

"What's the right flower to take to church, Annie?"

"Oh! sober flowers that smell of the earth, like."

"Ay! ay! Such as what?" asked Cupples, for he had found in Annie a poetic nature that delighted him.

"Oh! such as thyme and southern-wood, and maybe a bit of mignonette."

"Ay! ay! And so the common custom abuses you, young, bonnie lambs of the flock. Wouldn't you take the rose of Sharon itself, nor the fire-red lilies that made the text for the Saviour's sermon? Oh! na. You must be sober, with flowers bonnie enough, but smelling of the churchyard rather than the blue sky, which is the sapphire throne of Him that sat thereon."

"Well, but allowing that, you shouldn't make folk laugh, with a bonnie flower, but ridiculous for the size of it, except you give it room. A church is too small for it."

"You're right there, my dear. And I haven't been to the church at all. I have been to the hills."

"And what did you get there?"

"I got this upon the way home."

"But what did you get there?"

"Well, I got the blue sky."

"And what was that to you?"

"It *said* to me that I was a foolish man to care about the noises and the strifes of the world; for all was quiet above, whatever

Isn't that a bonnie ring of dead man's bells, Annie?

stramash they micht be makin' doon here i' the cellars o' the speeritual creation."

Annie was silent: while she did not quite understand him, she had a dim perception of a grand meaning in what he said. The fact was that Annie was the greater of the two *in esse;* Cupples the greater *in posse.* His imagination let him see things far beyond what he could for a long time attain unto.

"But what got ye at the kirk, Annie?"

"Weel, I canna say I got verra muckle the day. Mr Turnbull's text was, 'Thou, Lord, art merciful, for thou renderest to every man according to his works.'"

"Ye micht hae gotten a hantel oot o' that."

"Ay. But ye see, he said the Lord was merciful to ither fowk whan he rendert to the wicked the punishment due to them. And I cudna richtly feel i' my hert that I cud praise the Lord for that mercy."

"I dinna wonner, my bairn."

"But eh! Mr Cupples, Mr Turnbull's no like that aye. He's bonnie upo' the Gospel news. I wiss ye wad gang and hear him the nicht. I canna gang, cause Mrs Forbes is gaun oot."

"I'll gang and hear him, to please you, my lassie; for, as I said, I haena been to the kirk the day."

commotion they might be making down here in the cellars of the spiritual creation."

Annie was silent: while she did not quite understand him, she had a dim perception of a grand meaning in what he said. The fact was that Annie was the greater of the two *in esse;* Cupples the greater *in posse.* His imagination let him see things far beyond what he could for a long time attain unto.

"But what did you get at church, Annie?"

"Well, I can't say I got very much today. Mr Turnbull's text was, 'Thou, Lord, art merciful, for thou renderest to every man according to his works.'"

"You might have got a good deal out of that."

"Ay. But you see, he said the Lord was merciful to other folk when he rendered to the wicked the punishment due to them. And I couldn't rightly feel in my heart that I could praise the Lord for that mercy."

"That's no wonder, my child."

"But eh! Mr Cupples, Mr Turnbull's not always like that. He's bonnie upon the Gospel news. I wish you would go and hear him tonight. I can't go, 'cause Mrs Forbes is going out."

"I'll go and hear him, to please you, my lassie; for, as I said, I haven't been to the church today."

"But do you think it's right to break the Sabbath, Mr Cupples?"

"Ay and no."

"I don't understand you."

"What the clergy call breaking the Sabbath isn't breaking it. I'll tell you what seems to me the difference between the like of your Mr Turnbull and the Pharisees—and it's a great difference. They bound heavy burdens and grievous to be borne, and laid them upon men's shoulders, but wouldn't touch them to carry them with one of their fingers: Mr Turnbull and the like of him bear their share. But the burden's none the less a heavy one and grievous to be borne."

"But the burden's not *that* grievous to me, Mr Cupples."

"There's no saying what you women-folk will *not* take a pleasure in bearing; but the passage refers expressly to the men's shoulders. And faith mine *will* not endure to be burdened with other folk's trifles. And so come along, dead man's bells."

Annie thought all this rather dreadful, but she was not shocked as a Christian who lives by the clergy and their traditions, instead of by the fresh Spirit of God, would have been. For she could not help seeing that there was truth in it.

But although Cupples could say much to set Annie thinking, and although she did find enlightenment at last from pondering over his words, yet she could have told him far deeper things than he had yet suspected to exist. For she knew that the goal of all life is the face of God. Perhaps she had to learn a yet higher lesson: that our one free home is the Heart, the eternal lovely Will of God, than that which should fail, it were better that we and all the worlds should go out in blackness. But this Will is our Salvation. Because He liveth we shall live also.

Mr Cupples found in the missionar kirk a certain fervour which pleased him. For Mr Turnbull, finding that his appeals to the ungodly were now of little avail to attract listeners of the class, had betaken himself to the building up of the body of Christ, dwelling in particular upon the love of the brethren. But how some of them were to be loved, except with the love of compassionate indignation, even his most rapt listener Thomas Crann could not have supposed himself capable of explaining. As I said, however, Mr Cupples found the sermon in some degree impressive, and was attentive. As he was walking away, questioning with himself, he heard a voice in the air above him. It came from the lips of Thomas Crann, who, although stooping from asthma and rheumatism, still rose nearly a foot above the head of Mr Cupples.

"I was glaid to see ye at oor kirk, sir," said Thomas.

"What for that?" returned the librarian, who always repelled first approaches, in which he was only like Thomas himself, and many other worthy people, both Scotch and English.

"A stranger sud aye be welcomed to onybody's hoose."

"I didna ken it was your hoose."

"Ow na. It's no my hoose. It's the Lord's hoose. But a smile frae the servan'-lass that opens the door's something till a man that gangs to ony hoose for the first time, ye ken," returned Thomas, who, like many men of rough address, was instantly put upon his good behaviour by the exhibition of like roughness in another.

"I was glad to see you at our church, sir," said Thomas.

"Why so?" returned the librarian, who always repelled first approaches, in which he was only like Thomas himself, and many other worthy people, both Scotch and English.

"A stranger should always be welcomed to anyone's house."

"I didn't know it was your house."

"Oh, na. It's not my house. It's the Lord's house. But a smile from the servant-lass that opens the door's something to a man that goes to any house for the first time, you know," returned Thomas, who, like many men of rough address, was instantly put upon his good behaviour by the exhibition of like roughness in another.

This answer disarmed Cupples. He looked up into Thomas's face, and saw first a massive chin; then a firmly closed mouth; then a nose, straight as a Greek's, but bulky and of a rough texture; then two keen grey eyes, and lastly a big square forehead supported by the two pedestals of high cheek bones—the whole looking as if it had been hewn out of his professional granite, or rather as if the look of the granite had passed into the face that was so constantly bent over it fashioning the stubborn substance to the yet more stubborn human will. And Cupples not only liked the face, but felt that he was in the presence of one of the higher natures of the world—made to command, or rather, which is far better, to influence. Before he had time to reply, however, Thomas resumed:

"Ye hae had a heap o' tribble, I doobt, wi' that laddie, Alec Forbes."

"Naething mair nor was nateral," answered Cupples.

"He's a fine crater, though. I ken that weel. Is he come back, do ye think?"

"What do ye mean? He's lyin' in's bed, quaiet eneuch, puir fallow!"

"Is he come back to the fold?"

"Nae to the missionars, I'm thinkin'."

"Dinna anger me. Ye're nae sae ignorant as ye wad pass for. Ye ken weel eneuch what I mean. What care I for the missionars mair nor ony ither o' the Lord's fowk, 'cep that they're mair like his fowk nor ony ither that I hae seen?"

"Sic like's Robert Bruce, for a sample."

Thomas stopped as if he had struck against a stone wall, and went back on his track.

"What I want to ken is whether Alec unnerstans yet that the prodigal's aye ill aff; and—"

"Na," interrupted Cupples. "He's never been cawed to the

"You've had a heap of trouble, I reckon, with that laddie, Alec Forbes."

"Nothing more than was natural," answered Cupples.

"He's a fine lad, though. I know that well. Is he come back, do you think?"

"What do you mean? He's lying in his bed, quiet enough, poor fellow!"

"Is he come back to the fold?"

"Not to the missionars, I'm thinking."

"Don't anger me. You're not as ignorant as you would pass for. You know well enough what I mean. What do I care for the missionars more than any other of the Lord's folk, except that they're more like his folk than any other that I've seen?"

"Such as Robert Bruce, for a sample."

Thomas stopped as if he had struck against a stone wall, and went back on his track.

"What I want to know is whether Alec understands yet that the prodigal's always ill off; and—"

"Na," interrupted Cupples. "He's never been driven to the

swine yet. Nor he sudna be, sae lang's I had a saxpence to halve wi' him."

"Ye're no richt, frien', *there*. The suner a prodigal comes to the swine the better!"

"Ay; that's what you richteous elder brithers think. I ken that weel eneuch."

"Mr Cupples, I'm nae elder brither i' that sense. God kens I wad gang oot to lat him in."

"What ken ye aboot him, gin it be a fair queston?"

"I hae kent him, sir, sin he was a bairn. I perilled his life—no my ain—to gar him do his duty. I trust in God it wad hae been easier for me to hae perilled my ain. Sae ye see I do ken aboot him."

"Weel," said Mr Cupples, to whom the nature of Thomas had begun to open itself, "I alloo that. Whaur do ye bide? What's yer name? I'll come and see ye the morn's nicht, gin ye'll lat me."

"My name's Thomas Crann. I'm a stonemason. Speir at Robert Bruce's chop, and they'll direc ye to whaur I bide. Ye may come the morn's nicht, and welcome. Can ye sup parritch?"

"Ay, weel that."

"My Jean's an extrornar han' at parritch. I only houp puir Esau had half as guid for's birthricht. Ye'll hae a drappy wi' me?"

"Wi' a' my hert," answered Cupples.

swine yet. Nor he shouldn't be, so long as I had a sixpence to halve with him."

"You're not right, friend, *there*. The sooner a prodigal comes to the swine the better!"

"Ay; that's what you righteous elder brothers think. I know that well enough."

"Mr Cupples, I'm no elder brother in that sense. God knows I would go out to let him in."

"What do you know about him, if that be a fair question?"

"I have known him, sir, since he was a child. I perilled his life—not my own—to make him do his duty. I trust in God it would have been easier for me to have perilled my own. So you see I do know about him."

"Well," said Mr Cupples, to whom the nature of Thomas had begun to open itself, "I allow that. Where do you live? What's your name? I'll come and see you tomorrow night, if you'll let me."

"My name's Thomas Crann. I'm a stonemason. Ask at Robert Bruce's shop, and they'll direct you to where I live. You may come tomorrow night, and welcome. Can you sup porridge?"

"Ay, I can do that."

"My Jean's a wonder at making porridge. I only hope poor Esau had half as good for his birthright. You'll have a drop with me?"

"With all my heart," answered Cupples.

And here their ways diverged.

When he reached home, he asked Annie about Thomas. Annie spoke of him in the highest terms, adding,

"I'm glaid ye like him, Mr Cupples."

"I dinna think, wi' sic an opingon o' 'm, it can maitter muckle to you whether I like him or no," returned Mr Cupples, looking at her quizzically.

"Na, nae muckle as regairds him. But it says weel for you, ye ken, Mr Cupples," replied Annie archly.

Mr Cupples laughed good-humouredly, and said,

"Weel, I s' gang and see him the morn's nicht, ony gait."

And so he did. And the porridge and the milk were both good.

"This is heumble fare, Mr Cupples," said Thomas.

"It maitters little compairateevely what a man lives upo'," said Cupples sententiously, "sae it be first-rate o' 'ts ain kin'. And this *is* first-rate."

"Tak' a drappy mair, sir."

"Na, nae mair, I thank ye."

"They'll be left, gin ye dinna."

"Weel, sen' them ower to Mr Bruce," said Cupples, with a sly wink. "I s' warran' he'll coup them ower afore they sud be wastit. He canna bide waste."

"Weel, that's a vertue. The Saviour himsel' garred them gaither up the fragments."

"No doubt. But I'm afraid Bruce would have counted the waste by how many of the baskets went by his door. I'm surprised at you, Mr Crann, trying to defend such a miserable creature, just because he goes to your church."

"Well, he is a miserable creature, and I can't stand him. He's just a Jonah in our ship, an Achan in our camp. But I shouldn't speak so to one that's not a member."

"Never you mind. I'm old enough to have learned to hold my tongue. But we'll turn to a better subject. Just tell me how you made Alec peril his life for conscience sake. You don't burn folk here for not quite holding by the shorter Catechism, do you?"

And hereupon followed the story of the flood.

Both these men, notwithstanding the defiance they bore on their shields, were of the most friendly and communicative disposition. So soon as they saw that a neighbour was trustworthy, they trusted him. Hence it is not marvellous that communication should have been mutual. Cupples told Thomas in return how he had come to know Alec, and what compact had arisen between them. Thomas, as soon as he understood Mr Cupples's sacrifice, caught the delicate hand in his granite grasp—like that with which the steel anvil and the stone block held Arthur's sword—and said solemnly,

"Ye hae done a great deed, which winna gang wantin' its reward. It canna hae merit, but it maun be pleesant in His sicht. Ye hae baith conquered sin i' yersel, and ye hae turned the sinner frae the error o' his ways."

"Hoots!" interrupted Cupples, "do ye think I was gaun to lat the laddie gang reid-wud to the deevil, ohn stud in afore 'm and cried *Hooly!*"

After this the two were friends, and met often. Cupples went to the missionars again and again, and they generally walked away together.

"What gart ye turn frae the kirk o' yer fathers, and tak to a conventicle like that, Thomas?" asked Mr Cupples one evening.

"Ye hae been to them baith, and I wad hae thocht ye wad hae kent better nor to speir sic a question," answered Thomas.

"Ay, ay. But what gart ye think o' 't first?"

"Weel, I'll tell ye the haill story. Whan I was a callan, I took the play to mysel' for a week, or maybe twa, and gaed wi' a frien' i' the same trade's mysel', to see what was to be seen alang a screed o' the sea-coast, frae toon to toon. My compaingon wasna that gude at the traivellin'; and upo' the Setterday nicht, there we war in a public-hoose, and him no able

and the stone block held Arthur's sword—and said solemnly,

"You have done a great deed, which won't go wanting its reward. It can't have merit, but it must be pleasant in His sight. You have both conquered sin in yourself, and you have turned the sinner from the error of his ways."

"Heavens!" interrupted Cupples, "do you think I was going to let the laddie go reckless to the devil, without standing before him and crying *Careful!*"

After this the two were friends, and met often. Cupples went to the missionars again and again, and they generally walked away together.

"What made you turn from the church of your fathers, and take to a conventicle like that, Thomas?" asked Mr Cupples one evening.

"You have been to them both, and I would have thought you'd have known better than to ask such a question," answered Thomas.

"Ay, ay. But what made you think of it first?"

"Well, I'll tell you the whole story. When I was a lad, I thought to amuse myself for a week, or maybe two, and went with a friend in the same trade as myself, to see what was to be seen along a strip of the sea-coast, from town to town. My companion wasn't a great traveller; and on the Saturday night, there we were in a public-house, and him unable to to gang ae fit further, for sair heels and taes. Sae we bude to bide still ower the Sawbath, though we wad fain hae been oot o' the toon afore the kirk began. But seein' that we cudna, I thocht it wad be but dacent to gang to the kirk like ither fowk, and sae I made mysel' as snod as I could, and gaed oot. And afore I had gane mony yairds, I cam upo' fowk gaein to the kirk. And sae I loot the stream carry me alang wi' 't, and gaed in and sat doon, though the place wasna exackly like a kirk a'thegither. But the minister had a gift o' prayer and o' preaching as weel; and the fowk a' sang as gin 't was pairt o' their business to praise God, for fear he wad tak it frae them and gie't to the stanes. Whan I cam oot, and was gaein quaietly back to the public, there cam first ae sober-luikin man up to me, and he wad hae me hame to my denner; and syne their cam an auld man, and efter that a man that luikit like a sutor, and ane and a' o' them wad hae me hame to my denner wi' them—for no airthly rizzon but that I was a stranger. But ye see I cudna gang 'cause my frien' was waitin' for his till I gaed back. Efter denner, I speirt at the landlady gin she cud tell me what they ca'd themsels, the fowk 'at gathered i' that pairt o' the toon; and says she, 'I dinna

go one foot further, for sore heels and toes. So we had to stay put over the Sabbath, though we would fain have been out of the town before the church began. But seeing that we couldn't, I thought it would be but decent to go to the church like other folk, and so I made myself as smart as I could, and went out. And before I had gone many yards, I came upon folk going to the church. And so I let the stream carry me along with it, and went in and sat down, though the place wasn't exactly like a church altogether. But the minister had a gift of prayer and of preaching as well; and the folk all sang as if it was part of their business to praise God, for fear he would take it from them and give it to the stones. When I came out, and was going quietly back to the public, there came first one sober-looking man up to me, and he would have me home to dinner; and then there came an old man, and after that a man that looked like a cobbler, and one and all of them would have me home to dinner with them—for no earthly reason but that I was a stranger. But you see I couldn't go because my friend was waiting for his till I went back. After dinner, I asked the landlady if she could tell me what they called themselves, the folk that gathered in that part of the town;

ken what they ca' them—they're nae customers o' mine—but I jist ken this, they're hard-workin' fowk, kind to ane anither. A'body trusts their word. Gif ony o' them be sick, the rest luiks efter them till they're better; and gin ony o' them happens to gang the wrang gait, there's aye three or four o' them aboot him, till they get him set richt again.' 'Weel,' says I, 'I dinna care what they ca' them; but gin ever I jine ony kirk, that s' be the kirk.' Sae, efter that, whan ance I had gotten a sure houp, a rael grun' for believin' that I was ane o' the called and chosen, I jist jined mysel' to them that sud be like them—for they ca'd them a' Missionars."

"Is that lang sin syne?"

"Ay, it's twenty year noo."

"I thocht as muckle. I doobt they hae fared like maist o' the new fashions."

"Hoo that?"

"Grown some auld themsel's. There's a feow signs o' decrepitude, no to say degeneracy, amo' ye, isna there?"

"I maun alloo that. At the first, things has a kin' o' a swing that carries them on. But the sons an' the dochters dinna care sae muckle aboot them as the fathers and mithers. Maybe they haena come throw the hards like them."

"And syne there'll be ane or

and says she, 'I don't know what they call them—they're no customers of mine—but I just know this, they're hard-working folk, kind to one another. Everyone trusts their word. If any of them be sick, the rest look after them till they're better; and if any of them happens to go the wrong road, there's always three or four of them about him, till they get him set right again.' 'Well,' says I, 'I don't care what they call them; but if ever I join any church, it'll be that church.' So, after that, when once I had got a sure hope, a real ground for believing that I was one of the called and chosen, I just joined myself to them that should be like them—for they called them all Missionars."

"Is that long ago?"

"Ay, it's twenty years now."

"I thought as much. I expect they've fared like most of the new fashions."

"How's that?"

"Grown quite old themselves. There's a few signs of decrepitude, not to say degeneracy, among you, isn't there?"

"I must admit that. At the first, things have a kind of a swing that carries them on. But the sons and the daughters don't care so much about them as the fathers and mothers. Maybe they haven't come through the hardships like them."

"And then there'll be one or

two crept in like that chosen vessel of grace they call Robert Bruce. I'm sure he's enough to ruin you in the sight of the world, however you and he may fare at head-quarters, being all called and chosen together."

"For God's sake, don't think that such as him give any token of being one of the elect."

"How was he admitted then? They say you're very particular. The Elect should know an elect."

"It's the money, man, that blinds the eyes of them that have to sit in judgement upon the applicants. The creature professed, and they were only too willing to believe him."

"Well, if that be the case, I don't see that you're so far ahead of folk that don't make so many pretensions."

"Indeed, Mr Cupples, I fully believe that the displeasure of the Almighty is resting upon our church; and Mr Turnbull, honest man, appears to feel the weight of it. We have more than one instance in the Scripture of a whole community suffering for the sin of one."

"Do you know any instance of a good man being debarred from your set?"

"Aye, one, I think. There was a half-wit that longed to sit down with us. But what could we do? We couldn't know whether he had saving grace or not, for the

cudna speyk that a body cud unnerstan' him?"

"And ye didna lat him sit doon wi' ye?"

"Na. Hoo cud we?"

"The Lord didna dee for him, did he?"

"We cudna tell."

"And what did the puir cratur do?"

"He grat."

"And hoo cam' ye to see that ye wad hae been a' the better o' a wee mair pooer to read the heart?"

"Whan the cratur was deein', the string o' his tongue, whether that string lay in his mou', or in his brain, was lousened, and he spak' plain, and he praised God."

"Weel, I can *not* see that your plan, haudin' oot innocents that lo'e Him, and lattin in thieves that wad steal oot o' the Lord's ain bag—gie them a chance—can be an impruvment upo' the auld fashion o' settin' a man to judge himsel', and tak the wyte o' the jeedgment upo' 's ain shouthers."

"man couldn't speak that a body could understand him?"

"And you didn't let him sit down with you?"

"Na. How could we?"

"The Lord didn't die for him, did he?"

"We couldn't tell."

"And what did the poor fellow do?"

"He wept."

"And how did you come to see that you'd have been all the better of a greater power to read the heart?"

"When the man was dying, the string of his tongue, whether that string lay in his mouth, or in his brain, was loosened, and he spoke plain, and he praised God."

"Well, I can *not* see that your plan, keeping out innocents that love Him, and letting in thieves that would steal out of the Lord's own bag—give them a chance—can be an improvement upon the old fashion of setting a man to judge himself, and take the blame of the judgement upon his own shoulders."

CHAPTER LXXXI

Annie began to perceive that it was time for her to go, partly from the fact that she was no longer wanted so much, and partly from finding in herself certain conditions of feeling which she did not know what to do with.

"Annie's coming back to you in a day or two, Mr Bruce," said Mrs Forbes, having called to pay some of her interest, and wishing to prepare the way for her return. "She has been with me a long time, but you know she was ill, and I could not part with her besides."

"Weel, mem," answered Bruce, "we'll be verra happy to tak' her hame again, as sune's ye hae had a' the use ye want o' her."

"Well, ma'am," answered Bruce, "we'll be very happy to take her home again, as soon as you've had all the use you want of her."

He had never assumed this tone before, either to Mrs Forbes or with regard to Annie. But she took no notice of it.

Both Mr and Mrs Bruce received the girl so kindly that she did not know what to make of it. Mr Bruce especially was all sugar and butter—rancid butter of course. When she went up to her old rat-haunted room, her astonishment was doubled. For the holes in floor and roof had been mended; the sky-light was as clean as glass a hundred years old could be; a square of carpet lay in the middle of the floor; and cheque-curtains adorned the bed. She concluded that these luxuries had been procured for Mr Cupples, but could not understand how they came to be left for her.

Nor did the consideration shown her decrease after the first novelty of her return had worn off; and altogether the main sources of her former discomfort had ceased to flow. The baby had become a sweet-tempered little girl; Johnnie was at school all day; and Robert was a comparatively well-behaved, though still sulky youth. He gave himself great airs to his former companions, but to Annie he was condescending. He was a good student, and had the use of *the room* for a study.

Robert Bruce the elder had disclosed his projects to his heir, and he had naturally declined all effort for their realization. But he began at length to observe that Annie had grown very pretty; and then he thought it would be a nice thing to fall in love with her, since, from his parents' wishes to that end, she must have some money. Annie, however, did not suspect anything, till, one day, she overheard the elder say to the younger,

"You don't push, man. Go through to the shop and get a lump of red candy-sugar, and give her that the next time you see her alone. The likes of her knows what that means. And if she takes it from you, you may have the run of the drawer. It's worth while, you know. Them that won't sow, won't reap."

From that moment she was on her guard. Nor did she give the youth a chance of putting his father's advice into operation.

Meantime Alec got better and better, went out with Mr Cupples in the gig, ate like an ogre, drank like a hippopotamus, and was rapidly recovering his former strength. As he grew better, his former grief did draw nearer, but such was the freshness of his new life, that he seemed to have died and risen again like Lazarus, leaving his sorrow behind him in the grave, to be communed with only in those dim seasons when ghosts walk.

One evening over their supper, he was opposing Mr Cupples's departure for the twentieth time. At length the latter said:

"Alec, I'll stay with you till the next session upon one condition."

"What is that, Mr Cupples?" said Mrs Forbes. "I shall be delighted to know it."

"You see, ma'am, this young rascal here made a fool of himself last session and didn't pass; and—"

"Let bygones be bygones, if you please, Mr Cupples," said Mrs Forbes pleasantly.

"Indeed not, ma'am. What's the use of bygones but to learn from them how to meet the bycomes? You'll please to hear me out; and if Alec doesn't like to hear me, he must just sit *and* hear me."

"Fire away, Mr Cupples," said Alec.

"I will.—For those that didn't pass in the end of the last session, there's an examination in the beginning of the next—if they like to take it. If they don't, they must go through the same classes over again, and take the examination at the end—that is, if they want a degree; and that's a terrible loss of time for the start. Now, if Alec'll set to work like a man, I'll help him all that I can; and by the gathering again, he'll be up with the rest of the fleet. Faith! I'll sit like Death in the spectre-bark, and blow into his sails all that I can blow. Maybe you don't know that verse in *The Rhyme of the Ancient Mariner*? It was left out of the later editions:

'A gust of wind sterte up behind,
And whistled through his bones;
Through the holes of his eyes and the holes of his mouth,
Half-whistles and half-groans.'

"There! that's spicy—for those that like ghostliness."

That very day Alec resumed. Mr Cupples would not let him work a moment after he began to show symptoms of fatigue. But the limit was moved further and further every day, till at length he could work four hours. His tutor would not hear of any further extension, and declared he would pass triumphantly.

The rest of the summer-day they spent in wandering about, or lying in the grass, for it was a hot and dry summer, so that the grass was a very bed of health. Then came all the pleasures of the harvest. And when the evenings grew cool, there were the books that Mr Cupples foraged for in Glamerton, seeming to find them by the scent.

And Mr Cupples tried to lead Alec into philosophical ways of regarding things; for he had just enough of religion to get some good of philosophy—which itself is the religion of skeletons.

"You see," he would say, "it's part of the machine. What a person has to do is to learn what pinion or steam-box, or piston, or great water-wheel he represents, and stick to that, defying the devil, whose work is to put the machine out of gear. And so he must grind away, and when Death comes, he'll say, as Andrew Wylie did—'Well run, little wheel!' and take him away with him somewhere or other, where, maybe, he may make choice of his own machine for the next trial."

"That's pretty cold doctrine, Mr Cupples," Alec would say.

"Well," he would return with a smile, "go to your friend Thomas Crann, and he'll give you something much better. That's one of the most extraordinary men I ever met. He'll give you divine philosopy—a great deal better

| sicht better nor mine. But, eh! he's saft for a' that." | than mine. But, eh! he's soft for all that." |

Annie would have got more good from these readings than either of them. Mr Cupples was puzzled to account for her absence, but came to see into the mother's defensive strategy, who had not yet learned to leave such things to themselves; though she might have known by this time that the bubbles of scheming mothers, positive or negative, however well-blown, are in danger of collapsing into a drop of burning poison. He missed Annie very much, and went often to see her, taking her what books he could. With one or other of these she would wander along the banks of the clear brown Glamour, now watching it as it subdued its rocks or lay asleep in its shadowy pools, now reading a page or two, and now seating herself on the grass, and letting the dove of peace fold its wings upon her bosom. Even her new love did not more than occasionally ruffle the flow of her inward river. She had long cherished a deeper love, which kept it very calm. Her stillness was always wandering into prayer; but never did she offer a petition that associated Alec's fate with her own; though sometimes she would find herself holding up her heart like an empty cup which knew that it was empty. She missed Tibbie Dyster dreadfully.

One day, thinking she heard Mr Cupples come upstairs, she ran down with a smile on her face, which fell off it like a withered leaf when she saw no one there but Robert the student. He, taking the smile for himself, rose and approached her with an ugly response on his heavy countenance. She turned and flew up again to her room; whither to her horror he followed her, demanding a kiss. An ordinary Scotch maiden of Annie's rank would have answered such a request from a man she did not like with a box on the ear, tolerably delivered; but Annie was too proud even to struggle, and submitted like a marble statue, except that she could not help wiping her lips after the salute. The youth walked away more discomfited than if she had made angry protestations, and a successful resistance.

Annie sat down and cried. Her former condition in the house was enviable to this.—That same evening, without saying a word to any one, for there was a curious admixture of outward lawlessness with the perfect inward obedience of the girl, she set out for Clippenstrae, on the opposite bank of the Wan Water. It was a gorgeous evening. The sun was going down in purple and crimson, divided by such bars of gold as never grew in the mines of Ophir. A faint rosy mist hung its veil over the hills about the sunset; and a torrent of red light streamed down the westward road by which she went. The air was soft, and the light sobered with a sense of the coming twilight. It was such an evening as we have, done into English, in the ninth Evening Voluntary of Wordsworth. And Annie felt it such. Thank God, it does not need a poetic education to feel such things. It needs a poetic education to *say* such things so, that another, not seeing, yet shall see; but that such a child as Annie should not be able to feel them, would be the one argument to destroy our belief in the genuineness of the poet's vision. For if so, can the vision have come from Nature's self? Has it not rather been evoked by the magic rod of the poet's will from his own chambers of imagery?

CHAPTER LXXXII

When she reached Clippenstrae, she found that she had been sent there. Her aunt came from the inner room as she opened the door, and she knew at once by her face that Death was in the house. For its expression recalled the sad vision of her father's departure. Her great-uncle, the little grey-headed old cottar in the Highland bonnet, lay dying—in the Highland bonnet still. He was going to "the land o' the Leal" (*loyal*), the true-hearted, to wait for his wife, whose rheumatism was no chariot of fire for swiftness, whatever it might be for pain, to bear her to the "high countries." He has had nothing to do with our story, save that once he made our Annie feel that she had a home. And to give that feeling to another is worth living for, and justifies a place in any story like mine.

Auntie Meg's grief appeared chiefly in her nose; but it was none the less genuine for that, for her nature was chiefly nose. She led the way into the death-room—it could hardly be called the sick-room—and Annie followed. By the bedside sat, in a high-backed chair, an old woman with more wrinkles in her face than moons in her life. She was perfectly calm, and looked like one, already half-across the river, watching her friend as he passed her towards the opposing bank. The old man lay with his eyes closed. As soon as he knew that he was dying he had closed his eyes, that the dead orbs might not stare into the faces of the living. It had been a whim of his for years. He would leave the house decent when his lease was up. And the will kept pressing down the lids which it would soon have no power to lift.

"Ye're come in time," said Auntie Meg, and whispered to the old woman—"My brither Jeames's bairn."	"You're come in time," said Auntie Meg, and whispered to the old woman—"My brother James's child."
"Ay, ye're come in time, lassie," said the great-aunt kindly, and said no more.	"Ay, you're come in time, lassie," said the great-aunt kindly, and said no more.
The dying man heard the words, opened his eyes, glanced once at Annie, and closed them again.	The dying man heard the words, opened his eyes, glanced once at Annie, and closed them again.

"Is that ane o' the angels come?" he asked, for his wits were gone a little way before.

"Na, weel I wat!" said the hard-mouthed ungracious Meg. "It's Annie Anderson, Jeames Anderson's lass."

The old man put his hand feebly from under the bed-clothes.

"I'm glad to see ye, dawtie," he said, still without opening his eyes. "I aye wantit to see mair o' ye, for ye're jist sic a bairn as I wad hae likit to hae mysel' gin it had pleased the Lord. Ye're a douce, God-fearin' lassie, and He'll tak care o' his ain."

Here his mind began to wander again.

"Marget," he said, "is my een steekit, for I think I see angels?"

"Ay are they—close eueuch."

"Weel, that's verra weel. I'll hae a sleep noo."

He was silent for some time. Then he reverted to the fancy that Annie was the first of the angels come to carry away his soul, and murmured brokenly:

"Whan ye tak' it up, be carefu' hoo ye han'le 't, baith for it's some weyk, and for it's no ower clean, and micht blaud the bonnie white han's o' sic God-servers as yersels. I ken mysel there's ae spot ower the hert o' 't, whilk cam o' an ill word I gied a bairn for stealin' a neep. But they did steal a hantle that year. And there's anither spot

"Is that one of the angels come?" he asked, for his wits were gone a little way before.

"Na, indeed!" said the hard-mouthed ungracious Meg. "It's Annie Anderson, James Anderson's lass."

The old man put his hand feebly from under the bed-clothes.

"I'm glad to see you, pet," he said, still without opening his eyes. "I always wanted to see more of you, for you're just such a child as I would have liked to have myself if it had pleased the Lord. You're a sensible, God-fearing lassie, and He'll take care of his own."

Here his mind began to wander again.

"Marget," he said, "are my eyes shut, for I think I see angels?"

"Ay they are—close enough."

"Well, that's very well. I'll have a sleep now."

He was silent for some time. Then he reverted to the fancy that Annie was the first of the angels come to carry away his soul, and murmured brokenly:

"When you take it up, be careful how you handle it, both because it's quite weak, and because it's not over clean, and might spoil the white hands of such God-servers as yourselves. I know myself there's one spot over the heart of it, which came of an ill word I gave a bairn for stealing a turnip. But they did steal a lot that year. And there's another spot upon the

upo' the richt han', whilk cam o' ower gude a bargain I made wi' auld John Thamson at Glass fair. And it wad never come oot wi' a' the soap and water—Hoots, I'm haverin'! It's upo' the han' o' my soul, whaur soap and water can never come. Lord, dight it clean, and I'll gie him 't a' back whan I see him in thy kingdom. And I'll beg his pardon forbye. But I didna chait him a'thegither. I only tuik mair nor I wad hae gi'en for the colt mysel'. And min' ye dinna lat me fa', gaein' throu the lift."	right hand, which came of too good a bargain I made with old John Thomson at Glass fair. And it would never come out with all the soap and water—Heavens, I'm babbling! It's upon the hand of my soul, where soap and water can never come. Lord, wipe it clean, and I'll give him it all back when I see him in thy kingdom. And I'll beg his pardon besides. But I didn't cheat him altogether. I only took more than I would have given for the colt myself. And mind you don't let me fall, going through the sky."

He went on thus, with wandering thoughts that in their wildest vagaries were yet tending homeward; and which when least sound, were yet busy with the wisest of mortal business—repentance. By degrees he fell into a slumber, and from that, about midnight, into a deeper sleep.

The next morning, Annie went out. She could not feel oppressed or sorrowful at such a death, and she would walk up the river to the churchyard where her father lay. The Wan Water was shallow, and therefore full of talk about all the things that were deep secrets when its bosom was full. Along great portions of its channel, the dry stones lay like a sea-beach. They had been swept from the hills in the torrents of its autumnal fury. The fish did not rise, for the heat made them languid. No trees sheltered them from the rays of the sun. Both above and below, the banks were rugged, and the torrent strong; but at this part the stream flowed through level fields. Here and there a large piece had cracked off and fallen from the bank, to be swept away in the next flood; but meantime the grass was growing on it, greener than anywhere else. The corn would come close to the water's edge and again sweep away to make room for cattle and sheep; and here and there a field of red clover lay wavering between shadow and shine. She went up a long way, and then crossing some fields, came to the churchyard. She did not know her father's grave, for no stone marked the spot where he sank in this broken earthy sea. There was no church: its memory even had vanished. It seemed as if the churchyard had swallowed the church as the heavenly light shall one day swallow the sun and the moon; and the lake of divine fire shall swallow death and hell. She lingered a little, and then set out on her slow return, often sitting down on the pebbles, sea-worn ages before the young river had begun to play with them.

Resting thus about half way home, she sang a song which she had found in her father's old song-book. She had said it once to Alec and Curly, but they did not care much for it, and she had not thought of it again till now.

> Ane by ane they gang awa'.
> The gatherer gathers great and sma'.
> Ane by ane maks ane an' a.
>
> Aye whan ane is ta'en frae ane,
> Ane on earth is left alane,
> Twa in heaven are knit again.
>
> Whan God's hairst is in or lang,
> Golden-heidit, ripe, and thrang,
> Syne begins a better sang.

ENGLISH

> One by one away they're called,
> The gatherer gathers great and small.
> One by one makes one and all.
>
> Ever as one departs from one,
> One on earth is left alone,
> Two in heaven receive their own.
>
> When God's harvest's gleaned ere long
> Golden-headed, ripe, and strong,
> Then begins a better song.

She looked up, and Curly was walking through the broad river to where she sat.

"I kent ye a mile aff, Annie," he said.

She looked up, and Curly was walking through the broad river to where she sat.

"I knew you a mile off, Annie," he said.

"I'm glaid to see ye, Curly."

"I wonner gin ye'll be as glaid to see me the neist time, Annie."

Then Annie perceived that Curly looked earnest and anxious.

"What do ye say, Curly?" she returned.

"I hardly ken what I say, Annie, though I ken what I mean. And I dinna ken what I'm gaun to say neist, but they say the trowth will oot. I wiss it wad, ohn a body said it."

"What can be the maitter, Curly?"—Annie was getting frightened.—"It maun be ill news, or ye wadna luik like that."

"I doobt it'll be warst news to them that it's nae news till."

"Ye speyk in riddles, Curly."

He tried to laugh but succeeded badly, and stood before her, with downcast eyes, poking his thorn-stick into the mass of pebbles. Annie waited in silence, and that brought it out at last.

"Annie, when we war at the schule thegither, I wad hae gien ye onything. Noo I hae gien ye a' thing, and my hert to the beet o' the bargain."

"Curly!" said Annie, and said no more, for she felt as if her heart would break.

"I likit ye at the schule, Annie; but noo there's naething i' the warl but you."

Annie rose gently, came close to him, and laying a hand on his arm, said,

"I'm richt sorry for ye, Curly."

"I'm glad to see you, Curly."

"I wonder if you'll be as glad to see me the next time, Annie."

Then Annie perceived that Curly looked earnest and anxious.

"What do you say, Curly?" she returned.

"I hardly know what I say, Annie, though I know what I mean. And I don't know what I'm going to say next, but they say the truth will out. I wish it would, without having to say it."

"What can be the matter, Curly?" —Annie was getting frightened.—"It must be bad news, or you wouldn't look like that."

"I expect it'll be worst news to those it's no news to."

"You speak in riddles, Curly."

He tried to laugh but succeeded badly, and stood before her, with downcast eyes, poking his thorn-stick into the mass of pebbles. Annie waited in silence, and that brought it out at last.

"Annie, when we were at school together, I would have given you anything. Now I have given you everything, and my heart to the boot of the bargain."

"Curly!" said Annie, and said no more, for she felt as if her heart would break.

"I liked you at the school, Annie; but now there's nothing in the world but you."

Annie rose gently, came close to him, and laying a hand on his arm, said,

"I'm right sorry for you, Curly."

He half turned his back, was silent for a moment, and then said coldly, but in a trembling voice,

"Don't distress yourself. We can't help it."

"But what'll you do, Curly?" asked Annie in a tone full of compassionate loving-kindness, and with her hand still on his arm. "It's hard to bear."

"Lord knows that.—I'll just have to struggle through it like many another. I'll go back to the pig-skin saddle I was working at," said Curly, with a smile at the bitterness of his fate.

"It's not that I don't like you, Curly. You know that. I would do anything for you that I could do. You have been a good friend to me."

And here Annie burst out crying.

"Don't cry. The Lord preserve us! don't cry. I won't say another word about it. What's Curly that such a one as you should cry for him? Faith! it's nearly as good as if you loved me. I'm as proud as a turkey-cock," averred Curly in a voice ready to break with emotion of a very different sort from pride.

"It's a sore thing that things won't go right!" said Annie at last, after many vain attempts to stop the fountain by drying the stream of her tears.—I believe they were the first words of complaint upon things in general that she ever uttered.

"Is't my wyte, Curly?" she added.

"Deil a bit o' 't!" cried Curly. "And I beg yer pardon for sweirin'. Your wyte! I was aye a fule. But maybe," he added, brightening a little, "I micht hae a chance—some day—some day far awa', ye ken, Annie?"

"Na, na, Curly. Dinna think o' 't. There's no chance for ye, dear Curly."

His face flushed red as a peony.

"That lick-the-dirt 's no gaun to gar ye marry the colliginer?"

"Dinna ye be feared that I'll marry onybody I dinna like, Curly."

"Ye dinna like him. I houp to God!"

"I canna bide him."

"Weel, maybe—Wha kens? I *daurna* despair."

"Curly, Curly, I maun be honest wi' you, as ye hae been wi' me. Whan ance a body's seen ane, they canna see anither, ye ken. Wha cud hae been at the schule as I was sae lang, and syne taen oot o' the water, ye ken, and syne—?"

Annie stopped.

"Gin ye mean Alec Forbes—" said Curly, and stopped too. But presently he went on again—"Gin I war to come atween Alec Forbes and you, hangin' wad be ower gude for me. But has Alec—"

"Na, nae a word. But haud yer tongue, Curly. Ance is a' wi' me.—It's nae mony lasses wad hae tell't

"Is it my fault, Curly?" she added.

"Devil a bit of it!" cried Curly. "And I beg your pardon for swearing. Your fault! I was always a fool. But maybe," he added, brightening a little, "I might have a chance—some day—some day far away, you know, Annie?"

"Na, na, Curly. Don't think of it. There's no chance for you, dear Curly."

His face flushed red as a peony.

"That lick-the-dirt's not going to make you marry the college man?"

"Don't you be afraid that I'll marry anyone I don't like, Curly."

"You don't like him. I hope to God!"

"I can't stand him."

"Well, maybe—who knows? I *daren't* despair."

"Curly, Curly, I must be honest with you, as you've been honest with me. When once a person's seen one, they can't see another, you know. Who could have been at the school as I was so long, and then saved from the water, you know, and then—?"

Annie stopped.

"If you mean Alec Forbes—" said Curly, and stopped too. But presently he went on again—"If I were to come between Alec Forbes and you, hanging would be too good for me. But has Alec—"

"Na, not a word. But hold your tongue, Curly. Once is all with me.—It's not many lasses would have told you such a thing. But I know it's right. You're the only one that has my secret. Keep it, Curly."

"Like Death himself," said Curly. "You *are* a fine lass."

"You mustn't think ill of me, Curly. I have told you the truth."

"Just let me kiss your bonnie hand and I'll go content."

Wisely done or not, it was truth and tenderness that made her offer her lips instead. He turned in silence, comforted for the time, though the comfort would evaporate long before the trouble would sink.

"Curly!" cried Annie, and he came back.

"I think that's young Robert Bruce been to Clippenstrae to ask after me. Don't let him come farther. He's an uncivil fellow."

"If he gets by me, he must have more feathers than I have," said Curly, and walked on.

Annie followed slowly. When she saw the men meet she sat down.

Curly spoke first, as he came up.

"A fine day, Robbie," he said.

Bruce made no reply, for relations had altered since schooldays. It was an evil moment however in which to carry a high chin to Willie Macwha, who was out of temper with the whole world except Annie Anderson. He strode up to the *colliginer*.[1]

---

[1] COLLIGINER (Scots): college student

"I said it was a fine day," he repeated.

"Well, I said nothing to the contrary," answered Bruce, putting on his English.

"It's the custom in this country to make what answer a man has the sense to make when he's spoken to civilly."

"I considered you uncivil."

"That's just what a bonnie lassie sitting yonder said about you when she prayed me not to let you go a step nearer to her."

Curly found it at the moment particularly agreeable to quarrel. Moreover he had always disliked Bruce, and now hated him because Annie had complained of him.

"I have as much right to walk here as you or any one else," said Bruce.

"Maybe; but even college students don't always get their rights. One right sometimes rides upon the top of another. And Annie Anderson has a right not to be disturbed, when her uncle, honest man, is just lying waiting for his coffin in the house yonder."

"I'm her cousin."

"It's small comfort any of your breed ever brought her. Cousin or not, you shan't go near her."

"I'll go where I please," said Bruce, moving to pass.

Curly moved right in front of him.

"You won't go by me. I have licked you before for ill-treating her; and I will again if you go a step nearer to her. She doesn't want you. Faith I will! But I would rather not fight in front of her. So just come back to the town with me, and we'll say no more about it."

"I'll see you damned!" said Bruce.

"Maybe you will, being likely to arrive at the spot first. But in the meantime, if you don't want her to see you licked, come down into that hollow, and we'll just settle off hand who's the best man of the two."

"I won't move a step to please you or any one else," returned Bruce. He saw that his safety consisted in keeping within sight of Annie.

Curly saw on his part that, a few steps nearer to where Annie sat, the path led behind a stunted ash-tree. So he stepped aside with the proverb,

"He that will to Coupar, maun to Coupar."[1]

Without deigning a word, Bruce walked on, full of pride, concluding that Curly's heart had failed him. But the moment he was behind the tree, Curly met him from the other side of it. Then Bruce's anger, if not his courage, rose, and with an oath, he pushed against him to pass. But the sensation he instantly felt in his nose astonished him; and the blood beginning to flow cowed him at once. He put his handkerchief to his face, turned, and walked back to Glamerton. Curly followed him at a few yards' distance, regretting that he had showed the white feather so soon, as, otherwise, he would have had the pleasure of thrashing him properly. He saw him safe in at the back-door, and then went to his own father's shop.

---

1   "He that will to Coupar, must [go] to Coupar": a proverb meaning a wilful person will have their way

After a short greeting, very short on Curly's part,

"Heavens, Willie," said his father, "what's come over you? You look as if some lass had said *na* to you."

"Some lasses' *no* is better than other lasses' *ay*, father."

"Indeed, maybe laddie," said George; adding to himself, "That must have been Annie Anderson—no other."

He was particularly attentive and yielding to Willie during his short visit, and Willie understood it.

Had Annie been compelled, by any evil chance, to return to the garret over Robert Bruce's shop, she would not indeed have found the holes in the floor and the roof reopened; but she would have found that the carpet and the curtains were gone.

The report went through Glamerton that she and Willie Macwha were *coortin'* (courting).

CHAPTER LXXXIII

Thomas Crann's conversation with Mr Cupples deepened both his annoyance and his grief at the membership of Robert Bruce. What was the use of a church if such men as he got into it, and, having got in, could not be got out? Had he been guilty of any open *fault*, such as getting drunk, for one solitary and accidental instance of which they had excluded one of their best and purest-minded men, they could have got rid of him with comparative ease; but who so free of fault as Bruce? True, he was guilty of the crime of over-reaching whenever he had a chance, and of cheating when there was no risk of being found out—at least so everybody believed—but he had no faults. The duty, therefore, that lay upon every member, next to the cleanness of his own garments—that of keeping the church pure and unspotted—was hard to fulfil, and no one was ready to undertake it but Thomas Crann. For what a spot was here! And Thomas knew his Lord's will.

Neither was the duty so unpleasant to Thomas's oppositive nature, as it would have been to a man of easier temperament.

"Jeames Johnstone," he said, "the kirk maks nae progress. It's no as i' the time o' the apostles whan the saved war added till't daily."

"Weel, ye see," returned James, "that wasna *oor* kirk exacly; and it wasna Mr Turnbull that was the heid o' 't."

"It's a' the same. The prenciple's the same. An' Mr Turnbull preaches the same gospel Peter and Paul praiched, and wi' unction too. And yet here's the congregation dwin'lin' awa', and the church itsel' like naething but bees efter the brunstane. *I* say there's an Ahchan i' the camp—a

"James Johnstone," he said, "the church makes no progress. It's not as in the time of the apostles when the saved were added to it daily."

"Well, you see," returned James, "that wasn't *our* church exactly; and it wasn't Mr Turnbull that was the head of it."

"It's all the same. The principle's the same. And Mr Turnbull preaches the same gospel Peter and Paul preached, and with unction too. And yet here's the congregation dwindling away, and the church itself like nothing but bees after the brimstone. *I* say there's an Achan in the camp.—a

Jonah i' the vessel—a son o' Saul i' the kingdom o' Dawvid—a Judas amo' the twal'—a—"

"Hoots! Thomas Crann; ye're no pittin' a' thae gran' names upo' that puir feckless body, Rob Bruce, are ye?"

"He's nane feckless for the deevil's wark or for his ain, which is ae thing and the same. Oot he maun gang, gin we tak' him by the scruff o' the neck and the doup o' the breeks."

"Dinna jeist, Thomas, aboot sic a dangerous thing," said James, mildly glad of one solitary opportunity of rebuking the granite-minded mason.

"Jeist! I'm far eneuch frae jeistin'. Ye dinna ken fervour frae jokin', Jeames Johnstone."

"He micht tak' the law upo's for defamin' o' 's character; and that wad be an awfu' thing for puir fowk like us, Thamas."

"Aye the same thing ower again, Jeames! Shy at a stane, and fa' into the stank . That's the pairt o' a colt and no o' a Christian."

"But arena we tellt to be wise as serpents?"

"Ye wad tak' a heap o' tellin' upo' that heid, Jeames."

"Ow, 'deed ay! And I'm no my lane, Thamas. But we *are* tellt that."

"The serpent turned oot an ill cooncellor upon ae occasion ower well to be remembert by Adam's race."

"The words stan' as I say," persisted James.

Jonah in the vessel—a son of Saul in the kingdom of David—a Judas among the twelve—a—"

"Heavens! Thomas Crann; you're not putting all those grand names upon that poor feckless body, Rob Bruce, are you?"

"He isn't feckless for the devil's work or for his own, which is one and the same thing. Out he must go, if we take him by the scruff of the neck and the seat of the trousers."

"Don't jest, Thomas, about such a dangerous thing," said James, mildly glad of one solitary opportunity of rebuking the granite-minded mason.

"Jest! I'm far enough from jesting. You don't know fervour from joking, James Johnstone."

"He might take the law upon us for defaming his character; and that would be an awful thing for poor folk like us, Thomas."

"Always the same thing over again, James! Shy at a stone, and fall into the ditch. That's the part of a colt and not of a Christian."

"But aren't we told to be wise as serpents?"

"You would take a heap of telling upon that head, James."

"Oh, indeed aye! And I'm not alone, Thomas. But we *are* told that."

"The serpent turned out a bad counsellor upon one occasion too well to be remembered by Adam's race."

"The words stand as I say," persisted James.

"You're not to make the serpent your counsellor, man. But once you know your duty, you may well take example by him how to carry it out. Did you ever see an adder lying over a stone as if he was nothing but a stick himself, biding his time? That's me, in the Scripture sense. I'm only waiting till I see how. A body mustn't do ill that good may come, though wow! it's a great temptation sometimes; neither must he neglect to do right for fear that ill may follow."

"Ay, that's true. But you needn't burn the house to rid the rats. I expect you'll get us all into over-hot water; and a body needn't take the skin off for the sake of cleanliness. Just take care, Thomas, what you're about."

Having thus persisted in opposing Thomas to a degree he had never dared before, James took his departure, pursued by the words:

"Take care yourself, James, that in saving the right hand you don't send the whole body to hell. It was always your danger. I never got bold counsel from you yet."

"There's more virtues in the Bible than courage, Thomas," retorted James, holding the outer door open to throw the sentence in, and shutting it instantly to escape with the last word.

Thomas, abandoned to his own resources, meditated long and painfully. But all he could arrive at was the resolution to have another talk with Mr Cupples. He might not be a Christian man, but he was an honest and trustworthy man, and might be able from his scholarship to give him some counsel. So he walked to Howglen the next day, and found him with Alec in the harvest-field. And Alec's reception of Thomas showed what a fine thing illness is for bringing people to their right minds.

Mr Cupples walked aside with Thomas, and they seated themselves on two golden sheaves at the foot of a stook.

"What you said to me the other day, sir," began Thomas, "has stuck fast in my crop, ever since. We must have him out."

"Na, na; better let him sit. He'll keep down your pride. That man's a judgement on you for wanting to be better than your neighbours. Don't try to escape judgement. But I'll tell you what I would have you do: Make much of him. Give him enough rope. He'll go from bad to worse, you may be sure. He'll turn to stealing at last."

"To the best of my belief, sir, that's not to come. He's stolen already, or I'm much mistaken."

"Ay! Can you prove that? That's another matter," returned Cupples, beginning to be interested.

"I don't know whether I ought to have mentioned it to one that wasn't a member, though; but it just came out of itself like."

"Sae the fac' that a man's a member wha's warst crime may be that he is a member, maks him sic precious gear that he maunna be meddlet wi' i' the presence o' an honest man, wha, thank God, has neither pairt nor lot in ony sic maitter?"	"So the fact that a man's a member whose worst crime may be that he is a member, makes him such precious gear that he mustn't be meddled with in the presence of an honest man, who, thank God, has neither part nor lot in any such matter?"
"Dinna be angry, Mr Cupples. I'll tell ye a' aboot it," pleaded Thomas, than who no man could better recognize good sense.	"Don't be angry, Mr Cupples. I'll tell you all about it," pleaded Thomas, than who no man could better recognize good sense.

But the Cosmo Cupples who thus attracted the confidence of Thomas Crann was a very different man from the Cosmo Cupples whom first Alec Forbes went to the garret to see at his landlady's suggestion. All the flabbiness had passed from his face, and his eyes shone clearer than ever from a clear complexion. His mouth still gave a first impression of unsteadiness; no longer, however, from the formlessness of the loose lips, but from the continual flickering of a nascent smile that rippled their outline with long wavy motions of evanescent humour. His dress was still careless, but no longer neglected, and his hand was as steady as a rifleman's.

Nor had he found it so hard to conquer his fearful habit as even he had expected; for with every week passed in bitter abstinence, some new well would break from the rich soil of his intellect, and irrigate with its sweet waters the parched border land between his physical and psychical being. And when he had once again betaken himself to the forsaken pen, there was little reason to fear a relapse or doubt a final victory. A playful humanity radiated from him, the result of that powerfullest of all restoratives—*giving* of what one has to him who has not. Indeed his reformation had begun with this. St Paul taught a thief to labour, that he might have to give: Love taught Mr Cupples to deny himself that he might rescue his friend; and presently he had found his feet touching the rock. If he had not yet learned to look "straight up to heaven," his eyes wandered not unfrequently towards that spiritual horizon upon which things earthly and things heavenly meet and embrace.

To such a Cosmo Cupples, then, Thomas told the story of Annie Anderson's five-pound note. As he spoke, Cupples was tormented as with the flitting phantom of a half-forgotten dream. All at once, light flashed upon him.

"And sae what am I to do?" asked Thomas as he finished his tale.—"I can pruv naething; but I'm certain i' my ain min', kennin' the man's nater, that it was that note he tuik oot o' the Bible."

"I'll put the proof o' that same into yer han's, or I'm sair mista'en," said Mr Cupples.

"You, Mr Cupples?"

"Ay, me, Mr Crann. But maybe ye wadna tak proof frae sic a sinner against sic a sanct. Sae ye may keep yer sanct i' yer holy boasom."

"Dinna gang on that gait, Mr Cupples. Gin ye can direc' me to the purification o' our wee bit temple, I'll hearken heumbly. I only wiss ye war ane o' us."

"I'll bide till ye hae gotten rid o' Bruce, ony gait.—I care naething for yer sma' separatist kirkies.—I wonner ye dinna pray for a clippin' o' an auld sun that ye micht do withoot the common daylicht. But I do think it's a great shame—that sic a sneak sud be i' the company o' honest fowk, as I tak the maist o' ye to be. Sae I'll do my best. Ye'll hear frae me in a day or twa."

Cupples had remembered the inscription on the fly-leaf of the big Bible, which, according to Thomas Crann, Mr Cowie had given to Annie. He now went to James Dow.

"And so what am I to do?" asked Thomas as he finished his tale.—"I can prove nothing; but I'm certain in my own mind, knowing the man's nature, that it was that note he took out of the Bible."

"I'll put the proof of that into your hands, or I'm much mistaken," said Mr Cupples.

"You, Mr Cupples?"

"Ay, me, Mr Crann. But maybe you wouldn't take proof from such a sinner against such a saint. So you may keep your saint in your holy bosom."

"Don't go on that way, Mr Cupples. If you can direct me to the purification of our wee temple, I'll listen humbly. I only wish you were one of us."

"I'll wait till you've got rid of Bruce, anyway.—I care nothing for your small separatist churches.—I wonder you don't pray for a clipping of an old sun that you might do without the common daylight. But I do think it's a great shame—that such a sneak should be in the company of honest folk, as I take most of you to be. So I'll do my best. You'll hear from me in a day or two."

Cupples had remembered the inscription on the fly-leaf of the big Bible, which, according to Thomas Crann, Mr Cowie had given to Annie. He now went to James Dow.

"Did Annie ever tell ye aboot a Bible that Mr Cowie ga'e her, Jeames?"

"Ay did she. I min' 't fine."

"Cud ye get a haud o' 't?"

"Eh! I dinna ken. The crater has laid his ain cleuks upo' 't. It's a sod pity that Annie's oot o' the hoose, or she micht hae stown't."

"Truly, bein' her ain, she micht. But ye're a kin' o' a guairdian till her—arena ye?"

"Ow! ay. I hae made mysel' that in a way; but Bruce wad aye be luikit upon as the proper guairdian."

"Hae ye ony haud upo' the siller?"

"I gart him sign a lawyer's paper aboot it."

"Weel, ye jist gang and demand the Bible, alang wi' the lave o' Annie's property. Ye ken she's had trouble aboot her kist, and canna get it frae the swallowin' cratur'. And gin he maks ony demur, jist drap a hint o' gaein to the lawyer aboot it. The like o' him's as fleyt at a lawyer as cats at cauld water. Get the Bible we maun. And ye maun fess't to me direckly."

Dow was a peaceable man, and did not much relish the commission. Cupples, thinking he too was a missionar, told him the story.

"Weel," said Dow, "lat him sit there. Maybe they'll haud him frae doin' mair mischeef. Whan ye jabble a stank, the stink rises."

"Did Annie ever tell you about a Bible that Mr Cowie gave her, James?"

"Ay she did. I remember it well."

"Could you get a hold of it?"

"Eh! I don't know. The fellow has it in his own clutches. It's a sad pity that Annie's out of the house, or she might have stolen it."

"Truly, being her own, she might. But you're a kind of a guardian to her—aren't you?"

"Oh! ay. I have made myself that in a way; but Bruce would always be looked upon as the proper guardian."

"Have you any hold upon the money?"

"I made him sign a lawyer's paper about it."

"Well, you just go and demand the Bible, along with the rest of Annie's property. You know she's had trouble about her chest, and can't get it from the swallowing creature. And if he makes any demur, just drop a hint of going to the lawyer about it. The like of him's as scared at a lawyer as cats at cold water. Get the Bible we must. And you must bring it to me at once."

Dow was a peaceable man, and did not much relish the commission. Cupples, thinking he too was a missionar, told him the story.

"Well," said Dow, "let him sit there. Maybe they'll keep him from doing more mischief. When you stir up a swamp, the stink rises."

"I thought you were one of them. You mustn't let it out."

"Na, na. I'll hold my tongue."

"I care nothing about it. But there's Thomas Crann just eating his own heart. It's a sin to let such a man live in such distress."

"Indeed it is. He's a good man that. And he's been very kind to our Annie, Mr Cupples.—I'll do as you say. When do you want it?"

"This very night."

So after his day's work, which was hard enough at this season of the year, was over, James Dow put on his blue Sunday coat, and set off to the town. He found Robert Bruce chaffering with a country girl over some butter, for which he wanted to give her less than the market-value. This roused his indignation, and put him in a much fitter mood for an altercation.

"I won't give you more than fivepence. How are you today, Mr Dow? I tell you it has a goo[1] (*Fren. goût*) of turnips or something worse."

"How can that be, Mr Bruce, at this season of the year, when there's plenty of grass for man and beast and all creatures?"

"It's not for me to say how it can be. That's not my business. Now, Mr Dow?"

Bruce, whose very life lay in driving bargains, had a great

---

[1] GOO (Scots): A strong, unpleasant taste. The Scots word has been retained here due to its similarity to the French goût.

dislike to any interruption of the process. Yet he forsook the girl as if he had said all he had to say, and turned to James Dow. For he wanted to get rid of him before concluding his bargain with the girl, whose butter he was determined to have even if he must pay her own price for it. Like the Reeve in the Canterbury Tales, who "ever rode the hinderest of the rout," being such a rogue and such a rogue-catcher that he could not bear anybody behind his back, Bruce, when about the business that his soul loved, eschewed the presence of any third person.

"Now, Mr Dow?" he said.

"My business'll keep," replied Dow.

"But you see we're busy tonight, Mr. Dow."

"Well, I don't want to hurry you. But I wonder that you would buy bad butter, to please anybody, even a bonny lass like that."

"Some folk like the taste of turnips, though I don't like it myself," answered Bruce. "But the fact that they aren't a favourite with most folk, brings down the price in the market."

"Turnips are neither here nor there," said the girl; and taking up her basket, she was going to leave the shop.

"Wait a bit, my lass," cried Bruce. "The mistress would like to see you. Just go in to her with your basket, and see what she thinks of the butter. I may be wrong, you know."

So saying he opened the inner door, and ushered the young woman into the kitchen.

"Now, Mr Dow?" he said once more. "Is it tobacco, or snuff, or what is it?"

"It's Annie Anderson's chest and all her gear."

"I'm surprised at you, James Dow. There's the lassie's room upstairs, fit for any princess, whenever she likes to come back to it. But she was always a wild lassie, and a regular vagabond."

"You lie, Rob Bruce," exclaimed Dow, surprised out of his proprieties. "Whoever you say that to, don't say it to me."

Bruce was anything but a quarrelsome man with other than his inferiors. He pocketed the lie very calmly.

"Don't lose your temper, Mr Dow. It's a grave fault that."

"Just you deliver up the bairn's effects, or I'll go to those who'll make you."

"Who might that be, Mr Dow?" asked Bruce, wishing first to find out how far Dow was prepared to go.

"You have no right whatever to keep that lassie's clothes, as if she owed you anything for rent."

"Have *you* any right to remove them? How do I know what'll become of them?"

"Well, I'll be off to Mr Gibb, and we'll see what can be done

dune there. It's well known over all Glamerton, Mr Bruce, in what manner you and your whole house have borne yourselves to that orphan lassie; and I'll go into every shop, as I go down the street, that is, where I'm known, and I'll just tell them where I'm going, and what for."

The thing which beyond all others Bruce dreaded was unremunerative notoriety.

"Heavens! James Dow, you don't know joking from jesting. I never was the man to set myself in the face of anything reasonable. But you see it would be cast up to all of us that we had driven the poor lassie out of the house, and then flung her things after her."

"The one you've done. The other you shan't do, for I'll take them. And I'll tell you what folk will say if you don't give up the things. They'll say that you both drove her away and kept hold of her clothes. I'll see to that—*and more besides.*"

Bruce understood that he referred to Annie's money. His object in refusing to give up her box had been to retain as long as possible a chance of persuading her to return to his house; for should she leave it finally, her friends might demand the interest in money, which at present he was bound to pay only in aliment and shelter, little of either of which she required at his hands. But here was a greater danger still.

"Mother," he cried, "put up Miss Anderson's clothes in her box to go with the carrier tomorrow morning."

"I'll take them with me," said Dow resolutely.

"You can't. You haven't a cart."

"You get them put up, and I'll fetch a barrow," said James, leaving the shop.

He borrowed a wheelbarrow from Thomas Crann, and found the box ready for him when he returned. The moment he lifted it, he was certain from the weight of the poor little property that the Bible was not there.

"You haven't put in Mr Cowie's Bible."

"Mother! did you put in the Bible?" cried Bruce, for the house-door was open.

"No indeed, father. It's better where it is," said Mrs Bruce from the kitchen, with shrill response.

"You see, Mr Dow, the Bible's lain there so long, that it's just our own. And the lassie can't want it till she has a family to have worship with. And then she'll be welcome to take it."

"You go upstairs for the book, or I'll go myself."

Bruce went and fetched it, with a bad grace enough, and handed over with it the last tattered remnants of his respectability into the hands of James Dow.

Mr Cupples, having made a translation of the inscription, took it to Thomas Crann.

"Do you recall what Bruce read that night you saw him take something out of the book?" he asked as he entered.

"Ay, quite well. He began with the twenty-third psalm, and went on to the next."

"Well, read that. I found it on a blank leaf of the book."

Thomas read—'*Over the twenty-third psalm of David I have laid a five-pound note for my dear Annie Anderson, after my death,*'—and lifting his eyes, stared at Mr Cupples, his face slowly brightening with satisfaction. Then a cloud came over his brow—for was he not rejoicing in iniquity? At least he was rejoicing in coming shame.

"How could it have been," he asked after a brief pause, "that Bruce didn't fall upon this, as well as you, Mr Cupples, or didn't scratch it out?"

"'Cause it was written in Latin. The man hadn't the wit to suspect its contents. It said nothing *to* him, and he never thought it could say anything *about* him."

"It's a fine thing to be a scholar, Mr Cupples."

"Ay, sometimes."

"They say the Miss Cowies are great scholars."

"Very likely.—But there's one thing more I'd like from you. Can you tell the day of the month that you went home with your praying friend?"

"It was the night of a special prayer-meeting for the state of

Glamerton. I can find out the date from the church-books. What am I to do with it when I have it, sir?"

"Go to the bank Bruce deals with, and ask whether a note bearing the number of those figures was paid into it upon the Monday following that Sunday, and who paid it. They'll tell you that at once."

But for various reasons, which it is needless to give in this history, Thomas was compelled to postpone the execution of his project. And Robert went on buying and selling and getting gain, all unaware of the pit he had digged for himself.

CHAPTER LXXXIV

One Sunday morning Mr Cupples was returning from church with Alec.

"Ye likit the sermon the day, Mr Cupples."

"What gars ye think that?"

"I saw ye takin' notes a' the time."

"Gleg-eed mole!" said Mr Cupples. "Luik at the notes as ye ca' them."

"Eh! it's a sang!" exclaimed Alec with delight.

"What cud gar ye think I likit sic havers? The crater was preachin' till's ain shaidow. And he pat me into sic an unchristian temper o' dislike to him and a' the concern, that I ran to my city o' refuge. I never gang to the kirk wi'oot it.—I mean my pocket-buik. And I tried to gie birth till a sang, the quhilk, like Jove, I conceived i' my heid last nicht."

"Lat me luik at it," said Alec, eagerly.

"Na, ye wadna mak' either rhyme or rizzon o' 't as it stan's. I'll read it to ye."

"Come and sit doon, than, on the ither side o' the dyke."

A dyke in Scotland is an earthen fence—to my prejudiced mind, the ideal of fences; because, for

One Sunday morning Mr Cupples was returning from church with Alec.

"You liked the sermon today, Mr Cupples."

"What makes you think that?"

"I saw you taking notes all the time."

"Sharp-eyed mole!" said Mr Cupples. "Look at the notes as you call them."

"Eh! it's a song!" exclaimed Alec with delight.

"What could make you think I liked such nonsense? The fellow was preaching to his own shadow. And he put me into such an unchristian temper of dislike to him and all the business, that I ran to my city of refuge. I never go to the church without it.—I mean my pocket-book. And I tried to give birth to a song, which, like Jove, I conceived in my head last night."

"Let me look at it," said Alec, eagerly.

"Na, you wouldn't make either rhyme or reason of it as it stands. I'll read it to you."

"Come and sit down, then, on the other side of the dyke."

A dyke in Scotland is an earthen fence—to my prejudiced mind, the ideal of fences; because, for one thing, it never keeps anybody out. And not to speak of the wild bees' bykes in them, with their inexpressible honey, like that of Mount Hymettus—to the recollection of the man, at least—they are covered with grass, and wild flowers grow all about them, through which the wind harps and carps over your head, filling your sense with the odours of a little modest yellow tufty flower, for which I never heard a name in Scotland: the English call it Ladies' Bedstraw.

They got over the dyke into the field and sat down.

"Ye see it's no lickit eneuch yet," said Mr Cupples, and began.

"O lassie ayont the hill!
Come ower the tap o' the hill;
Or roun' the neuk o' the hill;
For I want ye sair the nicht.
  I'm needin ye sair the nicht,
For I'm tired and sick o' mysel'.
  A body's sel 's the sairest weicht.
O lassie, come ower the hill.

Gin a body cud be a thocht o' grace,
  And no a sel' ava!
I'm sick o' my heid and my han's and my face,
  And my thouchts and mysel' and a'.
  I'm sick o' the warl' and a';
The licht gangs by wi' a hiss;
  For throu' my een the sunbeams fa',
But my weary hert they miss!

  O lassie ayont the hill!
  Come ower the tap o' the hill,

>   Or roun' the neuk o' the hill,
>   For I want ye sair the nicht.
>
> For gin ance I saw yer bonnie heid,
>   And the sunlicht o' yer hair,
> The ghaist o' mysel' wad fa' doun deid,
>   And I'd be mysel' nae mair.
>   I wad be mysel' nae mair,
> Filled o' the sole remeid,
>   Slain by the arrows o' licht frae yer hair,
> Killed by yer body and heid!
>   O lassie, ayont the hill! etc.
>
> But gin ye lo'ed me, ever so sma'
>   For the sake o' my bonnie dame,
> Whan I cam' to life, as she gaed awa',
>   I could bide my body and name.
>   I micht bide myself, the weary same
> Aye settin' up its heid,
>   Till I turn frae the claes that cover my frame,
> As gin they war roun' the deid.
>   O lassie, ayont the hill! etc.
>
> But gien ye lo'ed me as I lo'e you
>   I wad ring my ain deid knell;
> Mysel' wad vanish, shot through and through
>   By the shine o' your sunny sel'.
>   By the shine o' yer sunny sel,
> By the licht aneath your broo,
>   I wad dee to mysel', and ring my bell,
> And only live in you.
>
> O lassie ayont the hill!
>   Come ower the tap o' the hill,
> Or roun' the neuk o' the hill,
>   For I want ye sair the nicht.
>   I'm needin' ye sair the nicht,
> For I'm tired and sick o' mysel';
>   A body's sel 's the sairest weicht!
> O lassie, come ower the hill."

ENGLISH

"O lassie beyond the hill!
Come over the top of the hill;
Or round the side of the hill;
For I want you here tonight.
   I'm needing you here tonight,
For I'm tired and sick of myself.
   A person's self's the sorest weight.
O lassie, come over the hill.

If a person could be a thought of grace,
   And not a self at all!
I'm sick of my head and my hands and my face,
   And my thoughts and myself and all.
   I'm sick of the world and all;
The light goes by with a hiss;
   For through my eyes the sunbeams fall,
But my weary heart they miss.

     O lassie, beyond the hill!
     Come over the top of the hill,
     Or round the side of the hill,
     For I want you here tonight.

For if once I saw your bonny head,
   And the sunlight on your hair,
The ghost of myself would fall down dead,
   And I'd be myself no more.
   I would be myself no more,
Once on the cure I'd fed,
   Slain by the arrows of light from your hair,
Killed by your body and head.
       O lassie, beyond the hill! etc.

But if you loved me, though just for a day
   For the sake of my bonny dame,
When I came to life, as she went away
   I could bear my body and name.
   I might bear myself, the weary same

>   Forever lifting its head,
>   Till I turn from the clothes that cover my frame,
>   As if they were round the dead.
>   O lassie, beyond the hill! etc.
>
>   But if you loved me as I love you,
>   I would ring my own death knell;
>   Myself would vanish, shot through and through
>   By the shine of your sunny self.
>   By the shine of your sunny self,
>   By the light beneath your brow,
>   I would die to myself, and ring my bell,
>   And only live in you.
>
>   O lassie, beyond the hill!
>   Come over the top of the hill,
>   Or round the side of the hill,
>   For I want you here tonight.
>   I'm needing you here tonight,
>   For I'm tired and sick of myself;
>   A person's self's the sorest weight!
>   O lassie, come over the hill."

"Isn't it rather metaphysical, Mr Cupples?" asked Alec.

"Ay, it is. But folk are metaphysical. True, they don't always know it. I would to God I could get that self of mine safe beneath the ground, for it just sometimes torments the life out of me with its ugly face. It and I just stand and scowl at each other."

"It'll take a heap of Christianity to lay *that* ghost, Mr Cupples. That I know well. The lassie wouldn't be able to do it for you. It's too much to expect of her or any mortal woman. For the soul's a temple built for the Holy Ghost, and no woman can fill it, were she the Virgin Mary over again. And till the Holy Ghost comes into his own house, the ghost that you speak of won't go out."

A huge form towered above the dyke behind them.

"You had no right to listen, Thomas Crann," said Mr Cupples.

"I beg your pardon," returned Thomas; "I never thought of that. The sound was so bonnie, I just stood and listened. I beg your pardon.—But that's not the right thing for the Sabbath day."

"But you're having a walk yourself, it seems, Thomas."

"Ay; but I'm going over the hills to my school. And I mustn't stay to gossip with you, for I have a good two hours' travel before me."

"Come home with us, and have a mouthful of dinner before you go, Thomas," said Alec.

"Na, I thank you. It does the soul good to fast a bit one day in seven. I had a snack, though, before I left. What am I bragging of! Good day to you."

"That's an honest man, Alec," said Cupples.

"He is," returned Alec. "But he never will do as other people do."

"Perhaps that's the source of his honesty—that he walks by an inward light," said Cupples thoughtfully.

The year wore on. Alec grew confident. They returned together to their old quarters. Alec passed his examinations triumphantly, and continued his studies with greater vigour than before. Especially he walked the hospitals with much attention and interest, ever warned by Cupples to beware lest he should come to regard a man as a physical machine, and so grow a mere doctoring machine himself.

Mr Fraser declined seeing him. The old man was in a pitiable condition, and indeed never lectured again.

Alec no more frequented his old dismal haunt by the seashore. The cry of the drowning girl would not have come to him as it would to the more finely nervous constitution of Mr Cupples; but the cry of a sea-gull, or the wash of the waves, or even the wind across the tops of the sand-hills, would have been enough to make him see in every crest which the wind tore white in the gloamin, the forlorn figure of the girl he loved vanishing from his eyes.

The more heartily he worked the more did the evil as well as the painful portions of his history recede into the background of his memory, growing more and more like the traces left by a bad, turbid, and sorrowful dream.

Is it true that *all* our experiences will one day revive in entire clearness of outline and full brilliancy of colour, passing before the horror-struck soul to the denial of time, and the assertion of ever-present eternity? If so, then God be with us, for we shall need him.

Annie Anderson's great-aunt took to her bed directly after her husband's funeral.

Finding there was much to do about the place, Annie felt no delicacy as to remaining. She worked harder than ever she had worked before, blistered her hands, and browned her fair face and neck altogether autumnally. Her aunt and she together shore (*reaped*) the little field of oats; got the sheaves home and made a rick of them; dug up the potatoes, and covered them in a pit with a blanket of earth; looked after the one cow and calf which gathered the grass along the road and river sides; fed the pigs and the poultry, and even went with a neighbour and his cart to the moss, to howk (*dig*) their winter-store of peats. But this they found too hard for them, and were forced to give up. Their neighbours, however, provided their fuel, as they had often done in part for old John Peterson.

Before the winter came there was little left to be done; and Annie saw by her aunt's looks that she wanted to get rid of her. Margaret Anderson had a chronic, consuming sense of poverty, and therefore worshipped with her whole soul the monkey Lars of saving and vigilance. Hence Annie, as soon as Alec was gone, went, with the simplicity belonging to her childlike nature, to see Mrs Forbes, and returned to Clippenstrae only to bid them good-bye.

The bodily repose and mental activity of the winter formed a strong contrast with her last experiences. But the rainy, foggy, frosty, snowy months passed away much as they had done before, fostering, amongst other hidden growths, that of Mrs Forbes' love for her semi-protégée, whom, like Castor and Pollux, she took half the year to heaven, and sent the other half to Tartarus. One notable event, however, of considerable importance in its results to the people of Howglen, took place this winter amongst the missionars of Glamerton.

CHAPTER LXXXV

So entire was Thomas Crann's notion of discipline, that it could not be satisfied with the mere riddance of Robert Bruce. Jealous, therefore, of encroachment on the part of minister or deacons, and opposed by his friend James Johnstone, he communicated his design to no one; for he knew that the higher powers, anxious to avoid scandal wherever possible, would, instead of putting the hypocrite to shame as he deserved, merely send him a civil letter, requesting him to withdraw from their communion. After watching for a fit opportunity, he resolved at length to make his accusation against Robert Bruce in person at an approaching church-meeting, at which, in consequence of the expected discussion of the question of the proper frequency of the administration of the sacrament, a full attendance of members might be expected.

They met in the chapel, which was partially lighted for the occasion. The night was brilliant with frosty stars, as Thomas walked to the rendezvous. He felt the vigour of the season in his yet unsubdued limbs, but as he watched his breath curling in the frosty air, and then vanishing in the night, he thought how the world itself would pass away before the face of Him that sat on the great white throne; and how the missionars of Glamerton would have nothing to say for themselves on that day, if they did not purify themselves on this. From the faint light of the stars he passed into the dull illumination of the tallow candles, and took his place in silence behind their snuffer, who, though half-witted, had yet shown intelligence and piety enough for admission into the community. The church slowly gathered, and at length Mr Turnbull appeared, supported by his deacons.

After the usual preliminary devotions, in which Robert Bruce "engaged," the business of the meeting was solemnly introduced. The only part which Thomas Crann took in it was to expostulate with the candle-snuffer, who being violently opposed to the wishes of the minister, and not daring to speak, kept grumbling in no inaudible voice at everything that came from that side of the house.

"Hoot, Richard! It's Scriptur', ye ken," said Thomas, soothingly.	"Heavens, Richard! It's Scripture, you know," said Thomas, soothingly.

"Scriptur' or no Scriptur', we're nae for't," growled Richard aloud, and rising, gave vent to his excited feelings by snuffing out and relighting every candle in its turn.

At length the further discussion of the question was postponed to the next meeting, and the minister was preparing to give out a hymn, when Thomas Crann's voice arose in the dusky space. Mr Turnbull stopped to listen, and there fell an expectant silence; for the stone-mason was both reverenced and feared. It was too dark to see more than the dim bulk of his figure, but he spoke with slow emphasis, and every word was heard.

"Brethren and office-beirers o' the church, it's upo' discipline that I want to speak. Discipline is ane o' the main objecs for which a church is gathered by the speerit o' God. And we maun work discipleen amo' oorsels, or else the rod o' the Almichty'll come doon upon a' oor backs. I winna haud ye frae particulars ony langer.—Upon a certain Sawbath nicht i' the last year, I gaed into Robert Bruce's hoose, to hae worship wi' 'm.—I'm gaein straucht and fair to the pint at ance. Whan he opened the buik, I saw him slip something oot atween the leaves o' 't, and crunkle 't up in 's han', luikin his greediest. Syne he read the twenty-third and fourt psalms. I cudna help watchin' him, and whan we gaed down upo' oor k-nees, I luikit roon efter him, and saw him pit something intil's breek-pooch. Weel, it stack to me. Efterhin I fand oot frae the lassie Annie Anderson, that the book was hers, that old Mr Cowie had given it to her upon his death-bed, and had told her besides that he had put a five pound note between the leaves of it, to be her own in remembrance of him, like. What say you to that, Robert Bruce?"

"It's all a lie," cried Robert, out of the dark back-ground under the gallery, where he always placed himself at such meetings, "got up between yourself and that ungrateful cousin of mine, James Anderson's lass, who I have kept like one of my own."

Bruce had been sitting trembling; but when Thomas put the question, believing that he had heard all that Thomas had to say, and that there was no proof against him, he resolved at once to meet the accusation with a stout denial. Whereupon Thomas resumed:

"You hear him deny it. Well, I have seen the Bible myself; and there's this inscription upon one of its blank pages: 'Over the twenty-third psalm of David,'—I told you that he read that psalm that night—'Over the twenty-third psalm of David, I have laid a five pound note for my dear Annie Anderson, after my death!' Then followed the number of the note, which I can show those that want to see. Now I have the banker's word for stating that upon the very Monday morning after that

efter that Sunday, Bruce paid into the bank a five poun' note o' that verra indentical nummer. What say ye to that, Robert Bruce?"

A silence followed. Thomas himself broke it with the words:

"That money he oucht to hae supposed was Mr Cooie's, and returned it till's dochters. But he pays't intil's ain accoont. Ca' ye na that a breach o' the eicht commandment, Robert Bruce?"

But now Robert Bruce rose. And he spoke with solemnity and pathos.

"It's a sair thing, sirs, that amo' Christians, wha ca' themsel's a chosen priesthood and a peculiar people, a jined member o' the same church should meet wi' sic ill-guideship as I hae met wi' at the han's o' Mr Crann. To say naething o' his no bein' ashamed to confess bein' sic a heepocreet i' the sicht o' God as to luik aboot him upon his knees, lyin' in wait for a man to do him hurt whan he pretendit to be worshippin' wi' him afore the Lord his Maker, to say naething o' that which I wadna hae expeckit o' him, he gangs aboot for auchteen months contrivin' to bring that man to disgrace because he daurna mak' sic a strong profession as he mak's himsel'. But the warst o' 't a' is, that he beguiles a young thochtless bairn, wha has been the cause o' muckle discomfort in oor hoose, to jine him i' the plot.

Sunday, Bruce paid into the bank a five pound note of that very identical number. What say you to that, Robert Bruce?"

A silence followed. Thomas himself broke it with the words:

"That money he ought to have supposed was Mr Cowie's, and returned it to his daughters. But he pays it into his own account. Don't you call that a breach of the eighth commandment, Robert Bruce?"

But now Robert Bruce rose. And he spoke with solemnity and pathos.

"It's a hard thing, sirs, that among Christians, who call themselves a chosen priesthood and a peculiar people, a joined member of the same church should meet with such ill-usage as I have met with at the hands of Mr Crann. To say nothing of his not being ashamed to confess such hypocrisy in the sight of God as to look about him upon his knees, lying in wait for a man to do him hurt when he pretended to be worshipping with him before the Lord his Maker, to say nothing of that which I wouldn't have expected of him, he goes about for eighteen months scheming to bring that man to disgrace because he daren't make such a strong profession as he makes himself. But the worst of it all is, that he beguiles a young thoughtless child, who has been the cause of much discomfort in our house,

It's true eneuch that I took the bank-note frae the Bible, whilk was a verra unshuitable place to put the unrichteous mammon intil, and min's me upo' the money-changers i' the temple; and it's true that I paid it into the bank the neist day—"

"What garred ye deny't, than?" interrupted Thomas.

"Bide a wee, Mr Crann, and caw canny. Ye hae been hearkened till wi'oot interruption, and I maun hae fair play here whatever I get frae yersel'. I didna deny the fac. Wha could deny a fac? But I denied a' the haill affair, i' the licht o' wickedness and thievin' that Mr Crann was castin' upo' 't. *I* saw that inscription and read it wi' my ain een the verra day the lassie brocht the beuk, and kenned as weel's Mr Crann that the siller wasna to be taen hame again. But I said to mysel': 'It'll turn the lassie's heid, and she'll jist fling't awa' in murlocks upo' sweeties, and plunky, and sic like,' for she was aye greedy, 'sae I'll jist pit it into the bank wi' my ain, and accoont for't efterhin wi' the lave o' her bit siller whan I gie that up intil her ain han's.' Noo, Mr Crann!"

He sat down, and Mr Turnbull rose.

"My Christian brethren," he said, "it seems to me that this is not the proper place to discuss such a question. It seems to me

to join him in the plot. It's true enough that I took the bank-note from the Bible, which was a very unsuitable place to put the unrighteous mammon into, and reminds me of the money-changers in the temple; and it's true that I paid it into the bank the next day—"

"What made you deny it, then?" interrupted Thomas.

"Wait a bit, Mr Crann, and be calm. You have been listened to without interruption, and I must have fair play here whatever I get from yourself. I didn't deny the fact. Who could deny a fact? But I denied all the whole affair, in the light of wickedness and thieving that Mr Crann was casting upon it. *I* saw that inscription and read it with my own eyes the very day the lassie brought the book, and knew as well as Mr Crann that the money wasn't to be taken home again. But I said to myself: 'It'll turn the lassie's head, and she'll just fling it away in crumbs upon sweeties, and plunky, and suchlike,' for she was always greedy, 'so I'll just put it into the bank with my own, and account for it afterwards with the rest of her money when I give that up into her own hands.' Now, Mr Crann!"

He sat down, and Mr Turnbull rose.

"My Christian brethren," he said, "it seems to me that this is not the proper place to discuss such a question. It seems to me likewise ill-judged of Mr Crann to make such an accusation in public against Mr Bruce, who, I must say, has met it with a self-restraint and a self-possession most creditable to him, and has answered it in a very satisfactory manner. The hundredth psalm."

"Steady, sir!" exclaimed Thomas, forgetting his manners in his eagerness. "I haven't done yet. And where would be the place to discuss such a question but before a meeting of the church? Call you that the public, sir? Wasn't the church established for the sake of discipline? Such things aren't to be ironed out in a hole and a corner, between you and the deacons, sir. They belong to the whole body. We're all wronged together, and the Holy Ghost, whose temple we should be, is wronged besides. You at least might know, sir, that he's withdrawn his presence from our midst, and we are but a candle under a bushel, and not a city set upon a hill. We bear no witness. And the cause of his displeasure is the accursed thing which the Achan in our camp has hidden in the County Bank, besides many other causes that come home to us all. And the world just scoffs at our profession of religion, when it sees such a man as that in our midst."

"All this is nothing to the point, Mr Crann," said Mr Turnbull in displeasure.

"It's to the very heart of the point," returned Thomas, equally displeased. "If Robert Bruce saw the inscription the day the lassie brought home the book, will he tell me how it was that he came to leave the note in the book till that Sabbath night?"

"I looked for it, but I couldn't find it, and thought she had taken it out upon the way home."

"Couldn't you find the twenty-third psalm?—But just one thing more, Mr Turnbull, and then I'll hold my tongue," resumed Thomas.—"James Johnstone, will you run over to my house, and fetch the Bible? It's lying upon the drawers. You can't mistake it.—Just have patience till he comes back, sir, and we'll see how Mr Bruce'll read the inscription. I would have made nothing of it, if it hadn't been for a friend of mine. But Mr Bruce is a scholar, and will read the Latin to us."

By this time James Johnstone was across the street.

"There's some foul play in this," cried Bruce, out of the darkness. "My enemy must send for an outlandish speech and a heathen tongue to insnare one of the brethren!"

Profound silence followed. All sat expectant. The snuff of the candles grew longer and longer. Even the energetic Richard, who had opposed the Scripture single-handed, forgot his duty in the absorbing interest of the moment. Every ear was listening for the footsteps of the returning weaver, bringing the Bible of the parish-clergyman into the half-unhallowed precincts of a conventicle. At a slight motion of one of the doors, an audible start of expectation broke like an electric spark from the still people. But nothing came of it. They had to wait full five minutes yet before the messenger returned, bearing the large volume in both hands in front of him.

"Take the book up to Mr Turnbull, James, and snuff his candles," said Thomas.

James took the snuffers, but Richard started up, snatched them from him, and performed the operation himself with his usual success.

The book being laid on the desk before Mr Turnbull, Thomas called out into the back region of the chapel,

"Now, Robert Bruce, come forward, and find out this inscription that you know all about so well, and read it to the church, that they may see what a scholar they have among them."

But there was neither voice nor hearing.

After a pause, Mr Turnbull spoke.

"Mr Bruce, we're waiting for you," he said. "Do not be afraid. You shall have justice."

A dead silence followed the appeal. Presently some of those furthest back—they were women in hooded cloaks and *mutches*—spoke in scarce audible voices.

"He's not here, sir. We can't see him," they said.

The minister could not distinguish their words.

"Not here!" cried Thomas, who, deaf as he was, had heard them. "He was here a minute ago! His conscience has spoken at last. He's fallen down, like Ananias, in the seat."

Richard snatched a candle out of the candelabrum, and went to look. Others followed similarly provided. They searched the pew where he had been sitting, and the neighbouring pews, and the whole chapel, but he was nowhere to be found.

"That would have been him, when I heard the door bang," they said to each other at length.

And so it was. For perceiving how he had committed himself, he had slipped down in the pew, crawled on all fours to the door, and got out of the place unsuspected.

A formal sentence of expulsion was passed upon him by a show of hands, and the word *Expelled* was written against his name in the list of church-members.

"Thomas Crann, will you engage in prayer," said Mr Turnbull.

"Na, not tonight," answered Thomas. "I'm like one under the old law that had been burying the dead. I've been doing necessary but foul work, and I'm defiled in consequence. I'm not in a right spirit to pray in public. I must go home to my prayers. I hope I mayn't do something myself before long that'll make it needful for you to dismiss me next. But if that time should come, spare not, I beseech you."

So, after a short prayer from Mr Turnbull, the meeting separated in a state of considerable excitement. Thomas half expected to hear of an action for libel, but Robert knew better than venture upon that. Besides, no damages could be got out of Thomas.

When Bruce was once outside the chapel, he assumed the erect posture to which his claim was entirely one of species, and went home by circuitous ways. He found the shop still open, attended by his wife.

"Preserve us, Robert! what's come over you?" she exclaimed.

"I had such a headache, I was forced to come out before all was done," he answered. "I don't think I'll go any more, for they don't conduct things altogether to my liking. From now on I won't bother with them."

His wife looked at him anxiously, perhaps with some vague suspicion of the truth; but she said nothing, and I do not believe the matter was ever alluded to between them. The only indications remaining the next day of what he had gone through that evening, consisted in an increase of suavity towards his grown customers, and of acerbity towards the children who were unfortunate enough to enter his shop.

Of the two, however, perhaps Thomas Crann was the more unhappy as he went home that night. He felt nothing of the elation which commonly springs from success in a cherished project. He had been the promoter and agent in the downfall of another man, and although the fall was a just one, and it was better too for the man to be down than standing on a false pedestal, Thomas could not help feeling the reaction of a fellow-creature's humiliation. Now that the thing was done, and the end gained, the eternal brotherhood asserted itself, and Thomas pitied Bruce and mourned over him. He must be to him henceforth as a heathen man and a publican, and he was sorry for him. "You see," he said to himself, "it's not like a slip or a sin; but an evil disease cleaveth fast unto him, and there's small chance of him ever repenting now. All has been done for him that can be done."

Yet Thomas worshipped a God, who, if the theories Thomas held were correct, could at once, by the free gift of the Holy Spirit, generate repentance in Bruce, and so make him fit for salvation; but who, Thomas believed, would not do so—at all events, *might* not do so—keeping him alive for ever in howling unbelief instead.

Scarcely any of the "members" henceforth saluted Bruce in the street. None of them traded with him, except two or three who owed him a few shillings, and could not pay him. And the modifying effect upon the week's returns was very perceptible. This was the only form in which a recognizable vengeance could have reached him. To escape from it, he had serious thoughts of leaving the place, and setting up in some remote village.

CHAPTER LXXXVI

Notwithstanding Alec's diligence and the genial companionship of Mr Cupples—whether the death of Kate, or his own illness, or the reaction of shame after his sojourn in the tents of wickedness, had opened dark visions of the world of reality lying in awful *unknownness* around the life he seemed to know, I cannot tell,—cold isolations would suddenly seize upon him, wherein he would ask himself—that oracular cave in which one hears a thousand questions before one reply—"What is the use of it all—this study and labour?" And he interpreted the silence to mean: "Life is worthless. There is no glow in it—only a glimmer and shine at best."—Will my readers set this condition down as one of disease? If they do, I ask, "Why should a man be satisfied with anything such as was now within the grasp of Alec Forbes?" And if they reply that a higher ambition would have set him at peace if not at rest, I only say that they would be nearer health if they had his disease. Pain is not malady; it is the revelation of malady—the meeting and recoil between the unknown death and the unknown life; that jar of the system whereby the fact becomes known to the man that he is ill. There was disease in Alec, but the disease did not lie in his dissatisfaction. It lay in that poverty of life with which those are satisfied who call such discontent disease. Such disease is the first flicker of the aurora of a rising health.

This state of feeling, however, was only occasional; and a reviving interest in anything belonging to his studies, or a merry talk with Mr Cupples, would dispel it for a time, just as a breath of fine air will give the sense of perfect health to one dying of consumption.

But what made these questionings develop into the thorns of a more definite self-condemnation—the advanced guard sometimes of the roses of peace—was simply this:

He had written to his mother for money to lay out upon superior instruments, and new chemical apparatus; and his mother had replied sadly that she was unable to send it. She hinted that his education had cost more than she had expected. She told him that she was in debt to Robert Bruce, and had of late been compelled to delay the payment of its interest. She informed him also that, even under James Dow's conscientious management, there seemed little ground for hoping that the farm would ever make a return correspondent to the large outlay his father had made upon it.

This letter stung Alec to the heart. That his mother should be in the power of such a man as Bruce, was bad enough; but that she should have been exposed for his sake to the indignity of requesting his forbearance, seemed unendurable. To despise the man was no satisfaction, the right and the wrong being where they were.—And what proportion of the expenses of last session had gone to his college-accounts?

He wrote a humble letter to his mother—and worked still harder. For although he could not make a shilling at present, the future had hope in it.

Meantime Mr Cupples, in order that he might bear such outward signs of inward grace as would appeal to the perceptions of the Senatus, got a new hat, and changed his shabby tail-coat for a black frock. His shirt ceased to be a hypothesis to account for his collar, and became a real hypostasis, evident and clean. These signs of improvement led to inquiries on the part of the Senatus, and the result was that, before three months of the session were over, he was formally installed as librarian. His first impulse on receiving the good news was to rush down to Luckie Cumstie's and have a double-tumbler. But conscience was too strong for Satan, and sent him home to his pipe—which, it must be confessed, he smoked twice as much as before his reformation.

From the moment of his appointment, he seemed to regard the library as his own private property, or, rather, as his own family. He was grandfather to the books: at least a grandfather shows that combination of parent and servant which comes nearest to the relation he henceforth manifested towards them. Most of them he gave out graciously; some of them grudgingly; a few of them with much reluctance; but all of them with injunctions to care, and special warnings against forcing the backs, crumpling or folding the leaves, and making thumb-marks.

"Noo," he would say to some country bejan, "tak' the buik i' yer han's no as gin 'twar a neip, but as gin 'twar the sowl o' a new-born bairn. Min' ye it has to sair mony a generation efter your banes lie bare i' the moul', an' ye maun hae respec' to them

"Now," he would say to some country bejan, "take the book in your hands not as if it were a turnip, but as if it were the soul of a new-born child. Remember it has to serve many a generation after your bones lie bare in the mould, and you must have respect to those that come after you, and not abuse their fare. I beg you won't mangle it."

The bejans used to laugh at him in consequence. But long before they were magistrands, the best of them had a profound respect for the librarian. Not a few of them repaired to him with all their difficulties; and such a general favourite was he, that any story of his humour or oddity was sure to be received with a roar of loving laughter. Indeed I doubt whether, within the course of a curriculum, Mr Cupples had not become the real centre of intellectual and moral life in that college.

One evening, as he and Alec were sitting together speculating on the speediest mode of turning Alec's acquirements to money-account, their landlady entered.

"Here's my cousin," she said, "Captain McTavish of the *Seahorse*, Mr Forbes, who says that before long he'll be wanting a young doctor to go and keep the scurvy off his men at the whale-fishing. So of course I thought of my own first, and ran upstairs to you. It'll be fifty pounds in your pocket, and plenty of rough pranks that the like of you young fellows like, though I can't say I would like such things myself. Only I'm an old wife, you see, and that makes the difference."

"Not that old, Mistress Leslie," said Cupples, "if you wouldn't lie."

"Tell Captain McTavish that I'll go," said Alec, who had hesitated no longer than the time Mr Cupples took to say the word of kind flattery to their landlady.

"He'll want testimonials, you know."

"Wouldn't *you* give me one, Mrs Leslie?"

"Indeed I would, if it were of any account. You see, Mr Alec, today's not yesterday, and this session's not the last."

"Hold your tongue, and don't rub a sore place," cried Mr Cupples.

"I beg your pardon," returned Mrs Leslie, submissively.

Alec followed her down the stair.

He soon returned, his eyes flashing with delight. Adventure! And fifty pounds to take to his mother!

"All right, Mr Cupples. The Captain has promised to take me if my testimonials are satisfactory. I think they will give me good ones now. If it weren't for you, I should have been lying in the gutter instead of walking the quarter-deck."

"Well, well, bantam. There's two sides to most obligations.—I'm librarian."

The reader may remember that in his boyhood Alec was fond of the sea, had rigged a flagstaff, and had built the *Bonnie Annie*. He was nearly beside himself with delight, which continued unjarred until he heard from his mother. She had too much good sense to make any opposition, but she could not prevent her anticipations of loss and loneliness from appearing. His mother's trouble quelled the exuberance of Alec's spirits without altering his resolve. He would return to her in the fall of the year, bringing with him what would ease her mind of half its load.

There was no check at the examinations this session.

CHAPTER LXXXVII

Mrs Forbes was greatly perplexed about Annie. She could not bear the thought of turning her out; and besides she did not see where she was to go, for she could not be in the house with young Bruce. On the other hand, she had still the same dangerous sense of worldly duty as to the prevention of a so-called unsuitable match, the chance of which was more threatening than ever. For Annie had grown very lovely, and having taken captive the affections of the mother, must put the heart of the son in dire jeopardy. But Alec arrived two days before he was expected, and delivered his mother from her perplexity by declaring that if Annie were sent away he too would leave the house. He had seen through the maternal precautions the last time he was at home, and talking with Cupples about it, who secretly wished for no better luck than that Alec should fall in love with Annie, had his feelings strengthened as to the unkindness, if not injustice, of throwing her periodically into such a dungeon as the society of the Bruces. So Annie remained where she was, much, I must confess, to her inward content.

The youth and the maiden met every day—the youth unembarrassed, and the maiden reserved and shy, even to the satisfaction of the mother. But if Alec could have seen the loving thoughts which, like threads of heavenly gold (for all the gold of heaven is invisible), wrought themselves into the garments she made for him, I do not think *he* could have helped falling in love with her, although most men, I fear, would only have fallen the more in love with themselves, and cared the less for her. But he did not see them, or hear the divine measures to which her needle flew, as she laboured to arm him against the cold of those regions

> Where all life dies, death lives, and nature breeds,
> Perverse, all monstrous, all prodigious things.

Alec's college-life had interposed a gulf between him and his previous history. But his approaching departure into places unknown and a life untried, operated upon his spiritual condition like the approach of death; and he must strengthen again all the old bonds which had been stretched thin by time and absence; he must make righteous atonement for the wrong of neglect; in short, he must set his inward house in order, ere he went forth to the abodes of ice. Death is not a breaker but a renewer of ties. And if in view of death we gird up the loins of our minds, and unite our hearts into a whole of love, and tenderness, and atonement, and forgiveness, then Death himself cannot be that thing of forlornness and loss.

He took a day to go and see Curly, and spent a pleasant afternoon with him, recalling the old times, and the old stories, and the old companions; for the youth with the downy chin has a past as ancient as that of the man with the gray beard. And Curly told him the story of his encounter with young Bruce on the bank of the Wan Water. And over and over again Annie's name came up, but Curly never hinted at her secret.

The next evening he went to see Thomas Crann. Thomas received him with a cordiality amounting even to gruff tenderness.

"I'm right glad to see you," he said; "and I take it very kindly of you, with all your grand learning, to come and see an ignorant man like me. But Alec, my man, there's some things that I know better than you know them yet. He that made the whales is better worth seeking than the whales themselves. God's works may swallow the man that follows them, but God himself's the hiding-place from the wind, and the covert from the tempest. Set up no false God—that's the thing that you love best, you know—for like Dagon, it'll fall, and maybe brain you in the fall. Come down upon your knees with me, and I'll pray for you. But you must pray for yourself, or my prayers won't be of much avail: you know that."

Yielding to the spiritual power of Thomas, whose gray-blue

eyes were flashing with fervour, Alec kneeled down as he was desired, and Thomas said:

"O thou who madest the whales to play i' the great watters, and gavest unto men sic a need o' licht that they maun hunt the leviathan to haud their lamps burnin' at nicht whan thou hast sent thy sun awa' to ither lands, be thou roon' aboot this youth, wha surely is nae muckle waur than him 'at the Saviour lo'ed; and when thou seest his ship gang sailin' into the far north whaur thou keepest thy stores o' frost and snaw ready to remin' men o' thy goodness by takin' the heat frae them for a sizzon—when thou seest his ship gaein far north, pit doon thy finger, O Lord, and straik a track afore't, throu' amo' the hills o' ice, that it may gang throu' in saf-ety, even as thy chosen people gaed throu' the Reid Sea, and the river o' Jordan. For, Lord, we want him hame again in thy good time. For he is the only son of his mother, and she is a widow. But aboon a', O Lord, elec' him to thy grace and lat him ken the glory o' God, even the licht o' thy coontenance. For me, I'm a' thine, to live or dee, and I care not which. For I hae gotten the gueed o' this warl'; and gin I binna ready for the neist, it's because o' my sins, and no o' my savours. For I wad glaidle depairt and be with the Lord. But this

eyes were flashing with fervour, Alec kneeled down as he was desired, and Thomas said:

"O thou who madest the whales to play in the great waters, and gavest unto men such a need of light that they must hunt the leviathan to keep their lamps burning at night when thou hast sent thy sun away to other lands, be thou round about this youth, who surely isn't much worse than him that the Saviour loved; and when thou seest his ship go sailing into the far north where thou keepest thy stores of frost and snow ready to remind men of thy goodness by taking the heat from them for a season—when thou seest his ship going far north, put down thy finger, O Lord, and stroke a track before it, through among the hills of ice, that it may go through in safety, even as thy chosen people went through the Red Sea, and the river of Jordan. For, Lord, we want him home again in thy good time. For he is the only son of his mother, and she is a widow. But above all, O Lord, elect him to thy grace and let him know the glory of God, even the light of thy countenance. For me, I'm all thine, to live or die, and I care not which. For I have gotten the good of this world; and if I'm not ready for the next, it's because of my sins, and not of my savours. For I would gladly depart and be with the

Lord. But this young man has never seen thy face; and, O Lord, I'm just afraid that my countenance might fall even in thy kingdom, if I knew that Alec Forbes was down in the ill place. Spare him, O Lord, and give him time for repentance if he has a chance; but if he has none, take him at once, that his doom may be the lighter."

Alec rose with a very serious face, and went home to his mother in a mood more concordant with her feelings than the light-heartedness with which he generally tried to laugh away her apprehensions.

He even called on Robert Bruce, at his mother's request. It went terribly against the grain with him though. He expected to find him rude as of old, but he was, on the contrary, as pleasant as a man could be whose only notion of politeness lay in *licking*.

His civility came from two sources—the one hope, the other fear. Alec was going away and might never return. That was the hope. For although Bruce had spread the report of Annie's engagement to Curly, he believed that Alec was the real obstacle to his plans. At the same time he was afraid of him, believing in his cowardly mind that Alec would not stop short of personal reprisals if he should offend him; and now he was a great six-foot fellow, of whose prowess at college confused and exaggerated stories were floating about the town.—Bruce was a man who could hatch and cherish plans, keeping one in reserve behind the other, and beholding their result from afar.

"Ay! ay! Mr Forbes—so you're going away among the train-oil, are you? Have you any share in the take?"

"I don't think the doctor has any share," answered Alec.

"But no doubt you'll put to your hand, and help at the catching."

"Very likely."

"Well, if you come in for a barrel or two, you may count upon me to take it off your hand, at the usual price—to the *wholesale* merchan's, ye ken—wi' maybe a sma' discoont for orderin' 't afore the whaul was ta'en."

The day drew near. He had bidden all his friends farewell. He must go just as the spring was coming in with the old well-beloved green borne before her on the white banner of the snowdrop, and following in miles of jubilation: he must not wait for her triumph, but speed away before her towards the dreary north, which only a few of her hard-riding pursuivants would ever reach. For green hills he must have opal-hued bergs—for green fields the outspread slaty waters, rolling in the delight of their few weeks of glorious freedom, and mocking the unwieldy ice-giants that rush in wind-driven troops across their plains, or welter captive in the weary swell, and melt away beneath the low summer sun.

His mother would have gone to see him on board, but he prevailed upon her to say good-bye to him at home. She kept her tears till after he was gone. Annie bade him farewell with a pale face, and a smile that was all sweetness and no gladness. She did not weep even afterwards. A gentle cold hand pressed her heart down, so that neither blood reached her face nor water her eyes. She went about everything just as before, because it had to be done; but it seemed foolish to do anything. The spring might as well stay away for any good that it promised either of them.

As Mr Cupples was taking his farewell on board,

"Ye'll gang and see my mother?" said Alec.

"Ay, ay, bantam; I'll do that.—Noo tak care o' yersel; and dinna tak leeberties wi' behemoth. Put a ring in's nose gin ye like, only haud oot ower frae's tail. He's no mowse ."

So away went Alec northwards, over the blue-gray waters, surgeon of the strong barque *Sea-horse*.

CHAPTER LXXXVIII

Two days after Alec's departure, Mr Bruce called at Howglen to see Annie.

"How are you, Mistress Forbes? How are you, Miss Anderson? I was just coming over the water for a walk, and I thought I might as well bring the money with me that I'm owing you."

Annie stared. She did not know what he meant. He explained.

"It's well on to a year that you've had neither bite nor sup beneath my humble rooftree, and as that was to make up for the interest, I must pay you the one seeing you won't accept the other. I have just brought you ten pounds to put in your own pocket in the meantime."

Annie could hardly believe her ears. Could she be the rightful owner of such untold wealth? Without giving her time to say anything, however, Bruce went on, still holding in his hand the dirty bunch of one-pound notes.

"But I'm thinking the best way to dispose of it would be to let me put it to the rest of the principal. So I'll just take it to the bank as I go back. I can't give you anything for it, as that would be breaking the law against compound interest, but I can make it up some other way, you know."

But Annie had been too much pleased at the prospect of possession to let the money go so easily.

"I have plenty of ways of spending it," she said, "without waste. So I'll just take it myself, and thank you, Mr Bruce."

She rose and took the notes from Bruce's unwilling hand. He was on the point of replacing them in his trowsers-pocket and refusing to give them up, when her promptitude rescued them. Discomfiture was manifest in his reluctant eyes, and the little tug of retraction with which he loosed his hold upon the notes. He went home mortified, and poverty-stricken, but yet having gained a step towards a further end.

Annie begged Mrs Forbes to take the money.

"I have no use for it, ma'am. An old gown of yours makes as good a frock for me as I can ever want to have."

But Mrs Forbes would not even take charge of the money—partly from the pride of beneficence, partly from the fear of involving it in her own straits. So that Annie, having provided herself with a few necessaries, felt free to spend the rest as she would. How she longed for Tibbie Dyster! But not having her, she went to Thomas Crann, and offered the money to him.

"'Deed no, lassie! I winna lay a finger upo' 't. Lay't by till ye want it yersel'."	"No indeed, lassie! I won't lay a finger on it. Lay it by till you want it yourself."
"Dinna ye ken somebody that wants't mair nor me, Thomas?"	"Don't you know somebody that wants it more than me, Thomas?"

Now Thomas had just been reading a few words spoken, according to Matthew, the tax-gatherer, by the King of Men, declaring the perfection of God to consist in his giving good things to all alike, whether they love him or not. And when Annie asked the question, he remembered the passage and Peter Peterson together. But he could not trust her to follow her own instincts, and therefore went with her to see the poor fellow, who was in a consumption, and would never drink any more. When he saw his worn face, and the bones with hands at the ends of them, his heart smote him that he had ever been harsh to him; and although he had gone with the intention of rousing him to a sense of his danger beyond the grave, he found that for very pity he could not open the prophetic mouth. From self-accusation he took shelter behind Annie, saying to himself: "Babes can best declare what's best revealed to them;" and left Peter to her ministrations.

A little money went far to make his last days comfortable; and ere she had been visiting him for more than a month, he loved her so that he was able to believe that God might love him, though he knew perfectly (wherein perhaps his drunkenness had taught him more than the prayers of many a pharisee) that he could not deserve it.

This was the beginning of a new relation between Annie and the poor of Glamerton. And the soul of the maiden grew and blossomed into divine tenderness, for it was still more blessed to give than to receive. But she was only allowed to taste of this blessedness, for she had soon to learn that even giving itself must be given away cheerfully.

After three months Bruce called again with the quarter's interest. Before the next period arrived he had an interview with James Dow, to whom he represented that, as he was now paying the interest down in cash, he ought not to be exposed to the inconvenience of being called upon at any moment to restore the principal, but should have the money secured to him for ten years. After consultation, James Dow consented to a three years' loan, beyond which he would not yield. Papers to this effect were signed, and one quarter's interest more was placed in Annie's willing hand.

In the middle of summer Mr Cupples made his appearance, and

was warmly welcomed. He had at length completed the catalogue of the library, had got the books arranged to his mind, and was brimful of enjoyment. He ran about the fields like a child; gathered bunches of white clover; made a great kite, and bought an unmeasureable length of string, with which he flew it the first day the wind was worthy of the honour; got out Alec's boat, and upset himself in the Glamour; was run away with by one of the plough-horses in the attempt to ride him to the water; was laughed at and loved by everybody about Howglen. At length, that is, in about ten days, he began to settle down into sobriety of demeanour. The first thing that sobered him was a hint of yellow upon a field of oats. He began at once to go and see the people of Glamerton, and called upon Thomas Crann first.

He found him in one of his gloomy moods, which however were much less frequent than they had been.

"How are you today, old friend?" said Cupples.

"Old as you say, sir, and not much further on than when I began. I sometimes think I have profited less than anybody I know. But, eh, sir, I would be sorry, if I were you, to die before I had got a glimpse of the face of God."

"How do you know I haven't had that glimpse?"

"You would look more solemn like," answered Thomas.

"Maybe I would," responded Cupples, seriously.

"Man, strive to get it. Give Him no rest, day or night, till you get it. Knock, knock, knock, till it be opened to you."

"Well, Thomas, you don't seem so happy yourself, after all. Don't you think you may be like one that's trying to see the face of which you speak through a crack in the door, instead of having patience till it's opened?"

But the suggestion was quite lost upon Thomas, who, after a gloomy pause, went on.

"Sin's such an awful thing," he began; when the door opened, and in walked James Dow.

His entrance did not interrupt Thomas, however.

"Sin's such an awful thing! And I've sinned so often and so long, that maybe He'll be forced after all to send me to the bottomless pit."

"Heavens, Thomas! don't speak such awful things," said Dow. "They're dreadful to listen to. I'll wager He's as kind-hearted as yourself."

James had no reputation for piety, though much for truthfulness and honesty. Nor had he any idea how much lay in the words he had hastily uttered. A light-gleam grew and faded on Thomas's face.

"I said, he might be *forced* to send me after all."

"What, Thomas!" cried Cupples. "He *couldn't* save you! With the Son and the Spirit to help him? And a willing heart in you besides? Faith! you've a greater opinion of Satan than I gave you the discredit of."

"Na, na; it's not Satan. It's myself. I wouldn't lay more blame upon Satan's shoulders than his own. He has enough already, poor fellow!"

"You'll be of old Robbie Burns's

opinion, that he 'might perhaps still have a stake.' "[1]

"Na, na; he has none. Burns was no prophet."

"But just suppose, Thomas—if the devil were to repent."

"Man!" exclaimed the stonemason, rising to his full height with slow labour after the day's toil, "it would be cruel to make *him* repent. It would be too hard upon him. Better kill him. The bitterness of such repentance would be too terrible. It would be more than he could bear. It would break his heart altogether.—Na, na, he has no chance."

The last sentence was spoken quickly and with attempted carelessness as he resumed his seat.

"How do you know that?" asked Cupples.

"There's no such word in Scripture."

"Do you think He must tell *us* everything?"

"We have no right to think anything that He doesn't tell us."

"I'm not so sure of that, Thomas. Maybe, sometimes, he doesn't tell us a thing just to make us think about it, and be ready for the time when he will tell us."

Thomas was silent for a few moments. Then with a smile—rather a grim one—he said,

"Here's a curious thing now.—There's neither of you converted,

---

[1] i.e. a chance. (Robert Burns, in the last verse of his poem "Address to the Deil" speculates that Satan might yet repent and be spared.)

and yet your words strengthen my heart as if they came from the realm above."

But his countenance changed, and he added hastily,

"It's a mark of indwelling sin. To the law and to the testimony—Go away and leave me to my prayers."

They obeyed; for either they felt that nothing but his prayers would do, or they were awed, and dared not remain.

Mr Cupples could wait. Thomas could not.

The Forlorn Hope of men must storm the walls of Heaven.

Amongst those who sit down at the gate till one shall come and open it, are to be found both the wise and the careless children.

CHAPTER LXXXIX

Mr Cupples returned to his work, for the catalogue had to be printed.

The weeks and months passed on, and the time drew nigh when it would be no folly to watch the mail-coach in its pride of scarlet and gold, as possibly bearing the welcome letter announcing Alec's return. At length, one morning, Mrs Forbes said:

"We may look for him every day now, Annie."

She did not know with what a tender echo her words went roaming about in Annie's bosom, awaking a thousand thought-birds in the twilight land of memory, which had tucked their heads under their wings to sleep, and thereby to live.

But the days went on and the hope was deferred. The rush of the *Sea-horse* did not trouble the sands of the shallow bar, or sweep, with fiercely ramping figure-head, past the long pier-spike, stretching like the hand of welcome from the hospitable shore. While they fancied her full-breasted sails, swelled as with sighs for home, bowing lordly over the submissive waters, the *Sea-horse* lay a frozen mass, changed by the might of the winds and the snow and the frost into the grotesque ice-gaunt phantom of a ship, through which, the winter long, the winds would go whistling and raving, crowding upon it the snow and the crystal icicles, all in the wild waste of the desert north, with no ear to hear the sadness, and no eye to behold the deathly beauty.

At length the hope deferred began to make the heart sick. Dim anxiety passed into vague fear, and then deepened into dull conviction, over which ever and anon flickered a pale ghostly hope, like the *fatuus* over the swamp that has swallowed the unwary wanderer. Each would find the other wistfully watching to read any thought that might have escaped the vigilance of its keeper, and come up from the dungeon of the heart to air itself on the terraces of the face; and each would drop the glance hurriedly, as if caught in a fault. But the moment came when their meeting eyes were fixed and they burst into tears, each accepting the other's confession of hopeless grief as the seal of doom.

I will not follow them through the slow shadows of gathering fate. I will not record the fancies that tormented them, or describe the blank that fell upon the duties of the day. I will not tell how, as the winter drew on, they heard his voice calling in the storm for help, or how through the snow-drifts they saw him plodding wearily home. His mother forgot her debt, and ceased to care what became of herself. Annie's anxiety settled into an earnest prayer that she might not rebel against the will of God.

But the anxiety of Thomas Crann was not limited to the earthly fate of the lad. It extended to his fate in the other world—too probably, in his eyes, that endless, yearless, undivided fate, wherein the breath still breathed into the soul of man by his Maker is no longer the breath of life, but the breath of infinite death—

> Sole Positive of Night,
> Antipathist of Light,

giving to the ideal darkness a real and individual hypostasis in helpless humanity, keeping men alive that the light in them may continue to be darkness.

Terrible were his agonies in wrestling with God for the life of the lad, and terrible his fear lest his own faith should fail him if his prayers should not be heard. Alec Forbes was to Thomas Crann as it were the representative of all his unsaved brothers and sisters of the human race, for whose sakes he, like the apostle Paul, would have gladly undergone what he dreaded for them. He went to see his mother; said "Hoo are ye, mem?" sat down; never opened his lips, except to utter a few commonplaces; rose and left her—a little comforted. Nor can anything but human sympathy alleviate the pain while it obscures not the presence of human grief. Do not remind me that the divine is better. I know it. But why?—Because the divine is the highest—the creative human. The sympathy of the Lord himself is the more human that it is divine.

And in Annie's face, as she ministered to her friend, shone, notwithstanding her full share in the sorrow, a light that came not from sun or stars—as it were a suppressed, waiting light. And Mrs Forbes felt the holy influences that proceeded both from her and from Thomas Crann.

How much easier it is to bear a trouble that comes upon a trouble than one that intrudes a death's head into the midst of a merry-making! Mrs Forbes scarcely felt it a trouble when she received a note from Robert Bruce informing her that, as he was on the point of removing to another place which offered great advantages for the employment of the little money he possessed, he would be obliged to her to pay as soon as possible the hundred pounds she owed him, along with certain arrears of interest specified. She wrote that it was impossible for her at present, and forgot the whole affair. But within three days she received a formal application for the debt from a new solicitor. To this she paid no attention, just wondering what would come next. After about three months a second application was made, according to legal form; and in the month of May a third arrived, with the hint from the lawyer that his client was now prepared to proceed to extremities; whereupon she felt for the first time that she must do something.

She sent for James Dow.

"Are you going to the market to-day, James?" she asked.

"Indeed I am, ma'am."

"Well, be sure and go into one of the tents, and have a good dinner."

"Indeed, ma'am, I'll do nothing of the sort. It's a sin and a shame to waste good money upon broth and beef. I'll just put a snack in my pocket, and that'll bring me home as well as all their kale. I can stand anything but waste."

"It's very foolish of you, James."

"It's your pleasure to say so, ma'am."

"Well, tell me what to do about that."

And she handed him the letter.

James took it and read it slowly. Then he stared at his mistress. Then he read it again. At length, with a bewildered look, he said,

"If you owe the money, you must pay it, ma'am."

"But I can't."

"The Lord preserve us! What's to be done? *I have but thirty* hained up i' my kist. That wadna gang far."

"No, no, James," returned his mistress. "I am not going to take your money to pay Mr Bruce."

"He's an awfu' cratur that, mem. He wad tak the win'in' sheet aff o' the deid."

"Well, I must see what can be done. I'll go and consult Mr Gibb."

James took his leave, dejected on his mistress's account, and on his own. As he went out, he met Annie.

"Eh, Annie!" he said; "this is awfu'."

"What's the matter, Dooie?"

"That schochlin' cratur, Bruce, is mintin' at roupin' the mistress for a wheen siller she's aucht him."

"He daurna!" exclaimed Annie.

"He'll daur onything but tyne siller. Eh! lassie, gin we hadna len' 't him yours!"

"I'll gang till him direcly. But dinna tell the mistress. She wadna like it."

"Na, na. I s' haud my tongue, I s' warran'.—Ye're the best cratur ever was born. She'll maybe perswaud the ill-faured tyke."

Murmuring the last two sentences to himself, he walked away. When Annie entered Bruce's shop, the big spider was unoccupied, and ready to devour her. He put on therefore his most gracious reception.

"Hoo are ye, Miss Anderson?

I'm glad to see you. Come into the house."

"No, I thank you. I want to speak to yourself, Mr Bruce. What's all this about Mrs Forbes and you?"

"Great folk mustn't ride over the top of poor folk like me, Miss Anderson."

"She's a widow, Mr Bruce"—Annie could not add "and childless"—"and lays no claim to be great folk. It's not a Christian way of treating her."

"Folk *must* have their own. It's mine, and I must have it. There's nothing against that in the ten tables. There's no gospel for not giving folk their own. I'm no missionar now. I don't hold with such things. I can't beggar my family to keep up her great house. She must pay me, or I'll take it."

"If you do, Mr Bruce, you won't have my money one minute after the time's up; and I'm sorry you have it till then."

"That's neither here nor there. You would be wanting it by that time anyway."

Now Bruce had given up the notion of leaving Glamerton, for he had found that the patronage of the missionars in grocery was not essential to a certain measure of success; and he had no intention of proceeding to an auction of Mrs Forbes's goods, for he saw that would put him in a worse position with the public than any amount of quiet practice in lying and stealing. But there was every likelihood of Annie's being married some day; and then her money would be recalled, and he would be left without the capital necessary for carrying on his business upon the same enlarged scale—seeing he now supplied many of the little country shops. It would be a grand move then, if, by a far-sighted generalship, a careful copying of the example of his great ancestor, he could get a permanent hold of some of Annie's property.—Hence had come the descent upon Mrs Forbes, and here came its success.

"You'll have as much of mine for yourself as'll clear Mrs Forbes," said Annie.

"Well. Very well.—But you see that's mine for two and a half years anyway. That would only amount to losing her interest for two and a half years—altogether. That won't do."

"What will do, then, Mr Bruce?"

"I don't know. I want my own."

"But you mustn't torment her, Mr Bruce. You know that."

"Well! I'm open to anything reasonable. There's the interest for two and a half—call it three years—at what I could make of it—say eight per cent—four and twenty pounds. Then there's her arrears of interest—and then there's the loss of the overturn—and then there's the loss of the money that you won't have to lend me.—If you give me a quittance for a hundred and fifty pounds, I'll give her a receipt.—It'll be a great loss to me!"

"Anything you like," said Annie.

And Bruce brought out papers already written by his lawyer, one of which he signed and the other she.

"You'll remember," he added, as she was leaving the shop, "that

to pay ye no interest noo excep' upo' fifty poun'?"	I have to pay you no interest now except upon fifty pounds?"
He had paid her nothing for the last half year at least.	He had paid her nothing for the last half year at least.

He would not have dared to fleece the girl thus, had she had any legally constituted guardians; or had those who would gladly have interfered, had power to protect her. But he took care so to word the quittance, that in the event of any thing going wrong, he might yet claim his hundred pounds from Mrs Forbes.

Annie read over the receipt, and saw that she had involved herself in a difficulty. How would Mrs Forbes take it? She begged Bruce not to tell her, and he was ready enough to consent. He did more. He wrote to Mrs Forbes to the effect that, upon reflection, he had resolved to drop further proceedings for the present; and when she carried him a half-year's interest, he took it in silence, justifying himself on the ground that the whole transaction was of doubtful success, and he must therefore secure what he could secure.

As may well be supposed, Annie had very little money to give away now; and this subjected her to a quite new sense of suffering.

CHAPTER XC

It was a dreary wintry summer to all at Howglen. Why should the ripe corn wave deep-dyed in the gold of the sunbeams, when Alec lay frozen in the fields of ice, or sweeping about under them like a broken sea-weed in the waters so cold, so mournful? Yet the work of the world must go on. The corn must be reaped. Things must be bought and sold. Even the mourners must eat and drink. The stains which the day had gathered must be washed from the brow of the morning; and the dust to which Alec had gone down must be swept from the chair in which he had been wont to sit. So things did go on—of themselves as it were, for no one cared much about them, although it was the finest harvest that year that Howglen had ever borne. It had begun at length to appear that the old labour had not been cast into a dead grave, but into a living soil, like that of which Sir Philip Sidney says in his sixty-fifth psalm:

"Each clodd relenteth at thy dressing,"

as if it were a human soul that had bethought itself and began to bring forth fruit.—This might be the beginning of good things. But what did it matter?

Annie grew paler, but relaxed not a single effort to fill her place. She told her poor friends that she had no money now, and could not help them; but most were nearly as glad to see her as before; while one of them who had never liked receiving alms from a girl in such a lowly position, as well as some who had always taken them thankfully, loved her better when she had nothing to give.

She renewed her acquaintance with Peter Whaup, the blacksmith, through his wife, who was ill, and received her visits gladly.

"For," she said, "she's a fine douce lass, and speyks to ye as gin ye war ither fowk, and no as gin she kent a'thing, and cam to tell ye the muckle half o' 't."

"For," she said, "she's a fine pleasant lass, and speaks to you as if you were other folk, and not as if she knew it all, and came to tell you the greater half of it."

I wonder how much her friends understood of what she read to them? She did not confine herself to the Bible, which indeed she was a little shy of reading except they wanted it, but read anything that pleased herself, never doubting that "ither fowk" could enjoy what she enjoyed. She even tried the *Paradise Lost* upon Mrs Whaup, as she had tried it long ago upon Tibbie Dyster; and Mrs Whaup never seemed tired of listening to it. I daresay she understood about as much of it as poets do of the celestial harmonies ever toning around them.

And Peter Whaup was once known, when more than half drunk, to stop his swearing in mid-volley, simply because he had caught a glimpse of Annie at the other end of the street.

So the maiden grew in favour. Her beauty, both inward and outward, was that of the twilight, of a morning cloudy with high clouds, or of a silvery sea: it was a spiritual beauty for the most part. And her sorrow gave a quiet grace to her demeanour, peacefully ripening it into what is loveliest in ladyhood. She always looked like one waiting—sometimes like one listening, as she waited, to "melodies unheard."

CHAPTER XCI

One night, in the end of October, James Dow was walking by the side of his cart along a lonely road, through a peat-moss, on his way to the nearest sea-port for a load of coals. The moon was high and full. He was approaching a solitary milestone in the midst of the moss. It was the loneliest place. Low swells of peat-ground, the burial places of old forests, rolled away on every side, with, here and there, patches of the white-bearded canna-down, or cotton-grass, glimmering doubtfully as the Wind woke and turned himself on the wide space, where he found nothing to puff at but those same little old fairies sunning their hoary beards in the strange moon. As Dow drew near to the milestone he saw an odd-looking figure seated upon it. He was about to ask him if he would like a lift, when the figure rose, and cried joyfully,

"Jamie Doo!"

James Dow staggered back, and was nearly thrown down by the slow-rolling wheel; for the voice was Alec Forbes's. He gasped for breath, and felt as if he were recovering from a sudden stroke of paralysis, during which everything about him had passed away and a new order come in. All that he was capable of was to cry *wo!* to his horse.

There stood Alec, in rags, with a face thin but brown—healthy, bold, and firm. He looked ten years older standing there in the moonlight.

"The Lord preserve's!" cried Dow, and could say no more.

"He has preserved me, ye see, Jeamie. Hoo's my mother?"

"She's brawly, brawly, Mr Alec. The Lord preserve's! She's been terrible aboot ye. Ye maunna gang in upo' her. It wad kill her."

"I hae a grainy sense left, Jeamie. But I'm awfu' tired. Ye maun jist turn yer cairt and tak' me hame. I'll be worth a lade o' coal to my mither ony gait. An' syne ye can brak it till her."

"The Lord preserve us!" cried Dow, and could say no more.

"He has preserved me, you see, Jamie. How's my mother?"

"She's very well, Mr Alec. The Lord preserve us! She's been terrible about you. You mustn't go in upon her. It would kill her."

"I have a grain of sense left, Jamie. But I'm awfully tired. You must just turn your cart and take me home. I'll be worth a load of coal to my mother anyway. And then you can break it to her."

Without another word, Dow turned his horse, helped Alec into the cart, covered him with his coat and some straw, and strode away beside, not knowing whether he was walking in a dream, or in a real starry night. Alec fell fast asleep, and never waked till the cart stood still, about midnight, at his mother's door. He started up.

"Lie still, Mr Alec," said Dow, in a whisper. "The mistress'll be in her bed. And if you go in upon her like that, you'll drive her daft."

Alec lay down again, and Dow went to Mary's window, on the other side, to try to wake her. But just as he returned, Alec heard his mother's window open.

"Who's there?" she called.

"Nobody but me, Jamie Doo," answered James. "I was half way to Portlokie, when I had a mishap upon the road. Bettie put her foot upon a sharp stone, and fell down, and broke both her legs."

"How did she come home then?"

"She had to come home, ma'am."

"Broke her legs!"

"Heavens, ma'am—her knees. I don't mean the bones, you know, ma'am; only the skin. But she wasn't fit to go on. And so I brought her back."

"What's that in the cart? Is it anything dead?"

"Na, ma'am, devil a bit of it! It's living enough. It's a stranger lad that I gave a lift to upon the road. He's worn out."

But Dow's voice trembled, or—or something or other revealed all to the mother's heart. She gave a great cry. Alec sprung from the cart, rushed into the house, and was in his mother's arms.

Annie was asleep in the next room, but she half awoke with a sense of his presence. She had heard his voice through the folds of sleep. And she thought she was lying on the rug before the dining-room fire, with Alec and his mother at the tea-table, as on that night when he brought her in from the snow-hut. Finding out confusedly that the supposition did not correspond with some other vague consciousness, she supposed next that she "had died in sleep and was a blessed ghost," just going to find Alec in heaven. That was abandoned in its turn, and all at once she knew that she was in her own bed, and that Alec and his mother were talking in the next room.

She rose, but could hardly dress herself for trembling. When she was dressed she sat down on the edge of the bed to bethink herself.

The joy was almost torture, but it had a certain qualifying bitter in it. Ever since she had believed him dead, Alec had been so near to her! She had loved him as much as ever she would. But Life had come in suddenly, and divided those whom Death had joined. Now he was a great way off; and she dared not speak to him whom she had cherished in her heart. Modesty took the telescope from the hands of Love, and turning it, put the larger end to Annie's eye. Ever since her confession to Curly, she had been making fresh discoveries in her own heart; and now the tide of her love swelled so strong that she felt it must break out in an agony of joy, and betray her if once she looked in the face of Alec alive from the dead. Nor was this all. What she had done about his mother's debt, must come out soon; and although Alec could not think that she meant to lay him under obligation, he might yet feel under obligation, and that she could not bear. These things and many more so worked in the sensitive maiden that as soon as she heard Alec and his mother go to the dining-room she put on her bonnet and cloak, stole like a thief through the house to the back door, and let herself out into the night.

She avoided the path, and went through the hedge into a field of stubble at the back of the house across which she made her way to the turnpike road and the new bridge over the Glamour. Often she turned to look back to the window of the room where he that had been dead was alive and talking with his widowed mother; and only when the intervening trees hid it from her sight did she begin to think what she should do. She could think of nothing but to go to her aunt once more, and ask her to take her in for a few days. So she walked on through the sleeping town.

Not a soul was awake, and the stillness was awful. It was a place of tombs. And those tombs were haunted by dreams. Away towards the west, the moon lay on the steep-sloping edge of a rugged cloud, appearing to have rolled half-way down from its lofty peak, and about to be launched off its baseless bulk into

"the empty, vast, and wandering air."

In the middle of the large square of the little gray town she stood and looked around her. All one side lay in shade; the greater part of the other three lay in moonlight. The old growth of centuries, gables and fronts—stepping out into the light, retreating into the shadow—outside stairs and dark gateways, stood up in the night warding a townful of sleepers. Not one would be awake now. Ah yes! there was light in the wool-carder's window. His wife was dying. That light over the dying, wiped the death-look from the face of the sleeping town. Annie roused herself and passed on, fearing to be seen. It was the only thing to be afraid of. But the stillness was awful. One silence only could be more awful: the same silence at noon-day.

So she passed into the western road and through the trees to the bridge over the Wan Water. They stood so still in the moonlight! And the smell from the withering fields laid bare of the harvest and breathing out their damp odours, came to her mixed with the chill air from the dark hills around, already spiced with keen atoms of frost, soon to appear in spangly spikes. Beneath the bridge the river flowed maunderingly, blundering out unintelligible news of its parent bog and all the dreary places it had come through on its way to the strath of Glamerton, which nobody listened to but one glad-hearted, puzzle-brained girl, who stood looking down into it from the bridge when she ought to have been in bed and asleep. She was not far from Clippenstrae, but she could not go there so early, for her aunt would be frightened first and angry next. So she wandered up the stream to the old church-forsaken churchyard, and sat on one of the tombstones. It became very cold as the morning drew on. The moon went down; the stars grew dim; the river ran with a livelier murmur; and through all the fine gradations of dawn—cloudy wind and grey sky—the gates of orange and red burst open, and the sun came forth rejoicing. The long night was over. It had not been a very weary one; for Annie had thoughts of her own, and like the earth in the warm summer nights, could shine and flash up through the dark, seeking the face of God in the altar-flame of prayer. Yet she was glad when the sun came. With the first bubble of the spring of light bursting out on the hill-top, she rose and walked through the long shadows of the graves down to the river and through the long shadows of the stubble down the side of the river, which shone in the morning light like a flowing crystal of delicate brown—and so to Clippenstrae, where she found her aunt still in her night-cap. She was standing at the door, however, shading her eyes with her hand, looking abroad as if for some one that might be crossing hitherward from the east. She did not see Annie approaching from the north.

"What are ye luikin' for, auntie?"

"Naething. Nae for you, ony gait, lassie."

"Weel, ye see, I'm come ohn luikit for. But ye was luikin' for somebody, auntie."

"Na. I was only jist luikin'."

"What are you looking for, auntie?"

"Nothing. Not for you, anyway, lassie."

"Well, you see, I'm come unlooked for. But you were looking for somebody, auntie."

"Na. I was only just looking."

Even Annie did not then know that it was the soul's hunger, the vague sense of a need which nothing but the God of human faces, the God of the morning and of the starful night, the God of love and self-forgetfulness, can satisfy, that sent her money-loving, poverty-stricken, pining, grumbling old aunt out staring towards the east. It is this formless idea of something at hand that keeps men and women striving to tear from the bosom of the world the secret of their own hopes. How little they know what they look for in reality is their God! This is that for which their heart and their flesh cry out.

Lead, lead me on, my Hopes. I know that ye are true and not vain. Vanish from my eyes day after day, but arise in new forms. I will follow your holy deception;—follow till ye have brought me to the feet of my Father in Heaven, where I shall find you all with folded wings spangling the sapphire dusk whereon stands His throne, which is our home.

"What do ye want sae ear's this, Annie Anderson?"

"What do you want as early as this, Annie Anderson?"

Margaret's first thought was always— "What can the body be wanting?"

"I want you to take me in for a while," answered Annie.

"For an hour or two? Oh ay."

"Na. For a week or two maybe."

"No indeed. I'll do nothing of the kind. Let them that made you proud, keep you proud."

"I'm not proud, auntie. What makes you say that?"

"So proud that you wouldn't take a good offer when it was in your power. And then they turn you out when it suits themselves. Gentle folks are far from gentle! I'm not going to take you in. There's David Gordon wants a lass. You can just go and find work like other folk."

"I'll go and look after it at once. How far is it, Auntie?"

"Going and giving away your money to beggars as if it were dust, just to be a grand lady! You're none so grand, *I* can tell you. And then coming to poor folk like me to take you in for a week or two! Indeed!"

Auntie had been listening to evil tongues—so much easier to listen to than just tongues. With difficulty Annie kept back her tears. She made no defence; tried to eat the porridge which her aunt set before her; and departed. Before three hours were over, she had the charge of the dairy and cooking at Willowcraig for the next six months of coming winter and spring. Protected from suspicion, her spirits rose all the cheerier for their temporary depression, and she went singing about the house like a *lintie* (linnet).

As she did not appear at breakfast, and was absent from the dinner-table as well, Mrs Forbes set out with Alec to inquire after her, and not knowing where else to go first, betook herself to Robert Bruce. He showed more surprise than pleasure at seeing Alec, smiling with his own acridness as he said,

"I expect you haven't brought home that barrel of oil you promised me, Mr Alec? It would have cleared off a good sheaf of your mother's debts."

Alec answered cheerily, although his face flushed,

"All in good time, I hope, Mr Bruce. I'm obliged to you for your forbearance, though."

He was too solemn-glad to be angry.

"It can't last for ever, you know," rejoined Bruce, happy to be able to bite, although his poison-bag was gone.

Alec made no reply.

"Have you seen Annie Anderson to-day, Mr Bruce?" asked his mother.

"Indeed I haven't, ma'am. She doesn't often trouble us with her company. We're not grand enough for her."

"Hasn't she been here to-day?" repeated Mrs Forbes, with discomposure in her look and tone.

"Have you lost her, ma'am?" rejoined Bruce. "That *is* a pity. She'll be away with that vagabond, Willie Macwha. He was in the town last night. I saw him go by with Baubie Peterson."

They made him no reply, understanding well enough that though the one premise might be true, the conclusion must be as false as it was illogical and spiteful. They did not go to George Macwha's, but set out for Clippenstrae. When they reached the cottage, they found Meg's nose in full vigour.

"Na. She's not here. Why should she be here? She has no claim upon me, although it pleases you to turn her out—after bringing her up to notions that have just ruined her with pride."

"Indeed I didn't turn her out, Miss Anderson."

"Well, you should never have taken her in."

There was something in her manner which made them certain she knew where Annie was; but as she avoided every attempt to draw her into the admission, they departed foiled, although relieved. She knew well enough that Annie's refuge could not long remain concealed, but she found it pleasant to annoy Mrs Forbes.

And not many days passed before Mrs Forbes did learn where Annie was. But she was so taken up with her son, that weeks even passed before that part of her nature which needed a daughter's love began to assert itself again, and turn longingly towards her all but adopted child.

Alec went away once more to the great town. He had certain remnants of study to gather up at the university, and a certain experience to go through in the preparation of drugs, without which he could not obtain his surgeon's diploma. The good harvest would by and by put a little money in his mother's hands, and the sooner he was ready to practise the better.

The very day after he went, Mrs Forbes drove to Willowcraig to see Annie. She found her short-coated and short-wrappered, like any other girl at a farmhouse. Annie was rather embarrassed at the sight of her friend. Mrs Forbes could easily see, however, that there was no breach in her affection towards her. Yet it must be confessed that having regard to the final return of her son, she was quite as well pleased to know that she was bound to remain where she was for some time to come.

She found the winter very dreary without her, though.

CHAPTER XCII

Finding herself in good quarters, Annie re-engaged herself at the end of the half-year. She had spent the winter in house work, combined with the feeding of pigs and poultry, and partial ministrations to the wants of the cows, of which she had milked the few continuing to give milk upon turnips and straw, and made the best of their scanty supply for the use of the household. There was no hardship in her present life. She had plenty of wholesome food to eat, and she lay warm at night. The old farmer, who was rather overbearing with his men, was kind to her because he liked her; and the guidwife was a sonsy (*well conditioned*) dame, who, when she scolded, never meant anything by it.

She cherished her love for Alec, but was quite peaceful as to the future. How she might have felt had she heard that he was going to be married, I cannot take upon me to say.

When her work was done, she would go out for a lonely walk, without asking leave or giving offence, indulging in the same lawlessness as before, and seeming incapable of being restrained by other bonds than those of duty.

And now the month of April was nearly over, and the primroses were *glintin'* on the braes.

One evening she went out bare-headed to look how a certain den, wont to be haunted by wild-flowers and singing-birds, was getting on towards its complement of summer pleasures. As she was climbing over a fence, a horseman came round the corner of the road. She saw at a glance that it was Alec, and got down again.

Change had passed upon both since they parted. He was a full-grown man with a settled look. She was a lovely woman, even more delicate and graceful than her childhood had promised.

As she got down from the fence, he got down from his horse. Without a word on either side, their hands joined, and still they stood silent for a minute, Annie with her eyes on the ground, Alec gazing in her face, which was pale with more than its usual paleness.

"I saw Curly yesterday," said Alec at length, with what seemed to Annie a meaning look.

Her face flushed as red as fire.—Could Curly have betrayed her?

She managed to stammer out,

"Oh! Did you?"

And then silence fell again.

"Eh! Alec," she said at length, taking up the conversation, in her turn, "we thought we would never see ye again."

"I thought so too," answered Alec, "when the great berg came down on us through the snow-storm, and flung the barque upon the floe with her side crushed in.—How I used to dream about the old school-days, Annie, and finding you in my hut!—And I did find you in the snow, Annie."

But a figure came round the other corner—for the road made a double sweep at this point—and cried—

"Annie, come hame direcly. Ye're wantit."

"I'm coming to see you again soon, Annie," said Alec. "But I must go away for a month or two first."

Annie replied with a smile and an outstretched hand—nothing more. She could wait well enough.

How lovely the flowers in the dyke-sides looked as she followed Mrs Gordon home! But the thought that perhaps Curly had told him something was like the serpent under them. Yet somehow she had got so beautiful before she reached the house, that her aunt, who had come to see her, called out,

"Losh! lassie! What hae ye been aboot? Ye hae a colour by ordinar'."

"That's easy accoontet for," said her mistress roguishly. "She was stan'in' killoguin wi' a bonnie young lad an' a horse. I winna hae sic doin's aboot my hoose, I can tell ye, lass."

Margaret Anderson flew into a passion, and abused her with many words, which Annie, so far from resenting, scarcely even heard. At length she ceased, and departed almost without an adieu. But what did it matter?—What did any earthly thing matter, if only Curly had not told him?

Now, all that Curly had told Alec was that Annie was not engaged to him.

So the days and nights passed, and Spring, the girl, changed into Summer, the woman; and still Alec did not come.

One evening, when a wind that blew from the west, and seemed to smell of the roses of the sunset, was filling her rosy heart with joy—Annie sat in a rough little seat, scarcely an arbour, at the bottom of a garden of the true country order, where all the dear old-fashioned glories of sweet-peas, cabbage-roses, larkspur, gardener's garters, honesty, poppies, and peonies, grew in homely companionship with gooseberry and currant bushes, with potatoes and pease. The scent of the sunset came in reality from a *cheval de frise* of wallflower on the coping of the low stone wall behind where she was sitting with her Milton. She read aloud in a low voice that sonnet beginning "*Lady that in the prime of earliest youth.*" As she finished it, a voice, as low, said, almost in her ear,

"That's you, Annie."

Alec was looking over the garden wall behind her.

"Eh, Alec," she cried, starting to her feet, at once shocked and delighted, "dinna say that. It's dreidfu' to hear ye say sic a thing. I wish I was a wee like her."

"Weel, Annie, I think ye're jist like her. But come oot wi' me. I hae a story to tell ye. Gie me yer han', and pit yer fit upo' the seat."

She was over the wall in a moment, and they were soon seated under the trees of the copse near which Annie had met him before. The brown twilight was coming on, and a warm

"That's you, Annie."

Alec was looking over the garden wall behind her.

"Eh, Alec," she cried, starting to her feet, at once shocked and delighted, "don't say that. It's dreadful to hear you say such a thing. I wish I was a little like her."

"Well, Annie, I think you're just like her. But come out with me. I have a story to tell you. Give me your hand, and put your foot upon the seat."

She was over the wall in a moment, and they were soon seated under the trees of the copse near which Annie had met him before. The brown twilight was coming on, and a warm sleepy hush pervaded earth and air, broken only by the stream below them, cantering away over its stones to join the Wan Water. Neither of them was inclined to quarrel with the treeless country about them: they were lapped in foliage; nor with the desolate moorland hills around them: they only drove them closer together.

Time unmeasured by either passed without speech.

"They told me," said Alec at length, "that you and Curly had made it up."

"Alec!" exclaimed Annie, and looked up in his face as if he had accused her of infidelity, but, instantly dropping her eyes, said no more.

"I would have found you out before a day was over, if it hadn't been for that."

Annie's heart beat violently, but she said nothing, and, after a silence, Alec went on.

"Did my mother ever tell you about how the barque was lost?"

"No, Alec."

"It was a terrible snow-storm with wind. We couldn't see more than a few yards a-head. We were under bare poles, but we couldn't keep from drifting. All in a moment a huge ghastly thing came out of the gloamin' to windward, bore down on us like a spectre, and dashed us on a floating field of ice. The barque was thrown right upon it with one side stove in; but nobody was killed. It was an awful night, Annie; but I'm not going to tell you about it now. We made a rough sledge, and loaded it with provisions, and set out westward, and were carried westward at the same time on the floe, till we came near land. Then we launched our boat and got to the shore of Greenland. There we set out travelling southwards. Many of our men died, do what I could to keep them alive. But I'll tell you all about it another time, if you'll let me. What I want to tell you noo's this.—Ilka nicht, as sure as I lay doon i' the snaw to sleep, I dreamed I was at hame. A' the auld stories cam' back. I woke ance, thinkin' I was carryin' you throu' the water i' the lobby o' the schuil, and that ye was greitin' upo' my face. And whan I woke, my face was weet. I doobt I had been greitin mysel'. A' the auld faces cam' roon' me ilka nicht, Thomas Crann and Jeames Dow and my mother— whiles ane and whiles anither— but ye was aye there.

"Ae mornin', whan I woke up, I was my lane. I dinna ken richtly hoo it had happened. I think the men war nigh-han' dazed wi' the terrible cauld and the weariness o' the traivel, and I had sleepit ower lang, and they had forgotten a' aboot me.

was thrown right upon it with one side stove in; but nobody was killed. It was an awful night, Annie; but I'm not going to tell you about it now. We made a rough sledge, and loaded it with provisions, and set out westward, and were carried westward at the same time on the floe, till we came near land. Then we launched our boat and got to the shore of Greenland. There we set out travelling southwards. Many of our men died, do what I could to keep them alive. But I'll tell you all about it another time, if you'll let me. What I want to tell you now's this.—Every night, as sure as I lay down in the snow to sleep, I dreamed I was at home. All the old stories came back. I woke once, thinking I was carrying you through the water in the school lobby, and that you were crying upon my face. And when I woke, my face was wet. I suspect I had been crying myself. All the old faces came round me every night, Thomas Crann and James Dow and my mother—now one and now another—but you were always there.

"One morning, when I woke up, I was alone. I don't rightly know how it had happened. I think the men were nigh-hand dazed with the terrible cold and the weariness of the travel, and I had slept too long, and they had forgotten all about me. And

And what think ye was the first thocht i' my heid, whan I cam' to mysel', i' the terrible white desolation o' cauld and ice and snaw? I wantit to run straucht to you, and lay my heid upo' yer shouther. For I had been dreamin' a' nicht that I was lyin' i' my bed at hame, terrible ill, and ye war gaein aboot the room like an angel, wi' the glimmer o' white wings aboot ye, which I reckon was the snaw comin' throu' my dream. And ye wad never come near me; and I cudna speak to cry to ye to come; till at last, whan my hert was like to brak 'cause ye wadna luik at me, ye turned wi' tears i' yer een, and cam' to the bedside and leaned ower me, and—"

"Sae ye see it was nae wonner that I wantit you, whan I fand mysel' a' my lane i' the dreidfu' place, the very beauty o' which was deidly.

"Weel, that wasna a'. I got mair that day than I thocht ever to get. Annie, I think what Thomas Crann used to say maun be true. Annie, I think a body may some day get a kin' o' a sicht o' the face o' God.—I was sae dooncast, whan I saw mysel' left ahin', that I sat doon upon a rock and glowered at naething. It was awfu'. An' it grew waur and waur, till the only comfort I had was that I cudna live lang. And wi' that the thocht o' God cam' into my heid,

what do you think was the first thought in my head, when I came to myself, in the terrible white desolation of cold and ice and snow? I wanted to run straight to you, and lay my head upon your shoulder. For I had been dreaming all night that I was lying in my bed at home, terribly ill, and you were going about the room like an angel, with the glimmer of white wings about you, which I reckon was the snow coming through my dream. And you would never come near me; and I couldn't speak to cry to you to come; till at last, when my heart was like to break 'cause you wouldn't look at me, you turned with tears in your eyes, and came to the bedside and leaned over me, and—"

"So you see it was no wonder that I wanted you, when I found myself all alone in the dreadful place, the very beauty of which was deadly.

"Well, that wasn't all. I got more that day than I thought ever to get. Annie, I think what Thomas Crann used to say must be true. Annie, I think a man may some day get a kind of a sight of the face of God.—I was so downcast, when I saw myself left behind, that I sat down upon a rock and glowered at nothing. It was awful. And it grew worse and worse, till the only comfort I had was that I couldn't live long. And with that the thought of God

and it seemed as gin I had a richt, as it war, to call upon him—I was sae miserable.

"And there cam' ower me a quaietness, and like a warm breath o' spring air. I dinna ken what it was—but it set me upo' my feet, and I startit to follow the lave. Snaw had fa'en, sae that I could hardly see the track. And I never cam' up wi' them, and I haena heard o' them sin' syne.

"The silence at first had been fearfu'; but noo, somehoo or ither, I canna richtly explain 't, the silence seemed to be God himsel' a' aboot me.

"And I'll never forget him again, Annie.

"I cam' upo' tracks, but no o' oor ain men. They war the fowk o' the country. And they brocht me whaur there was a schooner lyin' ready to gang to Archangel. And here I am."

Was there ever a gladder heart than Annie's? She was weeping as if her life would flow away in tears. She had known that Alec would come back to God some day.

He ceased speaking, but she could not cease weeping. If she had tried to stop the tears, she would have been torn with sobs. They sat silent for a long time. At length Alec spoke again:

"Annie, I don't deserve it—but *will* you be my wife some day?"

came into my head, and it seemed as if I had a right, as it were, to call upon him—I was so miserable.

"And there came over me a quietness, and like a warm breath of spring air. I don't know what it was—but it set me upon my feet, and I started to follow the rest. Snow had fallen, so that I could hardly see the track. And I never came up with them, and I haven't heard of them since.

"The silence at first had been fearful; but now, somehow or other, I can't rightly explain it, the silence seemed to be God himself all about me.

"And I'll never forget him again, Annie.

"I came upon tracks, but not of our own men. They were the folk of the country. And they brought me where there was a schooner lying ready to go to Archangel. And here I am."

Was there ever a gladder heart than Annie's? She was weeping as if her life would flow away in tears. She had known that Alec would come back to God some day.

He ceased speaking, but she could not cease weeping. If she had tried to stop the tears, she would have been torn with sobs. They sat silent for a long time. At length Alec spoke again:

"Annie, I don't deserve it—but *will* you be my wife some day?"

And all the answer Annie made was to lay her head on his bosom and weep on.

CHAPTER XCIII

Is it worth while, I debate with myself, to write one word more?—Shall I tie the ends of my warp, or leave them loose?—I will tie them, but no one needs sit out the process.

The farm of Howglen prospered. Alec never practised in his profession, but became a first-rate farmer. Within two years Annie and he were married, and began a new chapter of their history.

When Mrs Forbes found that Alec and Annie were engaged, she discovered that she had been in reality wishing it for a long time, and that the opposing sense of duty had been worldly.

Mr Cupples came to see them every summer, and generally remained over the harvest. He never married. But he wrote a good book.

Thomas Crann and he had many long disputes, and did each other good. Thomas grew gentler as he grew older. And he learned to hope more for other people. And then he hoped more for himself too.

The first time Curly saw Annie after the wedding, he was amazed at his own presumption in ever thinking of marrying such a lady. When about thirty, by which time he had a good business of his own, he married Isie Constable—still little, still old-fashioned, and still wise.

Margaret Anderson was taken good care of by Annie Forbes, but kept herself clear of all obligation by never acknowledging any.

Robert Bruce had to refund, and content himself with his rights. He died worth a good deal of money notwithstanding, which must have been a great comfort to him at the last.

Young Robert is a clergyman, has married a rich wife, hopes to be Moderator of the Assembly some day, and never alludes to his royal ancestor.

THE END.

APPENDIX:

LITERAL ENGLISH TRANSLATIONS OF ALL THE SCOTS POEMS THAT APPEAR IN ALEC FORBES

POEM 1 (p. 130)

There came a man to our town end,
And a woesome man was he;
With a snub nose, and a crooked mouth,
And a cock in his left eye.
And much he spied, and much he spoke;
But the burden of his song
Was always the same, and over again:
There's none of you all but's wrong.
You're all wrong, and all wrong,
And altogether all wrong;
There's not a man about the town,
But's altogether all wrong.

That's not the way to bake the bread,
Nor yet to brew the ale;
That's not the way to hold the plough,
Nor yet to drive the mill.
That's not the way to milk the cow,
Nor yet to wean the calf;
Nor yet to fill the meal-chest—
Ye know not your work by half.
You're all wrong, &c.

The minister wasn't fit to pray,
And let alone to preach;
He neither had the gift of grace,
Nor yet the gift of speech.
He reminded him of Balaam's ass,
With a difference you may know:
The Lord he opened the ass's mouth

APPENDIX

The minister opened his own.
He's all wrong &c.

The poor precentor couldn't sing,
He grunted like a swine;
The very elders couldn't pass
The ladles to his mind.
And for the ruling elder's grace,
It wasn't worth a horn;
He didn't half uncurse the meat,
Nor pray for more tomorrow.
He's all wrong, &c.

And always he gave his nose a twist,
And always he crooked his mouth;
And always he cocked up his eye,
And said, "Be careful now."
We laughed behind our palm, man,
And never said him nay:
And always he spoke—just let him speak!
And always he said his say:
You're all wrong, &c.

Said our goodman: "The creature's daft;
But wow! he has the chatter;
Let's see if he can turn a hand
Or only look and grumble.
It's true we musn't trust to him—
He's fairly cracked with pride;
But he must live, we cannot kill him—
If he can work, he shall bide/stay."
He was a' wrang, &c.

It's true it's but a laddie's turn,
But we'll begin with a small thing;
There's all those weeds to gather and burn—
And he's the man for everything."
We went our ways, and let him be,
To do just as he might;
We think to hear no more of him,

Till we come home at night;
But we're all wrong, &c.

For, Lord! ere it was dinner-time,
The sky was in a flame;
The smoke rose up, as it had been
From Sodom-flames, I vow.
We ran like mad; but corn and byre
Were blazing—woe's the fate!
As if the devil had brought the fire,
To make another hell.
'Twas all wrong, &c.

And by the blaze the man stood,
With his hands beneath his tails;
And always he said—"I told you so,
And you're to blame yourselves.
It's all your fault, for you're all wrong—
You'll maybe own it at last:
What made you burn those devilish weeds,
When the wind blew from the west?
You're all wrong, and all wrong,
And altogether all wrong;
There's not a man in all the world
But's altogether all wrong."

POEM 2 (p. 141)

"O let me in, my bonnie lass!
It's a long road over the hill;
And the fluttering snow began to fall,
As I came by the mill."

"This is no change-house, John Munro,
And you needn't come any more:
You crooked your mouth, and slighted me,
Last Wednesday, at the fair."

APPENDIX

"I slighted you!" "Above the glass."
 "Curse the hateful mouth
That made the lying word to pass,
 By wrapping it in the truth.

The fact was this: I couldn't bear
To hear your bonnie name,
Where great mouths were opened wide
With lawless mirth and shame.

And all I said was: 'Heavens! Let sit;
She's but a child, the lass.'
It turned the spate of words a bit,
And let your fair name pass."

"Thank you for nothing, John Munro!
My name can go or stay;
It's not a tone of drunken words
Would turn my head aside."

"O Elsie, lassie of my own!
The drift is cold and strong;
O take me in one hour, and then
 I'll gather me and go."

"You're good at coaxing/wheedling, Jock Munro.
For you heed not false and true:
Go in to Katie at the Mill,
She loves such like as you."

He turned his foot; he spoke no more.
The sky was like to fall;
And Elsie's heart grew great and sore,
At sight of the driving snow.

She laid her down, but not to sleep,
For her very heart was cold;
And the sheets were like a frozen heap
Of snow about her folded.

APPENDIX

She rose very early. And all outside
Was one broad winding sheet;
At the door-sill, or window-sill,
Was never a mark of feet.

She crept all day about the house,
Slow-footed and heart-sore,
Always peeping out like a frightened mouse,—
But Johnnie came no more!

When soft the thaw began to melt
Away the ghostly snow,
Her heart was softer than the thaw,
Her pride had taken a fall.

And she across the hill would go,
Where the sun was blinking bonnie,
To see his old Mother in her cot,
And ask about her Johnnie.

But as along the hill she went,
Through snow and slush and wet,
She stopped with a choking cry—
'Twas Johnnie at her feet.

His head was smothered beneath the snow,
But his breast was mostly bare;
And 'twixt his breast and his right hand,
He clasped a lock of hair.

'Twas golden hair: she knew it well.
Alack, the sobs and sighs!
The warm wind blew, the lark flew,
But Johnnie wouldn't rise.

The spring came over the westward hill,
And the frost it fled away;
And the green grass looked smiling up,
None the worse for all the snow.

And soft it grew on Johnnie's grave,
Where deep the sunshine lay;
But, long ere that, on Elsie's head
The golden hair was gray.

POEM 3 (p. 240)

As I was walking on the strand,
I spied an old man sit
On one old rock; and always the waves
Came washing to its foot.
And always his lips went muttering,
And his eye was dull and blue.
As I came near, he looked at me,
But this was all his say:
"Robbie and Jeannie were two bonnie bairns,
And they played together upon the shore:
Up came the tide 'tween the moon and the stars,
And parted the two with an eerie roar."

What can the old man mean, said I,
Sitting upon the old rock?
The tide creeps up with moan and cry,
And a hiss almost like a mock.
The words he mutters must be the end
Of a weary dreary song—
A dead thing floating in his brain,
That the tide will not let go.
"Robbie and Jeannie were two bonnie bairns,
And they played together upon the shore:
Up came the tide 'tween the moon and the stars,
And parted the two with an eerie roar."

What parted them, old man? I said;
Did the tide come up too strong?
'Twas a fine death for them that went,
Their troubles weren't long.
Or was one taken, and the other left—

APPENDIX

One to sing, one to weep?
It's sore, right/very sore, to be bereft,
But the tide is at your feet.
"Robbie and Jeannie were two bonnie bairns,
And they played together upon the shore:
Up came the tide 'tween the moon and the stars,
And parted the two with an eerie roar."

Maybe, said I, 'twas Time's gray sea,
Whose drowning's worse to bear;
But Death's a diver, seeking you
Beneath its choking tide.
And you'll look in one another's eye
Triumphing over gray Time.
But never a word he answered me,
But over with his dreary chime—
"Robbie and Jeannie were two bonnie bairns,
And they played together upon the shore:
Up came the tide 'tween the moon and the stars,
And parted the two with an eerie roar."

Maybe, old man, said I, 'twas Change
That crept between the two?
Hech! that's a drowning awfully strange,
One worse than one and all.
He spoke no more. I looked and saw
That the old lips couldn't go.
The tide unseen took him away—
Left me to end his song:
"Robbie and Jeannie were two bonnie bairns,
And they played together upon the shore:
Up came the tide 'tween the moon and the stars,
And took them where parting shall be no more."

POEM 4 (p. 439)

"Sweep up the floor, Janet;
Put on another peat.

APPENDIX

It's a calm and starry night, Janet,
And neither cold nor wet.

And it's open house we keep tonight
For any that may be out.
It's the night between the Saints and Souls,
When the bodiless go about.

Set the chairs back to the wall, Janet;
Make ready for quiet folk.
Have everything as clean as a winding sheet:
They come not every week.

There's a spale upon the floor, Janet;
And there's a rowan-berry:
Sweep them into the fire, Janet,—
They'll be welcomer than merry.

Then set open the door, Janet—
Wide open for who knows who;
As you come through to your bed, Janet,
Set it open to the wall."

She set the chairs back to the wall,
But one made of the birch;
She swept the floor,—left that one spale—
A long spale of the oak.

The night was calm, and the stars sat still
Aglinting down the sky;
And the souls crept out of their earthy graves,
All dank with lying by.

She had set the door wide to the wall,
And blown the peats rosy red;
They were shoeless feet went out and in,
Nor clumped as they went.

When midnight came, the mother rose—
She woud go see and hear.

APPENDIX

Back she came with a glowering face
And wilting with very fear.

"There's one of them sitting before the fire!
Janet, go not to see:
You left a chair before the fire,
Where I told you no chair should be."

Janet she smiled in her mother's face:
She had burnt the rowan red,
And she left beneath the birchen chair
The spale from a coffin lid.

She rose and she went to the kitchen,
Always shutting door and door.
Three hours went by ere her mother heard
Her foot upon the floor.

But when the gray cock crew, she heard
The sound of shoeless feet;
When the red cock crew, she heard the door,
And a rush of wind and wet.

And Janet came back with a wan face,
But never a word said she;
No man ever heard her voice loud out,
It came like from over the sea.

And no man ever heard her laugh,
Nor yet say alas or woe;
But a smile always glimmered on her wan face,
Like the moonlight on the sea.

And every night 'tween the Saints and the Souls,
Wide open she set the door;
And she mended the fire, and she left one chair,
And that spale upon the floor.

And at midnight she went to the kitchen,
Always shutting door and door.

When the red cock crew, she came to the inner room
Always wanner than before—

Wanner her face, and sweeter her smile;
Till the seventh All Souls' eve.
Her mother she heard the shoeless feet,
Said "she's coming I believe."

But she came not through, and her mother lay;
For fear she couldn't stand.
But up she rose and to the kitchen she went,
When the golden cock had crowed.

And Janet sat upon the chair,
White as the day did dawn;
Her smile was a sunlight left on the sea,
When the sun has gone away.

POEM 5 (p.466)

When Andrew from Strathbogie went,
The sky was lowering dreary;
The sun he wouldn't lift his head;
The wind blew low and eerie.
In his pocket he had a coin or two,
I vow he hadn't many,
Yet Andrew like a linnet sang,
For Lizzie was so bonny!

O Lizzie, Lizzie, bonny lassie!
Bonnie, saucy hussy!
What right had you to look at me,
And drive me daft and dizzy?

When Andrew to Strathbogie came,
The sun was shining rarely;
He rode a horse that pranced and sprang—
I vow he sat him fairly.

And he had gold to spend and spare,
And a heart as true as any;
But his look was down, and his sigh was sore,
For Lizzie was so bonny!
O Lizzie, Lizzie, bonny hussy!
You've turned the daylight dreary.
You're straight and rare, you're false and fair!—
Hech![1] old John Armstrong's deary!"

POEM 6 (p. 559)

One by one they go away.
The gatherer gathers great and small.
One by one makes one and all.

Always when one is taken from one,
One on earth is left alone,
Two in heaven are knit again.

When God's harvest is in ere long,
Golden-headed, ripe, and full,
Then begins a better song.

POEM 7 (p. 582)

"O lassie beyond the hill!
Come over the top of the hill;
Or round the corner of the hill;
For I want you sore tonight.
I'm needing you sore tonight,
For I'm tired and sick of myself.
A person's self's the sorest weight.
O lassie, come over the hill.

If a person could be a thought of grace,
And not a self at all!

---

1   HECH (Scots): an exclamation (in this case akin to a sigh of sorrow)

APPENDIX

I'm sick of my head and my hands and my face,
And my thoughts and myself and all.
I'm sick of the world and all;
The light goes by with a hiss;
For through my eyes the sunbeams fall,
But my weary heart they miss!

O lassie beyond the hill!
Come over the top of the hill,
Or round the corner of the hill,
For I want you sore tonight.

For if once I saw your bonnie head,
And the sunlight on your hair,
The ghost of myself would fall down dead,
And I'd be myself no more.
I would be myself no more,
Filled of the sole remedy,
Slain by the arrows of light from your hair,
Killed by your body and head!
O lassie, beyond the hill! etc.

But if you loved me, ever so small,
For the sake of my bonnie dame,
Whan I came to life, as she went away,
I could bear my body and name.
I might bear myself, the weary same
Always setting up its head,
Till I turn from the clothes that cover my frame,
As if they were round the dead.
O lassie, beyond the hill! etc.

But if you loved me as I love you I would ring my own death knell;
Myself would vanish, shot through and through
By the shine of your sunny self.
By the shine of your sunny self,
By the light beneath your brow,
I would die to myself, and ring my bell,
And only live in you.

APPENDIX

O lassie ayont the hill!
Come ower the tap o' the hill,
Or roun' the neuk o' the hill,
For I want ye sair the nicht.
I'm needin' ye sair the nicht,
For I'm tired and sick o' mysel';
A body's sel 's the sairest weicht!
O lassie, come ower the hill."

DISCOVER MORE OF G.K. CHESTERTON'S FAVOURITE MACDONALD BOOKS!

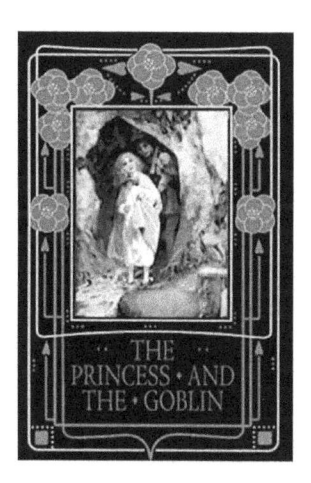

FIND THESE AND MORE MACDONALD CLASSICS AT
theroomtoroam.com